WIVES AND MISTRESSES

Also by Suzanne Morris

GALVESTON
KEEPING SECRETS
SKYCHILD

WIVES

AND

MISTRESSES

Suzanne Morris

DOUBLEDAY & COMPANY, INC.
GARDEN CITY, NEW YORK
1986

Library of Congress Cataloging-in-Publication Data
Morris, Suzanne.
  Wives and mistresses.
  I. Title.
PS3563.O87448T49 1986   813'.54   85-25235
ISBN: 0-385-19099-9

In memory of my father Frank M. Page,
whose love for Houston inspired this novel
AND
for my friends the Cornelius C. Sullivan family,
who provided me the special place for it.

Acknowledgments

Since I began researching the background for this novel in 1979, I have become indebted to many people for help and support. Some of them are no longer living. I am pleased, nonetheless, to include their names among the others here.

In Houston: Mrs. Doris Glasser, Head; Mrs. Lorraine Jeter, Librarian; and all the staff of the Texas and local history department, Houston Public Library; Mrs. Barrie Scardino, former Architectural Archivist, Houston Metropolitan Research Center, Houston Public Library; Mr. Stephen Fox, Fellow of the Anchorage Foundation of Texas; Mrs. Cornelius C. Sullivan; Dr. Thomas M. Biggs; Mr. Harris Masterson; the late General Maurice Hirsch; Mrs. Lydia Jerrell; the late Miss Kate Ebdon; the late Mrs. Rosa Tod Hamner; and my father, the late Frank M. Page.

In New Orleans: Mr. Collin Hamer, Head, Louisiana division, New Orleans Public Library; Mrs. Florence Jumonville and Ms. Judith McMillan, Historic New Orleans Collection; the late Mrs. E. E. Allgeyer; Mrs. G. S. Kennedy, Jr.; Mrs. Audrey McCrary; Ms. Bryce Reveley, Textile Consultant; and Mr. and Mrs. Walter Moses. For their cordial hospitality and assistance, I am especially thankful to Mr. and Mrs. Edward Gilly.

I am very much indebted to my cousin Sharon Frederick, her husband David, and their daughters Regina and Courtney of Teague, Texas, who welcomed me into their home for working vacations and gave me their love and support.

I am grateful to Mrs. Nancy May for typing the manuscript, and to Mrs. Karen Giesen for proofreading. Last, but by no means least, I want to express my heartfelt appreciation to Susan Schwartz and Al Zuckerman.

Contents

Nothing is so strong as gentleness,
nothing as gentle as real strength.
    —St. Francis de Sales

Alvareda

1887–1901

PART 1

Chapter 1

It will soon be daylight, and this night of silent vigil in the house my father built will be over at last. Yet, will I go away from here any less his prisoner than before? Can any of us whose lives he touched really escape his evil?

Now and then I close my eyes and imagine that the child lying close to me rises from her bed, pulls back the veil of mosquito netting which encloses her, and, smiling at me with a toss of her curls, dances around my chair. When I open my eyes the stark truth mocks me. The doctor was here until shortly after midnight and said that Elzyna might never walk again. I watched from an upstairs window as the lights on his buggy moved like a pair of fireflies down the narrow path, then disappeared into the thick shroud of trees that surround this place in the wilderness. And I stood at that window for a long time, thinking of the insidious web of circumstances that began before I knew anything about the house or the life my father structured for himself, and inevitably brought disaster not only to Elzyna but to all of us.

It was in a little town not so far from here that I grew up. Harrisburg, Texas, was then—as it is now—an ugly collection of streets and buildings, bereft of design or style. The grass grew tall over many of the city blocks, and the streets were unpaved and dusty. Two bayous—the Brays and the Buffalo—intersected near the middle of town. Down the center ran the main thoroughfare of Broadway, and in the southeast corner was the Glendale Cemetery, where heroes of the Texas Revolution were buried alongside less distinguished people.

There were a few saloons, a couple of grocers, a post office, a school for all grades, and a blacksmith. There were several boardinghouses, and a few grand homes such as the one where the Charles Milby family lived and the one at the corner of Broadway and Sycamore where I lived with my father and sister. Papa built the house shortly before the Civil War, and it might have been a happy place for a while. From the time I could remember, it was not. It was a two-story house with a third-floor attic, which later became my father's quarters, and where, from a small oval window, he could look down upon the yard. It had deep windows with art glass in the second story, a vine-covered gallery on the ground floor that wound around the side of the house, a pitched roof with ridge cresting and one tall central brick chimney. The yard was shaded with old magnolias and surrounded by an iron fence.

Inside the house was well furnished, as might be expected of the home of a prosperous family. Fine clothing filled the wardrobes and dressers; the larder was well stocked with food. Yet I spent many a late afternoon out on the front gallery looking across the street at the one-story cottage of a railroad family and wishing I lived there. The children wore hand-me-downs and ran around dirty most of the time. But there was laughter there, and when the father came home in the evening after working in the shops, he gathered the children in his arms and rode the youngest piggyback all the way up the walk and into the house. I wished I could follow them inside and eat leftover stew around their table.

I will never forget January 5, 1887, two days after my seventeenth birthday. Surely there was never a day less fit for walking home from school; yet of necessity I was doing just that. My arms were loaded with school books. My hands were cold and wet in spite of a pair of gloves. The chilly wind penetrated my woolen coat and the wet mush underfoot soaked through my boots. The ice hung on shrubs and fences, and slickened the dead yellow grass that surrounded the houses. The trees—the only features of natural beauty in the town—were black and barren skeletons which reminded me of how much I disliked this time of year. The fact that I had not been picked up from school, two blocks down and one block over, indicated that Papa was gone from town. Of this I was thankful, for at least the house would be peaceful once I arrived.

Nearly home, I passed by the Leider house and glanced up at the porch. Until several years ago, the Leiders lived in a large home with lawns that swept down to the edge of Buffalo Bayou. Then, Mr. Leider was discovered to have a mistress. My father led the church committee that exposed them.

After that Mr. Leider and the woman disappeared. There was a tale circulated that was never proved, but was never doubted either, that they ran away together. Mrs. Leider soon moved her family to a lesser house—the one that I was passing now—and took in boarders. David no longer lived at home. But he was there today, on the front porch, talking to a tall, distinguished-looking man about to depart. I thought the man might be a prospective boarder.

I did not want David to see me looking. I faced ahead as soon as I realized they had both noticed me. I failed to see a dip in the muddy street and, missing my step, fell forward, my books sailing from my hands. I do not believe I have ever been so painfully embarrassed. The guest had come down off the Leider porch and was now lifting me to my feet. Our eyes met. Then we were both speaking at once: he to inquire as to my well-being; me, to apologize for my clumsiness and offer thanks. The jumble of words this produced caused him to stop and smile. "I'm afraid you've spoiled your coat," he said.

"It doesn't matter," I stammered.

He told me his name was Neal Gerrard, then said, "Let me see you home."

"No, thank you. I live just there." I pointed toward our house up the street, noticing that my half-sister Olivia had stationed herself at her upstairs window and now peered down at us. Olivia was Papa's daughter by his first wife. At thirty-seven her youthfulness was gone. Her wide brown eyes were lackluster. She wore her hair pinned up in back, and the unruly strands of gray that now invaded it made a frizzy patch of the bangs she wore above her forehead. Her shoulders were round and fleshy; her breasts were a wide and fulsome plain that rose and fell with her breathing. She was old enough to be my mother, and most of the time she treated me accordingly.

Neal must have seen her too, for he paused a moment, then looked at me. "Well, then, here are your books . . . unless you would let me carry them for you."

"Oh no, good day," I said, already hurrying away.

"But what's your name?"

"Alvareda. Alvareda Cane."

He tipped his hat. Once I looked back, and he was still standing there, his long hands driven deep down into his overcoat pockets. He did not look like a prospective boarder. He was too smartly dressed, like a businessman from Houston, or Galveston perhaps.

Once inside the house, I rushed to a front parlor window, rubbed a clear place in the mist, and looked out. I could still see his tall figure, doubling back toward the Leider home.

Olivia was soon beside me. "Who was that?"

"Just a nice fellow," I told her, still looking out the window. "Isn't he handsome?"

She considered. "Not as handsome as David. He's a little on the thin side, don't you think?"

I had been thinking of the kind hazel eyes and the high cheeks, reddened by the cold wind, and the lock of brown hair that tumbled down his forehead as he straightened me up. I could close my eyes and feel the warmth of his arms—"No—that is, well, there was something about him."

"Come along. Let's get you some dry clothes and hot tea."

Olivia's rooms were not only the warmest, but also the prettiest in the house. They were decorated in the cheerful colors of mauve and turquoise, with sheer panels over the windows and light-colored wallpaper and carpets, white woodwork, and a beautiful gas fixture fashioned into a bouquet of glass tulips from which the gaslights shone hazily. Potted palms took to the effusive light in these rooms, and there were at least a half dozen stationed around the floor. Everywhere—on benches and chairs, and stacked on windowsills—were taffeta pillows with deep flounces, and a velvet drapery with gold tassels separated the sitting room from the bedroom. Near the windows on the east side, there stood an easel with a portrait of my father and her mother on their wedding day.

We sat on peacock chairs with a tea table between us. Olivia's Haviland tea service was her pride and joy. This and her other "pretty things," as I called them, were the only source of glamour left in her life. Not until I was thirteen did she allow me to enter her room at will. Her white Persian cat—appropriately named Fluff—now hopped upon her knees and stretched, settling down in the hearth-warmed lap of her mistress. Olivia stroked her, and she purred and curled up her tail. Outside it was sleeting again, and the window near us was open slightly at the bottom, producing a pleasant waft of cold air to temper the heat of the fire. Glad to be in out of the weather, I looked lazily out the window and relived the few short moments with the kind stranger all over again.

"What are you thinking of?"

"Oh, just that man I met today. He told me his name, Neal Gerrard," I said, enjoying the sound of it as it rolled off my tongue.

"It was kind of him to come to your aid. I suspect he is a good deal older than you are, though."

I glanced at her. "Why were you spying on us?"

"I wasn't spying. I was worried about you. I must have looked out a dozen times, wondering what kept you. I was about to hitch up Papa's bays and come after you, regardless of how he feels—"

"I wonder if Mr. Gerrard will come back again."

"Probably not," she said quickly. "I mean, there is little to bring people to Harrisburg these days, and now with even the railroad shops moving, Papa says—"

"I know, sister. He's talked of nothing else for weeks."

Papa resented Houston's growth. He was born in upstate New York and as a young man was lured to Texas by newspaper ads that promised holders of script in land companies some acreage upon arrival here. Papa bought some and, in 1834, traveled down to clear and farm his land. But he found the script did nothing except allow a man the privilege of looking for a piece of land to buy. He made his way to Harrisburg and decided the ten-year-old city, with its navigable stream and sawmills, would prosper. He became a land agent, traveling all over the territory to find suitable tracts for those who, unlike him, could afford to buy.

He was here two years later when the battle for Texas independence was waged, and now, more than fifty years later, he still had his soldier's uniform. Many times I had heard the story of his heroic deeds because when he was drinking heavily he forced us to sit at the dining room table and listen to him for hours.

Harrisburg was razed by Mexican troops during the revolution, but Papa, like some others, returned to rebuild what he had lost. Eventually two brothers, John K. and Augustus C. Allen, came from New York to Texas to build a city, and they tried to purchase land in Harrisburg through Papa, by then a well-established agent. However, Harrisburg land was tied up in litigation since its founder's death and wasn't to be sold to the Allen brothers or anyone else. The Allens went five miles upstream and staked out a town on the swampy banks of Buffalo Bayou. They named it Houston, in honor of the hero of the Revolution. Almost at once, Harrisburg began the long and painful process of withering. The recent removal of the railroad shops to their new location in the Fifth Ward of Houston was the deathblow. I did not want to talk of Papa's most recent sore subject now.

"Well, you never know. Maybe he travels around, like David," I said of Neal.

Olivia replaced her china cup in its saucer and wiped the biscuit crumbs from the corners of her mouth. She put down her napkin lingeringly, then looked across at me. "Don't start thinking of boys again, Alvareda. You know how Papa feels."

"But I'm seventeen now. It isn't the same as two years ago, when David—"

"I understand. But as long as you live in Papa's house, you must abide by his rules. Be thankful you have a beautiful home and nice clothes to wear."

"Yes, sister. But surely Papa doesn't expect me always to stay here."

"Sh. Have some more tea now, before it gets cold."

I shrugged in defeat and looked out the window again. It would have been nice if Olivia could have treated me more as a sister. She had once been courted by young men, so surely she sensed how I was feeling right now. Yet I suppose her attitude was understandable. She had been forced to assume matronly duties at such an early age. Her own mother died of yellow fever during the Civil War, and for several years there was no one except Olivia and Papa in the house. Then in 1869 Papa married my mother, and in late 1876 came the tragedy which took my mother's life. Olivia was then twenty-six years old. She was once and for all established in her role as my substitute mother and Papa's companion and confidante, for he never married again. Now that I was nearly grown, she was often caught between her wish to see me happy and her fierce loyalty to him, because in our household the two could not be mixed.

Papa returned home in one of his bitter moods that evening. His work took him to all parts of the state, and he often traveled to places accessible only on horseback. Today he had ridden through icy rain. He was both exhausted and wet when he came through the door. Olivia and I stood by nervously as he shed his outer garments and rolled up his sleeves. I do not believe I have ever seen a man who so completely crowded a room. He had a strapping body that showed little wear from age. He had very little gray in his auburn hair and a pair of unruly eyebrows above dark, suspicious eyes. At best, he was coldly cordial toward me; at worst, he was downright brutal.

He ordered a glass of whiskey now. Olivia was busy disposing of his wet garments, and signaled me to fix his drink. I walked into the dining room and nervously took the top off the decanter on the sideboard. Reaching for a glass, I upset the decanter top and sent it crashing to the floor. Seized with terror, I put my hands behind me and turned to the door. Papa had heard the noise and stormed in. "What have you done now, daughter? Broke my best decanter?"

"I'm sorry, Papa, I—" I stammered breathlessly.

"Get out of here, you clumsy—"

My whole body was suspended, numb. My limbs were icy. I could not have moved, even in obedience to his bitter direction. Olivia drew up behind and interrupted him. Softly she said, "Papa, Alvareda took a fall today. I'm sure it has upset her."

He did not stop to inquire of my well-being. He simply sent me a look of contempt. He ordered Olivia to pour the drink and remember to have the broken article repaired. At Olivia's nod, I fled from the room and up the stairs, my heartbeat a frenzied whacking in my breast.

I shut the door to my room and stood for a while with my hand still on the knob, trying to collect myself. At last I fell on the bed and lay there motionless. How could Papa hate me so? I lamented, even while I felt sure I knew the answer. Sometimes I thought he would like to kill me.

Finally I turned over and opened my English literature book. I was staring blindly at the page in front of me when I heard Olivia and Papa approach the landing on the second floor, where the stairway makes a sharp right turn, then listened to their footfalls up the next flight. They were going up to Papa's quarters, at the top of the stairwell, directly above my room. Often they passed the long evenings up there, and if I stayed awake long enough, I would sometimes catch a note of laughter, though I could never make out what they said to each other.

I lay there for a long time before finally I began to concentrate on the book in front of me. Why was that area kept so secret, I wondered? I would not have expected to be welcome during their conversations, but the fact that the door was always locked, Papa keeping one key and Olivia keeping the other, seemed unnecessary unless there was something in the room Papa did not want me to see. Not for the first time, when left to my own thoughts, my fear of Papa, my rationalizing of his motives toward me, gave over to resentment at being denied entry into his life. I was like an outsider. I did not belong. I might have been a boarder taken in by a family who had suffered a financial setback and regarded with condescension as a paying guest. For as long as I could remember I had felt this way. Yet I could remember nothing before my mother's death when I was not quite seven, and had only sketchy recollections of things outside of that up to the age of ten or eleven. Olivia had often said that Papa used to be different, happy. When she was a child he bought her a pony and taught her to ride. He took her on trips with him as well. She still had geegaws and trinkets picked up in exotic places like New York City and Philadelphia. He had never taken me anywhere. When did he change? The probable answer, though Olivia had never admitted as much, was with the death of my mother. And my mother and I resembled one another so strongly that I was a constant reminder in more than one way that his second wife, as well as his first, had been taken from him.

Before putting out the light, I read ten pages in the section on English poets, gaining nothing from them because my mind kept returning to the difference between me and Olivia. Surely her situation was better than mine, yet, was she any happier? Earlier today, with her plump shoulders and head silhouetted against the burning log fire, her cheeks especially rosy from the heat, she reminded me of herself as a young woman. When I was not yet tall enough to reach to the top of the wheels on Papa's buggy, Olivia was one of the belles of Harrisburg. She had been courted by a young law student—though he was by no means her only beau—and, just before my mother's death she had become engaged to him. On the afternoons when he would call, I could still remember her standing in the parlor, with her music propped upon the stand, practicing the violin, tapping her foot to keep time. She wore little spectacles with black wire rims when practicing because she was terribly nearsighted. I believe the regimen helped to pass the time and therefore settle her nerves, for she would station me near the window to watch for Mr. Nelson, as she referred to him. Now and then she would stop suddenly and ask, "Is he coming yet?" Then, when I assured her there was no sign of him, she would straighten the eyeglasses and remind me to be sure she had time to remove them before he approached the door, for she was mortified at the thought that she might be seen in them. Then she would resume her playing.

Actually, she was one of the prettiest girls in town. Though we favored in some ways—both of us having light brown hair and deep-set brown eyes—she was always on the chubby side, while I was destined to frailty. Inheriting my mother's stature, I was as tall as Olivia by the time I was fourteen. My cheekbones were high and angular, my mouth small, and my complexion a little darker than Olivia's.

After Mother's death, Olivia broke her engagement, and I never saw Mr. Nelson again. I can remember on many nights going to bed to the sound of Olivia's weeping and sniffling in the bedroom next to mine. I felt so terribly sorry for her. In my youthful perception, she had suffered a loss of her loved one as I had in my mother's death. I had no idea the two losses had any connection.

Later, about the time I reached my eleventh birthday, she was courted by a widower with three young boys. Again, it seemed a marriage was in the offing. Again, however, the wedding did not take place. I believe it was shortly after that, she switched her quarters to the larger rooms that our parents once shared on the east side of the house and began to select new decorations. Many of her mother's things were placed in there. My mother's possessions were stored away. Papa removed himself to the third floor, which before that time had not been finished off. From the day he moved in there, the door was kept locked. I had not even seen the rooms since I played with my dolls under the rough underside of the hip roof during the days it was an attic.

I looked around me now. Even in the darkness my small room was drab. There was a bed and a dresser, a desk, a wardrobe, a table and lamp. All were old before I got them. Maybe I should redecorate, I thought. Suddenly I was seized with the fear that I was beginning to think like my sister, as though my destiny were sealed in this house along with hers. I did not want this to be true, and spent much of the night unable to relax into sleep.

I did not see or hear from Neal Gerrard over the following three weeks. Each day on my way home from school, I glanced at the Leider house. No one was out on the porch; no carriage or buggy awaited to indicate the presence of a visitor inside. I quickly looked ahead again, minding my step, and tried not to think about him. Not since David had I entertained any real affection for a young man. The first obstacle, of course, was Papa. But aside from that, there was really no one in my small class at school who was interesting to talk to, and the same people I went to school with, I went to church with as well. Harrisburg was so small, my life so confined, it had been easy to put off thinking about boys.

Yet Neal had awakened something in me. . . . I shook my head. No. He had probably already forgotten me. I was nearing completion of my final school year, and would soon be preparing for examinations and writing essays. There would be much to occupy my mind and make me forget Neal Gerrard as well, I thought.

Then one day our class went by train to Houston to see a matinee performance of Mary Goodwin's, *Sis* at Pillot's Opera House. No sooner had the gaslights dimmed and the curtain risen when I heard a voice behind me say, "Mind your step. We have icy streets in Houston, too."

I glanced around to see Neal smiling at me. "Good afternoon, Mr. Gerrard," I faltered, then quickly looked ahead. I was so excited at seeing him again I could barely contain myself. Still, if I were to be caught speaking with a man in the audience . . .

I leaned back a little, brought my fan to my face, and whispered, "What are you doing here?"

"I saw you outside in the ticket line. My office is not far from here. May I see you home when the performance is over?"

Clearly this man was not accustomed to dealing with a schoolgirl. I shook my head. "No. I have to go with the class by train. . . . But I wish I could."

"When may I call on you then? This evening? Tomorrow?"

"No. I'm awfully sorry, but I have to say no. At least—"

"Well?"

I could think of no solution, and struggled in silence. Finally, in a desperate attempt to keep him from giving up and leaving, I leaned back and whispered, "I didn't know you were from Houston."

"I was born in Galveston. I've only been here for a year."

I considered what effect this might have on Papa should I gather the courage to ask his permission to let Neal call on me. Papa felt all men from Houston were slick rascals, after a fast dollar, and swelled up with pretension. He did not associate with them, and surely wouldn't allow me to. However . . . Neal wasn't *from* Houston originally. Even if he did work here now. . . .

"Well, when may I call?"

"Oh, I just don't know—"

"You don't want to see me?"

"No. I mean, yes, I do, very much," I faltered, and fanned myself rapidly.

"Then say when. I'll come any time you say."

Suddenly I knew. "My sister and I come to Houston each Saturday to shop, then I have a piano lesson at twelve o'clock. I could try and meet you somewhere around one o'clock. I mean, I am sure it would be all right for us to have a stroll together." I wasn't really sure at all. My heart was beating faster and faster.

"Do you know where the Cotton Exchange Building is?"

"Across from the Hutchins House, isn't it?"

"Meet me there, at Travis and Franklin, one o'clock sharp."

I nodded. I was aware of Neal's slipping out behind me. I looked surreptitiously down the aisle to see if anyone were watching, but apparently everyone was engrossed in the comedy being portrayed on the stage. I tried to look equally intent. "One o'clock sharp," he had said, just like a businessman. Almost a command. As though he didn't like to be kept waiting. Oh dear, how was I going to manage this? I shouldn't have let my great desire to see him again overcome my good sense. Yet . . . maybe somehow I could keep the appointment. What would I wear? I went through my wardrobe mentally, featuring myself as looking worldly, sophisticated. What could I put on that would make me look older? He would not want to be sporting around with a young—

All at once there was a burst of laughter and applause, and the curtain descended with a loud thud on the first act. The girl seated to my right— Mathilda Harcourt—looked at me strangely. I forced down my fan, which I had been holding in front of me with a death grip, and began to clap with everyone else. My hands were icy cold. I sat there through the next hour oblivious to the play.

Chapter 2

I had quickly concluded that I would have to confide in Olivia about my plan to meet Neal, and by the time our train pulled into the station at Harrisburg that Thursday evening, had practiced over and over my appeal for her help. Since I could never be sure how she would react to anything that Papa might question, I had to be very careful when speaking to her to make all seem perfectly harmless.

I had less than two days to win her over, and repeatedly tried to broach the conversation, then lost courage and fell silent. The best possible moment would have been tea time on Friday, and all through the school day I braced myself. Yet when I walked in the door with my books in my arms, Olivia was putting on her hat.

"I have to run an errand for Papa. I'll be home by five," she said. Then she noticed my crestfallen face. "Bad day at school?"

"No." I leaned back against the table.

She brushed my cheek with a kiss as she passed. "I have to rush." She went out toward the stable, then doubled back. When I saw her approach, I thought she had decided to take time—

"Sister, it wouldn't be David Leider you wanted to talk to me about, would it?" she asked.

"No. Why?" I said, surprised.

"He stopped by yesterday, while I was out in the yard. You were at the post office, but of course I didn't tell him where you were."

"What did he want?"

"He . . . well, he just asked about you. He said he was leaving town and would come by when he returns," she said, and looked at me again as though to assure herself I was as innocent as I seemed.

I shrugged.

"Of course, I was not rude," she said, "but I gave him no encouragement."

Then she paused before asking, "You wouldn't either, would you? You know how Papa feels about David."

"No. Of course not. Olivia, what I wanted to—"

"We'll talk when I get back," she interrupted, and walked out.

I lingered in the kitchen for a few minutes, thinking of David. I did not want him to call on me any more than Papa did. It wasn't because of his father—that was not David's fault, though Papa condemned him as well. It was something else entirely.

One day after we had been seeing each other for a while, David and I went canoeing on the bayou. Olivia was up on the banks, but she was reading a book, and her parasol hid us from her view now and then as we moved slowly along, past one elbow curve or another. David had not kissed me yet, and that day as he looked at me, I knew that he was going to. I was excited . . . fluttery inside as we both moved toward the center of the boat. I will never forget with what sweet promise he slipped an arm around my waist and lifted my face in his large, boxy hand, yet how soon the hand closed in a vise-like grip and the kiss turned into something unexpected . . . his tongue thrust inside my mouth, moving around, pushing hard, his arm around me so tight it hurt my ribs. After I struggled free he looked pleased, as though he did not realize I was not ready for that kind of embrace. I felt demeaned . . . used . . . and therefore swelled up with anger I could not quite understand and uncomfortable at the prospect of being alone with him any longer. He had taken my silence as we glided back up the bayou to be consent. He smiled at me expectantly, his big arms working the oars back and forth against the current. I looked away, grateful for the cool breeze against my hot face. Catching Olivia's eye, I waved at her in relief. When I finally got home I washed my mouth and face and stood before the basin trembling, wondering suddenly if there was something wrong with me because my first kiss from a young man had made me feel violated.

It was only a short time after that, the Leider scandal happened and David and I saw each other only once more, briefly, to say good-bye. He tried to kiss me again; I pretended to be worried we would be seen, and hurried away.

I shook my head now. I was not concerned with David anymore, and did not want to think about that day. What bothered me was that the only time to talk to Olivia about Neal would be while she cooked dinner this evening. She did not favor distractions during this chore, because she was intent on preparing perfect meals. Yet, there might not be another chance.

I went up to my room and opened my wardrobe. Everything was either too childish-looking or too dressy, or not dressy enough. The streets of Houston could be intolerable in January, and after a heavy rain the brick pavement on one street often washed over to the next. But by and large the people who strolled along the boardwalks past the collection of stores and banks and other businesses were dressed nicely. Normally I wore a dark skirt and a

white shirtwaist, with a jacket if weather suggested, because this was acceptable fashion at the Mozart Conservatory of Music where I had my piano
lessons. But for this coming Saturday I wanted to discard the usual attire and
narrowed the selection down to three possibilities. A silver-gray camel's-hair
dress with dark gray velvet coat was one. Yet the stand-up collar was stiff and
sometimes scratched my neck. Another was a dark blue grosgrain skirt that
fell in wide pleats, with a pleated silk vest in front. Yet the one time I had
worn this outfit was to a reception at the Hutchins House for music students,
and it seemed too fussy with its lace cuffs and collar. The last was a walking
suit of brown suede velvet with a coat of brown plaid and a round hat of
suede felt trimmed with a small ostrich plume.

After holding up each costume in front of me for what seemed the hun-
dredth time, I finally decided on the brown. The shoes I wore with it were the
most comfortable for walking, and somehow it seemed more grownup than
the others. Yet it was conservative, and less likely to draw Papa's attention
should he see me come or go.

When Olivia returned, I closed the wardrobe doors and hurried to the
kitchen. I did not know how many minutes I would have to present my case
before Papa walked in, and I certainly could not afford the risk of his learning
my plans beforehand.

Olivia was braising a piece of beef when I walked in. "Sister, I need to talk
to you."

She looked up, frowning. "I've still got biscuits to make and peas to shell
and cook. Couldn't it wait?"

"No. Actually I just need to tell you something. It won't take long."

"Well then?" she said. Her face was rosy from the heat of the stove. She
stood with her spoon poised in the air.

"I happened to see Neal Gerrard while in Houston yesterday at the play,
and he asked if he could take me for a stroll tomorrow after my music
lesson."

She placed the spoon on the table and wiped her hands on her apron. Then
she paused motionless with knitted brow. Had I sounded too serious after all?
Why did she consider so long?

"So Mr. Gerrard is a Houston man?"

"Not from Houston, but Galveston. He only works in Houston."

"I see. Well, I don't know——"

"It would only be for a little while, sister, and I owe him a thank-you for
what he did for me."

"I suppose . . ." she said slowly. "But you know we're taking the wagon
tomorrow because I have to get flour and sugar, and we have to be back at
three, or Papa——"

"I know. It's just a stroll, though. Say it's all right, please."

She looked at the clock. I knew the time was running out. She'd say something definite, just to get it over with. Again, I braced myself. "All right, I suppose it would do no harm just to walk with the gentleman a little."

A wave of relief passed over me.

I have never known anyone more proud of his chosen profession than Neal Gerrard. On that first Saturday, when I arrived giddy with excitement in my brown velvet Sunday best, he first took me on a tour of the Cotton Exchange Building and assured me that only in the basement where there was beer drinking and billiard playing could a lady not venture at the risk of compromising herself. He said this with a wink, taking my arm in his.

The business of the exchange was conducted primarily on the second floor of the building, the top floor merely a gallery for looking down upon the bustling activity taking place on the marble tiles below. Above were elegant chandeliers, and surrounding the building were French plate glass windows. Chairs and big brass spittoons were strategically placed. The huge blackboards, on which was noted the latest information on prices in all the cotton markets, the telegraph station nearby, the reading room, where one could look through volumes of printed information on the subject of cotton—all of these were, according to Neal, at the very pulse of the greatest industry in the world. And on any given workday, with the exception of Saturday afternoon, which was relatively quiet, the building was alive with excitement of businessmen selling and purchasing the commodity, puffing on their cigars and consulting with each other along the gallery railing.

Cotton was the recognized king of commerce in this part of the country, and the Cotton Exchange Building was the pride of Houston. As we stood in the gallery talking, I remembered three years ago, when the handsome brick building was completed, how my father laughed with contempt at the great zinc cotton bale that embellished the roof.

"Do you work for the Exchange?"

"No, but I spend a lot of time here. I'm a cotton factor."

I knew nothing about the cotton industry, and except that one of Papa's clients worked in it, I could not have even asked an intelligent question. "Is that like a commission merchant?" I queried, remembering the client's occupation.

"Not exactly. A factor has more of an investment in the cotton because he advances interest-bearing loans of anywhere from 80 to 90 percent of the current market value, then he hopes the price will go up rather than down when it's time to sell.

"Say, how would you like a tour of my sample rooms, where the buyers come to make bids?"

I glanced at the big electric clock across the floor. "I'm not sure I have time. I have to meet my sister at Pillot's before two o'clock."

"It's just over on Main, not too far from the wharves, but do you know, you've looked at that clock more times since we walked in here than I've looked at it since they put it up there. Are you afraid she'll go home without you?"

"Not exactly."

We both hesitated.

"You see, my father is very strict," I then explained. "I've wanted to tell you that since the first day we met. If we aren't home on time, he wants an accounting of every moment we're overdue. I'd not only be in trouble, but I'd get Olivia in trouble too."

"Why is he so worried about you? Is he afraid someone might steal you away from him?"

"Oh, something like that. . . ."

"I see. Well, I might," he declared, smiling.

I lowered my eyes, hardly believing the flood of emotions inside me. I loved the way he talked to me, the way he made me feel so . . . important to him. There was a quality of strength and masculinity about Neal that made me wish he would never let go of my arm. Finally I looked up at him, searching for something to say that would not betray my excitement. "Why did you come here to go into business, rather than stay in Galveston?"

"Have you ever heard of a man named Charles Becker?"

"No."

"My father and a lot of other merchants in Galveston backed him in the mayor's race early last year. He made a lot of talk about breaking up the wharf monopoly and finding a better water supply for Galveston after the big fire in '85. All this took place at the time I was laying out plans for my business."

"Then suddenly Becker bowed out of the race, and—"

"Why? Was he losing?"

"Quite the contrary. He seemed headed for victory. No one really knows why he backed out. There was a statement made about his health, but none of us took much stock in that because before long he was practicing law again and the last time I passed him by on the Strand, he tipped his hat and looked fine to me.

"I think there may have been a—well, a private matter—that his opponents learned about. And when they threatened exposure, he dropped out. Of course, that's popular conjecture down there, but a scandal can ruin a man's career. It's too bad, but that is the way of life."

Somehow the word "scandal" seemed especially ominous when he uttered it. I remembered the episode about Clifton Leider, and how his family had been ruined because of his misdoings. Mrs. Leider often lowered her gaze or looked away when we passed her on the streets of Harrisburg, and there were always people standing aside, whispering as they looked in her direction.

"I suppose so . . ." I agreed with Neal. "And when Mr. Becker gave up, you came here?"

"That's right. As long as the Wharf Company has a grip on the port in Galveston, it puts a damper on the future for cotton. Here we have rail connections better than anywhere in this area of the country, plus business leaders who believe in growth as a way for all of us to profit.

"I don't mean to sound like a walking advertisement, but there is a way of thinking here that is different from other towns. It's wide open. In a few years, I can foresee a deep-water port for Houston. When that happens, we'll be connected from both sides, by sea and by rail. There will be no limit then, although we probably won't ever have a big manufacturing center unless the price of fuel gets a lot cheaper."

"Some people think it's foolish for Houston to expect Buffalo Bayou to ever be anything."

"That's backward thinking."

"Yes, you must be right," I said, not telling him that I was borrowing a remark from my father. When we stepped off the curb to cross Prairie, a reckless man driving an open buggy whizzed around the corner, throwing mud from under his wheels. We both turned around with a start, and when we did I noticed Olivia following us at a discreet distance.

She never said she'd do that, I almost blurted out in anger.

"What is it?"

"Nothing." He took my arm again.

"You didn't get muddy, did you? Fool of a driver . . . they ought to do something about—"

"No. I'm all right. Let's go on."

We walked on silently for the next few blocks. I felt Olivia had betrayed me. Did this mean she had told Papa about my meeting with Neal as well? Would she go home tonight and join him in his third-floor rooms to report on us? Luckily Neal didn't know Olivia, so he'd never realize we were being "chaperoned." What would he think of a girl who, at the age of seventeen, couldn't even stroll the streets of Houston without her sister following? It was downright degrading. . . .

We had reached Neal's offices high up on the third floor of a red brick building with a decorative wrought-iron porch over the ground floor. In the windows were lettered, "Clayton O'Neal Gerrard—Cotton Factor," then, in another window, "General Warehousing."

We climbed the stairs up to his quarters, and he showed me the sample room (stating it was not large enough and he needed more space) where four men in their shirt sleeves picked over fleecy white cotton samples spread out on rows of long tables.

He walked with me up and down, explaining the process. "From these samples we 'grade' the lot. "The quality is dependent on so many things—

whether we get too much rain in the fields, or too much cold, or too much hot weather at the wrong time, to name a few—we just have to sell what we get.

"Someday I'd like to have my own compress. It's an expensive undertaking, but profitable. Every grade has to be compressed, so it doesn't matter which—

"I'm sorry. I have a terrible habit of getting carried away with shop talk."

I laughed. "It's all right. Obviously, you're very taken with it. I'd like to hear some more one day, but I'd better be on my way now."

"May I walk you to Pillot's?"

"Oh, you really don't need to. I can go alone."

"But I'd like to."

"All right, then," I said, hoping Olivia was there by now, hoping when I introduced them he did not then realize she had been following us.

We walked back toward the front, passing Neal's office: a small alcove with a rolltop desk piled with papers. "How did you get to know David Leider?" I asked him.

"His uncle is a seller in West Texas. I thought I might do a little business with him, and he directed me to David. David represents him in the spot market. That day in Harrisburg was the first time I'd met him. Have you known him long?"

"All my life. Everybody knows everybody in Harrisburg. And a couple of years ago, he courted me . . . just for a little while. He is a few years older than I am."

"How old are you?"

"Seventeen. And you?"

"Twenty-seven," he said, but was more interested in talking about David Leider.

"Was that why you stopped seeing him, because he was too much older?"

"Oh no," I said quickly. "When you like someone, I don't think age makes a difference." My own transparency almost made me blush.

"Then, what was the matter with David?"

I hesitated, then finally said, "He . . . well, he's a little self-centered, that's all." After what Neal said about scandal, it would have seemed cruel to David for me to tell about his family troubles. And I didn't want to tell Neal either that I was almost relieved when Papa stepped in between us, that I was by then . . . wary . . . of David, because I could not tell Neal why. It would be much too embarrassing.

"That's a good quality in a businessman if he tempers it properly," Neal was saying.

"Oh, I don't think of David as a businessman, actually."

"Really? I should think he would be a natural. He knows a lot about cotton; he has some good contacts. I'll probably be seeing more of him in the future. Here." He placed a fluffy cotton boll in my hand. I brushed it against my cheek and vowed silently never to part with it.

"Can I meet you again, next Saturday?" he asked.

"I'll try to come, yes. We'd better hurry," I told him, and as we made our way back up the street, I thought of the consequences if we arrived late.

"Is that your sister, up there in the wagon?"

"Yes," I said, relieved, but at the same time embarrassed that we did this sort of thing, bringing our wagon into town on Saturdays, like two country bumpkins. "Good afternoon, Miss Cane," he said to Olivia. "Fine day, isn't it?"

Olivia nodded, her lips tightly pursed. I hurried around to the other side, and Neal gave me a hand, then put his arms around my waist, and lifted me up. The wagon was high and cumbersome, not made for ladies in nice dresses. I sat down and looked at him. He spoke to both of us. "Next Saturday I'd like to take Alvareda down to the wharves at the foot of Main to see the barges loaded with cotton. Why don't you come along as well, Miss Cane?"

We had not even discussed this actually, and I had to admire Neal's perception of the situation. Surely Olivia could not object to that. Yet she was unyielding. "I can't promise we'll be in Houston next Saturday, Mr. Gerrard, though your offer is generous. Good day." She flicked the reins and we bumped forward. Neal tipped his hat and I raised an arm to wave. Halfway down the block I was still looking back at him, and while Olivia tried to get me to talk about him, I didn't want to share him with her. I wanted to savor privately everything that had just taken place. "Well I might . . ." he had said. I might steal you away. . . . And he had lifted me into the seat. I could still feel his hands around my waist.

I might. I might steal you away. . . .

We arrived at home on time and Papa made no comments, but after having been in the company of someone so enthusiastic, so kind and considerate, it was difficult to be around him. The only way I could get through the following week was to keep clear of him as much as possible, avoid saying anything that might give away my recent rendezvous, and concentrate on the next Saturday. That is, presuming there would be another Saturday with Neal.

I had decided not to say anything to Olivia about this till late in the week. Nor did I reveal that I knew she'd taken it upon herself to chaperone us secretly. Perhaps if I let her continue to do so, she would feel that she had the situation under control and wouldn't try to stop it. More than anything I did not want it to stop. Even if I were not really alone with Neal, it was better than not seeing him at all. During Friday tea I asked, as casually as possible, "Will we be going to Houston tomorrow?"

"Yes, I suppose so. We haven't much to do except your music lesson. I doubt we could stay afterward. Papa would . . . well, since there is no real reason to . . ." her voice drifted off.

On many Saturdays we had nothing to do beyond my music lesson. So intent on seeing Neal again, I'd failed to remember that. I held my empty teacup between my hands. This was not going to be easy. "Just let me stay long enough to meet Neal and tell him I can't visit the wharves. It would be discourteous not to," I said.

"I suppose so," she said. "All right. But you'll have to be quick."

I knew from her answer she had not gone behind my back and alerted Papa.

"And, sister, on Saturdays when we stay later, couldn't I see him?"

"And leave me to do all the shopping alone? That isn't fair."

"No, I know it isn't, but—well, didn't you ever feel that you just wanted to see someone?" I begged. Then I remembered something else. "I used to stand watch for you when Mr. Nelson was expected to pay you a call. Couldn't you do this for me, now?"

She sighed heavily, in resignation. "All right. I suppose I can't deny you that. As long as it doesn't go any further."

"Oh, it won't," I promised, kissing her cheek. "It's just that he is so interesting and nice to talk to."

"It isn't like with David?" she asked, searching my face.

"No, it isn't like that at all," I said. And in some ways, that was the truth.

I know Neal must have cared for me early, or he surely would never have pursued such a limited courtship: an hour together two or three times a month, to be spent walking, talking, poking in and out of the shops on Main Street, or sitting together over a cup of hot chocolate in the ice cream emporium. I scarcely thought of anything but him, from one week to the next, and those Saturdays when I could not spend an hour with him made the day miserable and the two long weeks on either end seem an eternity. I could hardly believe he could be so happy to see me whenever we met; after all, he must have courted many more interesting girls than me. Finally I asked him, "Why do you go on seeing me? I've so little to offer someone like you."

He considered for a few moments, then said, "The first time I saw you, that day in Harrisburg, when I helped you up from your fall, I thought you had the sincerest eyes I had ever looked into.

"And every time I see you again, I seem to get more fascinated. Aside from all that, and maybe because of it, you are a lovely lady. I'm very proud to have you on my arm."

I looked away in shyness but said, "All those things you see in me are the things I see in you, Neal."

He would have kissed me then, I am sure, but for the fact we were standing in the middle of an aisle at Pastoriza's store, purchasing a tin of spiced tea for Olivia. It seemed the kindest declaration of feelings there could be, and I went over it again and again till I saw him the following week. I think he had been searching for a place where we could really be alone, because on that Saturday we ducked into the back of Christ Episcopal Church and sat down in a pew. I thought of Olivia, somewhere close by and no doubt wondering what in the world we were doing in a church. Shortly Neal said, "I figured this might be the only place your sister wouldn't follow us."

I looked up. "Oh, I'd hoped you didn't know she kept watch on us," I said. "She's even begun to shop during my piano lesson, so that she won't miss a moment."

We both smiled, then laughed at the unorthodox quality of our meetings. Suddenly Neal got very quiet, pulled me close, and kissed me. His arms were firm around me, but the kiss was gentle and tender. When he released me, he raised a hand and placed the palm lightly against my cheek for a moment. Like his kiss, the touch of his hand made me feel warm and tingly. I reached up and closed my hand around his. A smile began at the corners of his eyes, and he looked into mine for a long moment, as though considering something. When finally he rose and reached for my arm, my heart was pounding excitely; my knees would barely hold up under me.

I don't know how long we would have gone on meeting like that. I suppose that something was bound to change shortly, one way or another. I was falling in love with Neal, and he was with me. Should I have accepted a proposal of marriage, there would have been Papa to deal with, but somehow, together, we might have been able to make things turn out differently. We could have prepared the way, surely. We might have even persuaded Olivia to help, if we approached her in exactly the right fashion. I don't know. I just know that, because of a coincidence, perhaps serendipitous, perhaps inevitable, everything went wrong.

Chapter 3

Because of his work, Papa subscribed to newspapers all over the state—the Dallas *Morning News*, the San Antonio *Express*, the Galveston *Daily News*, and the Houston *Daily Post*—for possibilities in land sales and purchases. Of course, he was interested in the items pertaining to real estate. But he also noted the arrivals of new people in town who might want to buy property, and departures of citizens bound for different cities who wanted to sell.

Therefore, he scanned personal sections, and society columns, writing down interesting tidbits in his little green leather notebook.

One Monday evening toward the end of March, when Papa seemed otherwise in an amiable mood, he produced a section of the Houston *Daily Post* at the dinner table, held it high in front of him, and read aloud, "A certain smart-looking couple have been seen regularly on the streets of Houston lately. The young man's name is often to be heard around the floor of the Cotton Exchange. The lady on his arm, we are bound to disclose, is a resident of Harrisburg." It was typically "mysterious" society column news.

For a moment, I didn't take in its full implications. Then "Harrisburg lady" hit me, and I sat stockstill, my hand around a water goblet. Olivia took the paper from Papa's hand and read it silently, her expression unchanging. Then she passed it to me. I read it over, my temples throbbing with every word. Perhaps up to that time Papa was merely speculating on the possibility at hand. However, after I continued to stare at the little item—so innocent, yet so intimidating—I am sure he felt certain he was correct. I said nothing. I couldn't have spoken if my life depended on it. I looked across at Olivia, terrified of what she might say. There were any number of ways she might word her statement, and make herself look innocent while indicting me.

At last she shrugged. "Must have been one of the Grey girls." She kept her voice remarkably even, much more so than I could ever have done.

Papa rose from his chair. My eyes widened. I looked fearfully toward Olivia. She sat there silently, her lips pursed. Papa walked over toward my chair and stood behind me. I would not dare look around at him. I could scarcely breathe.

"Surely your sister is right," he said calmly, and then I felt him close a hand around the back of my hair. I bit my lip and closed my eyes. He pulled at my hair just a little and said, "Neither of my daughters goes about with Houston people, isn't that so, Alvareda?" He pulled harder and my head went back. "Eh?"

I swallowed hard and touched my throat. "No, no, Papa."

"That's right," he said, and held my hair a little longer. I kept looking straight ahead, too terrified to move.

At last he released me and made his way back to his own chair. He wiped his mouth with his napkin, took a sip of water, and said, "All the same, it has occurred to me we're not likely to be needing anything from Houston for a while. If we do, I can stop off on one of my trips and pick it up."

I could not speak. Olivia said, "But what about Alvareda's music lessons, Papa? She is doing so well—"

"With the end of school approaching, she will be too busy. Write her teacher a note, and tell her Alvareda will see her next fall."

"Yes, Papa," she replied.

There was nothing in the world I would rather have done than to leave the table and flee to my room. Yet, such was the discipline under Papa's roof that I would not have even dared ask to be excused. Instead I sat through the whole meal, pushing my food around the plate, scarcely lifting the fork to my mouth. Had I spoken a word, I would have burst into tears right there.

Later that evening Olivia slipped into my room, where I sat weeping uncontrollably. She soothed my quaking shoulders and tried to dry my tears. "He can't do this!" I snapped in a whisper.

"Sh. There, there, Alvareda. Time will heal your sorrow. You're lucky Papa didn't decide on a showdown tonight. He could have been much more direct."

I pulled away. "He has no right to ruin my life. Why should he care if I have some happiness?"

"He's afraid of ambitious men, especially when they come from Houston. Sometimes people . . . take advantage of others who have money."

"Neal may be ambitious, but I'm sure he doesn't want Papa's money. Anyway, how does Papa know anything about Neal? Olivia, did you tell him?"

"Certainly not," she said. "How could you think I would betray a confidence?"

"You could, if you thought it would please Papa enough."

She stood up. "I won't let you speak to me this way. You're cruel and unfair. Look what I did tonight, suggesting the Grey girls. Honestly, I—"

"I know, I know. I'm sorry. It's just that I don't know how else Papa arrived at the conclusion that Neal was ambitious."

"Papa thinks all young men in Houston are ambitious, or they wouldn't be there. That's all I meant."

"All right. I'm sorry. Thank you for what you did." I sat and thought for a few minutes. Papa found fault with David for one reason, with Neal, obviously, for another, even though they had never met. Would there always be something wrong with anyone I chose for a companion?

"Olivia, I want to ask you something. Did Papa send your Mr. Nelson away all those years ago?"

"No. That is, not exactly."

"Then why did you break your engagement?"

"Papa needed me. He had you to raise, and with your mother gone, it just seemed best."

I did not believe that. "Did Papa regard Mr. Nelson as ambitious? Where was he from?"

She shook her head. "Enough of this. I made my own decision."

"Then why can't I make mine?"

"You're so young—" she began. She sat down and smoothed the hair back from my forehead, as she had done since I was a child in need of comfort. The gesture was no source of comfort now.

"I'm as old as you were when you had your first suitors."

"I know. It's just that Papa doesn't want you spending your time . . . that is, he—"

We were going in circles. "It's something else altogether, isn't it?" I said. "Papa is trying to ruin my life, to get back at me, isn't he?"

"Of course not. How could you say such a thing?"

"He hates me. You know why."

"Alvareda, please don't go on like this," she begged. She looked as though she, too, might begin to cry.

"But you know I am right. That's the only explanation for the way he is behaving now. He doesn't want me to be happy. Regardless of whom I meet, Papa will stand in the way. Regardless of how old I am, he will step in and prevent marriage. He did it to you because he wanted companionship. He will do it to me out of hatred."

"You are beside yourself. Let's get a cloth and bathe your face."

I took in a breath. I could not let it end like this. "Olivia, can I at least send Neal a note, just to explain—"

"Our household affairs are none of his business."

"I didn't mean that. I want to let him know. I can't leave him wondering. What has he done to deserve that?"

She sighed. "Write it now, and I'll give it to the carrier in the morning. I have some other mail to post as well."

I sat down at my desk and began to write with trembling fingers, "Dear Neal. I'm sorry that I cannot see you anymore. It was very nice, but—" then my pen remained poised in the air. I could not do this. My mind raced in search of a solution.

"Well?" said Olivia.

"Yes, I'm almost through," I finally told her, and completed it. Another idea had just occurred to me. I signed it, "Yours sincerely, Alvareda Cane." I picked up an envelope and addressed it to his office. I put no return in the corner. Then I handed it to her. "You can read it if you wish."

She slipped it into her pocket. "Does that make you feel better?"

"Yes. Thank you, sister."

When she was gone I went back to my desk. I had intentionally directed the note to the wrong address. If I were reasonably lucky and Olivia didn't realize the error, and if delivery were delayed because it went to the wrong address first, then I just might be able to . . .

I sat up very late, devising another, much longer, note. I told Neal exactly what had happened, and that I did not know what to do but that I wanted to go on seeing him more than anything I had ever wanted in my life. I read it over before signing it, "Love, Alvareda." Love. Should I alter it? "Yours," or "Ever yours"? No. I would leave it. It was the most daring thing I had ever read, much less written. And the most daring part was yet to come. I slipped into bed and put out the light. I could hear Olivia and Papa going up the stairs to his quarters.

I laid there for a long time worrying about getting the second letter to Neal, hopefully before the first arrived. Finally it occurred to me I might intercept the first and exchange it for the second. I would wait to hear Olivia's steps down from Papa's room, then for her to fall asleep. Then I could sneak into her room and search out the letter and make the switch.

. . . But suppose she noticed the new one was fatter? Maybe I should rewrite it, shortening it. But then, what if she caught the changed address? No. Too risky. I'd have to go through with my first plan, hastily plotted while she was waiting. This simply could not be done without risk of something going wrong. One must weigh the possibilities, choosing the less dangerous route, that was all. . . .

Shortly after eight o'clock the next morning I arrived at my school desk with the four-page letter tucked safely inside my skirt pocket. My eyes kept traveling to the clock on the wall. Frequently they were to be met by the stern gaze of Mr. Burns. I would quickly drop them, feel my heart thumping, and try hard to concentrate on the paper in front of me. Now and then I felt my pocket to be sure the letter was still in place. I had the terrifying feeling that it might have dropped out and that, in a moment Mr. Burns would start down the aisle with his pointer and make a stab for the letter. If that should happen . . . or if someone else should discover it . . .

The only opportunity to mail the letter was between twelve and twelve-thirty, during our lunch break. We were not allowed to leave the grounds except by express permission following a note from home. I would have to sneak away early, while the others were busy eating, and get back before anyone missed me.

If I were caught . . . if I were caught . . .

At five minutes past twelve I emerged from the campus on the far side of Baraca Hall, and started quickly down Medina Street toward the post office. With every step I looked about me, fearful Papa would pass by in his buggy, or Olivia would be out and about doing her errands. I looked straight ahead. One block, two. At last I reached the post office, knowing I still had to face Mr. Brumaker, the postmaster, who knew Papa. He might notice the letter was addressed to a cotton factor and assume I had written a letter for Papa, which Olivia often did. What if he mentioned it to Papa? I walked faster and faster. If that happened, if that happened . . . Papa had not used a strap on me since I was thirteen. I could envision him meeting me at the door with a firm grip on the handle. Oh, heavens, I must be losing my mind. Until now I had not thought of so many things going wrong. . . .

At the post office there were several people waiting in line. One of them, I knew. Mrs. Caldwell, with her tall gray braids and fruit-laden hat, was one of the town gossips. I could never do such a thing as mail a letter during the lunch hour at school without her taking note. There was no surer way of getting the information back into Papa's hands. I stood outside at the window and waited till she was at the counter. Then, while she and Mr. Brumaker were busy discussing the best way to send her brown package to Knoxville, Tennessee, I slipped in and put the letter in the slot right at the corner, where there were several other pieces, all waiting to be ushered into the oblivion of a huge mail sack. . . .

When finally I made it back to campus I stood outside against a wall and took deep breaths. Apparently I was safe. From here I could see across the wide field. Most of the students were gathered at the edge of the field close to Mr. Milby's potato patch, feeding a baby goat from a bottle.

"Alvareda. What are you doing here?"

I nearly jumped out of my skin. It was Mathilda Harcourt, who had rounded the corner and nearly run into me. She eyed me suspiciously.

"I—oh, just resting," I said, trying to steady my voice.

"Are you all right?"

"Of course."

"Could you straighten my bow?" she asked, turning around. "I'll be glad when we graduate and won't have to wear these big bows anymore. That little monster Teddy Radcliffe jerked on it and nearly pulled it off."

"There," I said, giving it a horizontal pull.

"Thank you," she said, then paused. "Well, are you coming inside?"

"Yes. I am coming."

Just before the bell sounded, I walked back to my desk and sat down. Not till Mr. Burns began his lecture on the River Nile did I chance to relax my breath.

Two days passed. I tried to maintain a state of calm. Over and over again I thought of my letter. Maybe I should not have revealed so much about my father in it. Maybe I should not have signed it with, "love." I blushed at the thought of my recklessness now. Maybe at this moment Neal was passing the pages around his office, giving all his employees a chance to laugh at my expense.

No. Neal would not do that. Even if he felt he was too busy to trouble any further with me, he would not be insensitive to my predicament. Yet he might surmise that if my father were such a strange person, perhaps I would one day inherit his strangeness. Neal was from a normal, happy family, after all. Many Saturdays, when he left me in Houston, he caught the train to Galveston and spent the balance of the weekend at his parents' home. They had parties, invited people over for an evening to play whist. They went down to the beach for oyster roasts. They went to dances. He probably courted several girls in Galveston, none of them with the stigma of a father who would not accept even the best of people if it meant his daughter might be happy . . . might build a life of her own apart from the self-imposed isolation of his home. . . .

Chapter 4

For several weeks Papa had been busy putting together a complicated deal in which four partners were proposing to buy several hundred acres of rich farmland from a well-to-do widow. The acreage was located down in South Texas, and Papa had made many trips to the site, gathering volumes of information on water and mineral rights, railroad rights-of-way and other contributing factors. Most evenings he spent in his office downstairs, and oftentimes Olivia sat in there helping him long after I turned out my lamp.

On Thursday night—two days after I had mailed my letter to Neal—Papa sent Olivia out early, claiming he was having a difficult time with one section of the proposal, and he would call her in when he was ready to dictate it. His voice had an edge of irritation as she emerged. She closed the office doors, rolled her eyes as though she were glad to escape for a little while, and said, "Sister, play the piano while I work at my embroidery, will you? It will help to calm my nerves."

If she had a need for calming, it could not have compared with mine. The last thing I wanted to do was play the piano in front of someone expecting a reasonably good performance. I sat down reluctantly, opened the music, and proceeded to do a halting job on one of Beethoven's most flowing compositions. Three times I faltered, stopped, and started again. Olivia looked up from her embroidery in mild consternation. I was just at the point of giving up and asking to be excused when the doorbell rang. My hands froze on the keys and I looked up.

"What now? We weren't expecting anyone tonight," Olivia said, "and my lap is full of yarn."

"I'll go," I said, and rose from the bench. All the way to the door I thought it was going to be David, come back to town. Then I opened it and there stood Neal.

"What are you doing here?" I gasped, and stepped out on the porch, pulling the door behind me.

"Are you all right? I got your note this afternoon and came as soon as I could get away. I don't understand your father. Why is he so—"

"Who is it, sister?"

I lifted my hands in futility. "It's Mr. Gerrard," I told Olivia through the door, then after a moment's hesitation disobeyed my father's unexpressed wish. "Please come in, Neal."

Olivia was standing in the foyer, holding her ball of yarn. "Good heavens, Mr. Gerrard. What brings you here?"

"I'd like to speak to Mr. Cane, please."

"I'm afraid that isn't possible," said Olivia. "He's very busy just now."

"I won't take much of his time."

"It would be inadvisable to disturb his concentration," Olivia insisted.

"Then I'll wait till he's finished," said Neal.

I stood there, looking from one to the other. I could not believe Neal was so stubborn. His face was set with determination.

"Perhaps, if you have some business with my father, you might make an appointment in a day or two," said Olivia. For so many years she had filtered out unwanted guests, like a palace guard, saving an untold number of embarrassing scenes. Yet now, at last, she had met someone who was not to be frightened or put off with excuses. Neal said, "Perhaps you might just ask him if he would mind seeing me."

Olivia was floored. "My dear Mr. Gerrard, you can't just barge in like this and expect—" she began, but by this time Papa had overheard the argument and opened his office doors.

"What's going on?" he bellowed.

"Excuse me, sir," said Neal. "I'd like to have a word with you." And to Papa's obviously great surprise, Neal advanced toward his office door. I stood there with my hand against my mouth. Neal was no match for my father. Something terrible was about to happen. Olivia's eyes met mine, and we both followed Neal down the hall. As we drew up to the open doorway, I heard Neal introduce himself. He offered his hand across Papa's desk. Papa did not accept the handshake. I wanted to cringe with shame at Papa's rudeness.

"I can see you're busy, so I will get right to the point," Neal said, withdrawing his hand. "I've been seeing your daughter for some weeks now, and I just wanted you to know that my intentions are completely honorable. I apologize for having caused you alarm."

"So you are the one who has been flaunting my daughter around the streets of Houston."

"We have been seen in public together," Neal agreed.

"Behind my back—"

"I did ask permission to call, but Alvareda felt you might disapprove. Her sister can tell you that we've done nothing more than walk together, for an hour or less, on some Saturdays."

Papa looked at Olivia, who now stood behind me in the doorway. "So you've been involved in this conspiracy as well."

"Yes, Papa," she answered faintly.

"There has been no conspiracy," Neal corrected him. "I met Alvareda quite by accident several months ago, when I was here in Harrisburg on a business matter, and since then we've come to know and admire each other.

"As I was about to say, I wouldn't be taking her time unless she were important to me. And I hope I can continue to see her, now that you understand my intentions."

Papa considered a few moments, and I realized with a sickening feeling that he was about to draw me into a trap. "Just what made you think that you had caused me alarm?"

If Neal was nonplused, he didn't show it. "Alvareda sent word that you had forbidden her to come to Houston and see me any longer."

I looked at Olivia, and knew she was trying to remember whether I had been so explicit in the note she mailed to Neal.

"Oh?" said Papa. "I don't recall telling her to send word to that effect."

Olivia intervened. "Alvareda wrote a note and I mailed it, Papa. She simply wanted to let him know she wouldn't be meeting him anymore, out of courtesy."

"Well I must say it's kind of the three of you to decide to let me know what is going on in my own household."

"I'm sorry, Papa. This is all my fault. Don't blame Olivia," I said. "And I never let Neal know that it wasn't permissible for us to take walks together in Houston."

"Is there some reason why Alvareda should not be able to keep company with me?" Neal began. "If you doubt my character, I can assure you—"

"Mr. Gerrard, there is nothing you can say about your character that will make any impression on me. Alvareda is a seventeen-year-old schoolgirl who doesn't know her own mind. She is easily impressed, I now find."

"I don't follow you," said Neal, but I could see that he did.

"Harrisburg is a small town compared to Houston. I'm sure you enjoy showing off in front of an innocent young lady who has never been anywhere. I'm sure you enjoy having her look up at you and show her amazement. I do not confuse what you are doing with 'honorable intentions' for one minute. When you grow tired of her—"

"I beg your pardon," said Neal. "If you cannot realize from what I've said so far that I intend to marry your daughter, if she'll have me, then it's because I've tried to put my feelings to you too carefully. The truth is that, before I received that letter today, I'd planned to discuss marriage with Alvareda this coming Saturday."

"Oh my goodness," I whispered, and sank into a chair.

Papa's mouth was slightly open. I wasn't sure, once he recovered, whether he would laugh with contempt or take Neal by the collar and throw him out. He took a deep draw on his cigar, stamped it out with prolonged emphasis, then finally looked at Neal. "I still make the decisions that govern her life, and I expect to for some time. I never gave her permission to be courted by you, and I certainly have no intention of letting her marry you."

Neal turned to me, as though he expected me to say something in support of his plea, but I could not make the words come forth. I sat dumbly in my chair.

"You see, my daughter only awaited my intercession to be rid of you," Papa said innocently. "Show him out, Alvareda."

I stood up. "No, Papa, that isn't true. I do want to marry Neal. It's only that . . . I don't want to displease you."

Papa's lip curled into a smile of victory. "Well, at least you know when to put first things first. Now, get this Houston hooligan out of my sight before I throw him out and take a strap to you."

Had Papa not threatened me, had he been able to withhold his normal sarcasm at that moment, Neal might have reacted more calmly. As it was, he took a step forward and put his face close to Papa's. I could see the high color rising to Neal's cheeks. My heart was beating wildly. Papa's explosive temper was a well-known fact. I was at once afraid he might hurt Neal, and afraid Neal was angry enough to overcome him. When Neal spoke, his voice was low and even. "I'll thank you to be man enough to step out into the street if you wish to call me names. As far as I am concerned, Alvareda can leave with me as soon as she can pack a bag, and if you so much as lay a finger on her, you'll have to deal with me first."

Papa raised a hand. I gasped. Olivia, however, was there in the fraction of a second, placing herself between them. "Wait, Papa. Let me have a word with you in private. Alvareda, conduct Mr. Gerrard into the parlor."

I placed my hands on Neal's rigid arm. "Come, please," I entreated. At last he allowed me to walk him out of the room and close the door. Once in the parlor, I offered him a glass of port, which he refused, and I told him I was terribly sorry for all this.

"It's all my fault," he said. "I should not have lost my temper. I never meant to mention the fact I was going to propose marriage, either, till he made me so angry.

"Look. Come with me tonight. We'll go to Galveston. You can stay with my parents until we can arrange the ceremony. We can be married in just a few days." He was still breathing hard, as though he truly had just engaged in a physical quarrel.

Everything was happening too quickly. I felt like a person who arrived late at the railroad station and now ran to catch up with the train she was supposed to have boarded. Galveston . . . marriage in a few days . . . "I can't, Neal. I'm not ready, and you aren't either."

"But I can't let you stay—"

"Believe me, I'll be all right. Papa just . . . it's just that he can't seem to stand the thought of me . . . well, getting married. And tonight, you arrived at a bad time, you see."

"But who knows what will happen now? And where do we go from here? Don't you realize he is going to make life even more miserable for you than before? Don't you see that after what just happened, he'll do anything to keep you from me?"

"Oh, I don't know what to do. Everything is such a mess."

Olivia soon came through the door. "Papa has made a decision," she said, and cleared her throat. "If you will promise not to contact each other in any way until Alvareda graduates at the end of May, then, if you both feel strongly about each other, Papa will not stand in the way of your marriage . . . after a suitable period." She paused. "You must understand, Mr. Gerrard, that all this was quite sudden. Certainly you can appreciate a father's eagerness for his daughter to complete her education before making a decision about her life."

I was amazed that Papa should have become so reasonable. Apparently Neal was too, but viewed it differently.

"Could I speak privately with Alvareda?" he said.

"Of course," she said. "But let me caution you both not to do anything foolish." She made no move to let us be alone.

"Let's go out on the porch," I said. "It's so stuffy in here."

Olivia watched us pass as though she were afraid we might try and run away.

Outside Neal sat on the rail and took my hands. "Alvareda, come with me now. What he's asking is preposterous. If he really intended to give his permission, what good would it serve to keep us apart?"

"Maybe he just wants to give us time to think. Oh, Neal, you can't imagine how generous his offer is. He's accustomed to having his way in everything. I would have never dreamed he would back down like this."

"You're not saying you believe him?"

"Oh, I know it's hard to understand, but now I see I was wrong about everything. You see, I never asked Papa if you could call on me because I was so sure he'd disapprove, and Olivia agreed. Now that I look back, I could probably have prevented all this if I'd only approached him about it at the beginning.

"But we angered Papa by sneaking around. Then when you came in tonight, so unexpectedly, it was the final insult."

"So you think he has made a complete about-face in his thinking, and that he is going to suddenly become a reasonable, cooperative person? You're fooling yourself."

"No, I didn't say that. But Olivia can be very convincing with him. What she has done is made him realize that he can't win this battle. Short of locking me up, he couldn't keep me from you. And except that we've injured his pride, he doesn't want to keep me from having my own life. After all, he has Olivia. It simply boils down to the fact that we made him furious. I think he recovered his reason very quickly."

"Still—"

"Trust me, please," I begged.

He sighed. "Perhaps you're right. You know him better than I do." He let go my hands and put his arms around my waist, pulling me to him and hugging me. It was a long time before he spoke. Finally he said, "I'm so impatient. Every day I deal in a business where time is vital. Everything has to work in harmony right down to the last detail. I spend most of my time coordinating schedules and watching figures that are subject to change in a moment. If I don't react quickly, I can lose my shirt.

"I guess I expected to work things out for us in the same way." He held me from him. "Do you really love me?"

"Of course I do. My major concern was that you might not love me."

He smiled. "I must say I had envisioned telling you differently than I did."

I lowered my eyes. "It's all right. What you did tonight was heroic. I feel . . . oh—"

"What is it, darling?"

"I feel I am just so much trouble. You must love me a lot to put up with these circumstances."

He lifted my chin. "I believe I fell in love with you the moment I first saw you. The only thing that could have stood in my way would have been you not loving me back." He paused, then added, "I'm going to give you such a good life. You're going to be happy, I promise."

"I know," I told him. "Go now, before Papa has a chance to change his mind."

He hesitated and looked up at the door. Then he put his arms around me and kissed me. I did not want to let him go, and almost wished things had worked out so that I did go with him now. Everything about him made me feel safe and confident. I stood there on the edge of the porch with my arms folded, watching him until he'd climbed into the buggy and driven away, and the horse's hooves were but a muffled beat growing fainter and fainter in the distance.

Olivia was not around when I walked back into the house. The doors to Papa's office were pulled closed, and I listened but could hear no voices inside. I walked into the parlor and found Olivia's sewing things on the chair. The piano was still open, with the sheet of Beethoven propped above the keys. How long ago it seemed that we sat here, before the doorbell sounded. In the space of less than an hour, my whole life had changed.

I assumed Olivia had gone to bed. I tidied up and turned out the lamps, then walked into the hall toward the stairs.

The shaft of light from beneath Papa's office doors beckoned to me. I wondered if I should say something to him. I had never experienced Papa's changing his mind so dramatically about anything that concerned me. Did he expect me to thank him? Perhaps what happened tonight meant he had faced up to the fact I was a grown woman and it was time to treat me differently. I had no idea what was in his mind, how he regarded this development—

"Is that you, Alvareda?" He startled me. I brought a hand to my breast and took a breath. There was no inflection in his voice that told me what to expect. I eased the door open like a maid who has been caught stealing from the pantry.

"What do you want?" he asked evenly.

"I just wanted to say—uh—thank you, Papa," I faltered. Then I turned to go, afraid of getting into a conversation with him.

"Wait a minute, come in," he said. I clenched my hands and obeyed. When I walked in, I saw Olivia sitting in the corner near his desk. "You seem to think I've done you some sort of favor. But let me ask you, what can your friend Gerrard do for you? Has he any money?"

"I—I'm sure he can provide for me."

"I'm going to do some looking into this, to see if he's all he claims to be."

"I don't understand what you mean," I said faintly.

"For instance, how old is he?"

"Twenty-seven."

"And never married. That seems a bit peculiar, doesn't it?"

I could not form a word to reply. I looked at Olivia, helplessly.

"Papa, Mr. Gerrard has been establishing his business. He probably—"

"Aha!" he cut her off. "I intend to find out why he could not find a bride in all of Houston."

Now I was approaching tears. "I don't believe he was looking. We met by accident and . . . and fell in—" My voice choked on the last word.

He leaped on it. "What's that you say? Love? You think he is marrying for love? Don't fool yourself. He's too ambitious for that. Olivia almost made the same mistake twice, didn't you my dear?" He focused his eye on Olivia. She lowered her head.

"The trouble with both of you is that you don't know how good you have it, or how much I've protected you from the world out there. If you did, you'd never speak of leaving."

At that moment I wanted more than anything not to cry in front of Papa . . . not to appear weakened by his onslaught. I blinked back my tears.

"We'll see, we'll just see about Mr. Gerrard," he threatened.

When finally I lay down in bed that night, my whole body felt sore from the tensing of muscles throughout the evening, and my tears, no longer in check, escaped and rolled down my cheeks. In the distance I could hear the whistle of the late night train pulling out of Harrisburg, and I wondered if I'd already missed out on my chance of happiness. Neal had never seemed so far away, and his appraisal of Papa now echoed in my mind.

Chapter 5

After that night I would not dare to mention Neal's name in Papa's presence, for fear he might take that as a breach of the promise we made to keep apart from each other. Papa was a wizard at twisting words as well as situations, and I hoped that by keeping quiet I could avoid the risk of his changing his mind.

For a while Papa did not bring up the subject of Neal, and as the days wore on I grew a little more confident. Then one evening he began talking quite freely about Neal. And while I could see that many of his ideas had their roots in questions answered by Olivia, albeit innocently, his remarks were so cunningly phrased that he soon had me wondering whether I was about to make a serious mistake, and kept me constantly upset.

"So your meeting was quite by accident?" he began. I bit my lip and nodded, afraid of what was coming. "Did you know that on the very day your hero rescued you from your fall on the icy street, he had no end of questions to ask David Leider about you? David's mother says that he stayed long past his appointment, quizzing her son.

"Now, doesn't that seem a little odd? Here he is, this prosperous young businessman, suddenly come upon a young girl whose house is the finest one in all Harrisburg. His eyes feast on it for a time. And no doubt David gladly educates him on the state of her father's income. So he decides this might be worth pursuing, and goes about learning something of her habits . . . when she might chance to be in Houston, which is easy enough to do, if you talk to a few people in Harrisburg . . . who would be her chaperone . . . Then, surprise! He—"

"Papa, if you think Neal is after your money, you're wrong. He's perfectly capable of—"

"Oh, is he now? Did you know he left Galveston owing everybody in town?"

I could feel the color rising to my cheeks. I knew that was a gross exaggeration, but must be gentle in my correction. "His father made him a loan to begin his business. I don't see anything wrong in that."

"Well even if that were all, it would be sufficient to make you proceed with caution in getting to know him. Cotton factoring calls for an enormous amount of capital. I mean, a factor is almost like a bank. You either have to have a lot to begin with, or keep borrowing more until you get yourself established. How long did you say he'd been at it?"

"A year."

"Well, it takes a lot longer than that to start making any money. Look around at the others—Cleveland, Longcope, Taylor, House—they've been around for years."

"Everyone has to begin somewhere, Papa," I said, trying to keep my voice even but too shaken to succeed very well.

"Certainly. But Mr. Gerrard has been in this business just long enough to be in a real squeeze for money. And now along comes the daughter of a property agent who seems to be well off. . . ."

Later, when I was alone in my room trying to study, my mind kept returning to all he had said. Rude as he was, and knowingly or not, Papa had already begun to touch on the one really weak spot in my determination. He had brought into focus—as he would over and over in various ways as time went by—my own inadequacies. What could anyone find so interesting about me? Neal was sophisticated. I was the little country girl who brought her wagon into the big city to pick up provisions. Why pursue a romance with me? What if he did need money? He'd have to stay away from girls whose fathers made money in cotton, because they would suspect his motives right away. And in Houston, as Neal himself pointed out, most of the wealth came from cotton. In Harrisburg, he might find someone whose wealth did not depend on cotton. . . . Papa was mistaken, of course. Yet . . . there was no fault in his logic.

On another night, at the dinner table, Papa asked me whether I knew that the Gerrard wholesale grocery business in Galveston had lost money in the past year.

"No, I didn't," I said, growing uncomfortable. I wondered how he had gotten this information.

"It's a fact, yes, and all that money gone to cotton factoring in Houston, just now when the elder Gerrard needs it most. It's a pity. Of course, under the circumstances I suppose if it would have seemed a good idea for Neal to become a part of his father's business, he would have. Strange, isn't it, that he'd come all the way to Houston, and even change his field. Of course, there are many cotton factors in Galveston and their Cotton Exchange is older and better than that one in Houston. Yet, for some reason, the young Gerrard must go away. . . ."

I looked pleadingly at Olivia. I did not believe I could take much more of this. She cleared her throat and said, "Alvareda needs to get to her studies, Papa." I hurried to my room.

One morning at breakfast, Papa said, "And how did Mr. Gerrard's father distinguish himself in the war? I find no record that he did."

"If you mean in the Texas independence war, he was not here. He migrated in the forties from England." I started to add that Neal's mother was full-blooded Irish but decided to keep silent. I was not sure how Papa felt about the Irish. Then I remembered something else: "Mr. Gerrard aided General Magruder during the battle at Galveston during the war with the Yankees."

"Ah," he said, "a mighty scrap with little real significance."

I could not imagine what possible difference any of this made now, but I only sighed and excused myself from the table, claiming I'd soon be late for school.

Sometimes Papa's remarks were more subtle, and on many occasions he said nothing at all while I remained proned and ready for an attack on Neal's character. The effect was exactly the same. I wound up with my stomach in knots.

Perhaps most interesting of all, in between the verbal assaults, he took the greatest care to be charming. One night, he even complimented both Olivia and me on the dinner. Our eyes met across the table in awe.

Each night I went to bed and wondered. Was Papa so bad, after all? If I changed my mind and decided not to marry, would he begin to treat me as he treated Olivia? Would he confide in me? Invite me to join him and Olivia at night in his quarters? Treat me like an adult?

Oh, if only I could see Neal, talk to him just once, for reassurance! I longed for the touch of his hand in mine, the special smile he gave me, the look in his eyes that told me even more than his words that he was all the wonderful things Papa tried to refute. If I closed my eyes, I could almost feel the touch of his lips on mine. Yet, of course, my need for Neal's comforting presence and my failure to be able to obtain it was something already foreseen by Papa as part of his plans for me.

Chapter 6

One afternoon in late April Olivia and I went down to sit together on the banks of the bayou. This was the first day of weather that foretold of the new season. It was as though spring had crept up in the night and made magic on the garments of bleak winter, causing it to vanish. Suddenly the grass was sprouting green; the trees and bushes were budding. The massive cypress trees formed a dense, green curtain over the bayou and the only noise was the call of crickets and bullfrogs, and locusts.

I was feeling especially well and optimistic that day, probably because I had finally, out of sheer exhaustion, slept soundly the night before. I sat with my feet crossed and leaned back on my hands. I lifted my head back and breathed in the wonderful spring air. At last I said, "In a way, I will miss Harrisburg."

"Oh?" said Olivia. She had brought a little wicker stool to sit on, and held her parasol to shade her eyes from the sun.

"It's so peaceful here, compared to Houston. There, everything seems to be always in motion; everyone walks with a quick step. It seems much farther away than five miles. . . . Not that I dislike the hustle bustle. I'd love living anywhere with Neal."

Olivia changed the subject. "Sister, Papa wanted me to find out if there is anything special you wish for as a graduation present."

I was surprised and pleased at his kind solicitude. I could think of nothing I wanted for graduation except Papa's blessing on my marriage to Neal, and this I dared not ask. Finally I answered, "I do not need anything special. Let Papa choose."

"Good. I believe he is considering something quite remarkable," she said.

On the night of graduation exercises Papa and Olivia gave me a silver vanity set and a huge basket of roses. The vanity set had my initials—"AC"—engraved on it—and the roses were lovely. I thanked them for both, but could not see what was remarkable about either of them. Papa gave me several moments of discomfiture before he produced a slender envelope from his pocket, a winning smile on his face.

I opened it and pulled out a steamer ticket and itinerary for a tour around the world. New York to London . . . Paris . . . Rome . . . Vienna. . . .

I looked up at both of them, at a loss for words. Olivia quickly said, "All three of us would go, of course. Think of it: six months. We'd be gone till Thanksgiving!

"That is, unless—well, Papa, I think we've managed to surprise her."

"I—I hardly know how to begin to thank you. I—but—"

Papa's smile had already vanished. "You can be thankful for the fact I finally completed the sale in South Texas I worked on for so long, not that it was any help the night you and your Houston friend barged in on me while I was working on the proposal."

"Yes, I'm—well, I don't know what to say."

"Think of it later, sister. We'll be late for the ceremony."

"Did you receive a gift from your Mr. Gerrard?" Papa asked.

"No, sir."

"Ah, well, just as I thought. Let's be going. Maybe he'll appear at Baraca

Hall tonight. There was an announcement in the Houston paper this morning."

While there was no reason to expect Neal at the ceremonies, Papa succeeded in causing me to look around expectantly all through the speeches and presentations, hoping for a sign of him. Mary Blessing's fiancé was there, and five out of the other seven girls in the class were accompanied by gentleman friends. Faye Winslow, a graduate of two years ago who came to see her brother graduate tonight, sported a beautiful emerald ring and bragged of her wedding in August. I felt left out. I wanted to tell them, "I have someone, too. . . ."

The evening was tarnished even further when we returned home before ten o'clock and went to bed, Papa and Olivia claiming they were tired out after a short reception with punch and cookies. This should have been an extended evening of celebrating, concluded with a cake and candles. Maybe even champagne. Neal should have been a part of it, congratulating me on my diploma.

Of course, he may not have seen the notice in the paper.

If he had, he may have been fearful of displeasing Papa by appearing at Baraca Hall.

Still, why was I here, lying in bed too excited to sleep, and not a soul around to share the occasion?

He should have come, that's all.

I slept till nine o'clock the next morning and awoke with a clear mind at last. I opened the envelope and read the itinerary again. All my life I had heard and read of faraway places, seen pictures of the Eiffel Tower, Buckingham Palace, gondolas churning down the canals in Venice. Never had I dreamed that I would someday visit any of these exotic places. Travel was for "worldly" people, not people who lived in Harrisburg and got no farther than Houston on Saturday afternoons.

Until just then I had been ready to hand back the ticket because of my promise to marry Neal. Now I realized I should be *going* because of my commitment to Neal. When I returned, I would be far more capable of moving in the same circles as the man I was marrying. Neal spent his fifteenth summer in Europe. He would find me much more interesting if I, too, had visited there. His absence last night proved he was past the point of remembering the importance of a high school graduation. He was, in so many ways, years ahead of me. Yet, after I'd had the experience of travel, I could hold forth with confidence in front of people of his kind. Papa may have hoped to make me forget about Neal while overseas, but he would actually be preparing me for marriage to him. Probably Neal himself would see it from this standpoint. . . .

I dressed unhurriedly, glancing out the window now and then in hopes of seeing Neal, then somewhat relieved when I did not. Today was a workday after all. Maybe he would not come till tonight. Oh, why had we not been more specific in our plans?

The day stretched out long before me. It might be evening when he came. I sat down to breakfast at ten o'clock, and before I had taken the first bite, the doorbell rang. Olivia answered while I sat there, staring down at my plate of eggs, my chest drawn tight with apprehension. In a moment she peeked around the dining room door. "It's Mr. Gerrard. I told him you could speak with him in the parlor."

I walked slowly there, as one might approach a prison cell. What would I say to him? My head bowed, I opened the door timidly. I could see, across the floor, his long narrow feet, slightly apart. I knew he was looking at the portrait of Olivia's mother, his hands dug deeply in his pockets. I stood a moment longer, then looked back toward the stairs. Olivia was poised half-way up, her hand on the rail, looking down on me in expectation. I took a deep breath and walked in.

Unlike me, Neal was exuberant, full of confidence. He looked handsome in his light gray suit and dark blue tie. Just as I had been poised for nearly two months in expectation of an attack on Neal's character by Papa, I was poised now for Neal's launch into the subject uppermost in our minds. Instead he drew me near and kissed my cheek, then said, "I've been admiring this lady in the painting. Your mother?"

"What? Oh no. Olivia's mother." The portrait was always an eye-catcher. The background was almost black, and her fragile face and pale shoulders appeared almost to spring forth from it. She had been a beautiful woman.

"I didn't realize you were half-sisters. No wonder I couldn't find a resemblance to you in this."

"I look like my mother. We have no pictures of her down here. They are in my father's room . . . or at least, I— Neal, let's go outside and sit in the yard."

"Yes," he said, and sighed. I realized then that he was apprehensive too. We walked through the sun room and out the side entrance. Maybe he is going to call it off, I thought. He doesn't want to talk about it. He'll lead into it gently.

I sat down on a wooden lawn chair and he leaned on the table nearby. It was a beautiful day. The cool morning air was pleasant, the breeze soothing across my face. "You look well," he said, then considered, "maybe just a little thinner."

"You look well, too," I said, and wrapped my fingers around the arm of the chair. Oh, let's get this over with.

"I've been traveling a lot, visiting clients. In fact, I just returned on the morning train from Corpus Christi, and came straight here."

"Oh . . . oh. I hadn't realized you traveled a lot in your work."

"This time of year I drum up business, then I have to be back here and ready when the season begins." He paused. Then, "Alvareda, something is wrong. What is it? Why don't you look at me?"

"Nothing. Nothing is wrong."

"Are you packed? We can be in Galveston by lunchtime if we hurry."

I turned to face him. "Now? I hadn't realized you wanted me to go with you today."

"But you said we'd be married right away. I've arranged for you to stay with my parents till the wedding." He smiled and reached for my hands. "I have so much to tell you. I've leased a furnished house on Franklin Avenue as of June 15. It's very convenient—just two blocks from Courthouse Square, and close to my office. We can live there until we decide where we want to settle permanently. I think you'll really—" He stopped. His eyes were puzzled. "What is it?"

I cleared my throat and pulled my hands away, gripping the chair arm. "It's just that, I don't think we had exactly the same thing in mind. I thought . . . we'd be married . . . a little later. I expected to live here until then." I took in a breath and shifted in the chair.

At length he said, "I see. . . . All I have thought about for these weeks is how fast I can get you away from here. I just assumed you understood we'd go today."

"No. I didn't understand that at all," I said softly. There was a large lump forming in my throat.

He folded his arms in front of him, and looked away from me. "You've changed your mind, haven't you? I knew it the minute I saw you."

"No. It's just that I've felt so rushed. And confused. Papa—" I stopped.

"What?"

"Nothing." I didn't want to tell him of the things Papa said of him. Now that I was in his presence again, I didn't want him to think I even listened for a moment, or was the least affected by them. "I've been doing a lot of thinking, as I'm sure you have. Neal, I don't know if I can . . . can adjust myself to your life. I feel so . . . so . . . inexperienced."

"I see." He still would not turn to me.

"And now Papa wants to take me on a world tour. We'd be away six months. I'd get to see Vienna, Rome, all kinds of places. I was thinking that, when I came back, I'd be more prepared to be your wife. Can you understand?"

"Perfectly." He turned around now. His face was hard, as it was that night he confronted Papa in his office. He began to pace back and forth. "Now, try to see it from my standpoint. I met you last January, and we carried on the most unusual courtship, while you were frightened all the time of making a wrong move, watching the clock for fear you'd be one minute late.

"One day I walked into my office and saw a letter from you on my desk. In it you wrote at length about the cruelty of your father, his completely unreasonable views about my courting you. His threats if you should continue, I read between the lines.

"So I came here that night, and within five minutes I knew there was a real basis for the desperation you felt. You knew already that I cared for you very much. I wanted to take you away that night."

He raised a finger and shook his head. "But you persuaded me to wait. And so, for two months, I've lived night and day wondering what was going on here. Strange courtship indeed! I couldn't see you at all. But I waited just the same." He stood still and looked at me again. "And now you're asking me to wait another six months, while your father takes you thousands of miles away so that he can poison your mind about me? I'm supposed to conduct my business day by day worrying about your welfare? Wondering what next your father will devise to keep us apart, once you return? . . . "Well, is that what you expect?"

Almost without realizing it, I had begun to cry. I tried to stop, but the tears kept filling my eyes and streaming down my face. He handed me his handkerchief.

"Oh, you don't know how it has been, how confusing—"

"Can't you see that is precisely why your father kept us apart? How could you not see that?" He sat down in a chair nearby and leaned toward me.

"How can you be so certain my father is horrible?" I demanded. I could not look at him directly.

He raised his hands in futility.

I dried my eyes. "You are quite as stubborn as he is," I said, letting out a breath.

"Alvareda, don't do this. Come with me now. I can't take you on a world tour just yet, but I promise someday I will."

"You miss the point."

He stood up. "No, it is you who misses the point. I've had as much as I can take of waiting. I won't wait and worry any longer."

"You would if you really loved me. Then you'd be willing to wait."

"If you loved me, you wouldn't ask me to wait."

He came toward me and took my hand. "Good-bye, Alvareda."

I kept holding onto his hand, my eyes pleading with his, till he moved away and pulled his hand free. "Neal, please," I called, my voice choked. I watched as he walked across the lawn and down to the front where his buggy awaited him in the street. With every step he took, I prayed he would turn and come back. How could he leave me?

When he was gone, I felt a terrible wrenching inside, the undeniable signal of my own mistake. I felt empty and washed out. Yet I could not bring myself to run after him. What he asked of me seemed overwhelming.

I sat there for an hour or more, leaning back and shading my eyes from the sun. It seemed so final. Of all the things I least expected in the past two months, it was that we would part in this way. I tried to think ahead. Soon we'd be gone to Europe, and I would be trying to forget. And when I returned, there would be no Neal. If we went on Saturday shopping trips again, I would be trying to escape a chance meeting with him: looking over my shoulder while crossing the intersection, looking about as we rode in the wagon, then, seeing someone who resembled Neal, looking straight ahead in order to avoid the possibility of meeting his eyes.

There might someday be another man. Olivia met another man. She did not love him as she had loved Mr. Nelson, I didn't think, because she seemed less upset when they broke off their engagement.

Maybe that sort of love that she had with her Mr. Nelson comes only once. Maybe that was why she sent the widower with three sons away.

I closed my eyes. He will come back . . . he will come back and say he is sorry and that he will wait. I will sit here for a while longer and listen for his approach. He'll say that he can't live without me, that he will wait six years if necessary, that there will never be anyone else for him. Listen to the birds calling. Hear the chirrup of crickets. Hear the children calling to each other as they play in the street. He will come back . . . once he thinks about it . . . he will come. Is that the sound of the horse's footfall?

I opened my eyes. Nothing. I looked up at the house. In the upstairs window I could see Olivia, gazing down upon me.

Into the afternoon, he did not return. I stood up in my room and looked down upon the lawn, staring at the chair in which I had been sitting and the table nearby where he had stood. I went over our words again, trying to think of one phrase that might suggest he was not giving up on me. There was nothing. The afternoon closed, the shadows fell, and evening began. Olivia knocked on my door. "Dinnertime," she said.

"I'm not hungry," I told her.

"You and Neal . . . did you set a date for the wedding?"

"No. We called it off . . ."

"Oh . . . it's a pity. But sometimes things work out for the best."

"Yes. Sometimes they do."

"Well, I'll leave you alone then."

When she was gone I lit my bedside lamp, opened up a book, and stared vacantly at it. I was still sitting there when the clock in the hall struck nine. Papa and Olivia had not bothered me at all. They were sensitive to my feelings, I thought.

After a while I remembered the cotton boll that Neal gave me the first time we spent an hour together in Houston. I went to the drawer in my dresser where I'd put it carefully away. I picked it up and brushed it across my cheek. And that was when I heard the sound of Olivia and Papa on the stairs. I listened until the door had been opened and shut, then I began to think it would be nice if they would invite me to join them in there. It seemed to me that I had earned the right to be treated as an equal now, that they might have stopped by my door and said to me, "Alvareda, join us for a while. We'll have a little glass of wine and talk about the trip."

Maybe they were waiting for me to show a desire to be with them.

However, I'd been told explicitly never to come up there.

But that was long ago. Maybe now things were changed. They'd been going up there together by long habit. They probably would not even think that I might want to join them.

I replaced the cotton boll and walked out the door. As soon as I put a foot upon the flight of stairs leading up to my father's rooms, my pulse quickened. This seemed unnatural. The stairs were half the width of the others, and the passage was dark. There was but one small gaslight, right at the top by the door. Halfway up, I paused. I almost turned and walked down. Yet now I could hear voices. In fact I would need to be just a bit closer to understand everything they were saying. I lifted my skirt. Just four or five more steps now. . . . Once I finally reached the door, I had not the courage to knock, but stood there, frightened as ever of breaking a household rule, or raising the fury of my father. I was afraid to go down. I looked below. You could only see the first few steps from here. What if I fell and went tumbling down to the second-floor landing? They would know then that I was eavesdropping. Papa would—

I heard my name mentioned. I drew up to the door, curiosity overtaking fear. "He couldn't have done us a bigger favor than failing to show up last night," Papa was saying. "But it was that trip that clenched it."

"Yes, Papa."

"Do you think we can cancel it without having her start this thing up all over again?"

"I'll see, Papa. I don't know how much she was counting on it."

"Well, do something quickly. The departure date isn't far away, is it?"

"No, Papa."

"You know, I don't have unlimited funds, though some people seem to think that I have."

"Yes, Papa."

"Look what I've already put out in the past year alone."

"I know."

"It will take at least half of this commission to cover the balance. I must be a damned fool for trying to do all I do."

"No, Papa, you just have a deep sense of loyalty."

"It's nice to have at least one of you acknowledge that. But I can only do so much. Confound Alvareda, I just get that goddamned Leider family out of my hair, and she falls for a Houston rascal."

"Papa, I do think you worry too much about that."

"Nonsense. Any fool can see in which direction Houston is growing."

"I suppose you're right."

I brought a hand to my mouth. There was much I didn't understand about what they said, but one thing was clear: I had been willing to forego my happiness with Neal in the frail hope that Papa had really changed toward me, that we could start anew with each other; all the time he and Olivia were making a mockery out of my feelings and plotting to cheat me. I had been right in the beginning; Neal had been right all along.

I took the steps down as quietly as I could, then fled to my room. It was too late to catch an evening train tonight and, even if I could, I had no idea how to find Neal's bachelor quarters once I got to Houston. I'd simply have to wait out the night and catch the seven o'clock train in the morning. I packed a bag, put on my traveling suit, and sat down in a chair by the window. There I stayed, all through the night, part of the time chastising myself for my idiotic behavior of the morning, part of the time praying that Neal would understand and forgive me.

And what if he would not?

I'd simply have to take that chance.

At six the next morning I put on the light, combed my hair and straightened my suit. I would slip out quietly. I had no wish to stage a confrontation, especially as it might delay my getting to the station. Yet I was not really afraid of being caught. I felt strangely calm about leaving, now that I knew where I stood with Papa and Olivia. I was putting on my hat when the door opened and Olivia looked in.

"Sister, where are you going? I noticed the light—"

"I'm going to Neal."

"But I thought—"

"You were wrong." I shoved a pin through my hat.

"I must tell Papa," she said breathlessly.

"Go ahead. But that won't stop me. And Olivia, here's my steamer ticket. You'd have been after it later, anyway."

Her eyes widened. She stood there a moment, as though unsure what to do. Then she turned and left. I now had just a few minutes to make it to the train station. I picked up my bag and walked down the front stairs. As I was about to turn the knob on the front door, I heard Papa's voice on the stairs behind me.

"Stop there! Who gave you permission to leave?"

My knees nearly buckled under me. I drew up my shoulders and turned around. I will never forget how he looked standing there, filled with rage. His face was florid, ear to ear. Olivia stood behind him.

"Papa, I'm leaving," I said faintly, then gulped. I could feel the blood pulsing behind my eyes.

He took three steps down. "I'm warning you, don't go out that door. I'm through trying to reason with you."

"But you promised you wouldn't stop me."

"Don't you dare defy me." He raised a hand and I swung backward, protecting my face. Olivia was very quick. She placed her body between us and told Papa, "No, not again. Don't do it. Let her go."

He stared at Olivia as though she had brought him to his senses. Then he shot me a glance that was full of contempt. "You've never been anything but a goddamned nuisance, Alvareda—"

"I'm sorry, Papa. I'm sorry for . . . ruining your life. Truly I am." I could feel tears smarting behind my eyes. I had a death grip on the valise.

"If you leave this house now, you may never come back into it again as long as I am alive. What's more, as soon as you walk out that door, you can consider yourself disinherited. Now! See how sincere your beloved Mr. Gerrard is. See if he wants to marry a penniless little waif."

I looked up at Olivia, my heart sagging with pain. Was I never to see my sister again? I wanted to cry out to her for some reassuring word, yet she put a finger on her lips and lowered her eyelids, shaking her head.

I took in a shallow breath and turned the knob on the door. Slowly I opened it, frightened with each fraction of a second that Papa would come down and stop me, but still unable to move in quick motions. When I finally shut it behind me I stood there for several moments, taking in gulps of air. I felt I was at the edge of a cliff, as indeed in a way I was. Finally I gathered the courage to step off the porch. As I walked down toward the gate, and just as I reached for the latch, I heard Olivia's voice behind me. I turned.

She was standing at her window, waving her handkerchief. Fluff was standing on the sill. "Good-bye, sister."

I took a step forward, but she shook her head. "No, don't. Be happy. Forgive Papa, and at least consider he has prepared you for the worst."

"But when will I see you?"

"We'll meet someday. Go now."

I nodded. Tears streaming down my face, I put down the valise, cupped my hands to my mouth, and blew her a kiss. Leaving Olivia was the most difficult thing I had ever done. I wiped the tears from my eyes and picked up my valise. I must think only of getting to the station on time. . . .

When I finally sat down in the train car, I thought, as I had many times through the night, of the words I overheard Papa say. Oh, I was so thankful to be away. . . . Yet, what of Olivia? Would she be all right now that Papa had lost in his bout to foil my plans? Would Papa blame her? I thought of Olivia, seated in her pretty room, all her pretty things around her. I knew exactly the price Papa paid to keep her, and how close he had come to imprisoning me as well.

Chapter 7

I arrived at Neal's office building at half-past eight o'clock, and looked up at the gold lettering on the windows: Clayton O'Neal Gerrard—Cotton Factor. Now it seemed overpowering, forbidding as it had not before, when I stood here with him. I waited for a long while in indecision. All around were sights and sounds of the morning. Newspaper carriers were tooling around on their bicycles, their baskets loaded with rolled-up copies of today's *Post*. Shopkeepers were sweeping out their stores, and talking to each other as they worked. Bright-colored awnings were being rolled out above the boardwalks. Up ahead was a bakery wagon, the smell of fresh-baked bread wafting behind it and drawing a trail of hungry dogs, tails wagging. Business people strolled down the boardwalk, on the way to their offices. All of them seemed so confident, as though everything in their lives was going all right, and this was just an ordinary day.

I took a deep breath and walked up the stairs, having no idea what Neal would be doing, whether or not he would be there. He might be at the Cotton Exchange Building by now. He might not even come into his office today. He might . . . might even have left town again. Why hadn't I thought of all this before?

I opened his door and stood just inside. I couldn't see him from there, and my heart sank. Then someone behind me said, "Can I help you, miss?"

I turned around to face a clerk on his way to the sample room. "Is Mr. Gerrard in this morning?"

"Yes, ma'am. Right there in the back. Shall I take you to him?"

"No, no," I said quickly. "I don't want to bother him if he's busy. Just tell him, please, that Miss Cane is here to see him, and will be in his office waiting."

He nodded and smiled. I watched him walk toward the back, then I saw Neal emerge to the right of two other men who were dressed in suits, their coats on. Neal was in his shirt sleeves, explaining something and touching the fluffy cotton samples on the table. Oh, he must have buyers in. What a terrible time for me to show up. I went into his office and sat on a chair in the corner. I put my valise on the floor, then in my lap, then on the floor again. I wrung my hands. Oh, truly this was worse than when he approached my door in Harrisburg yesterday. As if I had not already caused him enough trouble. . . .

Finally, he came to the front. He stopped briefly to show the clients out, then walked into his office. I was up on my feet at once. "Neal, I've been wrong about everything. Please forgive me," I blurted out.

He shut the door behind him. He stood there, looking at me. Finally he said, "What changed your mind?"

There seemed so much to tell, I didn't know where to begin, though I had been rehearsing all the way from Harrisburg. "I always loved you. There was never any doubt of that. But I thought you should understand how I felt." No, this wasn't working. I couldn't make what I wanted to say come out. I sighed, then began again, "For all of my life, I have wanted to please my father. I was thinking while on the train this morning, that it is almost like a sickness—I can remember so many times, trying to do things for him, making him presents, bringing home good school reports to make him proud of me. And nothing ever worked. It was always more than evident that somehow I'd fallen short, that he didn't like what I'd done.

"He never seemed to want to touch me. He wouldn't take me on his lap, wouldn't hold my hand, wouldn't . . . wouldn't kiss me. Wouldn't talk to me, except to reprimand me for something.

"Well, I guess most people would have gotten the idea a lot earlier that it is futile trying to make someone love you. But I could never really give up. And the awful truth is, I still can't say that I ever will because I know I am at least partly responsible for the way he feels. You see, my mother died in an accident—she fell to her death, and it was my fault—"

Neal looked puzzled, and opened his mouth to speak, but I shook my head.

"Don't ask any questions of me now. Maybe someday, but not now. . . . So over the past few weeks, he has seemed different toward me. He has come just far enough to make me believe he might really forgive me. He might really be able to love me after all. You see, I would have given anything as long as there was some chance. But I wouldn't anymore. At least I've learned my lesson about that."

"But you still haven't told me what happened."

"Last night I overheard him talking to Olivia. He never really planned to take us abroad . . . it was just a trick to keep me from marrying you. I realized as they talked that he had not changed toward me after all, that I had been stupid to believe in him for a moment. . . . I packed a bag and waited up through the night, to be sure of catching the early train."

I took a deep breath. He might as well know it all. "When I walked out the door Papa said I could never come back once I left, and that he intended to disinherit me. I—I felt you should know that."

For a while he considered me silently. Then he said, "But still you came."

I nodded. "Can you forgive me?"

"Come here," he said, and I went into his arms and wept so hard, for such a long time, that at last he pulled out his handkerchief to dry my eyes. Then he smiled and said, "You know, Alvareda, I believe you are the greatest boon that the cotton handkerchief trade has ever known."

"Oh, Neal, I'm so happy," I told him, and cried some more.

The wedding was planned for three weeks hence.

From the moment I listened to Neal talking to his mother over the telephone I sensed more strongly than ever the wide difference in the way we had been brought up. "We'll be there by lunchtime," he was saying. "No, I don't really think Alvareda is ready to meet anyone today," glancing at me. "Um-hum. Tomorrow or the next day. No, Martin and Josephine will be all right, but not anyone else." He turned from the telephone to reassure me, "Just my brother and his wife for dinner tonight."

"Oh, I must look a fright," I said as he hung up.

"You look as if you could use one good night's rest before my mother's social circle is loosed on you. Don't be afraid to tell her 'no' if you feel she is pushing you. She has been anxiously awaiting your arrival for two months."

"But I did not bring any decent clothes, only what I could carry."

He took me in his arms again and kissed my forehead. "Don't worry. You can shop in Galveston."

"Oh . . . all right," I said, reminded that I was bringing nothing to this marriage, not even the proper clothing.

The Gerrard home was a block off Broadway. Built on a corner lot, it had twice as much yard as surrounded the other houses up and down the block. Above the tall front stairs was a deep veranda that covered all sides except the back, and made a wide circle at one edge, enclosing the big dining room. This room, with windows all around, was not like our dining room: formal and austere. It was a central gathering area for family and friends on both important and everyday occasions. The Gerrards, I soon learned, often had family visiting—favorite aunts, old maid cousins, uncles who lived far away, even distant relations occasionally from Britain. The chief difference in the house where I grew up and this house was the pleasant atmosphere that pervaded it.

Neal's mother was tall and slender. She had high cheeks and hazel eyes, and dark hair parted down the center and wound into braids in the back. Neal resembled her more so than his father, who was stocky, with light, wavy hair and blue eyes. They were both waiting on the front stairs when we arrived. Mr. Gerrard took both my hands in his, and shook them warmly; Mrs. Gerrard opened her arms to hug me. She hustled me inside, up the stairs, and showed me to the room above the dining room. This room was also surrounded by windows, and as the roof above was surmounted by a cupola, the ceiling went up to a point. From the center hung a gas fixture that had recently been electrified. Mrs. Gerrard turned it on for me to see. "It's a trend," she said. "It won't be long before the whole island will be electrified."

And so there was another difference. The Gerrards were progressive, trying out new things. My father would probably be dead before we would have electrified lights in our house.

Mrs. Gerrard plumped the pillows on the big bed and said, "Lunch will be ready in an hour. Why don't you just relax and sleep till then?"

"You're very kind," I said.

"We're so glad to have you," she said. "Neal has spoken of nothing but you for months. He is very proud to have you for his bride." Then after a pause, "I understand your mother is no longer living."

I nodded. "But I do have a sister who has been like a mother to me."

"Is that so? Well, we must arrange for her to stay with us during the wedding parties."

"I'm afraid . . . afraid she won't be able to attend the wedding."

"Have you asked her?"

"No, but she is very devoted to my father and, perhaps Neal told you—"

"He did. But I think you should invite her anyway. There is some notepaper in the desk there. Why don't you write her? You might find she will surprise you."

"Yes, ma'am."

"Rest now. I'll be back in an hour."

The gulf breeze blew soothingly across me as I lay down on the big bed, yet for a while I was much too wound up to relax. I could not believe I was here, and Harrisburg seemed very far away, almost like a foreign country. I could not get over the kind and loving ways of Neal's parents. Here I was, suddenly transported and plunked down in the middle of their busy lives, and yet they had made me feel they had nothing else to do but fuss over me. No wonder Neal was so sure of himself. He had always known he was surrounded by love. He never had to worry he would make a mistake and forfeit his family's affection. . . . Still savoring all these pleasantries, I finally dozed into the first carefree, untroubled sleep I had enjoyed in a very long time.

Neal did not exaggerate his appraisal of the social life of his family in Galveston. Two days after I arrived I began entertaining callers. And because Josephine and I were about the same size, I was loaned two afternoon reception dresses made for her, with slight alterations. For the first round of callers, I wore an apple green faille gown with an embroidered cream satin front, cream silk stockings, and pale green slippers. I wore Mrs. Gerrard's three-strand pearl choker, bracelet, and earrings. Though the clothes did not belong to me—even my wedding gown would be borrowed from Josephine—I felt grown up and lovely.

I sat for hours in a bustle chair in the front parlor—the only formal room in the house—while friends of the family, mostly ladies, many of them elderly, trooped in to meet me and leave their cards on the silver tray near the door. Among the early callers were two younger ladies, Miss Bettie Brown and her sister, Mrs. Mathilda Sweeney. I had been hearing about the Brown family since I met Neal. They lived a few blocks away in a huge red brick Italianate villa on Broadway, and Bettie had traveled all over the world. She was dramatic to watch, filling the room with her presence. She wore her light-colored hair in a high crown of curls, and spoke with great authority. Mathilda, the younger of the two, was prettier, in a soft, pleasing way, and quiet and reserved. Bettie chatted with Mrs. Gerrard for a few moments, then suddenly whipped around to face me with a piercing gaze. I took in a breath. She narrowed her eyes and said, "You're awfully young, aren't you?"

"I'm seventeen," I said quickly.

She paused momentarily and inclined her head, still studying me. "You're marrying into a fine family. If Neal were a little older, I would have snatched him for my own. He had a terrible crush on me when he was still in knee pants." With that the inimitable Miss Bettie made a wide turn. The train on her aquamarine afternoon dress swept the floor, and she opened her fan. "I dislike long visits," she said. "They get so boring. We'll see you at the wedding, Miss Cane."

Mrs. Sweeney smiled. "I'm certain Mr. Gerrard is lucky to have found Miss Cane," she observed, then said to me, "Ask Bettie to show you some of her paintings one day. She's very good—has studied in Vienna—and her work lines the walls at Ashton Villa."

I promised I would.

As they were leaving, two other women were coming in. The parade went on into the early evening. Neal said it was important to his mother that I meet people, and she did not want any of her friends on the island to be left out.

"And you? Is it important to you?" I asked, thinking he probably did not care very much for this custom. I was quite wrong.

"It's very important, and as soon as we get settled in Houston, there are a lot of people there that I want you to meet."

That was the first time, through the months that we had known each other, that I realized Neal definitely expected something from me. Always he had made it clear that he had so much to give. I began to worry if I could measure up to his expectations.

Following the suggestion of Neal's mother, I had written to Olivia several days after my arrival, sending her the address in Galveston and inviting her to the wedding. After I had been away from home even this short period of time, Olivia's destiny seemed to me cruel, more so than ever. I hesitated at length before writing that Neal and I were very happy, and that his family were kind to me. I chose every word carefully, so as not to make thoughtless comparisons, when in fact I could have produced page after page of details.

Halfway into the second week, amid preparations for the ceremony that had turned the house into a beehive of activity, the busy doorbell sounded once again. "I'll answer," said Josephine. "Probably another gift."

This delivery was no different, except that it came all the way from Harrisburg. There were several boxes, a letter for me, and a large trunk. I looked at the letter. "Dear Sister, I know you will understand that I cannot be at your wedding, though it would give me such happiness to see you wed to Mr. Gerrard.

"I am sending you some things I know you will need, and a little gift from me. I hope it will do.

"Fluff and I miss you. In the afternoons about the time you used to come home from school, Fluff stands in the window looking out. Papa has been away some, but will be back tonight. I must go and fix his dinner. Lovingly, your sister Olivia."

I reread the letter, my eyes about to spill over with tears. It was so brief, yet said so much about Olivia's life, and but for the good fortune of meeting Neal, mine too. Oh, how I missed her! I wished so much she could come to the wedding, and the knowledge she could not even think of such a thing because of Papa twisted now like a knife inside me.

I followed the boxes and trunk up to my room, and shut the door. In the trunk was the biggest part of my wardrobe, including dresses and shirtwaists, handbags and shoes and hats. In one large box was my collection of books and articles from my desk. In another was my selection of music for piano. And in the last box I opened, there was a satin case which held a long white silk sleeping gown and a matching robe. Around the bodice and sleeves was an elaborate display of hand embroidery, in the palest shade of blue thread. The robe was held together with a blue satin sash that tied into a bow in front. It was the most beautiful sleeping apparel I had ever seen, and she had even included a matching pair of white slippers, with embroidered toes.

She must have been working on this since the beginning of my courtship with Neal. "Oh, sister," I sighed, and held the gown against my breast. I could not wait to tell Neal about the present when he arrived this evening. Yet, as soon as that thought occurred to me, another followed it.

"Oh, I could not show him this!" I gasped, and looked in the full-length mirror nearby. My face was crimson.

All afternoon I was preoccupied with the prospect brought home by Olivia's gift. When all the celebrating was over, and the ring had been slipped on my finger, something new would be expected of me. . . . Yet I had no firm idea of what exactly I was to do. Neal had once said he wanted a big family, and I, too, wanted children. But that had been before we had declared ourselves to each other, so it had no serious implications then; suddenly, it had more than one. I knew that men were made differently from women, and that was because in conceiving children the man passed the seed into the woman. But it had never occurred to me until now that you had to be at least partially unclothed to accomplish that, and . . . even worse . . . it must be horribly embarrassing, for how could it not be? And also . . . I reasoned . . . painful. All at once I was terrified.

I said nothing of my fears that night when Neal arrived from Houston. We attended a dinner party and were rushed to make it on time. It lasted till very late, extending my excuse for not opening the subject uppermost in my mind. For several nights after, I could not bring myself to say anything, though there were moments when I might have, when we were on a buggy ride or talking together out on the wide front veranda.

Then, two nights before the wedding we visited in the home of Martin and Josephine. Martin resembled Neal's father as much as Neal resembled their mother. Josephine was a pretty woman with thick brown kinky hair, a high forehead, and wide-set blue eyes. Their home, just a few blocks from the beach, was airy and cool, modest and friendly. We played whist until ten o'clock, then stayed for Josephine's specialty of cherry torte. It was as wonderful as Martin predicted, but having followed the hearty supper prepared by Neal's mother, it made both Neal and me feel overstuffed. Neal suggested we take a long walk down the beach. It was a beautiful moonlit evening with a pleasant breeze across the water, and Neal seemed in especially high spirits as we strolled down toward the Beach Hotel. He confessed the beach was his favorite place in the world. He came here often to think and, as he put it, "to get my bearings." Then he said, "Less than three weeks ago, I thought my wedding day would never get here. Are you as anxious as I am for all this to be over? Finally, we can get settled down in our house on Franklin." He paused. "Well?"

"I—uh, of course."

"It seems an eternity since last March, doesn't it?"

"Oh, to be sure. . . ." I could not tell him what was weighing on my mind.

We soon approached the huge clapboard resort hotel. It was teeming with people, walking, leaning against the rails surrounding the wide promenades, playing barefoot out on the beach and alighting from buggies, around the front drive. The whole rambling structure was ablaze with lights, and lilting music came from a band of musicians who were jammed into the small bandstand.

Suddenly Neal said, "Come on, let's dance." He took my hand and we ran all the way to the dance floor and joined the other couples doing the two-step.

The fact that I had never danced in my life was not a matter of great concern to either of us. Neal was soon leading me smoothly around and for an hour we danced everything from polkas to waltzes until my feet ached and my heart pumped. I had never spent that length of time in Neal's arms, and when at last the band played "Auld Lang Syne" and the long strings of lights went out, we danced even longer while Neal hummed a tune and held me closer than before. Finally, laughing and out of breath, I said, "Don't you think we ought to go home before your mother starts to worry?"

"I suppose you're right," he said reluctantly, and arm in arm we started back down the beach toward home. The surf was beautiful under the moonlight, one wave forming a wide arc as it played out on the beach, to be overtaken by still another, and another, over and over, the noisy splashing followed by brief silence. Neal was still in a playful mood, and not to be hurried home. When I told him I had never realized how swell it would be to grow up by the water he stopped walking and said, "Have you ever run barefoot along the beach and let the water splash over your feet?"

"No. I had never even seen Galveston beach until three weeks ago."

He was amazed. Then I saw a twinkle in his eye. "I'm afraid there is a serious gap in your education. Now. You sit here." He placed his arms around my waist and lowered me down upon a rock.

"What are you doing?"

He said nothing, but began to unlace my boots, then removed them. Next he said, "Oh, your stockings. I forgot. Take them off."

"Neal, I—do you think it's proper?"

"I have no idea whether or not it is proper. But I will turn away while you take them off."

He turned and folded his arms. I looked around to see if anyone was coming, then cautiously rolled the stockings down and slipped them inside my discarded shoes. "There," I said, and got up.

"Come on," he said, taking my hand. We ran splashing down the beach for quite a ways, laughing like young children just let out of school for summer vacation. Finally he stopped, lifted me up, and swung me around. "Oh, I do love you, Alvareda."

"Let me down," I protested, laughing.

He let me slowly down and, holding me still, began to kiss me longingly, with more urgency than ever. I had never experienced such passion. I was as amazed with myself as I was with Neal. Sooner than Neal, however, I became alarmed and pulled away. We stood facing each other, the waves splashing at our feet and surrounding them, then speeding on.

"I'm sorry," he said at last, and took a deep breath.

"It's all right, Neal. It's just that—"

"What, darling?"

"Neal, I have to ask you something very important."

"Anything," he said, wiping his brow.

I hesitated, almost losing my nerve. Yet if I didn't blurt it out, right now, I would never be able to work up the courage again. "I just have to know . . . what you expect of me, after we're married."

"Just go on being the way you are, that's all."

I shook my head. I despaired of appearing hopelessly dumb. "I know how children are conceived—" I began. "I mean, I suppose that's just one of those things you have to do . . . embarrassing or not . . . isn't it?" I looked away.

He looked at me as though considering how he might answer, then after a few moments he smiled and said gently, "That isn't exactly right. Let's walk." We walked in silence for a while, just at the edge of the surf. Then he said, "First of all, I love you."

"I love you too, Neal."

"When a man loves . . . when two people love each other, they must find ways of expressing that love, not just in order to have—" he began, then after a long pause added, "Just now, when we kissed, didn't you feel there must be something more?"

"Yes. . . ." I said slowly. It was just beginning to dawn on me that my feelings for Neal . . . the physical stirring . . . was connected with all this.

"Well then, just trust me."

"I do," I told him, but the feeling of discomfiture was returning.

We walked a few more steps. "Does this mean . . . it isn't going to hurt?"

He sighed. "It probably will at first, but not for long."

Not for long . . . well . . . that was something, anyway. "Neal, just answer me one more thing. Will you, that is, do we have to, oh!" I stopped and turned to him. "Do we have to be undressed in front of each other?"

I think he was astonished. "Yes," he said.

"Completely?"

"Yes," he said. His tone was definite.

"Oh, dear!" I turned from him and hurried down the beach.

He caught up to me and took my hand.

"Oh, Neal, sometimes I feel so . . . at such a disadvantage. I am afraid I might fail you."

He hesitated before replying. "I don't believe you ever could."

"But—"

"All right." He winked. "Didn't I teach you how to dance tonight?"

"Yes."

"I'll teach you how to be a married lady—a happy one."

I suddenly felt better about everything. "Neal, not just tonight, but whenever you touch me I . . . I get a warm feeling in the pit of my stomach. Oh, I shouldn't have said that."

He threw back his head and laughed, then put an arm around me. "Alvareda, I have a feeling you're going to keep me awfully busy."

I married Neal on June 18, 1887, and if I live to be a hundred I will not forget a single detail of our wedding night because I knew more happiness than I had known throughout my previous life.

There were so many candles in the bedroom, on tables, beside the big canopied bed, and on the dresser nearby. The whole room was bathed in a warm glow. I changed in the small dressing room, putting on the white silk sleeping gown, and brushing my hair, then pulling it up with a pale blue ribbon. My heart was pounding wildly and my fingers trembled.

I opened the door and walked out into the bedroom, where Neal stood awaiting me, bare to the waist. His shoulders and chest were broader than I'd realized, and below them his body tapered down to a slender waist. He took my hands and smiled at me, then said, "Are you still afraid, Mrs. Gerrard?"

I nodded. I could not speak.

"Don't be," he said. He took the ribbon from my hair. I could feel the weight of the hair tumble down my back. He gently lifted off the gown, then stood back, holding my hands away from my body and lacing his fingers in mine. He looked at me as one might observe a fine work of art. "You are the most beautiful sight I ever hope to see," he said, and brought my hands to his lips.

From that moment my fears subsided, because everything he had told me was true. He took me in his arms and began to kiss me eagerly, his mouth, his tongue caressing my mouth, my face, my neck, and moving down softly to capture my breasts and my nipples, awakening in me the same stirring that had been only a hint in my body before this night, but that sprang from deep inside me. As his hands splayed out and moved along my ribs and spanned my waist, then lingered on my hips as he kissed me deep down in the patch of hair where lay the very center of my desire for him, I caught my breath and leaned forward, closing my arms around him, knowing suddenly what this ritual of touching and loving and joining together would be. He lifted his head and looked into my eyes. I nodded and kissed him feverishly, my hands encircling his face. He raised up then, lifting me with him, and carried me to bed and laid me down. He turned aside and took off his trousers, then faced me and paused. My heart leaped at the beautiful sight of him, and I held out my arms. He lay down and kissed and fondled every inch of me again and again, until I was aching with readiness, before finally lifting his body up and lowering himself into me. I do not remember more than one brief instant of pain, even that first time. He paused for one breath, two. I held him tightly and pulled him against me, wanting this moment more than any ever before in my life, and soon all I could feel was a wonderful sensation of release in my own body unlike anything I had ever experienced, like the smashing of waves upon a shore, again and again; and at last the surge of his warm semen into me like the rushing of water down a hill. For several moments we both lay still, locked in each other's arms. Then he pulled up and looked at me tenderly, searching my eyes. I smiled at him. "I love you," I said, and kissed him, already wanting him again.

When finally we slept, the candles were burned down to nubs, and before my eyes closed, I promised myself I would always live up to his expectations as he had more than lived up to mine. It seemed to me as I lay in the circle of his arms, that no one and nothing could ever come between us, and for the first time in my life, I felt completely safe.

My father had lost his grip on me, or so I thought.

Chapter 8

Neal was up at half-past five every weekday morning. I rose with him, brewed fresh coffee, and had breakfast on the table by the time the newspaper arrived at half-past six. During the meal he pored over the closing prices of cotton, the weather and crop reports, and the opinions of Cargill & Richardson on the state of the industry. By seven o'clock he was ready to put on his hat, tuck the newspaper under his arm, and kiss me good-bye. He seldom returned for lunch, usually stopping by the Cotton Exchange to check on current prices of the day and take care of other business, then joining business acquaintances at the oyster saloon next door or at some other dining room.

My days were busy with household tasks—I had a cleaning lady twice a week but did all the cooking and a lot of the other chores myself—and I also loved the house and was constantly making something for it, from lace curtains for the front parlor to embroidered pillow shams for our bed. Our home was neither fancy nor large, and probably seemed a curious design to most people because all of the downstairs rooms opened off a long narrow hall behind the small foyer at the left end of the house front. It had very little yard in front, but a nice expanse in back, shaded by a big pear tree that was sagging with ripe fruit when we moved in, and a great old pecan that bore a substantial harvest every fall. I could not begin to count the mornings when I enjoyed the sunrise through the kitchen window while making hot biscuits for Neal. I had never known the simple pleasure of caring for someone who appreciated me. All day long I missed my new husband and thought of ways to please him. I could not wait for the sound of the back door to open in the evening, and would drop whatever I was doing and rush to meet Neal.

The cotton season formally opened in the latter part of July, when the first bale from South Texas arrived in Houston to be weighed in on the floor of the Exchange and treated with customary celebration. Shortly before that, factors and commission merchants began arriving back in town from summer vacations, and the calendar began to fill with evening socials for husbands and wives, and daytime coffees and at-homes for women. I was more than grateful for the short period of training for these activities I'd received in Galveston. Life with Papa had not prepared me for any kind of normal existence, and it seemed strange to look back and realize in what isolation the three of us lived, never entertaining callers, never accepting invitations, showing no hospitality to outsiders. Now I had my own calling cards printed. Now I had weekday afternoon at-homes in which people stayed for an hour or two of pleasant chitchat and light refreshments. And apart from getting acquainted with cotton people, I got to know others when we joined Christ Episcopal Church, where Neal had attended some while a bachelor, and had taken me the first time we shared a private moment together. There were benefit luncheons, meetings of the Ladies Parish Association, parties at the rectory for couples in the parish. Neal was soon serving on three or four committees at once, often hosting a meeting in our home.

There was nothing missing from our life except children, and by the end of September I knew I was expecting. Neal was jubilant. I was, too, though now I felt obliged to be in contact with Olivia and Papa again. In all these months I had not seen or heard from them. I had written three times in the early weeks of my marriage, but none of my letters was answered and finally I gave up.

I was both hopeful and reluctant about sitting down to write to them about the baby. This would be Papa's first grandchild. Regardless of how cruel he had been, he surely had the right to get to know this child, I reasoned. And perhaps . . . perhaps this might be just the chance I had always hoped for to gain his love and acceptance.

I started many letters over the next few weeks, only to throw them away finished or unfinished. Neal could not understand why I felt I must write. One night he said, "You are just letting yourself in for another disappointment."

His remark struck me wrong. "That is easy for you to say. As soon as we learned I was expecting, you picked up the telephone and called your family long distance. Why shouldn't I want to include my family?"

He shook his head. "That is not the point. You keep hoping to win your father's love, and the idea that an expected grandchild might warm his heart is very naïve. But do whatever you wish."

"I will. And you'll see that I am right."

The next morning I mailed a six-page letter in which I tried to state gently that, while I was sorry to have caused Papa so much heartache, my marriage was a completely happy one, and that Neal was very good to me and a fine provider. Then I broached the subject at hand and told Papa and Olivia that it would give me great pleasure to bring the baby for them to see, and to have both of them attend the christening on the appointed day.

I read the letter over a number of times, to be sure I sounded confident and assured about my life, and about their positive decision to share in this happy event. I ended with, "I await your early reply. Love, Alvareda."

No reply came.

To his credit, Neal did not remind me I had been wrong. One chilly fall evening as we sat quietly before a log fire, he suddenly realized tears were streaming down my face. "Come here," he said, and took me on his lap. "You know that my family loves you like a daughter. You had my father wrapped around your finger the first time he saw you." Then he smiled and put his arms around my abdomen. "It's going to be hard enough to keep from spoiling the child with just one set of adoring grandparents.

"Promise me you will not let your father upset you anymore. We both have so much to be thankful for."

"Oh, I know," I said, and nuzzled close to him. We sat for a while longer, basking in the warmth of the fire and of each other. Finally he began to kiss me and said, "Should I start carrying you up the stairs now that you're nearly four months along?"

"I don't know. Are we going upstairs?"

"Yes, if I can wait that long."

I giggled and observed, "I feel certain we're going to have a houseful of children."

In late October Neal was called out of town on business from Tuesday evening till Friday night. It was the first time we had been apart, and through the week I spent equal time sitting in a chair, tears of misery washing down my face, and occupying myself with chores in order to keep from dwelling on how much I missed him. Around five o'clock on Thursday evening I began the task of snipping dead leaves off the houseplants, having run out of anything else to do. I was in the parlor, working on the Boston fern, when I heard a knock at the door.

I was not expecting company, and a rush of hope that Neal might surprise me by returning early sent me hurriedly to open the door, slipping the scissors in my apron pocket as I went.

I almost didn't recognize David Leider. He had grown a moustache and beard, and his frame was a little more filled out than the last time I saw him. That difference was not disturbing; his obvious state was. I had never seen him so distracted; his eyes were grave; his tie, loosened. When he took off his hat, his hair lay in clumps as though he had been running his fingers through it.

"Alvareda, let me come in," he begged. He had been drinking; I could tell from his voice. My heart beat a little faster. I was not at all certain I should allow him in.

"I suppose," I said at last. "There's coffee on the stove."

"No, I don't want any." He stood just inside the door. "Is it true, what I heard just now at the Cotton Exchange? You've married Neal Gerrard?"

For a moment I just gaped at him. Now that I realized the reason for the sudden visit, my knees felt weak under me. I hoped we could get it over quickly, and he would leave. I folded my hands and stood across from him. "It is," I assured him.

"But how could you have done that to me, Alvareda?"

His impertinence angered me. "You have no right to ask me that. I had no commitment to you."

"But you did. I counted on you. You led me to believe you would be my wife. I can't believe you've betrayed me."

He sounded like a child, furious to have had his toy taken away from him. But you can't deal with a grown man in the way you can a child, and I was more frightened by the moment because I didn't know how far this would go. I tried to humor him. "I owe you my thanks . . . since the day I met Neal he was standing on your porch in Harrisburg. We were married this summer in Galveston," I explained and smiled. I could feel my lips trembling.

He kept studying my face, as though trying to understand what I was really trying to tell him. David could never believe the simple truth unless it pleased him. "You did it just to please your father, Samuel, didn't you?" he charged.

"I did not," I replied, as calmly as I could. Of course, he would not accept this, for believing otherwise was much kinder to his conceit.

His expression softened just a little. "But surely you understood how much I loved you. I'd have done anything for you. All you had to do was give me time."

I would have given anything for Neal to walk through the door at that moment. "David, what happened between us was over long ago, when Papa insisted I not see you anymore. I thought you would have realized that, especially by now."

He was completely perplexed by my rejection. "Why would you choose Neal Gerrard over me, if not to please Samuel? What does Neal have that I lack?"

Gentleness, I almost said, and goodness. But that would have drawn him on and I didn't want that. "I really think you had better leave," I said firmly. But the conviction that I could make him do so was missing from my voice, I could tell as I uttered the words. Tears of frustration were burning behind my eyes. I felt trapped. I looked away. "Please, just go."

He mistook my feelings.

His voice became softer. He stepped forward and put his hand on my arm. I shifted away. "Listen, I told you when Samuel ran me off that I would be back, that I wouldn't take that from him. You were young; I realized that. But you should have waited."

What he said about promising to return was true. Yet I had not considered his intentions binding because Papa's authority was absolute. And because, while I felt terribly sorry for David after what had happened to his family and didn't want to injure his feelings more, I knew then I did not love him, or trust him, and felt secure in the armor Papa had provided me against him.

"I made no promise to you," I said. I was about to tell him, further, that Neal had won my love, not him, but he interrupted.

"I came to see you, more than once. Olivia always stood in the way, and I couldn't stay around Harrisburg waiting for my chance to come. A man has to spend most of his time getting ahead, especially when his family has been ruined."

If you had been the kind of man Neal is, you'd have come through the front door just like he did, instead of sneaking around, I mused. . . .

"I came on the evening of your graduation," he continued, "and Olivia told me you were leaving on a tour of Europe, and would not be back till around Thanksgiving. I asked if I might try again then . . . she didn't answer. But I waited anyway, thinking you were far away, when you were really here.

"Alvareda, look at me now." He turned my face toward his. "I know you love me; you always have and you always will." He moved his hand around my head.

"Leave me alone, or I'll hit you," I warned. He smiled. I pulled away. He wrapped his other arm around me and pulled me against him. I felt panicked that he could be doing this to me again. As his lips touched mine I felt a wave of revulsion that nearly made me gag. I suddenly remembered the scissors. I reached into my pocket and pulled them out, but my hand was so shaky I sent them clattering to the floor. The noise alerted him. He relaxed his hold just enough. I twisted out of his arm and kicked his shin. When he grabbed his leg I slapped his face with all the force I could summon.

He glanced down at the scissors, then up at me, as though he could not fathom what had happened. "You get out of my house right now, and don't ever come back," I said. He was no angrier than I was now, and I didn't feel afraid of him anymore.

He picked up his hat and pointed his finger at me. "You've just made the biggest mistake of your life. I loved you enough to overlook what your father did to my family; having you was worth that much to me. But that's all over now."

"I don't know what you're talking about," I said. I was trembling all over; my voice shook. "My father is not responsible for your troubles."

"That's what he would like for you to think, but he did a lot more than just bring my father to ridicule in the church."

I looked at him, puzzled.

"After my father left Harrisburg, his business in ruins, good old Samuel stopped to see my mother and 'list' our house. Too bad, he could not find a buyer that would pay the price she was asking. So he took it off her hands for a good deal less than it was worth, and hired her to run the boardinghouse.

"I found out he turned around six months later and sold that property for three times what he paid her for it—at the time it looked like a railroad track was to be laid nearby."

"But, David, he had no way of knowing that—"

"Oh, he knew all right. He was one of the people involved with the railroad company. You don't have to believe me. I can show you the proof. I'd have sued Samuel if I'd had any legal grounds. But he managed to be sure he stayed just within the law."

I shook my head. "You're a liar. If you really had proof, you would have confronted him with it," I told him.

He took a step forward. His voice was low, and more threatening than ever. "Don't you think I want to? But my mother still lives in Harrisburg. She is employed by him, remember, and she has other kids to raise."

I did not know what to say to him. I knew that my father was mean and cantankerous, but I could not believe he was dishonest. David was just unable to face the truth about his father, that was all. And regardless, he had no right to take out his feelings about Papa on me, or to think he could bargain with my affections.

"Whatever happened between you and my father has nothing to do with me," I said. "I suggest you take it up with him, and leave me out of it."

"Oh, I intend to. You had better hope your father is as fine a man as he would have you believe because I'm going after him now. If there is anything at all I can get on him, I'll destroy him."

I could not believe his viciousness. "Get out," I said, and pointed to the door.

I sat in the parlor for a long while after he left, trying to collect myself. I was thankful that my own instincts had guided me away from him long ago, yet now I was more afraid of him than ever. Since he was angry at me as well as Papa, would he try to hurt both of us . . . maybe even Neal as well?

The thought sent a shudder through me. Oh, surely not, I told myself, for how could he? I would not mention David's visit to Neal, I decided. It would wind up with Neal confronting him and that would just arouse more trouble for all of us, and might make David even more determined to get even.

I looked at the scissors, still on the floor, and the whole specter of David's forcing himself on me played itself over again in my mind. I had a sharp sense of loathing for him that I felt, all at once, I must get rid of. I drew a bath and scrubbed my face and body so hard the skin felt tender.

Chapter 9

One afternoon in early February, when I was homebound both because the weather was cold and nasty, and because the baby was soon expected, I received a message that my father was seriously ill. The short note from Olivia said that Papa had suffered some kind of seizure and, if I could make the trip to Harrisburg without endangering the child, to please come at once.

I tried but could not reach Neal, so I left a message at his office and boarded the five o'clock train. All the way there I fretted over the word "seizure." So vague . . . yet so onerous. And it must have been serious or Olivia would never have sent for me. She had nursed Papa through hundreds of illnesses. He was often exposed to fevers and colds and sore throats because he traveled in terrible weather and often returned home wet and chilled to the bone.

Yet now he was sixty-eight years old. Perhaps his physical stamina was not a match for his strong will. He was the kind of man one would expect to live to a very old age. Indeed, I had been told that his father lived way up into his nineties. Yet, Papa had worked very hard for all of his life. Maybe this had taken its toll on his health. I remembered in that conversation I overheard last May, when he mentioned something to Olivia about not having unlimited funds, and said that his commission would not be enough to cover some balance he owed, or something of that sort. I could not recall exactly his words. I had been too preoccupied with my own situation to listen carefully. But now I had been married eight months, and I realized how hard Neal worked to provide for us. Papa was surely too old to work as hard as he did. . . . Had our way of life in Harrisburg placed an unfair burden on him? I had never thought we lived extravagantly, but perhaps I was simply naïve. . . .

When I arrived at the door, Olivia hugged me and burst into tears. "Oh, sister, I've missed you so," she sobbed. I held her close, but I did not cry. Her distraught state of mind bolstered me. She had always dried my tears. Now she needed my strength.

I took off my coat and hat. "Sit down and tell me what has happened."

"Oh, forgive me. I should have offered you something hot. In your condition, and after your long ride here. Wait. Let me brew some tea for us. Papa is sleeping now."

I sat down in the parlor and let her fix the tea tray. Perhaps the age-old ritual would steady her. It was very strange to be in this house again. Surely it had never been so close, dark and drab, so musty. Olivia's knitting basket was beside her favorite parlor chair. The piano I used to play was closed tight. I could look through to the foyer and see the hall tree. Papa's coat hung on one hook. His hat hung on another. How my heart used to contract when I would walk in and see his hat and coat there. My first thought was always one of concern over his mood.

Now . . . it seemed forever since I lived from day to day worrying about that. . . .

Olivia was pouring the tea. I asked her if Papa was here when the "seizure," as she called it, occurred.

She sat down and shook her head. "It was so puzzling. It happened yesterday evening. I came in from some shopping. I saw his coat and hat on the hall floor, as though he had thrown them down. I called to him. He didn't answer. I went into his office and found him behind his desk. His face was pale. He could not speak to me. I felt of his forehead. It was damp and cool. I don't believe I have ever been so frightened. I went for the doctor at once. He examined him and said he believed Papa had suffered apoplexy—a hemorrhage in the brain. We could only keep him quiet and watch him for the next twenty-four hours.

"I started to send for you then, but I . . . well . . . I couldn't decide what to do. I decided just to wait. The doctor felt nothing should be done to stimulate him. I—oh, I—"

"It's all right. I understand."

"We made up something of a bed on the sofa in his office. I know it isn't comfortable, but the doctor told me he should not be moved unless absolutely necessary."

"And that's where he is now?"

"Yes. He has not changed very much since the onset of the seizure. He has spoken. Now and then something intelligible comes out. But I don't know what he was doing when it happened, whether something brought it on, or whether it occurred without any provocation."

"You said he sometimes was intelligible. Did he call my name, by chance?"

"There was a time, early this morning, when I almost thought he was trying to say your name. But I wasn't sure. The doctor came around noontime. He said frankly that he did not know if Papa would survive. His heart is not strong since he had that last fever several years ago. And after all, he is getting older."

I sipped my tea. "Well, I suppose all we can do is wait."

"I do think that you ought to see him when he wakes up. I do not know if he will last through another night." She began to cry again. I realized for the first time that, while her life had been severely limited by Papa, there would be no center to it should he die.

"Is Neal coming here?" she asked, dabbing her eyes.

"Not at this point," I said. "I left a message that he should not come unless I sent a wire."

"Yes. I think that's best," she said, and although I knew what she meant, that she feared Neal's presence might be even more upsetting than mine, I allowed her to correct herself. "I mean, all we can do is wait, just as you said. No need for Neal to interrupt his busy schedule now."

"Olivia, there is something I want to talk to you about," I said. For a long time I had wanted to confide in her about David's upsetting visit last October. I told her all that he said to me. "Is there any truth at all in it?" I asked.

She was silent at length, then said, "Not at all, sister. David is just bitter, twisting things to suit himself. I wouldn't put any credence in anything he says about Papa. He hasn't bothered you any further, I hope?"

I shook my head.

"Well and good, then," she said with a nod. "You . . . surely you wouldn't say anything to Papa about it tonight. It might upset him."

"No, no, of course not. I haven't mentioned it to anyone except you, and I won't."

She smiled in approval, then shook her head as though in dismay at David's misguided ways.

Papa awoke at a little past eight in the evening, shortly after Olivia and I had eaten a light supper. Since the clock struck seven she had walked to his door regularly, to see if he was awakening. I did not follow her. I had the same feeling of reticence I had once entertained when considering a climb up the stairs to his third-floor quarters. Wherever he was, in whatever state, I dreaded that first moment of his acknowledgment of my presence.

Now she approached and said, "He is more coherent, I believe. I've told him you are here, and that I will send you in to see him."

"What did he say?"

"Nothing. But his eyes seemed to suggest he knew what I was talking about."

I took a deep breath and walked in. My first shock, as I stood at the side of his little makeshift bed, was the extent to which my father had aged. Surely his face had more lines now than when I last saw him. His eyes were sunk back, his forehead more prominent than I remembered, and his mouth tighter around his teeth. I wondered if my leaving him had so affected the steady downfall of his health. "Papa?"

He slowly turned his head and half opened his eyes. I thought I saw surprise registered there. His hands moved slightly on the blanket. "Why did you come back?"

"Olivia said you were ill, Papa. I was concerned about you."

"You . . . you—" His voice drifted off.

"What is it, Papa?"

"Ruined. Everything . . . ruined."

"What, Papa? Are you talking about my leaving? You have Olivia. She loves you more than anything."

He paused as though considering this. "No. It was you. Fool!"

I could hardly hear him, and was drawing closer without realizing it. His chest wheezed. I thought of what Olivia said about his heart being weak. I didn't know whether to stay or go. I wasn't sure he realized it was me.

"Followed me . . ." he began, then sighed. "I—I would have gone on—" he began, and his voice got very soft. I thought what I read on his lips was, "taking care of you." But I was not sure.

He was still for a long time. I began to think he had died, and I was horrified. I stepped back and turned to go for Olivia. Then I heard him say, "Get out. I don't want to see you anymore."

Tears sprang to my eyes. "All right, I'll go," I said. "But I'm not going to worry about you loving me anymore, do you hear?"

"Get . . . out . . ." he began, then it was as though a flash of pain went through him. He winced and caught his breath. I made for the door. Olivia appeared. "What is it? I heard your voice, sister."

I shook my head and fled from the room. I rushed to the kitchen and ran water over my hands and face. I was more angry than anything else—angry with Papa, angry with myself, angry with everything. I felt somehow that I would not speak to him again, that he would not get well. I feared that I had squandered my final chance with him. I should not have let him get me mad. I should have defied him by being patient and gentle. I stood there until Olivia came back. I was trying to steady myself, to do the best thing for the child I was carrying.

"Are you all right?" she asked.

"Yes. But I'd like to go home now. If there is any way we could reach Neal, I'd like very much for him to come and get me."

"Sister, there is icy rain outside. I think it would be safer if you stayed the night. I'll put you in my room. The bed is comfortable. I'm going to stay down here on the parlor sofa so that I can hear if Papa needs anything."

"All right," I agreed at length. I felt very tired. "I didn't even get a chance to talk to him about the baby."

"It's just as well," she said. "Let's go upstairs. I've already lit the fire. It's nice and warm up there. Come." She kept an arm around me all the way up the stairs, and turned down the bed while I changed into nightclothes. "It's nice to have you here," she said as I got into bed.

"It's nice to be with you again, in here. Your rooms have always been the only friendly ones in the house."

Indeed they had never seemed more hospitable. The candles were lit at the bedside. The fire flickered behind the grate. There was a rosy glow over all, and the bed linens were soft and warm. I remembered our many teatimes up here in front of the fireplace . . . our stolen moments of girl-talk and giggles in an otherwise drab existence.

She fluffed the pillows and straightened the coverlet. "If there is nothing else you need, I'll go downstairs now. Sister, I have wanted to tell you since you came to the door, you do look lovelier than I've ever seen you. It must be wonderful to have a child."

"It is. Come, let's see if the baby will give us a little kick." I drew her near and placed her hand on my abdomen. Nothing. We waited a while, but nothing.

She smiled. "Perhaps the baby is as exhausted as the mother." She kissed my cheek and went out of the room. I lay back on the pillows and looked at the fire. I had felt the baby moving shortly before I went in to see Papa, and that was the last time. I had never really paid attention to the amount of time in between the baby's movements. It seemed that, during the night, they usually went on and on. Often they awakened me and sometimes disturbed Neal's sleep as well.

I yawned at last and blew out the candles by the bed. It was going to be a lonely night without Neal, but I was so tired . . . so very tired. . . .

I slept till almost eight o'clock the next morning, and would have slept longer still, but Olivia came in and pulled the drapes open, letting in the morning light.

"Is the sun shining?" I asked, yawning.

"No. It's another gray day. I've brought you some tea." She walked over to the bed, and propped up the pillows behind me. I could see now that her eyes were red and tearful. "Papa?"

"He died sometime in the night. The doctor has already been here."

"Oh, sister," I said, and took her hands.

"Why don't you stay up here for a while, and get your bearings? Mr. Daigle will be here at ten o'clock, and I can make the arrangements. I suppose we'll have the funeral day after tomorrow, and probably by tomorrow he'll have Papa ready to . . . lie in state . . . in the parlor. What do you think?"

"Whatever you wish."

After she left the room, I lay there sipping my tea. What a cruel irony our last conversation had been. I went over it in my mind again and again. What he was trying to convey in his delirium I had no idea. It was all too clear, however, exactly what his feelings were for me. I was only sorry I had lashed out at him. I should never have done that. What if, by doing so, I had prompted his death? If my leaving all those months ago had begun a decline in his health, and my coming yesterday had posed too much of a strain on his failing heart, then had I not destroyed my father completely? It seemed almost as though I were born to this end. From the time I was six years old I had, step by step, created disaster for him.

Oh, Papa, I thought, and wept.

Early in the morning on the day before the funeral, the undertaker brought Papa's body back home to us. I was in the kitchen buttering bread for tea when I heard the doorbell ring, shortly followed by a few muffled words between Mr. Daigle and Olivia, then another interval before the sound of many shuffling feet, and quick phrases, "Careful there, don't hit that door facing." "That's it, just on the other side of that table." "No, a little more to the left. Is that right, Miss Cane?" It was as though they were moving in a large piece of furniture recently ordered for delivery. I heard more muffled conversation, then at last, the door closed. I wondered whether the casket was uncovered now. Was Olivia standing in front of it, inspecting the work on Papa's body? I didn't want to go in there. I kept buttering bread and lingering. I washed the knife and put everything away. I loaded the tea tray and stood beside the kitchen table for a while longer. Why should it be so hard to look at someone dead? Yet it was. It was no easier to face the prospect of seeing Papa's lifeless body than it had been all those years ago to view my mother.

"Come in and look," said Olivia as I finally emerged with the tea tray. I nodded reluctantly, took in a breath, and walked over there. The worst part was that first glance, which took in the whole setting: the long brown polished box with its brass handles, the table underneath, the white pillow and tufted lining that enshrouded him. Once I got past that, it was a little easier.

"I think he looks well, don't you?" said Olivia.

"He certainly looks peaceful," I said. His whiskers neatly trimmed, his hair combed back into place—a little too slick to his head to look natural, I thought, but did not say so—his starched white collar and black tie neatly in place, it was hard to believe that vigorous ball of energy could be stilled forever inside its shell. I could not help wondering what would become of Papa's soul. His attitude of superiority over others . . . his cruelty . . . his treachery. Would all this be forgiven as we were taught in Sunday School? Yet . . . who was I to judge? I had done my share of bringing him the grief that so changed and embittered him.

Olivia knelt and kissed him. I did not. I could not bear to come that close to death. Not now. I had sent a message to Neal that he should wait and come for the funeral. The weather made traveling hazardous, and Olivia needed my help, I told him. What I did not tell him was that I kept waiting for signs of life in my own body. I could not bear the thought that Neal would anxiously reach for the bursts of growing life that he had so looked forward to, and find stillness. Maybe in a few hours from now the baby would move.

If not in a few hours, then, during the night. If not then, maybe next day. . . .

In the afternoon while Olivia was busy talking to some people whom Papa had known, I became restless and decided to walk around. I mounted the stairs, thinking I would go into Olivia's sitting room and find a book to read. Then I came to the second-floor landing and stopped cold. I looked up toward Papa's rooms. They would now be exposed by the unquenchable daylight, their every nook and corner laid bare. Vulnerable. I wanted in some strange and morbid way to walk in there and look over his things. I wanted to pull out drawers and throw open cabinet doors. I placed a foot upon the narrow stairway, then paused again. What would Olivia say? Yet, indeed, what could she say? She had been the simple conductor of Papa's wishes during his lifetime. Now his death yielded her a toothless lion.

I looked down. I could hear the voices of visitors, in their customary funeral drone, all of them, I knew, eager to say just the right thing at a time when nothing was right. . . .

I felt giddy. I looked up again. Then, I seemed to glide with ease toward my father's sanctuary.

The door was unlocked. I pushed it slowly and looked timidly inside. Papa's bed was bare, the bedclothes gone, the pillows missing. It made me think of Mother's room after her death. I had walked into her room on the day of her funeral and I remembered nothing about the looks of her room except the bare bed, white and massive as an open plain.

I walked around, feeling already like an intruder who took chary advantage of the owner's absence. I opened his wardrobe. There were all the suits of clothes he owned, except the one he would be buried in. At the end of the rack hung his Texas uniform, in which he had taken such pride. I wondered why Olivia hadn't chosen it for him to be buried in. Down below, a neat row of polished boots. There were a dozen pair. I closed the doors. Next I walked over to his dresser, thinking how ordinary was his tonic water, his shaving brush and razor strop, his collar buttons, his hairbrush, his pocket knife. Why had he kept his rooms so secret? What had he to hide?

Perhaps his whiskey. He drank a lot of it. There was one empty bottle and one half-empty on a table near his bed. But that was no secret. He often drank in front of me, and by the time I was fifteen I realized there were mornings when he awoke in a stupor from having had too much whiskey the night before. He often grumbled through a breakfast that he hardly ate, then, if possible, he'd go back to bed and the house would be peaceful for a few hours.

Oh Lord, what we went through to get along with him!

I had looked over everything, and yet found nothing of significance. I walked over to his bedside then, and saw a photograph. I hadn't noticed it before because it lay flat, rather than upright. The frame support was broken on it. I picked it up. The face was of a woman I had never seen before. Or had I? It was difficult to tell. The face was in shadows because of the placement of the hat. It could even be my mother, I realized, though somehow I didn't really think that was the case. The forehead was a little wide; the eyes larger. I held it in my hand for a while, considering. Finally I put it down. There was no date on it. It might even have been a portrait of his own mother, or of his first wife, Olivia's mother. Did it agree with the painting downstairs? It was hard to tell. I thought of something else. Where were the pictures of my mother, which I had felt so sure must be kept up here?

I went about opening drawers. I burrowed my hand under articles of clothing and linens, plunged my fingers into packets of paper, looked through old wallets and inside small boxes and envelopes. Nothing. All at once I was aware of time passing. I hurried out and quickly descended the stairs. I kept wondering why there were no pictures of my mother. It wasn't till much later in the day that I realized there may never have been any.

She was the daughter of a poor farmer. Probably the family didn't have portraits done, and maybe she and Papa simply overlooked having any made later. One day I would ask Olivia.

I felt a little guilty as we spent the remainder of the day together for having sneaked about rather than simply stated my intentions and opened my father's door. Yet I also felt slightly disappointed for, at the time, it seemed there was nothing significant about Papa's room except his fetish for privacy.

At the graveside service in Glendale Cemetery, while the soughing February wind caused the tall trees to sway and the burial flowers to list and flutter, Olivia became overwrought. She had to be supported by Neal on one side and another kind man on the other. I felt sorry for her now, in her black mourning dress and bonnet. What would she do? For a while she would busy herself with matters of his estate—it had been left entirely to her, as expected—but what then? I looked at Neal, and felt a rush of gratitude for our lives together. We would return to Houston that night, to our cheery home with its organdy curtains and small yard, and talk of the child so soon to come as we went about our own routine. For Olivia there was no one; only a big old empty house.

I did not feel well during the final weeks of pregnancy, and there were no real signs of life. Now and then I would awaken during the night, sure I had felt movement. Or was it only a dream? It never happened during the day. On the Monday after Easter, our first child—named Alice Marie for my mother —was stillborn. Despite the fact I had suspected this, I was not in any way prepared. Instead of the thrilling moment when the doctor raised the child in front of me, pinched and red, bellowing its claim to life, there was the moment when the doctor whisked the infant into wrappings held by the nurse and, speaking in hushed tones, not letting me see my child at all, closed the

door behind the nurse as she took the child away. I raised up in bed, screaming, "No! No, let me see, I want my baby!" and in moments Neal was there,
holding me in his arms while I furiously beat my hands against his chest,
crying out again and again, then at last, in defeat, falling limply on his shoulder, weeping until I was completely spent, the helpless protest left to smolder.
He kept holding me, rocking me in his arms, tears rolling down his cheeks.

From the moment I was calm again and able to think, I wondered if all the
happy months of marriage to Neal, all our pleasant anticipation about the
baby, were only a surreptitious force gathering to shatter me. Or did I cause
this, in those final moments with Papa?

For a long time I could not talk about it, could not adequately express the
feeling there was a deep cavern hollowed out inside me now, and my guilt lay
at the bottom of it. Although he, too, was grieving, Neal tried to strengthen
me. Mrs. Gerrard came immediately and stayed with us for two weeks. She
said she had lost four babies in her childbearing years, and, as in my case, the
doctor said she was perfectly healthy and must simply try again. It had been
after these heartaches that Neal was born. I spent much time recovering up in
our bedroom, gazing out the window. Finally one evening Neal came home
from work and said, "It's time to snap out of it, darling. I have two tickets to
Grey's Opera House tonight—there's a comedy playing—so let's get dressed
and go."

"I don't feel like it," I said dourly.

"Alvareda," he sighed, and sat on the edge of the bed. "You have to get
over this and go on."

I glanced at him. "That's all right for you, but you don't know what I've
been through."

"She was my daughter, too," he said in an injured tone.

I paused a moment and looked at him. Over the weeks I had been oblivious
to his feelings, sometimes speaking sharply to him, sometimes taciturn. What
he was voicing now I had seen in his eyes for a while. He could understand
my grief, but not my resentment. I had never been able to bring myself to tell
him the details of my mother's death because remembering was too painful. I
could still see my father's stricken face. I could not speak of it now. Yet he
deserved to know at least what I believed to be the reason for the death of our
child. I took in a deep breath. "Neal, do you believe people are sometimes
punished for things . . . that is . . . if someone did something terrible,
then maybe God would . . . oh, I just don't know how to tell you this." I
could not look at him anymore. Tears filled my eyes.

He gently turned my face toward his. "What is it, darling? You can tell
me."

"That last time I saw Papa, I was so terrible, I—"

"What do you mean?"

"I was . . . so in hopes he would forgive me for Mama's death, say he loved me, and when he wouldn't I just couldn't stand it. I yelled at him, told him I didn't care if he loved me anymore. Oh, Neal, I never felt a sign of life from the baby after that." I shook my head. "That's why I can't help believing that losing Alice Marie was punishment, and I'm so afraid now. I close my eyes at night and all I can think of is this happening again and again, that every time I carry a child there will be tragedy at the end, and I don't know if I can stand it, Neal——"

He placed his hands on my shoulders. "Alvareda, calm down and listen to me. Were your father an ordinary man, he would not have withheld his love from you because of an accident, no matter how serious. Can't you see you're punishing yourself? You are not being punished at all. And I don't believe for a minute this will happen to us again. Look, now, you've just had too much all at once. I'm here now and I love you. We'll have other children. We'll go on with life."

"Oh, Neal, are you sure?" I asked, holding both his hands as though they were my only rescue. I was so grateful for the kind of man he was, the wealth of understanding he always gave me. I kissed his fingers and hands again and again, and pulled him close to me. He began to kiss me, and to fumble with the fastenings on my dress. I needed to know that I was still beautiful to him, that what happened had not placed something between us that he could cover with kind words but not camouflage in the way he expressed his love to me. Each of these things I did not fully realize until he'd worked the dress off my shoulders and arms, and slipped down the tight-fitting chemise under it. My breasts were still somewhat enlarged for the child who did not live to suckle them. I was so afraid that the sight of me might remind him of the failure we'd been through. When he looked at me I turned my face away. He turned it back. His eyes were wet with tears. "Oh, Alvareda, I love you so," he said, and buried his head against me.

I put my arms around him and whispered, "I've needed you so badly, Neal. It's like a terrible aching inside me."

He rose and lifted me against him. It felt so good to absorb his warmth, to feel his heart beating against mine. Hurriedly we both undressed and fell into bed, grasping each other feverishly. It had been such a long time since we had made love. When I felt his flesh enter mine I knew such complete comfort that I did not want it ever to end.

I slept peacefully that night, for the first time since Papa died, and in the morning I awoke thinking about the photograph I found in his room, and wondering who it was.

Chapter 10

I had been too preoccupied with myself to pay attention to Neal's business concerns. There were a number of serious considerations in his mind that I was not aware of till later.

One was that he was no longer happy with the amount of traveling he had to do. As a bachelor he had not minded spending much of his time out of town. Now he wanted to be home with me. As soon as possible, he wanted very much for us to have another child, for he realized that was the only thing that could truly lift me out of the doldrums. Then, should I find I was expecting, he did not want to leave me alone during the months before childbirth. Apart from all that, his business was growing rapidly; he was forced to spread himself too thin.

He did not speak to me about his plan to resolve the problems he faced. Yet one night as we cleared away the dinner dishes, he said, "Did you hear that David Leider is getting married?"

At the mention of his name my pulse quickened. "No," I told him, and cleared my throat.

"He's marrying March Bennett's daughter, Carlotta."

The name clicked into place. Her father was a prominent cotton merchant who was responsible for several railroads to Houston. It was Carlotta who often accompanied her mother to Lyceum board meetings. I remembered once being in a group of ladies sipping coffee at some affair or another. They knew the Bennetts, and one said that Carlotta was getting to the age where her failure to be married was worrisome. Another lady had said it was hard to understand. Carlotta was such a pretty girl. The first offered that she was very proper and starchy. Perhaps too much so.

And that was the girl David Leider was to marry.

Neal almost voiced my thoughts when he said, "Marriage might be a good stabilizer for David."

"Yes, you're probably right."

That was the end of the conversation. It was some months later before I heard that March Bennett was retiring, and I asked Neal if David was to take over the factoring and compress business, or did Mr. Bennett have a son prepared to step in and take over. Neal knew more than I would have expected, but I did not place any significance on it at the time.

"David will take over. None of March's sons are interested in cotton. Two of them are attorneys living out of state, and one, I think, is a doctor out near San Antonio."

"I wonder when the wedding will take place."

"In December, I understand."

"Sounds as though you're in touch with David quite a lot," I said, feeling nervous.

"No, just the grapevine, mostly. The other day I had a brief chat with March at the Cotton Exchange. He said he is very pleased about the marriage, and is also pleased about David taking over the firm. He feels that David has a lot of ability."

Well, that sounded a little less serious, I thought, relieved. Though David's vindictive attitude toward Papa was surely of small importance now that Papa was dead, I still felt very uncomfortable at the thought of David being around Neal. I hoped they could keep their mutual involvement in the cotton industry at a distance.

One night in the fall of 1888, Neal came home from work and said he had a surprise. "David and I are forming a partnership."

"Oh?" I felt I'd had the wind knocked out of me. I put a platter of meat down on the table and sat down in a chair.

"I guess you could tell I had been thinking about this for months," he began.

No, I had not guessed. . . .

"The one thing that held me back for so long was David's failure to marry. Frankly, I wouldn't take in a business partner who was not married."

"Stability," I echoed, a lump rising in my throat.

"Yes. I always felt David had everything that would make him a good partner to me—he is less of an administrator, finds paperwork bothersome. But he is a whiz at persuading people—better than I am—and thanks to his uncles, he has many, many contacts. . . . What's the matter? I thought you'd be glad."

"Oh, I—it's just, I'm so surprised," I stammered.

He took my hand across the table. "Best of all, David carries a suitcase as naturally as a turtle carries a shell. He can do some of the traveling, so that I can spend more time with you."

I squeezed his hand and managed a small smile. I believe he was truly caught up in his own optimism too much to realize how I was feeling.

He continued, ". . . and it'll be a good beginning for us, with the Bennett business added to mine."

I nodded. If March was as smart as people believed, he wouldn't leave his business to someone like David by himself . . . . oh Lord, David Neal's partner. Every time I thought of it—

". . . with David to handle selling, I'll have more time to see to the administrative side of the business." He ate a few bites, then began to tell me about the compress business. It hurt me to be unable to respond the way he expected; yet when it came to David I could not conjure up any but the most negative feelings. If only he had discussed this with me beforehand, rather than surprising me. . . .

". . . The compress is far out, north of the city, but I won't have to be out there too much. We're bringing in David's first cousin from Brazoria to be office manager and accountant. He has experience, and David thinks highly of him. When David is in town, he can help oversee things out there.

"Oh yes, the Bennetts are throwing a big to-do next month to honor David and Carlotta. A lot of cotton people will be there. He wants to announce the merger that night."

He reached for my hand again. "Darling, you've got to stop dwelling on the past and look forward to the future. Try to work up some of that enthusiasm that means so much."

I smiled again and told him I would try, and was somehow relieved he applied my strange response to the wrong reason.

The party was held on the very evening we had received the wedding invitation in the mail and it was not till I read the fancy engraved card that I realized David was marrying into a Roman Catholic family. The ceremony would be held under the towering spire of Annunciation Church. It had always seemed to me that Catholics took their religion with special seriousness. To my knowledge, David had not stepped inside a church since the scandal in his family. Had this young woman changed his mind? If so, maybe she had a more profound influence on him than I first expected.

I certainly hoped so, and I tried to concentrate on the positive side of this development. Yet, as the day wore on and the time came to dress for the party, I was as nervous about seeing David again as ever. I had chosen a deep blue velvet dress with wide ruffles of ecru lace around the neckline and sleeves, and fringing the velvet tiers that made up the short train. I would wear a small headpiece of tiny flowers intertwined in lace and velvet ribbons. Neal stood in front of the mirror fiddling with his bow tie while I adjusted the headpiece and pinched my colorless cheeks in the vain hope of improvement. I was preoccupied and did not realize he had been talking to me. In a moment he said, "Well, don't you agree?"

"With what?"

"Never mind. What's the matter with you? You're so distracted lately."

"Nothing. I'm just fine."

He paused, then turned from the mirror and faced me. "You look so pretty tonight. And I really think that getting out again is going to be good for you. It'll put some color in your cheeks."

I nodded and he reached for my cape on the bed. "Hurry up, we'll be late," he cautioned, and kissed my cheek as he put the cape on my shoulders. "I know it's rough, and I appreciate your making the effort tonight more than you could imagine."

As we went down the stairs I felt guilty for letting him continue to think that only the loss of our child affected my feelings about that night. Yet, what good would it do now to correct his notion?

In Houston almost everything revolved around Main Street. On the north end were the business offices and banks, terminating with the wharves at the foot of the street. In the central blocks were retail stores, small and large. On the southern end of Main were many of the most beautiful houses in the city, formidable structures with two or three stories, towers, long upper galleries, and wide promenades. Many of the homes were built by cotton people, and the March Bennett home, between Polk and Clay, was among the most pretentious.

Surrounded by a tall fence, the two-story dark brown brick structure was fronted by a wide-open railed porch. There were striped canopies on the big windows on the second story, and a tall pitched roof with brick chimneys climbing up both sides. On this night there were lights in all the downstairs windows, and a long line of fine carriages in front. There were twenty-four couples in attendance, and the party had already been written of in the morning *Post* as "the most important event of the social season, excepting of course the Z. Z. Club's Society Ball." Oh, how I wished I could have stayed at home, yet I simply had to overcome my feelings. The appearance of the four of us tonight would establish the merger's stability in front of others in the cotton industry. I could only hope that David had become as sincere as Neal thought him to be, or that perhaps I had misread David because of the circumstances we were in, and he was a much better man than he had revealed to me.

At the first of the evening, I truly thought I had been unfair to David. When we arrived, the guests were mingling, with champagne and little plates of hors d'oeuvres in their hands, being greeted and made comfortable by the hosts. March Bennett was a wiry little man with fuzzy hair, almost like an elf. Mrs. Bennett was a bit taller than her husband, with dark hair and large eyes. She wore a huge flower on her shoulder and rows and rows of pearls. David and Carlotta were busy posing for a portrait in the drawing room.

Carlotta favored her mother, except that she was a tiny human being. As I watched the picture being made, I was struck by the great difference in size between Carlotta and David. He towered over her, looking more like a father with his young daughter than a fiancé with his bride. She wore a dress of Nile green with a sash of black ribbon, and tiny pink flowers at the waist and in her auburn hair. She had an expression that was hard to describe. Worldly? Not exactly. I could not pinpoint it. She looked up at David with obvious adoration and now and then, as the photographer made an adjustment to the camera, she would say something to him and he would lean down as though very interested, and answer her. He seemed to be enchanted with her.

As they finished with their picture taking, David spotted us and came over while Carlotta was delayed with someone else. He shook Neal's hand, then took both my hands in his. "Well, Mrs. Gerrard, I can see that marriage has agreed with you."

I smiled through a frozen glare and offered congratulations on his engagement, then, to my relief, Neal struck up a conversation with David about business, saving me from the task of making small talk.

Just after we sat down at the long dining table, March Bennett stood up and summoned everyone's attention. He offered a toast to David and Carlotta, then he asked all four of us to stand and announced the partnership. "At the opening of 1889, the firm of Bennett, Gerrard, and Leider will open its doors in offices now occupied by Mr. Gerrard." Then, with an attempt at humor he added, "As soon as Molly and I have moved away to Wimberley within a year or two, I will extract my name from the firm and leave these fellows to their own devices. While they concern themselves with the procurement of a deep-water port in Houston, I will be quietly fishing for bass and hope we are all successful in our ventures. . . ."

On and on he droned. To me his words seemed condescending toward David and Neal, and I remembered in one of our recent talks, Neal said March Bennett was known to be "fluffed-up with pride."

After the waiters passed around trays with raisins and fruits, crackers and Edam, and poured claret wine, the small orchestra hired for the evening began tuning up for dancing in the large room across the foyer. Neal and I, Carlotta and David had been asked to lead off the dancing, and once several songs had been played and most everyone was on the floor, David approached and begged permission to dance with me.

As we worked our way to an empty place on the floor, I felt the life drain out of me. David put an arm around my waist and lifted my hand to waltz. "You don't seem pleased to see me tonight, Mrs. Gerrard," he said.

"We did not part on the best of terms last time we met," I told him.

We twirled around. "That should not worry you," he said.

"I suppose not, not now anyway," I replied. Without meaning to I was seeking reassurance from him, and I hated myself for it. He sensed this as quickly as a hunting dog sniffs out a wild deer in the wood, and smiled.

"Well, a person can't undo the past, they say, and besides, the future looks interesting. By the way, what do you think about the partnership?"

I could have slapped him. "I think—I think it will be as good as what you both put into it, and I have no doubt Neal will more than do his share."

He nodded. "Certainly no one could argue those points. Of course, after what I've already done for the firm, you could hardly call me a piker."

It took me a few moments to realize what he was talking about. Then I said, "Forgive me, but I can hardly see marriage to Carlotta Bennett as a personal sacrifice."

He threw back his head and laughed. "Oh, Alvareda, I have always appreciated the way we understand each other." He pulled me a little closer.

I decided to try to appeal to his kinder side. "She seems to adore you. I hope you'll appreciate *that,* and be good to her."

He held me away, smiling. "I do believe you're playing the devil's advocate, my dear. And I'm certain you'll be standing by to remind me when I slip from the pedestal on which my wife has me placed."

"You can depend on it."

We danced through a few more bars in silence. I was beginning to feel a little more comfortable, and to remember that David might have more than his share of shortcomings, but he had always respected someone who would keep him in check. Really, he was no more than an overgrown child. . . .

"Where will you and Carlotta set up housekeeping?"

"We've leased a house on Crawford, around the corner from Dr. Blake's house."

"That isn't but a few blocks from where we live."

"Well, don't worry, Mrs. Gerrard, it won't be long before we move. When the Bennetts pack up for Wimberley, Carlotta can move into this house. It's part of her inheritance."

"It seems you've come a long way from Harrisburg."

"It will never be far enough."

"Will your mother come for the wedding?"

"Yes, I finally persuaded her, though it took all the charm I could muster." My brow lifted in puzzlement.

"She doesn't care for people like my future in-laws."

"Why?"

"She doesn't like Catholics. But I assured her she needn't worry about that. I told the Bennetts I'd agree to a Catholic wedding, and that I would adopt the faith. But I didn't promise to be a *good* Catholic."

The music had stopped. I did not want David to think of me as an adversary, not when so much depended upon the four of us getting along. As we walked back to the edge of the floor I said, "When you and Carlotta return from your honeymoon trip, you must join us for dinner at our house. By the way, where are you going?"

"We board a train for California within an hour after the wedding reception. We'll be gone for two weeks, visiting Carlotta's brother."

"Oh, that's very nice," I said, yet thinking it odd to spend a honeymoon visiting relatives.

"I wanted to take my bride to Boston for a honeymoon without any family around, but my wishes were overruled."

Carlotta drew near and took David's arm. He smiled down at her and patted her hand. How phony he is, I thought, and felt the brief interlude of my own growing confidence that David had changed ebb away from me like the couples that now glided, arm in arm, back toward the dance floor.

It was shortly before Christmas when the Leiders returned from California, and we had them to dinner on a Saturday evening. Neal was brimming with things he wanted to talk over with David—in a little more than two weeks the joint firm would begin. I was like a child looking forward to Christmas, as I had been last year. This was to be our second Christmas together and therefore the second happy Christmas in my life.

I was in hopes that David and Carlotta would be happily married, and we could make this evening the beginning of an enjoyable association with them. If David found happiness with his new wife, he would no longer have any excuse for causing me misery.

I had decorated the table with holly and candles. I had Mrs. Masterson's recipe for chicken pie and Olivia's recipe for pecan cake. I worked for two days to make the house and the dinner gay. When the Leiders arrived there were candles in the windows and the smell of cinnamon and cloves in the air. The two of them, however, immediately dampened my spirits and Neal's too. They were anything but aglow with happiness.

When Neal and I had returned from a week's honeymoon in New Orleans a year and a half earlier, we were teased by his family for never being more than two feet apart. The Leiders, on the other hand, did not seem to be able to get far enough away from each other. We drank hot wassail by the parlor fire. Carlotta sat down in a chair near the fire. David sat at the far end of the sofa. They were cordial at best. We asked about the stay in California. Carlotta explained her brother had a big ranch and she went horseback riding everyday. "I went fishing in the brook," said David, and Carlotta added that one night they cooked trout over an open fire outside, for supper. "It was cold, but crisp and beautiful out there," she said. "I wouldn't mind living in California and maybe I shall someday."

This was uttered almost threateningly toward David. He ignored her and asked Neal about business. I was thankful for the release, and found myself trying to think up subjects we might discuss safely through dinner, then through dessert and coffee. Before Carlotta and David arrived I wondered if I should have asked them to come earlier than seven o'clock. Now the clock said a quarter past seven and I wondered how I would endure the long evening ahead.

Through the meal we managed polite talk about parties coming up around town, but then Carlotta told us she was not sorry she missed this year's Society Ball because on the way to the ball last year she dipped the train of her dress in the mud. She missed out on the evening and her dress had to be thrown away.

"Dear, dear," mocked David. Carlotta glared at him.

Taking a signal from Neal, I excused myself to cut the cake and invited Carlotta to come in the kitchen with me. I was not sure whether Neal was again looking for a relief of tension in the air, or he wanted me to try and find out from Carlotta what was wrong between her and David. As it turned out, Carlotta saved me the anguish of probing for information I was not sure I wanted to obtain.

As soon as we walked in she pulled out her handkerchief, sat down at the table, and started to cry. I put an arm around her shoulder. "What is it, Carlotta?"

"He hates me. Can't you see? We haven't had a happy moment in the sixteen days since we married."

I sat down across from her and asked her what seemed to be the trouble.

"He didn't want to go to California. He pouted the whole time."

I did not find that difficult to believe, especially after what David said to me earlier. "Well, maybe you just need some time to yourselves. Sometimes family can interfere without realizing it."

"I don't want to be by myself with David. I can't stand him."

I did not know what to say to her. I kept thinking of all the fanfare, the huge wedding at Annunciation with a stream of attendants, Carlotta in her gorgeous wedding gown with its fourteen-foot train . . .

"What is it that makes you feel so?"

She sniffed into the handkerchief and dried her eyes. "We have very different ideas about marriage, that's all."

"Well, I suppose in time that can be worked out. Maybe you should just talk to David. You might find he is more understanding of your views than you think."

She looked at me as though I were a maniac. "Understanding!" she said. "He is an animal."

I stood up to cut the cake. I really didn't want to hear any more. Yet it was obvious she had been gathering courage to have her say since we walked in the kitchen.

"He thinks that we should share the same bedroom. He thinks that . . . that I should not mind undressing right in front of him."

"Oh dear," I breathed.

"My mother and father have been married for thirty-five years and she has never done such a thing."

"Carlotta, don't you think—"

"I told him to do whatever was necessary, then to get away from me. I have never denied it is my place to bear children, but I do not think I need to do anything at the expense of my personal dignity."

I must have turned a deep shade of red. Seldom have I been so embarrassed, or so at a loss for reasonable words. I did not know how to help her without divulging things that were none of her business. Yet I somehow felt that she wanted me to, in order to reassure she was within her rights. I put down the cake knife and sat down again. "Carlotta, don't you think you're being a little harsh? I mean, David has dignity too. And he is very proud, you know."

"I have not asked anything unfair of him," she said stubbornly.

"Perhaps that is true," I finally agreed. "But if you are to stay married, each of you is going to have to bend a little."

"Well, you can be sure I won't. And if he doesn't like it, just let him try and divorce me."

It was in that moment I was finally able to pinpoint the element I saw in Carlotta that evening at the party. The word to describe Carlotta's expression was *hard*. Her eyes were like iron.

Through dessert I kept thinking how sad it was that Carlotta's mother had so misled her about marriage; on the other hand, perhaps David had been less than gentle in his treatment of her in the bridal chamber. I thought of his forcefulness with me, and I felt my face grow hot. I lowered my eyes and took a bite of cake.

David reminded Carlotta of her wish to tell Neal a story about someone in Galveston, and soon Carlotta was dominating Neal's attention. As she talked, I rose to remove the dessert plates, and David picked up the cups and followed me.

In the kitchen I thanked him for helping and said, "I can handle the rest. Why don't you go back to the table and—"

"Alvareda, why is it my presence always bothers you?"

"It—it doesn't," I faltered. "No more so than ever." I plunged the plates into soapy water and tried to look very busy.

He paused at length, then said, "I know what has been on your mind, but don't worry. I'm going to make Neal a good partner."

You had better, I thought, but said, "I'm sure you will." I went on washing the plates, glad for an excuse not to look at him.

"Then why are you so uncomfortable tonight? Did Carlotta tell you all our secrets?"

"She . . . she mentioned there were problems. I really don't think it's any of my—"

"Well, at least she was disturbed enough to talk to someone. Maybe there is some hope for her."

It irritated me that he should feel it was all Carlotta's fault. "Maybe you should be a little more patient . . ." I told him. "I know that isn't easy for you."

He was silent for a few moments, then said, "Is Neal patient?"

Now I was really angry. I glared at him. "That's none of your business."

"Oh, why so touchy?"

I ignored him. He moved a little closer.

I had to get out of there. I dipped my hands in the pan of clear water and, reaching for the towel I said, "No marriage is perfect. You just have to work things out."

"Does this mean there are problems in the Gerrard household, too?"

I wiped my hands. "David, I don't know what you're leading up to, but I can assure you—"

He touched my arm. "Alvareda, let's face it. We both made a mistake—I could see it in your eyes at the table—but it isn't too late to change all that. We could—"

I shot him a look of contempt and pulled my arm away. "You have more nerve than good sense. And you couldn't be more mistaken about my marriage. I warned you once to keep your hands off me. Next time you bother me, I'll tell Neal."

"Oh, will you?" he said, smiling.

"You can be sure of it."

I hurried toward the door, then I took a breath and paused. "Had I known Neal planned to take you as a partner, I would have told him then I don't trust you. Since I didn't get that chance, I think we had better come to terms with it right now. You leave me alone and I'll stay out of your business."

He came close to me and barred my way. "Hold on, Alvareda. I know where I can find somebody who will welcome my attentions."

I shot him a cold glance. "As I said, I'll stay out of your business. Choose anyone you want for your mistress. It makes no difference to me."

He smiled. "Oh, I have a feeling it will make a whole lot of difference before I'm through."

"Get out of my way."

When finally they left, I felt completely exhausted. Neal and I stood arm in arm on the front porch, waving good-bye. "The marriage is a disaster, isn't it?" he observed.

"It appears so."

"I noticed both of them found a way to get you alone."

"Yes," I said weakly. I had not realized he was paying that much attention. I told him what Carlotta said to me, and that David—"David, well, I think he just wanted me to try and talk with her as a friend."

He shook his head. "We would be wise to stay out of it, and let them work it out for themselves."

"Yes, I think you're right," I told him and walked back inside.

I lay in bed for a long time that night, trying to fight down a growing sense of dread about David. Why was he so sure that his extramarital activities were significant to me, when I had made it clear I did not want him?

Again, I tried to forget it. Olivia was right when she said he was just bitter. Yet . . . I turned toward Neal and moved close to him. When his arms encircled me I felt safe again.

Chapter 11

The partnership between David and Neal worked well for a while. David spent a great deal of time traveling around, bringing in new accounts and keeping in touch with old ones, getting acquainted with customers of March Bennett and widening the area of business so much that they were soon cramped for space in their quarters on Main and had to rent the top floor of another building around the corner on Travis.

David did not bother me and I grew more and more confident that his threats were groundless. He and Carlotta seemed resigned to each other, and the four of us spent evenings together frequently. If they seemed to be heading toward a battle, we simply cut the evening short. And I made certain I did not get caught alone with David again.

It was not long before Carlotta discovered she was expecting a baby. She said nothing at first, nor did David. One night we had several couples over for cards, and Carlotta came into the kitchen to help me with refreshments. It was a balmy April evening, and she had worn a white shirtwaist made of some kind of filmy material. She was leaning over a tray of cups, filling them with coffee. I suppose it was the way the light caught the contour of her figure that made me guess. "Carlotta, you're expecting, aren't you?" I blurted out.

She looked up as though I'd accused her of stealing a spoon off the tray. "Yes."

"That's wonderful," I said, and caught her in a hug. "When will the baby arrive?"

"Around August."

"My goodness, that's soon. When are you and David going to announce it? How about tonight?"

"Oh, I'm much too embarrassed."

I breathed a sigh and began to cut the lemon pie. "You have no idea how lucky you are. If I were to be in your shoes, I'd shout it to the rooftops."

"I'm sorry," she said. "If the coming of children had anything to do with love between two people, you and Neal would have many, and probably you will. As it is with David and me, I told you a long time ago I would do my part. I'm praying hard for a boy."

"Oh? For David's sake?"

"And mine. Every woman owes that to her husband. After that's over, she has fulfilled her duty to the family name."

"What if it is a girl?"

"I will be terribly disappointed, that's what." She picked up the tray and walked through the door.

There was no announcement. Finally David told Neal in private and the whole event was treated as though it were something to be ashamed of. It angered me because it seemed so unfair. I would have given almost anything for one healthy child, boy or girl, and yet month after month I faced another disappointment. Carlotta viewed the matter as though it were a necessary inconvenience. Her parents brought over stacks of baby gifts, and March Bennett talked about the expected grandchild with pride. But Carlotta went into confinement at the end of May and if I chanced to see her, she said nothing about the baby. Neal told me that David never spoke of the child either.

One hot morning at the end of August, David arrived at the office and told Neal that Carlotta was in labor. Neal called me at home. "Shall I go over there?" I asked him.

"David says Mrs. Bennett is there, and March is downstairs pacing the floor."

"I see. I'll wait then. Call me if you hear of anything I can do."

In truth I was almost relieved. As the months had gone past I had begun to wonder what my feelings would be when I saw Carlotta's child. I had heard some women who were unable to bear children became distraught at seeing someone else's new baby. Hardly a day went by lately when I did not dwell at least for a few moments on the sorrowful experience of the stillbirth of Alice Marie. What if, seeing the Leiders' baby, I began to sob? That would be terrible. I went around in a nervous state all day, hoping Neal would be home before I was asked to go to the Leiders, so that he could go with me, or maybe I would not have to go over there till the next day.

The telephone rang at three o'clock. Mrs. Bennett said, "The baby is here. It's a girl." She sounded tired, or perhaps disappointed. I could not tell which.

"Is Carlotta fine, and the baby healthy?"

"Oh, certainly," she said, as though anything less would have been unheard of.

I was not sure what to say. "Shall I come over, or would it be better to wait till tomorrow?"

She considered at length, then said, "I think it would be nice if you come now. Carlotta regards you as a very good friend. You might sit with her while I rest."

"Very well," I told her, thankful in a way that the decision had been taken from me.

When I arrived Carlotta was napping. The nurse in her gathered cap and long apron took me on tiptoes to the crib near Carlotta's bed. "Can I pick her up?" I whispered.

The nurse nodded, though she obviously would not leave the room. She pulled back the mosquito bar. The little girl was reddened and her face still pinched. She had a fuzz of light-colored hair on her head. Her little hands moved in the air. I lifted her gently onto my shoulder, and put my hand on her back. It was the most wonderful feeling I had ever experienced. I could feel her heartbeat against my breast. She was soft and warm and full of life. I believe I could have gone on holding her through the evening. The nurse signaled me to put her down, but I shook my head. Not yet. Not yet. I took her to the rocking chair by the window and held her some more. I felt I'd been handed an angel. She gurgled and pushed against me, then relaxed again with her soft cheek against my neck. Tears came to my eyes, but they were tears of joy, not of sorrow for my own loss. I began to hum and to rock. After a while I looked up and realized Carlotta was staring at me.

"Oh, she's beautiful!" I said. "Congratulations."

Carlotta looked away. "It's a girl. I—I'll just have to try again, that's all."

I could not find adequate words to respond. I held the baby a few minutes longer, then carefully placed her back in the crib. She was growing fretful. The nurse came forward and said, "I think she's hungry, Mrs. Leider. Here, let's get you propped up a little bit. Are you comfortable now? Good. Come, little darling, that's it. . . ."

I slipped out the door and went downstairs to get my bag and gloves. I was standing in front of the hall mirror putting my hat on, when Mrs. Bennett appeared. "Did you see her?"

"Yes, and held her. She is an exquisite baby, perfect in every way. Carlotta and David are lucky."

"Did Carlotta tell you they are naming her Elzyna Rebecca, for my mother?" She spelled out El-zy-na, emphasizing the long "i" sound in the middle.

"No. What a beautiful name. Elzyna Rebecca Leider."

"Carlotta is a little disappointed she did not produce a son for David. But I told her just be patient—"

I could not stand any more of this talk. "Good evening, Mrs. Bennett. I have to get home and fix supper for Neal." I had ridden over in my buggy because I thought I might go down to the market before going home. But now I did not feel like going anywhere. I was so angry at David and Carlotta that I felt like horsewhipping both of them. It was nearly five o'clock. I rounded the corner at Crawford and Franklin and continued down toward our house. I was almost to the intersection at Caroline and Franklin when I

looked up ahead and saw David whiz by in his buggy on Fannin. I assumed
he was on his way to see his new daughter. On sudden impulse, I decided to
try to overtake him and talk to him before he went in there. Maybe I could
make him realize how fortunate he was to have a fine healthy daughter, and
stop this nonsense about placing all hopes in a male offspring. If he could only
open his heart and see . . .

He was not too far ahead once I reached Fannin. I called to him, but he did
not hear me. He was driving his buggy awfully fast. Well, I thought, maybe he
is eager to see Elzyna after all. Yet when he reached the Crawford intersection
he did not turn. He continued south down Fannin. I almost turned back, then
decided to go on. I thought he was taking another direction home, or maybe
had a stop to make.

On he drove, past Capitol then Rusk and Walker. At McKinney Avenue he
turned to the left and started east. I could not imagine where he was going
now. I kept going a little farther, and with every block I was drawn more
from curiosity than purpose. He could be going to the Howes' at Austin and
McKinney. Mrs. Howe was the granddaughter of John Harris, who founded
our hometown. Possibly David knew them. Yet he passed by the two-story
house with double galleries and lattice work, and continued. I tapped the
whip to the horse's flank and hurried on, keeping a block's distance between
us. I had ceased to think of the lecture I was going to give David, and would
not have known what to say to him had I overtaken him at this point.

Still I drove, speculating along the way on where he might be going, aware
that I had no right to meddle, but unable to make the decision to turn around
and go home. Still ahead, there was the home of Captain Hutcheson in the
1400 block, then, four blocks farther, between Chenevert and Hamilton, the
Pillot home, where Neal and I had once attended a reception. We had remarked to each other how far out it seemed, almost like a country home. Was
David going there?

The street noises were lessening, the trees growing more dense. LaBranch
. . . Crawford . . . Jackson. The street was almost deserted now. I began to
feel nervous. I should turn back. Yet . . .

Now he was nearing the Pillot house . . . now he passed it by. I followed.
The two iron dogs stationed in front of the house looked ferociously real.
They seemed almost poised to lunge at me as I hurried past. Foolish . . .
two lifeless objects, incapable of moving. . . .

Dowling . . . St. Charles . . . Live Oak. On went David. Now the buildings were fewer and fewer. Neal and I had driven out here after the Pillot
reception, just out of curiosity. There was little out here in the way of commerce except small grocery stores which doubled for saloons, and, here and
there, a boardinghouse. Residences were few and far between and, after another six or seven blocks, it was as though civilization dropped off. From
York Street on, across the railroad tracks, the street was a dirt road lined with

oak trees. It was about here Neal and I had turned back. I slowed down now. The only sound was the muffled beat of the horse's hooves.

David had never tarried, not at a saloon, not at a residence. I pulled the horse to a stop on the other side of the tracks. One moment . . . two . . . A wild rabbit leaped across the path in front of me, and the horse lifted his feet and bleated loudly. I heard myself, "Sh! Sh!" I looked all around me. There was no David. There was nothing but quiet. Darkness was gathering. I felt uneasy. Surely a few miles on the other side of the wilderness ahead of me was Harrisburg . . . unless I'd completely lost my sense of direction. And maybe I had. I started to turn back.

Then I heard a sound up ahead. Through the trees a horse and rider sprinted, the underbrush crackling beneath. After a few moments, nothing. I got down out of the buggy and walked forward. I was no more than twenty feet from a clearing. Dead leaves and twigs crackled under my feet as I made my way through thick vines and underbrush. I felt something grab and pull at me. I brought my hands to my mouth in horror. Then I realized I'd caught my skirt on a thorny vine. I carefully dislodged the stubborn thorns, one by one. My heart was pounding. Yet if I went just a bit farther I could at least find out what was out here, and where the rider was going.

Uncertainly, I went on. . . .

Finally I reached the edge of a large piece of property surrounded by a wooden slat fence. Down to the left the unpainted fence continued farther than I could see. To the right it went perhaps a hundred feet, then turned a corner. Shortly after the corner there was a gate, and the gate had been left open. I picked up my skirt hem and tiptoed to the end of the fence, around the corner, approaching the gate. I should leave, I told myself, my heart beating rapidly. The dirt path inside the gate was well tended, the vines along the ground trimmed back. What if someone . . . ? . . . Yet . . . I pushed on the gate, but stood still again, afraid to step through it. Ahead of me was another group of trees, and through them I now saw a house. It was a rude structure, two stories, with a little stoop in front, and windows on each side. To the left of the path near the stoop was an oak tree that stood apart from the rest, and from a huge limb of this tree hung a swing. A swing. . . .

I took in a breath and narrowed my eyes. I walked in a little farther. I stopped and reflected. I had a queer feeling. . . . No, it could not be. I shook my head. Suddenly I heard a crunching noise. I wheeled around to left, to right. Nothing. I put my cold hands against my throat. I could feel the pulse pounding in my neck. Oh, this was madness. I had no business here. Yet now that I had seen the swing my curiosity was redoubling. I just had to investigate a little farther. I moved up several more feet and craned my neck forward. Toward the back of the house I could see the edge of some sort of outbuilding—a large barn or stable. The rider had disappeared, and there was no sign of David either. I kept standing there, staring at the house. I could not dismiss the peculiar feeling I'd been here before. Yet, why would I have been? This was far away from everything. There was a pervasive quiet that made me feel I had been chopped off from civilization. The cottage looked lonely, forlorn. . . .

Abruptly, a light came on in the windows. My eyes widened. A chill ran up my spine like a frightened cat scaling a tree. No one came out.

I stood there as though pinned to the ground, afraid to stay, afraid to go. One moment . . . two . . . still nothing. I obviously had come upon someone's country cottage. They were in there now, perhaps looking out at me. Lucky they didn't shoot me. That would teach me to interfere in the lives of others. If Neal knew I had come here, he would be furious, I thought nervously. I turned to go, and took a few steps. Then a voice behind me said, "Afternoon, Alvareda."

I jerked around. "David!" I gasped. My arms flew to my chest. He was on the porch stoop, arms folded, smiling. "What are you doing here?" I stammered.

"Seems to me that ought to be my question," he said, walking toward me.

"I—I was trying to catch up with you . . . in town . . . I wanted to tell you how . . . how lucky you are to have a beautiful daughter. It's none of my business, I know. But—but Carlotta seems to feel she let you down." My voice was choked and unconvincing.

"She did, but not by having a daughter," he said evenly. His manner was so relaxed, it occurred to me he had known I was following him for a very long way back.

"Well, then . . . Look, I'm sorry for all of this. I don't know what came over me. I've got to go home now."

"You're lying," he said.

"I beg your pardon?"

"You must have known about this place, or why would you have followed me? You knew exactly where you were going. You just wanted to be sure you knew what I was doing."

"I don't know what you're talking about. I've never been here in my life . . . that is, I don't believe I have. And certainly I am telling you the truth about today."

He didn't believe me. He took my arm and nudged me forward. "Come on, I want you to meet someone. Try telling her you don't know anything about her."

"David, I— David, please."

He had a grip on my arm and was forcing me forward. We walked up the path and to the door. He opened it as though he had some claim to the house and came here regularly. Once in, he called out, "Amanda, where are you? Samuel Cane's daughter Alvareda is here."

A few moments passed before she came in. I looked around me. The house was simple but furnished very nicely. There were two rooms in front with a large open passage in between. I saw no stairway, so it must have been on the back of the house. I looked in the room on the right. There was a corner fireplace, a very pretty one with carving on it. Again I had a strange sense that I had been here before.

"She doesn't seem to be home," I said dourly to David.

"Oh, she's here. She has been for a ride and is upstairs changing."

At last she appeared at the other end of the open passage. She was an attractive young woman with black hair parted down the center and pulled into a knot in back. She had pretty, very light skin and green eyes.

"Did you call, darling? What is it?" I heard her say, then she noticed me and stopped. She looked at David quizzically.

"Mrs. Gerrard, formerly Alvareda Cane," said David.

"Oh," she said faintly. "Show her to the library, David. I'll bring in the coffee."

When we were seated I demanded, "Who is she? I mean, apart from being a very close friend of yours."

"You really don't know?" he asked, and he suddenly looked full of mischief, as though he were enjoying my discomfort more and more.

"Of course not. It's getting late. I've got to get home."

The woman returned with the coffee and sat down. "You don't recognize me, do you?"

"I don't believe we've met."

"My name is Amanda Cane. We did meet once, when we were children."

"I . . . I don't understand. Are we related?"

She took in a deep breath and looked at David. He nodded. "We are half-sisters, Alvareda. Samuel Cane was my father."

The allegation struck my ears like a discordant piano note.

"That's—that's the most absurd—" I shifted my eyes toward David. "How could you—"

"Wait a minute," he interrupted. "There is proof."

I sat back in the chair and brought a hand to my chest. I could hardly get my breath. My heart was pounding. I tried to collect my thoughts. There had to be some mistake, that was all. None of this had any real connection with me.

Amanda had retreated to a little cabinet nearby. Opening the glass doors, she pulled out a framed photograph and brought it to me. I stared at it. It was my father, all right, and he was pictured next to a woman. The woman that I had seen in the photograph beside his bed? Certainly the resemblance was unmistakable. Weakly I handed the picture back to her. "I think you owe me an explanation."

"It's simple really. My mother's name was Eva Longworth. They met in

Brazoria in 1870, while he was traveling on business. She was widowed by the war, and had no children.

"They were very much in love. The problem was, he was already married . . . unhappily, I might add, though surely you must know that. He built this house for her, out where there was no danger of their being found out. I was born soon after. And here my mother and I stayed."

"And your mother—where is she now?"

"She died some time ago."

I was too taken aback to ask any further questions for a while, but finally I thought of one. "You indicated we had met. When, and where?"

"You came here when you were a child. Just before . . ." she paused and glanced at David ". . . before you turned seven. We took turns swinging out there under the oak tree."

"My father brought me?"

"No. Your mother brought you. We were kept busy outside while our mothers talked. Your mother had somehow learned about my mother and me. I am sure they had a lot to say to each other."

So many things were going through my mind just then: my father's words just before his death about being followed. Everything being ruined. He had not been thinking of me. He had been thinking of my mother. In fact I now wondered if he did not mistake me for her during the whole visit, if he was not more delirious than Olivia and I realized. Olivia. "Does my sister know about all this?"

"Olivia has known for as long as I can remember," she said. "We are in frequent contact."

I had a strong feeling many things were going to make sense to me now, as soon as I had time to sort them out in my mind. "I'd like to go now," I told her.

She nodded.

David rose and walked with me to the door. "I'll see you to your buggy," he said.

I sent him an icy glance. "I think that's a very good idea."

As we walked toward the gate I was trembling all over. "And how did you find out about Amanda?" I demanded.

"I told you I was going after Samuel. I trailed him out here one day to see what he was up to. By the time I was able to put two and two together, the old—he was dead. A while later, I came out and introduced myself to Amanda. I didn't have too much trouble convincing her to talk to me."

Now something clicked in my mind. "You were speaking of Amanda that night in the kitchen, when we—"

"I was uncertain whether you knew about her. And I still wanted you—"

"Does Carlotta know about any of this?" I interrupted.

He shook his head.

I took in a long breath. "Do you realize what Neal would do if he found out?"

He smiled. "I was kind of figuring we might keep it to ourselves."

I considered him for a few moments. "You wanted me to find out about Amanda, didn't you? You wanted to hurt me because you could not get back at my father."

He said nothing.

"You realize you have to give her up, don't you? This can only lead to—"

"I won't give her up."

"But you have a family to look after, a beautiful child. What about your responsibilities?"

"I'm through with Carlotta. Oh, I'll stay married to the cold bitch, but I'll be damned if I'll confine myself to her bed. I'd as soon sleep on the North Pole."

"Neal must never, never find out about any of this. Do you understand?"

"I could not agree with you more."

He helped me into the buggy. I flicked the reins and moved slowly away. In a moment I heard David call my name. I stopped and looked around. He was smiling. "You could have prevented all this, you know."

I just looked at him.

"If you had only had enough faith in me to be my wife, I would have considered myself repaid for all Samuel did."

I felt such contempt at that moment I could not express it. I turned around and signaled the horse to move on.

For the first few minutes of the trip I could think only of the terrible realization that my father loved someone else, and not my mother. And all my life I had thought he hated me because I took her from him. Now Neal's words after the birth of Alice Marie came back to me. Papa's feelings for me had to stem from something else, but what? Oh, if only I had discovered Amanda before his death, I could have confronted him without fear. There might be so much I could have learned. . . .

As I neared the railroad tracks, the point to which Neal and I once ventured out of such innocent curiosity, I began to think of him: what he had said the very first day we walked together in Houston about how scandal can ruin a man's career. And that night on the beach, when he said he did not think I could ever let him down . . . as though I were not capable of that. And his mother had said Neal was so proud to have me as his bride. Yet all the time my father was supporting another family, hidden away between Harrisburg and Houston. I was so ashamed. . . . Perhaps I ought to tell him everything, get it out in the open now. Yet, what if he looked at me with understanding but profound disappointment, and I could see his love for me vanish from his eyes as he realized I was to be a burden instead of the helpmate he had so counted on when he chose to spend his life with me? No,

I could not stand losing his love, our marriage surviving only on his loyalty. I would keep the secret from him, though I hated this deception most of all.

As I neared the pleasant sight of lights in the windows of my home on Franklin Avenue, I had a very disheartening feeling that I had just made a pact with the devil, and that my father would be smiling in satisfaction could he know what a position his treachery had placed me in.

PART 2

Chapter 1

It seemed forever since our little ship had pulled away from the docks at Harrisburg and begun the long narrow passage up Buffalo Bayou to Houston. The ceiling of trees above us was so dense that now and then the sunlight was extinguished altogether. Sometimes we moved so close to the cypress knees and thick, gnarly underbrush that it seemed we could not clear them. It was a primitive waterway of elbow curves and sloping banks. Yet, people like Neal and David and other Houston merchants were already drawing plans to widen, deepen, and straighten it into a fifty-mile channel all the way to the Gulf of Mexico, adequate for use by huge oceangoing vessels in relaying cargo all the way to the Houston wharves. If their efforts failed, our railroad lines would soon be rerouted to Galveston; our barges would be outmoded; commerce would bypass our city, leaving it to wither and die like Harrisburg.

For three years now, since early in 1891, Neal and David had been members of the Ship Channel Committee of the Houston Cotton Exchange. The committee worked tirelessly to help our representatives in Congress get notice for Houston's appeal. Recently the committee chairman received a letter from a senator who wanted to come to Houston and bring two other congressmen and their wives. Regardless of its less than official status, this meeting, which began with a bayou cruise, was regarded as a high priority by the committee. Carlotta and I, with help from the other wives, had worked to put together a luncheon at the four-story wooden pavilion at Magnolia Park, so that the visitors could look out over the water as they enjoyed their meal. The yacht now carrying us down the bayou to the park, with its flag-lined canopy and wicker chairs, belonged to a committee member.

Early on the trip I had moved around and chatted with the ladies on board, but we had little in common since I had no children and most of these women either had several children, or even grandchildren. Carlotta, on the other hand, was born and reared for this sort of entertaining. She could tell them much about Houston beyond what I knew, and she also could chat about the antics of her children. Following the birth of Elzyna in 1889, Carlotta produced another daughter—Patricia—in 1890.

The years had not brought Carlotta and David any closer. She remained determined to do her part as a wife in accordance with her views; he remained discreet, but obstinate, about continuing to pay regular visits to Amanda Cane. Whether she was the only woman he called on I don't know. He spent many evenings at the Turf Exchange, gambling and drinking in the company of other Houston businessmen. Otherwise he continued to travel a lot, and was every bit as involved in the cotton business as Neal.

It seemed to me at times David was like two people. He never let Neal down as a partner, and often surpassed the expectations Neal entertained when they began. The factoring side of the business was stronger than ever. The compress facility had almost doubled in size, and now was comprised of three brick warehouses, five sheds for cotton storage, plus the compress, pickery, and other machinery, all sitting on a four-acre site by a railroad track near Houston Heights. Neal had increased the area from two to four acres, and there was now room for even further growth. In two more years, the debt owed on the improvements would be paid and they would begin to realize the hoped-for level of profit. Their operation was well respected in the industry; nothing could go wrong, or so we thought.

I suppose Neal realized that David was less than faithful to Carlotta, but he did not know about Amanda or the house way out past the foot of McKinney Avenue, and he did not know about my father's secret life. This knowledge was shared only among David, Amanda, Olivia, and me. Olivia had been relieved, I think, when I told her I had learned of it. And she had long since known what David was up to. She told me only that she was sorry, and that she had tried hard to protect me from the truth. I would still go to Harrisburg to visit Olivia once or twice a month. We did not speak of the situation very much, neither of us really caring to discuss something that could not be changed, and might be a source of conflict between us if we allowed ourselves to delve too far beneath the surface.

Now and again I tried to persuade Olivia to sell the house in Harrisburg and live with us. Living alone had not been good for her. She had never found any interests beyond those she had before Papa's death, never developed new friends or started to go places regularly. She was becoming old beyond her forty-four years, and was often absent-minded and preoccupied. She seemed oblivious to the fact the house she lived in was in serious need of repairs, and would not even spend the money to have the exterior repainted. It was gradually turning from a fine structure into an eyesore. The shrubs had grown out of proportion, and the vines that used to grow around the front porch were no longer in check. They now obscured the porch completely, covered the front of the house and part of the sides. Yet Olivia would say only, "That can wait, sister," if I urged her to do something to improve the state of the house. Possibly it was hard for her to imagine any urgency. She rarely went out, and the inside of the house looked much the same as when Papa died.

The Leiders had moved into the Bennett home on Main three years ago, Carlotta first having extensive remodeling done. We still lived on Franklin Avenue, though Neal had recently purchased some property on Main a few blocks south of the Leiders'. He had expressed a desire for a big home and planned to spend around seventy-five hundred dollars. "Isn't that a lot of house, just for the two of us?" I asked, and he smiled and told me to be patient, that someday we'd fill it up with children.

By far the greatest consolation to both of us in the absence of children, however, was Elzyna. She was almost like our own. When she was an infant I visited the Leider home frequently just for the joy of holding her and playing with her. Once she was able to walk, she came to me as soon as I entered the room, or begged to be taken on Neal's lap. As soon as she was old enough, we took her places, and she often stayed overnight. I loved her very much, but I also felt sorry for her. She was not treated like her sister Patricia, whom Carlotta seemed to accept more easily in spite of her failure to be male. Patricia was a precocious little girl who was mainly concerned with herself. She demanded more attention and therefore received it, while Elzyna remained shy and reserved. Patricia looked like her mother, with auburn hair and freckles and a petite build. Elzyna, with blond hair, pale blue eyes and creamy skin, looked more like the Leider side of the family. Once she said to me, "Mommy says I'm awfully tall to be a girl, and my feet are longer than hers when she was my age. Am I going to be big?"

"I don't know," I told her honestly. "Your grandmother Leider—she died when you were too small to remember—was a tall woman and she was beautiful. You remind me of her a lot." Even as I uttered the response, it struck me that perhaps one reason Carlotta shunned Elzyna was because of this physical resemblance to David's family.

I could see that Elzyna was starving for the kind of love and attention she should have found at home, but there was little I could do about it. Neal treated her with far more warmth than David, who seemed aloof and rarely took her in his arms. When she stayed with us, Neal carried her on his back and fixed her hot chocolate at bedtime. If thunder should rumble in the night, Neal was the first to awaken and go to comfort Elzyna in her room.

While enjoying Neal's company immensely, Elzyna would have done anything to have gotten the same or even half the amount of attention from her own father. More than once I watched as David came to fetch her in the afternoon, and when she reached up to hug his neck, he would extend her a limp embrace and a too-quick kiss on the cheek. He always seemed to be in a hurry, but the subtle way he put distance between them was reflected in her crestfallen face, quickly followed by a look of resignation. At every opportunity I tried to reassure her of his love. It was all I could do.

I would not discuss Elzyna with David because I could envision the angle at which the conversation might turn. He might remind me of his unhappy marriage and that he continued to occupy the same residence as Carlotta purely out of a sense of obligation to Neal and to me. He might say that if he loved the mother he might be more inclined to love the child. He might suggest that if I were so interested in his being a good father, I would allow everything kept secret to come into the open so that he could be divorced from Carlotta and marry Amanda Cane and start another family.

No . . . I did not discuss Elzyna with her father very much. I was hamstrung by my own dependency on him. . . .

The captain sounded the bell as we rounded the last curve in the bayou before docking at Magnolia Park, and I rushed to be helped out of the ship before the others so that I could hurry up the pavilion stairs and make sure all the preparations were ready. So many people had helped. Carlotta had not only served as a graceful hostess aboard ship, but had also arranged flowers for the long table and provided place cards for all the guests.

Local merchants provided refreshments and on the stroke of noon, we sat down to platters of steaming hot fried oysters and potato puffs, bowls heaped high with coleslaw, and long loaves of hot buttered bread.

There was much enthusiastic conversation about the waterway. The visitors were clearly impressed, and I had never seen Neal and David enjoy themselves more. It was nearly three before the gathering was over and nearly four o'clock when we arrived back in Houston at the train station. Through a flurry of compliments and thanks, we escorted the visitors to the platform just in time for their departure. We were waving to them as they passed us by in the train, when suddenly I realized I was weary to the bone and my feet ached. I turned to Neal, and started to ask if he was ready to go home. Then we both noticed a young man rushing across the concourse in our direction. I heard Neal say to David, "Look, it's Walter. What's he doing here?" They both walked quickly toward him. The man, dressed in his work clothes, his head bare, was talking excitedly and gesturing with his hands while David and Neal listened. One moment . . . two . . . Carlotta and I looked at each other. Then Neal came back to me. "There's a fire at the compress. David and I will take our buggy. You go home with Carlotta," he said, and took off running.

I looked at Carlotta in astonishment. "Let's go."

"Home?" she said.

"No. To the compress. Hurry."

The location of the compress had been a source of concern to Neal from the time he and David took it over. While it had perfect access to the railroad tracks, it was farther out than the city water mains reached. From the Union Depot you took Preston, all the way out twenty blocks to Washington, then another twelve blocks down Washington, past the Inman Press, and the county hospital. The Gerrard-Leider Press was just beyond the hospital. As we drove block after long block, I kept thinking how impossible it would be to get help quickly enough to put out a fire before it grew to monster proportions. Surely the steamer engines could not get there fast enough to stop anything as incendiary as burning cotton. Worse, this time of year the warehouses and sheds were heaped with the season's yield. The farther we went, the worse I imagined the fire to be. When finally we crossed the bridge near Phoenix Iron Works, just before reaching Washington, I could see the black smoke and the tongues of fire lapping the air. The sky above the compress was amber.

"Holy Mary, it looks like a whole city is in flames," Carlotta gasped.

We were still two blocks away when the horse whinnied and balked, and pitched backward. It was all I could do to get him turned forward and pulled into a dark alleyway. We jumped down and together managed to tie the reins to a post while the horse continued to toss and wrestle. We ran from the buggy, both of us holding our skirts above our knees. There were guards posted around the premises, holding people away. I could see neither Neal nor David anywhere. We had no choice but to stand by helplessly and view the spectacle. Plumes of smoke ascended into the air as though pushed up by giant bellows constantly at work. Flames leaped hundreds of feet and threw sparks above them. Interspersed with the roar of the flames were the shrieks of birds which circled above, confused and panicked, their wings flapping wildly as they struggled to soar higher. You could hardly breathe for the smoke, hardly see for the burning in your eyes. Carlotta and I stood first dabbing our noses with handkerchiefs, then holding the cloths in front of our noses and mouths. The heat was so intense that we took steps backward again and again, unable to stand any closer. The fire took over shed after shed, warehouse after warehouse, as sidecars became flaming vessels of cotton bales. Still it spread angrily as a starved beast desperate for prey.

How long since the steamers arrived, I did not know. Firemen fought boldly, in spite of the fact their means to extinguish the fire were sadly inadequate. The property was flaming from end to end, walls falling; roofs caving in. It seemed to go on forever. I wondered if all the workmen had gotten out safely. There were already ambulance wagons there, but the attendants were waiting along with us. I could not understand why Neal and David did not appear. Carlotta said they were probably on the other side of the yard. Still, why would they stay back there, rather than coming up here?

The fire continued to rage. It would be, in fact, half-past five o'clock before they would finally extinguish it. Shortly before that time someone drew up to the ambulance attendants and talked and pointed toward the back of the yard. The attendants picked up a litter and ran forward, soon disappearing around the corner. I was gripped by a fear I had never experienced before. I grabbed Carlotta's hand. We both stood transfixed for what seemed an eternity, neither of us daring to speculate on whom the rescue squad might have gone after. When finally they emerged again, there were two firemen carrying the litter and the attendants hurrying behind. They were some distance from us, through the crowds. I could not make out anything of the cargo. All that was visible was the long brown blanket. The last to emerge, walking behind the others, was David.

I caught my breath.

"Stay here. I'll go and find out," said Carlotta.

"No. I'm coming," I said.

We pushed past the crowd of onlookers, were delayed by the guards until we finally convinced them of our identity. Finally we entered the grounds where the ambulance wagon was waiting. They were just closing the doors when we arrived. David looked at us but didn't speak. His clothes were torn, his face blackened from smoke.

"Is it Neal?" I begged.

He nodded. "A wall collapsed on him."

I opened my mouth to speak, and everything went black.

Chapter 2

When I awoke I was looking into a gas fixture with four lights at the top and four at the bottom. I blinked, and I heard Carlotta's voice. "Are you awake, Alvareda?" She sounded far away. Something very heavy was around my hand. She spoke again. "Alvareda, it's Carlotta. Are you coming to?"

Then I realized she was quite near, holding my hand tightly. A hospital nurse in white gown and ruffled cap was just behind her. "Wake up, Mrs. Gerrard. You're at county hospital."

Then I remembered. I sat up with a start. "Neal! Is he all right? Where is he?"

"Sh. Try to calm down," said Carlotta. "The doctors are with him now."

"Let me out of here. I have to see him."

"You can't, I'm afraid," said the nurse. "Sit still and I'll bring you some cool water."

"Carlotta, do you know anything? Please, for heaven's sake—"

"Neal is all right as far as I know. He . . . he was not burned at all, and suffered only minor abrasions, the doctor told us. But he has some broken bones. His right leg received the worst blow. He has several fractured ribs. But the important thing is that he is alive and there is nothing wrong with him that won't mend. The doctors are setting the broken bones and seeing to the cuts and bruises."

"Oh, thank God," I said, then felt dizzy and lay down again. "When can I see him?"

"It'll be a while yet."

"How long have I been here?"

"Only a little while, less than an hour."

"Oh, how could I have stayed like that for so long?"

"You had already been through a taxing day, then the fire, then the shock of seeing Neal. The body has a limit, you know. I've thought of a couple of things. You might want to call Neal's personal doctor to look at him, and move him—if it's safe, of course—to a hospital closer to home. I'm sure the facility out here is fine, but it is a long way and they may want to watch him closely for several days."

"Yes, that's good. Let's call Dr. Morant. Neal doesn't have a doctor here, but Dr. Morant looked after me when I was expecting Alice Marie and we both liked him. I think he's connected with St. Joseph's."

"Good. I'll look into it for you. Also, you'll want to contact Neal's parents. The fire will be in the newspapers, you know. You don't want them to see the story before you've talked with them."

"Of course you are right. Have you any idea how it happened?"

"Yes, David told me it started in one of the sheds. Around four o'clock, a locomotive passed by and threw a spark into it—at least, that is what they think, and it seems fairly certain because there was nothing else in there to start a fire."

I thought of the cruel irony: as we waved good-bye to the visitors leaving town in one locomotive from Union Station, another locomotive was speeding us toward disaster.

". . . David and Neal went around to the back when they got there. David said the firemen were just then getting their hoses unrolled. Neal went into the building where the records are kept, to try and salvage them. When he came out, he passed by one of the other brick buildings. Its wall collapsed on him."

"He should have never risked going in there."

"Yes, but I guess it seemed safe enough at the time."

"Is there anything left now?"

"Not much. One warehouse is standing, down at the far end, but it only had around two hundred and fifty bales stored in it. The press, the pickery, all the machinery, everything else is gone, not to mention the cotton stored. David says it's going to be a mess, figuring it out. He's contacting the insurance people now."

"We're so fortunate he wasn't hurt as well."

"Yes. In a few minutes they'll let you see Neal. Then we're going to take you home. Here, let me help you with your shoes."

"I'm not leaving without Neal."

"But you have nothing with you, no nightclothes . . . why not go home for tonight and rest? You can come back tomorrow."

"No. I couldn't possibly leave him."

It was after seven o'clock when they finally let me in to see Neal. He had been taken to a room in which there were several beds, but none of the others were occupied. The sight of him moved me to tears. His head was bandaged, his ribs were wrapped, the broken leg was elevated in its cast, and he had bandages over much of his arms. Only his hands and part of his face were uncovered. I squeezed his hands and leaned over and kissed him.

"Oh, sweetheart, I've been crazy with worry. Are you all right?" he asked.

"Of course I am," I said. Big tears rolled down my cheeks and plopped onto the bed covers.

"Whenever I close my eyes, all I can see are the flames. But they tell me no one else was hurt."

"That's right."

"We've got a lot to be thankful for. Who was it said we needed a compress?"

I smiled. "It was perhaps not one of their better ideas, was it?"

"Is there anything left?"

"Not much, I'm afraid. David is still here, if you want to talk to him now."

"Yes, I'd like to, please. Don't go far, though, promise?"

"I promise."

Carlotta was correct about the newspapers. The next morning while sitting at Neal's bedside I read of the catastrophe. Not much was reported that David had not told us, yet the extent of it seemed greater than what David had said. Some of the estimates of the loss would fall short once the loss was fully calculated; others would prove accurate. Reading about it made it seem more real than living through it.

Following a colorful description of the fire, there were several paragraphs about the heroic efforts of Neal to salvage the records, and the injuries he suffered as a result. There were even a few words about my fainting spell. I did not like this. It was as though I were being examined against my wishes, and made me feel just as I had felt long ago when a reporter wrote on the society page about my courtship with Neal, alerting my father in the process.

I laid the paper aside, determined that if there were any way to avoid it, I would never have my name appear in the newspaper again.

Neal was transferred to St. Joseph's Infirmary within four days, and Dr. Morant undertook his care.

He said the healing process would be long—once Neal was released and sent home it would be months before he walked again, and only then with crutches at first, then probably a cane for a while before he was completely recovered. Somehow it all seemed ominous when I imagined it affecting our lives over the months ahead. Yet Neal's physical recovery would soon be overshadowed by something far worse.

When he came home, I converted the downstairs parlor to a bedroom and collected his trade journals and newspapers, plus a stack of new books from Baldwin's, to keep close at hand. I knew it was going to be hard to keep him entertained. He was concerned about the dropping price of cotton—now at three cents a pound—and the effect on business in general since the compress was out of operation. He was worried about the expense of rebuilding when the firm was already in debt. Yet it must be done quickly because the insurance proceeds would only go so far, and delays would be expensive.

One night he said, "I've got to contact Nat Jobron so that he can work up a clear picture of our financial situation. I've been trying to get David to bring the books to me for three days. Damn, it's frustrating to be stuck in this cast."

"Oh, darling, we're so lucky you weren't hurt any worse. Just try and be patient," I told him.

He sighed. "It isn't only that. I've never been happy with the way Pete handles the books out at the compress, and it's a sure bet he doesn't have things up to date right now, just when I need them the most. In fact, I've decided to bring all the accounting back to my office downtown so I can be sure it is done right. I'm really tired of putting up with David's cousin."

"You intend to fire Pete?"

"Yes."

"What will David say?"

He looked as though I had insulted him. "I really don't care what he says." Then he softened. "Oh, I'm sorry. I didn't mean to be so rude. It's just that all I do is sit here and think of all the things that needed to be done even before the fire, not to mention since. And the very ledgers I was carrying when I almost got killed, I can't get my hands on now."

I drew close and kissed him, and took his hands in mine. "I'm glad to have you near, even if you are an old fussbudget."

That night I lay in bed thinking. I had never been any real help to Neal, yet my household duties were not great either since we had no children. Obviously, the load of accounting duties would be a burdensome one. Why couldn't I do this for Neal? He could train me while resting at home. It would give him a sense of progress, and it would be good for me to learn to do something new. As I thought about it, the idea seemed more and more appealing. By morning I was eager to approach Neal about it.

I took his breakfast to him—hot biscuits, eggs and bacon, and our own pear preserves—and tried not to rush him as he ate, although I was growing more and more impatient to talk to him. Finally I took the tray, refilled his coffee cup, and drew my chair near him. "I have the most exciting idea," I began, and tried hard to infect him with my enthusiasm.

He listened attentively, but I was certain before I finished telling him that he wouldn't agree. He shook his head at last. "No, I don't want you to be involved in the business," he said.

"But there isn't much for me to do at home. I'd have time, and I know I could do it well. Math was easy for me in school and—"

"You'll have plenty to do, once we build our new house."

"But, Neal, I still think—"

"Honey, I appreciate it, but I just don't believe it would work."

"Couldn't I at least try?" I pleaded.

"No. That's final."

I was crushed. I had not felt that sting of rejection since I lived with Papa. It was as though Neal felt I didn't have any ability to help. I picked up my embroidery and got very busy, not once looking up, and the more I sat there, the more hurt I felt. I did not deserve to be treated like a child, but I could see now that was how he viewed me. . . . I took a few stitches. I was just someone he took care of, not a helpmate. . . . I had no children . . . was of no real importance to anyone . . . just decoration, like a vase on the mantelpiece. Oh, I was so angry. My hands were now shaking. Finally I pricked my finger with the needle and cried out in pain. I looked up at Neal. He opened his mouth to speak. I threw down the embroidery hoop and ran from the room in tears.

All through the day I stayed busy at household tasks, hardly speaking to Neal. He kept looking at me as though to assess my mood, but I looked away. Already I felt a little guilty for adding to his many concerns. He looked so helpless, his leg still hoisted up in a cast, his ribs bandaged. Still . . . all the more reason he should welcome my help.

Early that evening as I fluffed the pillows under his back, he caught my hand and said, "Alvareda, I didn't mean to hurt your feelings. I'm sorry."

That helped some, but not much. "It's all right," I lied, and drew my hand away. I waited a moment to see if he had reconsidered. Yet the next thing he said was, "Would you remind David about the ledgers?"

My stomach tightened, as though to sustain a blow. "Certainly," I said tacitly. Then I let out a breath and said, "As a matter of fact, I could use an outing. I think I'll hitch up the buggy and go over there right now."

He nodded.

"I'll be home before dinnertime."

I had not seen much of David since the fire. He had on his shoulders the whole burden of the business, plus the added responsibilities brought on by the fire. I assumed he was just forgetful of his promise to Neal with so much to worry about. When I arrived Carlotta said that David was busy working, and she retreated to a little room behind the front parlor to tell him I was there. When she returned she said, "He'll be out in a minute. How about a cup of tea?"

I told her I would like that, then I heard Elzyna's footsteps on the stairs, and in a moment she was rushing into my arms. "I drew a picture for Uncle Neal," she soon told me and went off to get it.

I glanced up to see David standing there. He looked tired and distracted. His collar was unbuttoned and his sleeves were rolled up.

"What's the hurry about the ledgers?" he asked.

"Oh, good evening, David. Neal needs to get a financial report done."

"Well, I'll get them to him soon," he said, then took a breath before reminding me, "I've been a little busy, as you can imagine."

"I know that. Since Neal's confined, he has nothing to do but sit around and worry about things. He just asked me to remind you. I can come down to the office and pick them up tomorrow, if you like."

"No, that won't be necessary," he said quickly. "I'll bring them over."

"All right, thank you."

He nodded and walked out.

I couldn't blame him for being defensive, I reasoned afterward. Yet Neal could not help being impatient either. Oh, I would be so glad when things were back to normal again.

The next evening David delivered a portion but not all of the books. He said Pete was still getting the recent ones updated. I was busy nearby in the dining room while he and Neal talked, and I soon overheard Neal say, "You just don't have enough time to do a good job of supervising Pete out there, and it's obvious he can't manage himself very well. . . ."

When David left he looked upset, but didn't argue with Neal's decision. I saw him to the door, and told him good night. As he stepped out he turned and said, "I've got to talk to you. Right now."

I closed the door and went out on the porch with him. "What is it?" I said. I was certain he was going to try and get me to persuade Neal not to fire his cousin.

"I need your help," he said. "I've—borrowed a little money from the company. I was going to pay it back before Neal realized it was gone."

I winced and dug my fingernails into my palms. "Yes . . ."

"Well, the fire messed up everything, you see. I've been busy these past few days trying to compare the recent bank statements with the ledgers, so that I could arrive at the exact amount."

"I—I don't quite follow you," I said quietly. I gripped the porch rail with one hand and leaned back against the pillar.

"Well, if the deposits to the bank didn't quite match up to the receipts, Pete would let it go till I could right it again. But I haven't . . . well, I've lost a little at the Turf Exchange lately, and, well, here and there."

Oh, Lord. Anything but this. "How much altogether?"

"Around nineteen hundred."

"Nineteen hundred dollars?" I gasped. That was nearly equal to Neal's annual salary.

He nodded.

It took me several moments to overcome the shock of what he said and reflect on the beginning of this discussion. Then I said, "I can't imagine how you think I could help you. I have no money."

"Well, I haven't either, that's for sure."

"What about Carlotta?"

"She wouldn't help me, for one thing, and for another, her father would find out and that would ruin us all."

I lifted my hands. "I can't believe this," I said, and yet in my heart I realized this was what I had always somehow dreaded. "I think it would be best to go to Neal and explain. Maybe he'd understand—"

His mouth curved into a mocking smile. "Oh, Alvareda, you are so naïve."

"What do you mean?" I countered.

He sighed. "Neal may indulge you like a loving father, but I can assure you he has not the same charity toward me."

The term "loving father" hit painfully close to home, but with David's problem to deal with, my own wounded feelings toward Neal seemed less significant just then.

"Well then, why did you get yourself in such a fix? You've always had just as much income from the company as Neal."

"Neal keeps a tight rein on money. He hasn't declared a bonus since we formed the partnership; the only thing he wants to do is put all the profits back into the business. When are we supposed to get something for ourselves?"

He sounded like a greedy little boy waiting his turn in line for a lollipop. I was surprised that David was not happy with the way Neal ran things, and he was no doubt right about Neal's reaction. Neal would consider him a thief.

Yet, that was David's problem, not mine. "You're going to have to face Neal sooner or later. You might as well get it over with," I said, and started for the door, hoping against hope this would be the end of it. He put his hand in front of me. My pulse was beating like rain on a tin roof.

"Just a minute, Mrs. Gerrard," he said. His tone had changed from one of supplication to warning.

I turned toward him. My knees felt weak. "What is it?"

"I think you will help me."

I hesitated. The hair stood up on my neck. Finally I said faintly, "I told you, I have no money."

"Then go to your sister. Olivia has plenty of money."

I twisted around. I wanted to slap his face. "How dare you!"

"You owe me this and so does she."

I looked at him coldly. "This obsession with getting back at my father has gone far enough. You must know there is a limit to how far I'll go—"

He smiled and said, "Oh, is there? You might say the same is true of me."

"Get out of my way."

"I could hurt you, you know. You and Neal. If Neal finds out what I've done, I won't have anything to lose."

I had not thought of that. Suddenly the whole circumstance of Amanda and all the deceit we had practiced for years flashed across my mind. I bit my lower lip. I could scarcely get my breath. He continued, "If the partnership splits up I'll tell everything about your father that I know. I'll tell all about Amanda and me, and how you've known about it all this time. Before I'm finished the Gerrards and Canes will be linked together as the laughingstock of Houston, and it will be a lot nastier than the ridicule my father suffered because of your old man."

"You wouldn't," I cried softly, and rested my forehead on the door. Please, God . . .

His face was near mine. I closed my eyes. He spoke in my ear. "Alvareda, I never wanted to hurt you, not like you hurt me, but for God's sake you've got to do this for me now. If you will, I promise I won't make the mistake again. I'll work harder than ever in the cotton business, you watch and see if I don't, Alvareda, you've got to see it my way. . . ." In a moment I felt the brush of his lips on my neck, and my eyes flew open. I raised my hand to slap him, then, in the fraction of a second, realized that was the mistake I always made with him. This time I would remain calm.

I looked at him. My voice quavered as I spoke. "Did you know that I hate you? That you have done nothing but make my life miserable from the first day we met?"

"No, I don't believe that. I'll never believe it. You're just stubborn."

I pushed him aside and shook my head. "I have to think. I don't know what to do right now."

"Can you tell me tomorrow? I've got to get the rest of the books to Neal before he suspects—"

I shook my head again. "I don't know."

"Alvareda, think of it sensibly. If you help me, no one gets hurt."

"It seems to me you've already done considerable damage."

I walked into the house and shut the door. Neal had been busy poring over the books and had not realized how long I had been out there. I passed him by and went into the kitchen. Then I fixed a cup of strong tea and sat down at the kitchen table to drink it while salty tears streamed down my face.

Over the next few days I struggled as I have never struggled with a problem in my life. I went over the conversation with David from beginning to end again and again, so many times I was sick to death of it. First I tried to rationalize what would happen if I refused to help. He had made what he intended to do very clear. How much of it he could carry out I had no idea, and the damage was difficult to predict. Yet Neal's own words when first we met haunted me still: a scandal can ruin a man's career. . . .

Would David do it? Was he that vicious? I did not know. I knew he was vindictive, but just how far he would go when challenged I could never be sure.

And what if he did everything he claimed he would? Would Neal ever believe in me again? Oh, it just seemed such a foolish chance to take right now when anything would hurt Neal twice as badly because of the fire. Maybe if this had been discovered at another time the firm could overcome it, but now, when Neal faced losing so much, was it fair to risk it?

On the other hand, what might happen if I agreed to help David? His insistence he was not really stealing seemed sincere, though I was sure that any thief asking for help would be equally convincing. And maybe I did owe him a debt from his viewpoint. The question was, would this be the end? If so, then giving him the money was truly wise. If not, there might be no end to the nightmares to follow.

Finally I realized I could not make this decision alone. Ironically, the only person who could advise me was Olivia. I went to her house in the afternoon and explained the whole predicament. She sat quietly as I talked, looking slightly away from me and stroking Fluff. When I finished she drew in a deep sigh and looked into my eyes. "So David has been stealing from the firm."

I nodded, then stopped and shook my head. "Maybe that is what bothers me the most. I'm not sure. He claims that Neal refuses to enjoy the profits they make, so he 'borrowed' in order to support his . . . expensive habits."

"David always was extravagant," she said.

"I was wondering, sister, why did he so quickly think to turn to you for help?"

She knitted her brow and sat back to think. Finally she said, "Thanks to Amanda, he has no doubt come to believe Papa was worth a great deal more than he was. Amanda has always spent freely. Clothing, jewelry, travel. . . ."

"Travel?" I repeated, surprised.

She nodded. "Papa sent her to England once, to visit some cousins there. And she was taken by her mother to San Francisco, New York, Chicago. . . . She still travels."

I must have looked as stunned as I felt. I was thinking of my own aborted trip around the world, all those years ago.

". . . and there is the house in Galveston."

"Galveston?"

"It's only rented, of course, while the house out on McKinney is owned by the estate. But Papa wanted her to have an opportunity for social life. He had arranged for that house just before he fell ill. She spends a lot of time there now."

I was amazed I had never seen her in Galveston, but then we went only on weekends as a rule, and did not venture far past the Gerrard home and the beach. I was shaking my head.

"So you can see there isn't a lot of money to spread around."

"It appears Papa favored Amanda even above you. I wonder why he did not marry Amanda's mother after my mother died."

"He—well, I can assure you he had his reasons."

"Protecting his name, most of all," I said.

She looked away.

"But, Olivia, look how he made you live. Surely you must have resented the difference."

She shook her head. "Papa needed me. I was important in his life. I looked after things for him, saw to his needs."

"Well, I can tell you that it makes *me* furious."

"You can't complain, Alvareda. You fell in love and married the man of your dreams. Everyone has to have some unhappiness. You suffered yours early and got it over with. Be thankful for it."

I sat back in my chair. I still had not received the answer I came for. "What do you think we should do?" I asked her. If this went on much longer I would be crying again.

She considered awhile and said, "I think that if we help him now, he'll come back for more."

I sat forward. "The trouble is, if we don't, he will hurt Neal, and I don't think I could live through that. . . ." My eyes filled up. I wiped them and looked away from her.

"But he might steal again from Neal, then what?"

I shook my head. "I don't know. At least Neal is taking over the accounting. David will not have access to the books anymore."

She nodded as though this satisfied her, then said, "Do you think Neal suspects David is dishonest?"

This had not occurred to me. "No . . ." I said slowly. "At least, I don't think so. Oh, when I think that I could have prevented all this years ago, if I had only spoken out. I never dreamed David's hatred of Papa could wind up infecting our lives this way."

Olivia began to stroke Fluff again and leaned back in her chair, deep in her own thoughts. She was silent for a long while. Finally she looked at me and said, "You know, I've made a great many mistakes in my lifetime."

"Oh, don't blame yourself for Papa's misdoings," I hastened to tell her.

"But I am guilty too, for having participated with him," she said, and put Fluff down on the floor.

All at once she seemed eager for me to go, as though she had things to do alone. She said, "Amanda has nearly drained me dry, and you have asked for so little. . . . I'm going to prepare a letter to the bank now. I wish this could be for you, and not David. But if it will help ease your problems, at least that is something."

"Thank you, sister."

She looked into my face, then reached over and kissed my cheek the way she used to do when I was a child. "Poor, dear little sister. This is all so unfair. . . ."

The change in her mood was puzzling, yet perhaps it was just that now the matter was settled, she wanted to dispose of it quickly, I reasoned. I sat quietly in a corner while she sat down at her desk, put on her spectacles, and dipped the pen in the ink well, then put the lines on paper. As I watched her I felt more miserable than ever at having to ask her for this. She was the only one of Papa's three children who had no real hope of providing for herself. And who knew how long she would live, what needs she would require in her lifetime? Had anyone ever thought of Olivia's needs before his own? As she completed the letter, removed her eyeglasses, and rose, I thought of those times she awaited her Mr. Nelson, aghast he might see her in her eyeglasses. Tears came to my eyes.

The image of my sister writing that letter stayed in my mind all the rest of the day, and that evening when I handed the money to David I felt a new revulsion for him well up inside me. "Don't expect me to ever do this for you again," I warned him, my throat constricted as his hand reached for the envelope.

"Oh, I never make the same mistake twice, you can be sure," he said.

"Just in case your memory fails you in the future, though, Amanda has spent most of Papa's estate by now. It isn't a bottomless well."

He nodded, then smiled. "I knew I could count on you."

"Keep in mind my reason for doing this is only to protect Neal, and I would not have done it if you still had access to the company records," I said. I realized I was saying too much, but I could not stop. When his expression clouded, I took in a breath of anxiety.

"My imagination is not limited to amassing wealth through the cotton business. You should know that by now, Alvareda." He brushed my cheek with the palm of his hand, and walked away.

I did not know what to make of that remark, and it was a long time before I did. All I felt then was an empty relief that I was rid of him . . . for now . . . and I ran the palm of my hand down my cheek, hard, as though to wipe him off me.

As soon as I walked into the house and saw Neal, I was filled with trepidation. The honesty that characterized his nature showed in his face as well, and was startling in its contrast to what I had just done. The greed and deceptions of my father had become like a deep pit of quicksand into which I had fallen and pulled others with me. And how far down would we be sucked before rescue came, or would we safely emerge at all?

Chapter 3

I did not see Olivia over the next few months. I was even busier now that Neal was at home from the hospital, and though I invited her to come over for tea or supper now and then, she refused. I thought it was because she knew our household arrangement was inconvenient for entertaining just now. Around Christmas Neal was able to discard his crutches. We dispensed with the bed in the parlor and began to live normally again. I had written to Olivia, inviting her to come with us for Christmas Day in Galveston. She wrote her refusal but added, "I am anxious to speak with you and Neal. Could you come over when you return from Galveston?"

Did I only imagine a tone of urgency about the note?

We returned from Galveston in the early evening and loaded the buggy for Harrisburg. There was now a good road all the way there from Houston, and we would be at Olivia's house by seven. I'd purchased a gown and slippers for her, some new eau de cologne and a pretty fan. We packed a tin of pecans from our tree as well, and some divinity and assorted cookies sent to her from Mrs. Gerrard.

It was a chilly night. Neal put the top up on the buggy and we folded blankets over our knees. As we drove along I reflected on Olivia's puzzling behavior when last we visited, and wondered if it had anything to do with her need to see us now. Surely she did not have some notion to bare her soul about Papa and David in front of Neal. So far, David had worked as hard as he had promised after I helped him, and he had not caused any more trouble, at least not to me. My heartbeat quickened as we neared Olivia's. . . .

From the moment I laid eyes on her I was glad we had come, for she had drastically changed. She had lost weight—her dress was a little too wide at the shoulders; her face was gaunt and there were dark crescents under her eyes. The big old house seemed more gloomy and cheerless than ever and accentuated the change in her. "Sister," I cried, and caught her in a hug.

She insisted on making a pot of spiced tea, and that we go upstairs to drink it by the fire in her sitting room. "I rarely sit in the parlor," she told us. "It's too cold and formal."

Not until we had taken our chairs before the glowing log fire did I realize Fluff was missing. "Where's Fluff?" I asked.

"Fluff died three weeks ago," she said, and at once her eyes were glassy.

"Oh, I'm sorry, sister. I know how much you miss her. If I'd known, we could have brought you a new kitten for Christmas."

"We could still do it," said Neal. "In fact, I think our neighbors down the street have a brand new litter."

"Oh no," she said. "I couldn't think of replacing Fluff."

"But you would fall in love with a new little kitten. They're so playful—" I began.

"No." She shook her head. "I don't want another pet now." There was a note of finality in her voice that alarmed me.

"There's something I must tell you both." She looked first at Neal, then at me.

"Alvareda, you deserve the truth, and I'm the only one who knows it." A queer little half smile played at the edge of her mouth. "I've struggled with it for years . . . and the time has come for me to have some peace of mind."

I leaned forward, not daring to draw a breath. I could not imagine what she would say, and all kinds of possibilities converged at once on my mind as I waited for her to continue.

She drew up her shoulders. "Sister, forgive me." Her eyes filled with tears and her voice grew unsteady. "You were not responsible for your mother's death, as you were led to believe."

"What?" I said, my voice sounding as though it came from someone else. Surely she was mistaken. That I caused Mama's death was one thing of which I was certain.

"Please let me explain. Papa and Alice had never gotten along very well. I've told you before that she came from a poor family. Papa was strange in some ways, even then. Early in the marriage he somehow got it into his head that she only wanted his money, that she did not love him."

"Do you think that was true?" I asked.

"No. I believe that Papa had not gotten over the death of my mother. He married too soon. He expected Alice to fill my mother's shoes, and of course that was impossible.

"I guess he couldn't see the truth, or couldn't admit it. So he'd accuse her of things, or blame her for what wasn't her fault. They quarreled constantly. Then—" She broke off and looked at me. I knew she had almost let it slip out about Eva Longworth.

"Then, that day when it happened, Alice and Papa had fought, violently. The two of you had been gone for the morning, and I had been out looking at a property with Papa. When we all got home, the argument started. You were outside playing.

"I remember they started downstairs, and argued all the way upstairs. I was in my room down the hall. I wanted to stay in there until they finished. I waited by the door for the shouting to stop. I had never heard either of them so angry. I peeped out my door. He was standing on the landing, two or three stairs above her. He suddenly turned and struck her hard with the back of his hand. She fell from there all the way down to the next stair landing. I could not believe my eyes. He ran down to her.

"Then . . . you walked in, screaming that you had broken your doll. Papa . . . Papa took the opportunity that was there. He told you you startled her and she fell. That was completely untrue."

The whole episode now rehearsed itself before me with painful clarity. I could see my father standing above my mother, and looking at me, saying in a choked voice, "You've killed her, child. You've killed her." I was gripping the chair arm. I had never dreamed—

"At first I was too frightened to say anything," she continued. "Then I began to calculate. If Papa went to prison for murdering his wife, what would become of you and me? We'd have no home. My Mr. Nelson would never marry me with such a blot on my family. He was a very proper Methodist."

She leaned back now, as though relieved to have unburdened herself. "So many times through the years I have come close to telling you the truth. But the longer a lie goes on, the harder it is to reverse it. It's like a disease.

"And when the two of you met, I thought, now sister can find real happiness. It won't matter about the lie if she has a happy marriage. I was wrong. I should have told you."

Neal took my hand. I said nothing, but stared into the log fire thinking. What Olivia almost said about Eva Longworth caused another element of her story to fall into place for me. That morning of my mother's death, she had taken me along to Eva Longworth's house so that I wouldn't be left alone. I was so young then I don't suppose she thought I would remember any of it. Just as Amanda said, they talked in the house while we stayed outside and took turns pushing each other on the swing under the oak tree.

Now I realized it was after we returned that she confronted my father about the affair with Eva and the child Amanda. . . .

I did not know whether to feel happy or sad. Olivia said, "You were a living reminder of what Papa had done. He felt terribly guilty and took it out on you. He was a lot more frightened of you than you were of him. He lived in constant fear you would realize the truth. I'm certain that's why . . . at least part of the reason . . . he drank so much."

"So he kept Alvareda terrified in order to stay in control," Neal observed.

She nodded slowly. "I suppose you would have to say that. . . . Sister, forgive me, please? It would give me such peace, to know that you would."

I could not register my feelings as quickly as she wanted me to. I needed time. "I guess you did what you felt you had to," I finally told her. She waited for the word "forgive," to be offered. I just could not, not yet.

"Could you just hug me?" she asked pitifully.

I reached across and held her for a moment. Only a moment. I felt drained. Finally I looked up at Neal. "Let's go. Tomorrow is a workday and it's getting late."

Olivia looked as though I had slapped her.

"Oh? Couldn't you stay a while longer? Or the two of you could spend the night with me and return early in the morning. It's so dark now. . . ."

She waited. Neal said to me, "Why don't you stay, dear? I could come back for you tomorrow after work."

"No!" I said, too quickly. I could not face that house tonight of all nights, nor Olivia either. "I want to go home with you." I turned to Olivia. "I—I have so much to do tomorrow. Perhaps I'll drive out one afternoon soon, when the weather is fine."

She nodded. I knew I had hurt her feelings, but I just couldn't help it, not then. All I could think of was the pain and heartache she might have spared me by just telling the truth earlier. Papa could not have suspended me in guilt all those years . . . could not have exacted my pitiful wish that he could have a change of heart and love me. At the moment I last spoke to him, it would have been so different. . . .

Once we were in the buggy, Neal tucked blankets around my lap and feet. "Don't you think you could say something more to her?"

I shook my head. It was so easy for him to stand away from my complicated family situation and view it objectively.

As we moved away I looked up at the house. Except for her upstairs window, it was shrouded in darkness, and I will never forget her figure posed there, outlined by the gaslight, her face looking down on us. She lifted a hand to wave, just as she had on the day I left home to marry Neal more than seven years before. I had the same feeling I had then, that she was truly a captive in her father's house. Yet what she related just now paralyzed my feelings of pity for her. I just wanted to get away.

I waved back and said, almost in a whisper, "Good-bye, sister."

On Thursday, February 14 of 1895, we awoke to the breathtaking sight of a thick mantle of snow outside, white and glistening as the sugar icing on the Valentine's cake I had baked the night before. It had begun around eight o'clock, while I was still in the kitchen. When we went to bed at midnight, we were convinced it would soon turn to rain. The ground was damp; the snow was icy. It was typical February weather. Yet in the night the north wind blew dry and the ground froze.

Neal rose at the usual time and parted the draperies in the bedroom. "Come look," he said. "I don't think we're going to make it all the way to Mother's for the dinner tonight."

The log fire had gone out; the room was freezing. I threw on a robe and hurried to the window. Neal wrapped his arms around me from behind. You could see beyond our backyard all the way over to Commerce Street and beyond, almost to the Bayou. Everything was laden with white. You could not even make out where Commerce cut between the houses. Clumps of snow couched on weather vanes, and lodged in every crevice on cupolas, steeples, and belvederes, and slid down to make a patchwork on rooftops. Trees and shrubbery were transformed into works of art as beautiful as when heavy with blossoms and leaves in springtime. Fences and gate posts were scalloped with gleaming white. Chimneys puffed up towers of smoke, soon to flatten and dissipate in the chilly air above. Icicles hung like pointed needles from our back fence and along the eaves of the barn. Still the flurries continued, twirling down and coating more thickly the layers already settled.

"I don't believe the snow in '86 was this beautiful," I told Neal. "Or maybe it was just that I was not with you, so it didn't seem so beautiful."

He held me tighter and nuzzled his face in my hair.

I looked up at him out the corner of my eye. "Surely you aren't going to work today?"

"I don't see how I can."

I smiled contentedly. "And there is no reason we need to be up so early, is there?"

"I can't think of one." He had begun to lift the hair up off my neck and kiss me, and work his hands inside my robe. Desire flooded over me like an ocean wave. When his fingers were laced around my breasts, warmly circling each nipple until it hardened with pleasure, I arched my back, stretched my arms around his neck, and brought my mouth to his. With one hand still around my breast, he reached down with the other to gently stroke between my legs, seizing me with delight. Even after all these years, I wanted him as fiercely as I had in the beginning, and so many months had passed since we were like this with each other, I could hardly wait as he lifted me up and carried me back to bed.

"I'll build up the fire," he said, putting me down and kissing my fingers. His eyes were glassy, suffused with love.

"No, not now," I begged. I raised up against him, then pulled him, laughing at me indulgently, into submission.

It was the first carefree day we had had in a long time. Neal locked the wheels on the buggy, and in our homemade "sleigh" we rode to the Leider house and picked up Elzyna, then took a tour of the city and stopped for hot chocolate before coming home. I did not think of Olivia till we returned in the late afternoon and darkness was falling. Suddenly I wondered if she had enough kerosene to keep the house warm. She'd not been herself lately and might have been careless about household details. Oh, you're being silly, I told myself. She is perfectly capable of looking after things. If she only had a telephone, though, so I could call her. . . .

Around six o'clock Neal called the depot and confirmed the trains were running. "If you like we could call Mother and tell her we'll be at the dinner after all. We could stay overnight and come back tomorrow."

"Good. I'll put the cake in the box. There are some Valentine presents by the door."

"Did you mail Olivia's card?"

"Yes."

"Did you write her a note like you promised?"

"Yes."

Neal had been after me since Christmas to write to Olivia and assure her I accepted her apologies. Yet it had taken me all this time to be able to frame the words that she so badly wanted to receive from me. What I finally had to realize was that she, more so than myself, suffered from the quarrel that ended in my mother's death. She lost the only man she ever truly loved, her Mr. Nelson. Although the mistaken belief that I had caused my mother's death brought me much anguish through the years, it had not crippled my ability to enjoy my life. I was so glad to know the truth at last, if for no other reason than that it simply helped explain my father's attitude toward me. Yet she had been right, too, in thinking I could have survived without knowing, for look whose strong arm I had to lean on now. And look how pitifully alone Olivia had remained. . . .

For a reason that I cannot yet identify, Olivia stayed on my mind all evening long. We arrived in Galveston at seven o'clock, and although it was past dark you could still make out the magnificent covering of snow everywhere. The whole island was like a fairyland. Neal's mother had the dining room fixed with valentine hearts and flowers, and everyone was in high spirits.

Yet I spent the hours preoccupied with Olivia. I went to bed around eleven, staying in the room which I had occupied before my marriage to Neal. He was up for a while longer, talking to his father and to Martin. I did not really sleep until he came to bed, not being accustomed to sleeping without him near. We both wound up oversleeping the next morning, and Mrs. Gerrard out of kindness left us alone.

At half-past nine, Neal awakened me. "I'm afraid we missed the early train," he said. He already had the newspaper and was reading about the snow. "Twenty-two inches total," he remarked.

"That must be a record," I told him. "Is it clearing now?"

"Beginning to," he said. "Mother's fixing breakfast for us. I think we can still make the noon train, and maybe then I can go on to the office."

It was nearly two o'clock before we finally walked through the door at home, and the telephone was ringing. It was Mrs. MacDonald, who lived behind Olivia on Medina Street. She had not seen Olivia since the day before yesterday, and she was worried. She had been calling repeatedly all day.

"She probably stayed in out of the weather," I suggested, my pulse quickening.

"Yes, but her milk was delivered this morning, and it's still on the back stoop."

At that my heart fell. "I'll be there as soon as I can," I told her. "Would you—no, never mind. Thank you very much."

I hung up the receiver and told Neal. "I don't know what this means, but I think you'd better go with me."

"She must be ill. She did not look well the last time we saw her. Why don't you call her doctor and have him meet us there? I'll get the buggy and meet you around in the front."

We took the train, for Neal feared Harrisburg Road might be impassable with so much snow still on the ground. I was growing more and more anxious, and impatient at waiting out the departure time for the train. No longer did the snow seem a pleasant change of pace; now its presence irritated me. As we chugged along in the train, past the countryside covered with melting snow, Neal tried to reassure me. "She's probably just not feeling well. Maybe she forgot about the milk."

"I do wish she would get a telephone. Today I'll insist. Situations like this prove the point."

"Right," he said, and took my hand in his. I believe the prospect that we would not find her alive was as much on his mind as on my own. We fell into silence. I kept thinking of the many times since yesterday that she had crossed my mind. I should have obeyed my instinct, dropped everything, and gone to her. By the time we drew up in front of the house I was in a state of agitation. Dr. Pillant was just arriving in his buggy, his aging figure dwarfed by mounds of woolen wrappings and a large hat. "I had two patients waiting when you called," he said. "I came as quickly as I could." The three of us approached the front door together, and found it locked. That was unusual in itself. People in Harrisburg didn't lock their doors unless they were going to be gone for a long time. . . . Neal banged on the door, and we awaited a response. None. He tried again, and still again, without reaction from inside. Finally I said, "Get a rock. Break the glass. We've got to get in."

"Let me check the back door first," said Neal. But he came back around the house shaking his head. "I think we can more easily break into the back," he said, and so we trooped around to the door that led into the kitchen, slushing through the melting snow. Mrs. MacDonald was leaning on the fence. She waved at us. When Neal finally got the door open, I was almost afraid to go in. I called Olivia's name as soon as I was inside. Nothing. The kitchen was as neat as always. A bowl of ripening oranges was in the middle of the table. The pungent smell of fruit rind pervaded the air. Nearby, a newspaper three days old and an empty teacup.

We went through the kitchen and down the dark hall to the stairway. Everything was perfectly in order. I heard the clock on the stairs strike the hour of four. I began to walk up, but Dr. Pillant said, "Wait, Alvareda. I know where her room is. I'll just have a look if you don't mind. I'll call you."

I turned around and sat down on the stairs, and looked up at Neal. "She's dead. I know she is."

"Sh. Wait, Alvareda."

We listened to him shuffle up the long stairs and down the hall toward the end. I heard the door open, then close. I strained my ears for the sound of a voice. Nothing. I kept staring into Neal's face. "I wonder if she got the Valentine card. I mailed it three days ago."

"We'll find out," he said. He looked up toward her room.

A few moments passed. I heard the door open again, and again the sound of Dr. Pillant's footsteps down the hall. I stood up and turned toward the landing to await his approach. Finally he appeared, shaking his head. "I'm sorry, Olivia is dead. I would guess she died last night. It appears she took too much . . . the bottle of sleeping medicine I prescribed a week ago is empty."

I slumped down on the stairs. Neal was beside me, reaching for my hands. "All right, honey?"

I shook my head. "I don't know. Let me just sit here awhile." I was cold on the outside, hot on the inside, trembling all over, my teeth chattering. Yet I could not cry. I stared out into nowhere, unable to grasp the very thing I had suspected.

I heard Neal ask Dr. Pillant to wait with me while he went upstairs, and I guess he was gone for several minutes. I had no concept of time passing. When he returned, he held the card and letter in front of me so that I could see she received it in time. I looked at the red valentines and cupids and filigree on the card and burst into tears. Neal put his arms around me, then quickly said, "You're freezing. I've got to get you warm, come."

He built a fire in the kitchen stove and wrapped blankets around me, as Dr. Pillant left the house to notify the undertaker. I sat there for a very long time, while Neal stood behind me, rubbing my shoulders and back soothingly. I looked around the kitchen—Olivia's domain—at all the hanging pots and pans, the spice rack on the wall, the rolling pin on the wooden board in the corner, the butter churn nearby. I could almost see her bustling around, her cheeks warm and rosy from the heat of the stove. How often she would pause and bring a finger to her chin and gaze around in assessment. Then she would focus on something she had forgotten, and hurry to look after it. How much of her energies were spent in this room! Tears rolled down my eyes, and I pulled Neal's handkerchief back and forth through my fingers.

At last I took a deep breath and looked at him. "I'm warm now. Let's go away from here."

I was strangely calm all the way back to Houston that night. Neal kept his arm around me, holding me close as I stared out the train window and watched the bleak, wet landscape go by. Dr. Pillant had told us she probably took an overdose of the sleeping medicine by mistake. That was what would be reflected on the death certificate. Neal and I both knew that was not the truth. I thanked him for his kindness.

On the train I asked Neal if he thought she had been contemplating suicide since before Christmas. "I keep thinking of her remark about how it would give her so much peace if I would only forgive what she had done."

"I don't know. I guess there are lots of things we'll never know about Olivia. But I had a feeling something was going to happen. That's why I insisted on your writing a note."

"I'm so glad she got it," I said, then thought again. "You don't think she awaited that response, then killed herself, do you?"

"I doubt it. I think she just lost interest in life. We might have seen it coming for years, the way she let things go and withdrew."

I counted up the years since Papa's death, and realized that he had died seven years ago almost to the day. When I told Neal, he said, "I hadn't thought of that. This may have been a very hard time of year for her to get through."

Yes, and even more so, I thought, because she continued to be pulled toward him by her loyalty, while knowing the damage she created. I remembered the day she gave me the money for David. "Sister really did love me deep down," I said suddenly.

"Yes, I know she did," Neal said. He squeezed my hand.

I had always sensed that. Yet I was not sensitive enough to imagine the hopelessness that must have lain underneath the smooth surface of her skin, much like the brown tufts of grass and the stark, barren tree limbs lie hidden beneath the white fantasy of snow.

Chapter 4

As the days went by and I overcame the shock of Olivia's suicide, I became more and more obsessed with figuring out whether there was something recent that had prompted it. My thoughts went back to the day we spoke of David's predicament. She regretted all the mistakes she had made, mentioned her guilt. Could guilt have led her to suicide? Surely not, because of her decision to tell me the truth about my mother's death. She said she sought peace of mind. It did not add up, not when there were still so many other things left hanging. . . .

Finally, when I met with her attorney, what he told me was like the planting of a seed in my mind. I began to think I knew what Olivia's true purpose was, perhaps the product of the grief and despondency that characterized her final years.

Because of his obsession with maintaining his upstanding name, Papa had put nothing in his own Last Will and Testament for Amanda, relying on Olivia's steadfast desire to obey his wishes and look after her. That enabled Olivia to leave what remained of the estate to me, without creating trouble from Amanda. If Amanda were to take legal measures now, to claim what she felt was her due from Papa's estate, she would have little or no convenient proof that she was his daughter, and the obvious question of why she did not bother to make a claim on the estate years earlier, after Papa died, would further dilute any case she might be able to bring forward.

All of this did not occur to me while I sat in Mr. Seaton's office. But in the middle of the night following my visit with him I suddenly awoke and sat bolt upright in bed. Olivia had paved the way for me to rid myself of Amanda once and for all, I reasoned, whereas she, because of her fierce loyalty to Papa, could not.

Did she do this on purpose, I wondered? Her will had been drawn in January of this year, 1895. Therefore it stood to reason this was what she had in mind. I lay down and figured. There would be some cash from the estate, how much had not yet been fully disclosed. The rest of the estate was in land, including the house in Harrisburg, the house out on McKinney Avenue, a large piece of land out in West Texas, and some acreage here and there over the rest of the state. Olivia knew that I could not very well tell Amanda to get off Papa's property and support herself, not without leaving myself open to blackmail. But I might just be able to buy her out with cash, and maybe some property. She surely was sensible enough to realize she could not live off Papa forever, that eventually the money would run out.

The only problem was that Neal had some expectations about Papa's estate. He was not able to sit in on the meeting with Mr. Seaton, the attorney, but afterward he remarked that we should probably take the cash in the estate and invest it in property in and around Houston.

I pretended to be busy shaking out the dust on the bottom of my skirt from the trip to Harrisburg, and said, "I don't know how much there is left by now. Probably very little."

He said, "I doubt that. Your father was an astute manager, there is no denying him that, and I'm sure he left a lot more than Olivia spent, considering the way she lived."

"Yes, of course," I said. We agreed to place her house on the market, then I quickly changed the subject.

Now the prospect of getting rid of the burden of Amanda Cane was wonderful to savor. The thought of her, feeding off Olivia like a parasite, was repugnant to me. I wished profoundly never to have to see her again, never to go out to that house again, once this was done. And I had to admit to myself that, with or without an exchange of money, I would never be satisfied until she was yielded powerless, and vanquished. For all I cared, the house she lived in could burn to the ground, although I realized that was foolish.

I would offer her a little money—not enough to be missed by Neal—and perhaps some property too, on the stipulation she not see David anymore. Only then would she really be out of my way.

Yet, what leverage did I have, if she refused? Would she or David come banging on our door one night, and tell Neal everything? I wasn't sure about Amanda, not then anyway. But David was vindictive. He might . . .

Still, he was also smart. He had as much at stake in keeping this from Neal as I had. He could hardly just pull out and take Amanda with him, not when the new notes at the bank were in his name as well as Neal's. . . .

For hours I thought of the possibilities. Next day while tidying the house for dinner guests in the evening, I was dusting off a bench in the hall, and, still preoccupied, I chanced to look up into the mirror above. My face wore a new expression. I no longer had the appearance of the young, innocent girl who ran from the clutches of her wicked father into the arms of Prince Charming. I now looked . . . what was the word? Sophisticated. Yes. And something more . . . cunning. Had this been a gradual change, or did it happen through last night as I contrived my plans? I kept staring . . . a strange feeling came over me. At last I turned from the mirror and sat down in a chair. I did not want to look anymore. For the first time in my life I had looked into a mirror and seen a striking resemblance to my father reflected there.

Early in March I met with Mr. Seaton for a final calculation of the estate. The cash value was more than I expected. There was almost fifteen thousand dollars. Neal had been right. It would be easier than I thought, I now surmised. I would offer her a quarter of the cash value. That was a hefty sum, but would leave enough to avoid rousing suspicion in Neal's mind. Apart from that, there was one piece of property that she might find appealing. . . .

Two days later, in the afternoon, I hitched up the buggy and rode out to see her. I had no idea if she was at home, but would go back as many times as necessary if not.

I did not feel as uneasy making the trip as I had before. The area was much unchanged. Past the Hutcheson place and then the Pillot house it was little populated, and beyond the railroad tracks, as much a wilderness as before. Yet I traveled it in daylight, full knowing what was at the other end. The only real unknown was how Amanda might respond to my proposal.

She did not look surprised as she opened the door and saw me there. "Come in," she said. "I was about to have some tea. I'll get a cup for you." She had been out for a ride. Her cheeks were red. She wore a dark blue riding costume with big buttons down the front and tight-fitting sleeves. Expensive-looking. I showed her a copy of Olivia's will, to let her know first that she had not been included. As I watched her read the long document, I thought with satisfaction that she bore no resemblance to Papa. When she finished, she handed it back. "Where does this leave me?" she said. She did not appear surprised, or shaken, as I hoped.

"You must have known, eventually, that Papa's support of you would no longer be possible."

She sat down and stirred her tea. She looked up at me and said, "Perhaps."

Her lack of discomfort over all this was redoubling mine. I tried to convince her I was now in control. I offered my proposal. She listened calmly, then leaned back and sighed. I sat there growing anxious, but kept quiet. At length she stretched her arms and laughed softly. She leaned forward and faced me directly. I do not believe I have ever seen such a treacherous look on anyone's face.

"Well?" I said, then cleared my throat.

"You can't make me give up David."

Somewhat relieved at the limp remark, I said, "Amanda, face the truth. David is not going to marry you, or he would have by now. You could take the money and go somewhere else, meet someone who could provide you a home and a living for a lifetime through marriage. You could have children . . . a family all your own."

"You could be mistaken about that," she said, yet I realized from the look on her face that my words had made an impression.

I leaned forward. "You're a beautiful girl, and still young. You won't be young forever."

She considered for a few moments, then asked, "How much is the property worth? The one in West Texas you mentioned."

"Around twelve hundred dollars, I believe," I told her, and as she paused, I thought my task was accomplished. I could not have been more wrong.

At last she said, "You may have a good point about David. He hasn't shown any real hurry to give up his wife for me." It occurred to me she had calculated many things before I came today. I said nothing, but sipped my tea.

"I may take you up on it, Alvareda, but I want it all."

"All? What makes you think there is any more?" I quickly asked. "You've spent a great portion of it over the years. You must know there is only so much to go around. I'm sure Olivia made you somewhat aware—"

She interrupted me. "Oh, but I have a much better idea of my own expenses than you have. You may think I'm frivolous, which I am to some degree, but I know what was there before Papa's death, and I have a pretty good idea what is left there now. You could triple that figure and still have a lot left over."

I'm sure I must have grown pale at that moment. "That's impossible," I said, thinking of Neal. I narrowed my eyes. "Moreover, I won't do it. If you were smart, you would take my offer, for it is a generous one. I am tired of you and David and all this deception. I've just about reached my limit."

She looked at me now, her expression hard. "Oh, have you, Mrs. Gerrard?" she snapped, then after a long pause, continued, "You thought I would just stay hidden away all of these years, and be glad for whatever I got, didn't you? Thought I'd keep quiet forever while you and Olivia enjoyed the luxury of a pedigree, and you married a man who would do anything for you—oh yes, David talks about you and your husband—and who only grows better off as the years go by?"

"I—I'm not sure I follow you—"

"David and I are somewhat alike, when it comes to recognizing opportunity, and I've known mine would appear for some time." She laughed. "I knew what you'd offer when you walked through the door."

Furious, I rose to my feet. "If you think you can threaten me, you're sadly mistaken."

She splayed out her fingers in front of her and calmly looked over her fingernails. Then she looked at me sidelong and smiled. "Sit down, Alvareda. I have something very interesting to tell you."

I do not believe I could have gone on standing at that moment if my life depended on it. I moved down uneasily, as one who takes a seat in the dentist chair.

"Our dear papa, Samuel Cane, was a cold-blooded murderer."

At first I thought she referred to my mother's death, then the words "cold-blooded" fell on me like an icy drizzle. I leaned forward.

"Remember when David's father was driven out of Harrisburg for adultery?"

"Yes," I said weakly, and gripped the chair arm.

"Just after Papa and his committee were finished, Clifton Leider did some investigating on his own. He followed Papa out here one night, and the next day in Harrisburg he presented him with what he found: me and my mother."

I looked away. I wanted to cover my ears and run.

She continued, "He told Papa that either he would go with him before the townspeople and announce what he was doing himself, or that he, Mr. Leider, would do it for him. I imagine he savored the idea of making Papa say those incriminating words himself.

"But that was a mistake. He should never have given Papa any time. Papa pretended to agree, of course, to what he demanded. This was a Saturday, and there was to be a meeting after church the next day. Papa said he would do it then."

I lowered my forehead on my hand. Oh God, I should have known, why did I never figure it out? As she went on, I thought of what Papa told Olivia so long ago, about getting rid of the Leider family. I assumed he meant only to get rid of my suitor. I was too involved in my own predicament to wonder if he meant anything else—

She leaned back in her chair. "I remember it all vividly," she mused, as though she enjoyed the story as a child enjoys a fairy tale. "It was a rainy night—lightning, thunder—and I was still awake when Papa came in. I listened to him tell my mother that he had followed Mr. Leider as he left, trailed him to where his mistress lived, a few miles on the other side of Harrisburg. I'm sure Mr. Leider could hardly wait to tell the woman what was going to happen.

"Papa shot them both dead, put them in the back of his buggy, and came here."

I shook my head in anguish.

"She wouldn't let him bury them on this property. It frightened her too much. He promised to get back in his buggy and find some other place. I have no idea where. He was in a state near panic when he arrived.

"Of course he knew she'd never tell. She worshiped the ground he walked on. He took such good care of her."

My breath came in gulps. I put a hand on my throat. "Did Olivia know?"

She nodded.

I realized then that Olivia probably had taken her life out of guilt after all. She would not have deliberately led me into this. Suddenly I realized something else and looked up. "And David? He never found out?"

She cocked her head to one side. "Up to now, I've never told a living soul."

"I see," I told her, for indeed I did. I kept sitting there, feeling the wind had been knocked out of me. I wanted to run far away and pretend none of this was true. Yet I was as involved as she was. "And your price for keeping the secret from now on is Papa's estate?"

She smiled. "You're very perceptive, Alvareda. You can have this house, and the other properties around here. To tell you the truth, I'm sick of this place. I want the money. I won't take less than ten thousand dollars, regardless of how much is left in Papa's estate."

"Very well," I said at last, took half a breath, and rose. I could not bear to look at her anymore, or to stay in that house. "But what guarantee have I that you will keep your end of the bargain?"

"Oh, if I don't, you'll probably hear about it from David."

No, no. This would not do. I quickly searched for a solution. "I'll pay you out in fourths, over, say, the next two years," I said at last.

She reflected long enough that at least I was certain she really wanted the money. Otherwise, I do not know what I would have had to bargain with. At last she said, "I want half now, and the rest you can pay in fourths."

I hesitated. Only so long as I owed her money could I count on her. "I'll give you half when you vacate this house, and I'll have the deed for the West Texas property at the same time. I'll pay you one installment per year." I started to ask her to send me her address, then realized the folly in that. "What day will you move out? I'll meet you here that morning."

"Give me a week."

I nodded. "And after that—"

"I'll probably go to Galveston for a while. I have friends there."

I caught my breath again. Galveston was too close. I shook my head.

"Don't worry. My friends in Galveston know nothing," she assured me.

"And you won't see David anymore?"

"I'll tell him I've agreed not to for certain compensations. I guess the rest is up to him."

I walked to the door and, feeling somewhat calmer, I turned and said, "When the money is gone, there won't be any more. I can't—won't—steal from my husband. So don't come to me again."

She smiled and said, "You'll just have to trust me, sister."

In that moment I knew all the frustration of an insect who has been pinned to a wall, and struggles helplessly. I would not have believed I was capable of the deep contempt I felt for Amanda. I thought of her greedy bargain again. What would I tell Neal?

The late afternoon breeze out in the yard felt good to my feverish face. I stepped unevenly off the porch and across the yard. When I got into my buggy I lingered for a while, trying to collect myself. At that point I was so distracted I was not certain I could drive myself home safely. I closed my eyes and sat still. Finally I gazed at the little rustic cottage, nestled in the shadows of the trees, where so much of my life was entangled. From the great long limb of the oak tree nearby still hung the swing which I had sat in briefly, long ago, not knowing all that this house would mean to me someday.

Samuel Cane, my father: a twisted man who would go to any lengths to achieve his destructive, self-serving goals. One of his daughters he had held captive in Harrisburg; one seethed with jealousy out here in her wilderness prison. Was I, the third, any more free than they were? I flicked the reins, and as I left to begin the long journey back to Houston, it struck me with a clang of desperation, that before, in dealing with David, I had been mopping up after the damage I knew my father had done. Now, through Amanda, I was dealing with Papa himself. I realized for the very first time that the sick, helpless kind of love I once felt toward my father had calcified into hatred.

If I had been afraid of David before, it was mild compared with what I suffered after Amanda was gone. Each time he walked into a room my pulse quickened. I searched his eyes to see if they portrayed a new signal. Had he seen her? Had she told him why she left? Had she told him more? Just as Amanda conveyed, even blackmail called for some trust.

One night David came by to talk to Neal and this time I did not try to avoid him. I simply had to know what he would say. Standing in the kitchen, I heard his footsteps approach, and the door swing open. I stood with my hands folded in front of me, and tried to look perfectly calm. He made light chitchat about all the rain he encountered on a recent trip to Central Texas, and he seemed so congenial that for a short while I was hopeful I had been right about the withering state of his feelings for Amanda, and that he was not angry with me for sending her away or for anything else. . . .

Then he remarked, "You know, Alvareda, once a man gets used to being on the road, distance doesn't mean much to him anymore. You don't really think you can keep me from Amanda if I want to see her, do you?"

His way of phrasing the statement seemed to indicate that I was right. The romance was cooling on its own. Finally I reminded him, "I helped you out once. Don't you think you have gone far enough to make me miserable?" I waited for his reply, hoping with all my heart it would tell me what I had to know.

"My dear Alvareda, what you gave me was merely a down payment. I still don't have what I really want."

"What *do* you want?" I hurled the words back at him.

"I'm surprised you haven't figured it out by now," he said, then walked out.

I paced from corner to corner about the kitchen, hands folded in front of me, trying to reconcile what he had just said with the truth about his father's death. His words and his manner indicate he knows nothing, I reasoned. Yet . . . "surprised you haven't figured it out," he had said. God have mercy, what did he mean by that? I stood still for a long time and studied the floor, tapping my foot.

Finally a chilling new thought occurred to me and I eased down into a kitchen chair. Amanda might have double-crossed me and told him, and together they conspired to keep quiet until she had all the money, then they would . . . would what? I thought of David's viciousness after the fire. If he was desperate enough he might do almost anything. My father had once cheated his mother out of her home. If David knew the extent of my father's crime beyond that, what could he do about it? File charges of some kind? Oh, I was so hopelessly ignorant about legal matters. Could he bring some kind of suit against Neal and me together, for damages to his mother? Ruin Neal and all he had worked so hard to achieve? No, he couldn't do that, not unless he had proof of the murder.

I pulled out my handkerchief and mopped my brow. Yes, that was a comforting thought. There was no evidence. I thought again. Amanda claimed there was none. What if she really did know where the bodies were buried? What if she had already told David the truth before I ever appeared at her door? He might have been in on this from the start. . . . Oh Lord, make this end, I prayed.

I had to get busy or I would go out of my mind. What time was it? I looked at the clock. After ten. It would soon be time to go to bed, and if Neal saw me in this state, he would know something was wrong. I picked up a cloth and began to scrub the kitchen table. Up and down the surface I went, both hands pushing the cloth, harder, harder, again and again. Suddenly the door swung open and my shoulders pitched violently backward, the cloth dropping from my grasp. "Oh, Neal! You startled me."

"Sorry," he smiled. "Is anything wrong?"

"No, of course not."

He shrugged. "I'm going up to bed."

"I'll be there soon."

After he was gone I took deep breaths, trying to collect myself and wondering if anything had shown in my face.

Chapter 5

The first week in April, when cotton season was slowing down, Neal and I left on a two-week vacation. By train we went to San Antonio, over to Austin, and then to El Paso. It was the first time we had been away since the fire, and we spent all our time sightseeing and playing, sleeping late and eating heartily. The trip was exactly what we both needed. When far away from home, it was easier for Neal to relax, and easier for me to believe everything would be all right, that regardless of what David said, he wouldn't go out of his way to see Amanda, and she was smart enough not to risk telling David what she knew.

Shortly after we returned, I began to suspect I was carrying a child. I had had so many disappointments, month after month, year after year, I was afraid I might be wishing so hard my imagination had taken over. I said nothing to Neal at first. It would not do to get his hopes up until I was certain.

In June I paid a call to Dr. Morant, whom I had not seen since Neal's recovery. He was a dapper man with a flock of gray hair and a soft voice, and a pair of unruly brows under a wrinkled forehead. I had always felt at ease with him. He completed his examination, then looked at me above his eyeglasses, gray eyes bright with pleasure. "You're going to be a mother, Mrs. Gerrard. I would predict, around the first of January."

"Oh, I can't believe it," I exclaimed, and rose from the examination table, clutching my heart.

He laughed. "I told you not to give up when you talked to me after Neal's accident. Now, get dressed and come sit down. I want to talk to you."

He folded his hands and looked across the desk at me. He wanted to know how I was feeling generally.

"I've been fine," I said, not mentioning the mental anguish I'd gone through. Then I paused at length before asking the question that had haunted me since the stillbirth of Alice Marie. I leaned forward and said, "But can you be sure it won't be the same as the first time? I mean, how can you be sure the baby is healthy?" I held my breath till he answered.

He shook his head. "I had a feeling you were going to be asking that." He removed his glasses and peered at me like a stern schoolmaster reprimanding a student. "I don't want you to spend a moment's worry over it. You're in fine health—I've never seen you look better. Try to stay calm, don't be afraid of moderate exercise, and eat the right foods. Your chances of bringing a healthy baby into the world are as good as any woman's."

I nodded.

He winked and smiled. "Come back and see me in a month."

He did not know that remaining calm was probably the tallest order he gave to me. Still, I think I had already developed that instinctive will of the mother to protect the unborn child that grows within her. I began that very afternoon to talk myself out of worrying about David and Amanda with all the determination that was within me. I also took the first of many long walks that would use up my energy in a positive way, and keep my mind at peace.

That evening when I told Neal he was not as surprised as I expected. He let out a shout of joy and picked me up and twirled me around. "I knew it! I just knew it. If I had had any idea this would have happened, we would have taken a lot more vacations." He let me down and covered me with kisses. Then he took my hands and looked into my face. "Should you stay in bed? Let me wait on you?"

I shook my head and smiled. "No, because if you do I shall grow fat and lazy, and you'll be sorry you married me."

He smiled at me, the way he often did, the smile beginning at the corner of his eyes and spreading over his face. "That is the one thing that will never, never happen, Mrs. Gerrard."

I put my arms around him and held on tightly as I thought of my father and all he had involved me in, and hoped with all my heart that Neal would always feel as he did in that moment.

I prayed nightly for a healthy child and followed exactly the doctor's instructions. I made regular trips to the city market to pick over the fresh fruits and vegetables in the stalls. When the cold weather came in December, I spent hours in front of the log fire, knitting blankets and sweaters and caps. On January 6, 1896, I felt the first grips of labor at six in the evening. Before midnight we had a healthy son. He had a fuzzy halo of golden hair, and was the most beautiful sight we had ever beheld.

We named him Gabriel.

Now Carlotta was jealous of Gabriel; I sensed this from the beginning. When she told me, eight months after his birth, that she was expecting another child, I prayed hard that she would bear a healthy son. Not only did I want this for the sake of the Leider family, thinking that it might help to bring them closer together. I was also very protective of Gabriel. I did not like the threat of anyone's jealousy cast in his direction. It seemed . . . well . . . perhaps the word is unlucky.

In February of 1897 Carlotta went into labor at seven o'clock in the evening. The trial was long and difficult. Not until noon of the following day was the baby born, a nine-pound son. Jordan resembled Elzyna as a newborn infant. Yet, unlike her, he cried endlessly the first time I held him, and Carlotta said he was the most fretful of the three children she had produced.

I laughed, and smoothed out the covers around him. "Looks like you have a fighter on your hands."

"What could you expect?" Carlotta said dourly. "He looks like his father. Probably he'll behave like him, too."

It did not sound like the kind of remark a mother would make of her newborn son, but then I knew Carlotta was tired from the strain of childbirth. I set his crib to rocking in hopes he would be lulled to contentment. "Is Jordan a family name?"

She nodded. "David's side. It was my choice. This is David's child. He should have a Leider family name."

From the tone of her voice, she seemed to be absolving herself of responsibility toward the infant. Again, I felt she was speaking from exhaustion, or perhaps I misinterpreted her remarks. As much as she had wanted this child, I could not believe she felt as bitter as she sounded.

All afternoon as I tended to my own son, my mind kept returning to Carlotta. Her attitude toward her children was hard to fathom. When Elzyna was born I had thought Carlotta simply resented the fact she was not the much wanted son. Yet now the son had been born and she seemed to resent him equally. Could it be they both reminded her of David, whereas Patricia took after the Bennett side of the family?

That seemed to make sense as I considered it. She continued to treat Elzyna like an interloper, rarely praising her, frequently reminding her of her failings, making unfavorable comparisons between her and her sister in front of others. Was her treatment of Jordan to be the same?

That evening David came over. Gabriel was already in bed. Neal was attending a vestry meeting at the church. I was in the dining room, with a set of house plans spread over the table. We had finally returned to the project of building our home. As I opened the door, I realized David had been drinking. Normally his grooming was immaculate. He owned twice as many suits of clothes as Neal, in varying fabrics and shades. Tonight the coat was rumpled; his tie was loosened. His hair was untidy. I had no choice but to invite him in.

"Congratulations on your new son," I said, wondering what he was really here for.

He nodded, but said nothing further.

I poured him a cup of coffee, and we sat down across from each other. "I—I'm a little busy right now. Neal is at a meeting, but he ought to be home pretty soon."

He smiled, enjoying my discomfort as he always had.

Then he glanced toward the dining room. "Busy on house plans?"

"Yes. You know, there are so many things to—"

"May I have a look at them?" he interrupted.

That was not the response I had hoped for. I nodded, and he followed me into the dining room. He stood behind me as I told him about the house. "It's about the size of the house I grew up in," I began. Red brick with gray and white trim, and galleries on both floors. "There will be a solarium at one end and a large parlor, here, opening into the dining room, at the other. In between there will be a curving stairway, just here. Upstairs Neal will have a study, and there will be six bedrooms with large bathrooms in between."

"Hm . . . and what's this here?" he asked, pointing. His breath nearly overpowered me.

"A big window, behind the staircase. It will be made of art glass, and the front door will have art glass too. I have to pick that out next week. Building a home is a lot of work, I find."

"I wouldn't know. I never had that experience," he said.

"Your coffee will get cold," I reminded him, and we returned to the parlor. I hoped he would drink it and go. "Have you been celebrating?" I asked with growing trepidation.

"Yes, in a way. Every man wishes for a son, doesn't he? Of course, it is always nicer if he can have it with the woman he loves."

I shifted in my chair.

"You know what Carlotta told me this afternoon?"

I shook my head.

"She told me that now she had fulfilled her 'obligation' to me. She invited me to move my things to a room down the hall."

"Oh . . ." I breathed.

"I told her it was no loss to me. She said she realized that. She said I had enough 'other women' to keep me busy every night of the week."

I raised an eyebrow.

He smiled. "Not to worry, Alvareda. Our secret about Amanda is intact. I understand from my daughter you still have her house."

"I still have the property, yes."

"You ever go out there?"

I was not certain where this line of questioning was leading. I just wanted him to go. "Not very often. We check on it now and then, and Elzyna seems to enjoy going out there with us."

"Oh? And Neal knows about it?"

"He—he knows it is a rental property from Papa's estate, and in fact it is. We've had two families there so far."

He paused, and I feared he would ask about the cash from the estate. I had told Neal the estate was diminished to a few pieces of property, and that most of the cash had all been tied up in these, and that Olivia had made some poor investments over the last few years of her life that absorbed a lot of the money.

Thankfully, David did not pry just now. He leaned back. "You knew that Amanda married a widower from Jefferson."

I told him that I did but did not say how much relief the news provided me. She had sent me the message through an attorney, and stated she would continue to rent the house in Galveston, but would spend most of her time in Jefferson. The installments of money I owed her should be sent to her Galveston address during the first week of March every year. There she would collect them. I had not told David about her plans to spend part of her time in Galveston, and was in hopes he would not find out. I changed the subject. "Maybe Carlotta is a little out of sorts. I understand she had a difficult time with Jordan—"

"For Carlotta, anything natural in *life* is difficult."

I wished he would leave. I knew he was drawing me into a trap. "You ought to go home and get some rest," I told him. "Perhaps things will look better in the morning."

He leaned back. "Did you know that Amanda's husband is sixty years old and walks with a cane?"

"No. How did you hear that?"

"Oh, I have my ways. He is a rich old son-of-a-bitch—"

"I really wish you would watch your language in front of me."

"Forgive me, Alvareda. But she could not have done better as far as money goes. Edward Choate is one of the richest people in that part of the state."

"David, it doesn't do much good to concern yourself with her. Now, I have a lot to do so—"

He leaned forward. "I have the most terrible habit of wanting things I can't have. I learned that when I lost out on you," he said.

I blinked and stared at him. There was something about the expression on his face that made me realize he was sincere. Always I had thought of myself as a pawn in his battle of wits with my father. I never for a minute believed he might really care for me. I didn't know what to say. At last I looked away and fiddled with the lace on my sleeve. "I—I think you had better leave now."

Oh, what a sharp instinct he had. He knew very well he had managed to say something to me at last that resulted in a feeling other than anger. "Alvareda?" he queried.

"Please, David," I said, still looking away.

He picked up his hat, ran his fingers through his hair, and shook his head in defeat. "Nine years. You know, Alvareda, it's a hell of a note to have got so far and then realize you were going in the wrong direction."

I was not about to pursue that remark. I only wanted him to go. I stood with my arms folded as he placed his hat on his head. I was aware all at once that David was beginning to grow slack around the jaws. His mouth was beginning to sag. What would he do, I wondered, when he was no longer attractive to women? I suddenly remembered David the way he looked while we were youngsters, a barefoot, raggedy ball of energy whom I looked up to. Now it was as though his whole life passed before my eyes. I felt a silly urge to cry.

Just as he went out the front door, I heard Neal coming in the back. "Was that David's buggy out front?"

"Yes. He came by to—to brag about his new son," I said quickly. That night as I lay in bed I felt more and more pity for David. Life had cheated him. My father had done so much more damage to him than, thank God, he even knew, and the part of the truth he did know had led him to poor decisions. Tonight more than at any other time I truly grasped what a horrible disappointment his marriage had been, when perhaps it could have been so very different if Carlotta were loving and kind.

I moved closer to Neal and felt so grateful that he had come into my life when he did, that no matter what happened through the years, his mere presence meant warmth and safety to me. Of course I assumed that David's visit tonight would have no effect on that.

PART 3

Chapter 1

Sometimes the memory of a day is imprinted on the mind not because of a certain event by which a change is marked, but because in its simple regularity lies the last vestige of sameness, of things that once were, and will never be again.

Such a day was Friday, September 7, 1900.

It was a beautiful day. Temperatures had been up in the nineties all week, and when Neal awoke that morning he said, "I need some time off, and we could all use a dip in the Gulf before the season's over. Let's pack up and go to Galveston for the weekend. . . . We might stop by and see if Elzyna wants to go with us."

I did not want to go by the Leiders'. Lately every time we asked Elzyna to do something special with us, Carlotta was insistent that Jordan be included, and this always led to trouble because our boys did not get along well together. Jordan was a little bully who took joy in grabbing what belonged to Gabriel, and delighted in his fury. Perhaps he'd outgrow his meanness, still . . .

I pushed the covers back and rose from the bed. "Let's not this time. I want to hurry and get out of town before someone calls from the office and changes your mind."

Neal had been busier than ever. For a long time our trips to Galveston—indeed, anywhere—had been few and far between. While Neal's heart still belonged to the long Galveston beaches and the gentle surf he'd grown up with, his business interests were in the strongest competition with his native city since he moved to Houston in 1886. The Galveston bar now had twenty-five feet of water, winning its designation as a deep-water port. All the fears that the island city would surpass Houston as a center of commerce were nearing fruition, even though predictions of the phenomenal growth of the cotton industry had proven true, and the Galveston wharves were not adequate to handle the millions of cotton bales consigned to them. Congestion from the docks all the way up the railroad line was commonplace during the fall of the year.

The compress companies and storage facilities in Houston were burdened with thousands of bales of cotton that could not be moved to the crowded port at Galveston. The Gerrard and Leider Company alone was storing between ten and fifteen thousand bales. The downtown business district from the wharves to the railroad station was a chain of cotton-loaded cars and platforms.

Although overworked and frazzled because he was dividing his time between the drive for deep water and his own business, which depended so much on its success, Neal was as happy as ever I had seen him. We now had a spokesman on the Rivers and Harbors Committee in Washington, Congressman Thomas Ball, who was as determined as the Houston businessmen to force Congress to act. Furthermore, Neal's company was out of debt. Profits were building.

On the other hand, David did not seem to share his enthusiasm. Since the busy cotton season of 1898, Neal had complained more and more frequently that David was not carrying his load. Each time he brought up the subject I held a breath until I was sure he was not going to say that David was actually cheating the firm in some way. Then, in the final week of August this year, Neal had said, "I feel like I'm in business by myself again. I'm going to look into the possibility of offering to buy David out of the firm."

I felt a great sense of relief.

We crossed the railroad bridge into Galveston at half-past nine under a sky of azure blue with white clouds coursing through it like brushstrokes. We planned to spend the morning at Josephine and Martin's house, within an easy walk to the shore, then stay the night at Neal's parents'. As soon as we arrived to put down our suitcases, Neal's mother said there would be an oyster roast at the beach on Sunday, and asked if we could stay till it was over. We promised we would.

By ten o'clock I was sitting in Josephine's kitchen while she cut up boiled eggs and celery and onion for chicken salad. Neal and Gabriel were on their way to the beach. Since Gabriel's birth we had spent more time with Neal's brother and his family than before. I now had more in common with Josephine and while she often complained of gray streaks in her light brown hair —she was forty-four, and Martin was forty-six—there seemed no age difference between us when we were together. I felt more relaxed out on her front veranda, sharing mint juleps, or sitting at her kitchen table, than anywhere except in my own home.

Their home was the same two-story wooden cottage with storm shutters and a picket fence around the small yard they'd built as newlyweds. They had not built anything larger or fancier, although they could afford it, because they liked living near the beach and enjoyed their neighbors. Their daughter had finished school. Their two boys were twelve and thirteen, and had a number of friends on the block. They envisioned staying here for the rest of their lives. There was no reason to suppose anything could change their plans.

Josephine stood at the sink and spoke to me over her shoulder as she chopped and mixed. She was wearing an apron embroidered with red flowers that crisscrossed in back. The ceiling fan whipped around above us, and a loaf of bread baked early that morning sat plump and golden brown on the shelf of the stove. The sights and smells of Josephine's kitchen always gave me a warm feeling, and reminded me of all those times I had sat with Olivia as she prepared meals for Papa. . . .

She asked if we had found a new housekeeper yet. Ours had moved away to California in July. I told her we had not, and she mentioned the fact she had two names of Galveston ladies for us to interview. She gave me a slip of paper and I put it into my pocket.

"I'd like to have lunch out on the veranda, but the wind is so gusty, I wonder if we can," she said. Before I could reply the telephone rang in the hall. Josephine wiped her hands and went to answer. I was smoothing out the frosting on a chocolate cake, trying to gauge how much I need save for the top layer, when I caught the tone of her voice and stopped to listen. It was Martin calling. "Oh? We didn't know that," she said. "No, Neal and Gabriel are down on the beach right now. Well, it certainly doesn't *look* like a storm is anywhere near. Yes, I'll tell her."

I heard the receiver click, and her footsteps up the hall. When she returned she said, "Mr. Cline has hoisted the storm flags. And Martin says there was a small item in the *News* about a storm out in the Gulf. He has been trying to reach the weather office by telephone, but the line is continuously busy. . . . When did Neal say they'd be back?"

"He didn't say." I washed my hands and walked out on the front veranda to see if Neal and Gabriel were in sight. From here, if you listened especially for it, you could hear the surf pounding ashore. I was sure the storm flags were not up when we arrived at the train station, or we would have noticed. I gazed down the block. Two dogs frolicked in the street, one running circles around the other. The heat shimmered in the air. Except for the unusually gusty wind, it seemed a perfectly ordinary September day. Still . . . if they didn't come home soon, I would go down to the beach and fetch them.

I was about to go back into the house when I saw them round the corner. There was nothing I loved more than watching them together. Neal had not had the time to spend with his growing son that he would like to. When I thought of all the years when Neal was less busy than now, I felt regretful that it had taken so long to conceive our second child, that somehow I had robbed the two of them of many special times because my family burdens had kept me half upset all the time and in doing so delayed that most natural process of bringing children into the world.

It was not that Neal complained. When he came home at night from work, Gabriel met him at the door, ready to be tossed into the air and carried to the dining table on Neal's back. Often on Sunday afternoons we took Gabriel to City Park for a picnic or boarded the dummy train for Magnolia Park to go canoeing. Sometimes, when cotton season was keeping him especially busy, Neal would take Gabriel to the office with him on Saturday mornings. Gabriel talked incessantly, and Neal listened as though what he said was the most important news in the world.

Now as I watched them approaching hand in hand, Gabriel's blond hair blowing in the wind, I felt saddened. If Neal really did buy out David, would he have still less time to spend with his son? Were the opportunities for coming down here to be even less frequent?

They saw me now, and I smiled and waved. Gabriel ran up to show me the few seashells he had in his pockets, and Neal said the wind was so strong, the waves rolling in with such force, you really could not enjoy yourself. He was wet all the way up above his knees. When I told him about Martin's call, he looked up at the sky and considered. Finally he said, "I think we ought to go home. We're bound to be in for some heavy rains, even in Houston, and I need to fix that spot that leaks in the solarium. I wouldn't want to have to replace the floor from water damage." I nodded in agreement. The leaky solarium roof had been a problem since we moved into our house on Main at the beginning of 1898.

We stayed through lunch with Josephine, then went over to pick up our things at the Gerrards' home. Neal's father was now semi-retired—he had turned sixty-seven on his last birthday and finally conceded the business would probably survive if he came in only half days—and he drove us in his buggy down to the train station. He hugged the three of us before we boarded the train and said, "Remember, you promised Mother you would come back Sunday for the oyster roast."

"Unless the weather is bad," said Neal.

"Oh, it will have blown over by then. Bye now, my son."

I watched from the train window as Mr. Gerrard turned out onto Mechanic Street and started for home. The wind blew his hat from his head and sent it spinning down the street in front of him.

Chapter 2

We awoke early on Saturday morning, pulled the drapes and looked out the window. The sky was a beautiful shade of salmon with a luminous cast that made it seem strangely unreal. "I don't believe I have ever seen a sky like that," Neal said.

"I guess the storm blew elsewhere," I suggested.

"Perhaps," he said quietly, and went to call his family in Galveston again.

We had talked to Mr. Gerrard late on Friday afternoon, and all he could tell us then was that the winds were up to thirteen miles an hour, according to the weather office. He had only gotten through the one time because the lines were constantly busy. Later in the evening Neal called Martin. He had driven along the beach on his way home from work, and said the waves roared like thunder, smashing against the beach and sending sprays of water seven or eight feet high. He had passed Isaac Cline, the weatherman, observing the beach from his buggy, and Mr. Cline, holding his hat on his head, said it was a good thing the wind was blowing from the north, but he felt people should get to high ground in case the direction changed. "The waves were so noisy, and the wind so strong, I could not make out anything else he said."

"Are you going to take Mr. Cline's advice?" Neal asked.

"If it gets worse. It isn't all that bad yet."

"Don't wait too long. You can always go home if it turns out to be a false alarm."

When Neal told me what Martin said, I thought of the gentle surf at Galveston and our many expeditions down to the beach. I found seven- or eight-foot sprays hard to imagine. Yet Galveston had been the target of many serious storms. The last one, twenty-five years ago, brought waves that were themselves nearly eight feet tall. After that, the new houses built were lifted up eight feet off the ground to allow for the high water.

Neal made several attempts before finally getting a clear line to his father, and this must have rattled his nerves because after a brief exchange I heard him say abruptly, "Get on the train and come up here, before it's too late."

Apparently an argument followed. When he hung up, he turned to me and said, "It has begun to rain. Dad says they haven't been warned to leave the island. Martin and Josephine are coming up there as soon as they get their house secured."

That was the first time I felt a real sense of alarm. The memory of Josephine calmly chopping and mixing in her kitchen just yesterday, under the pleasant whirring ceiling fan, was displaced by the image of her scurrying around getting clothes packed for the children, ordering them to hurry, while Martin went from window to window, closing the storm shutters with loud thuds. Perhaps she would carry a few treasures upstairs to safety. There would not be time for many trips up and down. And all the while the waves a short distance from there pounding noisily ashore. . . .

"I guess that's all we can do for now," Neal said with a sigh. He then called the manager out at the compress and told him to secure the buildings and go home. No sooner had he hung up the telephone than a call came from the office that David had not shown up for an appointment with a customer in the sample rooms. The customer was waiting, not altogether patiently. Neal promised to come immediately.

By now the sky was dark gray and rain was driving down hard. Neal quickly dressed in his white shirt and suit. He pulled on his rubbers. I helped him into his mackintosh. Before he left he said, "Call Mother in an hour or so, to see what's happening. I'll be back as quickly as I can."

I kissed him good-bye and watched him hurry across the backyard to the stable. Gabriel came up from behind, rubbing his sleepy eyes. "Where's Daddy going?"

I picked him up and held him. "To the office, darling." We watched the horse and buggy issue from the stable. Neal banged shut the door, then led the reluctant animal forward down the drive. Rain splintered off the buggy roof.

"Why does Daddy have to go in the rain?" Gabriel asked.

"He had an appointment," I answered, but thought with irritation, because David didn't show up. "Come, I'll fix you some breakfast."

Shortly after ten o'clock Elzyna came to the door beneath a huge umbrella. I hustled her in out of the weather, and asked her why she'd come out on such a day. "I ran away from home," she announced indignantly, and sat down on a bench.

I was tugging on her rubber boots. I looked up. "Why?"

"Mother is mad at me and I just won't stand for it."

"What made her angry?"

"Last night I slept in the barn with Mindy so she wouldn't be afraid."

"Oh, I see. Why did you think your horse would be afraid?"

"Because the wind howled so. I explained it to Mother, but she said that was being foolish and she wouldn't let me. So I slipped out after she was asleep."

I smiled. "But obviously she awoke before you did."

"Yes. She told me I was very bad and sent me to my room. When she said I could come out, I told her I was going to stay with you forever."

We both rose and I put the wet boots aside. Elzyna at eleven years old stood five feet tall, and still had her long mop of blond curls. I kissed her forehead and told her she could stay all day, anyhow.

"Has my Daddy been here?"

"Why no. Was he supposed to be?"

"I don't know. He and Mother had a quarrel last night before dinner. He left and did not come home. Maybe he went out of town."

"Maybe so," I told her. Yet if he had been leaving town, why make an appointment in Houston for Saturday morning? "He'll probably be home when you get there tonight," I reassured her, although the way he had behaved of late I wasn't so sure. Aside from the other tensions inside the Leider household, David created more trouble by his growing affinity for drinking and gambling, and his undependability. Carlotta surely had more than her share of worries right now. I slipped out while Gabriel and Elzyna entertained each other—had it been left up to Gabriel, Elzyna could have moved in for keeps—and called Carlotta. I told her that Elzyna was here and she could stay overnight if it was all right.

"I suppose Elzyna told you her father was missing," Carlotta said.

"She—uh—she wondered if he were here, but I haven't seen him." I started to tell her he missed an appointment, but decided the less I said the better. Anyway, Carlotta needed to do the talking.

"There is no way in the world he can go on like he does and not eventually be found out. I personally would not lower myself to expose him, but someone else might."

"What do you mean?"

"Just what I said."

She went on complaining for a few minutes, then ran out of steam. After we hung up I wondered if she were trying to get me to signal David she was onto him. Carlotta loved to be mysterious. Perhaps I would tell him sometime, but right now I had other concerns. I put a call through to Mrs. Gerrard. The connection was poor; static punctuated our words.

"The wind is blowing a gale and the rain is so heavy you can't see two feet in front of you, but people are down on the beach having a great time in the breakers," she began. "A neighbor told me that Midway has never been busier. They're selling hot dogs and beer to the crowds."

"Are Martin and Josephine and the children with you?"

"Not yet, but I talked to them a few minutes ago. Martin wants to wait a little while. They have no water in their yard as yet, and he's borrowing extra time to nail some boards over the front door and the shutters he is able to reach."

"I'd feel better, and I know Neal would, if they would get up to your house as soon as possible."

"Oh, don't worry so. I don't believe this storm is going to cause as much mischief as the one in '75. And I know the builder who put up Martin's house. It's well constructed. The most they'll suffer is water damage if the water gets up as high as eight feet. But you know, we've been hearing about the possibility of this 'terrible' storm since yesterday, and nothing has happened yet except a lot of wind and rain."

I did not relish the thought of greeting Neal with the information his mother had just given me. It was past eleven o'clock. Surely he would be home soon.

An hour passed. Still he had not come. I called the office and was relieved to hear the sound of his voice above the sputter on the telephone line. "I'll be on my way within the hour," he promised, then asked about Galveston. When I told him the news he said, "Confound it, what are they waiting for? I'll call right now and see if I can get Martin."

We hung up. I felt more uneasy than before because Neal's concern had grown and his was based on experience. A remark he made once came to me now. We had been talking about the Galveston wharves and he said, "I don't care how much money they spend on getting deep water, the simple fact remains that there is just so much land area, and that's it. Galveston is too little for a deep-water port. If they were smart, they would spend that money on bulkheads to protect the island from storms."

Only now did I fully realize what he had been talking about. Galveston could not withstand any more of a beating than it took in 1875. If the wind shifted from the north and began to blow in the same direction as the waves, it could prove disastrous. Oh, surely it would not, I thought nervously, and made a pot of tea.

The wind raced by, humming louder, then softer, then louder again. I heard the glass in the solarium rattle. I went toward it and timidly pushed open the door. All around the glass panes were visibly moving in their frames. Outside the sky was black and the slanting rain struck like daggers. If a tree limb or a roof slate, or any piece of debris should be thrown against the glass, the solarium would come crashing down. Now I was thoroughly frightened. I closed the door and hurried to the parlor where the children were at play. I told them not to open the door to the solarium for any reason. Immediately both heads poked up and Elzyna asked why.

"It—it just isn't a good idea, that's all," I told her and walked away before she could further pursue the question. Right now the children were calm. I did not want to give them my fears. I went into the pantry where the kerosene lamps were kept and brought out all six of them. These had not been used since the days when we lived on Franklin Avenue, and the lamp chimneys were dingy with smoke and soot. I found some newspapers and began to clean them, trying to pass the time and calm my nerves. Two o'clock. Where in the world could Neal be? I would give him just a few minutes more before calling again. I filled the lamps with kerosene and placed them around the downstairs rooms. I started to put one in the big entrance hall but then I realized the tree outside, which now brushed against the window like a cloth wiping a dish, rammed through the window, could become a missile, sending glass everywhere and upsetting the lamp. A fire could begin. I went through the entrance hall and put the lamp in the parlor. I would not have believed there would come a day when I was afraid in my own home. And if it was this bad here, what was it doing in Galveston?

I called Neal. The line was open, but there was no answer.

I called Galveston. After nine tries I got through, though the connection was so scratchy I could barely make out Mrs. Gerrard's words. She told me that Martin and Josephine had not come, and that Mr. Gerrard had gone after them. Their telephone was dead.

Was it the connection, or did I now sense real fear in Mrs. Gerrard's voice? She told me there was water in the street in front of the house, and she knew there had to be much more where Martin and Josephine lived. "I couldn't keep Neal's father from going," she said.

"Maybe they will all be with you shortly," I tried to reassure her. I asked her if she had gotten kerosene lamps and placed them around, and if she had taken anything upstairs to safety. I was trying to help restore the calm I felt she was losing. Mrs. Gerrard had been one of my own strongholds through heartache and fear since the first time I met her. It was unsettling to realize she was reaching her limits. When we hung up I told her I would call again in an hour, that maybe by then this would be all over.

The only thing that kept me from completely going to pieces about Neal was the logic that if his parents' home was still in relative safety, then anything in Houston should be even safer because we were on higher ground and not in danger of high water. He would not have left the office to come home if he had not felt it was safe to do so. Neal was cautious, that I could depend on.

The children approached, running out of entertainments. I pulled out Gabriel's box of toy soldiers and Elzyna went to work on the embroidering she had begun one other rainy day while visiting with us. After working for a while, she looked up and said, "Do you think my father would leave and never come home?"

"Of course not. Your father loves you far too much to ever leave you."

She inclined her head this way and that, and took another stitch. Then she said, without looking at me, "He had promised to go with me and Mindy on a long ride today."

"Well, since the weather turned out so badly, he would have had to do that another day anyway."

"If he loves me, he would have said good-bye when he left."

"Perhaps he was just upset. You said he and your mother quarreled."

"Yes, but they quarrel all the time. And when they do, sometimes he leaves. But he is always home when I wake up in the morning."

It always pained me deeply to see Elzyna questioning David's love for her because I knew all too well how that felt. "Elzyna, your father brought you Mindy for your birthday this summer. That was a wonderful present. He would not have done that if he didn't love you very, very much." She did not know that David bought her the horse because I urged him to. Now with Jordan around, as well as Patricia, Elzyna was even further bereft of attention.

"I suppose you're right," she said with a sigh. "Do you think he is safe? The wind is blowing so hard."

"Of course he is. He may even be home by now."

After that she grew quiet. She was the kind of child who showed her concern by becoming withdrawn. Gabriel, on the other hand, was more and more talkative when feeling afraid. The times I took him to the doctor, he would nearly talk my ears off as we awaited the examination. At least he did not appear to be frightened as yet. He lined up his battle brigade, then knocked them all down and sat back on his heels laughing. I sat nearby in a rocker, looking out the window. The wind and rain could not go on much longer, I told myself, yet it seemed to be getting worse by the hour instead of better.

At three o'clock I called Galveston again. This time the line was dead. With a sense of panic I tried Neal's office again. Nothing. I went and stood by the window in the parlor. The street outside was quickly being covered with debris, and I could see big clumps of shrubs and flower stalks sailing by. The striped awnings on the house across the street were torn to ribbons. I thought of the storm flags hoisted on Friday in Galveston. They would be gone by now, long since flushed away from their poles and blown to oblivion, of no help to anyone.

Shortly after four o'clock, the lights went out. Murmuring words of reassurance to the children, I carried the one kerosene lamp already glowing around the rooms, lighting the others as I went. One by one, they lit up the downstairs chambers like torches light up the inside of a cave. The furniture cast mammoth shadows on the walls and ceilings. The children made sport of their own spectacular images moving across the walls.

I was growing possessed by a feeling that something had happened to Neal. I felt emptied out and vacant inside as I tried without success to talk myself out of what I feared. If he was gone from the office by two o'clock—the last time I got a line through—then there was simply no way he could not yet be home. Nearly three hours, assuming he had just walked out the door when I called. He had only to guide his buggy from one end of Main to the other. It simply could not take this much time.

He could have been hit by a piece of debris and killed.

The water on Main could be higher in places where drainage was poor. He could have drowned.

He could have run into something that he could not see and been killed.

He could even have—oh, surely he would not have—tried to make his way to Galveston, to bring his family back.

I began to pray. Losing Neal would be more than I could stand. I suddenly realized how vulnerable we all were, on what kind providence our lives continued from one day to another. I prayed for the Gerrards, for all the people in Galveston, for David Leider wherever he might be. I repeated these prayers over and over again as though my own sanity depended upon the exercise. All the while I realized any one or all of them might already be dead.

At six o'clock we all gathered in the parlor and the children ate plates of cold food by the light of the kerosene lanterns. I sipped tea to calm my nerves. I could hear the glass rattling in the solarium and behind the stairway. Whether any panes had blown out I had no idea, and would not go in there to see. The singing wind, the relentless rain, ground on my already taut nerves like a fiddle bow in the hands of a novice grinds across the strings. Gabriel had asked at least twenty times where his father was. Elzyna fretted more and more about her missing father. It was growing harder and harder for me to answer their pitiful questions with patience.

When they finished eating I took their plates and promised to bring them some of the chocolate cake Josephine had insisted we take home with us when we left her home yesterday. How long ago that seemed. . . . As I turned down the hall toward the kitchen I saw a light through the kitchen door glass and a great hulking shadow looming there. It frightened me so I nearly dropped the plates on the floor. I froze in place and watched the shadow move. One moment . . . two. Then with suddenness the door flung wide open. My mouth opened to scream, and the plates went crashing to the floor. Then, in the blink of an eye, I felt relief flood over me.

It was Neal. I ran to him.

While I fixed a plate of food for him, Neal sat at the kitchen table in his robe and house shoes. We exchanged information about the Gerrards. When I told him his father had gone to collect Martin and his family, he grimaced and shook his head. "But that was early," I said, "two o'clock anyway. I'm sure they all made it back just fine."

"My father is so stubborn," he said. "He ought to have realized Martin was capable of shepherding his family to safety."

I knew that too, but there was nothing that could be done about it now. "What time did you leave the office?" I asked, and he began to tell the three of us about his arduous journey home. He had not gotten away till half-past three because a slate from a neighboring roof sailed into one of the windows, and before leaving he had to secure that and the other windows with boards. He had not heard the telephone ring because he was far from his desk, clear at the back of the sample room. "That's one of the things that worries me most about Galveston," he said. "After that fire in 1885 they passed a city ordinance that building roofs had to be made of slate. When they come loose they make deadly weapons."

"What was it like down on Main?" I encouraged him to go on. I did not want him to start dwelling on the possibilities for people in Galveston.

"Signs have been blown off the buildings. A great big piece of the cornice on Kiam's Store is gone. Awning cloths have been ripped to shreds. When I left people were lined up inside the stores looking out the windows like spectators at a parade.

"There is a huge hole in the roof of the Capitol Hotel, and that big tree in front of the Presbyterian church is lying across the street diagonally. I had to go around it.

"Then, when I got farther down the road, I nearly ran into a trolley car that was stopped in front of me like a beached whale. The rain was blinding. I couldn't see the car until I was right up on it. I guess I'm lucky the horse didn't get killed and me with it."

I thought of how close he had come to each of the possibilities created in my imagination, and was thankful all over again for the answer to my prayers. He had not mentioned David, and I was afraid to say anything within Elzyna's earshot. She had asked Neal as soon as he got through the door whether he had seen her father. When he told her he had not, she drew up her shoulders in silence. Now, after waiting politely for him to finish his story about coming home, she looked him in the eye and said, "Uncle Neal, do you think my father is in Galveston?"

Neal and I stole a glance at each other. "No," he said. "I can't think of any reason in the world why he would be there."

I could think of one. Only one.

Around ten o'clock we fixed beds for the children on the couches in our room, on which they immediately fell asleep. We lay in bed rigidly, both of us too worried to fall into slumber. While I was worried about what the possibility of David's being in Galveston might mean—Amanda had been paid off last year—there was too much real danger to dwell on that now. All I could concentrate on was Neal's family.

Sometime before midnight the wind died down just enough to make us both aware of it. Neal went to the window to look out.

"The worst is over," he said. "I can see lightning way out there in the distance. That signals the end."

Neal would have dressed and tried to make his way to Galveston right then, but I persuaded him to wait till morning. At last we both slept and I do not know what thoughts had been in his mind before he finally dozed off. I had envisioned Neal's family safely inside his parents' house, and assumed

Martin and Josephine would return tomorrow to a house with some water damage. Now, with the wind and rain dying down, the fearsome storm did not seem so treacherous.

Chapter 3

By Sunday morning gossamer rays of sunshine hung like a curtain through the clouds. Neal started out early, determined to get to Galveston one way or another. Already, rumors up and down our block were spreading like the debris that awaited picking up all over the city. Some said there was not a building left standing on the entire island of Galveston. Some said there were over a hundred people dead. Someone said that Midway was already open again and people were swimming in the Gulf. I wondered who to believe.

As he left he kissed me and held me close, then warned, "I don't know when I will get back. There may be too much to do in Galveston to start back till tomorrow. As soon as the telephones are working again, I'll call you."

As it happened, his first trip was one of frustrating defeat. Along with several others, he boarded a G, H & H train which got no farther than LaMarque—fifteen miles this side of Galveston—before being forced to turn back because the tracks were washed out. From there he walked to Texas City, another fifteen miles, but he could not get across the bay to Galveston, and had to turn back again. His journey home took eleven hours, and the last leg of it brought him up Buffalo Bayou from Lynchburg in a yawl that someone else had abandoned.

He arrived after midnight. He had no shoes on. His feet were swollen and cut; his trouser legs were rolled up to the knees. He collapsed in exhaustion.

On Monday at ten o'clock he went aboard another train, one carrying food and water to the island. This time a successful connection was made by boat from Virginia Point, arriving on the island around noon. Several days passed before I saw him again, and by the time he returned I had learned, little by little, the horrifying details that suggested the magnitude of the disaster: Galveston as we knew it was no more. The storm had pelted it with winds up to a hundred and twenty miles an hour and drenched the island with a sixteen-foot tidal wave—twice as high as in 1875. The pleasant beaches along which we had so often strolled, where Neal had found such peace and composure throughout his lifetime, now provided berths from which wagons heaped with bodies were hauled out to sea and dumped. Every day the newspaper reports of the total number of people dead or missing increased: five hundred, eight hundred, one thousand, five thousand. Arriving at figures required many days of lifting the rubble of lumber and shingles and windows and doors that had been, until Saturday, houses with porches and fences. Over much of the island, the buildings left standing loomed like lonely, grotesque phantoms above a graveyard of twisted and battered remains.

Scarcely a family on the island was left intact, and on the night Neal finally came home, I learned the Gerrards were no exception. Martin and Josephine and the children had left for the safety of the home off Broadway only minutes before Mr. Gerrard began his trek through the flooding streets to find them. They arrived safely and with Mrs. Gerrard they awaited his return. He did not come. Some forty people spent the night in that home, as did hundreds of others in homes on the high part of the island. They could only trust that he had taken refuge nearby, and on Sunday morning Martin went out in search of him. He was not to be found.

In the whole week of searching after Neal arrived, his father still could not be found. Yet Neal would not give up hope. With eyes that were pools of the desperation he could not express in words, he looked at me and said, "There are so many possibilities. A lot of people had injuries to the head, and haven't regained their memories. Plenty of people are walking around stunned and confused.

"Others wound up a long way from the island, having ridden the floodtide miles and miles. I heard one woman had been carried thirty miles." His eyes widened with a plea for reassurance. "He will turn up, don't you think? He'll be just fine. I know he will."

I put my arms around him and cradled his head to my breast. I could not tell him that he was fooling himself. I could not let him see the tears welling up in my eyes. I kept thinking of his father just a week ago, waving good-bye to us as we pulled out of Galveston on the train.

Neal's mother refused to leave the house, and sat all the day long by a parlor window, awaiting her husband's return. She scarcely spoke, and at intervals would begin to weep softly. Then she would stop, dry her eyes, and look ahead through the window again. She kept a Bible nearby and now and then would open it and study it at length, then close it and hold it tightly while she closed her eyes in prayer. Josephine—to whom we talked daily once the telephone service was restored—said she had never seen anyone more determined. She and Martin and the children were now living there. Their own pleasant cottage with its picket fence had simply vanished. Josephine said that finding the street along which it once stood was no small challenge. Everything ran together in a field of scattered debris.

David had not come home, and I understood that Carlotta was having some sort of investigation conducted. While Neal helped in every way he could, David of course could not be his single concern. I said nothing to anyone of my own growing belief. Daily I checked the newspapers for the name of Amanda Choate or Amanda Cane among the dead or missing. Neither name appeared.

As soon as he came home, Neal threw himself into the massive effort of aiding storm victims, and I knew that in his heart lived the hope that the whereabouts of his father would emerge as the work went forward. Yet Mr. Gerrard had been wearing an old work shirt and trousers, which surely must have looked identical to the clothing worn by many of the men on the island. He had not taken his pocket watch—he did not want it to be ruined by the rain—and he was wearing no other jewelry. There was little promise of identifying him unless his eyeglasses were still in place.

The relief committee in Houston was in session around the clock at the mayor's office, and was responsible for collecting thousands of dollars to help the survivors, as well as trainload after trainload of cooked food and drinking water. They helped coordinate efforts from all across the United States to get provisions routed to the island, and served as a filter system as best they could to detain sightseers who had no real purpose on the island except to satisfy their morbid curiosity. I was astonished to think anyone would have the gall to want to go on a sight-seeing excursion around the island, but then I read in the newspapers of worse things: looters who stole rings and other jewelry from the bodies of victims still lying among the debris, and emptied their pockets of coins and valuables. I closed my eyes and tried not to think of Mr. Gerrard.

Neal was one of the chief coordinators of the relief work, and I worked with a group of ladies who were collecting clothing for women and children. Mrs. Qualtrough's group had a sewing room set up on the top floor of city hall, where we mended and sorted clothing when it came to us. Much of it could not be worn without buttons being replaced and rips sewn up. We also sorted piles and piles of shoes to be transferred to the island, and mended thousands of pairs of stockings.

On Thursday morning after the storm, I went along with others to help with the incoming trains bearing refugees. Those without a place to stay would have to be directed to hotels or private homes; those with family or friends awaiting them needed help in locating one another. Many unfortunate people were transferred directly to Houston Infirmary and St. Joseph's, and in a short time these hospitals were overflowing with storm victims. Uniformed members of the Caldwell Light Guard with the help of armed citizens stood guard to be sure that none except committee workers were allowed around the platforms.

I'm not certain what I expected to find when that first train roared into the station. Yet the sight was more overwhelming than I could have imagined. Somewhere between eight hundred and a thousand men, women, and children emerged on swollen, bare feet, their clothing torn to shreds, many of them half nude. Their bodies were bruised and cut as though attacked by vicious animals. A few had makeshift bandages wrapped around wounds; some had blankets draped around their bare shoulders. Many had no such amenities and looked as though the train had picked them up from where they stood in the aftermath of the storm's destruction.

One of the most touching sights was that of some relative or friend waiting to greet a poor, beleaguered party with open arms. But many of them desperately appealed for help in locating the telegraph office or the *Post*, in hopes of communicating with loved ones separated from them during the storm, who had a less than even chance of being alive. There was a smell about them all that could be likened only to burning flesh, and I realized it was the smell of death, redoubled by the hot, humid air. By the time I got home that evening, my own body reeked with it and I sat in a tub of hot soapy water for nearly an hour staring at the bathroom wall while visions of listless, vacant faces marched on and on across my mind. The idea of finding Mr. Gerrard among them, which I could not help entertaining anymore than could Neal, soon became nearly obliterated in the overpowering sight. I felt I'd been in a war zone.

On Friday I helped with a first aid station set up and manned by a group of women from the church. Two registered nurses were among us to treat minor wounds and administer aid to victims who fell faint. My job was folding bandages, and they disappeared almost faster than I could fold them. Sometime after the second train of the day arrived I heard my name spoken and looked up.

"David!" I gasped, and rose so quickly I nearly upset the table in front of me.

The nurse standing nearby had the presence of mind to help him into a chair, and I asked another of the ladies to fetch Neal from farther down the way. When I knelt down beside him, he leaned forward and put both his arms around me. He held me so tightly I could hardly breathe. In spite of everything that had happened between us, I could not help being grateful to see him safe. I heard him whisper, "Amanda is dead."

I caught my breath. I could say nothing.

He went on holding me like a frightened child holds his mother after waking from a bad dream, and I could feel his chest heaving and knew he was crying. I stroked his back and tried to comfort him.

After a few moments I looked up to see Neal standing above. "Look, David," I said, and moved away so that Neal could greet him.

"Hi, partner," Neal said, and embraced him warmly. I felt tears spring to my eyes.

The nurse motioned both of us away to do a cursory examination. David had escaped serious injury, though his feet were badly cut and one was blackened from the ankle all the way down to the toes. He had a cut about two inches long on one temple, and this was thickly scabbed over, making it difficult to judge how deep it was. His shirt and trousers were bloodstained and soiled.

"He ought to go to the hospital as soon as possible," the nurse concluded.

"I'll take him," Neal said.

"I'll call Carlotta," I offered.

We draped David's arm around Neal's shoulder, and they started down the long aisle of people. I went immediately inside the train station to a telephone. I had to wait some time before there was a line open, and when I reached her and told her David was safe, she fell silent.

"Carlotta?"

"Yes. I'm all right. When will he be here?"

"Neal's taking him to the infirmary, but he really isn't hurt badly. He'll bring him home afterward." I told her about his foot, the only serious worry.

"What if he should be crippled?" she said, and let the remark hang in the air between us. I wasn't sure whether she dreaded the thought for his sake, or was revolted at the prospect of being married to a crippled man, or perhaps believed it would serve him right. Finally she said, "I'll make a place for him to sleep downstairs."

I found myself groping for words. "Carlotta, maybe this is a chance to start anew."

"That's up to David," she said.

I sighed, and hung up the telephone.

I went back to folding bandages for a couple of hours, but was distracted now by what had just taken place. Amanda was dead. I couldn't believe it. How should I feel? I had no idea. I felt nothing except . . . perhaps . . . a sense of relief. Was that wicked? I didn't know. I didn't care. I picked up a length of white gauze. Amanda was dead. Then I put the gauze down and stood motionless, thinking. A door had just opened for me, and I felt a thrill run all through me. This would be the time to tell Neal everything, to get it all out in the open. Now that Amanda was dead and her secret with her . . . now that the partnership would be dissolved . . . now that the newspapers were busy with more dramatic stories than could be contrived from our business . . . now was surely the moment. I felt strangely elated . . . almost a physical sense that a burden was lifting slightly up and away from me.

I went home at two o'clock, and while the morning had been exhausting, I did not feel tired at all. I spent most of the afternoon rehearsing in my mind how I would phrase things, how explain my reasons to Neal for keeping the truth from him all these years. I counted up . . . it had started on the day of Elzyna's birth in August of 1889 . . . I could hardly believe how long this had drained me, how many developments had followed that only worsened it.

I would be busy at some routine or other, and suddenly find myself speaking aloud. More than once Gabriel paused to look at me in puzzlement, or to ask if I were talking to him. Through it all, I felt more and more confident. It was all so plausible. Perhaps if I had ever stacked one event next to the other in my mind, like one stacks books next to each other on a shelf, I would have gained the confidence to tell the truth sooner. . . . Neal would surely understand all this.

At seven o'clock Neal called from the hospital to say David was going to be all right, even his foot would heal completely, and that he would be home as soon as he delivered David to his family.

I hung up the telephone. Trepidations began. How long would it take for him to get here? I wondered. How would I broach the subject when he did? A quarter past seven. I took a ham out of the oven and put some potatoes on to boil. Full of nervous energy, I trimmed the crust on the apple pie I'd made, and brushed the top with cinnamon and sugar and egg white. I put it in the oven and went to freshen my hair. Half-past seven. I splashed cold water on my face and fussed with the tendrils of hair that hung limply around my face. I changed my dress. Eight o'clock.

I heard Gabriel greeting Neal excitedly downstairs, and the big front door close. My heart was beating wildly. I could still delay, I thought, some other time might be better. Yes, maybe. . . . No, I told myself. There would never be a better time than now. I put my hand on the balustrade at the top of the stairs. "Hello, darling."

After the supper dishes were done and Gabriel put to bed, we sat down to talk at last. Neal began to report on David's homecoming, and while I could not have chosen a better way to begin myself, I could feel my knees growing weak under the table as he spoke.

"The children were delirious with joy," he said. "Elzyna had fixed him a dinner tray with a posy on it. Carlotta was . . . well, she had the room all ready for him. She said now that David is home I can arrange to have people brought there who need a place to stay."

"Oh good," I said, appalled at the shakiness of my voice. I shifted in my chair and added, "I wondered why she had not before."

"I think she was afraid there might be an embarrassing scene when David showed up," he said, then paused to sip his coffee. I stirred my coffee absently, my hand icy cold.

"More pie?" I asked suddenly.

"Well . . . maybe just a little slice," Neal answered, and I was grateful for the diversion of rising to cut the pie and place it before him.

I sat down. I opened my mouth to speak, but fell silent. With every ounce of determination I could gather, I tried again, but failed. Oh, this was going to be much harder than I ever dreamed. Now that he was sitting across from me, I could envision his expression changing as I spoke—

"You were about to say?" he asked me.

I swallowed hard and put a hand at my throat. Now. "Neal," I said

abruptly, then paused before asking, "Did David tell you . . . any of the
. . . details?"

"He was visiting a lady friend, which won't surprise you any more than it
did me. They waited too long to get out of the neighborhood where she lived,
and they found themselves swept by the current like so many others. They got
separated. David watched her go under, but couldn't get to her in time to
save her. He later climbed up on a roof that was not much above water level,
and there he stayed. He said he was amazed to find after it was all over how
far he was from where he began. He spent the next two days trying to locate
the woman, and he finally found her, identified her by a piece of jewelry she
was wearing."

I took in a breath. "That must have been horrible."

"I think David is pretty shaken up. I don't know how long he had known
the woman. He did not say anything much about her. . . . I wish this would
convince David to straighten up. He has been lucky so far—I know for a fact
he has been involved with several women along his travels. One day he'll be
found out."

I cleared my throat. "What happens then?" I asked weakly, and looked
away.

"I don't know. I have too many other things to worry about right now."

Weighing this remark, I looked at him again. "Does this mean—do you
think you will still offer to buy him out?"

"Not for the time being. We are headed for a hard year after the storm. I'm
going to need all the help I can get."

With every phrase of his final assessment, I felt my own resolution dissolving. The burden now shifted itself onto me again. I released a long sigh.

"You look disappointed," Neal said.

"I—well—" I stammered. "I know how long you've wanted to get free of
David," I rushed, the curious phrasing unintended.

"Yes, but I'll just have to wait a little longer, I guess, thanks to the storm."

And that is exactly what I will have to do as well, I thought dolefully.

Five weeks passed before the final death toll had been placed at around six
thousand, and all the bodies under the rubble had finally been disposed of.
Plans for rebuilding the island, for constructing a massive granite seawall to
fortress it from the capricious nature of coastal weather, and for raising the
island itself to a level seventeen feet above the former level by pumping tons
of sand underneath it had begun.

Through it all, people went about the business of rebuilding their homes
and their lives, those who stayed proud of the fact. Martin's family continued
to live with Mrs. Gerrard, and Martin resumed the wholesale grocery business begun forty years earlier by his father.

Mr. Gerrard was among those who were never identified. Neal's mother finally gave up her watch by the parlor window and came to terms with her loss. Whether Neal found any such reconciliation, I had no way of knowing. With the same creeping anxiety with which we had all awaited the storm, I helplessly watched as my husband completely changed toward me.

Chapter 4

At first Neal's behavior was no different from what I expected. Both of us were busy with relief committee work through most of October. The sewing room was visited by an average of 350 people daily in need of clothing for their families, and by the time I returned home at night I was so tired, my back aching so much from leaning over the sewing machine and bending and reaching up to find items for people waiting in line, I wanted nothing but a tub of hot water to soak in and a warm bed.

Neal's committee handled more than thirty-three thousand dollars in funds sent to Galveston via Houston, and helped great numbers of people—particularly women with children who had lost their husbands in the storm—find employment throughout the state. One such woman, named Agnes Helmke, became our housekeeper. She alone survived out of a family of seven.

At the same time Neal was caught up in another tricky cotton season. The price of cotton had climbed again, to almost ten cents a pound, but there was heavy crop damage in Texas because of the spring rains, then the pounding effect of the storm winds and water, so that there was little top quality cotton received. Added to that was the problem of transportation. Nothing could be moved through Galveston until November because of damage to the port and shipping so, because Houston was still limited without its own deep-water port, we faced another blockade situation.

Neal's compress and storage facilities, having suffered minimum damage, were overloaded. In the storm the Bayou City Compress was torn to pieces. The Inman Press, nearby the Gerrard-Leider facility, was seriously damaged. W. D. Cleveland's warehouses suffered heavy damage as well, and the few other compresses in Houston shared the extra business. At least David was doing his part. He was not traveling except when absolutely necessary, and was putting in long hours of work. I knew from Elzyna that he was returning home each night, and apparently the atmosphere in the Leider home was at least one of relative peace, for Elzyna seemed happy and untroubled. I was thankful for this, because I knew it relieved the strain Neal was feeling.

Yet Neal was not sleeping at night. Often I would awaken in the early morning hours to find him gone from the bed. The first time this happened I found him in a chair by the window, looking out, lost in thought. I went over and knelt down beside him. "Something troubling you?"

"No, I'm fine. Just need to think. Go back to bed."

"Want some hot milk?"

"No, nothing. I just want to be alone."

I kissed his forehead and went back to bed. After the first two or three times, I stopped trying to get him to talk to me. It was difficult to do this, because he had always been ready to help me when I was troubled about something. Often I would await his return to bed, and reach for his hand. He would either clasp it for a moment, then turn the other way, or just ignore it.

With Gabriel he was much the same. He was always kind, yet he'd lost his playfulness, and if Gabriel wanted to ask a question or climb upon his lap, often as not he would say, "I'm busy right now. Go and play for a little while."

Watching this occur over and over again was more painful than his subtle rejection of me.

Neal went to Galveston at least once a week to check on his family and the progress on repairs of their home. I went with Neal now and then, taking things I had baked for them and bringing items from the Houston stores that they needed since there could be little or no shopping in Galveston. But I did not relish the visits. The Gerrard home itself had lost its warm, friendly atmosphere. The smells of damp, rotted wood, the sound of the workman's saw, and the general disorder was saddening.

Moreover, the whole island was still such a terrible mess that it was depressing to go down there. It seemed the rubble was endless and could never be cleared. Everywhere there were visible efforts to clean up and put things back together, the noise of saws and other machinery, yet it seemed an overwhelming amount of work before any results would show. I spoke with Neal several times about getting his mother to come to Houston and stay for a while. He tried, but she would not even consider it. Martin had to be there to continue their business. Josephine spent much of her time helping him. Mother Gerrard was not about to leave them or her grandchildren. And she was as taciturn as Neal. By the time we left, Gabriel was full of questions about the difference in the way everybody behaved at his grandmother's house, and I would have to deal with these all the way home on the train, while Neal sat gazing out the window.

For a long time I assumed he was simply reacting to the loss of his father, plus the pressures of business. Then, as time went on I began to wonder. It wasn't like Neal to remain upset. When we lost Alice Marie, he was the first to recover and look to the future. When the horrible fire claimed so much he had worked hard to build, he soon put that behind him. Surely he was grateful that only one member of his family was taken by the storm, and the rest were safe and well.

Yet he did not seem to be, and many times I thought it may well have been a blessing I was not able to confide my secret to him that evening I tried so hard. He was like a different person altogether. I did not feel confident of his understanding right now. There was no telling how he might react. I knew I must not look for another opportunity to tell him, perhaps not for a long time. And this was hard for me because it seemed that all my intentions were unraveling in front of me. Would the moment ever come again? And now that David was back at work, putting forth a great deal of effort from all appearances, would he eventually grow discontented again with the income he earned and create more mischief? Oh, surely not, I prayed.

Weeks passed. On many days Neal left for work before I rose, and failed to kiss me. Often I would awaken to the sound of the door shutting quietly behind him, and realize with a pang of dejection that he no longer cared to begin his day with an embrace. Nights were no different. His usual spontaneity was gone. He never reached toward me in bed.

Our home had turned almost as somber as the household I grew up in. Even Gabriel was quiet and withdrawn.

Finally one morning at breakfast in early December, I tried Neal's own tactic of downright insistence for change. "You're going to have to quit withdrawing from Gabriel and me," I told him. "I know you're grieving but you have to come out of this at some point. If you would only talk about it, tell me what you're feeling, maybe I could—"

He interrupted me coldly. "There's nothing to say," he declared, then rose from his chair without having touched the meal in front of him, tucked his newspaper under his arm, and walked out the door.

My nerves were under a strain as well as his. I started to cry because I felt bad about opening the subject when I did. I kept thinking, he hadn't even had breakfast. I should never have upset him the first thing in the morning. Why couldn't I hold my peace?

That night when he returned home I sat with him through our recently developed habit of silent meals, determined not to further irritate him. When we went to bed I moved close and began to kiss him. "No, not now," he said, and turned away. Perhaps it should not have made me angry, but it did.

For hours I lay there miserable, wishing I could say something yet afraid to say anything for fear it would only bring on more rejection. In the morning I awoke as he was dressing. I waited, eyes closed, till I heard him cross the floor and head for the doorway. When he reached for the knob I raised up and said, "Neal, sometimes I feel like I lost you in that storm."

He turned and looked at me as though I had hit him, then hesitated for a long moment, still looking at me. I had never seen so much unexpressed pain in his face. Finally, without a word, he turned and walked through the door, closing it behind him.

I fell back on the pillows and let the tears fill my eyes and splay down over my cheeks.

After that I found it natural to withdraw from my efforts at comforting him. All these years I had walked the tightwire posed by my father's misdeeds, caring only for the preservation of my life with Neal, for his feelings. Now with one angry storm it seemed that all of my efforts were swept away, and I wondered, what was it for? How strong was the marriage I tried so hard to protect?

Shortly after that David came by to pick up Elzyna, and while he was there I did something I will always regret. Elzyna and Gabriel were in the backyard playing with a hoop when he came, and instead of hurrying her off as usual, he sat down and had coffee with me. He was different that day, calmer, reflective. At first he spoke of the latest antics of Jordan—the only one of his children in whom he had ever taken an interest. Normally this irritated me, but that day I did not really mind. I was lonely for company. Finally he said, "I suppose you've told Neal all about me and Amanda."

"No," I said quickly, then looked down. "We haven't talked very much about anything lately. He has been busy . . . and . . . keeps to himself."

"I've been doing a lot of thinking myself lately. I guess you can't go through something like that storm without seeing your whole life a little differently."

"Oh?" I said. I still could not face him.

"I suddenly feel that Neal and I have something in common."

"What?" I blurted out, looking up.

"You might say I lost my father kind of like he did."

I began to finger the lace on my sleeve, fearing what might be about to come.

". . . you know, the disappearance. I spent a long time looking for my father, but I never found him, or his lady friend for that matter."

"Oh?" I said faintly, and touched my throat.

"There were just no clues at all. Finally I realized if he wanted to be found, he would be. My mother was very much against my looking for him, and so I finally abandoned the project . . . although through the years in my travels, I've continued to ask questions." He shook his head. "I suppose he's dead by now."

"Yes, probably he is," I said, relief flooding over me.

"Alvareda, I want to confess something," he said. His voice was kind, soft.

I looked away again. Oh, it was so much easier to deal with David as an adversary than in this fashion.

"Alvareda, please look at me," he said gently, and so I did. "I've been wrong to want to hurt you. I knew that the minute I laid eyes on you at the train station. I don't think I have ever been so grateful to get my hands on—to see anyone."

I turned aside and studied the kitchen wall.

"I just couldn't stand your turning me down all those years ago. Seeing you with Neal tore me up inside. All I could think about was getting you back. And every time I saw you it just got worse. After a while, I was determined to make you care for me so that I could turn away from you, and show you how it felt."

I kept looking away. My hands had begun to tremble. I began swinging my foot back and forth.

Finally he said, "Alvareda, did you ever care for me?"

I sighed and looked at him. "Oh, David, maybe I would have, but even before I fell in love with Neal you frightened me so. You were just too—too much like my father . . . that is, in some ways. Oh, why could you never see that?"

He seemed to consider this, then asked, "And now?"

"Oh, David," I said again, and shook my head. I wanted to tell him that he was no match for Neal, had never been. Yet I felt so terribly sorry for him, felt that he deserved the truth about what my father had done to his. I was suddenly tempted to tell him. Yet in that moment I could not find the words to declare anything.

"I want you to know that I didn't mean to hurt Neal either, not about the money anyway. I really would have paid it back."

I nodded.

"You and Neal . . . well . . . I hate to have to admit this, but you have always been like married people should be. I've always admired that."

The remark triggered all the tears waiting to come. I could have killed myself, but I could not stop crying.

He offered me a handkerchief. I took it and dried my eyes. "Is everything all right?" he asked.

"Of course," I told him.

"I'll go then," he said at last. He closed his hand around mine and pressed it. I didn't look up again. I waited until he was out the door, and then I wept some more. While I was still sitting there, Neal came through the door, talking to David over his shoulder about some papers he wanted to give him while he was here. Neal must have met David in the yard, I realized, and I dried my eyes.

I did not want Neal to know I had been crying, so I hurried up the stairs. Before I got to the top he called to me from below.

"What's the hurry? Anything wrong?"

"No," I told him. "Just a headache." I went into the bedroom and closed the door, hating myself for being trapped into lying to Neal once again.

When I think now how close I came to telling David the whole truth, I wonder what an effect it would have had on the events that followed. I cannot help believing that, whatever his response, it could not have been as terrible to bear as what inevitably happened.

Chapter 5

Four months after the storm, on January 10, 1901, another upheaval occurred which had effects as far reaching to Houston as the hurricane had to Galveston. Yet it was a plunge forward. The biggest oil discovery in the Western world occurred at a little hill called Spindletop, ninety miles east of Houston, when a well in a field that few people knew about and fewer believed in burst forth with a black plume that shot sixty feet in the air.

Up to that time, as far as I was concerned, oil was something we used to light lamps with. I knew of fields in Pennsylvania, and even as close as Corsicana, near Dallas. But from the beginning, this discovery had portent far beyond anyone's dreams or expectations. For reasons of which I was not quite certain in the days when first we began to read about it, Spindletop was the most exciting event to happen in this part of the country since Texas gained her independence from Mexico. When Neal brought in the newspaper on January 11, he was more animated than I had seen him in months.

"Why don't you go and have a look at it?" I asked him.

"I just may do that," he said, then left the room to call David.

Each day the news spilling out of the sleepy town of Beaumont, near the site of Spindletop, was more dramatic than the day before. People were crowding into the hotel lobbies, stores, offices, and on the street corners talking about the well. The early efforts at containing the flow of oil were hopelessly inadequate, and oil was shooting two hundred feet in the air and spreading all over the surrounding prairie. Meanwhile, syndicates were being quickly organized to buy up land surrounding the great phenomenon. Even people in Houston, normally absorbed in talk of the current cotton season, were crowding into the Capitol Hotel (which, as I understood, was undergoing a change in name to the Rice) and the Cotton Exchange Building, talking about oil, and organizing syndicates.

By the following Tuesday there was an editorial in the newspaper that made all of it more clear to me. The importance of Spindletop to Houston lay in the fact that it may be the heavy grade of oil that would be useful as fuel. If that was so, then our age-old problem of the high price of fuel such as coal would vanish. Fuel oil, in almost unbelievable quantities only ninety miles away, could be piped into Houston quickly and efficiently. Manufacturing industries formerly reluctant to build plants in Houston would now eagerly locate in our city limits. The potential for growth in Houston would zoom as never before.

Since the storm, the talk about Houston as an important deep-water port was taken more seriously than ever before. The achievement of the port, then, plus the rail center already well established and growing, plus the cotton spot market, and now a cheap fuel to enable us to entice huge manufacturing concerns, all added up to the potential for a city equal to New York or Boston. I now felt greatly excited myself.

Less than a week after the first report of the Lucas gusher, Neal and David boarded a morning train for Beaumont, and if I had to guess, I would have said Neal was far more excited when they left than David. Yet, Neal returned within a couple of days, after he had enough of the crowds, the pandemonium, and the endless talk of oil. David stayed on.

Neal looked as though he had not slept in weeks. He said the streets of Beaumont were filled with people and animals. The Crosby Hotel, across from the railroad depot, was more crowded than Houston's hotels after the storm refugees had come. Cots lined the corridors and men fought over the use of them. Neal had slept one night in a tent someone had put up around the corner from the Crosby. He paid ten dollars for a cot with a mosquito net. The other night he managed to get into a hotel room elsewhere in Beaumont. The small room, usually reserved for one or two guests, had cots lining it wall to wall. He counted sixteen of them. His overnight there cost him fifteen dollars. Neither night had been restful. At the hotel, the room was more a terminal than a sleeping place. All night long people came in and out. The saloons in Beaumont did not close their doors day or night, and he awoke at one point to find himself next to a fellow who smelled like a distillery and whose snoring sounded like a locomotive whistle.

"What about the gusher? Is it as tall as they say?"

"It could not be exaggerated, I don't believe. I wouldn't take anything for the experience of seeing it. They've got it better under control now, but still it is an awesome sight. You can see it for miles."

"What about David?"

"I lost track of him after the first night, and there is no finding anyone in that town. He'll get back when he can, I guess. Or, when he decides he has had enough."

For David, that time never came. From the moment he stepped out of the passenger car in Beaumont, he was infected with what people were coming to call, "oil fever." He came back to Houston and stayed only long enough to pack a bag, take care of a few things at the office, and buy another railroad ticket. For many weeks to come, we did not see much of him, and when he did spend time with us, he talked of nothing but oil and land and leases. Failing to get in on some of the early activity because he did not know who to talk to or how to go about it, he was not able to pick up a lease on a large tract of land for the price of a few dollars, as some had done. In many ways, he was like a child excited over a brand-new Christmas toy that was complicated to operate and failed to include instructions in its box.

Carlotta said, "David is going out of his mind over this whole thing. He's dying to get his hands on enough money to invest. I told him he wasn't going to use any of my money."

By April, the Spindletop field was a forest of derricks, and David finally had his chance to become wealthy as many others had done, going in with a few thousand dollars and coming out with a million. Through his travels back and forth, he had met two men from West Texas, and together with them he found a tract of fifteen acres on the hill that could be leased for seventy-five hundred dollars plus a fourth of the well to the farmer who owned it. It was not too far from the Lucas geyser and the profitable Beatty well which followed it. The figure arrived at for obtaining a drilling team plus the equipment to drill and transportation to the well site was roughly thirty thousand dollars. Each man was supposed to come up with one-third for his share, and they would meet back in Beaumont with cash in hand.

All this time, Neal had watched events unfold with interest. Although an impressive number of the wells drilled did pay out, many others did not. Oil was risky business, calling for thousands of dollars in investment, with a less than even chance the dollars would be multiplied. And if the investment did not pay off, you walked away without your original capital, sometimes in less time than it took for you to gather it. One night Neal shared a table at a dinner meeting with Jesse Jones, who had come to Houston several years ago and was now one of its greatest promotors. Neal had met him before, and immediately struck up a friendship because their basic philosophies were much the same. Mr. Jones, who was principally in the lumber business and in real estate, had been to Beaumont and made some money in trading leases, but the oil business wasn't for him, he said. When Neal returned from the dinner that night he said, "It was good to talk to someone who felt the same as me. I was beginning to think I was crazy for not sinking everything I own into an oil well."

Shortly after that David arrived at our doorstep in a state of great excitement. I will never forget that night. David's clothes had surely been slept in; the back of his coat was a mass of wrinkles as were his trousers. There was dust on the knees of his pants and the elbows of his coat, and dirt under his fingernails. His tie was hanging free and his shirt collar was unbuttoned. His hair was dirty and full of oil and dust. He had come straight to our house from the depot. Neal poured a drink for him, which he immediately downed, then asked for another. It seemed to me he was drinking twice as fast as usual, and he was clearly agitated. He was, I soon realized, afraid of what Neal's response would be to his proposal. "Sit down and stop pacing around," I told him as Neal left to refill his glass.

"I can't be still, Alvareda. I tell you, I've never seen anything so exciting in my life. There are millions just waiting to be made out there. All you have to do is punch a hole in that hill and up pops a geyser of oil. It's the greatest opportunity that ever came around. If Neal doesn't take advantage of this, he's—"

"I'm what?" said Neal, returning with his refill.

"Just hear me out, now," he said, and came to rest in front of the fireplace. "You know, I've been going down there for three months now. I didn't want to make any hasty moves because that's where you lose your shirt. I missed out on a few cheaper deals, but the one I'm going to tell you about tonight is not a bad one, and it's also low risk because of the location. I think this old farmer who wants to lease tried first on something that didn't work out. That's why he's eager to do business now."

"You mean, he drilled a well that was dry?" Neal asked.

"No," David quickly replied. "I mean, the group he optioned to couldn't come up with the money." He shook his head in dismay. "That's the confounding part. You've got to have at least a little to make a fortune. . . . Look, all we have to put in is ten grand apiece," he said, then paused before adding, "I'm counting on you to back me, Neal."

Somehow I had the feeling this plea had been practiced and practiced beforehand. In a way I could not help admiring David for his determination to strike out in this new venture. Daily there were newspaper stories about fortunes being made on that increasingly famous hill.

"Counting on? You mean, you've committed to this?" Neal asked.

David, trying hard to retain his air of confidence, but not quite succeeding, let out a long breath. "Yes."

"Well, if you can do it personally, I say, go ahead, and I wish you all success. But if you're looking to me as a backer, I don't have it right now. I just bought forty acres of real estate on the south side of Houston."

I knew of David's inability to finance his dream, and I felt deflated for him at that moment. I looked off to the side, embarrassed at having to watch Neal scuttle his plans.

"I'm not asking you to go out on a limb," he said. "I want us to do it together—let the firm put up the money, start up a new arm of Leider and Gerrard, if you want to. We've both worked hard for this—" he imposed, then stopped.

I glanced at Neal. He was shaking his head. Without taking exception to the "we" in David's phrase, he said quite simply that the firm couldn't do it just now. "Profits are down this year and there have been a lot of extra expenses, as you know. Or ought to."

"Oh, Neal, don't tell me you don't have it tucked away in an account somewhere. You always manage to come up with—"

"Damn it, David, you haven't the vaguest notion of our finances. You never have. I'm leveling with you. We can't afford to invest ten thousand dollars in oil right now. And even if we could, I'd want to do some investigating first."

David sat down and leaned back, and gulped down the rest of his drink. I sat rigidly in my chair, afraid of where this argument might lead.

"Well then, hock something, can't you? It wouldn't be for long. This well will pay out, I tell you. I'm convinced beyond a doubt. We'll have our money back before the middle of this season."

"No. I'm sorry. But that's final."

"By God, Neal, it's half mine, isn't it? Well, take my half out."

"I said we don't have it," Neal snapped. "We agreed that decisions over capital investment would be mine. And I tell you, there is no decision when you simply don't have it."

"Go to the bank then. You're on the Board now. Borrow it," said David. I looked from one to the other, filled with apprehension.

"Our bank doesn't make loans on oil wells. I can't ask them to do for me what they don't do for others."

"That damned bank is as back—conservative as you are," David said angrily, and rose to leave.

"Look, if you're really serious about this, maybe you'd like me to buy you out of the partnership. I can't do it now, but I might be able to by next year. You don't seem too interested in cotton anymore. I'm sure the oil business will still be around."

David looked as though Neal had popped him in the jaw. "But this deal won't. Good night, Alvareda. I'll find some other way."

When he was gone, Neal drew in a breath and said, "I think I'll have a drink on that one. Join me?"

"No. Yes. That is, a glass of sherry please," I said nervously, and sat down in a chair. I had never seen David and Neal quarrel before. Through the years, as many times as I heard Neal's complaints against David, and even heard David express his grievances, I had never been together with them in a room when such anger flashed. I felt thoroughly shaken and exhausted, and enormously relieved that David had left. What if they had wound up hitting each other?

Neal was handing me my drink. "Did you really mean that?" I asked abruptly. "You positively couldn't do it? Granted, David has gone beyond his rights, but surely—"

A faint glimmer of displeasure came into his eyes, and he looked at me for a moment before replying. "It used to be that the business decisions were left up to me. Now it seems no one cares to wait for my opinion."

His position angered me. "Maybe your need to control everything has gotten out of hand," I told him. "No one seems to be capable of making decisions except for you. Even after the fire, when I offered help, you treated me like a child, instead of your wife—Listen, I don't want to argue with you. I just think you ought to realize that sometimes you lord it over David as though he has no ability at all. I'm sure it must be frustrating for him."

He was silent for a while, then said, "I did not know you took such an interest in his welfare."

"Oh, Neal, I don't. Why is it I can't tell you anything anymore? Every time I say something you take it wrong. I wish—I wish—"

"What?"

I sighed. "That you had never taken David as a partner."

"Well that makes two of us." With that, he turned and walked out.

I stood there, trembling. Never had we left such a disagreement so unresolved.

I had a sense of forboding that night which kept me awake until nearly dawn. More than the argument between David and Neal, it was Neal's attitude that frightened me. His reference to my interest in David's welfare kept repeating in my mind. Why had he looked at me that way? What did he think I was up to? I told myself again and again that it was simply a product of the words which passed between us immediately before. Yet in my heart I felt an alarming certainty that was not it at all. . . .

Next to me Neal wrestled with sleep as well, but did not reopen our conversation. Just as I was dozing off around six, he rose from the bed, and in the daze of half-wakefulness, I remember he kissed me, and said he was leaving for the office. In my mind I held onto that one little kiss as though in it lay a slender hope for our marriage.

Chapter 6

When I finally opened my eyes it was ten o'clock. The pot of tea on the tray Agnes had placed beside the bed had grown cold. I yawned and put on my robe. I felt wonderful. Rested. I drew the drapery and looked out the window. Gabriel was playing out on the lawn and Agnes was nearby with a bowl of fresh peas in her lap. I opened the window and drew in a deep breath of air. Springtime. I reminded myself of the kiss Neal gave me as he left for work, and told myself everything was going to be all right now. The partnership would finally be dissolved. David would soon be too busy in his new pursuit to trouble us anymore. He would probably be out of our lives forever. The insistent voice arguing inside my head was easy to ignore in the light of day. . . .

I went downstairs to get some hot tea. The newspaper was on the edge of the dining room table. I looked over the headlines. The ever-present news of Spindletop dominated the front page. There was nothing really new these days, except the subject of the oil field. What could happen to displace this? I wondered idly, and thumbed through the pages.

Then the doorbell rang. Agnes was too far out in the yard for me to get her attention. My robe was heavy enough to be decent. I opened the door myself, and to my dismay found David standing there. Oh no, now what? I thought anxiously, and wished I had not gone to the door. David was better groomed this morning, but his eyes looked tired, his face pale. Apparently he had slept poorly.

I tried to get rid of him. "Neal is at his office this morning."

"I wanted to see you," he said, with a tone of urgency.

I gripped the doorknob and hesitated. "Oh, all right," I said at last. He followed me into the parlor and closed the door. I glanced at the door uneasily.

We sat down across from each other, and he began. "Everything has changed," he said. Then, too nervous to sit, he began to pace and rub his hands together. "It's the chance for a new beginning, if you're willing to risk it."

"You mean, in oil?"

"Yes. You know, the cotton people are not going to be running this town anymore. The future is right at the fingertips of people who go after oil. If I can get in early, I can be a part of something that is so big—so big—it makes the cotton business look like a game of jackstones on Sunday afternoon."

"You're entitled to your opinion," I said, annoyed.

"Opinion! You should be around those men buying up the leases down in Beaumont. They're rough and hard-drinking sons-of-bitches but by God, they're alive! And there is so much money being invested down there. Why, you don't think John Galey would come all the way down from Pennsylvania for a few barrels of lamp oil, do you?"

"I understand your excitement, but I don't see what it has to do with me."

He paused, with forced patience. "You know that the starched-collar, stodgy cotton business has never been for me. I was in it in the early days because it gave me something to do that kept me on the move. When Neal offered me the partnership, I still wasn't sure I wanted to be in that business for the rest of my life. But it was the only way to make any money.

"Always, something inside me was empty. But I thought it was just my foolish nature. I tried to be happy, and I did a damned good job for Neal.

"Yet . . . that was the trouble. I always felt I was doing a job for Neal.

Never for myself. And when he fired Pete, I realized he really considered himself the sole proprietor, always pushing his weight around. I never felt accepted as his equal, nor part of that whole group of capitalists. Their long meetings, their committees. Their endless campaign for a deep-water port. Oh, it bores me. And now, oil will make their dreams come true. Now those jackasses in Washington will listen. They want a port? They can have one. Oil money will buy anything they want."

"You should be telling all this to Neal."

He turned and gave me a cold stare. "I tried that, but Neal hasn't the vision I have. You knew that last night. I could see it in your face."

I looked down. "I don't believe that's it. If he had the money, he might invest it," I said. I didn't tell him what an argument we had after he left. I looked up at him again. "And you, why haven't you got some money put aside?"

He knew the answer to that as well as I did. "Up to this point, I've been foolish," he said. "I've spent my money because I was trying to buy the happiness I didn't get otherwise. But all that has changed now. Here's what I want you to do."

"Me?"

"Yes. Hear me out. I know you must have a lot of cash out of your father's estate. Neal is old-fashioned about providing for you. You must have kept it tucked away somewhere. All I need is ten thousand."

My heart quickened as though touched by an icy finger, but I knew I had to stand my ground. I shook my head. "There is nothing left except the McKinney property."

"Then let me use the property as collateral. I know where I can borrow it. I'll cut you in. Neal doesn't have to know."

I wanted to slap his face for that suggestion. I looked down and folded my cold hands in my lap. "No. That's impossible. I'm not going to have any more secrets from Neal." He was silent so I looked up and said, "Do you understand?" My voice was shaky. I felt as pinned down as I had when he approached me about money after the fire.

David's brow had relaxed, his mouth slightly open in astonishment. "But . . . you didn't tell him about me and Amanda. Even after it was over and you could have told him, you didn't. You've been keeping things from him for years. Why stop now?"

"I think you had better leave," I said hoarsely, then looked away.

"No, wait a minute," he said. "You led me on, last time we talked. I could see you were unhappy. You all but told me right out."

I shook my head miserably, realizing all at once his mistaken impression. "You're wrong," I said, raising my hands and looking at him.

He came closer and considered me. I believe he was just then beginning to realize that he could not persuade me to his thinking.

"You accused me of frightening you because I was so much like your father. And all these years, you've been holding me under your thumb, using me. You're far more skillful than he was, and a hell of a lot more subtle."

"I've been using *you?"* I repeated shrilly, anger crashing through all my trepidations.

"I've kept your secrets, lived with that bitch for the sake of appearances. I even let you send Amanda away. She'd be alive today if it weren't for you."

"You're accusing me?" I gasped. "How was I to know you would take up with Amanda again, meet her in Galveston? Don't try to blame me for that."

"Yes, but if not for you, we would have met out on McKinney Avenue, remember."

I wagged my head, furious. "If you hadn't married someone out of selfishness instead of love, you'd never have taken up with Amanda in the first place," I yelled.

"You think Amanda took the place of *love* missing in my life?" he demanded. Then his whole expression changed, and I realized he had not meant to let this out. I saw the truth for the first time, and my mouth opened in shock. My voice was very low when finally I spoke.

"It was you, wasn't it? Amanda was giving my father's money to you. How stupid of me not to guess. And when she ran short, you went right to the source, Olivia. . . . I was right about you from the beginning. You never cared for anyone but yourself. You simply made use of all the opportunities."

He looked as though he'd like to kill me. "Damn you, Alvareda. When are you going to admit that you love me?"

He broke off and stepped toward me, raising a hand. His eyes were alight with fury. I covered my face and turned away, certain he would strike me to the floor. Yet he grabbed both my arms and forced me to turn toward him. He put a hand around my chin and pulled me against him. I tried to turn my face from side to side, but I was as powerless against him as I had been the first time he kissed me. He closed his mouth on mine and pressed his tongue so hard I thought he would choke me. I was so filled with rage, had I been able to grab a weapon I know I would have killed him. Yet I could not move. I could not even breathe. I tried to lift my hands. He only pressed harder, then began to murmur, "Alvareda, Alvareda"—

Neal walked through the door.

"What the hell?" he said, and we both looked toward him. David stepped away and opened his mouth to speak, but Neal cut him off. "Get out of my house. I'll deal with you later."

David picked up his hat, looked at me, then stomped out of the room. I heard the front door slam. I collapsed in a chair. "That wasn't what it looked like," I said weakly, and looked up at him. I realized I was still in my robe, and caught my breath.

He stood there for a long moment, looking at me, and I knew that he did not believe me.

"Neal?" I began, but he walked right past me and up the stairs. I tried to collect myself, to organize my thoughts so that I could explain. If not for what had passed between us the previous night, he probably would not have jumped to conclusions. If not for all that had happened over the past few months, he would not have been so unreasonable. If not for . . .

After a few minutes I walked to the bottom of the stairs. I heard the bedroom door shut, and put a hand to my chest. When he approached the top of the stairs, he was carrying a suitcase.

"I'm going to Galveston," he said, and started down.

"But when will you be home?"

"I don't know," he said. "Where is Gabriel?"

"In the backyard."

He nodded, and passed me by like a chilly waft of air.

"Neal, if you'll only let me explain—there is so much I need to tell you—"

"There is no explanation necessary," he said, hardly missing a step. "I should have seen it coming a long time ago."

I was now too angry to defend myself. Through the blurred vision of unspent tears, I watched from the window as he stopped by and kissed Gabriel good-bye, then headed for the carriage house. When he disappeared inside, I murmured, "How could you? How could you?" I sat down on the stairs, dug my fingers into my palms, and wept bitterly.

Chapter 7

Somewhere far away a rooster crows and ushers in the morning. I realize with a start that I have dozed off, and the sunlight has stolen in and brightened the room around me. My eyes immediately move to the sight of Elzyna in her cocoon of netting. She is still sleeping quietly, not having stirred since the doctor laid her here last night. I feel my heart contract with sorrow, and I breathe a prayer that she might walk again. . . .

I see clearly now that I am largely at fault for what occurred during the past few hours. Had I only had the courage to tell Neal the truth from the beginning, instead of being controlled by a fear he might not love me anymore, none of this would have happened. Elzyna would be safe in her own bed at this hour. Oh, what I would give if only that could be true and all this would be but a frightful nightmare from which I would soon awaken. . . .

I did not hear from Neal after he left. Though I passed the day looking out the window, sure he would return and give me a chance to explain, sure that he must still love me, he did not come. I kept thinking of the day in 1887 when I could not bring myself to leave Harrisburg with him just at the moment he commanded. And I had sat the day long, waiting for him. Finally I had gone to him begging. . . .

But that time was different; I was the foolish one. This time, it was Neal who would have to take the first step toward making amends, before I told him what had been locked up inside me for so long. If that step was taken . . . if he ever came home to me again. It was painful to accept that, for all the deceits into which I had let myself be drawn, I was blamed for the only one of which I was not guilty.

I stayed at home through the night and most of the next day. When I could stand the suspense no longer, I decided there was no reason I had to be there. If Neal could leave, then so could I. Forcing animation into my voice, I suggested to Gabriel we spend a few days out at the house on McKinney Avenue. It had been without a renter for several months, and would be a good change of scenery just now.

Gabriel and I loaded some things in the buggy and left around three in the afternoon. I did not like leaving our home on Main untended, with no one knowing where I was. Agnes wasn't scheduled to be back until next Tuesday, and she had no telephone so I couldn't reach her. I called Carlotta and said that Neal was out of town, and told her of my plans. She must have conveyed them to Elzyna.

After leaving me, Neal had stopped by his office and tried to reach David, but David was already on his way back to Beaumont. Neal asked Carlotta to tell David upon his return that he needed to speak with him. When David returned, three days later and I gather not successful in his bid for a well, he called Neal's office and told him if he had something to say to him, he could come ahead, but he wasn't about to set foot in their office again.

Neal went to David's home, full of anger.

Carlotta had once said she would not lower herself to have David investigated, but that someone else might. The meaning of her prediction became clear late last night when she appeared at this door following the news of Elzyna's accident. Her father, March Bennett, chanced to discover David in Galveston during the summer of 1900, with a woman he could not see well enough to identify. Suspecting the worst, he hastened to alert Carlotta and insisted on hiring a private investigator. The investigator was busy on the case when the hurricane struck in September. He suffered serious injuries. Much later, when he tried to resume his work, he was halted. The storm destroyed not only people and buildings, but records as well. Thus far, he had only been able to pinpoint a piece of property far out, east of Houston. The few people who knew there was a house out there referred to it as the Cane place.

Carlotta knew that Cane was my maiden name, but at that point believed it was simply a coincidence because the name is a common one.

When Neal arrived at the door, he and David talked in one room while Carlotta eavesdropped from the next. And when Neal said to David, "If you ever come near my wife again, I'll kill you," Carlotta had her answer.

Neal was no sooner gone than Carlotta charged through the door and confronted David about his affair with me. She demanded he fall on his knees in the church's confessional and completely change his life.

He told her she was crazy, that he was never setting foot in a church again, and wanted a divorce.

She said she would not give him a divorce.

He stomped out and slammed the door. Elzyna was standing in the hallway, incredulous at what she had just overheard between her parents. Seeing her, Carlotta said, "Now you know all about your precious Alvareda. Your father's mistress. What do you think of people who commit adultery?"

Frantic with confusion and hurt, Elzyna saddled Mindy and began her disastrous journey out here. She was not too far from the edge of the yard when she was pitched from the horse, and there she lay for better than two hours before Gabriel and I took a walk in the cool evening breeze and chanced to hear her weak moaning.

When I think of all the years I tried so hard to keep a cloud of scandal from descending on our lives, to keep our names from being spread across a newspaper page above great columns of words for all to see, I realize with deep regret that I would gladly accept that in trade for the injuries caused by my own deceit to everyone involved, and especially to Elzyna.

We now await the morning visit of the doctor, in hopes he can accurately predict Elzyna's destiny, and I wish he could predict mine as well. I think of all the misfortune that has issued from this house my father built, and I wonder: Does it harbor deep within it the fertile seed of my father's evil? Will tragedy follow everyone who enters through its gate?

The inability to answer these questions has weighed on me throughout the long night and has led me at last to a decision. If Elzyna is doomed to go away from here without hope for complete recovery from her injuries, I will set fire to this house and watch it burn to the ground. I will never set foot on this property again, nor will I allow anyone else to walk here.

Elzyna
1905–1914

PART 1

Chapter 1

Hail Mary, full of grace; the Lord is with thee: blessed art thou among women, and blessed is the fruit of thy womb, Jesus. Holy Mary, Mother of God, pray for us sinners, now and at the hour of our death. . . .

There is a great deal for which to be thankful, and I must remember this tonight and every other night, and go on. If I should hear the sound of a train rumbling down the tracks a few blocks away, I must be strong enough to cover my ears and look into the comforting log fire, and not think of New Orleans and all I cannot have, all for which hope is gone. I must think of the children who, thank God, have not been harmed or taken from me. I must think of this house, which I have loved since I was a child. These are the major blessings. And there are the small, daily things, like sitting out on the porch in springtime and watching the four o'clocks bloom, and not feeling afraid anymore.

It would be easy to say all that happened within the past twenty-four hours was completely my husband's fault, that it all began the moment I met him in 1905—the year Patricia became engaged and appointed herself the role of matchmaker between me and Beryl Farrish in order to assuage her guilt for reaching the altar before her elder sister—but I know that all we have come to was as much my fault as Beryl's, and in truth was as inevitable as McKinney Avenue being paved and lined with houses, past those railroad tracks at York Street and farther, block by block: a suburban aisle through an arbor of oak trees.

The fact that as the firstborn Leider child I was not male displeased my mother. The soon-to-be obvious fact that I would be neither petite nor pretty was a second blow to her.

Alvareda and Neal Gerrard, my "auntie Reda and uncle Neal," were the only people who made me feel wanted and secure while I was growing up. As a child I often wished I could live with them, especially when there was a lot of arguing between my parents. Could I have won my father's love I would have placed it above all else, for he was my hero: handsome and winning when he wanted to be. When he smiled at me or stopped to talk to me, even for a few brief moments, I was lifted with pleasure. To the children at school I bragged about him, telling them all how important he was and that he traveled far and wide on business. One day when he happened to pick me up as school let out, dressed up in his fine suit and hat, I was so proud I could barely contain myself. Next day my status rose at school simply by virtue of my father's handsome looks.

When my mother called him an "adulterer" to my face when I was a child, I was shattered. Nothing in the Bible was more abhorred. The fact that Alvareda's name was linked with his in this matter was more than I could bear. I was too young and inexperienced to understand the meaning of that accusation seriously affected others whom I loved as well—Uncle Neal, even Gabriel. All I could think of as I tore out on my horse in fury was my mother's stricken face, and the realization that my devotion to my father and Alvareda had caused her grief. When I was pitched from Mindy as she vaulted a high thorny bush in our path, I believe I felt the first pangs of guilt before I even reached the ground. How wicked I had been for failing to appreciate my mother. This was my punishment.

Over the next year I struggled through a painful recovery. Again and again my mother said, "You are strong, Elzyna. For that you should be grateful. It may be all you have to rely on one day."

This was her way of helping me through the ordeal. It was the closest she could come to compassion. It was also the most complimentary thing she had ever said to me, and I savored and believed it accordingly.

Neal Gerrard, I later learned, paid for all the expenses of that year of my convalescence, for the lengthy hospital stays, for all the months of treatments that followed, for the back brace I learned to despise. He and Alvareda both felt they were to blame for my accident, that their household conflict spilled over to affect me. Alvareda spent a great deal of time with me as I recovered. Neal did not come, and I understood this because I knew he and my father had quarreled. I also knew that part of the quarrel was a misunderstanding. I was too young to get all this straight. The most important information I received was that Alvareda had nothing to do with my father's adultery. She was not bad, as Mother suspected.

One Sunday in the late summer after I learned I would be up to a short carriage ride, I begged Alvareda to take me to her house so that I could spend the day with her and Neal. She hesitated and looked very distressed. Finally she said, "You might as well know, Neal isn't living at home." Tears sprang to her eyes.

My astonishment grew as she explained he had gone back to Galveston, traveling to Houston only to get his work done, since the big quarrel that involved all of us.

"But, Auntie Reda, why doesn't he come home? I thought everything was okay now." I felt sick inside at the thought of them being angry at each other.

She turned away and wiped her eyes. "Oh, he thinks it is, now that everything is out in the open between us. He wants to come home, and I know that he loves me. Still . . ."

"What then?" It seemed to me there could be no further complication. If my parents loved each other the way the Gerrards did, I'd be the happiest person in the world.

"It isn't the way it used to be," she said finally. "I still—still can't talk to him."

Even at the age of twelve, I understood that. My parents got into an argument every time they talked. It was best if they didn't try to communicate.

"But Uncle Neal has always been easy to talk to."

"Not since he lost his father. And now . . . even after all we've been through, he continues to shut me out as though I'm incapable of the same understanding he has always . . . oh, I shouldn't be telling you this. I'm sorry."

I did not grasp it all, but I think I understood more than she realized. I made up my mind I was going to talk to Uncle Neal. I wrote him a letter at his office and asked him to come and see me while my father was out of town because I did not think I could ride all the way to his office and get up the stairs in my back brace. But if necessary, then I would try.

I did not see then that I must have frightened him with my determination. He soon came over.

When I saw him, I realized I could not possibly do what I set out to. Just looking at him, I burst into tears. He came over to the bed and held me close for a long time, just the way he used to when I was frightened of a storm. When he pulled away, I realized there were tears in his eyes, too.

"I don't understand why you and Auntie Reda can't be together," I said.

He sat nearby in a chair, and said, "It's what she wants."

"Then why is she so upset?"

He looked at me. "I—I don't understand what her problem is." He tried to smile. "Anyhow, it isn't anything for you to be worried about. You just need to concentrate on getting well, and—"

He sounded like my father when he wanted to get rid of me. Suddenly I knew what Alvareda was talking about. "Uncle Neal, Auntie Reda said you changed after your father died. Is it because you were very sad?"

I do not think he would have told me the things he did, then, except that he was more distraught than he let anyone know. He needed someone to talk to more than anything in the world and I think he forgot for a moment that I was a child. "It isn't that simple. Oh, if it only were. . . ."

He shifted in his chair. "I've never told anyone this before, but do you remember after the storm, I tried to reach Galveston but could get no farther than Texas City?"

"And you walked most of the way back home."

He nodded. "Yes. But another man was there, in the same predicament—unable to get across the water. He caught onto a railroad tie and paddled himself across. I almost did the same daredevil thing. The only difference was that his wife and daughter were over on the island. He had to risk his life because all that he had was there.

"But my family was here. If anything happened to me, I would have robbed Alvareda and Gabriel. When I realized that, I decided not to risk it. But I was confused about whether I was just being cowardly by not going on like the other man did, and I still hate myself sometimes."

He leaned back.

"But you did right, didn't you?"

"Maybe." He sighed.

I didn't know what to say. It was all too confusing. I just sat there, wishing I could comfort him, wishing I could get him and Auntie Reda together again.

Finally he said, "You know, there's something else. Sometimes I get so mad at my father that it makes me feel . . . guilty."

I understood that. Still, I said nothing.

After a few moments he continued, but he did not look at me. It was as though he was drawn inside himself, thinking things out. "Dad did a very foolish thing. He should have believed in my brother enough to know he'd have the sense to leave his home and go to shelter. He'd told him to already. He just couldn't let go—let Martin take charge. He'd be alive today if he hadn't tried to control everyone else's—" Abruptly he stopped, as though something had just registered with him. He looked at me and swallowed. At last he said, "I've got to go, honey. I've got some thinking to do." He kissed my cheek and squeezed my hand. "Thank you, sweetheart."

As he walked out, I wasn't sure why he was thanking me. But I suddenly had a good feeling inside, like everything was going to be all right again.

Within a few days Auntie Reda and Uncle Neal came back with Gabriel in tow and we all went for a carriage ride. I had not seen them so radiantly happy in a very long time, nor so affectionate. It was just like . . . I had to think . . . yes, it was just like before the storm. I felt wonderful inside. They took a long vacation in the fall and when they returned, Alvareda was expecting—their second son, Clayton.

Through the long legal process of severing their partnership, Neal and my father had gradually developed what might be described as "speaking terms." They never visited in each other's home anymore, though my mother and Alvareda would occasionally share a coffee hour during the day. I think that even this cool sort of courtesy extended between our families must have been brought about by the fact that I was caught in the middle of their fractured friendship.

Neal tried for a while without success to find a buyer for the compress operation, and it was not until late in 1904, that someone offered to buy him out completely. I was not told all the details, but apparently he made a handsome profit that enabled him to focus his attention on land and other types of investments.

Once the sale was complete, sometime in 1905, Neal kept a promise made to Alvareda before they married and took her and the children on an extended tour of Europe. I was then sixteen and approaching my high school graduation. Patricia soon met George Stanley, the son of an oil millionaire, and begged Mother for permission to be courted by him. Mother raised her eyebrow at me and wondered if by chance George had a friend who might be interested in courting Patricia's older sister. And that was what led me to Beryl Farrish.

I saw him first on a November evening in 1905, when Mother and I attended a party in the home of George Stanley's parents on Lamar Avenue. The house had a wide, open promenade all the way across the front, and for the occasion of the party, rows of potted palms had been placed on each side of the entrance way in the center.

As Mother and I approached the door I noticed a young man standing at the end of a row of palms, having a smoke. He was fairly tall, but not long-legged, and he was muscular around the chest and shoulders. He had straight dark hair, parted up the side, and his skin was more tanned than you might expect for that time of year. As we passed he nodded at me. I nodded in polite response. He took one further draw on his cigarette, and, still looking toward me, smashed the cigarette in the dirt around the palm. I did not think it was respectful to a host to do that, and he looked almost defiant about it—I had seen that same look on the face of my brother Jordan. But it did not seem important to me at the time.

Once inside the door Mother whispered, "Who was that young man?"

"I have no idea."

"From his expression, I would have thought he knew you, or perhaps at least would like to."

"I'm sure you are mistaken," I said.

She rolled her eyes. "Oh, Elzyna, show a little optimism, won't you?"

She had taken my refusal to make a formal debut in society more graciously than I would have expected, and I really think it was because she felt she could count on Patricia when the time came—Patricia was so much more social than I was—rather than that she truly understood my reticence. I did not like parties and social gatherings because they always made me feel left out. Although I never admitted as much to Mother, I had had a long talk with Alvareda before my decision, and she had told me it wouldn't be fair to go through the social whirl if I truly did not want to. She herself disliked all the society page coverage and all the big to-do, and she would never force a daughter of hers to participate in anything of that sort against her wish.

I tried to obey Mother's wish now. She no doubt felt I would never make any effort to socialize and meet eligible young men. "He looked like a nice person," I said congenially, thinking all the time that he had actually struck me quite the opposite.

There were about fifty people in the Stanley home that evening, and it was not until after the buffet supper while we took coffee and dessert in the huge drawing room, that I saw Beryl again. Patricia looked beautiful that night in a gown of wine lace embroidered over satin. It had a pleated satin flounce that accentuated her well-shaped hips, and a neckline that was just low enough to cause much arguing between her and Mother as the dress was being fitted. Patricia had milky skin and dark brown hair with auburn highlights. She was about Mother's size, but had a softer look about her with teasingly slanted green eyes and long lashes. I could not count the number of times Mother compared her favorably with me, convincing me I was awkward and large and plain. Only the Gerrards and, on a few rare occasions, my father, had refuted her appraisal up to that time. Patricia flitted by in her usual airy manner, with Beryl on her arm. "Elzyna, I thought I'd never find you, darling," she said. "I want you to meet Mr. Farrish, an architect who has joined Radcliffe, Winter, and Tulley. He just moved down from Chicago, and is getting into the Star Wheels."

"You two will have a lot in common," she added, and darted away to find George.

Beryl sat down. "Your sister says you bicycle, too," he said.

"I've been in the Ladies' Club for a year," I told him. "The exercise is good for my—for me." He nodded with interest, but said nothing. So I continued. "Did you ride in Chicago?"

"All the time, in tournaments, races, what have you. Ever heard of Albert Schock?"

"The cycling champion?"

He nodded. "Good friend of mine."

You are exaggerating, I thought, but said nothing. He smiled, and when he did his lips turned down in a kind of scowl. He had a cruel mouth, it seemed to me. Yet that night he was pleasant. We chatted for a while about bicycling trails in and around Houston, and I told him some of my favorites, through Magnolia Park, which had not yet been carved into a subdivision, and out the

Harrisburg Road. Then I said, "You must have lots of people to meet. You needn't waste your time with me."

He looked surprised. "Let me be the judge of that," he said and winked. Just then he seemed charming. I smiled, and told him the two clubs were bicycling out to the San Jacinto Battleground next Sunday.

"Well then, no doubt I'll see you there. Where do we start from?"

"In front of the post office at Harrisburg. It'll be an all-day meet. We're going to picnic at the battlegrounds."

"You don't say—in the middle of November? Doesn't it ever get cold and snow down here?"

"The last time was ten years ago."

To say that I was preoccupied with Beryl through the following week would not be true. He did cross my mind occasionally, though I was not, "swept off my feet," as they say. There was something about him that I could not quite pinpoint. That he was a Yankee made his manner seem at times too abrupt, too quick, unpolished. Yet it was something other than that. A quality about him that was . . . perhaps . . . just a bit off-center. Well, at the time it was not of great concern to me. When the day of the meet came around I traveled in a carriage to Harrisburg with some other girls, and everyone in the group—some twenty altogether—arrived about the same time and began to untie bicycles from the backs of the carriages. The ladies had new green and black banners for their handlebars and scarves to tie at the waist. The men had black and crimson jerseys, with big crimson bands around the sleeves.

I must say that Beryl looked striking in his jersey and when he surprised me by walking up and helping me untie my cycle, the other girls noticed that he was noticing me. And I liked the way this made me feel. "You look fetching today," he said, and I must have glowed. I had to look away. How transparent I must have seemed to him.

"Your tires are low," he said, and grabbed the pump nearby. As he sat back on his feet and pumped the tires, I watched the flexing of his arm muscles in rhythm with the wheezing air. Somehow I found it oddly disquieting and began to hum and fiddle with a wisp of my hair so that he might not guess. When he was done and relinquished the cycle to me, I thanked him and watched him walk to his own cycle and mount. I thought of the other ladies here with us today, and wondered why he would bother with me.

Beryl was an astute rider, but not a good team member. I could see at once, as ladies followed gentlemen along the dusty road leading out of Harrisburg, that he sought leadership again and again, pedaling past the others whenever he could, then whipping around to wait for them, like a pet dog will run out in front of its master a few feet, then circle and wait for him to catch up. The others didn't like Beryl; this I could see already.

I found myself defending him. "Maybe he isn't used to our ways yet."

Speed picked up and we all leaned forward over the handlebars, thighs and calves straining.

"Ah, I love a good ride on Sunday," he said, passing me by. "No need to go in formation now, though," he added, and pedaled up to the front of the line again. I supposed he was entitled to his opinion, though he was rude in the way he expressed it.

When finally we reached the San Jacinto River banks to open the picnic baskets, Beryl sought me out again. I'm sure he was lonely, not knowing very many people. There was a pleasant breeze across the river. I sat back on my heels and pulled out my hankie to wipe my face and neck. I wondered what to say to him now.

"You were right about the weather down here. Imagine working up a good sweat just a week from Thanksgiving. Say, what's so special about this place, anyway?"

"The battle of San Jacinto was fought here. It's where we won our independence from Mexico."

"Oh yes, after all those men died at the Alamo. That was pretty foolish, wasn't it? I mean, what good did it do?"

"You'd better keep your voice down. Most people are proud of the battle of the Alamo."

He smirked. "Well, at least part of the building survived. What's for lunch?"

There were baked ham sandwiches, fruit and cheese, spice cookies, and lemon punch. It was a most appetizing sight to all of us, for we were thoroughly winded and famished. Someone handed me a plate. I passed it on to Beryl and reached for an apple and a wedge of cheese.

"Is that all you're having?" he inquired between bites.

"I'm not really very hungry," I said, though my stomach was painfully empty.

Through the lunch there was much talk about a tournament to be held in Dallas in April. We spoke of having new uniforms made, arranging train rides in a group, seeking financial backing through the Houston Business League. I offered to talk with Uncle Neal, who had been an important member of the league for years.

Beryl looked up from his third sandwich. "I didn't realize you knew Neal Gerrard. My firm is working on a bid for a new building he's putting up downtown."

"He and my father used to be in business together. The Gerrards are like family to me," I told him, and I have to admit I enjoyed impressing him.

"It's always smart to have the right connections," he said, and I told him that my connections were an accident of birth, and there was no credit due me.

"Leider, Stanley, Gerrard. I bet you even know Jesse Jones."

"Not really. I met him once, at a party at the Gerrards'. Neal knows him pretty well. He has helped him finance some real estate deals through his bank."

We'd have two hours for relaxing or taking the pleasure boats on the river before returning to Houston. Many of us, who'd gone on the boats before, walked nearer to the banks and sat out over the water to while away the time. Though I did not ask him to, Beryl followed me to the river's edge and sat down nearby. I asked him how he came to study architecture.

"I liked to draw as a kid, and when I grew up architecture seemed a respectable field to go into."

"How do you mean, 'respectable'?"

He paused. ". . . My father thought drawing was for sissies, and he gave me a hard time of it."

"What did he want you to do?"

"I don't think he really cared, as long as it was considered 'manly.' He himself was a bricklayer."

"Is that why you became interested in cycling, because of him?"

His mouth curved up with the hint of a smile—or was it a sneer? "Strangely, it isn't. When I was an architecture student in college, one of my instructors was always making me look at a good design . . . not just buildings, but furniture, machines, anything and everything. He thought the bicycle was simply the most magnificent design in existence, and I came to agree with him. Clean lines, functional, nothing on it wasted."

"I never looked at it that way before."

"I had not owned a bicycle since I was a kid. I bought one, and began to ride."

"Do you have to go to college to be an architect?"

"No, but with some firms it gives you an edge. I went to the University of Illinois. That wasn't my first choice, but at least there I could work my way through, and it was a good school."

I wondered if his going to college was a means of gaining superiority over his father, but of course that was none of my business.

"I think that is very admirable . . . paying your way through college," I said. "What brought you to Houston?"

His brow lifted. "Is this a quiz?"

"I'm sorry. I didn't mean it to be," I said quickly, and blushed. "I'm just curious, that's all."

"I first went to Galveston, four years ago. I wanted to get my start while they were rebuilding the city. But no one wanted to listen to my ideas—Nicholas Clayton is thoroughly entrenched there, with his fussy wedding-cake style. I went to California where some of my classmates went, then . . . well . . . here and there.

"A friend of mine settled in San Antonio, and invited me down to see him.

While there I spent a lot of time out at the mission ruins, and I really developed an appreciation for the mission revival style."

"Mission revival?"

"Yes. They're doing a lot of it out in California, but most of the time it bears none but a romantic resemblance to the language of that style."

"Language?" I repeated. He was losing me.

"What they are trying to express in the design. . . . Anyhow, the missions of San Antonio really spoke to me! I could see the people living in them, making their food and clothing, creating their clay pottery, the whole community designed to be functional. I came to understand what the mission revival style was really all about. I want to do some of it here. I've been working like crazy in my spare time. With Houston growing in leaps and bounds, I know I can put that style forward. . . . What's the matter? You don't agree?"

Only then did I realize I had been frowning in opposition. "Oh, I don't know . . . the battle for independence from Mexico happened so recently I'm not sure it would be accepted here."

Quickly he said, "You can be sure it will when I get through. People have to realize the Mexican thing is over and done with."

You may think so, I mused . . .

"The time has come for mission architecture and I intend to see it put forward here."

I shrugged and changed the subject. It was clear he was convinced of his ideas, regardless of his recent arrival in Houston. Nothing I could say would change his mind. Maybe that was a good trait . . . persuasiveness . . . yet, with Beryl it was more than that . . . what was the word? Pushy. He seemed to feel he could boss customers around without their resenting him.

Wouldn't he get further if he won the admiration of Houston people before he tried to tell them what to do?

Soon after that, Beryl came to call and brought me a box of Whitman's Sampler candies. I thought that was kind of him, although I could not afford the indulgence of eating one. I invited him in to share coffee with Mother and me in the drawing room. He looked very nice that day in a deep brown tweed suit and a brown tie with flecks of gold in it. He was charming to Mother, and told her that he could not stop very long because he had to get back to work.

Mother nodded her approval and said, "I find that a very desirable quality in young men. My father was one of the bulwarks of this city. He worked very hard for most of his life, though now he has retired."

"And what sort of business was he in?" Beryl inquired.

"Cotton, as were all the important people in this town."

"Mother, I am sure there are other important fields of work," I began, in an effort to rescue Beryl's feelings as an architect.

The point was lost. Beryl said, "Oh, and then your husband followed in his footsteps."

"In a manner of speaking. But Mr. Leider went in partnership with Neal Gerrard. My father gave them their start when he retired."

That was not right, but she would never admit Neal Gerrard was successful before my grandfather stepped in. I had to watch myself for fear of contradicting my mother before others, so I kept quiet.

"I see," Beryl remarked with interest. He sat forward with his knees apart. I could make out the hard thigh muscles in his legs. I quickly averted my eyes. "Yet Mr. Leider left the cotton business to begin something new?" he asked.

"Yes . . . as Elzyna may have told you, he is now in the oil business."

"Well, well," he stated, and leaned back in his chair. "Isn't it so that Houston is a place of unlimited opportunities for getting ahead."

He rose to leave. Mother said, "At Christmastime we'll be having a small party to formally announce the engagement of my daughter Patricia to Mr. George Stanley. I do hope you can join us. Mr. Leider will be there."

"It will be my pleasure," Beryl replied, and kissed my mother's hand, then mine. As he took my hand he looked up into my eyes and winked. I did not appreciate that. It was as though he were acknowledging some sort of conspiracy between us against my mother.

When he was gone Mother, oblivious to the seduction, said, "What a charming young man he is. I hope you'll be kind to him."

The following week Beryl asked me to accompany him to Sunday church, and when I told him I was Roman Catholic he said, "I saw the crucifix on the wall of your drawing room. I'm Catholic, too."

Mother was elated at the news.

After that we saw each other three or four times over the next few weeks, and I always felt that he was less interested in me than in my getting to know about him. He seemed to have strong views on a lot of subjects all the way from architecture to politics and, through it all, I could scarcely overlook the fact that Beryl was smart and he knew where he was going. I had to admire him.

Three days before Christmas, when Father was at home, Mother hosted the promised gathering to congratulate Patricia and George. Patricia told me while we were up in her bedroom before the party began that Mother had tried to persuade her not to marry at least until she made her formal debut next year and was honored at the Society Ball. "She wants me to follow in her footsteps," said Patricia. "I told her we'd wait till my sixteenth birthday and no longer. To tell you the truth, I think that's unfair—the end of May, for heaven's sake."

"I think she is right," I said from the bed. "You are very young even to be thinking of marriage."

"I know, Zyna," she cooed. "And if you don't hold onto Beryl Farrish, I'll feel even worse that all this with George happened before you found your man."

"Don't worry about that," I told her. "I have no certainty that Beryl and I will get serious."

"Well, George and I already are, but don't tell Mother."

I blinked. "What do you mean? Becoming engaged is serious, and that's no secret from Mother."

She sighed with forced patience. "George has a devil of a time keeping his hands to himself and"—drawing up her shoulders in resignation—"I doubt very much if I can hold him steady much longer. . . . I'm not at all sure I want to."

"Patricia!"

She stood at the door now, and opened a little feather fan close to her face. "I may have Mother's looks, but I have father's blood."

With that, she walked through the door.

I sat there for a long while, thinking. Patricia had always been miles ahead of me when it came to boys, and no more so than now. I could not imagine ever having the nerve to proclaim what she just had . . . could not imagine letting a boy take liberties as she described. Yet something inside me made me feel happy she felt that way, even if it was wrong. It must be wonderful, I thought, to have someone desire you. . . .

I walked to the dresser and picked up my hair ribbons. In the mirror's reflection my cheeks wore a blush that did not come from a finger pinch.

Patricia's remark was only the first surprise of the evening. Beryl arrived a few minutes early and asked to speak to me alone. We went to a little sitting room at the back of the house, one of the few rooms not decorated for the holiday and prepared for receiving guests, and he walked about nervously for a few moments, remarking on one thing and another to do with structural details of our home. He didn't like its striped canopies and wide-open galleries—he detested wasted space more so than anyone I'd ever known—but he was impressed with the fine workmanship. Finally he turned to me and said, "I've just been given a raise."

"That's wonderful," I said. "Patricia told me you are considered one of the brightest young men with the firm."

"Oh, did she?" he inquired, and inclined his head as though wanting to savor the moment. "Well now, think of that!" He turned to the log fire and rubbed his hands together. Without looking at me, he continued, "You know, I'll be twenty-four years old next year. It's time for me to think about settling down."

"Good. I'm glad you'll be staying here."

"That isn't what I meant. The thing is—" he said, "I'd like you to marry me."

I stared at him in surprise.

"I thought, if you're agreeable, we could discuss it with your father since he is home tonight. Well?"

I looked away and folded my arms. "I don't know. We've known each other such a little time . . . and you've never said you felt—well, affection—for me."

"I know. There will be lots of time for me to say what I feel. But the truth is that there is more to marriage than just sentimentality. A man has to think of marrying the right kind of woman, the kind that will be a real helpmate to him. I have felt for some time you are that person."

It seemed a reasonable approach to marriage, but it did not conform to what every girl dreams in her heart. I should not have been taken by surprise . . . Beryl should have been more ardent from the beginning so that I would have looked forward to this moment. He should have taken me in his arms and said he could not live without me. I should have felt equally—

He interrupted my thoughts. "I feel certain we could be happy together."

I shook my head. "I need some time to think. This is very sudden, quite unexpected."

"Very well then," he said somewhat petulantly. "A day or two?"

"A week. Let's say—January 1."

"But will your father be here so that we can do this thing right? I mean, I suppose that is how it's done down here."

"Mother will be here. Father is the last person in the world to stand on ceremony. If Mother gives her permission, then it's all right. But I want to think about it. I want to be sure."

"Whatever you like." He came near me and pulled my hands toward him, then, holding them firmly, he kissed my cheek. He seemed awkward doing this, as though he felt he must in order to seal the bond. I did not think he really wanted to kiss me, not like George apparently wanted to kiss Patricia. Beryl was very controlled, not driven by passion. I recognized this but did not recognize the consequences of it. There were so many things about Beryl that I either observed or instinctively felt, but I was too inexperienced to know what they would mean to our future together. All I felt for the rest of that evening was a curious sense of loss, that my first proposal—perhaps my only proposal—of marriage would not be as I always imagined.

Yet I realized my romantic notions were not necessarily wise. On Christmas Day I spoke to Mother. I tried to present her with all the details of the past few weeks. I don't believe she heard beyond the first three or four sentences. To her mind, Beryl was everything he needed to be. "I should think you would jump at the chance, Elzyna," she said. "After all, he's a rising young architect—and, so I hear, extremely gifted. He has never been married before. He is Catholic."

"I know, Mother, but—"

"Listen, Elzyna," she said, and looked at me intently. There were hard lines around her mouth and between her eyes. Her hair was interspersed with gray. The years with my father had not been easy for her. "I made a grave error in marrying a non-Catholic and expecting him to change for me. It has been the single greatest source of trouble between your father and me. Had we come from the same faith, he would have assumed his position with me just as I expected him to." She leaned back. "Marrying someone raised in the faith is the most important thing. From that, all things spring and all matters can be worked out because there is common ground."

What she said made a lot of sense; not to my surprise, my father told me something quite different when we talked that evening. Father was still a good-looking man, though he was a bit heavier than he used to be and the skin around his face was slack. He didn't have a gray hair in his head. After I told him what was on my mind, he asked simply, "Do you love this young man?"

"I don't know, Father. That's why I feel confused."

"Does he love you?"

"I don't know—I suppose so. A man doesn't ask a woman to marry him unless he cares for her, does he?"

He looked as though he were not quite sure how to answer that. Then he said, "Just be sure of your feelings for each other. Everything else will work out. Remember, you have to face each other every night when he comes home from work. Be sure you want him around."

Not like Mother doesn't want you around, or you don't want to be around, I almost said.

"You don't need to have me tell you whether or not you can marry this man. That's your decision. You're old enough and, God knows, you've always been mature."

As usual, the confusion caused by my parents drove me straight to Aunt Reda. She did not really disagree with either of them, but was most concerned that not enough time had elapsed since I met Beryl and that I was unsure of my feelings. "I would like to say that if you had to ask if you love him, then the answer must be no. But I cannot. I was confused when Neal asked me to marry him. I loved him, yes, but I was still in hopes of pleasing my father. Therefore I didn't know what to do and I almost lost him in the process. . . . What I'm saying is that, given time, you will be certain. Why should you rush?"

"No reason," I said.

"Elzyna, you aren't afraid of losing him, are you?"

"No, that is, I don't think so."

"Good. Take your time. You are considering one of life's most important decisions."

"Aunt Reda, if I don't know if I love him now, but feel a certain—affection —for him, is that enough? Will love follow?"

"It could. That depends upon what sort of man he is."

"Well, I do care for him."

"Good, darling. That's the right beginning."

In the end, of course, my decision was based on something entirely separate from any advice I received. If Beryl's approach to marriage seemed logical, mine was just as illogical. One day before the week was up, I happened to come out of Levy's Department Store just in time to see Beryl at the corner, chatting with another girl.

I thought about it all afternoon and all night. I was seized with fear that he would lose interest in me. Who else would want me? And here he was: bright, handsome, promising in his chosen career. I should be flattered that he felt I would be an asset to his life, shouldn't I? And didn't I feel at times a sort of . . . tenderness . . . toward him? How does one define love, how judge when it has happened? I did not know. I had never loved anyone before. Boys didn't pay attention to me.

As Mother said, I'd be foolish not to jump at the chance. Why shouldn't we be happy? And even Alvareda admitted she had had reservations about marrying Neal.

By morning my decision was made. I told Beryl that afternoon, and he kissed my hand and smiled. Shortly after that we made an appointment to see Father Baratino after Sunday mass. He was an elderly man with thinning gray hair and a brow full of wrinkles. He had known my family—Mother, especially well—for years. I could not begin to count the number of times I had arrived home from school in the afternoon to find him visiting Mother, listening, I am sure, as she aired her marital problems.

Father Baratino seemed delighted about our marriage, and I could not help wondering if Mother had also aired her worries that I would never find a mate. Our visit with him was brief. The only difficult moment came when he asked us each to answer why we wanted to get married to one another. First he looked at Beryl.

"I knew Elzyna was right for me the first time we met," he said brightly. "And while she knows how much I care for her, I've been honest about the fact I think marriage is more than just sentiment."

When he answered that way, I thought maybe it was a sweet expression of the affection he was reluctant to otherwise allow. Perhaps, in some ways, he was shy, I hopefully supposed. It did not occur to me then that he was twisting the truth in order to make himself look smart and sincere.

Father Baratino was looking at me. "I—" I stammered, and gazed down at my hands. I couldn't tell him the truth about my reason for accepting Beryl's hand in marriage. Finally I said, "I have admired Beryl since we met. I don't think—that is, I feel—that love grows between two people, through their experiences together." I glanced quickly at Beryl, for reassurance. He smiled his approval.

Father nodded in agreement, apparently satisfied. "How soon would you like to be married?" he asked next.

"Oh, not soon," I blurted out, then gulped.

"But certainly before the end of the year," Beryl said, and smiled at me again, this time in a kind of cautionary way.

Father nodded and opened up his book of appointments. "I think a long engagement will be good for the two of you, give you plenty of time to know each other," he said, apparently noticing my reticence.

"How about December?" I suggested.

Beryl nodded. Father looked down the columns of his book. "All right. The fifteenth?"

We both agreed. I felt much better. As we left, Father took both our hands and, after leading us through a prayer, said, "You know, after years of visiting with couples who want to be married, I have learned not to say too much. As long as you understand that you're making a lifetime commitment—till death do you part—the rest of what I say rolls off like wax down a candle. People in love hear exactly what they want to." He smiled. "Let me know if I can help in any way. God bless you."

Two days later our engagement was announced in the *Post*. Mother had begun to make plans. I thought with encouragement of the length of time till December. I would know my feelings better by then, as Father Baratino pointed out. I could even back out if I felt I wanted to. Yet, almost immediately the obligations which would bind me to that reluctant commitment began.

Chapter 2

Neal sat on the boards of several international cotton organizations, doing what Alvareda described as "ambassador duty" for the industry. He often attended meetings both here and abroad, and in March of 1906 he took Alvareda with him to a meeting of textile industry leaders in Liverpool, after which they continued their travels for several weeks.

Shortly after their return, Alvareda asked me to come over because she had a present or two for me and she and Neal wanted to discuss a matter with me.

She had found some beautiful lace in Brussels, and brought home enough for me to use in my wedding gown and veil, "If you like. But don't feel you have to use it. I haven't seen the design of your dress, and it may not be suitable," she said.

I unwrapped the dark paper which enveloped the lace, and lifted it against the light. Even to my unpracticed eye, it was exquisite: slightly off-white in color; about three inches wide. Alvareda said that it was handmade, and was called point de gaze. "The shopkeeper told me how it was done, and that several ladies were involved in the process, each working on a different phase. I wish I could remember more, but I looked at so many laces that day, and they were all so beautiful. I could hardly decide which one."

"I've never seen anything more beautiful," I said.

"Again, don't feel you must use it if it doesn't work. This lace is often passed down from one generation to the next, they tell me. Perhaps some day it might go into a christening dress for one of your children. Oh yes, and I was told to keep it wrapped in dark paper, to prevent discoloration."

Neal spoke up then. "We've been discussing something else as a wedding present for you and Beryl."

"Oh, but the lace is more than generous. And of course I will use it. I hadn't even really begun to think about my gown. . . ."

"Alvareda and I want you to have the McKinney Avenue property."

I glanced at each of them in surprise. I had loved that place since I was a child, when I used to ride out there in the back seat of the buggy with Gabriel next to me. It was far away from everything . . . especially the cares of living at home. When we were there I would often push Gabriel in the swing in the oak tree nearby the house, and sometimes we'd have a picnic there. Many times I would pretend to myself that the Gerrards were my parents and the old rustic cottage was our home together. To think now that it was to be mine was almost like having my childhood fantasy come true.

"Oh, I don't know what to say—it's such a generous gift. To think—"

"The house is in need of some major repairs at this point," Neal interrupted, "but the city is moving out that way and it's a good piece of property. I was thinking Beryl might like to design another home to put there."

Alvareda spoke now. "My feelings have been mixed about the idea," she said. "Too many unfortunate events are connected with it in my mind. Yet . . . it's up to you."

I was sure she referred mostly to my accident in 1901, and reassured her that I had nothing but good memories of the place. "And besides, nothing has happened there in all these years. Look how many times I've been there, and have even taken the bicycle club out there three times."

She considered me for a long moment, then said, "Your argument is along the same lines as Neal's. Perhaps you're right." She smiled then and said, "You do seem taken with the idea."

"It's the most wonderful thing that ever happened to me," I said, but in truth I still could not believe it. Alvareda and Neal had always been generous with me, but this sort of gift was overwhelming . . . any young couple would be fortunate to receive a wedding cottage from their parents; surely this went far beyond the limits of close friendship. I thought of the small duplex on Caroline that Beryl and I had arranged to rent. I had felt content to begin our married lives in that modest quarter. Now this . . . I just kept shaking my head in disbelief, while Neal continued talking.

"There are four acres, you know, and though the property is not worth a whole lot right now, it will be someday soon. It would be a nice investment for the future. There is just one thing," he interrupted again. "I would like to have a condition put into the agreement when it is deeded over to you that it be in your name as an individual. And I would retain the first option to purchase should you ever decide to sell the property outright, rather than pass it to your children. At the fair market value, of course."

"But why would you want the property to be in my name only?"

"Because it would just be simpler. I knew someone in Galveston—well, it would just be easier, that's all. If Beryl objects, we can discuss it further." He smiled. "Perhaps he can 'indulge' me a little for wanting to give special treatment to someone who is like my own daughter."

Tears filled my eyes. "Oh, thank you!" I said and hugged them both.

Alvareda said, "Speaking of daughters, Neal and I are hoping for one around the end of the year."

"It's only fair," Neal quipped with a smile at Alvareda. "With two boys in the house, she gets all the attention."

I looked first at Neal, then at Alvareda. "You're expecting again!" I burst out, and clapped my hands.

Alvareda nodded. "I'm thirty-six years old, and may not have a houseful as I planned when I was younger. But at least maybe we can manage to have one or two more before I'm ready to retire to the rocking chair. It'll be fun to have a little one around again, now that the boys are growing up so fast."

"Well, congratulations!" I exclaimed, and hugged them both again. "Just think, all three of them can come over and visit, just like I have at your house. We'll have a big yard to play in, and I'll bake cookies for them . . . Oh! This is all too much," I said in delight, then added, "You've always made me feel so welcome in your home . . . I do so hope my home will be as happy and full of good times as yours."

"I'm certain it will," Neal said kindly.

Yet, was he really? I wondered as I drove home with my lace in the back of the carriage. The fact he wanted the house and property put in my name alone seemed to indicate he had misgivings. Perhaps, though, he was just exercising businesslike caution. After all, a gift of land was a serious responsibility. You would expect legal technicalities and such, wouldn't you? And

Neal was cautious about the way he handled all business matters, not like my father, who seemed constantly to be getting into some deal or other that didn't turn out right because a partner had failed him. Probably as a result, Neal had become one of the wealthiest men in Houston; my father was still seeking his fortune.

Beryl seemed to have a clear business head, too. If so, he would understand Neal's reasoning behind the legal structure of the gift of property. If he resented what Neal had in mind, then that might be a warning to me about the kind of person he was.

He proved to have no reservation about the gift, yet I was not certain whether he was showing good sense, or whether he was simply too interested in the prospect of an opportunity to build a new home of his own design.

We bicycled out there after mass on the very next Sunday—a beautiful spring day of blue skies and cool temperature. All the trees were sporting brilliant greenery, as though washed off and left in the sun to dry. Not too far past York Street and the railroad crossing, the road narrowed and the trees thickened. Beryl, who rode out front, called back to me, "Are you sure this place is going to build up?"

"That's what Neal says. It isn't too much farther."

When we finally arrived at the property, Beryl wanted to walk the whole fence line to see it all. As we walked and looked around I realized for the first time just how much area four acres comprised. Beryl would stop and look, and jot down notes on a pad. He said little to me; he hardly noticed I was around. When we had walked over most of the property, he stopped and turned. "I don't much like the placement of the house that's there now. The trees are nicer back in the northeast corner, and I think we might get better exposure to the breeze. What do you think?"

I'd always liked the trees around the house, especially the tall oak from which the swing was still hanging. "I'd never thought of putting a house in a different place. That would put our house front on a different road, wouldn't it?" I said.

"Oh, I don't know. I don't necessarily think a house has to front a street or road."

I looked at him in puzzlement.

"Don't worry, you'll see what I mean when I get the drawings done. I'm already getting some ideas. To my mind, the house needs to 'belong' in the place where it's located. All those monster houses out on Main Street have nothing to do with what Houston is all about, and certainly not Texas."

I had no idea what he was talking about. I thought a house was simply a building you put on a lot. I was beginning to feel uncomfortable with his line of thinking. I suggested we might have a look at the house already there. He agreed, but not with enthusiasm. "It looks like a box. Wonder who built this eyesore."

"Alvareda's father. You want to go inside? I have a key."

"I guess," he said.

As far as I knew, there had been no changes made to the original plan. Beyond the front entrance hall was a large open passage that ran from front to back. To the right of this was a small library. Beyond that was a dining room, then a butler's pantry, and, finally, a separate kitchen building. To the left of the passage was a parlor, and beyond that a room probably used as a bedroom or sitting room. Each room had a corner fireplace. All the rooms were narrow and small. Upstairs there were just the two bedrooms, one on either side, and a sleeping porch along the rear. I told Beryl about my accident, and how I'd been brought here afterward.

"When did you say this was built?"

"Around 1870 I think."

"Well, the construction is pretty good. We could keep it, and someday I could use it as a studio. I don't know though, it probably wouldn't be worth the trouble."

When we left the property that afternoon, Beryl was soon careening along on his cycle, deep in thought about the plans for the house he would build. The remarks he had made just now caused me to realize how little I knew about his architectural ideas. Of course I knew that, even now, his job sometimes frustrated him.

From what I understood, Beryl wanted a bigger say-so in the decision-making process at his firm. Yet he was young, too new with the firm for anyone to listen to him. He often said he felt they treated him like a clerk. I remembered how sold on himself he was when first we met, and I told him to be patient, his time would come. They'd pay attention to him eventually. He had told me Radcliffe, Winter, and Tulley won out over a big architectural firm in San Francisco for his employment, so surely they had ambitious plans for him.

Beryl worked on the design of our home through the spring and into the summer, and wouldn't tell me anything about it because he wanted to surprise me. He often made trips out to the property alone, often spent extra time at night and on weekends working on various elevations. One thing at least was comforting: he was conscious of expenses, and I must admit he had a sensible approach toward the practical side of living in a house. The sparse amount of information he gave me indicated this. He wanted to be able to stay within a twelve-hundred-dollar budget. That seemed reasonable to me, as the home built by the Gerrards several years ago on Main cost eight thousand dollars, not including the property, and it was a great deal larger and more formidable than anything we might live in.

Toward the summer's end, the wedding plans became the principal occupation of my time. Patricia and George had married on her birthday, and she soon confided she was expecting her first child in a little less time than propriety allowed. Mother was more relieved than distraught, I think, and Patricia obviously had no intention of letting anyone's whispers about her be of concern. I had already asked her to be my matron of honor, and when she told me about the expected child she said, "I'll understand if you want to ask someone else." I could see from the look in her eye that she truly worried about my feelings in all this. I remembered that evening long ago when she told me about the seriousness between her and George, and I suddenly felt a rush of affection toward her. I hugged her tightly and said, "I don't see why you shouldn't stand up for me. The baby will be here by then."

Big tears came into her eyes and she sniffed, "That's right, and I'll have almost a month to whittle my waist down to size. Oh, Zyna, I'm so glad you understand."

I patted her and held her against me for a very long time.

It was about that time Mother interviewed Anna Winston to sew for the wedding party and make my entire trousseau. Anna had been in our home before, some years ago, when her mother sewed for my mother. Anna was fifteen at the time. We had them stationed in a little room underneath the stairway, where they set up two sewing machines. Anna, who was dark-haired and exotic-looking even then, was in charge of sewing miles and miles of ruffles to put on the frocks her mother fashioned. Sometimes, when her legs became tired, I would crouch down and work the treadle for her. I thought it was great fun and was flattered that a pretty girl like her would notice me and let me help.

Now, at the age of twenty-two Anna sewed for many of the families in Houston. She was, if anything, prettier than before. Her skin was as beautiful, her figure well proportioned. She had a waistline that Patricia envied and a bustline that was shapely under the tailored, button-down shirtwaists that she always wore while working. She was soft-spoken and demure.

Mother went into detail with Anna about everything she wanted for me. I was to have ten pairs of knee-length panties with lace medallions sewn into them like windows. I would have five day dresses and two petticoats. Two party dresses made of organdy, net, and lace, with embroidery ruffling and edging on the full-length sleeves.

The wedding gown itself was to be copied from a Paris design, with the beaded Brussels lace over the whole bodice and draping down into the sleeves and behind into an eight-foot train. The lace would be fashioned into a headpiece as well, with a thin net veil attached to it.

Anna would station herself in the same room as before—under the stairs—beginning September first. She'd bring her Wheeler and Wilson sewing machine, the same she had used before.

Next Mother and I went to Cargill's to pick out the design for the wedding invitations, the calling cards, and "at-home" cards. The invitation list included four hundred names. The wedding was of the utmost importance to Mother. Patricia had insisted on a small, simple wedding, the reason for which later became apparent. My wedding was Mother's chance to show off.

We spent the last week in September picking out wedding flowers, talking with caterers about the reception to be held in our home on Main, and arranging for the music. Mother checked off item after item on her lengthy list. It did not occur to me to voice an opinion about some of the arrangements, only to nod and agree. Without realizing it, by the week's end I was feeling a little frustrated myself. I was like a toy puppet being pulled through the rehearsal before a performance. When Patricia pointed out that I was letting Mother bully me and she couldn't imagine why, I decided she was right, yet I said nothing to Mother about my feelings.

It was in this frame of mind that I saw the drawings Beryl had done of our wedding cottage. On the way out to the property, he emphasized that the design was not fussy, but clean and straightforward. Functional. People would look at our home as a model which could be followed in the design of other houses. It would be a chance for him to show off mission revival and how suitable it was to this climate, how harmonious with our heritage. One chance to see it done right, and people would forget any stigma connected with the Mexican flavor.

"I've been thinking we might develop the four acres into eight plots, with a house on each. Maybe five or six rent houses, and an apartment house. All done in mission revival."

I smiled at him, trying to hide my trepidations. I'd never envisioned my home as a "model" for others. And mission revival—I'd thought that was for commercial buildings, not residences. . . . And subdividing the property—oh, I could never consent to that.

Beryl had set up a large piece of board over two wooden sawhorses, and standing above, his shirtsleeves rolled-up, he opened out the sheaf of drawings for me to see. At first glance I felt my stomach contract. More than anything else, I believe it was the austerity of the design that took me back. The structure was to be made of concrete, plastered over and painted to look like white stucco. The roof was to be red tiles, to be repeated in the flooring of the interior. The front of the house was like a long, stark arcade with Roman arches. Between the first and second story there was no designation, just a towering wall at each end of the arcade. And inside, the main living room was to have a two-story ceiling. I said nothing as he explained the details, carefully turning the pages. Great open fireplaces were located in three places on the bottom floor and in one bedroom on the top floor. In the back was to be a Spanish-style courtyard and garden, with brick tiles and a fountain in the center. At one end, the end which was two stories high, he'd provided for a window which resembled the rose window at the San Jose Mission. I sighed and stepped back. He was silent for a moment. Then he said, "You don't like it."

"Oh, I—it's just that I—"

"No, say it. You hate it, don't you?"

"No, not exactly . . ." I faltered. "It's just that . . . well, I'm not accustomed to such a—"

"What, then?"

"Well, I expected something more traditional, I guess."

"Traditional?" he glared.

"Yes. You know, wood siding or brick. Galleries, gingerbread, art glass. I'm just an inexperienced—"

"Gingerbread! Galleries!" he cried, and from the look on his face I thought he would strike me. He stood staring at me for a few moments, then he raised his hand as though in total exasperation. He turned to the table, lifted the sheaf of drawings, and tore them in two. I reached out, but he went on tearing them into pieces, then he threw them on the ground and stomped them with his foot. "There's your wedding cottage, Elzyna! Have a good look at it."

"Beryl, I—please—I didn't realize—"

"You shut up. I'll knock you down if you lay a finger on them. Get in the carriage. I'll take you home."

All the way there I sat stockstill, tears smarting behind my eyes, trying to think of some way of apologizing, yet not sure who had been wrong. When we drew up to my house, he just stopped and said nothing. I got down out of the carriage and backed away. Still he said nothing. I was afraid to speak. He did not look at me or say anything about when he might see me again. He just flicked the reins and moved down the street, his mouth drawn in a tight line. I stood there for a long time, looking after him. I had never been so frightened by another human being. I turned toward the house and ran up the walk and inside. I took the stairs two at a time, my heart pumping as though it would burst from my chest. When I got to my room I banged the door shut and fell on my bed, sobbing frantically.

Chapter 3

I remained in my room for the rest of the afternoon and through dinner that evening, thinking I did not know Beryl Farrish at all. Today he had shown a side of himself that must have been there all the time, but which I'd never seen. He was but a fraction of an inch from striking me as though I were an animal. I shuddered again at the prospect. Were all men like this? Surely not. Even Father, when he grew completely exasperated with Mother, did not physically harm her. And Neal Gerrard. It was impossible to think Neal ever got mad enough to hit someone, especially Alvareda. What would he say if he knew of the scene that had transpired this afternoon?

I tried to be objective.

I had tripped clumsily over the most important thing in the world to Beryl. It was stupid of me to take exception to his architectural ideas. Perhaps one could argue with him on any subject except that. Yet, we were not just talking about a design. We were talking about a home in which I would live. I would be spending many more hours there than he would. Wasn't it important that I feel comfortable in my surroundings? Wasn't it true that I ought to have a say-so in its design?

Oh, I had so many notions about the sort of married life I wanted. Now I did not think Beryl's ideas about marriage were the same as mine. He wanted to use our home as a showcase for his talents. Perhaps all architects were the same. Perhaps they were all temperamental as well. Was an architect's wife expected to bend under about certain things that ordinarily were agreed upon by both parties? Was I going to have to change my concept of marriage in order to please Beryl? And if I did, then would we have a happy marriage, free of the sort of exchange between us today?

I had not reached a conclusion about this when, at eight o'clock, Mother knocked at the door. Beryl was waiting in the parlor downstairs. Mother did not ask if I wished to see him, even though she knew I was upset over something. She simply said, "Hurry up. Men don't like to be kept waiting too long. And give your cheeks a pinch or two. You're so dreadfully pale. . . ."

I struggled for a few moments, not knowing what I would say to him. Then I realized that he might have something to say to me. Maybe he'd call off the engagement. Maybe it was for the better, after all. I straightened my hair and tried to bring some blush to my cheeks. I went into the parlor and shut the door behind me. "Good evening," I said, and sat down across from Beryl. At the same time that I began to apologize for hurting his feelings today, he began to speak to me. So I stopped and listened to him.

"I've always been sensitive about my work, probably because my father was so brutal about my drawings when I was young."

"I—I'm sorry," I said. "That was cruel of him." It reminded me of my mother's constant reminders that I wasn't living up to her expectations.

"When you are a student of architecture," he continued, "you have to show your work to a group of teachers periodically—it's called a jury. There are usually five or six instructors there, to judge the merit of your design. Sometimes it goes pretty well; other times it seems they are out to humiliate you. They can be the most vicious group of tongues you've ever heard. After they spend an hour or so verbally assaulting your design, a design you worked on for weeks perhaps, you feel as though you have no talent, that you should never have dreamed of studying architecture, that you are a total failure. You feel like a fool."

He faced me now. "That was how you made me feel today, like a miserable fool."

"I'm sorry I made you feel that way. I didn't intend to. I know you are gifted; I guess I didn't think that your feelings could be hurt by someone like me, someone who knows nothing about it."

"Don't ever do that again."

"No, I won't. And if you want to build the house according to the design, do as you wish. It's all right by me."

He glared at me, then grimaced. "I never want to see that design again. I hate it now."

I looked into his eyes for a moment or two, then looked away. "Perhaps you don't want to see me again, either. If you want to call everything off—"

"I didn't say that I did. I came here to explain why you enraged me so. That was all. If you want to break it off—"

"No, no," I said quickly. "It—it would seem foolish for us to part over something we've worked out. I understand now how you feel. You have to remember, you are the first architect I've ever known."

He nodded. "I'll be going now. I'll talk with you tomorrow night after Star Wheels." He passed by me and touched my shoulder with his fingers, absently, as though I were a pet dog. He is without passion, I thought. It isn't by strong will that he rarely touches me. It is because he doesn't want to touch me. When he was at the parlor door he turned and said, "By the way, I've decided to remodel the house on the McKinney property rather than build a new one. I'll do something that you like, and I'll show you the rough sketches as soon as I have them. I'm going out there tomorrow and formulate ideas."

"You don't have to do that, Beryl."

"Oh, but I insist."

I heard the big front door open and close. I felt somehow defeated, though in some ways I had certainly won. Now I would have a say-so in the design of my home. I should be grateful Beryl had come around to my way of thinking. Yet—what was it?—I thought for a few moments, then I realized. I had done all the apologizing. Never once had he even acknowledged that he had behaved improperly. Yet, perhaps this was the only point on which he felt really sensitive, like an artist and his paintings, or a writer and his prose. Perhaps I just had to always honor his seriousness about his profession, then getting along with him would be easy. . . .

Mother came in and stood behind me. "What is it? Your first lover's quarrel?"

"Something like that."

She patted my shoulders. "Well, think nothing of it. Weddings make people tense and edgy. All this will be over soon, and you'll be together in your own home, happy as two love birds."

"Beryl isn't going to build a new home. He has decided to remodel the house already there."

"Oh? Is that why you quarreled? You had your heart set on a new house?"

I shook my head. "No, Mother. I didn't like his design."

"Oh? Why not?"

"It was too—too unconventional, I guess is the word."

She sighed. "I suppose that's an architect for you, wanting to show off a bit. Well, he'll get over it. It's a woman's place to keep a man rooted in reality. One day he'll thank you for it, you'll see. The important thing is that you were able to get your disagreement ironed out."

"I suppose."

"Elzyna, don't look so glum. There is too much to do, too much excitement to look forward to. The next three months will be the most exciting of your life. And don't forget, Anna Winston will be here first thing tomorrow morning to begin sewing your trousseau. The last of the fabric was delivered this afternoon—and not a moment too soon."

Beryl spent much less time on the redesign of the house on McKinney Avenue than he had on the new one. Within a few days he had the rough sketches ready to show me, and in two weeks we went back out to the property to go over the finished design. He had succeeded, at least, in pleasing one of us. I was amazed at what improvements he was able to make, how quickly he could consider all aspects of the original house and know how to retain the best, while dispensing with the less desirable. I had to study the drawing for a while before I could see exactly what he'd done. He had simply expanded each of the rooms so that they were no longer narrow, but wide, roomy chambers, and enclosed the kitchen. The open passage was now a hall with a staircase on the left side.

Above each fireplace he had designed intricately carved woodwork, and bookcases with glass doors would extend out on either side except in the dining room. In that room, the walls would be paneled in dark wood, and the ceiling would have exposed beams. There would be a large bay window in the side wall, and a built-in sideboard in the opposite wall. From the day I first saw that drawing, the dining room was my favorite of all rooms in the house. I featured china plates resting along the upper molding, and envisioned having gay dinner parties. Beryl had plans for modernizing the kitchen, and would add a bathroom downstairs and a long, screened-in porch across the back of the house.

He enlarged the upstairs bedrooms and added a third, all with built-in closets. He dispensed with the sleeping porch in the upstairs rear, and designed a small square sleeping porch above the front gallery that provided an interesting focal point. Indeed, it was the exterior that showed most of the changes. A deep gallery stretched all along the front of the house and the dining room side as well. Where the rooms had been expanded, the walls were windowed. In the center, with a small and graceful arch above, he had provided for French doors that called for leaded glass panels, and a transom above. The house was a masterpiece of symmetry. One looked from the foot of the walk up to the front, up four steps to see the pillared gallery—narrow, graceful pillars—to the front doors, and then the eye rose to the arch that surmounted the gallery and the small enclosed porch on the second floor. Along the roof line was handsome ridge cresting, and the fireplace chimneys on either side were tall and commanding.

I stood back and sighed. "It is beautiful. I would have never imagined this could come from that old house. Oh, thank you, Beryl. I'm going to make it the happiest place you have ever lived in."

"I'm glad that it pleases you. That's the most important thing, after all."

Something in his voice—perhaps it was only the lack of enthusiasm—made me feel uneasy. Yet I could not see how he could dislike it. I reached for his hand. He clasped mine absently, then let go. He didn't seem to want to discuss the house any further, though I could have spent the rest of the day planning each of the rooms, how they would be furnished, considering colors, carpet, curtains. When we got into the carriage he said, "Why don't you contract a builder and give him the plan? You can oversee everything. You have more time than I do."

I nodded in agreement. I was already beginning to envision the landscaping. How perfect a waist-high hedge around the yard would be, rather than a fence. And there would be a small iron gate in the center and . . . suddenly a wonderful idea occurred to me: white tiles just outside the gate at the curb, inlaid with black, no, blue, tiles that spelled out B. Farrish. And the year. 1906. I had seen that done once before, outside a home we visited on Caroline.

I opened my mouth to tell Beryl of my idea, then decided to surprise him. It seemed such a creative idea . . . surely it would thrill him.

Beryl remained silent as we drove. When we were back up into the busy section of McKinney, just past the Pillot house with the big iron dogs out front, I said, "Beryl, are you sure you really want to marry me?"

"Why would you ask me that?" he said, impatiently.

"Oh, I don't know. You never seem to want to—to hold my hand, or to kiss me."

"Of course I do. How silly you act."

When we pulled up in front of my house, he kissed my cheek, and as I must have looked as though I expected something more, he put his hand on my chin and kissed my lips, gently. Then he sat back and observed me, as if he awaited some sign of my satisfaction with what he had done. I wanted to tell him he missed the point, that I was not looking for a dutiful performance, but a sign he truly cared for me.

"I'll ask Neal for the name of a good builder, unless you prefer a certain one," I said.

"It makes no difference to me," he said. "Any builder could do that job."

There was a note of sarcasm in his voice that stayed with me long after he was gone. Why was it there never seemed to be real warmth between us, as there was between George and Patricia, or Neal and Alvareda? All we could ever reach was a sort of friendly truce. . . .

That evening my father was home. As I watched him slide my mother's chair forward at the dinner table—a scene repeated before me for all of my life—I sensed a great depth of coldness between them as though it were all crystallized in that one simple gesture. Neal would never perform that same courtesy for Alvareda without the affection they shared becoming apparent. If only for a moment, she would look up and smile at him, and he would wink affectionately, perhaps touching her shoulder fondly before going to his own chair. My father, if he looked at my mother at all, did so with a vacant eye. Time and time again, year after year, in a single motion at the table, there had been disenchantment. Estrangement.

Suddenly I saw my future with Beryl as clearly as I saw my parents now. We were not going to be happy at all. Our marriage was going to be like theirs.

I put a cold hand against my throat. "What is it, Elzyna?" Mother inquired. "You look as though someone struck you across the face."

"Nothing," I said.

How I wish I had acted on that overpowering instinct.

Chapter 4

While convinced I was about to make a terrible mistake, I was also getting farther and farther from the last hope of reversing it.

Fighting my better judgment, I ordered the tiles to be installed as soon as the concrete walk was ready to be poured, sometime in late October. I picked up the printed invitations, and the calling cards and invitations to call after the wedding: MR. AND MRS. BERYL WAYNE FARRISH, At Home, Tuesday evenings in January, from eight to eleven o'clock. No. 4001 McKinney Avenue. At home I sat down at the desk in my room and opened a box of wedding invitations. They were beautiful, engraved in silver on crisp cards of eggshell white. "Mr. and Mrs. David Lawrence Leider request the honor of your presence . . ." Somehow the wedding invitations seemed even more final than the "at home" cards that presented us as the happy couple, sitting at the fireside awaiting callers.

Looking at all the boxes in front of me, the lists of names and addresses that I was beginning to transfer onto the envelopes, and hearing the sound of the machine just below my room as Anna Winston sewed me into eternal commitment, I realized with trepidation that the wedding itself was taking me over. To back out now would be unthinkable. Mother would be humiliated beyond recovery.

On the other hand, I had not yet mailed the invitations. That, surely, was the final act from which there was no return. That would not happen for weeks.

From mid-October on, we were entertained at a whirl of parties, receiving gifts from cut glass to copper and brass, French plate mirrors and fine linens. Patricia and George gave us a Seth Thomas Eight-Day clock, an upright piano, and a handsome walnut rocking chair with a high cane back that was more comfortable to me than any chair I had ever sat in. All of these would be perfect in the library.

Mother and Father furnished the front parlor of our new home with bird's-eye maple, gave us a dining room table and six chairs of oak, and a Mikado Steel range complete with six burners, a huge oven, and a warming closet. Each of these things represented one further step toward the point of no return. I wore the mask of a happy bride-to-be, and no one, not even Alvareda or Neal, guessed that my stomach was churning as the days wore inevitably on, or that I looked at each day's calendar with a feeling of dismay.

On the last Friday in October we were given a dinner dance in the home of the Gerrards. That morning as Anna Winston took a few stitches on the dress I was to wear, we received a call that the tiles were laid. I immediately called Beryl to say I had something to show him out at the house, and he promised to come over as soon as he finished a project at work.

We bicycled out in the late afternoon. There was a stiff wind blowing; the sky was overcast and gray. The temperature was dropping at last—the first cold spell of the season. This was the first time I had been out here since the house really began taking shape, and as we neared it I felt a thrill of anticipation. The exterior was looking well. Large rectangular grayish-white bricks now replaced the old wood siding; the French doors with their leaded glass were in their frame, and looked exquisite. The transom was above. The box hedge had been planted around the yard, though it was low and the shrubs were wide apart and spindly. The iron gate had been set.

We parked our bicycles and I directed Beryl to the ceramic tiles. "Close your eyes now, and I'll lead you. This is your wedding present. I hope you like it." When I had him just in front of the brightly polished tile work, I said, "Now, open your eyes."

He obeyed me. I saw his lips move through B. FARRISH to 1906. He said nothing. "Do you like it?" I asked him anxiously. He looked at me with the coldest stare I have ever seen. "You've put my name on this?" he said, almost in a whisper, uplifting his arm to encompass the whole prospect in front of him.

"But—but this is our home, I thought you'd be pleased," I appealed with a gasp.

He said nothing else. He only looked toward the house silently. He cut a sad-looking figure of defeat as he stood there, the wind blowing his hair. I think perhaps, in that moment, he was every bit as regretful about our coming marriage as I was. The disappointment over the house simply brought his feelings into focus. He must have felt as captive as I did. Had we only faced each other then, I know we'd have parted for good.

"I'll have them taken up," I said at last, pushing the hair from my forehead.

"No, leave them," he said. "I want them there. They fit right into the whole effect."

How stupid of me not to realize he hated the house. Without another word, I mounted my cycle and rode off. I knew that under the thin guise of propriety that Beryl sported, there was an anger and rage lurking, the depth of which I could not yet begin to imagine. I felt panicked. Yet there were all the parties, the friends wishing us well, the gifts, the expectations.

When I got home, Mother poked her head out the bedroom door and told me to hurry up and take my bath. "The party begins in two hours, you know," she said, and shut the door.

I walked into my room and angrily shed my clothes. This was one time Beryl was not going to have the final word. We would be in the carriage together for the length of time it required to drive the six blocks to the Gerrard house. I would tell him what was on my mind and he could let me out and keep going all the way back to Chicago if he wanted to.

When he arrived, however, he might have been someone else. Gone was the angry smirk, replaced with a smile. He'd brought me a nosegay with trailing yellow ribbons. I took it from him and murmured a limp "thank you." Outside he helped me into the carriage and smiled up at me. "You are looking swell," he said, and went around to take his place beside me. He flicked the reins. We moved forward.

"I want to apologize, Elzyna. It was thoughtful of you to have the tiles done. And I was truthful when I said they are just right for the house."

I looked ahead, relieved to know he realized when he had gone too far. Finally I said, "I think you sometimes overlook the fact we are fortunate to have had a home and a piece of property given to us. Your whole attitude is quite ungrateful."

"Oh, I do appreciate the Gerrards, you can be sure of that," he remarked, then added, "even though the property is yours, not ours."

"Is that what you resent so much?"

"No, not at all. In Mr. Gerrard's place, I would have done likewise."

"What is it, then? I can't seem to do anything to please you," I went on.

"That isn't true. I have great admiration for you, Elzyna. I have told you that from the beginning."

"You have an awfully peculiar way of showing it."

"Look, I've apologized, haven't I?" he said, with a note of warning, as though he was trying to tell me he was tired of this bout, and it was time for me to be tired of it as well.

"If you don't really want to marry me, just say so."

"There you go again, Elzyna. Don't mistake my feelings for my temperament. I'm just hard to get along with now and then. I need someone to put me in my place, that's all. But . . . once I've apologized, I expect to go on as though nothing happened."

"I suppose that's reasonable," I heard myself saying. I didn't really feel that. I didn't know what I felt.

We had arrived. He turned to me and said, "There, now. Let's kiss and make up."

That was the first "normal" thing I had heard him say in a long time, but at the moment I didn't feel like kissing him. I was still too angry. He put an arm around me and pulled me toward him. He kissed me hard, his mouth moving over mine and straying down to my chin, and on to my neck. I pulled away. He released me and smiled. I didn't like the way he had forced himself on me. I didn't like his smile. I didn't for a moment think either was sincere.

"Come, put on a happy face, or you'll spoil the party," he said.

The party at the Gerrards' lasted until after midnight, and I was too exhausted when finally I went to bed to care about anything. I slept deeply until nine o'clock, when Mother came in the door and drew open the drapes. "Hurry up and get dressed. Anna is ready for you to try on your wedding gown this morning. And I must say I'm relieved, with only a little bit more than a month to go before it has to be finished."

A month to go. I felt my heart contract. My head felt heavy on my shoulders, and my back ached from the neck down, as it always did when I became tense. I dressed as quickly as I could and went downstairs. As soon as I walked into the sewing room, Anna threw the skirt over my head, laughing as it cascaded down to the floor. She worked on the skirt hem for half an hour, and as she worked, Mother glanced through the newspaper. Shortly she turned to the theater page and said excitedly, "Listen, Elzyna. Here's a synopsis of "Toast of the Town" that we'll see next Monday night. Oh, I do hope it's good—" To my relief we were interrupted by the ringing telephone.

Mother was gone for a few minutes, and when she returned she was pulling on her gloves. "It's Jordan, in trouble at school again. I have to go over there right away. He hit one of the other boys and gave him a nosebleed. Mrs. Kinkaid has threatened to dismiss him for good. I wish David would take that boy in hand."

"Thank goodness," I heard Anna murmur, apparently thankful as I was to have Mother out of the way. She sat back on her heels and surveyed the hem. "There now, I think that's going to be about right. Let's look at the bodice." She pulled it around me and pinned it up in the back. Then she observed me with her head tilted first to one side, then to the other, and said, "It's going to pull. I'm going to have to let out those darts a little. My dear, from whom did you inherit such a bosom? Certainly not your mother." Then, before I could respond to her remark, which I felt to be in poor taste, she said, "Down here at the waist it's much too loose. Let's measure you again. Aha! You've lost an inch in the past month. Too much running about." She pinned in the waist a little more, then told me to turn and look in the mirror. I don't know what came over me when I saw myself in the dress, a filmy white promise of the handsome creation it would be when finished. I caught my breath, then I began to cry.

"There, there, dear," said Anna, handing me a hankie. "What's the trouble?"

"Nothing, I'm fine," I said, and blew my nose. I collapsed on a little stool nearby.

"Want to talk about it?" she gently inquired. "I've sewed for a score of brides . . . most of them are nervous." She patted my hand.

"No, Anna. I'm fine, really," I said, pulling away. I believe she sensed I was putting her in her place by refusing to confide in her. "I am just tired," I told her. "I want to get out of this dress—are you finished?" In fact the vision of myself walking down the aisle on Father's arm was more frightening than anything thus far. Suddenly I felt I just couldn't do it. I felt like a sacrificial lamb, being offered up for all the presents and the parties, the good wishes of friends, the expectations of my mother. Yet, the invitations were not due to be mailed for two weeks. If I backed out now, there would be only the injured feelings of a few close friends to worry about, a large number of gifts to return. It would be better than apologizing to four hundred people.

Through the day I tried to settle on how to tell Mother. Every time I thought it through all the way to where she would respond, I shook my head. She would never understand. Once it occurred to me that I could enlist the help of Father Baratino, perhaps get him to talk with Mother. Yes, of course. He would be able to persuade her, surely. For a few minutes I felt uplifted by that hope. Then I thought again. Father had been listening to my mother's troubles for years. He knew how much all this meant to her. I knew for a fact she had discussed some of the arrangements with him. He may just as easily side with her as with me. Oh, why was I thinking about choosing sides? This was my life, after all.

Oh, I didn't know what to do. Regardless of what the priest said, I would still have to face her, and I was frightened of that. She might think I had betrayed her by going to him.

Next I thought of talking with Aunt Reda. She would know what to do. Yet, I must inevitably face Mother. If I talked with anyone else first, she would be even less open to my appeal.

That afternoon I approached her. I picked the wrong moment, I soon realized, for she was already upset over Jordan's being expelled this morning from Kinkaid School. He would not be readmitted until after the Christmas holidays, and I think she wondered what she was going to do with him in the meantime. Before we started to talk, she told me the return was conditional, and that Mrs. Kinkaid had not wanted to take him at all. Only through Mother's pleading, and her promise he would straighten up, would the schoolmistress allow him back on probation. "Oh yes, I nearly forgot," she said at last. "Stowers phoned this morning. The bedroom furniture is ready for delivery. I told them it would have to wait, like everything else, that you would call them when the house is ready. Oh, I am exhausted." I stood there with my hands gripping the back of the chair, trying to summon the nerve. Finally she said, "Why are you standing there like that, Elzyna? Sit down and have some tea with me."

I sat down and poured a cup of tea for each of us. My hands trembled just enough that she noticed.

"What's the matter with you?" she demanded, then, as though realizing the possibility I might be nervous, she sighed with patient effort. "Getting the jitters?"

"No. Not exactly, that is—"

"I know. Don't tell me Anna has messed up the dress."

"No. The dress is just fine. Beautiful."

"Well then, what? How you try me with your dillydallying. Come on, out with it."

"All right," I said, and drew up my shoulders. "Mother—Mother, I wonder what would happen if someone backed out of a wedding at this point."

She shot me a hard glance. "What?"

"I mean, things are just not right between Beryl and me. Or at least, I don't feel right about the marriage."

Her face was a study in bewilderment, and she laughed nervously and said, "Oh, Elzyna, you just have the jitters. I had them myself. I know what it is."

I thought if I heard the word "jitters" again I would go mad.

"No, Mother, it is more than that. I feel we raced into this too quickly.

Beryl is—well, I hardly know him. And I have begun to think he feels the same, but probably is reluctant to spoil all the plans. You don't think it's right to go on just because all the plans have been made, do you?"

She took another sip of tea, then looked across at me. "Do you think I don't know what you're going through? Now look. I've been intending to have this talk with you anyway," she said, and I realized she thought I was nervous about my wedding night. In fact, though that prospect had been vaguely on my mind since the night Beryl proposed, I was far too reluctant about the whole marriage to have started worrying about basic things. . . . I had always planned to ask Aunt Reda about what was expected of me. Yet as I became aware Mother had obviously done some thinking about what she was about to say, I felt a new sense of guilt because I had thought to bypass her on this issue.

She began, "I know you're not completely ignorant like I was, Elzyna." Then she shrugged and looked away. "I was so pitiful. And your father. Well! He had no understanding at all."

I sighed and leaned back in the chair. Would this turn into a long lecture about how my father had wronged her?

". . . the truth is, there is really nothing to it. Oh, I suppose some people might enjoy the act of . . . of intercourse," she said, and nearly blushed at the word. "But, you don't have to." She looked at me intently. "Your only real obligation is to produce children. Don't let your new husband . . . bully you. Make him treat you with respect."

This advice did not sound like what Patricia was talking about. It didn't even seem to agree with the few accounts I had read. Love was mentioned . . . feelings . . . closeness. . . .

Mother concluded, "See? As I told you, there really isn't much to it. The conceiving of children is rather cut and dried. It's the result that should be of concern. Now, do you feel better?"

I fingered the doily on the chair arm. If I had had nothing on my mind except the physical side of marriage, I don't believe her words would have brought the needed comfort. As it was, I now felt an added reluctance.

"I—it's more than that, Mother," I said. "I'm just afraid I'm making a mistake. I don't believe I love Beryl at all. And I don't think he loves me. Wouldn't it be better all around if we—"

"Love!" she interrupted. "What do you know of love at your age? Love comes in time. If you thought you were in love with Beryl, it would simply be a matter of infatuation. Many people have it at first, but it doesn't last."

"But at least people have some expectations of happiness when they marry. I don't believe we do."

"Happiness? No expectations of happiness, when you have a lovely home to move into, a man who has ample means to support you, a future that promises even more? Oh, child! How naïve you are."

"Mother, I'm sorry if it disappoints you, but I just don't believe I can go through with it."

She turned on me then; her jaw was set. "Disappoints me? My life has been a disappointment since I married David Leider. I've sacrificed all these years in the hope you and your sister and your brother could hold up your heads with pride in the streets of Houston. I've worked hard to be sure you met the right people, mixed with the right society—your father never cared about that, and you know it—so that when you were of the age to marry you'd find someone who would provide you a good, stable life. I wiped my brow in relief when Patricia married George. Jordan—from all early appearances—is completely hopeless. Your father has seen to that. And now you—you, with a gifted, handsome man to marry, hundreds of dollars already spent on your wedding—you want to back out because of some foolish intuition that you may not be happy in spite of all this? Don't insult me, Elzyna."

I was near tears. "Mother," I pleaded, "you know none of these things make for happiness. You have money of your own, a fine house to live in, but you're miserable by your own admission. Don't you care if I'm happy?"

She glared at me. The silence was deafening.

"You don't care, do you? You've never cared about my happiness," I accused, revelation crashing over me in waves. She was relieved to be rid of me. Her next statement confirmed it.

"How many Beryl Farrishes are going to be waiting around the corner for you, Elzyna? How many? It's all right, back out. Go over to Auntie Reda and Uncle Neal and tell them all your troubles. It's what you have always done. You say that I don't care for your happiness? What have you ever cared about mine? You should have been Alvareda's child. You never asked your sister and brother to go over there with you and you never wanted to come home. Well, tell the Gerrards that you're breaking off with Beryl. Maybe they can find someone else for you to marry. I wash my hands of you."

"Mother!"

"It's all right. Leave me now. I don't feel well."

I kept sitting there, staring blindly at the chair arm. I felt as though everything inside me had been emptied out, and what remained was a hollow puppet whose only purpose was to be manipulated for someone else's pleasure. I drew in a deep breath. My voice was barely audible as I murmured the words that my mother awaited, the words that I hated worse than any I had ever uttered. "I'll go through with it. I hadn't realized how . . . selfish . . . I was being. I'm sorry."

The room was filled with strained silence. I glanced up. She was looking at me, her lips pursed tightly, her expression quizzical as though she wanted more assurance.

"We'll be happy," I said. "I know we will. Why shouldn't we? Forget all that I said . . . you must be right. A simple case of jitters. I won't cause you any more concern, I promise."

"Very well," she said. She paused momentarily, then rose and walked out of the room, her shoulders erect, her head held high.

I rushed up to my room, two steps at a time, then fell on my bed and cried. I knew the price of my guilt for hurting Mother would be paid out over the rest of my life. And all the while I lay there, the sound of Anna Winston's sewing machine made music to the relentless march of time.

A few days later I picked up the neat bundles of wedding invitations and took them to the post office. In a way, seeing them swept off by the clerk into the oblivion of the other mail was strangely comforting. The time for backing out was over. At last, my indecision was at an end. I was as committed as I would be when Beryl and I stood before the priest and said our vows four weeks hence.

Outside the streets were crowded with visitors to the annual Not-Su-Oh Festival coming to a close, and littered with remnants of the elaborate parade float decorations, the confetti, the streamers. As I started to cross at the intersection, I heard a voice calling from behind and turned.

"Miss? Excuse me, miss." A man approached me with two young girls in tow who wore matching broad-brimmed hats and tailored coats. The man was not much taller than I was, and was of curious build. His head was just slightly too large for his body. His brown hair tumbled across his forehead. He was impeccably dressed, and his brown eyes, above a long Roman nose, were very kind.

"If you would not mind," he said, producing a handkerchief and mopping his brow, "I am looking for the corner of Franklin and Prairie. There is a shop there, and I have an appointment with the proprietor in five minutes." He spoke with a slight French accent, which I recognized only because I had a teacher from France my final year in school.

"Franklin and Prairie—that's a long way from here," I said, pointing. "I don't think you'll make it through all these people, not in five minutes."

"Oh, but we must try. Come along, *mes petites*—"

"My buggy is just up the block. I'd be happy to drive you there."

"Oh, but that is very kind indeed," he said cheerily. There was a note of childish wonder in his voice as well as the French accent.

When we were all in the buggy he said, "My name is Paul Philippe Savoy. Let me introduce my daughters. This is Renée, and Genevieve." The little girls nodded politely and smiled. Their cheeks were rosy. They were very fetching.

"You are here for the festival?"

"Yes. I have a lace shop in New Orleans. We provide some of the materials for the young ladies in the Not-Su-Oh court each year."

Genevieve, the younger girl, piped up, "I was the one who told my father that Not-Su-Oh was Houston spelled backwards."

He laughed and said, "And I haven't been able to get along with you since."

"It must sound awfully strange to people from other places. It's quite an exciting time here. All the parades and the parties."

He smiled. "It reminds me a little of our Mardi Gras. Have you ever come to Mardi Gras?"

"No, I've never been to New Orleans."

"I hope you will visit some day. I think you would enjoy it."

As we rode along, we fell into silence, and it occurred to me that it was a comfortable silence, not like I'd felt at other times . . . with Beryl, for instance. I thought of the wedding invitations, four hundred of them, now dispatched. . . . We had reached our destination. "Here we are," I said, and pulled on the reins.

The three of them climbed down from the buggy. The man reached into his pocket and pulled out a business card, which he handed to me. "If you are ever in New Orleans, come visit my shop. Let me return your hospitality."

"I will, and thank you," I told him.

I watched as they disappeared into the building, thinking what a nice family they were, how happy they seemed. I looked at the card: "Savoy Fine Lace and Linen Company." Under that, "Royal at Conti, Vieux Carré, New Orleans." And at the bottom, "Finest laces imported from France . . . Belgium . . . Italy."

When I later took out the contents of my bag to put them into another one, I picked up the card and looked at it again. When would I ever be in New Orleans? I probably ought to throw it away. Yet, I found I could not. The man was so kind. It seemed unkind just to pitch it away. I pushed it back down into my handbag, supposing I would never think of it again.

Chapter 5

December 15, 1906.

On the afternoon of my wedding Alvareda came over for tea and brought me a special present. "My sister gave me a similar gift and it meant a lot to me because . . . well, just open it."

Inside a large box was a white muslin gown and robe, trimmed with light blue velvet ribbons and blue embroidery. It was lovely, delicate as a flower petal. I held the gown up to me and then the robe, delighted.

"I'm glad you like it," she smiled, and took a sip of tea. "Well, tonight is the big night. Are you all ready?"

"I think so," I told her. The wedding gown worked on so diligently by Anna Winston had been pressed and hung on a hook in the wall nearby, its train carefully draped over a table to keep it from wrinkling. My valise was packed and sitting by the door. My hair was curled and in place.

"And when will the house be finished? I'm dying to see it."

"The contractor says at least four more weeks. After our trip to San Antonio, we'll live at the Rice Hotel."

She paused. I felt there was something on her mind, but she was having difficulty getting to the subject. She looked at me out of the corner of her eye. "Are you feeling happy?"

"Oh yes, yes I . . . just a little nervous. It's funny, but for some weeks people have been telling me every time I turn around that I'm having the jitters. Now at last I think I really am."

She smiled. "I certainly did. I was very frightened in fact, although I soon learned there was nothing to fear."

"I'm not afraid . . . exactly," I told her, and fingered the smocking on the nightgown so that I would not have to look into her eyes. I had dispensed with the idea of talking with her about the expectations I would be facing much later tonight. I now felt so badly about all the grief I had caused Mother, I could not bring myself to approach the subject with Alvareda. "It's just—well—I'm not exactly sure what I am supposed to do . . . that is, when Beryl and I are alone," I said. I started to mention Mother's remarks, but felt that would be like betraying a confidence.

"Don't worry, Elzyna," she said. "The greatest revelation to me was that Neal was the same person wherever we were . . . he led me gently through all the things I did not know."

I found that reassuring, till I thought of Beryl's violent streak. But then surely he was only that way about his work. . . . "Well, I think that if Beryl is as kind and understanding as Neal, I'll be all right."

"Of course you will," she said, and rose to hug me. "Just one more time, let me hold my little girl."

"Oh . . ." I sighed, and clasped her tightly. Had I told her all my feelings now, I would have completely fallen apart, and it was too late for that.

After she left I realized her main objective in coming was to reassure me without causing me embarrassment. Yet something in the back of my mind kept telling me that, while she told me the truth, she did not have all the information necessary to project anything about Beryl.

At six o'clock Mother and I drove to the church, Anna riding with us. Mother was wringing her hands. Father had not come home to dress, and she feared he would not show up. I patted Mother's arm. "Don't worry, Mother. There is plenty of time yet."

"Oh!" she laughed bitterly. "Fine thing, your having to reassure me."

In truth I was a lot less confident than I pretended. Through all the months of preparation, I had considered the possibility more than once that Father might do something like this. Yet I had hoped with all my heart he could be relied on because he loved me enough not to let me down. One recent evening he had cheerfully modeled his wedding attire for me, as though he were looking forward to having me walk down the aisle at his side. He had swept me into his arms and hummed a wedding waltz, and I had been thrilled by the moments of gliding around the parlor with him, thinking there was at least one happy prospect in all this: appearing on my handsome father's arm before a huge audience of people.

Now, I gazed out the carriage window at the dusty street under the darkening sky, and wondered if that experience were to be stolen from me. As if she picked up my train of thought, Mother murmured, "I suppose we could ask Neal to step in for him."

"Yes," I said with a nod, thankful that I could at least count on that.

Forty-five minutes before the ceremony, as we stood in the nearby parish house, Father still had not shown up. Neal was dispatched to find him, and this he did while Alvareda, in her striking long blue coat that defied anyone to guess she was so soon to deliver a child, stood nearby a window, looking out with concern. In less than twenty minutes, Neal accompanied Father through the door. Neal was attempting to look pleasant, but his jaw was set with irritation. Father was not completely drunk, but he was not sober either.

I took in a breath, wondering anxiously how he would behave. His moods varied when he drank, depending upon his frame of mind. He could be the epitome of charm; or, he could behave reprehensibly. I observed him for a few moments before I felt halfway at ease. He pecked Mother's cheek. That was a good sign, though she reacted like a block of ice. Then he kissed Alvareda's hand, and went around greeting everyone he saw convivially, smiling and nodding. As we lined up at the church door and Anna Winston straightened the long train of my wedding gown to the tune of the organ prelude, he took my arm and smiled at me. "You didn't think I would let you down, did you?"

"Of course not, Father," I lied nervously. He looped his arm around mine. Patricia handed me my rosary and flowers. She kissed my cheek, pulled my veil down over my face, and stepped up to begin the procession.

It may have been my worry over the state Father was in that preserved my equanimity as we progressed through the long mass. It gave me no time to dwell on the fact that, with every chord of the wedding march pounding out from the immense pipe organ, I was edging closer to that inevitable moment when I must face Beryl alone . . . must share his life forever. . . .

I looked ahead, down the long aisle. Father Baratino was awaiting us, smiling pleasantly. Beryl was just drawing near the foot of the altar. When I saw him, looking toward me in expectation, everything that had ever seemed extraordinary about the two of us marrying flashed through my mind to the cadence of my steps. Beryl was, on that night, more handsome than ever. In his wedding tails and stiff collar, with his dark hair combed neatly in place above the high color of his cheeks, he might have been awaiting a royal consort in some faraway kingdom. People would surely be thinking the groom was much better-looking than the bride. Why did he settle for Elzyna Leider?

Why indeed?

Father relinquished my arm. Beryl smiled at me, his head inclined as though he were trying to reassure me to take those final steps with him. Certainly he had never looked more confident. Never more pleased. I was like a lifeless doll, hardly hearing the words uttered by Father Baratino, almost missing the signals to turn this way or that. And when we knelt before the Virgin to pray, my knees felt so weak I did not think I would be able to rise again.

When the service was finally over and we had marched down the aisle to the deafening peal of wedding bells, we were hastily bundled into a waiting carriage. My massive gown was like a foaming ocean wave around me. Beryl pressed down the folds, leaned over and kissed me gently. "You do look lovely tonight," he said, and smiled.

Oh, how very sweet, I thought, and turned away shyly, my heart pounding. Perhaps this was not a mistake, after all. Perhaps . . .

We stood in a reception line in Mother's drawing room for almost two hours, and greeted more than three hundred guests. Father had started on champagne the moment we arrived. I kept watching him out of the corner of my eye, and Neal stayed closer to him than his own shadow. Oh, bless Neal, I thought. Bless him! After the ceremonious slicing of the wedding cake and the sumptuous buffet, of which I could not eat a bite, I signaled to my attendants and went upstairs to change into my traveling suit. We would spend this night in the Rice Hotel, leaving early in the morning for San Antonio from the station not far away. As I was putting my hat on my head and straightening my hair, Father knocked on the door and requested that we talk alone.

"Of course, Father. What is it?"

"Oh, a father just needs to talk to his little girl when she gets married," he said. You really could not tell he had been drinking at this point, except that his attitude was more expansive . . . his emotions were near the surface. His voice was steady. For this I was thankful. Suddenly he took my hands, and great tears welled up in his eyes. "You'll be all right, will you? Beryl will treat you right? I should have talked to him. I was a confounded jackass for not talking to him."

"It's all right, Father. I'm sure you've no need to worry."

"I almost hate to let you go, even if I have never been a decent father to you—"

"Oh, really—"

He shook his head. "No, I haven't. Of course, when Patricia married I didn't have to worry about her not knowing what she was getting into. But you're different. You've been more . . . sheltered . . . I guess that's the word. You can always come to me, if you have problems. Count on that, will you?"

I've never been able to count on you, I thought, but smiled anyway and said, "That's kind of you, Father. I will."

He nodded and kissed my cheek, then turned to leave, his chest swelled. I know he had satisfied himself that duty was done. I stood there wondering idly just what he would do if I ever really brought a problem to him.

I glanced in the mirror again, and took in a breath of determination. And I really felt more prepared than ever in that moment.

It was nearly midnight before we finally arrived at our hotel room. Baskets of roses and carnations lined the furniture tops in the little sitting room, and there was a bottle of champagne and a tray of cheese and fruit from the Gerrards. We opened the champagne and took a sip or two. Then Beryl said, "Are you happy?"

I nodded and smiled, my pulse drumming rapidly.

"That's good," he said, then added, "I guess it's bedtime, eh? You can change in the bathroom if you like, and I'll use the bedroom. I'll wait for you. Women are invariably slow when it comes to changing."

I forced another smile and went into the bathroom. I could hardly breathe for my nervousness. I closed the door and leaned over the valise, searching for my new nightdress. When I stood up I suddenly became dizzy. I sat down on the toilet and put a hand on my forehead. Oh, this was terrible. I was going to be sick. Any moment I . . .

"Are you all right, Elzyna?"

"I think so." One moment . . . two. . . . I felt better now. I wouldn't tell him I was this nervous. He might not understand. I washed my face and brushed my teeth. I undressed and put on the gown, taking special care to get the blue velvet bow straight. I stood before the door, my mouth dry, my hand on the knob, for as long as I reasonably could. Finally I took in a deep breath, drew up my shoulders, and turned the knob.

The room was bathed in soft lamplight. Beryl lay in the bed with his shoulders bare. I had hoped he would at least be in a nightshirt. "Come to bed, darling," he said with a pleasant smile, his arm extended.

Darling. He had not ever called me that before. I climbed in and lay there rigidly. Cut and dried . . . cut and dried. . . . Mother's words repeated in my mind like a bass chord banging on the piano keys. Beryl drew deeply on his cigarette and stamped it in the tray. I thought of that first night we met, the look in his eyes as he stamped a cigarette in a planter. Abruptly he turned over and began to kiss me. Not like he had before, but hungrily, his mouth wet, his hands searching all over me. He didn't lift the gown from me; he took hold of it and ripped it down the center. I stared at him, aghast. He went on kissing me, below my ears, on my neck, on my breasts, biting and sucking on my nipples as I gritted my teeth in pain. His mouth moved down farther, on my stomach, then down farther, between my legs. He paused a moment, then he suddenly shoved one finger into me hard, then pulled it out, and then he looked right into my eyes before lowering his head and lapping me again and again with his tongue. I gulped and dug my fingers into the sheets. I could do nothing but lie there limply, not knowing what would come next. Alvareda's, Patricia's, Mother's words flashed through my mind as I tried vainly to connect all this with anything I had been told. I believe if he had gone on touching me much longer I would have raised up screaming. Instead he stopped and looked up. "Aren't you going to kiss me back?"

"Oh," I gasped, and brought my hands to my face. "I'm sorry. I just didn't expect—it happened so fast—I—"

"Don't you want me?"

"Yes, I suppose, but couldn't you just—"

"Just what?"

"Go a little slowly. I—oh, dear. I didn't know it would be like this!"

I had insulted him. He lay back on the pillows and lit up another cigarette. He went on smoking for a long time without saying anything to me. I didn't know whether to pull the covers over me or just lie there, and I wondered if he knew that and if, perhaps, this was his way of punishing me for having been so clumsy with my words.

At last he said, "Well, what did you think we were going to do, play tiddlywinks?"

"No, Beryl, I'm sorry if I acted wrong. I just didn't know what to do. Forgive me?"

He shrugged. "It doesn't matter."

I continued to lie there rigidly while he went through three cigarettes unhurriedly. Then he switched off his lamp and said, "Let's forget it and go to sleep." He turned over the other way. A long time later I finally pulled the covers around me gingerly and switched off my lamp as well. He was quietly sleeping. I was lying there miserable. I was appalled at what had happened. Maybe I should have expected this, or just pretended to like what he was doing. But for now I was truly horrified. I looked at the ring on my finger and thought desperately, Oh no. . . .

It must have been nearly dawn when I was awakened. I had not been sleeping very long, I'm certain. I looked up to see Beryl above me. I could see his male parts now and I closed my eyes. "Just hold still," he said, and then in the blink of an eye I felt the piercing sensation of his flesh invading mine. I cried out in pain, then, with instinctive determination clasped my hand to my mouth. He closed his arms around me and pushed in again and again. It seemed forever and I have never experienced anything so painful outside of the day I fell from my horse and hit the ground on my back. Finally I felt a great push, stronger than those before it, then a warm flood that seemed to spread through the lower portion of my body. He lay there on top of me, completely spent, his forehead wet with perspiration. "There," he said finally, and pulled up. "You'd better get dressed. The train leaves in two hours, and we still have to go to mass."

I have never felt lonelier than on the morning we departed for San Antonio. Our heels clicked across the wide, nearly deserted floor of the Grand Central Depot, and outside along the boardwalk. The cold air chilled our faces and the morning fog swirled lazily about us. All the way to San Antonio Beryl gazed out the window solemnly, as though he wished he were bound for another place, with someone else. I sat next to him, silent and wide-eyed, like a child who has broken something valuable which can be neither replaced nor repaired.

Our time in San Antonio deepened, if possible, the damage already done. For more than a week Beryl explored again the old dilapidated missions while I sat either in the hotel room or awaiting him nearby with a picnic basket, trying to pretend enthusiasm where there was none. When he was ready we would cycle back, or sometimes to another ruin, and I felt he must be delaying the inevitable because he surely dreaded it as much as I did.

I tried hard not to be so rigid, but in truth I found my husband repulsive. His opinion of me seemed to be the same. His movements were hard and mechanical. He never caressed the length of my body. If I felt that first night he was simply using my body to his own ends, then I felt it to twice the degree after that. He never said he loved me. He hardly looked at me. He simply invaded me, again and again. It was as though he acted out of some sense of obligation to himself that I didn't quite understand, only sensed.

The physical pain continued, though I tried to mask it as well as I could. When we were on our way back to Houston, our wedding trip concluded, he suddenly looked at me and said, "You probably should see a doctor."

"Doctor?"

"Yes. To find out why I cause you such pain."

"Oh, if you really think so. Yes, all right."

The first thing I did after we had crossed the tiles at 4001 McKinney and opened the doors of our new home was to call and make an appointment with a doctor I'd never seen before. I couldn't bear the thought of going to our family doctor. The examination was not painful as I'd feared, and more dignified than I would have expected. Afterward the doctor said, "I see nothing wrong at all. You could be throwing up a barrier. Becoming tense."

I turned crimson, and looked away.

"Mrs. Farrish, describe the pain to me once again."

And so I did, likening it to the accident in 1901. This time he seemed to pay more attention, and questioned me about the accident itself. I told him about the treatment which followed.

"It's quite possible this pain is connected with your back injury. If so I really don't know what to tell you. Why don't you just see if it lessens over the next, say, month or two? Then if not, come and see me again."

I promised him that I would, yet I delayed. The next time I saw him, in early April, he confirmed my suspicion that I was expecting a child. It was the first happy moment I had enjoyed since my marriage. I only wished my happiness could have included the fact that Beryl and I would now be even further committed to our lives together.

PART 2

Chapter 1

Passersby along oak-shaded McKinney Avenue would often pause to admire the lovely home at 4001. The box shrubs around the lot on which the house nestled so peacefully were lush and neatly trimmed, and rose evenly with the waist-high iron gate in the center. Petunias, pansies, and marigolds bloomed through spring and summer along the front walk. Tall crepe myrtle bushes at each end of the porch were heavy with pink blossoms till the first frost. The grass was healthy and verdant. The wood house trim was painted every other year; the windows were kept sparkling clean; the porch was swept daily. Often children were seen playing in the front yard, and the swing that hung from the big oak tree was frequently occupied. Outer appearance suggested there was a happy, normal family dwelling inside. And in many ways, we were.

Senta, our firstborn child, was the source of her father's delight. When he picked her up in his arms, the warmth and tenderness that he had never shown to me spread over his face. Beryl always called her "my pretty little girl," and in fact she was very pretty, almost from the day she came into the world. She had curly platinum hair and big blue eyes. It was soon obvious she would be petite in size, for which I was especially thankful. From the time she could walk reasonably well, Beryl often took her down to City Park on Bagby Street, where together they would visit the animals in the small zoo and wade in the pond. On Sundays we dressed her up like a china doll, and he carried her proudly into the church for mass. For the express purpose of photographing her, Beryl bought a new Kodak camera. He built her a rocking horse and fashioned a beautiful cradle for her many dolls. Senta's favorite playmate was Lilly Gerrard, born shortly after my wedding. I was especially pleased at this for more than one reason. First of all, Lilly was pleasant to be around. She was an adorable child with wavy auburn hair and freckles, and her father's radiant smile. She was full of pep and as sweet as any child I've ever known. She had a very good effect on Senta's troublesome nature, and could often change a scowl into a smile on my daughter's face by making an enthusiastic suggestion. Otherwise, I was happy for their friendship because it gave Alvareda and me something very special in common and kept us in touch frequently when we might otherwise have drifted apart.

Her other children were so much older. Gabriel was practically grown, and planning to attend Harvard in the fall of 1913. The only time we ever saw him was when he came to fetch Lilly, who idolized him, after she had played at our house or attended a birthday party. He was blond and brown-eyed, and had an endearing toothy grin. At the age of fifteen, he had already grown to equal height with his father. He was popular and gregarious, and all of us felt he would be headed for some interesting and exciting career.

If we saw little of Gabriel, we saw even less of Clayton. Clayton was dark-haired, and pale-faced because he had little interest in outdoor activities. Unlike Gabriel he was neat and methodical. He had a somber personality, and was usually involved in a serious project of one kind or another. Clayton had few friends, and was so different from Gabriel that the two boys often battled between themselves and never seemed close. Yet Clayton did not seem to mind being a loner. He always earned the highest marks attainable in school. The fact that he seldom came over to our house with his parents was not a real disappointment to me because, as Neal admitted, Clayton seemed to regard everyone around him with condescension.

In the summer of 1909, our son John Hawthorn Farrish was born. He was as different from Senta as Clayton was from Gabriel, and I don't know how much of this was due to the fact that Beryl continued to dote on Senta, never really dividing his attention equally between the children. John seemed to be different by nature. He was always puny, given to colds and stomach upsets. When he was an infant he was colicky and would often cry at long intervals, especially at night. It seemed to me I never slept, not for the first couple of years of his life. I would lie awake prone for the sound of his voice, and hurry to the nursery before he awakened Beryl. I would sit in a rocker and hold him, sometimes until dawn, when he finally wore out and slept. This, more than any of several medicines prescribed for him, seemed to remedy the problem.

If John was more than ordinarily difficult part of the time, when he was feeling well he was the sweetest child ever, with a much more unselfish and caring nature than that of his sister. And since Beryl paid him so little attention, I paid him more. While Senta was upstairs with her dolls and dishes, I would be down on the library floor, playing with John. When I was outside working in the garden, he was playing nearby. When I took Senta to her dancing lessons at Monta Beach Studio, John sat on my lap for an hour, happily playing with a toy. All the other mothers around us remarked on what a fine child he was.

I did not get much relief from the care of our children. Sometimes Beryl took Senta to the office with him on Saturdays if he hadn't too much to do there, and once in a while my brother Jordan would come over in the afternoons and entertain John for an hour or two. I seldom asked Jordan to come. Though I never confessed this to Mother, I did not feel comfortable leaving him alone with John. There was something cruel about him, though nothing he did was absolutely mean. He teased John a lot. He'd offer him a cookie, then hold the jar high in the air and continue to say, "You wanna cookie, eh? Oh, do you wanna cookie? Here then . . . whoops! Up goes the jar again. Aw, big boys don't cry. Stop crying and I'll give you one. Okay, here we go . . . whoops!"

Though I called him to task several times, he would do it when I was outside and could not know what was going on. Once I heard him threatening John, telling him he'd lock him in a closet where a big bogeyman was waiting, and after I stopped him it took me a full hour to get the frightened John calmed down. John early developed a fear of the dark that Senta never experienced, and I could not say for certain but I suspected it came from something Jordan said to him. After a few weeks of Jordan's visits, I asked Mother to try and keep him busy some other way. I felt badly about this—oh, all Jordan's life it seems I've felt guilty about him!—he is my brother after all and I'm sure he doesn't mean to be so cruel. He just has a pathetic hunger for attention.

I was probably as content as I would ever have hoped in those three or four years when Senta and John were still babies. Between the two of them I was too busy to worry much about the state of my relationship with Beryl. I made an effort to stay out of his way and avoid displeasing him. I tried never to complain about anything. When he came home at night, he despised having toys around, so before he arrived I would tidy up. I tried as hard as I could to maintain peace at the dinner table, but sometimes accidents occurred and trouble erupted. Beryl would often put on his hat and leave right in the middle of the meal. Other times when the children made a lot of noise, he'd leave for a few hours. I would not have dared ask him where he was going or question him when he returned. But it seemed to me that by and large we got along as a family about as well as anyone else. Certainly our household was more peaceful than the one I grew up in.

One night in the fall of 1911, Beryl surprised me by saying, "We haven't seen the Gerrards lately. When are they coming over again?"

I had suggested inviting them to supper many times, but Beryl had little to say in their presence and I really did not feel he was comfortable around someone as accomplished as Neal. I also suspected he resented coming in so late on a well-established friendship, and perhaps he really was offended by the property they gave us being in my name only.

On the evening they came, Beryl was unusually buoyant and friendly. I remember thinking that this was just the kind of evening I had dreamed of when we first remodeled the house, in which we would entertain friends around our dining table and everyone would enjoy being in our home. When I retreated to the kitchen to cut the coconut pie and pour the coffee, the subject turned to Jesse Jones. I did not know at the time who brought up his name. When I came in with the dessert tray, Neal was talking about him. He had built the Houston Chronicle Building and the Bristol Hotel, and had even persuaded the Texas Company and Gulf Oil to move here and had erected buildings for each of them.

"Still, I believe he regards his lumber business as—" Neal continued, but Beryl interrupted.

"Could you arrange for us to have dinner together one night?"

Neal looked uncertain for a moment, then said, "I could certainly try."

Jesse Jones was considered by many to be the most important citizen in Houston. I could understand Beryl's wish to meet him. But I could not understand—and from Neal's expression I gathered he could not either—why Beryl wished to meet him in such a confined situation as he suggested. Granted, Mr. Jones was a builder of buildings, but he surely would not care to spend an evening chatting with someone who had not even reached the status of junior partner in an architectural firm.

Starting the next day, when Neal reported Mr. Jones would join all of us for dinner at the Brazos Court, Beryl was like a child when he learns he is to be taken to the circus. He slept fitfully, ate little, and spent much time lost in his thoughts. I questioned nothing, but remained puzzled.

Then, a few days before the scheduled dinner I read something in the newspaper that seemed to make sense of everything. Jesse Jones was about to take on the monumental task of remodeling the Rice Hotel and making it into a modern, first-class hostelry that would be large enough to house meetings and conventions on a grand scale.

It was very possible people in the architecture profession were already vying for the job of design, I realized. That was the reason for Beryl's eagerness to invite the Gerrards to dinner. That was why the subject of Jesse Jones came up during the meal. . . . Did Beryl think that Jesse Jones could be persuaded to engage the firm he worked for to design the new Rice, and make a special request Beryl be assigned to the job?

On the night of the dinner party as I sat brushing my hair before the mirror, Beryl walked up behind me and said, "New dress?"

"Yes. You like it?"

He inclined his head from left to right, then said, "Blue is a nice color for you. I must say, motherhood seems to agree with you."

"Oh, why is that?"

"You've put on a pound or two, haven't you?"

My hand stopped with hairbrush in mid-air. "Oh, do you think so? Do I look terrible? Oh dear, you won't be ashamed of me tonight, will you?"

"Of course not," he assured me; then he put his hands on my shoulders and said, "Tonight, just leave everything to me, will you? I know what I am doing."

"Of course."

He picked up his coat and walked out of the bedroom. I sat there for a moment or two, thinking how odd his request seemed. Why should he think I'd do otherwise?

I finished my hair, rose and looked at myself in the mirror. Tonight I would have to eat sparingly. Tomorrow I would begin the diet regimen long familiar: soft-boiled egg, coffee, orange juice, lean meat, and green vegetables. I already dreaded climbing on the scale. And what if this time I just continued to gain in spite of all efforts not to? I always feared one day this would happen. . . .

Houston had but few restaurants and the Brazos Court, an outdoor dining room at the Brazos Hotel, was one of the finest. The soft lights and the palms placed here and there gave it an atmosphere of intimacy, and the music from a string orchestra on the balcony above made the ebb and flow of table conversation smooth and devoid of awkwardness most of the time. The waiters were impeccable in their black tie and tails, and the menu was well known for its variety of seafood delicacies, from Spanish mackerel and pompano to oysters and shrimp.

The evening began well. Neal sat at one end of the table, Alvareda at the other. Beryl and I sat across from Mr. Jones. He was over six feet tall, and must have carried around two hundred pounds. He had a kind, boyish face with keen eyes, and his voice was surprisingly soft, his manner quiet and modest, reserved. I remembered early in the evening Neal had told us that Jesse was acquainted with many people, chummy with none of them. He had an air of distance about him, even while being humorous and warm. I liked him immediately. Like Neal, he had an uncanny way of putting people at ease. Neal was less talkative than usual tonight, obviously in deference to Beryl. As luck would have it, Mr. Jones was a bicycle enthusiast, so he and Beryl spoke warmly about notables in the bicycling world and Mr. Jones told us he'd built a racing track in Dallas next to the fairgrounds back in 1897 in the hopes of getting national racing champions to participate in meets. Then he chuckled and added, "The scheme lost money in the end, but I still had a lot of fun with it so I don't count it as a total loss."

It was at that moment, Beryl said, "I admire a man with nerve enough to take a risk. What did you have in mind for the Rice?"

Mr. Jones leaned forward and began, "What I want is a five-hundred-room hotel. And I think the present site of the Rice is just right. I want to draw conventions, business travel, pleasure—I want the hotel to service any and everything a hotel can."

"How many stories do you want?" Beryl asked him.

He rubbed his chin thoughtfully. "Well . . . I used to feel like ten stories was tall enough for any building—no finer city in the world than Paris, France, and that rule of thumb holds true there. But now my friend Carter has gone up to sixteen stories, so I'm thinking about eighteen stories."

"Have you done much thinking about the building style?" Beryl asked expectantly. My pulse quickened at the thought he might turn this into a sermon on the advantages of the mission style. . . .

"A little," said Mr. Jones. "I have some drawings. I usually have a few things in mind before I talk to an architect."

"I'd sure appreciate an opportunity to work on the design with you," Beryl said, and leaned back, hooking a finger in his suspender.

"Which outfit are you with? Neal told me, but I—"

"I'm on my own," Beryl corrected, without so much as a pause. "Up until a short time ago I worked with Radcliffe, Winter, and Tulley. But I resigned a week ago."

I was astonished. I started to speak, then remembered my promise to Beryl. I wanted to die. I looked at Neal, then at Alvareda. It was obvious they, like me, had been under the false impression Beryl would be representing the firm that employed him this evening.

Neal said, "This comes as a surprise, Beryl."

Beryl shrugged and said, "Radcliffe and his partners are too provincial for my taste. They will keep Houston in the dark ages of architecture. I decided I'd be better off alone."

"I see," said Mr. Jones. "Well, I don't see anything wrong with that. I never could work with partners myself. And I admire your pluck, Mr. Farrish. Not so many years ago, I decided to try my luck at borrowing money from banks. The first bank I went to in New York City loaned me twenty-five thousand dollars. So I tried another, asking for several times that. I got turned down, but I never did think there was anything wrong in trying. . . . Come by my office tomorrow. We'll look over the things I've written down together."

Mr. Jones preceded us on the way out of the Brazos Court, and it was his handsome bay mare and carriage that was brought around for him before ours arrived. We bid him farewell and stood on the curb with the Gerrards. "I didn't realize you'd quit Radcliffe," Neal said.

Beryl turned to him and evaded the question. "Well, I haven't actually quit. I've dropped some hints, though, that I'll probably just work until the end of the month. This has been in my mind for a long time." Before Neal could say anything he quickly added, "Hey, thanks for what you did for me. I think I see our buggy up ahead. Good night."

Neal nodded, and Alvareda stood there with her arm looped in his, looking confused.

"Well?" I demanded as we drove home. I was embarrassed beyond words. My face felt hot from ear to ear.

"Well, what?"

"Are you really quitting, or have you quit, or what?" I said with a glare.

"Neither. Look. This is the greatest chance I've ever had. I'm not going to give it away to those old heaps I work with. Why should I?"

"But, won't they know what you've done?"

"I don't see how. Nobody in that firm is in a league with Jesse Jones."

"None of them is even acquainted with him?"

"No. I've already checked. I've got enough sense to cover myself before I lie."

I sighed. "Well, at least you admit that's what you've done."

He turned to me then. His eyes were blazing like the lanterns on the front of the carriage. "What's it to you, eh? A man has to get ahead the best he can. Nobody is going to get in my way."

I was appalled by the extent of his treachery and said nothing else all the way home. I'd never felt so ashamed of anything, never more involved in something I had nothing to do with and would never condone. What could I say to Neal? What would Jesse Jones think of us if he found out? Oh, I'd be mortified. Yet I had no choice but to stand by my husband. That was the place of a wife, wasn't it? And if the threads of the secret began to unravel, as surely they must, I would then have to stand by Beryl as he suffered chastisement. Neal would not want anything further to do with us. He no doubt already felt his friendship has been abused. Beryl had placed me at odds with the people who were dearest in the world to me. Oh, in that moment I almost hated him.

That night as we undressed for bed he said, "Here's how we'll do it. It'll take me at least three weeks of working every spare moment. I have to get some good preliminary drawings done. I'll clear out the room in back of the parlor to work in. During the day I'll work at Radcliffe's as though nothing had happened. If Jones should call me at home, tell him I'm out on an errand or something. Then phone me immediately and I'll get back in touch with him.

"I can slip out around noon tomorrow to see what his drawings look like. I probably won't like what he has in mind. I'll have to persuade him to think my way."

I could hardly fathom the depth of his naïveté, but said nothing. The next morning, after Beryl left for work, I called Alvareda to apologize. I told her I had no idea he intended lying to Mr. Jones.

"Yes, I could see that," she told me.

"And Neal? Did he realize I would never have let Beryl—"

"Of course, darling. It's just that—"

My heart turned upside down. "Just what?" I asked, my voice hollow. I felt as though I were being led up a hill to be crucified.

"Frankly, we're both concerned for you. This could prove embarrassing."

"I know," I told her, somewhat relieved. "Just as long as you and Neal know that I wouldn't do a thing like that, and certainly not to the two of you."

"Elzyna, if the firm Beryl works for should find out, he'll most likely be fired on the spot. Does Beryl realize that?"

I took in a deep breath and began an uncomfortable explanation. "I know he must, but he has been so frustrated with the backwardness of that firm, I think he just seized the moment when it came. He knew that if Mr. Jones were to go through the firm, he'd be overlooked as designer. The project means so much to him. I suppose his behavior is at least understandable to some extent. . . ."

She was silent for a while, then said, "Well, don't let it bother you too much for now. There isn't anything you can do, and maybe things will work out."

"Yes, of course, you're right," I said.

In truth the next three weeks were the worst, the most anxious I had had since the weeks that preceded my wedding. I felt caught in a web, and at night I would dream of being in a series of tunnels through which there was no exit. I would start to the end of one, only to see it turned and led into another. I would toss and turn, and awaken. Half the time Beryl wasn't even in bed. He worked into the wee hours of the morning on the design. He never showed me the drawing, and he kept the door closed to the room where he worked. He did say that Mr. Jones wanted a roof garden restaurant, but he intended to design a large courtyard that would be a restaurant instead. And there would be an arcade on three sides of the building with tables upon it, overlooking the courtyard. I didn't have to ask him if he was doing a mission revival. I would have been astounded to learn otherwise.

During the day I lived in fear the telephone would ring and I would hear the voice of Jesse Jones at the other end. I didn't want to carry Beryl's lie any further. How would I disguise my voice when that slow, Southern drawl inquired of Beryl's whereabouts? Each evening when Beryl walked through the door, I would be wringing my hands in fear that he would announce it was all over, that Radcliffe or Tulley or Winter knew what he'd done and he was now unemployed. But night after night he arrived to give the children an absent hug and retire to his work room. It was as though nothing existed for him outside that room. All I could think of was that I would be so thankful when it was over. Maybe Alvareda was right, that somehow things really would work out. What could happen? Beryl might finish the design, and Mr. Jones might be delighted with it. After all, he was a native of Tennessee. He might not have the same aversion to designs echoing Mexican themes that Texans did. And if he liked it, he might never find out that Beryl had been lying about his employment. Beryl could simply leave the firm, keep quiet for a suitable time while he completed the final drawings, and emerge as the most important architect in Houston. The more time that passed, the more I was willing to lessen the strain of worry by following Beryl's original logic.

Three and a half weeks passed. Then one Saturday morning when my mind was occupied with other things, I heard the doorbell sound and opened the door to find myself staring into the face of Jesse Jones.

Chapter 2

It was a cold winter's morning. Mr. Jones was dressed in business suit, overcoat, and hat. His face was troubled, and I knew at once what had brought him here. My voice was weak and tentative when I greeted him. I could hardly force my lips into a smile. He asked to see Beryl, and I told him Beryl was out on an errand—I was telling the truth—and invited him in for some coffee. "I have only a few minutes before another appointment," he told me.

I could have taken the opportunity to allow some time for Beryl to prepare for his visit by convincing him he might be in for a long wait, perhaps he ought to return later or let Beryl call him on the telephone. Yet I did not. I was so anxious to have an end to this whole affair that I thought of nothing else. While he sat in the parlor I nervously prepared a coffee tray. I had no idea how I would disguise my shaking hands when I served it. Indeed, it seemed he should have been able to hear the loud pounding of my heart. I could hear his voice. Senta was carrying on a conversation with him. I would tarry a little longer, then . . .

Finally I took in a breath and walked in. I placed the tray on a table across the room and, with my back to him, poured us both a cup of coffee. He was such a large man. His hand around the coffee cup almost covered it. He told me he liked our home very much, and he felt the property out here would greatly increase in value one day. "There is more building going on out this way than I realized," he remarked.

"Yes, we now have two neighbors less than a block away, and I noticed some people walking around the property across the street just a few days ago."

"Well, you have a good number of shops out here—grocers, druggists, furniture. I notice Texas Welding has opened out here too. All this will one day connect together, along with Park Place down the interurban, and Magnolia Park."

He looked at his watch. I knew that small talk was painful for him, and wished Beryl would hurry up.

Eventually, the back door opened and Beryl came through to join us in the parlor. He was as pale as death. At least he hadn't tried to bolt when he saw Mr. Jones's unmistakable fine bay trotting horse with the carriage hitched to it, waiting at the curb. They excused themselves and went into the library, sliding the doors to a close behind them. I sat there with my cup poised in my hand, the coffee growing cold, listening as though my life depended on the outcome. I could make out only a phrase here and there as they talked. Mostly I heard the voice of Mr. Jones, slightly louder than when I had heard him speak before. He said something about practicing deceit, and at this my hand closed over the top of the cup I was holding. Something inside me collapsed like a house of cards. I heard what I thought was the name Tulley, though I wasn't certain. Each of these remarks came in between conversation I could not make out. I sat frozen in place, hardly taking a breath.

They talked for around ten minutes. At last I heard Mr. Jones say he didn't do business with people who didn't tell the truth—I heard the whole phrase clearly. Then apparently Beryl said something about the drawings he'd finished and Mr. Jones said no thank you, he didn't wish to look at them.

The door opened. Mr. Jones walked out with his coat and hat on his arm, nodded at me politely, and opened the French doors leading out on the porch. I stood peering blankly into the library. I could see Beryl sitting in there by the corner log fire, his head inclined forward, his hands gripping the edge of the couch. I feared his response should I say anything to him. Presently he rose and walked from the room. He glanced at me, eyes blazing, his face beet red, and then turned and walked out the doors in the wake of Mr. Jones. He closed the door so hard behind him I thought the cut glass would shatter from the leaded framework. I hurried to the door to see where he went. He had not taken a buggy; instead he was stomping with hands in his pockets down the front walk, across the tiles, and thence down the street. There were several saloons up McKinney toward town, and I felt certain he'd wind up in one of them. He did not often get drunk, but occasionally he would, and I was frightened of being around him because anything I said was taken as insult, and I never knew how to handle him.

In the afternoon Alvareda brought Lilly over to play with Senta and John while she went shopping. I'd completely forgotten they were coming. When I told Alvareda Mr. Jones had paid us a visit and his apparent intention, Alvareda offered to change her plans and take Senta and John home with her.

"Elzyna, are you all right?"

"Certainly," I said, but in truth the sensitive question nearly brought me to tears. "But perhaps today isn't a good time for the children to play." She understood, and squeezed my hand. Oh, the Gerrards were so normal. If we could just be half as normal as they were. . . .

It was eight o'clock before Beryl walked in the door, and to my great dismay he was greeted by two children whose faces were covered with chocolate. I had not yet had time to get them cleaned up after dessert and as soon as they heard the front door open, they both rushed to greet their daddy.

Beryl smelled so strongly of whiskey that even Senta pulled away after a brief hug. Beryl wove his way through the parlor and collapsed on a chair near the fireplace. While I had half expected him to return in this state, my nerves were no less frazzled. I was frightened of what he might say or do, almost frantic at the thought the children might see some display of the violence of which I knew he was capable. I helped them through their baths, hurried them upstairs—all the while evading their questions about what was the matter with Daddy—and put them to bed. Then I paused at the top of the stairs before going down, bracing myself for the conversation which was bound to take place as soon as I walked into the parlor.

To my surprise, Beryl was out cold, having moved over to the sofa. I pulled off his shoes and tie, covered him up, and went to bed. I was much relieved that I had been able to forgo talking to him. When he had slept off the whiskey, he would surely be much more rational and less apt to fly into a rage. I fell into a deep sleep of exhaustion.

Beryl slept till Sunday afternoon. I noticed him stirring, so I brought some coffee and sat down near him. I had never seen him look so awful. His unshaven face and uncombed hair, his untidy dress and bare feet, made him look like a pirate just in after a long voyage. He took a couple of sips of his coffee, and lay back on his arm. "The children looked like urchins when I came home last night. The least you could do is keep them clean when I'm around."

"I had no idea when you were coming home."

He sighed as one who feels there is no hope for the world.

His attitude angered me. He was the one responsible for all this. "Well, what happened with Mr. Jones?" I asked.

"You might have guessed, the deal is off. At least it wasn't a matter of his not appreciating my design. He wouldn't even look at the drawings."

That's all important, isn't it? I thought. Your work is really all that matters, above integrity, honesty, all the rest. Odd to realize this was truly the first time I had admitted that to myself.

"Tulley called him in and told him I had lied. I don't know how he found out. But he told Jones I was still employed with the firm and that any work I did would be under their auspices. He told him—well, anyhow, he told him the firm would consider it a fine opportunity to design his hotel for him. I can just see old Tulley with his glasses perched upon his nose and that gleam in his eye.

"Jones declined. I told him it was my exasperation with the firm that had forced me to do what I did, but I don't think he cared."

"Do you think they will . . . dismiss you?"

He smirked. "I'd be willing to bet my life on it."

"What'll you do?"

"I'll look for something else, of course. I won't have lost very much, that's certain."

There were not many architectural firms in Houston, and I wondered if there was some sort of grapevine among them. Father used to say it was hard to keep a secret in the cotton business, that word always got around. Was it the same among architects? I wondered uneasily.

On Monday Mr. Tulley fired Beryl as soon as he walked in the door. He told him that inasmuch as he had ruined the firm's chances of ever doing business with the most important builder in Houston, he would make sure Beryl never worked for any other architectural firm here again. Beryl seemed to take the news with equanimity. He brought home his design tools in a box and put them in the room he had been using to work. He stayed around for a few days, claiming he needed to do some thinking. This was understandable, I suppose. Yet not much time would pass before he had to have income of some kind. He did not make enough money at Radcliffe to allow us to put much away, and it seemed we went through our household money by the nickel and dime.

None of the living expenses were unreasonable, but the total equaled Beryl's pay each month, and it would not be long before the bank account would be depleted. I didn't want to bother Beryl with these worries because I felt he must have enough on his mind. While I resented the predicament he had placed us in, I felt that a man must be entitled to one mistake and perhaps he learned a good lesson. I could not have been more wrong.

Beryl checked with the other architectural firms in Houston, in hopes Mr. Tulley was bluffing, but he was summarily turned down for employment. He told me one night that if only we had enough money to get us by, he could go on his own, working out of our home. I had to shake my head. He knew as well as I did where the money went. He kept the bank book and wrote out the checks. Then he added, "I wish there were some way I could get some cash to live on for a while. It probably wouldn't take more than a few months to get going. Maybe you could ask your folks for a little help."

I shook my head. Beryl did not know that my parents lived off my mother's inheritance, that my father made little money and quickly lost what he made in his work as an itinerant oil man. If I borrowed from Mother she would immediately take over our affairs, and I did not want that. Patricia's husband George could not be looked to either. George had long ago made it clear he didn't believe in loaning money to relatives. I felt it was because he knew the kind of man my father was, and didn't want to be used by him.

Finally Beryl said, "I know what. We can mortgage this house and land."

"No!" I almost shouted, and shook my head as though Beryl had invited me to leap from the top of a tall building. I felt almost nauseated at the mere suggestion. This home meant more to me than anything in my life, save the children. The thought of jeopardizing it on a chance that something might come of Beryl's intention was intolerable. Immediately the terms of the agreement when I was given the house sprang to my mind. Had Neal foreseen we would come to this?

Perhaps I should not have reacted so harshly. Beryl looked at me and said, "Well, I guess that proves how much faith you have in me."

"I didn't mean that," I said limply. "It's just that, as of now, we have a home no one can take from us . . . we ought to hold onto it and not endanger it, don't you think?"

He shrugged. "Have it your way, Elzyna. You always do. There's only one thing for me to do, and that's go looking somewhere else. I suppose we can afford a train ticket, eh?"

"I could put off paying for Senta's dancing lessons a month or two, I guess. They might be understanding."

The next morning Beryl left on a trip that would cover San Antonio—his first choice—and Dallas, and up to Chicago—his last choice for reasons I did not quite understand. He said he would take the opportunity of visiting his parents, whom he had not seen since our wedding five years ago. He was gone the better part of three weeks, and each day I was half afraid he would call me from somewhere far away to say he'd gotten a job and that I should sell the house, pack up our children and belongings, and come. I did not want to. A woman is supposed to follow her mate wherever he leads her, but I did not want to go anywhere with Beryl. I could abide a marriage to someone I did not love as long as I could be surrounded by friends and people I did feel close to. The thought of going off somewhere with him, beginning in a new city, was revolting to me.

He did not call me long distance, or send a telegram, or even write a letter. He arrived back in Houston on a Sunday afternoon. He had not been able to find a job as an architect. That was all he told me. He would not elaborate.

Within three months we were behind on our bills and Beryl still had not found work. Finally one afternoon he noticed an ad about a bicycle repair shop for sale. "It wouldn't hurt to check into it," he said, and walked out the door with the newspaper tucked under his arm. When he returned he said the owner was pretty eager to sell. "He'll let me pay him off out of the profits. What do you think?"

I shrugged and said, "It's up to you."

At first I did not take the idea seriously, thinking only that at least it proved there was a way out of all the difficulties. I still believed that some-how, somewhere, he would wind up designing for a living.

For two or three days he sat around considering. Finally he told me he had decided to go through with it. I wanted to ask if he really thought this would make him happy; yet I could not. Obviously his happiness could not be allowed to weigh in the decision. I kept my peace.

Beryl took over the Houston Bicycle Shop soon after that, retaining the name. I felt relieved that most of our troubles seemed to be over.

Chapter 3

At first Beryl seemed content. He kept very long hours at the shop, six days a week, and returned home exhausted. When he spoke of the business, he did so with reasonable enthusiasm. He undertook the repair of automobile tires, the need for this service resulting from the poor condition of the city streets themselves. Beryl said he thought one of his employees—a man he called Buck—might soon be doing automobile repairs as well. Buck was especially good at mechanics, and the location of the shop seemed to make it a likely place for Houston business people to bring their automobiles. They could walk to their offices in the busy downtown section, and return at the end of the day. "Working on automobiles is the future for a business like this one," Beryl concluded. His reasoning seemed logical. Many people were now buy-ing automobiles. Neal and Alvareda had one and so did my father. Two of our neighbors had converted their barns to garages.

Beryl never referred to the shop as belonging to him, or to us. I did not stop to question his attitude. I was only thankful he brought home enough money to bring our bills up to date, and keep them in that condition. I was able to take Senta to her dancing lessons without fear of being called aside for a discussion of when I'd be able to pay the studio.

I tried to fulfill my duty as a helpmate to Beryl. I realized nothing could take the place of being able to pursue a career in architecture, so I endeavored to make his life at home peaceful and even enjoyable. I put a great deal of effort into making the evening meal a nice one and paid particular attention to John's table manners. If most of the table conversation amounted to Senta telling her father all about the day at school and what she had learned in dancing lessons, that was all right. We had few unpleasant incidents.

Fulfilling my role as a bed partner was sadly unimproved from the first weeks of our marriage. I still felt somewhat fearful whenever he turned toward me, although for what reason I could not say. I had become convinced that he was after some basic satisfaction that required no effort on my part other than just to endure being touched and caressed by someone for whom I had no real feelings. Sometimes the ultimate conclusion was still painful, but I tried very hard not to let him know this. It was not his fault I had a tricky back. There was nothing that could be done about it, so what was the point of making an issue of it?

I stayed busy. As soon as we were able to get a woman to come in and clean twice a week—we'd had to let the last one go because we could not pay her—I used the extra free time for big projects about the house. I bought wicker furniture for the front porch and repainted the wood trim, this time in a deep blue that enhanced the grayish white brick of the house, and matched the blue letters in the tiles at the curb. I made most of Senta's dresses, often thinking of my younger days of helping Anna Winston put yards of thread through ruffles. Wherever we went, Senta was the most fetching child in her fancy clothes and long stockings. People would stop us on the street and remark on what a pretty little girl she was, with her long blond sausage curls and hair ribbons, her rosy cheeks and blue eyes. She adored every moment of being admired by others. I would pull John in front of me and introduce him, so that he would get his share of attention. John always went around dressed charmingly as well in his little belted aprons and caps, but Senta captured attention wherever we went.

It is difficult to state when things began to change drastically. No one occurrence made the difference, but a number of elements combined. First of all, sometime in the latter part of 1912, two of Beryl's employees quit on the spot. He did not tell me, but experience led me to believe, that he was less than diplomatic with workers. "I'm not going to worry about it," he said that night. "I'll find two others. Buck told me he knew one or two buddies that might be interested."

At that point I had not met Buck, or perhaps I would have been more concerned. He indeed found two others like himself. Beryl employed them both and I heard no more about it for a while. Beryl decided to take his drawing tools and drawing board to the shop, and when things weren't too busy he would get some drawing done. I thought this was a good idea. He soon began to work a little later at night, and still later. At first the children and I would await him, dinner growing cold on the sideboard. When he finally arrived we would try to continue the evening as though nothing were amiss, though I felt it was. I thought I could detect whiskey on his breath, but wasn't sure. He began speaking regularly of Buck and Chip and Ted. Chip's "old lady" was "bitching again" because Chip got home late. Ted had a boat he took out on Sundays on Cedar Bayou. He'd fish and drink beer all day long. Buck had a new "broad" that he was spending all his money on. Beryl had to loan him ten dollars till payday.

I did not like the sound of any of this.

In many subtle ways, his whole phraseology was changing. It wasn't just the use of words that he had not used in front of me before. It was a way of putting things that indicated a kind of surliness in his whole outlook. I felt more and more uneasy.

He stopped wearing his coat at the dinner table. Even my father—probably the most untraditional man I had ever been around—honored this custom. "It's too damned hot in the house. You keep it like a damned oven," Beryl swore. Senta, who happened to be in the doorway, stared at him wide-eyed, then ran up the stairs.

"So now you're swearing in front of the children," I told him under my breath.

"Why don't you shut up," he retorted, and walked away.

I collected the dishes from the table and took them to wash, fighting down the urge to cry. I had tried so hard to make this one time of the day a special time. Apparently he had not noticed. I was angry, not only for what happened that evening, but for the patterns I could see developing. I spent the evening with a book in my hand but scarcely read a line of it. When I put the children to bed and tucked the covers around Senta she said, "Daddy said a bad word, didn't he?"

"He didn't mean to. It just—just slipped out. He was wrong to do that, especially in front of you."

"No he wasn't. My daddy can say anything he wants to."

I was astonished. I didn't know what to say. Finally I told her not to argue with me, and that I had better not ever hear her say bad words, regardless of what she heard.

She shrugged, pushed her lip out, and turned over with her Teddy bear.

That short exchange made me realize I'd better put a stop to the problems before they went too far. I went downstairs and sat across from Beryl, taking my sewing basket in my lap. When I spoke my voice was even and polite. I did not have any wish to begin an argument, though lately every time I opened my mouth I had a feeling one was about to erupt. "Is anything wrong at the shop?" I asked him.

He continued to read his newspaper. "Nothing unusual. Same old one-two."

"Are your new people working out all right?"

He put down the paper and glared at me. "A 'darned' sight better than the last two, I can tell you that."

"They're a little on the . . . crude side . . . aren't they?" I remarked. I pretended to be searching through the basket, to avoid meeting his eyes, while my heartbeat picked up speed.

"They may be, but they're good folks, as good as you are. Anyway, you wanted me to get my hands dirty, didn't you? Now that I do, you've decided I'm not good enough for you and your fancy dining room anymore."

I looked at him, anger rising. "That's not true and you know it. But lately you seem to have a sour, quarrelsome attitude, and your language is beginning to edge toward the gutter. That wasn't true before Chip and Ted came to work for you. Before they came, even Buck didn't seem so—"

"Buck's always been the same. He just likes women too much for his own good. I've told him he'd be better off if he stayed away from them, but he won't listen to the voice of experience." He flipped the paper up in front of him again, something that was to become a habit when he wished to infuriate me.

"Is that what you think of women?" I asked coldly.

I heard him chuckle.

The cavalier response wounded me even more than his words. "Have I made such a terrible life for you?" I demanded.

"Oh, you're just the greatest little wife in the world, Elzyna, warm in bed between the covers. I don't know how I'd get along without you."

I put the basket down with a thud and stomped furiously out of the room.

We went on like this for a period of weeks, right on the edge, like two fighters circling in the ring.

Then, one night Beryl did not come home for dinner. At nine o'clock I put the children to bed and sat down in the library with a book. At ten o'clock he still had not come. I began to feel uneasy. I went upstairs and undressed for bed. I lay there with the lamp lit until eleven, and there was still no sign of him. All my senses were keened for his arrival. I listened; I walked to the window and peered down toward the street below for signs of his buggy. Until this night I had never realized how many creaks and groans came forth from the house. Several times I was certain I heard something downstairs. I'd go to the stair landing and listen. Nothing. I'd go back and climb into bed. A few minutes later I'd repeat the trip to the window. The moon was bright. Up and down the block I could see silhouettes of the tall trees and dark yawning windows of the houses nearby. But no sign of an approaching trap. Finally, at half-past midnight I could stay awake no longer. I put the light out and lay down under the covers. I dozed fitfully over the next hour or two, growing more exhausted as the night drew on.

Around two in the morning I heard noises downstairs. I rose and went to the landing, my heart pumping. I could hear Beryl's voice along with several others, and someone was picking a tune on the piano. The dining room light was on. I continued to listen. In a few minutes the room fell silent and I heard a shuffling noise, followed by another and another. Then a thumping noise, and after a short interval, a mixture of squawks and crows in response to the hand of cards received.

It is hard to express the mixture of feelings I had upon my realization that my husband had brought his friends home to play cards for what was left of the night. At first it made me so angry I could scarcely bear to lie there and let it go on. I felt they had invaded my home. The dining room belonged to me, to us as a family. I could feature them down there with their cigarettes and whatever they were drinking. I could hear their profanity, their laughing, and anxiously hoped they disturbed me only because I was still awake. I certainly did not want the children awakened.

This feeling of helpless invasion continued as I lay there stock still, listening for every sound. Now and then I heard the creak of the swinging door to the butler's pantry. Now and then I heard the sound of the toilet flushing in the bathroom. I thought of the filthiness of the men downstairs, greasy and sweaty from a day of work and carrying who knew what kind of germ. Using my toilet . . . washing hands in my sink . . . wiping with my towels. . . . I wanted more than anything to stalk downstairs and order them out. Yet I could not summon the nerve. I lay there longer, smoldering. Finally I realized I was being very selfish. Perhaps I didn't like Beryl's companions, but this was his home too.

I turned over and put my arm behind my head. My back was beginning to ache. It served me right. Any understanding wife would just go to sleep and let her husband have a little fun. Beryl would probably expect a confrontation. I would surprise him and say nothing. That would dissipate some of the rage which had been growing between us. Perhaps he was testing me by bringing his friends here tonight. Perhaps he wanted me to react angrily, to give him the justification for unleashing all his feelings of resentment against me. Well, I would show him I am not as foolish as he thought. Then maybe he would not feel inclined to bring them over anymore . . . maybe. . . .

At seven o'clock I awoke to feel the warm sunshine on my face. Beryl had never come to bed. I rose and stretched. My back felt better. The children would be up within a few minutes, demanding breakfast. I felt exhausted and wished only for a cup of hot coffee. I slipped quietly down the stairs, and began to look around. Beryl was in his shirt sleeves and trousers, asleep on the parlor sofa. I didn't want to wake him. I had no idea what sort of mood he'd be in. I went through the hall to the kitchen and put the coffeepot on the stove, then I stepped into the dining room. At first it did not appear to be any worse than I'd feared. There were beer bottles and an empty bottle of bourbon on the table, and several trays full of cigar and cigarette butts. I turned and went to have a look at the bathroom. It, too, was relatively straight except that one of the nice linen hand towels was soiled and rumpled, lying on the floor. Beryl need never know what went through my mind.

I returned to straighten the dining room. I picked up a tray of ashes and discovered a cigarette butt lodged underneath where it had fallen from its place. There, in the oak dining table, was a deep cigarette burn.

I was so furious my eyes began to water. Had I not been so tired and edgy from the long night and the too-short hours of fitful sleep, I might have behaved more rationally. Yet I was beyond all ability to control my emotions, and I completely disregarded the violent nature of my husband's. I stormed into the parlor, shook him awake, and demanded he come to the dining room to view the damage.

"What the hell?" he blurted sleepily, then followed obediently. In his state of semi-wakefulness, he must have feared the house was afire. When he stood before the table gazing at the cigarette burn, I warned him, "Don't you ever bring your so-called friends here again."

He looked up at me as though I had surprised him. Then in the flash of an instant I knew I had made the fatal mistake of speaking my mind at the wrong moment. "Are you telling me what to do, you bitch?" he demanded, pushing my shoulders backward. He pushed me again, then again, as I tried to keep from falling and pleaded with him to stop. To the door and into the hall he pushed, then he raised the back of his hand and slapped me full across the cheek.

It felt as though the whole side of my face were on fire. I fell to my knees, my hands covering my head, pleading, "No, no, no! Please, leave me alone."

"Get up before I wipe my feet on your ugly face," he said, and then we both heard the voice of John from the landing.

"Mommy? What's wrong, Mommy?"

Senta stood next to him, silently watching. Beryl glanced at John, then back at me with an expression of revulsion. He turned and left by the front door, slamming it behind him.

I remained there in the hall, still on my knees, sobbing. John came running down with his Teddy bear in tow, to comfort me. I couldn't look at him. He kept trying to lift my face, calling to me, whimpering. I suppose he might have feared I was dying. Finally I took him in my arms and held him close. I could feel his heart beating as violently as mine. I looked up beyond him toward the top of the stairs, into the face of Senta. Her eyes were wide; her expression was queer . . . she was almost smiling.

Chapter 4

I told no one what had happened. I felt ashamed, like a child who has been brutally punished for some wickedness. The whole event was preposterous, my behavior as well as Beryl's. I was as wrong as he was, I told myself, for if I were not, then I must face the fact I was living with a monster. It was easier to learn a lesson and try to prevent any further such occurrence. Beryl was not himself, that was all. I should never have pushed him so far. It would not happen again, I thought, because the children had witnessed it. He must have been wondering how he would explain himself to Senta and John.

Just to be sure, I would not cross him again. I would get to know his friends, invite them to dinner, pretend to like them. I could have the table fixed, surely. Or, maybe I would leave it for now, just in case repairing it should anger him. I could pretend it was fine, that a little cigarette burn was nothing to be upset about. Not worth destroying the peace of our household.

I looked at my cheek. It was flaming red, and bruised right at the jawbone. I must stay in where people would not see me. I could not convince anyone I'd run into something or suffered some other mishap. Spring planting would have to wait for a week or so. I could not chance a neighbor's stopping by and seeing me. Did we have groceries? Yes. We could make out for a few days so I could avoid shopping. And what was on the calendar for the next two weeks? I flipped through the pages, my hand shaking. Next Thursday an at-home. I'd have to cancel that, say that I was not feeling well. There was something else. I feared that Senta might talk to children she played with. By the time she next saw Lilly she would probably have forgotten all about it, but there were her friends in dancing class, now having extra rehearsals for the coming recital, and she played daily with the neighborhood children. In fact, she would soon be dressed and downstairs, ready to begin the Saturday as usual.

"Senta, darling," I said as she walked into the kitchen. "Let's not talk about what happened this morning, all right? Daddy was upset. He didn't mean to hurt me. It was an accident." I hoped I sounded a lot more controlled than I felt.

"Yes, Mommy," she said, and yawned.

She's forgotten it already, I thought.

Once I had the children fed and out the door to play, I relaxed a little. I felt as though I'd built a fortress in anticipation of an enemy attack. All the entrances were barred. I was safe at last. I sat down in the library and drank coffee. It was hard to believe the number of plans I had made and the possibilities that had crossed my mind in the past half-hour. It seemed a full week had passed by. My only worry now was whether Beryl would come home in a drunken rage. Thankfully, it was short-lived. I was still sitting in my rocker when he came through the door. He passed by the library door without a word. In a moment I heard the bathtub faucet running. When he finished bathing, he went to bed and slept most of the day. He never said he was sorry for having hit me, or showed any concern over the wound to my cheek or to my feelings. Life went on as usual. We had a pleasant dinner that evening around the dining table that had been the subject of our quarrel that morning. And I told myself that everything would be all right now.

One day Jordan came over. Now fifteen and a student at Houston High, he stayed busy with his pals most of the time and rarely came to see us. What few conversations I had with Mother indicated he was still as hard to manage as ever, more so now that he was old enough to be expected to take some responsibilities. His grades were poor; he often got into fights that in turn got him in more trouble.

I offered him a piece of angelfood cake, which I'd made that morning, and sat at the kitchen table with him while he ate first one piece and then another, and downed a big glass of milk. It was obvious Jordan was not going to be a tall man, though all the family had assumed he'd be built like Father. He was a little on the lean side. He wore his straight blond hair parted down one side, and let it flop over his forehead, much to Mother's dismay. She also complained about his refusal to attend Sunday mass. "Not that I would be proud to be seen with him," she had remarked. "He never polishes his shoes and I can't remember when I last saw him in a necktie." He had brown eyes, almost amber they were so light, like candle flames, and his expression was watchful, distrusting. He loved to lean toward you when he talked to you, as though planning a conspiracy of some sort. He loved to make people think he knew something no one else did. He'd tell you something, then wink and lean back as though to measure your response. I regarded him with both sisterly pity and instinctive dislike.

Today he said he'd been down to the bicycle shop. "Thought maybe I'd pass the time of day was all," he said, and finished off the milk. Why there? I wondered. "And," he continued, tossing his head, "I wanted to see if Beryl would give me a job in the shop."

"Oh? Doing what?"

"Sweeping out, dusting merchandise, whatever he needs doing. Ya see, I want to get me a car. Saw a dandy little 1910 runabout that a fella wants to get rid of for two-fifty. Dad won't let me drive his new Haynes, and Mother won't give me any money to buy an automobile."

"What does a fellow your age need with an automobile?"

"Gotta have something to run around in. I got thirty-five saved up. The man who owns this runabout said if I have a job, he'll let me pay out the rest ten a month."

The man had more confidence in Jordan than I had. "Shouldn't you be saving money to help pay for college?"

He smirked. "Let Mother pay for that. She's the one who wants me to go. Besides, if Neal Gerrard can afford to send Gabriel all the way to Harvard, surely Mother can afford to send me to Sam Houston."

The reference to the Gerrard family did not really surprise me. Jordan had learned to disdain them from childhood, when Father was still blaming Neal for all his business troubles, often talking in Jordan's presence, and Mother made her jealousy of their growing wealth all too clear. You might have said Jordan was born and reared with resentment for the Gerrard family.

Still I reminded him, "Mother does not have the kind of money the Gerrards do, and she's only looking out for your interests in wanting you to get a good education."

He reached for another bite of cake. "I can get along without college. She just wants me to go because it will improve her status with society."

Unfortunately, I could not argue that point. "Well, what did Beryl have to say about your working for him?"

"He wasn't around."

"He may have been in the back, working."

"Nah. That fella Chip told me he was gone home for the day. He offered me a beer."

"He hasn't come home yet," I said, growing uncomfortable at the situation.

"That store sure is a mess. They need someone to clean up."

"I don't know how much Beryl can pay you. Business is slow right now."

"I don't need much for now. Just enough to make the payments. Would you mention it to him tonight, and let me know?"

I hesitated. "Ten a month seems a little steep, but I'll ask him."

I did not think Beryl would hire Jordan, but he did. Maybe it was his way of trying to do something nice for me. In any case Jordan wrecked the automobile within two months after he started driving it, and still had to pay the installments. He fell right in with the well-entrenched beer-drinking habits of Beryl's employees, and easily picked up their language as well. Most of this he managed to hide from Mother, but even so he was such a constant source of trouble that she counted the days until he would go to college in the fall of 1914. Somehow she felt that, if she could just manage to get him accepted into a school out of town, it would change him, cause him to mature. I wondered. . . .

Although there were no major flare-ups in our household, I never felt comfortable when Beryl was at home, and when he wasn't at home I wondered where he was, when he would arrive, and what sort of mood he would be in when he finally got there. It kept me on edge constantly, and I knew the children sensed it, too. John, normally a quiet, retiring child anyway, grew more so as time passed. He also clung to me more and more, seldom going more than a few feet from my side during the day, refusing to play with other children. Senta was another matter. If anyone could handle Beryl, she could. She would skillfully feel out his disposition when he came home. If he seemed unusually quiet, she'd wait a bit, then take him a picture she'd drawn just for him. He'd soon have her on his lap and she'd be talking away to him. If he seemed in a good mood, she'd beg him to take her down to City Park to play. He seldom refused. John would never go with them. Senta rarely saw Beryl

when he'd had too much alcohol. If he came home drinking—he often did—
she was usually in bed asleep. She was able to keep believing that her father
was a great hero who gave her dancing lessons, carried her on his back, took
her on his lap, listened to her endless stories, and loved to watch her dance a
routine from his easy chair. And I was thankful she was this way. I did not
want her to see her father as a villain, the way I had so often seen mine.

One afternoon I walked into the room where Beryl had once kept his
drafting board to look for a pair of sewing scissors that had disappeared.
When I crossed the floor toward the chest of drawers in the corner, I felt a
spongy sensation under my feet. I reached down and touched the carpet. It
was soaked. I felt around to see how far the water had gone, and traced a
large area from the center of the room to the outside wall. The legs of the
furniture resting on it were wet. Some boxes Beryl used for storage were also
wet on the bottom. I called a plumber, then began to move what objects I
could manage out of the area. When the plumber arrived he confirmed my
fears: a major pipe had cracked in the wall. Much of the wall would have to
be taken down and replaced. The carpet would also have to be replaced—
thankfully, the rug in this room was not an expensive one. Beryl would be
furious. It would give him just one more grudge against the house. The
plumber wrote an estimate of the job. A hundred and twenty-five dollars, not
counting the repainting of course, or the replacement of hardwood in the
floor. When he was gone I collapsed in a chair, defeated. I almost wished I
hadn't opened the door.

Later in the afternoon, in an attempt to lessen the blow by salvaging all
that I could and clearing away the wet things, I opened up the boxes and
went through them. To my utter dismay, one was full of drawings. All of the
drawings, rolled up and propped diagonally in the box, were water-soaked
around the bottom and limp. I laid them out in the vain hope they would dry
and not be destroyed beyond hope. The ink notes made in Beryl's neat hand
at the bottom were blurred into oblivion.

Next I opened the other box, expecting the same. This box, however, was
full of technical books about architecture, including a fine-looking dictionary
on architectural terms and a book entitled *The Seven Lamps of Architecture*
by John Ruskin, and another, *The Stones of Venice.* These both were ruined
for they were near the bottom. Others—notebooks with pages written in
Beryl's hand—had extensive notes about Bernard Maybeck, whom Beryl
greatly admired, and Frank Lloyd Wright, another of the architects he respected. I pulled everything out and began laying the books and papers out on
the tables, and finally ran across an envelope mailed to him from his former
employer, Radcliffe, Winter, and Tulley. It appeared the envelope had not
been opened before, though I could not at first be certain. The mucilage was
ineffective at this point. I opened it and looked inside. Several smaller envelopes, each addressed to Mr. Beryl Farrish, were there. I saw statements from

shops that had never been opened, one of which I recognized as a bill we paid after Beryl had left his job, for which we had to request a duplicate statement because we could not find the original. Apparently all this came to him in his office after his departure, and was finally forwarded to him. The postmark was some two months after he was fired.

I scanned the envelopes, convinced they might as well be tossed in the trash at this point in time. I replaced them in the larger envelope and set them aside. Then I noticed another envelope, from the University of Illinois. Thinking it might be important, I opened it and read the letter inside. As I read, I realized it was something not meant for me to see.

The writer was apparently a friend of Beryl's who was ahead of him in school, and had ultimately joined the staff at the university. He said that his efforts to reinstate Beryl in the architectural school of the university had been in vain. He said he was able to get his hands on a copy of the full report, as Beryl requested, without anyone's finding out. "As you can see, there's only the one incident included. Nothing about the other things." (I assumed he meant similar, less serious incidents.) He said he thought sometime he might go out West, and if he did he would do what he could to help Beryl out there.

I turned to the report feverishly, my hands trembling. It made me feel like a woman must feel upon discovery of a love letter written by her husband to another woman. The long report was a typescript, covering three fragile pages of foolscap. I read it fully—it was at times boring with endless detail— and at the end it was signed by the department head, the assistant head, and two instructors.

This was what brought my husband to Houston, I realized, alarm seizing me.

In his final year—indeed, his final three months of school, he had been dismissed because of misconduct and insubordination. He had apparently suffered one of those grueling juries he had told me about long ago, and reacted so reprehensibly that the school felt they must remove him at once. A highly respected visitor to the school had sat among the small jury analyzing his design. When several of them reacted unfavorably to what Beryl had done, he went into a rage, pulling the drawings down from the board and stomping them, calling the jury members insulting names, swearing at them. I could just see him! The honored visitor among the jury was none other than Bernard Maybeck.

It was late afternoon and the sun was disappearing, throwing shadows across the room. I put the letter and report down on my lap and sat thinking for a very long time. So many things made sense now. Questions I had never asked surfaced right along with their answers. Beryl came to Houston where he would not be known. From things I had heard him say, I could gather he simply bluffed his way into the firm of Radcliffe, Winter, and Tulley. Probably he showed them some of his designs and promised—but failed—to arrange to have transcripts sent from the university to back up his claims of credentials. In that firm, graduates of architecture school were treated with special preference, Beryl had told me when first we met. Perhaps they recognized his talent, but when it became apparent the information was not forthcoming, they simply shoved him aside to do unimportant things. That was why he could not get ahead, why he was so frustrated. Tulley—from all Beryl had said about him—might have much enjoyed lording it over him.

When he left on that three-week trip some time ago, he had not found employment, and this was why. Perhaps he hadn't even tried. In Chicago he had spent his efforts trying to be reinstated in school. They wouldn't allow it, and I could understand why. He must have been a dreadful embarrassment to them.

I was married to a scoundrel, a phony, an impostor. He'd left school and traveled slowly south, stopping here and there to gather ideas about where he might best settle and fit into society with his secret intact. He had never really wanted to be in Houston, but had used it as an opportunity he could not get elsewhere. Now that I thought about it, I had never seen any certificate or degree. I'd seen awards for competitions he had won while in college, but never his certificate for having completed the course. I had assumed he left it at his office downtown, and later carried it with him to his room in the rear of the bicycle shop. But it had never existed.

At first, after considering all this information and its obvious ramifications, I felt smugly that I could use this to advantage . . . next time he took a notion to strike me, I'd warn him. . . .

After a while I thought again. If I did, what good would it do? He was already discredited in Houston and could never practice architecture again. So how could I hurt him? He could not have given a care if I tattled to my family and friends, exposing him for what he was. He had another set of friends who were not impressed by people with finer education. If I confronted him, what was likely to happen was an unbridled quarrel which would end in further injury to me. Oh, he was much stronger than I, that I knew. I would not go up against him again for any reason.

The letter and report would remain a secret, as safe with me as they had been while hidden among his boxes. I placed my hands on my hot cheeks and bent forward. It was nearly six o'clock. The room was in near darkness. I was married to a man who threw over his entire career for the sake of displaying his anger. With his far lesser regard for me, what tragedy would we ultimately be brought to?

Chapter 5

Shortly before school let out for the summer of 1913, Alvareda called to say she'd like to stop by for a visit. I had not seen her for a long while because she and Neal had been traveling, and I could hardly wait for her to arrive. When I opened the door and she looked at me, her face clouded.

"What is it? You look positively awful. Have you been ill?"

"No. Come in," I said, and hugged her. I had not realized I looked any different. Perhaps it was only the faint light at the doorway. Yet when we sat down she kept gazing at me with concern. "You look so drawn. There are circles under your eyes. What is it?"

"Oh, I haven't been sleeping well, that's all. My back has given me some pain."

She leaned back. "Maybe you ought to see a doctor about the pain. It could be that you need to be x-rayed again. How long has it been since you last had it checked?"

"A while, but really it's better now. I slept well last night and the night before that."

She was silent for a few moments. She doesn't believe me, I thought. It was difficult to keep things from Alvareda. "I was going to ask you to keep Lilly while Neal and I go to New Orleans next month—he has a business meeting there—but I just had a better idea. Why don't you bring Senta and John, and come along with us? We're staying at the St. Charles. Neal has a meeting there."

"Oh, I couldn't, I—"

"Why not?"

"I couldn't leave Beryl here alone."

"Of course you could. He could take care of himself for a few days. Men are surprisingly capable when left to their own devices."

I shook my head. "Oh, I don't think Beryl would approve. Who would be here to cook his meals and look after things?"

She sighed impatiently. "You've never been away from him, not in—what is it now—better than six years? He might learn to appreciate you more, if you were away. Anyhow, it wouldn't hurt to ask him. The only reason I did not plan to take Lilly in the first place is because I was afraid she'd be lonely for company. I'll be busy at teas and get-togethers for the wives, and evening functions. We have developed several close friendships there, so we have visiting to do. If you were along, you and the children could just be tourists, go to the zoo, the museums, and enjoy yourselves—sleep late in the morning and take it easy. . . . You'd be doing me a favor."

"It sounds like fun, but I don't know—"

"Just promise me you'll mention it to Beryl. If he objects, then I won't press the point further. I won't mention anything to Lilly until you tell me."

She told me more about the plans, about leaving on the train and about the fine hotel, and she made it all very appealing. Yet, not until she had left and I had time to think about it did I begin to consider accepting the invitation. Maybe getting away from Beryl would be good for both of us. . . .

Through the day I was preoccupied with the idea, rehearsing in my mind just how I could best approach Beryl. It would cost so little, he could not object to that. And I could ask the cleaning lady to fix supper for him on the days she came. I could bake a ham and make some cold potato salad and leave it in the icebox, too. Surely he could not refuse. Yet . . . if only to spite me, I feared he would. From four o'clock till suppertime I listened for his arrival. If he came home late and drunk, then I'd have to forget all about mentioning it. I only hoped I would find him in a good mood soon enough to approach him. I could not ask Alvareda to wait for an answer very long.

Beryl came home for dinner that night, and I heard him cheerfully greeting Senta as I finished putting salad on the plates in the kitchen. The time was ripe, then. I felt giddy suddenly, like a young girl asking permission to be courted by her first beau. I realized that in the few hours since Alvareda was here, the trip—especially the excuse to get away from Beryl—had come to mean more and more.

As we sat down at the table I took in a deep breath, and began to tell him about it, trying to sound as though the idea held no more importance for me than the prospect of changing the washday from Monday to Tuesday.

"It's only for six days," I hastened to assure him. "Neal has rented a big suite, and we would stay in one of the bedrooms. You'd only be out the train fare, and a little mad money . . . for the children to spend, I mean."

At first he was silent, and I did not think he would bother to honor the suggestion with a reply. I felt deflated, and wished Alvareda had never invited me and that I had not allowed myself to get my hopes up.

It was Senta's begging that swayed him at last. "Please Daddy, please," she cooed. "Lilly is my best friend. We can go to the zoo and eat out in restaurants. I'll bring you a present." She kissed his cheek and threw her arms around him.

He smiled indulgently. "I suppose so, love, if it's what you want. I wouldn't mind being a bachelor for a few days."

I was thrilled, even though I realized Beryl would have never done anything so nice for me. I had never been farther from home than San Antonio, and that trip was ruined by my unhappiness. This time would be different. I wouldn't have to worry about pleasing Beryl, or being abused by him. For the length of the trip I could almost pretend to be someone else. Oh, it was going to be so exciting. I found myself humming "Dixie" while I washed the dishes.

For once I let the yard go, and spent all my spare time sewing for Senta and John. My own wardrobe was dowdy. Since we married I had not bothered to buy much clothing. It seemed the extensive trousseau made by Anna Winston ought to last a good long while. Yet the styles had changed. There was now less material in skirts, and there was a softer look about fashion than before. Fabrics being used were more lightweight; one saw many pastels in the fashions in the store windows. I considered buying some new things. Then I thought again. I didn't want Beryl to feel this was going to put him to a lot of expense. I did not want anything to happen that would cause him to change his mind about allowing us to go.

I went to the attic to pull out the valises that had been gathering dust since our wedding trip. How long ago it seemed! I certainly was looking forward to this trip more than the honeymoon trip. I knew next to nothing about New Orleans, yet the name itself was intriguing. I stopped. The man that was here for the Not-Su-Oh festival had a shop of some kind in New Orleans. What was it now? If I could remember, I might go by and purchase a little something there.

For the moment I forgot about it, but all afternoon it nagged at me. After supper when I sat down and dug my hand in my sewing basket, I remembered.

I put the basket aside and went upstairs. I felt guilty, as though I were doing something treacherous. I found the handbag I had been carrying that day so long ago. I quickly loosened the drawstring. And there was the card, nudged down at the bottom of the bag. "Savoy Fine Lace and Linen Company." I replaced the handbag and turned to go.

"Senta! You startled me."

"What are you doing, Mommy?"

"Nothing, darling. Just a little packing."

"What did you put in your pocket?"

"Oh, a card, darling. Let's go downstairs."

Without a word, Senta stepped aside to let me pass, never taking her eyes off me. It is curious to reflect, even at that early point, I felt a kind of instinctive fear of my daughter, as though, like her father, she held a certain power over my life. I told myself it was ridiculous, yet I could not quite slough it off.

We left Houston on June 11th on the night train, and crossed the Mississippi by ferry early the next morning. Much of the night it rained. John was terrified of the thunder and lightning, and of the noisy bumpy process of moving the train cars onto the tracks on the big ferry, and I was occupied trying to calm him down for the remainder of the trip, so it was not until we finally pulled into the station that I realized all of this was really happening to me. Six days . . . six days. . . . The air was cool and dank from the rain and the carriages pulling up to the station spattered muddy water in all directions. But now the sky was clear, and as we made our way down Esplanade Avenue and into the French Quarter, the sunlight spread out above the narrow streets of little two- and three-story buildings with their iron-lace balconies, making the spectacle as rich and glittering as the window of a confectionery. Suddenly I felt exhilarated. I blurted out, "Oh, thank you for bringing us. It's going to be wonderful, I just know it."

Neal smiled at me. "I've been all over the world, and this is still one of the most exciting cities I've ever visited. I never tire of coming here."

Neal and Alvareda agreed the St. Charles Hotel was even more elegant than the new Rice in Houston. Our suite was enormous. The sitting room was handsomely furnished, and had a large fireplace and deep windows with exquisite draperies and sheer lace panels. Off this room opened three bedrooms furnished with big brass beds, rosewood dressers, and full-length oval mirrors.

I believe I could have happily spent six days closed up in the suite, but the children kept me on the run constantly, shopping, picnicking in the parks, riding the streetcars, and sampling anything and everything to be had off a street vendor's cart.

It was not until the third day of our trip that I finally summoned courage to walk down to Royal and Conti Streets, to look up the man named Savoy. Before that I had searched through the directory, to be sure the shop was still listed. I had also begged Alvareda to go with me. She eagerly agreed, and hired a woman—a Mrs. Hester, whom she had used before—to sit with the children.

"It seems a lot of trouble, just to go to a shop," I said.

"Nonsense. It's always worth the trouble to have some fun and besides, I need to do some shopping."

Alvareda was so confident, so much more worldly than I was. I did not suppose she could realize how anxious I felt about what we were going to do. We looked at a street map, which indicated we were some five blocks away from Royal at Conti. We had to cross Canal, after which St. Charles Avenue became Royal Street, then walk farther, into the French Quarter, to Conti. It seemed a very long walk, one which would give me ample time to fend off nervousness, yet as we walked I realized the blocks were as short as the French Quarter streets were narrow. Once we crossed Canal, it was like walking into a tiny city unto its own, everything close together in miniature proportion, row after row of shuttered windows and doorways, hanging baskets dripping with verdant green ferns and purple bougainvillea climbing up balconies. Walking through it was even more enchanting than viewing it from the train station, but every time we passed a corner with its street lantern

high on a slender pole, I slowed my steps again. We must be almost there.
. . . "Alvareda, we needn't hurry, do you think?" I asked nervously.

She smiled at me and hooked her arm through mine. "This man named
Savoy must be quite remarkable."

I blushed. "No, it isn't that. I hardly remember how he . . . he looked
. . . it's just that, I don't want to embarrass myself. Suppose we don't tell
him who we are. We can just browse through his shop."

"But that isn't fair. You did something nice for him. Give him a chance to
be kind in return. New Orleans people are gracious, you'll see."

And then we saw the shop front ahead.

The red brick building, like so many we had seen, had a black iron lace
balcony and two floors above the street level with shuttered French windows.
The shop itself looked as elegant as I had imagined. It had a sign suspended
from chains above the door, with shiny gold lettering. There were bay windows on either side of the formidable front door, and a fan window above.
Every glass pane was bright and clean; every piece of brass, from door handle
to knocker, was highly polished. When we opened the door, a small brass bell
tinkled merrily above. Inside, where Alvareda preceded me undaunted, the
shop was tall and narrow, with drawers of deep mahogany, plush carpet on
the floor, and display cases down the center holding examples of bonnets and
christening dresses, dainty slippers and doilies, lingerie cases, parasols, and
fans. A crystal chandelier in the center threw muted light over all. Several
clerks assisted ladies sitting on stools at the counters along the sides. One
client, dressed head to toe in black, held a magnifying glass as she closely
observed a piece of black lace. She spoke to the clerk in French, and the clerk
responded in French.

I felt awkward and out of place. If not for Alvareda, I might have turned
and left the shop. Yet she was accustomed to entering a shop and being
waited on instantly. She had a look of authority that I doubted I would ever
acquire.

A clerk in lacy shirtwaist and black skirt approached. "Madame?" she
said, and began to speak in French. Alvareda stopped her, saying we spoke
only English and explaining that we had come to see the proprietor. "Monsieur Savoy is upstairs. May I tell him who wishes to see him?"

"Mrs. Farrish of Houston," Alvareda said, then looked at me. "No, it was
Miss Leider then, wasn't it?"

I nodded. The clerk looked slightly puzzled, but nodded and disappeared
up the tiny stairway at the back of the shop.

"Why are you frowning?" Alvareda whispered.

"I just feel so foolish. What if he doesn't remember?"

"Don't worry. I'll buy something. That will make up for any awkwardness,
I can assure you."

Minutes passed. We looked around as other clients and clerks talked quietly over fabrics and laces, some hidden in drawers, some brought from a room in back, wrapped in dark paper. Alvareda asked the clerk to show her a lace jabot. The clerk nodded and directed her to a stool. From behind the case she pulled out several small drawers, and selected three or four of the items.

At last I looked up to see Monsieur Savoy descending. He looked exactly as I remembered: the large head and shoulders on a smallish frame; the small feet, the lock of brown hair. I would have thought the approach of the proprietor of a shop would subdue the atmosphere. Instead, the room seemed to brighten when he entered it. He had a pleasant smile, and an almost lyrical voice. His brown eyes were puzzled. He did not remember me at all. And who could have expected him to?

"Did you wish to see me?" he said.

I know I must have grown flushed with excitement and nervousness combined. My hands were icy cold. "I did not mean to be a bother," I said quickly. "We met in Houston once; I gave you a carriage ride. But it was long ago."

He thought for a few moments, then his eyes lit up. "Yes, yes, now I remember. I had not enough time to make my appointment and you saved the day for me. How good it is to see you again. Excuse me for taking so long." He took my hand and made a little courtesy bow, glancing into my eyes as he did so, no doubt amazed at the temperature of my hand.

"Don't let me keep you. I only wanted to say hello. And I think Mrs. Gerrard is about to make a purchase," I said.

Alvareda looked around and introduced herself. Monsieur Savoy invited us for coffee, and she waved us on. "You go. I'll join you later."

I could have gone through the floor. I did not want to be left to conversation with this Frenchman. He put a hand on his chin and said, "Is this your first visit to New Orleans?"

"Yes."

"Have you had beignets? *Café au lait?*"

"No."

"My daughter Renée is making beignets upstairs—that is where we live. Come, let me take you to the courtyard in back. You can rest there while I tell Renée we have a guest."

"Oh, but it isn't necessary. I can come again, when you aren't so busy." The words rushed out like champagne uncorked.

"Not at all. I would have stopped anyway. I always do, this time of morning."

He opened a back door, and the sunlight streamed in. I would never have dreamed the little courtyard before me was hidden among the buildings. He showed me to a small iron table, and pulled out a chair for me. "It's lovely," I said.

"This is one of my favorite spots. I come here to get away from everyone and everything. It is my 'thinking place.' " He disappeared inside again. I let my eyes travel slowly around the area. It was small compared with others I had seen, and all around it were shutters with wide fan windows above. Through the rear was a wooden gate leading out to another street, and just beyond the street I could see another stairway, another iron lace balcony. It gave me the feeling this was a fairy-tale world that went on into infinity. The outside world of traffic and street noises did not exist on the same plane. If you went through the gate, and so to another little narrow street and another courtyard, you would not be working your way back toward the busy world because it was not there . . . there was only more of the same. . . .

I breathed a sigh and relaxed. I no longer felt nervous and concerned about whether I would be clever or charming. There were beautiful blooming things all around me. If Monsieur Savoy was a gardener, then we would have much to say to each other.

The door swung open. Out came Renée in her apron, carrying a large tray with silver urn, china cups, snowy cloth and napkins, and a silver basket lined with napkins, covering the piping hot beignets. She had grown into a fetching dark-eyed girl. She had hair to her waist, light brown and shimmering clean, held back with a band. She wore a light blue dress with a lace collar and dark stockings above her white shoes. "Come, Papa," she said, and Monsieur Savoy sat down and handed me a napkin.

"Papa, may I be excused from Grand'mère's today?"

"No. I am sorry."

When she was gone I said, "What a charming girl."

He nodded and smiled. "I'm proud of her. She will go to school in France next year, to study medicine. Of course, this is painful for Mère—my mother."

"Oh, I see. She lives with you?"

"No, no. She lives up on Esplanade Avenue in a great big house. Mère is a proud aristocrat," he said with a wink. "She rarely comes to the shop. . . . Here, eat while they are hot. You must first sprinkle them with the powdered sugar."

I did as he said and took a bite of the pillow-shaped donut. It was a little heavier than the doughnuts we ate at home, but seemed to melt away even before I swallowed it. Immediately I realized how fattening it must be. Monsieur Savoy was filling my cup with *café au lait,* hot milk and coffee at the same time. "I will not need to eat again today," I told him.

He laughed. "In New Orleans food is regarded as a precious jewel, every meal a feast. That is why I am heavy around here," he said, patting his waist.

"I don't like to think what I would be like after living here for a while. I have enough trouble already. I've always been too large."

"Too large?" he said in surprise. *"Mon Dieu!* Your carriage is statuesque. Today's fashion was created with you in mind—the large hats, the tiered skirts and soft bo-deece. You ought to let me make something up for you. A tea dress of batiste and val lace, pearl buttons and a little train. It would look *élégant* on you."

Never had anyone's words made me feel so attractive. I smiled. "It would be nice, but beyond my budget, I'm afraid. How did you come to be in the lace business?"

"My cousins started the shop in 1870, and I took it over in 1895 when they returned to France. Now they broker for me overseas."

"Then you don't have to go there to buy lace?"

"Oh yes, I go twice a year. But they deal with the factories and the convents. It saves me a lot of time and trouble. Before I took over the shop, I worked as a tailor down on Chartres Street."

"How long have you been in this country?"

"I was born here. My mother was married twice—first to a Frenchman, in France, and after he died, to my father, who was a Creole. She met him while visiting here. After he died she decided to stay and look after me and my daughters. A few months before my father died, my wife passed away."

"Oh, I am sorry."

He shrugged. "It was very hard at first, but life continues." He took a sip of coffee, then added, "I worry only for the girls, especially Genevieve. They have only me and their grand'mère. And she is strict with them, too much so. So many customs, so many rules. That is why we don't live in the same house. *Mon Dieu!* I could not bear that any more than the girls could," he laughed.

"How old is Genevieve?"

"Twelve. She is a good little girl. Both my children are good to their father. And we have a good life together here. When Renée goes next year, I will miss her very much. But I must let her go—like a little bird, she must learn to fly. Do you have children?"

"Two. My husband spoils our daughter. Our son is constantly at my side."

"It's always so. Fathers and daughters, mothers and sons. Have another beignet."

"Oh, I mustn't—"

"Come, come. In Houston you can watch your figure. Enjoy New Orleans while you can."

I told him I had certainly enjoyed sitting in his courtyard, and we talked of flowers, for he was interested in gardening though he only supervised the work done here. He said, "In the afternoons when I am not too busy, I come here again to watch the four o'clocks bloom. They are my favorites because they bloom late, when everything else in the garden has closed up . . . . they bring a spot of color as the daylight fades."

I had seen four o'clocks before—they were related to the bougainvillea—but I had never thought of them in this way. It seemed to me unusual that a busy shopkeeper still had time to consider the beauty of a simple flower, and it seemed to me, too, that Monsieur Savoy was a more attractive man than I had realized. We lingered over coffee far longer than I expected, talking of one subject then another. He had not been back to the Not-Su-Oh festival since the year we met, but thought he might be going this fall. He thought it would be nice if he could take my husband and me out to dinner while in Houston.

I looked down, not knowing quite what to say. I did not like being reminded of Beryl in this setting. I did not think that an evening spent with Monsieur Savoy and Beryl would have any chance of success. "That—that is nice of you," I murmured, then I told him I must go.

He picked a gardenia from the bush nearby and handed it to me. "These are just beginning to bloom. In two weeks, the fragrance in the courtyard will be almost overpowering."

I put it to my nostrils and smiled. "You're very kind," I said.

When we returned to the shop a clerk told me that Mrs. Gerrard had gone on to keep an engagement at eleven. It was now half past that hour. "Oh dear, I've taken too much of your time," I said, suddenly ill at ease again and wishing Alvareda had signaled me she was leaving.

"Not at all. Come, I'll show you some beautiful lace." And so we spent till one o'clock inside the shop. He seated me near the back and showed me one piece of finery after another, pausing only now and then to ask a question, or give some advice to a customer. He began by showing me a piece of narrow val lace—which he explained was so called for the village in France called Valenciennes, where it originated. The shortened name resulted from the inability to pronounce such a name, he said. "There are two kinds, one handmade; one, machine made. They look much the same. Can you tell?"

I looked at the two pieces and told him I could not.

"Here—see the ground, the net part? Machine-made val lace has a diamond-shaped ground. Handmade has the honeycomb ground."

"I wish I had brought my wedding veil. I'd like for you to see it. It's point de gaze from Belgium."

"Ah, and I would like to. Point de gaze is the finest lace there is, to my mind. Take good care of it. Here. I'll show you how it is made."

He brought out a piece about the same width as mine, and explained the tedious process. "One woman makes the flowers, one makes the ground, one makes the leaves, another sews it all together. It takes six or seven women around six months to produce about one and a half yards."

He wrapped it up and replaced it in the drawer. I wanted so much to buy something from his shop. I glanced around, trying to think of something I could afford, that Beryl would not be furious with me for buying. Suddenly I knew. "Monsieur Savoy, I wonder if I could order a dress made for my daughter Senta, to have her picture made."

"Of course. How old is she?"

"Nearly six."

He nodded. "Could you bring her with you tomorrow, so that we can measure her?" He tapped his pencil on the counter. "And I might suggest a French bonnet, too. We have some upstairs that just arrived—"

"I'm not certain I can persuade Senta to take time off from her vacation for such a chore."

"Very well, then. Send the measurements to me." He wrote down what he would need on the back of a business card, and handed it to me.

"It has been a very interesting day," I told him. "Thank you for taking so much time with me."

"The pleasure has been mine." He took my hand as I rose from the stool and walked me to the door. "Your hand is warmer now," he smiled. "Enjoy your stay. *Bonjour.*"

"Good day, Monsieur Savoy."

All the way back to the hotel I thought of Monsieur Savoy. The hours had flown. We had walked into the shop shortly after ten. It would soon be two o'clock. Did he take this much time with every visitor? Or, was it possible he simply enjoyed my company as much as I enjoyed his? Well, no matter. I'd probably never see him again. But if I never had another happy moment in New Orleans, I would always savor the trip. Monsieur was truly a gentleman. One could not feature him ever being angry or crude. Not like—no, no, it was wrong to make comparisons. I mustn't let myself think about him. I would not take Senta back tomorrow, and maybe I should not send the measurements. I would have to think about that, consider the expense. I had not even asked about the cost of a dress, not to mention a bonnet. I had allowed myself to be carried away by the moment. I reminded myself that the French shopkeeper had no interest in me beyond a need to reciprocate a kindness of years ago, and he had more than done that today.

The next three days were much the same as the first two except that, occasionally while watching the children at play, my mind would return to the hours spent with Monsieur Savoy. As we traveled home on the train, speeding further and further away from New Orleans, the Frenchman with his elegant shop, his smiling face and gentle manner became smaller and smaller in my mind, until at last he seemed the object of the fairy-tale setting which, in reality, did not exist at all.

Our train pulled into Houston at nine o'clock in the evening, and it was past ten when we finally arrived home. I looked anxiously toward the house wondering in what state we would find Beryl. Cautiously I turned the door handle and looked in. He was not in the front parlor. I could hear a strange voice from the library. "We're home," I called hesitantly.

Beryl walked through the door. He did not appear to have been drinking, and was obviously glad to see us. My heart was flooded with relief. Senta leaped into her father's arms and began to tell him excitedly about New

Orleans. John went up to Beryl for a kiss, then retreated to my skirt tail. Then the visitor appeared.

"This is Joseph West, an old friend from school days," said Beryl. I nodded and extended my hand. Immediately the name was familiar, but I could not think of why. He was small and lean, with thinning hair. His eyes were dark and the brow above was discerning and expressive. He was informally dressed —in black jersey and well-cut trousers—yet he was immaculately groomed. His hair was neatly trimmed; his fingernails were smoothly manicured. There was something very different about him. "Are you from Illinois?" I asked.

He smiled and said he was, then added, "The word 'from' is more than appropriate. I'm stopping here a few days, on my way to California. I've accepted a position at Stanford."

"Joseph will be our house guest for a few days," said Beryl. There was no glare of warning in his eye as I might have expected.

"I hope I won't be imposing, but Beryl insisted."

"Of course. We're glad to have you," I told him, uncertainly. In fact I was too tired for entertaining and hadn't stocked the pantry since before we left for New Orleans. Moreover, I was surprised Beryl entertained while I was away. Surely he would have found it easier to ask Mr. West to stay in a hotel. Oh well, I would not make an issue of any of this, even in private. Such a cultured gentleman was a great improvement over the kind of friends Beryl had been keeping lately and I wanted him to realize I welcomed Mr. West. Yet, it struck me as odd that after all these years an old school friend would look up Beryl, who didn't even practice his profession anymore. . . .

As it happened, Joseph West was a pleasure of a house guest. At his own request, he occupied the little sleeping porch upstairs. Each morning I found his bed made neatly and the room in order. After breakfast he helped clear the table before leaving with Beryl. They spent the days sight-seeing and looking at various buildings around town, while Beryl's employees supervised the store. They never invited me and the children to come. I did not mind. I had plenty to do after having been away a week. The yard needed my attention more than anything, and I spent much of the days working in the flower beds and bushes. Though the name Joseph West tugged at my memory, I could not place it.

Within a few days the trash basket in the library was full of rough sketches of furniture designs—apparently Mr. West's main interest—and one morning as I emptied it, I found a note near the bottom on a piece of heavy stationery. I noticed it was from Joseph West to Beryl, dated two weeks previous. "I expect to arrive on the twelfth at nine o'clock, but don't bother meeting my train. The timing is perfect for me, for I will have more than two weeks before I have to be in California. I'm so glad you thought to write me. . . ."

I stared at the signature for a few moments, then realized where I had seen it before. It was at the bottom of the letter about Beryl's dismissal from school. I found the letter and compared. Yes, this was the man who tried to help Beryl.

I thought about it some more. The date mentioned in the note was the day after I left for New Orleans. For some reason, the men wished to visit alone. Though I puzzled over it for a while, I finally dismissed it. Could Joseph West do something to help Beryl now, I would hear about it soon enough. Perhaps he was talking to people he knew in Houston.

Joseph was with us eight days in all, and the only problem we encountered was with Senta. She was extremely jealous of anyone taking up her father's time. She was constantly on Beryl's lap when he was at home, insisted upon sitting by him at the dinner table, and at nighttime could barely be gotten to bed. She begged to be allowed to stay up until her father went to bed, and when that failed she insisted Beryl tuck her in. This he did, uncomplainingly, and would often sit up there with her until she went to sleep. What a good father he can be when he wants to, I thought. Maybe now, since things had been going smoothly for nearly a month, everything would be better.

On the morning Beryl took Joseph West to the train station, I took Senta's measurements so that I could order a dress from Monsieur Savoy. It might be expensive, but she would never have an opportunity to have another. It would be a keepsake, like a wedding veil or a christening gown. Alvareda and Neal had already mentioned they would return to New Orleans in January and would like for us to join them again. I had refused because I could not imagine leaving Beryl so soon again, especially since his attitude was much improved. Further, I did not feel right in imposing on them again. I would simply ask Alvareda to pay my respects to Monsieur Savoy while in New Orleans, and pick up Senta's dress.

Along with the measurements, I sent a one-page letter to Monsieur Savoy, explaining that the dress would probably be a First Communion dress and should have a little cape to match, plus the French bonnet. Otherwise, I would leave the design . . . "to you," I wrote. Then I looked at it and decided to change it to read, "in your capable hands." When he hears from me this time, I mused, he will probably remember me. But perhaps vaguely. Maybe I should have thanked him again for the refreshments. Maybe I should have asked about his daughters, his mother. Now that I began to think about it, the letter seemed cold and impersonal. Why had I not made it warm, conversational?

Finally I paused. What difference did it make? Why was I worrying about the letter? I was only ordering a dress, after all.

Two weeks after I mailed the letter, I received a response written in Monsieur Savoy's own hand. As I read the message in the tall, slanted scrawl, I realized he had not forgotten anything about my visit. He said that he could have the dress ready much sooner than January, but that he was going on a buying trip in September, and would like to take that opportunity to shop especially for the fabric and lace. He said that he usually took his outstanding orders along on trips, with that object in mind. He would wait until then to work on a design, but he did feel that flounces were always good for a little girl for they gave her growing room. And maybe two liners, one petal pink and one white, to make the dress more versatile.

His enthusiasm sang forth from the page. He asked if there were any chance I might come to New Orleans in January. I read the letter three times, including the closing, *"Meilleurs voeux.* Paul Philippe Savoy." And I thought: Oh, if only I could say yes. If only I could see him again.

Chapter 6

Through the summer of last year and up into the fall, I felt I had some control over our situation at home. If I did certain things, these would result in certain others. If Beryl brought home his employees for a night of card playing—he soon fell again into this habit—I would not complain as I cleaned up after them the next morning. If Beryl came claiming his conjugal rights, I cooperated as fully as one can when there is no feeling of warmth or affection. I built a little shell around me that he could not penetrate with words, and when he sometimes apologized for one thing or another, I always told him it was all right, that I knew he didn't mean it. And that was what I told myself. Beryl provides a living for us, I would remind myself. He has never been cruel to the children. In fact, if anything, he is overindulgent. He doesn't mean to be cruel to me, it's only that he is frustrated by his failed career. One day everything will change.

Inevitably, I was tripped up when something out of the ordinary occurred. It had to do with Senta. She was now in first grade at Holy Sacrament Catholic School, and while she was a sharp little pupil—she was advanced in arithmetic and spelling, and could read on the third-grade level—she was a troublemaker, and never made a high mark in deportment. The nuns at the small school felt she might be bored. I felt that, while that might be true, she was also spoiled. She was sassy to me and to others, and threw fits when things did not go her way. I tried to discipline her, but Beryl ruined everything I tried to accomplish by siding with her.

On this occasion, she became angry when another little girl mistakenly got hold of a drawing she had done. On the playground later, Senta pushed her down and pulled her hair. This was the final straw for Sister Johanna Marie, and she called me at home to ask me to come to the school. Unfortunately, I was not there. Next, Sister called Beryl at the bicycle shop, not knowing his temperament and his devotion to Senta. Beryl, who had begun drinking early in the day, came storming up to the school to defend his daughter. I was told nothing of the incident that night.

The next morning Sister called me again, this time reaching me. I hurried down to the school for a conference. Sister sat across from me at her big wooden desk with a picture of the Virgin and a crucifix on the wall behind her. Her hands were folded as though to offer prayer. She had been an educator for many years, and had seen many children enter and leave the halls of Holy Sacrament School. Today her eyes were kind and ageless, but her chin was set in determination. She told me everything. With each detail, I felt my heart beat a little faster.

"Often a father finds it difficult to see his daughter objectively," she said, "but frankly Mr. Farrish behaved quite unreasonably." Then she considered a moment before continuing. "Mrs. Farrish, I hope you will understand my asking this question—does your husband have a drinking problem?"

I was mortified. To think, how I had worried about concealing this from family and friends. And now to have the head of Senta's school discover it. I did not know what to say to her. "Oh no," I lied, my voice faint. "I'm sure you were mistaken about his having been drinking. You must understand that he is so fond of Senta. In his eyes, she can do no wrong." Sister continued to look at me, her expression unchanged.

"It's unfortunate you didn't reach me at first. But now that I know, I'll have a serious talk with her. And if this kind of thing happens again, please contact—"

"Mrs. Farrish, you are aware of our problems with Senta. I'm afraid if this kind of thing ever happens again, we'll have to dismiss her. I'm not at all sure this is the right school for your daughter. I've thought of double promoting her, but I'm afraid her immature behavior prevents it. If it were only boredom, but . . . well, we'll let the matter go for now."

"Very well, and thank you so much for understanding. I feel certain I can correct Senta's behavior."

All the way home I could see Sister's face. Nothing I said impressed her; my lies did not fool her. Beryl probably smelled like the Southern Select brewery. And Sister knew I was powerless to control or "correct" my daughter. A less experienced school administrator might have believed me and had faith in my ability to change my daughter; Sister Johanna Marie was seasoned, however. From the moment I arrived home till Senta returned at the end of the school day, I considered how best to get across to her the necessity for change. I could not threaten her with anything. Punish her in any fashion and she would run to her daddy. I was trapped. I would have to try and reason with her.

When she got home I gave her milk and cookies at the kitchen table, then told her that I had found out what had happened at school. I told her the consequences Sister had laid out should she misbehave again. While telling her this, I suddenly realized this was exactly the sort of behavior that got her father kicked out of the university. I came very near telling her this, and stopped myself just in time. Finally I said, "What do you intend to do about your behavior?"

She cocked her blond head and sent me a warning glance. "No one is going to take my drawings and get away with it."

I sighed. "But people make mistakes, Senta. Angela didn't know it was your drawing."

"She should have. Next time she will."

I glanced up and shook my head helplessly. "Senta, do you like having friends?"

She shrugged, and took a sip of milk.

"How many friends do you have?"

"Lilly is my friend. She always does what I tell her."

"Is that how you count someone for a friend?" I asked, exasperated. "I mean, of course Lilly is your friend. But she is your friend because she loves you and you love her back, because you enjoy things together."

Another shrug.

"How many friends do you have at school?"

She thought. "I don't really like anyone at school. They're all dumb."

"Oh, I think you're wrong. You may be a little advanced in some subjects, but you aren't so smart if you don't know how to behave."

She tossed her sausage curls. Clearly, she was bored with this conversation and I was getting nowhere. Without the threat of punishment hanging out there in front of her, she knew I had no power over her. At last I said, "Let me give you some advice. Nobody likes a little smart aleck. Nobody likes a troublemaker. If you don't straighten up, you won't have any friends, and if you are dismissed from school, you'll simply have to go to another school and face the same problems there. I sometimes wonder if you realize how lucky you are to attend a fine school like Holy Sacrament. If you don't appreciate it enough to behave, then they'll find a little girl who does appreciate it to take your place. And you will be humiliated—ashamed—to be put in another school because you were bad. Do you understand? You're only hurting yourself by your poor conduct."

"So what? Daddy says you have to be smart to get anywhere. I'm smart. He says friends don't matter, no one ever did anything for him. Anyway, whatever happens, Daddy will take care of me. . . . Can I go play now?"

I waved her away. There was no reasoning with her on the subject of her father.

At the door she turned and said, "I got two hundreds today, in arithmetic and handwriting."

I was too exasperated to respond. Because I got nowhere with Senta, I seethed all afternoon. Beryl and I simply had to come to terms with her behavior before it grew any worse. I was anxious for him to get home so that we could talk about it. At seven-thirty I realized he would probably come in very late, and be in no shape to talk. Still, I could not give up, nor did I want to put it off. I wanted to get it over with, and tonight. By then I was too angry to be completely reasonable. I finally went to bed at eleven, but I sat up against the pillows, waiting, till two in the morning. Then I heard noises downstairs, and realized I'd fallen asleep. Beryl and his entourage were playing cards again.

I picked up a book and started reading. At four o'clock I finally heard the front door open and shut, and Beryl on the stairs. I was bone tired and impatient, angry with Senta, angry with him. I confronted him with the problem when he walked in the door.

"So, put her in another school," he said flippantly.

"And what then? What happens when she misbehaves there? Move her again? When are you going to make her behave?"

"There's nothing wrong with her behavior. That old bitch who heads up the school ought to be taken out and drowned, along with those other hooded old bags she works with."

"Oh, can't you see you've spoiled her miserably? I can't discipline her. She knows you will defy me every time."

By now he had sat down on the bed. He looked around at me and said, "Who are you to tell me how to raise my daughter? How could anyone like you understand someone like Senta?"

"What do you mean by that?" I snapped.

"Senta is a beautiful, headstrong little girl. She is the kind that always gets what she wants because she has the gumption to demand it. You don't have to worry about Senta. She's just like me. I only hope she'll have sense enough not to marry a weak sniveling fool like I did."

That was it. I'd reached the end. I got close to his face. "Oh, you're such a great success, are you? Is that why you got kicked out of school?"

There was a moment of intense silence, when I realized I had said more than I intended to, and a multitude of conclusions came together in his mind. He put his hands on my shoulders and shook me. "What are you talking about?"

"I'm sorry! Don't! You're hurting me. Stop it."

"How did you know about that? Did Joseph tell you?"

"No. I found out by accident, from a letter he wrote to you," I said almost in a whisper, and clenched my hands.

"So, you also open other people's mail, do you? You stinking bitch, I ought to kill you," he said, and knocked me in the chin with his fist. The blow was so hard I fell from the bed, and I think he would have gone on hitting me except that I just scooted underneath the bed and lay huddled with my face protected. I had never been so shocked, never so completely terrified. My teeth began to chatter, my shoulders to shake. The lower part of my face felt as though it had been shattered like a piece of glass.

He was shouting at me, "Get out from under there or I'll pull you out, I'll —" He broke off. Senta herself was banging on the door. "Daddy, Daddy! What's the matter? Let me in!"

I stayed there, sobbing, praying in whispers, "Please, God, please, please. . . ."

Beryl opened the door slightly. Then, in a voice that had grown amazingly calm, he told Senta, "I was telling Mommy about something that happened at work. I didn't mean to get so loud. I'm sorry. Go back to bed, honey."

"Could you tuck me in, Daddy?"

He paused. "Yes. I'll be there in a shake. Run along now, sweetheart."

This seemed to satisfy her. At least I was relieved she had provided a break in Beryl's rage. He stood at the door momentarily, then at last he walked out and closed it softly behind him. I waited while he stopped by Senta's room, not daring to move, fearing he'd come back and hit me again. At last I heard the leaded glass doors downstairs open and shut.

I emerged from under the bed and crawled back up on the mattress. There I stayed till the sun shone through the window, my body quaking for a long while until I finally managed to breathe deeply, and, at last, to become still. Calmer now, I began to reflect. How stupid I had been to provoke this. Why could I not do the right things to keep peace? What an awful, clumsy way to confront someone with the mistakes of his past. For the first time in all our years of arguing, I was ready to take full blame. I could not imagine where we might go from here. I went to the dresser and peered into the mirror at my sore chin. It was feverish to the touch, but I did not think the jaw was broken, only bruised. The whole area was already swollen. I went downstairs for a hot, wet towel. I had no idea how large the area would become before it started to go down. And now we were edging close to the holidays. Stupidly, I had invited my family over for Thanksgiving dinner, everyone including Patricia and George and their family.

Well, I would simply cancel dinner, pretend to be sick. I would not see anyone until my chin was healed. I fixed the children's breakfast, and went to bed. I had to leave Senta in charge of John for an hour or two. I simply could not stay up any longer and Beryl had not shown up as yet. I fell asleep at eight o'clock, and did not awaken till two in the afternoon.

When I went downstairs I found a large box in the front parlor. At the bottom right-hand corner there was, stylishly lettered in gold, "Savoy Fine Lace and Linen Company."

I opened the box in astonishment. Here was the dress and bonnet for Senta, wrapped in deep purple paper. It could not have been more beautiful, with pin tucks across the bodice, elbow-length sleeves with lace medallions, and four flounces edged in chantilly lace. The two liners were there, petal pink and white. The big ruffled bonnet had an exchangeable ribbon as well.

As I was looking at it in wonder, Beryl walked in from the kitchen. I looked up in alarm. "Oh—oh, I didn't realize you were back."

He said nothing. His rage appeared to be spent. I hesitated, then placed my hand on the box. "Were you here when this arrived?"

"Yes, and it's a good thing, since you were sleeping the day away. The man said it was for Senta."

My heart skipped a beat. No delivery man would have known that. I tried to sound unconcerned. "Oh? Who delivered it?"

"I never saw him before. He had a little girl with him."

Oh dear, I thought, Monsieur Savoy and his daughter Genevieve. I remembered he had said he might come again to Not-Su-Oh. Apparently the dress was ready so he decided to bring it himself.

"Did he say anything?"

"He asked for you. I told him you weren't here. That was about all. He didn't leave a card or anything."

I could just feature it. There was Beryl, in his work pants and knitted underwear, unshaven, hair uncombed. No wonder Monsieur Savoy had not left his card. Lucky he did not come in, and see the mess from last night's card game. I was so embarrassed. I knew I would never hear from him again. I kept standing there.

"Friend of yours?" Beryl said.

I paused. "No," I told him. "I'd ordered this dress while in New Orleans. I thought it would come through the mail."

He shrugged, and started to walk out. "Wait, Beryl," I said. "I'm sorry about last night. I've known about the university for a long time. I did not want to tell you because there seemed no point. Yet, when it comes to Senta, I think we have to be realistic. I don't want her to get into trouble. I'm sure you will agree with that."

He turned and scowled at me. "What do I care if you know what happened at the university? They were all fools, dangling their diploma in front of me and making me dance for it. The day will come when I'll show them up for what they are. And as for Senta, she'll take care of herself." He left the room.

I looked down at the beautiful dress and thought, This was made with a little angel in mind. Wearing it, Senta will look the part. But God have mercy on her. She's anything but an angel.

Chapter 7

As the days went by, it bothered me more and more that Monsieur Savoy had received such a true impression of the way we lived. I did not like him to think he had wasted his time and effort to create something beautiful only to turn it over to a family that must have appeared almost . . . seedy. One sensed that he cared greatly about every article that went out of his shop. He had included a long set of printed instructions about the care of Senta's dress in the box. The last of these encouraged me to contact the shop if I had any questions.

Savoy dealt in articles to be passed from one generation to the next. When he arrived at our doorstep, he must have expected a family inside who lived like normal people.

Instead there was Beryl. Oh, how I hated all this. Without knowing what I would say to Monsieur Savoy, how I would explain without appearing totally foolish, I felt I must see him again and at least try. I called Alvareda and told her I had changed my mind and would join them in the trip to New Orleans. I was not sure how Beryl would react, nor did I care. When I told him, he only shrugged and said, "Going down to see your friend?"

I pretended not to know who he was referring to. "What are you talking about?"

He smirked. I know he was thinking what an absurdity that I should have captured the interest of another man. "Go wherever you like," he said. "Senta could use a departure from her dull routine. I assume you mean to take her."

"Of course," I told him. "And John . . . unless he is sick like he was most of last winter. Then we'll all stay home."

Beryl walked out the door. I began to pray that John would stay well.

We left for New Orleans on the morning train January 2, 1914. I had decided not to bring the wedding veil. All that had happened made me uncertain if Monsieur Savoy would still care to occupy his time examining it. The frozen weather outside formed a filmy vapor all over the window glass and Alvareda and I sat in the dining car, over steaming cups of coffee. At first we talked of the children. Gabriel had just returned to Harvard after his first Christmas vacation since he went away. Clayton had been double promoted once, and his teachers were inclined to double promote him again, but Alvareda and Neal stepped in and prevented them from doing so because they felt he was too immature and had enough trouble developing friendships as it was.

"It reminds me of our problems with Senta. At least he is not spoiled in the way she is, thanks to Beryl," I told her.

She paused, then changed the subject. "What made you decide to come?" she asked.

"Oh . . . I don't know. I just felt like getting away," I told her. "When Monsieur Savoy brought Senta's dress by, I wasn't even there to receive it. I just wanted to extend my thanks."

"But you could have done that with a note," she said. "Elzyna, is everything all right at home?"

"Certainly."

"Is Beryl still enjoying his business?"

"To the extent he can enjoy anything other than design. Why the questions?"

"I just wonder about you. You never talk to me anymore, not like you used to. Yet you don't seem . . . well, you don't seem happy."

"Oh? Well, I would tell you if anything was troubling me. As to happiness, I have my share of blessings. I don't forget that."

She continued to look at me for a long moment, then apparently decided not to pursue the questions any further. I was grateful. I longed to confide in Alvareda, to tell her all that had happened between Beryl and me, yet I did not want to force her into sharing my troubles because there was nothing she could do to help.

I had intended to go to Savoy Fine Lace and Linen as soon as we arrived. Yet I lost courage. It was within an hour of closing time, I rationalized, and Monsieur Savoy would be much too busy. Best to go early in the day. Yet I mustn't arrive at the usual time for coffee, or he would feel obligated to invite me to join with him in a cup. Perhaps he drank it upstairs in his quarters in the wintertime, and if so I would really be intruding.

When I awoke the next morning, a bleak one of gray skies and threatening rain, I almost put it off again. So easy just to stay in the hotel suite and let the children play with their toys. The log fire was warm and cheerful.

Yet, if not to see Monsieur Savoy, for what had I come all this way? I got up, arranged for Mrs. Hester to sit with the children, and dressed. For Christmas Alvareda had given me a beige-colored batiste blouse, with lace inserts coming to a point down the front, and a high collar with lace ruffle and lace ruffles on the long sleeves. She had bought it for me last time we were here, while I sat with Monsieur Savoy in the courtyard. I put on the blouse and chose a dark green suit which he had not seen. How foolish I am, I thought.

He would not notice the suit, and would notice the blouse only because it came from his shop.

I felt very nervous as I finally walked down Royal Street. I had failed to realize before that this part of the street was more exclusive in every way than other blocks. Fine antique shops, one after another, were lined up on both sides. People who walked the streets—and there were not many on this kind of day—were well dressed. They alighted from fancy landaus and expensive automobiles. As I walked I felt more ridiculous, and more alone. When Alvareda was with me it was different. She lent me her air of command, at least on the outside.

When I reached the entrance to Savoy's, my stomach was in knots. Alvareda was right. I could have simply written him a note. And probably would have seemed far more sensible. I timidly pushed on the door. Still time to—

"May I help, madame?" said a clerk.

"Yes, I would like to speak to Monsieur Savoy, please."

"I am sorry, but Monsieur Savoy is not available this morning. Perhaps I can help you."

Now I felt even worse. "Perhaps I could come back another time, if he isn't here."

"He is upstairs, madame, but very busy. You see, Mardi Gras is soon, and he has much to do before time for the big parades and parties. He gave explicit orders he did not want to be disturbed. . . . Perhaps I could show you something."

"No . . . no, it's all right. I needed to speak with him," I told her, trying to sound dignified, as though I had an important errand.

"I see. Would you like to leave a message?" she asked, drawing out paper and pen.

"All right. Yes." I sat down on a stool and tried to think how to express my feelings in three or four lines. The clerk had discreetly walked away, thank goodness. I did not want to take too long, else she would think I was as foolish as I probably was. "Dear Monsieur—" I began, "I stopped in to say thank you for my daughter's lovely dress. Sorry I missed you while you were in Houston." I stopped. Should I add, "Perhaps another time"? No. There would be no other time. The clerk was looking toward me now. I hastily wrote, "Sincerely yours, Elzyna Farrish." I folded the note and stuffed it in the envelope. I nodded toward the clerk and rose.

"I'll see that he gets it," she promised. "Good day."

The bell above the door tinkled merrily behind me as I left. I started down Royal. I wished I could disappear into a hole in the street. How stupid. I should never have come. I crossed the street and walked down the next block. Foolish, foolish woman. Alvareda must have realized my motives. I was so afraid he would think less of me because of Beryl that I came all the way here just to reassure him. He could not interrupt his busy schedule for that. How ridiculous. I was so angry with myself. It served me right. It—

"Mrs. Farrish?"

I turned. Hastening down the block, without a coat, his shirt sleeves rolled up, the measuring tape dangling from his neck, was Monsieur Savoy. I waved and waited. I have never been so happy to see anyone in my life, even while I still felt perfectly ridiculous.

He drew up and took both my hands in his. "Why didn't you tell the clerk who you were and insist on seeing me?"

"I didn't want to bother you. I can imagine how busy—"

"Nonsense. One is never too busy to see a friend, especially one from far away. Come, we'll stop and have some coffee."

I suddenly realized he must be freezing. "Poor Monsieur Savoy, I'm so sorry to have dragged you into this weather."

"Please call me Paul. Everyone does," he said.

"You may call me Elzyna," I quickly told him, excitement rippling over me. We walked down the block and into a little shop which had a big bakery shelf and a few tables. We sat down and ordered coffee. I could not think what I would say next. He smiled at me. "It's so good to see you again."

I told him about Senta having her picture made in the dress, about Alvareda having given me the blouse, which he recognized at once. I asked him how his holiday had been and he said they had had dinner as usual with his mother. All the while we spoke of trivial things, I was aware of him in a way that I had not been before. His arms were stocky and, I could see in the absence of sleeves, covered with brown tufts of hair. His hands were surprisingly small and delicate for such a . . . was the word brawny? . . . physique. He expressed much with his hands as he talked. I had not noticed that before either. He had dark brown, magnetic eyes framed with thick lashes, and there were moments as we talked when I felt as though his gaze sank all the way into me, and would have to force my eyes away then let them travel back again. There was also a sympathetic quality about his voice that made me want to tell him what truly was in my heart. When there was a pause, I said, "I apologize for the inhospitable way you found us when you were in Houston. I was not feeling well that morning and—"

He smiled and nodded. "The . . . gentleman . . . who answered the door told me that. That was . . . Mr. Farrish?"

I knew by the stilted phrasing that he was puzzled by Beryl. I nodded. "He was not at his best either," I explained. "He—he had been up with me in the night, you see."

He nodded politely. "Well, I should have telephoned first, but I really did not want to bother you except to deliver the dress. I'm so glad Senta likes it. It's similar to a design I did last year for another little girl's First Communion," he began. I still was frustrated by the impression he received of us. I took the opportunity to further explain Beryl.

"My husband is a designer, too," I said, and explained that Beryl was an architect. Then because I did not want to lead into something that would force me to lie to him, I said, "He is very gifted, but right now is not working at designing. He owns a small repair shop. Someday I hope he'll be able to design again full time."

He considered me thoughtfully. "Yes, it is frustrating not to be able to pursue one's chosen profession."

I looked down. "Yes. He is very, very frustrated," I said without thinking. Then I looked up and stopped. I feared he guessed so much more than I was telling him. I looked away. "To tell you the truth, I was so embarrassed when you came and saw—I didn't want you to think that I—we—I knew how much trouble you had gone to, how hard you had worked on the dress. I was afraid you would think that it would not be taken care of or appreciated. I was afraid you would think I was rude for not even having the courtesy to come downstairs and greet you. I—" I stopped and drew in a breath. I could have killed myself. . . . "I've taken up too much of your time. I really must get back." My fingers clutched my handbag.

"Elzyna, did you come all the way here just to apologize?"

"Yes, and now I feel more ridiculous than ever. I can't imagine what you must think of me," I said. In a moment I would be crying. Oh, if only I could just get away.

He reached for my hands. "I am so flattered and pleased you would think that much of me."

I rose from my chair. I had to get out of here.

"Could I see you again? Tonight, perhaps?"

"Oh, I couldn't possibly. That would not be—"

He clicked his tongue thoughtfully, then said, "How about you and the Gerrards? You could be my guest at dinner. Please say you will."

I looked at him again. "I would have to ask them. They may have other plans," I said, yet hoping they would not.

"Will you call me later and let me know? Just tell the clerk who answers the telephone your name, and they will connect you with me."

I nodded, and turned to go.

"You look even more lovely when distressed, Madame Farrish. *Bonjour.*"

"He is only trying to be kind," I told Alvareda when we both sat by the fireside in the suite that afternoon. A message had been delivered that Paul Philippe Savoy would be "in line" at Galatoire's at half-past seven, unless I instructed him otherwise.

Alvareda raised her brow. "Then he is most remarkably kind," she said.

"And look, he did not even give you a chance to call with your answer before he confirmed the appointment."

"I explained that you and Neal probably had other plans."

"No. Tomorrow night we're to meet Prissy and Wallace LeCourt, but tonight Neal has a stuffy business dinner. He has been looking for an opportunity to get out of it. . . . Of course, if you would rather go alone with—"

"Ah, you know I could not do that," I protested, color rising to my cheeks. She nodded and smiled.

When Neal arrived we asked him what was meant by "in line."

"Exactly what it says," he answered. Galatoire's was a favorite place of cotton men in New Orleans and Neal had been there before. He explained that reservations were not accepted, and as there was no place inside to stand in line—much less sit and wait for your table—you must stand outside, regardless of the weather, regardless of how important you were, and wait till they could seat you. "Once when I was here for a spring meeting, the line stretched around the block. I only hope it doesn't tonight. We'll all have pneumonia tomorrow."

"Do you think we should go?" I asked him.

"Of course," he said, then laughed. "Alvareda has spent so much money in his shop, we deserve a dinner. I'm sure Savoy thinks we had to haul our money to New Orleans in a cotton car." He closed his arms around her from behind, and playfully winked.

"Shush, Neal, what should we wear?" Alvareda asked, laughing, then reached up to kiss his cheek.

"Dress to the hilt," he said. "Galatoire's looks like an oversized barber shop, but they have the best food in New Orleans. I guess people dress up out of respect for the culinary fare."

The fact that Galatoire's was also Paul's favorite place became evident as soon as we walked into the brightly lit hall with its ceiling fans and mirrors along the wall. We followed the narrow maze between tables to a spot in the center. A waiter named Renaud quickly approached and bid Paul good evening. He offered menus but Paul begged our permission to order for the table, then spoke in rapid French to the waiter, awaiting suggestions then settling on oysters Bienville, pompano amandine, *pommes de terre* soufflé, and a bottle of his favorite white wine.

He looked at us. "Renaud says the pompano is very nice today. It's always best to listen to his advice." Then he looked at me. "Are you hungry, Mrs. Farrish?"

I had been wondering how I would manage to touch a bite of food. My heart was in my throat. I smiled uncomfortably. He looked at Neal and Alvareda. "This woman is amazing. She never eats. Well, don't worry. I ordered the potatoes with just you in mind. They are puffed up with air, very light. Let's have a toast, shall we?"

We were at Galatoire's till after eleven o'clock. Each time someone passed our table whom Paul knew, he would stop and introduce each of us. Paul and Neal seemed genuinely to enjoy each other for a reason I should have guessed beforehand: a common interest in cotton.

Yet they were also alike in their politeness toward Alvareda and me, drawing us both into the conversation. I soon relaxed and began enjoying myself. I had grown up around cotton people, listening to stories at my grandfather Bennett's knee, listening to Neal and my father talking about the business. I had no trouble joining in with intelligent remarks and questions. It had been so long since I sat at a dinner table and felt my presence was appreciated and enjoyed. I had almost forgotten, since my marriage to Beryl, how gentlemen converse at the table. I remembered—painfully still—our dinner with Jesse Jones at the Brazos Court. How different this evening was from that. How very, very pleasant. I noticed Paul smiling at me and was seized with guilt.

Before we left Paul said, "Have you been to the French Opera House? They're doing *Carmen* right now, and I've been told it's very good. Why don't you join me there tomorrow night?"

I opened my mouth to decline, but Alvareda was too quick for me. "Neal and I have an engagement with old friends tomorrow night, but why don't the two of you go?"

Again, I started to protest, but Paul said, "If you have never been to the French Opera House, you must take the opportunity. I would not feel I had shown you New Orleans if you denied me that pleasure."

I looked at the Gerrards, then at him. "All right. I suppose we could go."

When we parted that evening Paul kissed my hand and said, "I will come for you at seven tomorrow evening. Promise you won't change your mind."

I could not tell him how eager I was to go; nor how uncomfortable I was becoming because of my growing fondness of being with him. I nodded my promise. Yet, somewhere I had to put a stop to this. Either he was simply going out of his way because he had taken note of the amount of money spent by the Gerrards in his shop, or he was toying with my affections. How convenient, from his point of view, for what could be more safe for a man than to keep company with a married woman who is too far away from home for her husband to object?

As I lay in bed that night, trying to fall asleep, I continued to think of Paul. I wished I could allow myself to believe he sincerely cared about spending time with me. Yet if he did, what good would it do?

I do not believe there is any way of explaining the effect one's physical presence has on another. Alvareda always said that when Neal walked into a room, she immediately wanted to be near him and scarcely noticed anyone else, that she had felt that way always. Beryl, for all his handsomeness, held no such magic for me. I had been so puzzled by the fact that he left me cold, I had always wondered if there were something wrong with me. Now I knew there was someone whose appearance made my heart leap with joy. I was not sure, however, that Paul felt it for me. Until I could be sure, I must not risk becoming the victim of my own feelings. And if the Frenchman felt toward me as I felt toward him, then what?

In the huge French Opera House, the box seats were small and companions of necessity sat very close to each other. I sat especially close to Paul, for throughout the production, all in French, he whispered explanations in my ear. I suspected he remained closer to me than necessary, and at the end, caught up in the emotion of the story and the music, he suddenly was clasping my hand, tightly. When the curtain fell, he seemed reluctant to let go. All at once we looked at each other, and the feeling between us was not happy, but poignant, seeing a potential for fondness while knowing it was defeated before it even began.

I did not care to have dinner after the opera, as he offered. I asked him if we could walk back to the hotel. The evening was moonlit and beautiful, crisp and cold. We walked next to each other for a few yards. He looped his arm through mine. We walked a little farther. He pulled me closer to him. At last he said, "How long can you stay this time?"

"We leave on Saturday."

He winced. "I have to take Mère to Iberville tomorrow, and won't be back till Sunday."

I was crushed. "Oh? Well, thank you for the time we've had. I won't forget these evenings. They are the two most exciting in my life."

He looked at me without speaking. Finally he said, "Neal Gerrard says he comes back for meetings frequently. Next time he comes, you come with him and . . . and bring your wedding veil. You will need some advice about caring for it. It is surely an heirloom."

I nodded and sighed, and looked away.

"What is the matter? Have I made you unhappy? You do not want to return?"

"Of course I do . . . more than anything. It's just—Paul, why do you want me to come back? You surely have many . . . more interesting . . . people to spend your time with."

He thought for a few moments, then said, "The word is not 'interesting,' but 'sophisticated.' And being sophisticated does not necessarily cause endearment. . . ."

I thought of Beryl.

"I ask you to return because I like to be with you . . . because, well, because I sense that if one looked behind your eyes, he would find the same goodness that I see in your face and hear in your voice. And I have learned

. . . in the years since my wife died . . . that it is a quality not often to be found."

I was embarrassed. I smiled. "They say that Frenchmen know how to flatter . . . how to be charming . . . better than anyone else."

"Is that so?" he laughed. "I always thought that was true of Americans. Perhaps it is you who flatter me, Elzyna."

We were at the hotel now. "Say you will come back. Give me something to hope for."

"Very well," I said. "I will try."

It was not until the train ride home that I had an opportunity to talk to Alvareda alone about what had occurred. I told her most everything, careful always not to read more than was present in Paul's words and gestures.

She gazed out the window for a long while, then at last she looked at me. "The man is falling in love with you," she said. "I sensed it at Galatoire's. Now you've confirmed it."

"Oh no. He seems to care for me, but—"

"Why is it so impossible that he might love you? It took Neal and I no less time to fall in love. One doesn't explain love. It simply happens."

"Oh, but it isn't right, not for us," I said, miserably.

"Maybe it isn't, but I would have done anything to be with Neal because I loved him. I want you to have the same experience that I have had. It is what I have wished since you were a little girl."

The remark brought me close to tears. How many times in my life had I reached out and found Alvareda's hand ready to take mine? How often had she and Neal understood my problems when my own parents refused? "Oh, Alvareda, I love you so," I said, clutching her hand.

She patted my hand. "Just quit worrying about whether what you feel is right or wrong. Everything will work out."

"Oh, but if Beryl knew—"

"I don't know what he would think or say. It has nothing to do with him. Everyone deserves at least one chance to feel what you feel for Monsieur Savoy."

"Oh, but I feel so—so guilty."

"Guilty of what? Tell me the truth, Elzyna, have you had one happy moment since the day you married Beryl Farrish?"

I shook my head sadly. My eyes were beginning to fill with tears. "If only we'd met earlier, if only—"

"Quit saying 'if only.' We return to New Orleans in April and again in October. Take this chance to find happiness with your Frenchman," she said. And then I noticed there were tears in her eyes as well. She caught me in a hug.

I leaned back and sighed. That may be all there is to look forward to in my life, I thought. But if that's all there is, then I will simply take it and be grateful for it. And whatever misery Beryl may deal, I will be thinking of seeing Paul—even if it can only be in friendship—and that will make it bearable.

Chapter 8

We returned to Houston to find Beryl had purchased a Packard automobile. He noted my astonishment and told me that a man came into the shop to have a tire fixed and, while there, told him he was looking for a buyer because he was about to purchase a new Overland. Beryl so admired the design of the long, low-slung runabout with its gleaming black exterior and deep maroon leather seats that he made the man an offer of nine hundred dollars.

It seems curious to look back now at his delight with that automobile. As he pointed out the lines and features from one end to the other, he might have been speaking of a fine architectural style. He insisted the children and I board for a joy ride, but after once around the block of starts and jolts, and much horn honking, John was screaming at the top of his lungs in fright. So Beryl dropped us off at the house and put Senta in the front seat with him. They were gone a full hour, and she returned with a look of exuberance and something else—perhaps she seemed more worldly.

From that time on, Beryl took Senta for a ride almost daily. Rather than cycle down to City Park, they now rode in the Packard. This meant that John did not get to go. I felt sorry for him. I also felt that Beryl relished the opportunity to be alone with Senta as much as she adored having her father to herself. I can remember so many times watching them drive to the end of the block, and seeing Senta's golden curls blowing in the wind.

I was glad to see Beryl happy. From all I gathered the bicycle shop was still not too busy, and when Jordan ran out of odd jobs to do, he was kept busy shining up the Packard. He lived for the moment Beryl would say, "Hey, pal, why don't you take her for a little spin. But don't put a scratch on her or I'll wring your neck, eh?"

He never offered to teach me to drive, as Neal had taught Alvareda. Yet I didn't care. I was happy to get around in the buggy, and I was also content to dream of my next trip to New Orleans.

And there was no question in my mind that I would get back, somehow, whether Beryl approved or not. During the day, as I went about my chores, I thought only of Paul. Even while a part of me kept hesitating at the thought he might care for me, I relished every moment of dreaming that possibility could be true. I believed then that my own daydreams were enough to satisfy me. If I only imagined the things he might say, the things we might do together, then I never had to face the disappointment of learning he hadn't really cared after all.

As often as I counted the days till April, I dreaded the actual fact of seeing him again for fear I had let my imagination blow it all out of proportion. And what if it were true that he cared for me deeply? The possibility occurred to me often but I did not pursue that train of thought. There were too many consequences to face. I closed it out and only went on with my comfortable fantasies. As long as I was home in Houston this was easy to do.

Beryl and I got along fairly well until shortly before the trip was to take place. Then one night he came home with problems that might have led most anyone to drink. Business was nearly at a standstill at the shop. He didn't know how long it could continue. He was going to need some money soon. He ended with the proposition that I sell off the land. It was the first time he had brought up that subject in a long while.

His obvious failure to consider other glaring possibilities made me angry. We were due to leave for New Orleans in a week. I did not want to face this now. Finally I suggested, "Maybe there is some other way. Maybe you could let go a couple of your employees."

He grimaced. "That's it, think of yourself. You don't think those fellows need a living too, do you? In all the world, there is only Elzyna who matters."

"I didn't mean that. I thought it was normal to cut down the work force when business is off."

"Well that won't help much anyway. I don't guess you'd want me to let your little brother go."

I looked at him hard. "He ought to be the first to go."

This surprised him. "It still wouldn't help much," he said. "The fact is, I have some bills that need paying. I'm a little in debt right now."

That statement made the hair rise on my neck. "Just how far in debt?"

"Oh, two or three thousand. I could get by with a thousand right now, fend off the bill collectors until business picks up."

"How is business going to pick up when you run it like you do? You know how often people go by only to find the door locked, or to find your employees running the shop between rounds of beer. Who are you kidding, Beryl?"

I should not have said all that, not because it wasn't true, but because such words were as dangerous as the sword which marks off the boundaries before a duel.

Beryl surprised me by saying with a shrug, "Well, are you going to help me or not?"

"I don't know. I'll think about it while I'm in New Orleans. I'll let you know when I get back."

"You're going to New Orleans? When I've just told you how much debt we owe?"

Fear gripped me. "The—the trip will cost almost nothing," I faltered. "I always help out with Lilly so that Alvareda is free to do other things. You know that.

"Besides, you have your automobile to amuse you. The children and I deserve something nice for ourselves now and then." I turned to go. He was behind me in a moment, his hand on my shoulder. My chest muscles drew together like a fist. I could say nothing. "You're getting awfully sassy, aren't you, Elzyna? What the hell is so wonderful about New Orleans, anyway? Maybe I ought to come along and find out." His voice was like a growl.

"You're welcome to," I lied. I felt my heart contract at the thought he might really be serious.

He released my shoulder, "Maybe I would enjoy a little time off. Why don't you buy me a train ticket?"

I wanted to tell him he'd been "off" for all our years of marriage, but I stopped myself just in time. After a moment's pause I said, "I don't suppose you've considered selling the Packard?"

"No, I hadn't, and I'm not going to. I need that car."

"Why? You got along without it before."

"That's right. But I think it's high time I had some consolation in my life. God knows, anyone married to you would need something as a consolation."

I was halfway up the stairs. I turned and looked down at him, clutching the stair rail. "Maybe that's what the trips to New Orleans are for me. Consolation," I told him unsteadily.

"What have you got down there, eh? A lover?"

I almost froze on the spot. "Of course not," I said.

"I'll admit it is pretty laughable," he said, and walked out the door. I stood there for several minutes, my hand on my breast, taking in gulps of air. Then I hastened upstairs to the attic, flung open the door, and grabbed the suitcases frantically, as though the train to New Orleans were about to depart without me.

I spent the evening packing. At last I gently placed the wedding veil on top, this motion helping to keep me from losing heart. Then I lay awake for much of the night, my usual concern for Beryl's whereabouts almost overshadowed by a new one: the ring of truth in Beryl's laughter and his words. Wasn't he right? Wasn't I being a fool if I thought for one moment Paul Philippe Savoy might really care for someone like me?

As long as I was at home, New Orleans seemed to me a precious jewel in a box that I could take out and observe with delight now and then. Yet when we arrived on April 21 I remembered what a big place it was, much bigger than Houston, and that just the mere fact that I was in the city did not mean

I would see Paul, not unless I let him know I was here and he then made some indication he was still as eager to see me as I was to see him.

As it happened, however, I was saved the trouble of letting him know of my arrival. The cotton meetings Neal attended were always written about in the *Times Picayune,* and when Paul noticed the April dates of the one up coming, he had called the hotel and left a message at the desk for me. "Would you and Mrs. Gerrard and the children like to join Genevieve and me for a picnic down at the lake? Genevieve has learned to cook, and is eager to show off her skills. Call me when you arrive. *Toujours.* Paul."

I could not hide my pleasure.

Walking up to the room, Alvareda said, "See, what did I tell you? You are being pursued."

I was still smiling, holding on to the message as though it were a priceless treasure. "Can we all go on the picnic?"

"I wouldn't dream of it. You go, and take the children. That won't look the least bit strange."

And so by twelve o'clock all six of us were riding down St. Charles Avenue in Paul's small landau, with a huge cloth-covered basket sitting on Genevieve's lap. Genevieve was slight in build with dark brown hair like her sister's, except that it was full of natural wave. She had freckles across her turned-up nose and green eyes. For the picnic lunch she had spent much effort preparing a creole gumbo, small bread loaves, fresh strawberries with a flavored cream, and chewy pecan pralines.

On the way Paul confided, "You must eat some of everything today, or else Genevieve will be wounded to the heart."

I promised him that I would.

"Each time you come, it seems to me you are losing weight."

"I have not stood on the scales lately, but I'm sure you must be mistaken. All my life I have envied beautiful, slender women."

He turned to me and smiled. "How funny you are, Elzyna, always thinking you are not pretty. I find that very hard to understand."

I appreciated his words more than I could say. "If you think I am pretty, then I will simply enjoy the compliment."

He laughed. "But still you won't believe that I speak the truth. Well! I will not stop trying to convince you, no matter how long it takes."

I smiled and thought that if I could depend upon seeing him twice a year forever, I would consider my life a happy one.

Lake Pontchartrain was an amazing sight to the eyes of one accustomed to the narrow, meandering Buffalo Bayou. You could not see all the way across it—Paul told me it was twenty miles—and the water pitched and foamed as though caught by a tempest. The wind bade the small oak trees nearby to lean toward the water, and pelicans were perched one to a broad piling with determined holds.

Paul took off his tie, unbuttoned his shirt collar, dispensed with coat and vest, and rolled up his shirt sleeves. While the girls commenced with their own play some distance away, Paul played with John, hoisting him up in the air over and over again, while John begged for more, giggling and laughing and running circles in delight. There was nothing I could think of I would rather be doing than watching Paul with John. "Don't let John wear you out. He doesn't often have the chance—he loves to play."

"There we go, John, down again. Let me catch my breath." He came over and sat down on the bench next to me, stretching his legs and leaning back.

"I told you so," I laughed, and handed him a glass of tea.

"Ah! It's as much fun for me as for him," he said, then paused. "It's so uncomplicated when children are young. Their needs are simple, and you don't have to worry that you are making a mistake with them."

"Oh, but I think we can make serious errors when they are young. I worry constantly about Senta. She's so terribly spoiled."

"*Mon Dieu!* Wait until she finishes school. Then the worries begin."

"Oh? How so?"

"Renée. I do not want to put her on that boat to France next month to continue her studies. It is the hardest thing I ever had to do."

"But why?"

"I am very much afraid we will soon be at war."

In my wildest imagination, I never would have expected him to say that. "War? Whatever makes you think that?"

"Oh, it's inevitable, has been for years. The Kaiser is an absolute fool. Unpredictable as a crazy man, which I think he may be. Now and then my relatives send clippings from the papers over there. It is like a powder keg, awaiting a match."

"Oh, Paul, you frighten me."

He looked across at me. "I don't mean to, but it has to be faced. Of course, I don't know. I have lived with this worry for years, and nothing has happened so far. Perhaps it won't. Maybe it is just that I am caught between wanting my daughter to have her greatest dream come true, but at the same time, afraid to let her go out into the world. Her schooling there will take many years. Before even entering the Sorbonne in Paris, she will study outside of Marseille for at least a year." He smiled. "You see? That's what I mean by complicated."

"I think you are wonderful for wanting her to go and study medicine. It's such an important endeavor. My parents only wanted me to find a husband. There was never any question of higher education."

"Well I must admit, there have been times when I have almost wished she would not be so serious about this idea of becoming a doctor. It would be easier if she stayed here and married a fine Creole gentleman. Mère has been promoting such an idea all year."

I looked out across the water. "It is not so easy to tell beforehand how fine a man will be."

He looked at me, as though he expected me to go on. When I did not, he finally added, "People are like lace, you know. Sometimes you have to look at them closely for a long time before you can detect whether they are what they appear to be, or only a misrepresentation.

"On the other hand, some of us have a more practiced eye, and can distinguish quality more quickly." He winked. "We must go. I have to get back to the shop." He took my hands. His grip was strong and firm. I rose. He waited a moment too long before he relinquished my hands and called to the children. I looked away and reached for my gloves. I thought how nice it would be if we could stay here together, on the banks of the lake, forever. I thought how comforting it would be if his hands were extended to mine each time I felt afraid.

In the afternoon it rained. Alvareda was attending a ladies' tea, and the children and I stayed in the suite relaxing. The girls sat in the middle of the bed and cut out Alice in Wonderland paper dolls, while John took a nap, and I sat nearby in a lounge chair flipping through the pages of a magazine and thinking of Paul's last words. He had invited me to come to the shop tomorrow morning so that he could see the wedding veil. I was considering what I might wear. Since Beryl had purchased the Packard, I had felt no hesitation about purchasing some new clothing. I had added two new skirts to my wardrobe, and three waists, all on sale at Foley's. Afterward I'd stopped at Levy's—always my favorite store—and bought a becoming white linen dress with pleated mono bosom and lace inserts at the bottom edge of the elbow-length sleeves, around the waist, and collar. I'd also stopped at the millinery department and purchased a large straw hat with white roses around the crown. This I would wear tomorrow. . . . Senta looked over at me and said, "Why does Monsieur Savoy always invite us to go places with him?"

I looked up, startled. "Oh . . . he's just nice, I suppose. And of course we are customers from out of town so he takes special care to see that we enjoy the city."

Apparently satisfied, she returned to her paper dolls. But then she said, "I think Genevieve is snooty."

Lilly, who was gamboling around in her petticoat and stockings, paused a moment to ask, "Why? I think she's nice."

"She has all those pretty bonnets to wear, better than we have. And she doesn't like our games very much."

I put down my magazine. "Senta, Genevieve is older than you are. I think she makes a great effort to be nice to you and Lilly. And as to her clothing—

remember, her father is in the business of finery. Of course she has more bonnets and dresses than you have."

"Well, they don't have a Packard. I know because I asked her."

I sighed. She continued, "I hope we don't have to see her anymore."

"I'm afraid you will. Tomorrow I'm going to spend some time shopping at Savoy's. I want to see about buying a lace tablecloth for the dining table . . . and I have something else to show—"

She looked at me with what I had come to regard as her own special look of challenge. "You could buy a dumb tablecloth in Houston. You don't need to go to the Savoy shop for that."

I began to feel uncomfortable, and closed the magazine before replying. "All the same, I am," I told her. "Renée will take all of you to a puppet show while I am busy."

Lilly bounced on the bed gleefully, and said, "Oh boy, a puppet show, Senta!" but Senta continued to look at me, inclining her head. "What if I don't want to go? Puppet shows are not any fun."

I narrowed my eyes at her. "Don't be sassy. You're going anyway. Renée will bring you to the shop after the puppet show."

"I don't like this trip like the others. We have to do everything you want to do. It isn't fair."

I ignored her and looked again at my magazine, my pulse beating a little faster now. I must be careful of what I say to Senta, I thought nervously. I wished profoundly I did not have to deal with her through this. At times it was almost as though Beryl were here, watching me.

In the morning I put on the white linen dress and the straw hat, and pulled on a pair of white gloves. I picked up the carefully wrapped wedding veil and tucked it under my arm. When I looked in the mirror I wondered if I were too dressed up. I decided not and turned to go. Lilly, with her bouncing auburn curls and freckled face, looked up at me and said, "Aunt Elzyna, you look like you're ready for the Easter parade."

By ten o'clock, Paul and I were sitting out in the small courtyard. He spread the veil over the table between us to have a look at it in the natural light. Clearly he was impressed. "One of the nicest pieces of point de gaze I've seen. You said it came from Belgium, didn't you. Yes, the color tone is slightly different from the piece I showed you, made in France. Well, well, well. It is exquisite! Here, let me put it on you and see. . . ."

"Oh, you really don't have to—"

He was already removing my hat. "Yes, yes, here we are." He put the headpiece in place and carefully arranged the veiling around my shoulders. "You must have been a beautiful bride."

At that moment a clerk came through the door, and upon seeing me in the veil she began to make over the spectacle even more than Paul. Soon the rest of the clerks were admiring the veil and French superlatives were mixed with enthusiastic words that I understood. One clerk came toward me with a large mirror, saying to the others, "Let her see how lovely she looks. Move away now."

And whether because I was always in a state of nerves when Paul made over me, or because of the unexpected development, the whole situation began to resemble a bad dream from the moment I saw myself in the veil and the white dress I'd so carefully chosen for this morning. All I could think of was the tragedy of the marriage, beginning with all the misgivings I had beforehand, and then the wedding, my father coming so late and speaking to me after the ceremony. Then the terrible wedding night that followed. Everything flashed before my eyes in quick succession. "No, no take it off," I said suddenly. I was just on the point of becoming ill.

Paul reached over quickly and removed it. He dismissed the clerks and then sat down and took my hand. "Are you all right?" he inquired gently.

I started to nod, then shook my head. Tears filled my eyes. I could not believe I had somehow lost control. I was so embarrassed I wanted to die. "You must think I am crazy," I said.

"Not at all, but I am wondering what troubles you so? Is it sentiment for a happy day?"

I looked into his kind eyes and could not lie to him. "Oh—oh no," I said. "I wish it were that simple."

"What then?"

I hesitated before answering. "Do you remember the first time we met? I was coming from the post office. I had just mailed my wedding invitations. Except for meeting you, it was a horrible day—a realization that I had to go through with a marriage that I had never really wanted. . . . And I should never have done it."

He looked less than surprised. "Oh, I never meant to say that to anyone. I certainly shouldn't be bothering you with it. I'm all right now, really I am. Let me just have a sip of coffee. There. I want to buy a tablecloth of Venetian lace. Will you show me one?" I said.

He paid no attention. "Chérie, I have always suspected you were unhappy. I am sorry."

"I'm not completely unhappy. These trips to New Orleans bring me happiness. You have been so kind to me. You have no idea how much I appreciate it."

He looked as though I had saddened him.

"I must go now. It might be just as well if I didn't come again. I feel that I've—"

"No," he said, and put his fingers on my lips. "Do not say you won't come again. I live in hope you will come. Elzyna, I—" he began, then he leaned toward me and put his hands around my face. He began to kiss me lightly, gently, as one caresses a disappointed child in need of comfort. Then he rose up and pulled me up with him. He wrapped his arms around me and kissed me with an urgency I would have scarcely dared to dream he felt. Every part of me responded with a warmth that must have been welled up in me for all of my life. When he released me at last I was almost too dumbstruck to move. Then suddenly I realized the enormity of what we had just done. In a state of confusion I hurried to the door, with him following quickly behind.

"Forgive me, *chérie,* forgive me. I have cared for you all these months. I did not mean to—"

I could not look at him, but I caught his hand in mine and held it tightly. "No, Paul. You owe me no apology. I only wish with all my heart we could—" I began and then, just ahead of me in the doorway, Senta appeared.

To this day I do not know how long she had been standing there.

Chapter 9

I have never felt so guilty.

As we rode home on the night train, it seemed to me that I had swung the pendulum of my marriage in the opposite direction. Never had Beryl been guilty of seeing other women—not as far as I knew, anyway. Never had he spoken of our marriage to others in terms of its not being happy. I felt that I had undermined the integrity of our commitment to each other in a way that was unforgivable. If I was no worse than he was, certainly I was now equal. And how much had Senta seen? She said nothing to me, and I could certainly say nothing to her. I felt the only true defense was to behave as though there were nothing to hide. If she witnessed the embrace between Paul and me, then she would surely feel compelled to let me know about it. Much as I loved Senta, I knew she took great joy in making me feel uncomfortable. It was only a matter of time. . . .

I looked out the window at the darkening sky. I must go to Confession as soon as we returned, must promise God never to let this temptation conquer me again. Over and over again I rehearsed the words, "Bless me, Father, for I have sinned. . . . Bless me, Father, for I have sinned. . . . Bless me, Father, for I have—"

Alvareda sat down beside me. "I just got Lilly to sleep, so that makes all three. What's troubling you, dear?"

I told her what had transpired with Paul. She took my hand. "I feel responsible for this," she said. "I had not meant anything to happen that would cause you misery. I only wanted you to be happy."

I continued to look out the window. Finally I said, "Until I met Paul, I was convinced there was something wrong with me, that I was . . . cold . . . to men. Now I know that I am not. There must be more of my father in me than my mother. But where does that leave me? What can I do about it?"

She only smiled and sighed. Then she said, "What do you want to do about it?"

"If I were the kind of person I should be, I would never come to New Orleans again. I would go home and have a private confession, and go on about my business, never looking back. That would be the right thing."

"Yes, it would, Elzyna, if your first commitment is to your marriage."

"Perhaps I won't come again, then," I said, but could not bear the thought. "Oh yes, I will. Oh, I don't know what to do!"

"There is an easier way out of this, you know."

"What then, tell me."

"You could divorce Beryl Farrish."

The suggestion amazed me. "Divorce! Oh no, that's unthinkable. I could never do that. My faith forbids it. You know that. I knew when I chose to marry Beryl that, whatever came, my life would always be with him. I could never consider divorce."

She sighed. "Would the church annul your marriage? If they knew—"

"Knew what? Why are you looking at me that way?"

"Some time ago, Senta came over to play with Lilly. She told her that she had seen her father strike you to the floor. I was so furious! I told Neal, and he was outraged, but said that we mustn't interfere with your life unless you came to us for help. He was right, of course, but I have to confess to you that since then I have despised your husband. I'm sorry, but that's the truth. If he did that once, he might do it again."

I could say nothing. Her words had taken a leap over the whole incredible drama of being Beryl's wife. If I told her everything, then I would only feel more guilty than I had when we sat down and began to talk. I knew that I had to base any decisions I made on my own conscience. Regardless of what Beryl did, I had to face myself.

Alvareda patted my hand. "Whatever you do, remember to look to Neal and me for help."

"What would you do if you were me?"

She thought for a moment, then said, "Elzyna, I've already been through something like what you are going through now. My father made a prisoner of me. The first chance I got, I ran away from him. Had I made the mistake of entering the house of another ogre, believe me I would have run away from him as well. No one will ever treat me unkindly again."

I shook my head. I simply could not think of leaving Beryl.

At home, I tried not to think of Paul, but of course I thought of him constantly. Oh, such gentleness. Such immaculate poise. The very smell of him was heady fragrance for me. And those sweet, tender kisses. I might live a lifetime on them. He would be surprised at how little it took to make me happy inside, and my resolve was stronger by the day.

Then in May, Alvareda called to say she had something that I must pick up. Paul had called long distance to ask if he might write to me at her address. "I waited until I actually got a letter before telling you. Here is the evidence your Frenchman thinks of you when you are far away."

In spite of all my talking good sense to myself, I tore open the letter eagerly, hands shaking, heart pounding. *"Ma chérie,"* he began, "How I wish you could be here. I am sitting in the courtyard in the late afternoon. The four o'clocks are blooming and they form a bushy pink border along two sides of the courtyard. I think of you whenever I see them because they bloom the most beautifully when the other flowers are closing. What I have ceased to find in women since my wife passed away, I now find in you, and it is late, *chérie,* late in the afternoon for both of us.

"Please do not let me frighten you away by my arduous expression of feelings for you. If you can offer me nothing but friendship, I will understand and try to remember that in itself is a blessing to be treasured among all others.

"It is difficult for me to think of you as unhappy. I want to do something to turn your unhappiness into the pleasure that you deserve.

"I understand that it is you who have all the decisions to make. I will wait, nonetheless, for your return in October regardless of the conditions. *Toujours,* Paul."

I folded the letter and held it to my breast. Then I unfolded it again and read each line over again, once, twice, three times. I put the letter inside its envelope deep down in my pocket and sat for a long time in thought. I could take this letter and draw strength from it. But that was all I could do. I still had to face the fact that, despite my poor marriage, I was not free to change anything. When I envisioned myself going back, seeing Paul again, the road to New Orleans led only one way: to more unhappiness. However much joy I found in him, I still would have to come home to Beryl. Oh, Paul was so right. It was late for us . . . too late. I would treasure Paul's letter and his feelings always, but I would not go back to New Orleans. And for now, I would not write.

Over the summer my decision held. Yet when toward the end of the summer, we received the news that Germany had declared war on France, I decided at last I must write to Paul. He had been so worried about Renée. And now she must be in France. What must he be going through? I penned a lengthy letter, expressing my concern. Within a week I had a reply from him. At that point I believe he was still somewhat confused about what to do. He could not get his family to come over here. Mère's aging brother, with whom Renée was living, was in poor health and could not travel. Paul was not sure that Mère was up to the move over there. He was truly caught in the middle of a situation over which he had no control. On top of it all, there was the shop to consider. He could not just walk out. He had extended himself financially for the coming season, and could not afford to lose that much money. He also felt he might need money in the coming months, to send to his family in France. Renée was safe, he assured me. He ended his letter on a note of hope that perhaps the war would not go on very long.

Never before reading that letter had I felt as though I wanted to see Paul in order to comfort him. But now my heart went out to him. The tone of the letter lacked his usual confidence and enthusiasm. He spoke to me as one distressed appeals to a close friend. I promised I would come to New Orleans in October. I said nothing about this to Beryl.

I had been so sure that I had finally learned how to put up with Beryl and that there was nothing he could do that would surprise me further. Then one night in September our lives jackknifed. He had not come home by the time I went to bed, and I lay there for three hours with an unusual sense of doom that I could not explain other than the fact that the weather was horrible. It was lightning and thundering. I could hear the horse bleating in the barn, and the limbs of the big oak tree out in front were creaking and groaning. The end of the farthermost limb was brushing the screen of the sleeping porch upstairs. I wondered it did not wake the children with its scratching. It certainly made my hair stand on end.

Toward half-past one I dozed off, and in the next hours I spent equal amounts of time falling asleep and waking up wide-eyed at some new sound. I wished it would begin to rain. At least it would muffle the labored moaning of the old house. Finally I heard noises coming from downstairs and I opened my eyes. The power was out. The room was a black void except for the shafts of light from the distant lightning coming through the window. I lay there a while, listening. The noises continued. As there was no light in the house, Beryl could not be sitting in the dining room drinking unless he had lit a candle. And if he had lit a candle, then I needed to go down there and be sure he had the sense not to set the house afire.

Finally I got up and threw on a robe. I took a candle from the drawer by the doorway and started downstairs, first checking on John and Senta. John had at some point gone in and gotten into bed with his older sister. I would soon be thankful for this.

I walked carefully down the stairs. There was a small glow of light coming from the dining room. "Beryl, is that you?"

"Come in, Elzyna," he answered. It was Beryl, all right, and his voice told me he had been drinking. I sighed and went through the door, carrying the candle out to the side. I sat down across from him at the table. I could now see a bottle of whiskey, nearly empty, and a glass. At least he could not drink much more. The candle he had lit on the table was nearly burned down.

"There is a kerosene lantern in the butler's pantry," I said. "Let me get it. Isn't this weather dreadful?" I was trying to sound perfectly normal, though I felt anything but normal and I had a suspicion that there was something wrong that I had yet to learn about.

"No, sit down," he said. He sat there in silence for a while, gazing off into space, sipping from his glass. He reached for the bottle and emptied it. Whiskey sloshed outside of the glass and down on the table. I recognized the trap and kept quiet.

We must have sat there half an hour as I waited for him to begin a conversation, or fall asleep, all the while the lightning flashed outside, the thunder rattled the window glass. He did neither. Finally I said, "I believe I'll go back up to bed, if you don't mind."

"It doesn't matter what you do now," he said. "Go ahead."

I did not like the phrasing, nor the sound of his voice. I would do everything in my power to be conciliatory. I thought he might have money troubles again. After returning from New Orleans in April, I had asked if the outlook was better and he had said it was, and with summer coming business would probably pick up even more. Yet he had warned me he might still need some help with money, and I had quickly changed the subject before he suggested again we mortgage the house. "Did you want to talk about something? I now asked. "Problems at the shop again?"

"Who the hell cares? The shop can burn down for all I care."

I kept my shaking hands beneath the table and tried to steady my voice. "Listen, Beryl, I know how much you despise the shop," I began. "I know what your feelings are toward me. I . . . well . . . I want you to know how much I appreciate the way you have stood by us for all these years.

"If"—I continued, and when I said this I was thinking of those few shared moments with Paul—"If you would like to leave, I would not hold it against you. I know how unhappy you are. You've always been a good provider, working at something you did not like, taking responsibility for me and the children. In that respect, you have been one of the finest, most loyal people I've ever known." I paused to get my breath. He stared at me, the hint of a smile at the edges of his mouth as though he were letting me talk myself into a corner.

"We—we could get along all right," I stammered. "We have this home and all its furnishings. We'd get by. I could find some way to bring in an income.

"You could leave, go someplace else and find a new beginning." I closed my mouth. I could not believe what had just poured forth from me. I felt a hollow sensation at the pit of my stomach. Beryl was silent for a few moments. The rain began at last, with three or four hard plops on the roof, then a sudden violent drenching that nearly obliterated our voices.

"Oh, I'm going all right," he said. "But this time I'll do it my way. I'll make the rules, Elzyna. There won't be anything left when I go."

Fear crept up me like cat claws. "What do you mean? I don't understand," I said faintly.

"Just don't you worry about it. Go on back up to bed. Go to sleep. Your worries are almost over." He raised his glass to me and smiled. I was afraid to go, afraid not to. My knees felt weak. He had never spoken this way before. I needed time to think about what he might mean by all this, I—

"What are you waiting for, Elzyna? Go ahead. Go back upstairs. I'll be up after a while."

With his face above the dying candle flame, he looked like the age-old childhood notion of the devil. I think now that I will always remember that look, because what happened next would weld it into my memory. I picked up my candle and reluctantly turned to go. As I swung around toward the dining room door, the light in my hand swept across the sideboard. And there, in place of the soup tureen and the silver tea service that usually occupied the area, was an arsenal of neatly arranged weapons, including two rifles and a collection of knives. On top of the snowy cloth, they might have been a museum display. At once I felt the life suck out of me. I gasped and brought a hand to my mouth, then wheeled around at Beryl. He was smiling, raising his glass to me.

I hardly remember clambering up the stairs. All I could think of was getting the children out to safety, and yet, Beryl blocked the way to the exit. I could not even use the telephone because it was in the downstairs hall, right outside the dining room. At the top of the stairs I stopped and tried to collect myself. Beryl's words came back to me like the swift slicing motions of a knife. ". . . there won't be anything left . . . your worries are almost over." We'd have to go out over the roof. It was the only way. I had one hand wrapped around the balustrade, one gripping the candle. I went to Senta's room and pushed on the door. I first approached Senta. I pressed my hand to her mouth and woke her. "We have to leave right now. If you say a word, I will paddle you. Do you understand?"

Her eyes wide, she nodded.

Next I repeated the process with John. Then, while they both sat upright, gazing at me in puzzlement, I handed them their house shoes and robes. While they put them on, I went to the door and looked at the landing. There was no sound from downstairs, only the hard rain and the rumble of thunder. I signaled for the children to follow me, and we all held hands and tiptoed across the hall to my bedroom. I locked the door behind us. I looked out the front window, trying to gauge the risk. Then I motioned them toward the window and raised up the frame. The wind howled and the rain poured in on us. Senta was now growing obstinate. "Why can't we go down the stairs? Tell me, Mommy, where's Daddy anyway? What about him?"

I turned toward her. "Shh!" I glanced uneasily toward the locked door, realizing it could be hiding Beryl from us, as well as us from him. I looked back and squeezed her hand hard, to remind her of my warning. "We're going out on the roof and down the limb of the oak tree. "It is safe enough, if you are careful," I said, praying I was right. "Just grab the limb and hold on, and climb forward, then down."

"But we can't see," Senta insisted.

She was right. It was so terribly dark—no streetlights; no moonlight; only the sudden perverse flashes of lightning. "I'll go first, and you send John, then you follow last."

I climbed out, made my way toward the limb, and reached down to feel it. The limb was as slick as though coated with grease. What now? I thought, nearing panic. I carefully crossed the roof and climbed back into the window. Inside, I paused to get my breath and think, my eyes on the bedroom door. I did not know how much time we had. If Beryl should come banging on the door, I must surround the children with my arms, and scoot all of us under the bed, out of range. . . .

Finally I had an idea. "All right, we're going another way," I said. I pulled the spread and the sheets off the bed and began to tie the ends together. I pulled two more sheets from the drawer, all the while listening for footsteps on the stairs . . . the doorknob being tested. . . . When I had sufficient length I tied one end around Senta's waist and the other to the window handle. "Watch your step. The roof is slippery. When you reach the ground, untie the sheet from around you and wait right where you are. Help John when he gets down, and untie the knot from his waist. If you run off I'll—I'll paddle you. Do you understand?"

"Yes, but where's my daddy?"

"Daddy is—he isn't home. There is someone downstairs, a prowler in the house. Hurry, now."

Senta sat on the edge of the porch roof. The wind twirled her hair around her head. It seemed such a long, long way to the ground. I slowly eased her down, praying with every tug on the makeshift rope, envisioning her leg or arm being broken. My eyes were trained for the sudden appearance of Beryl below. He might have tried the bedroom door . . . felt the draft from the open window at his feet . . . any moment . . . any moment. . . .

When Senta was safe on the ground, she removed the sheet from around her, and I pulled it up, murmuring a prayer of thanks. I repeated this with John. "This is like in *Peter Pan,* isn't it, Mommy? Not scary at all?"

"Oh, John, my fine, brave boy," I said, and hugged him tightly. He stepped to the edge and sat down. He looked at me, pushing his windblown hair from his face. I nodded, then lowered him carefully, my heart constricted; please, God, hold John in your hand, he is so frail. . . . When he was down, Senta unlooped the sheet from his waist and I pulled it up. I was really afraid it would not hold my weight, and if I fell, I would be of no use to the children. I dispensed with the sheet and went to the far edge of the porch roof, above the shrubbery. I did not take time to consider the possible danger. I wrapped my robe around me and jumped into the shrub. It gave under me like mattress springs. I clambered out, shivering now in my thoroughly soaked clothing. Motioning the children back, I carefully made my way to the corner of the porch and peered across. All clear. Suddenly the wicker swing jerked on its chains as a gust of wind caught it, startling me so I nearly screamed out. I brought a fist to my mouth. I've got to hold on, I told myself, we're almost there. . . .

I signaled the children to come to me, and huddled them close. Like a family of urchins we raced together across the yard to the barn. I threw open the door and hitched up the horse and we boarded the buggy. I coaxed the reluctant horse from the safety of his barn, praying his whinnying would not alert Beryl. I whipped him all the way to the street. We went the length of McKinney Avenue in absolute darkness and driving rain, all the way up to Main, where thankfully the streetlights were burning. It took us at least half an hour before we were pulling up to the Gerrard house and I was pounding on the front door, tears of relief flooding my eyes and streaming down my face.

Chapter 10

After the children had been given dry clothing and were sound asleep, Alvareda and Neal and I sat together and talked. There seemed no point in trying to cover up the troubles we had in our home any longer, and it gave me a feeling of welcome release to be able to talk about it all calmly, knowing they would not be judgmental or begin to take over my life as I knew my own family would have done. Alvareda's eyes never left my face. She held my trembling hands to comfort me. Neal paced around in his bathrobe, arms folded, stopping now and then to look at me, then to pace and listen some more.

"I only hope John doesn't get sick from this," I said at last.

"He's warm and safe," Alvareda reassured me. "Don't worry about that for now. I think what you did was very courageous."

"Oh, thank you for saying that. I only did what seemed the sensible thing at the time. I don't know what I'll do now. I'm almost surprised Beryl hasn't called here or come after us."

Neal sat down. "If he did not hear you leave, he might have passed out in his chair. He could still be there."

"Yes, I suppose you're right." There was a comforting thought. Being here, wrapped up in blankets, was even more comforting. I looked down. "Oh, I just hate to face him again."

"I think someone should look in on him after a while," Neal said, thoughtfully.

For a moment his meaning didn't register. Then, when it did, I glanced up at him. "Oh dear, if he took his life, I'd never forgive myself."

Alvareda sighed. "Forgive yourself for what?"

"For just looking after myself. For not thinking to telephone the police, or a hospital, or something. I don't know what you do in such a case."

"You did no wrong," Neal said. "You can't work out Beryl's problems for him. I really think the only sensible thing to do is to stay here for a few days at least. I'll contact my attorney about what to do legally. You've got to get him out of the house, assuming he was only bluffing, or just out of his head, and didn't really do anything to harm himself. I'm not sure how that should be done. You have to be careful, or the ramifications can be very difficult."

I shook my head. "Oh, it all seems so overwhelming right now. I need to think about so many things—"

"Right now you need to get some rest," said Alvareda.

Neal built a log fire in the guest room and I lay down between the covers and tried to relax. I was stiff from head to toe, still poised as though awaiting a banging on the door or the ring of the telephone. After a while, Alvareda peeked in the doorway and said, "Still wound up?"

I nodded.

"I've brought you some hot milk with a little brandy in it." She put it down beside the bed and put her arms around me. "There isn't anything we can't handle together. Now, get some sleep."

"I will . . . just being here makes me feel so much better."

Whether from the effect of the warm beverage on my body, or simply the fact that the sky outside the window was brightening rapidly and it would soon be twenty-four hours since I slept, I finally dozed off. I do not think I ever truly relaxed; certainly I do not remember dreaming. I simply woke up, my eyes wide, and looked at the clock. Half-past eleven.

I could hardly believe last night had really happened.

I put on the robe Alvareda had loaned me, and walked down the stairs. It was a beautiful, sunny day. Through the huge glass window along the stairway, I could look out and see the children playing on the back lawn. All three of them—John, Senta, and Lilly, were frolicking. For them, it was just another day of play. How nice that they should be so oblivious to grief and sorrow, I thought. For them, each new day was a new beginning. It was too bad to have to outgrow that wonderful innocence.

Alvareda was in the big living room reading the newspaper. When she saw me, she said, "You look better. Sit down. I've kept the coffee warm. . . . Oh yes, and Neal has gone to consult with his attorney."

"Oh, I wish he wouldn't—"

"He is just trying to help you get prepared before you make any decisions, that's all."

When she returned with a cup of coffee, she said, "And there is one more thing. Your mother telephoned earlier, to speak to you. Apparently Beryl called her."

I winced. "I hadn't meant to draw her into this. What did she say?"

"She didn't say very much to me. Only that Beryl was very upset when he called, wondering what had become of you and the children. He thought you might have gone to her house. She told him of course that the chances were good you had come over here."

"So by now he knows where we are."

"Yes. But don't let that upset you. You can stay here as long as you like before even so much as talking to him."

"I wonder what he told Mother about our reasons for bolting suddenly."

"He—I gather he told her nothing except . . . he said he had planned to leave on a hunting trip this morning . . . was all ready . . . but now he was so upset over you that he just could not go."

"A hunting trip?" I repeated.

"That's what he said."

I shook my head and sipped the coffee.

"I told Carlotta you were sleeping, that I would have you call her when you awakened. As far as I am concerned, as tired as you were, you could be sleeping still. It may be hours before you awaken," she said demurely.

"I may as well get it over with." I walked into the hall and called Mother. The first thing she said was, "Get down here right away. I need to talk to you."

"Mother, I'm hardly dressed for paying a call."

"Very well. I'll come there."

"Come ahead," I said, and hung up the telephone.

Mother was dressed up in a dark suit and hat and gloves when she appeared. She was apparently running late for a luncheon, but felt that she must get "all this straightened out" before she would have any peace. I do not believe I expected her to show me much sympathy, yet a lot of what she said surprised me and indicated she must have had many thoughts about Beryl and me before now, and had formulated some opinions which she managed to keep to herself. Before now.

She asked we be allowed to talk in private. She was so stiff and businesslike with Alvareda, it was hard to imagine they had known each other for many years.

She pulled off her gloves and began. "Beryl is beside himself. He told me that he realized at times he was difficult to get along with, but that you and the children are his whole life."

"And you believed that?"

"Of course I did. Hasn't he stuck by you? After all the disappointments he has suffered, he has remained at home, making a living until the day he can get a break in the profession he so deeply cares about."

"He won't ever get back into architecture, not here anyway, probably not anywhere."

She narrowed her eyes. "Why not?"

I still did not want to tell her all of it. I did not know how she might use it, and I did not have time to think about all the consequences that might ensue. I simply said, "He was fired."

"Oh? What for?"

"What does it matter? It was long ago. It was over . . . over his work. He was . . . insubordinate."

"Insubordination? Well, that's not much of a crime. If you had only offered him your help and support, I'm sure he could have gone to work somewhere else, or eventually built up his own firm. With all the building going on, don't tell me Houston doesn't need gifted architects."

Her words about help and support had truly angered me. "What could I have done?" I demanded.

"You could have asked for help from Neal. That's what. He can get anything done that he wants to in this town."

I just shook my head.

"All you have ever done is find fault with Beryl. You never offered him encouragement."

That thoughtless remark finally set me off. "Just when did you ever once offer my father encouragement? All my life I've listened to you find fault with him. And now you're telling me—"

"Shut your mouth, Elzyna. Your father is an adulterer. He has been seeing other women since right after we married. I have given him far more than he deserves."

I stared at her. She had traipsed ever so unknowingly over my affections for Paul that I was unable to open my mouth for a long moment. Finally I looked away and said, "And just what do you propose I do?"

"You go home, of course, what else?" she began, then paused before continuing. "No one ever said marriage is all sweetness and light."

"Do you realize he was drunk—he is often drunk—and he made strong indication last night he intended to take his life and kill me and his children as well?"

"He told me that when you saw the guns and hunting knives, you went into hysterics. He didn't say anything about making threats. Did he threaten you?"

I sighed. "Not in so many words. Perhaps you think I should have run the risk of staying around, when I feared for my own safety, not to mention that of the children."

She raised a hand. "I'm not denying what you did was called for. But if your husband has a drinking problem, why haven't you encouraged him to do something about it? There are treatment centers for alcoholism right here in Houston."

"I could never even get him to admit he had a problem. I can't imagine his changing his mind now."

"Oh, but that man is desperate to keep his marriage together, you can be sure of that. This may just be the thing that he needed to make him see the error of his ways. You owe him at least the chance, don't you think?"

I remembered sitting in her parlor long ago and listening to him convince her of what a fine, upstanding young man he was. Apparently his ability to do so had not changed.

"All right, Mother, I'll talk to him," I said at last, and remembered a similar conversation years ago when I'd made up my mind to back out of the wedding and she finally tortured me enough to force me to go against my will.

She patted my hand. "Now you're showing some good sense. Things will change in your life. I'll telephone this evening to see how you are doing. I assume I'll find you at home."

I nodded.

"Perhaps you ought to see Father Baratino. He has been immensely helpful to me. Just the other day—"

"Perhaps," I interrupted, to hasten her away. The thought that I should so thoroughly follow in her footsteps by relying on Father Baratino's counsel to console me was repugnant beyond words.

Satisfied her task was done, my problems dispensed with, she turned and went through the door.

After she left, Alvareda and Neal both came in. I was thankful all over again to be sitting in their home, rather than Mother's. I did not get a chance to tell them what I had promised to do before Neal began to tell me about the legal advice he had received.

"I can't say it is very encouraging," he began. "But certainly it can be gotten through. First of all, there is really nothing you can do except file for divorce. Otherwise, if you try and force him to leave, you're in for all kinds of trouble. And divorce doesn't come easy either. You are likely to have to bring out a lot of things that you would just as soon leave private. There is no way to keep it out of the courtroom, or the newspapers, if you have any hope of being granted what you ask. Legally, Beryl has done nothing wrong. He comes home regularly and provides you a living. There is no adultery involved, not unless you haven't told us something—"

I shook my head.

"As far as a court of law is concerned, what happens under your own roof is simply your word against his, and a man who provides for his family is accorded a lot of understanding when it comes to quarreling with his wife."

And what if Senta had told Beryl about my embracing Paul?

In the end I called Beryl and told him I would like to come home and talk with him. He was most amiable. When I told him I wanted the knives and guns out of the house, and never to be brought home again, he said, "I've already taken them down to the shop. Chip and the fellas took them hunting." He emphasized the last word.

Neal drove us home. I asked that he not come in. He said, so as not to alert the children, "I have an errand farther out McKinney. When I'm through I'll double back and head for home."

I nodded my understanding of his signal. He had already made me promise before we left his house that if Beryl started to drink, I would call him immediately, or just call a taxi and return.

Senta piped up from the back, "Is my daddy at home yet?"

"Yes, darling. He is at home."

"Did he scare the prowlers away?"

"Yes. It's all over now."

Neal pulled up at the curb and opened my door. He leaned over and kissed my cheek. "I'll send the carriage back this afternoon. If you need anything, call me. I love you, honey."

If I had said anything I would have burst into tears.

Beryl opened the door for us and kissed the children. He might have kissed me too, but I turned away and went into the library. While the children were sent upstairs to change clothes, we talked. Even then, it seemed a strangely abbreviated conversation with all we had between us. He told me that if I thought he needed treatment for his alcohol problem, he would concede to that. "Sometimes I say things that I shouldn't, out of anger," he said. "But I'm really only angry with the way things have gone for me . . . it isn't your fault. . . . I'll try not to take it out on you anymore."

"I guess that's fair enough," I said, lifelessly. I went upstairs to change.

Monday morning Beryl made an appointment with a physician at a private hospital out in the Heights, and set up a two-week program to begin near the end of October. This coincided with a portion of the time we were to be in New Orleans, and I had told him that evening of my return that I intended to go. He had only nodded his assent, I assume out of an effort to treat me considerately.

While Beryl came home nightly on time, and sat at the dinner table with us, behaving with model courtesy and thoughtfulness, I counted the days until my visit with Paul. That anything other than friendship might exist between us I had already disregarded. But at the same time, I had promised I would come to New Orleans and I also felt well within my rights to get away from home for a few days. If I were going to give Beryl another chance, little as I thought it would do any good, then I at least deserved some enjoyment in my life. That was all I would allow myself to hope for in anticipation of the trip.

Just before I pulled out the valise to pack, Beryl said, "I don't really know that I need help after all. I seem to be doing all right so far. Haven't had a drink for weeks."

My pulse quickened. "I—I think you ought to go through with it. Maybe they can help you out with the reasons it became a problem in the first place."

He shrugged. "Maybe you're right."

I felt sick when I got up the next morning. All night long I had worried about Beryl changing his mind about the hospital. I assumed then that was the reason for my upset the next morning. But then it happened again the next day, and the next. And at last I realized that I was expecting a third child. I did not even tell Beryl before we left. I have never felt so downcast in my life, nor closer to being finally and fatally trapped.

Chapter 11

There was a note of melancholy about that last trip to New Orleans that had not characterized our trips before. My reasons for feeling sadness were plain enough: my pregnancy would prevent my coming back to New Orleans for a full year, even if Paul were there. And the chances that he would be awaiting my return seemed almost nonexistent.

But that wasn't all. Alvareda had just received a letter from Gabriel, who was very much involved in campus political meetings and debates about the war raging in Europe. He swore that if we were to enter into the war at any point, as he felt convinced we would, he would be the first to sign up for duty. "Neal has already written him that Wilson will not let that happen. But it frightens me still that Gabriel may be right. She sighed and leaned back. "Oh, it is terrifying to think I might really have to watch my son go away to some foreign land . . . and fight. I remember in '98 when everyone was talking about fighting in Cuba and Teddy Roosevelt formed his Rough Riders, I felt so smug that my child was safe from all that."

"Alvareda, don't worry. Surely the war won't reach us. Paul says the monarchies in Europe are all going to topple, but I don't see why that should affect us all the way over here."

She shook her head. "Oh, I know so little about these things."

"So do I," I said, and patted her hand.

"Gabriel is coming home soon for a week or so, for the opening of the Port. I don't think I've ever been so anxious to see him. Oh yes, I've been so worried about him, I almost forgot to tell you we could not get our suite at the St. Charles this time. The hotel was nearly full—apparently several meetings are going on at the same time. So I've arranged two rooms for you at the Palais Dauphine, right near the center of the Vieux Carre. The agency told me it is small, and quite elegant."

"Oh, you should have told me. I could have stayed at home. I don't like your having the extra expense. I feel such a burden already—"

"I knew you would feel that way, and that was why I put off telling you. After what you have been through, I was determined you should have this trip no matter what. And the expense doesn't matter. Neal feels exactly as I do."

I kissed her cheek. "What would I do without the two of you?"

"And let me care for the children a little more this time. Honestly, I am tired of ladies' luncheons and afternoon teas. I'm eager for some outdoor activities. You can spend more time relaxing in your room. I know you don't rest well at home."

How much of this shift of plans was coincidence, how much contrived? I do not know. It was one of the few questions I did not ask of Alvareda. I was especially glad for her thoughtfulness because within the next few hours I would realize how greatly I was needed by Paul.

I did not see him till the afternoon of our arrival, for he had been tied up all morning with prospective buyers for his shop. As soon as he saw me, he took my hands and said, *"Bonjour,* Elzyna. I was so afraid you would not come." He kept holding my hands and looking at me. I wanted so much to put my arms around him and hold him near. Yet I could not.

Finally I began, "Oh, Paul, I've been so worried about you." Tears sprang to my eyes.

He kissed my hands, then smiled and said, "Your hands are always cold, and always I want to warm them up in my own. I remember the very first day you walked into my shop, your hands were freezing."

I managed a smile. "I was more excited at seeing you again than I'd even admit to myself."

He laughed and said, "What the mind denies, the body will reveal. I'll tell you something: that, plus your beautiful eyes, got my attention immediately. . . . Come, let us walk for a while; stay close to me, please."

And so we strolled down Royal Street, my arm looped tightly in his. "You are going to sell the shop, then?" I said, trying not to sound as bleak as I felt. If he sold the shop, then he might leave New Orleans forever. . . .

He shook his head. "I am trying, but so far without success."

"But I can't imagine why," I said. "It's such a wonderful business, and obviously there is a great demand for what you have." I felt sorry for him. He looked worried. His voice was not as merry as it had been before.

"People looking to buy a business may have the same instincts that I have," he said. "I am afraid the days of fine lace are coming to a close."

"I can't believe you are serious," I said.

"Things are changing rapidly. Neal and I discussed this when we had dinner not so many months ago. Cotton is threatened as well. Fashions are changing. Less material is used than before."

"Paul, when you sell out, what will you do?"

"I must go to France. I cannot stay here while my daughter is there, and the only way I can be sure of helping my family is to get my hands on money, and take it there. We may even have to leave France for a while, and move perhaps to England. I do not know. My information comes from many sources."

"And what if the war is soon over?"

"I don't know. Perhaps we will come back. Perhaps not. Right now I can only plan for the immediate future." He stopped walking and looked at me. "Oh, Elzyna, I was so afraid you would not come back again."

I sighed. "It would be my last trip anyhow. I am expecting another child."

He stared at me. "And does this make you happy, *chérie?*"

"Happy?" My voice echoed. I shook my head. "No, no it doesn't." I walked on.

Paul was busy with the visiting buyers for the rest of the day and that evening. He asked me to accompany him and Genevieve to Mère's the following afternoon. And that evening, to join him for dinner again, just the two of us. I told him I would be glad at least to join him for dinner, "but I'm afraid I would be interfering with your visit to your mother's home. Perhaps I shouldn't."

"No, please," he said. "I have been telling her all about you. She wants to meet you." He stopped again to look at me. "And we have so little time together. If I must spend a few hours with her, then I want you to be there with me. . . . And if you do not want me to—to be more than your friend, then I will do what you wish."

I shook my head. "It isn't what I want. It is what must be."

"Then you will have to rely completely on yourself. I am not as strong as you are."

I looked away. I could feel my strength quickly ebbing.

Madame Renée Josephine Savoy lived in a house that was more ostentatious than it appeared from the street. Among her friends of the Creole aristocracy, she had lived on Esplanade Avenue since her marriage to Paul's father in 1870. On the way there I had told Paul, "I had always assumed your mother lived in the Garden District. I thought that was where the wealthy New Orleans people lived."

He laughed. "Do not say Garden District to *Mère*. She will throw you out of her house. Only *les Américains* live in the Garden District. The Creoles would never accept them on Esplanade."

"Well, thank you for saving me that *faux pas*. Which is the only French term I know."

The mood lightened. We laughed and rode merrily down the street in an open carriage. It was a gay, sunny October afternoon. I felt good, and more lighthearted than I had since my arrival. Genevieve sat in the back and complained. "Grand'mère always makes the children sit and listen to her play the piano," she said.

"The grown-ups have to suffer that as well," Paul reminded her.

"But at least you get to go into the best dining room for refreshments. The children have to sit on those little gilded chairs that are too high and my feet don't touch the floor. And we have to drink that awful claret wine with water in it and eat those horrible cookies. Oh, I hate Thursday afternoons!"

"Quiet, Genevieve. You will frighten Mrs. Farrish and she'll insist we return her to the hotel. Give her the present you brought for her."

"Oh, all right, Papa." She leaned toward the floor for a moment, then emerged with a little sack of seeds. "They're four o'clocks. Papa says you have never seen ours when they are blooming, so I bought you some seeds. You can plant them in your own garden."

"That was thoughtful, Genevieve. I shall plant them as soon as the ground warms up in spring."

"Here we are," said Paul. "Mind your manners, Genevieve."

When he handed me down from the carriage, he said, "Don't be afraid of Mère. She is quite harmless."

We did not actually greet Madame Savoy until we had gone through greetings with several others, starting at the front door with its etched glass window and lace curtain. And I do not remember any of their names. I was much too enchanted with the house to pay attention. Beyond the front with its iron-lace balcony, the two-story structure was long and narrow—shotgun, as Paul termed it. The stairway leading to the second floor was right inside the door and not separated from the parlor. Up those stairs there were three graduated windows of beautiful stained glass, the flower designs picking up pink and yellow and green as the sunlight poured in. Across from them, on the opposite wall, was a beautiful carved wood fireplace that was dwarfed by the tall ceiling of the parlor. On each side of this were tall windows with ornately carved cornice boards from which hung rose damask drapes and sheer lace panels. Madame Savoy sat at the back of the room, holding out her hand for kisses and greetings. She wore navy blue lace, with a very high, stiff collar, and a little lace doily on her hair. She had been a beautiful woman in her day, that was clear. Her dark eyes seemed to penetrate right through me as I greeted her. Genevieve curtsied. "How are your lessons?" she asked.

"Very good, Grand'mère, I got an 'A' in French yesterday."

She nodded her pleasure. Then she turned to me. "Paul tells me you are from Houston. Is Houston a place of saloons and guns, as I often hear?"

"Mère," Paul began.

"It's all right," I said. "No, Madame Savoy, in fact next month the Port of Houston officially opens. Big ships will bring cargo into our city. It's really quite civilized. And I have never shot a gun in my life."

Her eyebrows lifted. She turned away from me rudely.

How much she is like my mother, I thought, her response to my words driving through me like a nail.

"Let us go," Paul said. "Mère is not quite herself today." He looked into the second, inferior dining room. I could see the legs of the gilt chairs. "Come, Genevieve," he said. I heard a chair scrape across the floor. Genevieve appeared, thankful for the reprieve. In moments we were leaving Madame Savoy's house.

On the way home the atmosphere was subdued. Finally I said, "I'm afraid I must have said the wrong thing. Oh, I knew I shouldn't have come."

"I apologize for my mother's proverbial rudeness. One can never trust her. I think sometimes she really does forget herself."

"It's all right."

"No, it isn't. But tonight we will make up for it."

We were to have dinner together at the Court d'Orleans. As this was one of the most elegant restaurants in the Quarter, I planned to wear the nicest dress I had. When we got back to the hotel and I tried it on, however, I realized it was much too large. I had had no idea I was losing so much weight. Paul was right in his observation. While it was a delightful surprise, one I had never before experienced in my life, it produced a serious problem. There was nothing hanging in the wardrobe that would be nice enough for the evening with Paul. I was still puzzling over it when Alvareda walked in with the children.

"This calls for a shopping trip," she said gleefully. "We have just two hours. Hurry up. I'll ask Mrs. Hester to stay with the children."

Alvareda knew just where to go. Marks-Isaacs had the best millinery department in the city, but their ready-to-wear was not first class. Holmes might be a place to buy a dress, but if one wanted something original, the Liberty Shop was the best choice. We arrived at half-past three. I took six dresses to the fitting room and chose the fifth one. Surely every woman deserves to feel beautiful at least once in her lifetime, and, beginning with the moment the hooks and covered buttons were all fastened and I turned and looked into the mirror, I felt transformed. The effect was startling. Alvareda clapped her hands. "That's it!" she cried. A thrill went through me from head to toe. The dress was a soft, mauve pink. The silk skirt was narrow, falling just below the ankles. Over this there was a sheer tunic reaching to the knees and folding in front like a coat. The waist and bodice were tight-fitting, draped over with a sheer jacket with elbow-length sleeves. The whole effect was one of soft filminess, almost dreamy. The dress was a perfect fit, two sizes smaller than I normally wore. Alvareda hurried me out of it and into my street dress, then downtown to Marks-Isaacs where we chose a hat with a wide brim and pink roses around the crown. We stopped at the glove department, then in the shoe department for satin pumps. It was half-past five when we arrived back at the hotel, where the desk clerk said I'd had a telephone message from Beryl. I looked at Alvareda nervously. "I'll join you up in the room. . . ."

The only telephone was near the hotel desk. I held the telephone close to my ear and turned away. When I reached Beryl it was obvious he was drinking. My heart fell. He was scheduled to enter the hospital tomorrow. The way he was talking, I seriously doubted he would make it by himself. "When are you coming home?" he said.

"We'll be back on Saturday," I told him. I felt as though there was a vise gradually closing in on me.

"Oh, well I was hoping it would be sooner. But I guess I'll be all right."

"You don't sound all right. What's the matter?"

"Nothing. I'm perfectly fine. Since you aren't here, I thought I'd go out on the town tonight with Chip and Buck. You know, a kind of celebration before they lock me up tomorrow."

"Beryl, stop talking as though you are going to jail. This was your decision, and as far as I'm concerned, a wise one."

"Then why aren't you here?"

I hesitated, guilt stabbing me. "This trip was planned long ago. You know that. We discussed it before I left and you agreed I should come."

"If you cared anything about me, you would have stayed."

I held my breath. There was nothing I could say.

In a moment he added, "But don't worry. I'll get Chip to take me over there. Maybe I won't even go home tonight."

I hung up the receiver and looked toward the desk clerk, who, at least from all appearances, had not eavesdropped on my conversation. Even if I left now, I could not be home in time to make any difference in the way Beryl behaved. He was too far gone for that already.

"Thank you," I said to the clerk. He glanced at me and nodded. I walked slowly upstairs to the room, my feet like weights under me. Alvareda was awaiting me expectantly. "His voice is strange," I told her. "But he is still making sense. I suppose I should not have come," I said quietly, and ran my fingers over my beautiful dress, hanging nearby.

"Do you really think it would have made a difference?"

"I don't know."

"Stay and enjoy yourself as best you can. If he doesn't go into the hospital tomorrow, you can always persuade him to go after you return home."

I looked at her. "I'm going to stay because I want to see Paul. But I'm afraid my spirits have fallen to zero. I may not be very good company," I said. Then, "Oh, why?" I asked, and tears of frustration filled my eyes. Alvareda took me in her arms to comfort me, as she had done since I was a child.

Neal came to fetch Alvareda at seven o'clock. I was then dressed and trying to compose myself for the evening ahead. He took my hand. "You are absolutely glowing," he said. "You look as lovely as a debutante on her way to the party of the season." Then he kissed my forehead. "Don't worry. Things at home will work out. You go and have a good time."

Paul arrived at half-past seven with flowers, which I pinned to my waist. He looked so handsome. He wore a light brown suit and vest and a dark brown tie, the color of his eyes. The moment I saw him, my mind flashed back to what awaited me on McKinney Avenue in Houston. I made a brave attempt at cheerfulness, but my real mood was all too apparent. He took my arm and we walked down the hall. *"Bien-aimé,"* he said, "I have never seen you look more beautiful, but why so sad?"

"It is nothing; I am fine," I assured him.

Paul looked even more at home in the setting at the Court d'Orleans than at Galatoire's. The room was very intimate, with small tables and wine-colored velvet chairs, pink cloths on the tables, and candles and flowers on every one. From the background came the sounds of violin music. Paul ordered a bottle of a French wine that I had never tasted before, and soon the impeccable waiter returned with it, and placed crusty loaves of French bread and butter on the table. We talked for an hour before Paul ordered food. He thought that his mother had saddened me by hurting my feelings, and began to explain about her. "You must understand Mère," he said. "She knows nothing beyond tradition; times change, but Mère is secure in doing things the same as always. After my father died she sat behind the lattice at the French Opera for five years. Five years! She went from deep mourning into midi-mort after two years, and has been there ever since.

"But anyhow, Mère is old and trying to hold on to stability. She won't hear of leaving for France until All Saints' Day. Every year we make a pilgrimage to my father's gravesite. We put white chrysanthemums on the grave, and this year she feels we must whitewash the vault for we may not be here next year . . . or the next. Please forgive her."

The wine and Paul's humorous description of his mother had restored my mood to some degree. I smiled across at him. "She could not be too horrible, and managed to have a son as kind as you."

"Ah, Elzyna. It would be difficult to be unkind to you."

I thought of Beryl. "You have been so good for me, Paul," I said. "You could not imagine how much I appreciate having seen New Orleans with you."

He leaned a little closer and took my hand. "Will you let me show you Paris? You would love Paris. It is gay and happy all of the time. The people there are hardly aware there is a war. Even the threat of attack by the Germans could not convince them to dispense with their sidewalk painting, their coffee houses, their singing and merrymaking. And it looks now as though the city will be safe, thank goodness! Paris is a world all its own."

"I hear the women are the most beautiful in the world."

"That is a story perpetuated by the French! It is the fashion that is beautiful. Parisian women are no more lovely than Americans. Believe me, were you to walk down the Champs Élysées right at this moment, you would have every Frenchman forgetting the woman on his arm and staring at you."

"Paul, do you have someone in Paris, someone that you see when you are there?"

"No. I have only Elzyna, in New Orleans. And if I go on holding her hand much longer, I will want to kiss her again. And if that happens it may frighten her so much that she will refuse to spend every day she is here with me. How long do we have, Elzyna?"

"Till Saturday," I lamented.

"Elzyna, I have declared myself to you in all the ways I know. Do you care for me at all?"

"Yes, yes. You know that I do." I looked down. "It is cruel to tease me as you do."

"You mistake me. If I thought there was any hope in the world that you would come to Paris with me, I would stop in Houston before I sail, and wait while you pack your belongings."

"You have no idea how much I long to go with you. If only, that day so long ago when we met, I had known what would happen all these years later, I would never have mailed those wedding invitations."

"If I had known what I know now, I would have retrieved them from the post office myself."

I pulled my hand away and shook my head. "Oh, this is wrong. I should not be here with you, saying these things."

"Elzyna, have you any idea how much you are torturing me?"

I looked into his eyes. I shook my head again. But at last I realized what he meant. Until then, my own refusal to believe that anyone could care for me had posed a barrier between us so that I could see only what I was feeling. We had reached a point where we either went forward together, or we parted forever. I do not know how much of what followed that night was a result of the immediate situation at home, how much resulted from Paul's knowing that he would not be in New Orleans very long, but I know in that moment I finally reached a decision.

He ordered the meal. Like all New Orleans meals, it was a banquet before us, the waiter serving with pride and awaiting signs of our delight. We sat silently, neither of us eating much. I felt my heart was lodged just beneath my throat. I knew what was going to happen as surely as I knew I would never see Paul in Paris, perhaps never see him again after I left this time. At eleven o'clock we rose from the table and looked at each other.

"A lady is with the children. I must discharge her," I said. He nodded, then came behind me and helped me up from my chair, brushing my neck with his lips. I did not want to think. I wanted only to complete the feelings we had shared from the first time I walked into Paul's shop and saw him. Arm in arm, we walked back to the hotel. My heart was beating so loud I could have sworn everyone we passed could hear it. We went silently up to the two rooms on the third floor. I went next door and dismissed Mrs. Hester. The children were sleeping soundly. Thank God. I passed from that room, through the adjoining door, and into my own. I looked at Paul, then turned and locked the door. I took off my hat and gloves, and turned back toward him. I did not feel afraid. He held out his arms. I can remember being enfolded in a way that almost took the breath from me. The warmth that emanated from him was like a current that flowed into and through me. We held each other for a long moment, and then I raised my arms and began to take the pins from my hair so that, one by one, the heavy curls uncoiled and fell around my shoulders. I looked at him. His eyes were full of adoration; I did not think I had ever seen a face so caring, so splendid in its lack of conceit.

His gentle touch as he turned me around was itself like a caress. One by one, he carefully unfastened the buttons down the back of the pink dress, talking to me, telling me how much he loved me. But then, as the dress fell like a cloud to the floor I thought for one brief instant of the first night with Beryl, of the violence, the nightdress being torn down the front. And at once I was almost paralyzed by the memory of it, and could not unhook the corset that surrounded me. I felt nauseated and brought a hand to my forehead. Tears sprang to my eyes.

"What is it, _chérie?_" Paul asked.

"Nothing, nothing," I said, but kept facing forward.

"It is not what you want?"

"Yes it is, more than anything. I just—"

He turned me around. "You are afraid to trust me?"

"No, that is, I don't think so. Or perhaps I am. But I want to, do you understand?"

He nodded. "I think so. Your husband was not . . . caused a bad experience?"

"Yes . . . yes. Please, just hold me."

"Poor Elzyna," he murmured. He put his arms around me and stroked my back, patiently, lovingly, long enough for me to get Beryl out of my mind and release the clutch of the appalling memory.

Finally I began to breathe regularly and, sensing the change he laughed and said, "I do not know how women endure these corsets. It must feel like being wrapped up in sticks."

I laughed, and then laughed some more, and felt immensely better for his healing sense of humor.

"Come, let me," he said, and drew me over to sit on the edge of the bed. He knelt down. He reached up under the frilly drawer legs and removed the garters, rolling down the stockings, one by one. Each time he closed a hand around my ankle to remove a stocking, I felt a sudden, surprising thrill of desire that began there and traveled up over me. He put the stockings aside. He rose and began to unhook the corset from around me. He did this in a relaxed, methodical way that made me think for a moment how many times he must dress and undress the forms in the sewing room above his shop. Yet I was aware he was making an effort to put me at ease, and I felt grateful. He said, "At least ladies' corsets are not as poorly designed as they used to be . . . nowadays they are a little softer. There." He unbuttoned the shift underneath and opened it like a window. He looked at my breasts. I did not take a breath. His eyes met mine. "Ah, such élégance, Elzyna," he said hoarsely. "You are more lovely than I dreamed, and I have dreamed of this moment so often."

That simple, loving appraisal filled me with such confidence, I almost forgot myself entirely. He leaned forward and kissed each breast and nipple tenderly. I felt treasured, glorified, and could not wait for him to explore the rest of my body. Together we pushed down the shift and removed the ruffly drawers, all that was left to cover me. His tongue ran over his lips and he swallowed. I reached up and loosened his tie, unhooked the buttons of the neat collar, and helped him off with his shirt. I plunged my hands into the thick tufts of dark hair that covered his chest and shoulders. "Oh, Paul," I whispered. That any human could be so masculine, yet so sensitive, was the paradox that had drawn me to him from the beginning. "I want you to touch me . . . to kiss me everywhere," I said, as though for him to do so would eradicate the scars placed on me by Beryl. He put his arms around me and lowered me down on the bed. He began to unfasten the buttons on his trousers. When he was finished undressing himself and I looked at him, I caught my breath. The thick tufts of hair went all the way down his stomach and surrounded his organ. I looked into his eyes and smiled, thinking suddenly that the only good thing Beryl had done for me was to prepare me for the sight of another man.

He lay down beside me and continued to make love to me, with more patience, I think, than he really felt. I had never experienced the flood of arousal I felt that night, from the lambent fingers that softly traced a path all over me and finally reached down to explore the crevice between my legs. A sharp pang of desire charged through me. He brushed me with his lips, sweetly, playfully, all the way from there back up to my breast. He paused, looked up at me, and said, "I remember when we first were getting to know each other, how you felt you were not pretty—too large. Have I managed to dispel that terrible misapprehension?"

"Yes, oh yes," I said.

"Such fulsome, beautiful *poitrines*, so feminine," he remarked. He kissed them again and again, surrounding each nipple with his tongue; then, acknowledging the firmness there he glanced up and sighed. *"Bien-aimé,* are you ready? I do not think I can hold on much longer."

I smiled and closed my arms around him. He pulled up and arched himself above me. I held him tightly and lifted my hips to receive him, and once he was inside me I felt one pulsating burst after another, and a sense of supreme fulfillment that I had never once experienced in all the years of my marriage. When I felt his fluid roll out into me I wished with all my heart that my body could have been ready to conceive a child.

We had only the one night.

It was a cruelly short amount of time, yet it was long enough for me to know a joy that I had thought would forever be denied me. We held each other all through the hours till morning, and all I could think of was how little time there was left till Saturday. Maybe, I thought, or perhaps even dreamed, maybe there would be a news bulletin in the morning that the war in Europe was over and Paul would not have to leave.

At seven o'clock I was awakened by a knock at the door. I threw on a robe and hurried to answer before the children were awakened in the next room. This time it was a telegram. Beryl had been hurt in an automobile accident and was at St. Joseph's Infirmary. His condition was stable, but I should return home at once.

"Naturally," I whispered, and thought bitterly, You win . . . you win. I tore the telegram into little pieces, and stood at the door gazing vacantly ahead, unable to put one thought next to another, until I felt Paul's hands on my shoulders from behind. *"Chérie,* what is it? What has happened?"

I will never forget Paul's face as my train went steaming out of New Orleans on that same day. I had placed a burden of worry on him that was unfair. I was so eager that he completely understand how much I loved him and how deeply I hated to leave him that I said too much. I told him details of my marriage that I never meant to share with him. He is like Neal, I find. One begins to talk with him and finds a deep well of understanding and compassion in his eyes that invites the further speaking out of anything grievous. He begged me not even to go. He said that if I would stay, he would arrange to put us up here and we would travel to France with him whenever he was able to go. I could not, of course, agree and I felt he was basing too important a decision on the sorrow he felt at the time for my predicament. We arranged for Alvareda to keep the children till they returned on Saturday. Senta screamed and demanded to be taken to her father. I had to slap her at last to calm her down. To my surprise, John was the more subdued at being left. He let Alvareda hold him in her arms when I told him good-bye. Then Paul took me to the station and kissed me good-bye.

The conductor was calling, "All aboard." Paul kept holding my hands. "When will I see you again?"

Through a blur of unspent tears, I shook my head. "I don't know . . . soon, I hope."

I boarded the train and walked to a vacant seat. I looked out the window and threw him a kiss. The engine roared and the whistle blew. We moved away. He stood on the platform waving his hat, and I could still see him when we were far down the tracks. When I could see him no more I moved back in my seat and let the tears spill down my cheeks until my head ached and I could hardly open my eyes.

It was almost impossible to believe how one perfectly beautiful night could have so great a bearing on complicating an already serious situation. Now I was truly torn. I could no longer spend hours imagining what it would be like to have Paul tell me of his love for me, or how it would be to find completeness in that love. Now that my dreams of this had come true, the responsibilities were like ripples in a pond. Had he been less of a man, we would have said an easy good-bye that morning. But had he been less of a man he would have never won my heart. Now whatever happened to me involved him. And on top of everything else there was the complication of an expected child.

Of one thing I was certain: I would not take my night with Paul into the confessional. That anything so beautiful could be a sin I would not accept. Much more the sin was to have lived for years with a man I neither loved nor trusted. No, I was not going down on my knees because of last night, not for anyone. I would renounce my faith before that, I now realized, my hands folded tightly together. All at once it struck me for the first time in my life that I felt a deep sense of rebelliousness at the strictures placed on me by my faith and painfully administered by my mother. I felt almost physically ill . . . I must not dwell on this any longer. . . .

When finally I arrived at the infirmary at seven on that evening, and saw Beryl in his bandages, lying in bed, I was torn with guilt. He had been the passenger in Chip's truck, and was thrown forward. He might have gone through the windshield and been killed, but he hit the dashboard with his chest. He had no broken bones, but was very bruised and had many cuts. He was terribly sore. To move his hand or his arm, even to turn his head, brought excruciating pain. The doctor said he would suffer headaches probably for a long while.

"If you had been here, this wouldn't have happened," he said to me.

At the remark, my anger surpassed my guilt. I wanted to slap his irresponsible face. Still I said calmly, "I know. But it's fortunate you were not hurt worse."

"Where are the children?"

"I left them with Alvareda. I didn't know what I would be facing when I got here, and I felt it was better."

"This is a hell of a run of bad luck, eh? Aren't you going to kiss me?"

I leaned forward and gently kissed his forehead, my heart, my whole body, recoiling inside.

Beryl was in bed for the next two weeks, and up and around on a strictly limited basis for another two weeks after that. During that interval, I became, if possible, more confused than ever. All Beryl wanted to talk about was how we ought to try and make a go of our marriage. He claimed the accident had knocked sense into him, that it made him realize the value of having his family, and that we had been selfish not to try harder to get along. Maybe we really did love each other. I cringed when he said this. By now I was certain I could never love him. All I thought about, day and night, was Paul. Every day I expected to get word he was moving. I did get two letters the first of November saying the shop had been sold at last. He was now finalizing arrangements. He would get in touch again. He loved me. He worried about me and the children constantly.

I wrote him back and assured him everything was going peacefully at the present time, and that he should not worry for our safety. I said that I loved him too, and that this was the hardest period I had ever experienced. That I was trying hard to know the right thing to do for all of us. Had I been without children, the decision would have been so easy. But now with two, and another coming, I knew deep in my heart that I should at least try and salvage my marriage for their sakes.

Senta nursed her father like a professional. She was always doing something for him, straightening his pillows, dancing for him, hugging him, bringing him flowers. And Beryl even seemed to notice John more. He was kinder toward him, more affectionate. One day I told him what I had put off revealing, that we would be parents again. That seemed to give him renewed conviction about our marriage. While I despised that prospect, I finally had to realize he was probably right. I was only thankful for now I did not have to suffer being touched by him. I did not know how I would ever bear that again.

There was an aspect of Beryl's convalescence that was very unpleasant. The bicycle shop had suffered terribly over the past year, and now it was worse. In his absence, people began to learn they could reach him at home about the collection of bills. First there were one or two calls, then they came more and more frequently. Beryl kept telling me he would tend to it when he was up and around again. But that seemed a long time off to me, and in the meantime I had to answer the telephone calls, some of them nasty.

I decided, finally, to talk to Neal about selling him the lots around our house. I did not tell Beryl. Somehow I was not ready to admit to him that I was finally going to do what he had wanted me to do for years. At least I felt I could get enough to keep our household bills paid till Beryl was better, and pay off what bills his shop was owing. Maybe we could get along on the money till Beryl was well enough to get back to work. And maybe, with his more responsible attitude, he would make a go of his business along with his marriage.

The first thing Neal said when I consulted with him was that he felt I should put the money in a separate account. He did not really want to buy the property. He would rather I keep it, and loan me some money to get me past the rough spot. But I felt he had done far too much for me. I was not up to facing more responsibilities for debts of friendship.

Finally he agreed. But he said, "I really wish you would hold the money in another account. Just to be sure Beryl has changed as much as he claims."

"I couldn't," I said. "I feel so guilty about things already, I just couldn't do it."

He wrote me a check to advance a small part of the funds. It would be December before anything could be finalized on the property.

The first week in November Alvareda called to say she had just received a wire for me, from Paul. There was something onerous about a telegram, as opposed to a letter. Telegrams were meant to be speeded on their way; information in them was urgent. I felt certain this one contained the information that Paul was leaving for France immediately. Perhaps by now he was already on the ship. I made an excuse to Beryl, who was lying down on the parlor sofa with one leg propped up, and rushed over to the Gerrards'.

I read through it and looked up at Alvareda. "He's coming here. He wants to talk to me. Oh, what should I do?"

She read over it. "He'll be here November 10. That's the day of the port opening. You must meet him, and tell Beryl you are attending the opening with us. There will be crowds of people in Houston. You could arrange to have him come here . . . while all of us are at the opening. We'll be gone till very late. Neal rides aboard the *Windom* when it pulls into the channel, and that night there is a parade down Main Street. You could be alone here—"

"No . . . no," I said. "It is better we do not. It will only make it harder. I will send him a wire and meet his train. We will talk at the station."

"But, Elzyna—"

I shook my head miserably.

The station was jammed with people that Tuesday morning. President Wilson was due to press a pearl-topped button in Washington at noon, which would through some device using telegraph wires cause the explosion of a cannon at the Turning Basin in Houston, and that would be the official signal for Neal Gerrard and others like him to see their long-held dream of a deepwater port in Houston come true. The daughter of the mayor of Houston would stand on the platform of a ship, and throw white roses from a basket into the Turning Basin, christening the Port of Houston. A band would strike up "The Star-Spangled Banner." There would be a twenty-one-gun salute. Great oceangoing ships would now plunge down the channel that had begun as a quiet, narrow meandering waterway named simply, Buffalo Bayou. It was a happy day for thousands of people. It was the saddest day of my life.

There was no place for us that day. Houston was even more crowded than it had been the first time I met Paul, at the same time of year in 1906. He put his arms around me and kissed me. I did not want to let him go, and held him so tightly I could feel his heart beat against mine. At last we walked through the hordes of noisy, high-spirited people, all the way down to Courthouse Square, where we found a vacant bench in the bright morning sunshine, and sat upon it to talk about our uncertain futures. As much as I treasured this moment of just being near Paul, I did not want to have the conversation I knew we must. Tears pressed against my eyes like water pressing against a weak spot in the dam, yet I felt I must not let go. . . .

As Paul began to go over his plans, it was as though his voice was already coming from far away. ". . . I have booked passage for December 14. In the meantime, I have traveling to do, closing out accounts, settling affairs for Mère in Baton Rouge. . . . Come with me today, or join me in New Orleans before we leave. Once in France, we—"

"Paul, I cannot go," I said softly, my voice almost choking on the words. I told him what had occurred over the past few weeks. "I do not love my husband, but for the sake of the children I owe him this one chance to change and be a decent husband and father."

He argued further. I looked away and shook my head, my heart collapsing. He turned my face toward his. "Please, Elzyna," he begged. "People do not change because of an accident. He will revert. You have no idea what it has been like, wondering daily when he might turn again and abuse you further. Please come with me now while there is still time. I beg you."

I could not tell him yes, although I would have given almost anything to do so. Yet, looking into his tender, hopeful eyes, I could not bring myself to refuse. Finally I told him to let me think about it, that I would write and let him know of my decision. I really did not believe I could in good conscience change my mind. I took his hands in mine. "I will always love you, no matter what happens," I said, the tears now springing forth and spilling down my cheeks. "Paul, I wish this child in my body were yours. Then it would be easier, whatever I decide, whatever becomes of us."

He wiped the tears from my cheeks. *"Ma chérie,* please come. I will be waiting for your letter that tells me when to meet your train. Don't rob us of this one chance for happiness."

I walked back to the station with him and waited the short interval until the next train doubled back for New Orleans. In reverse positions from just a few weeks ago, we said good-bye again. The train roared off. I stood waving with my hat, watching through a veil of tears, until long after I could see the train no more.

Chapter 12

Hail Mary, full of grace; the Lord is with thee: blessed art thou among women, and blessed is the fruit of thy womb, Jesus. Holy Mary, Mother of God, pray for us sinners, now and at the hour of our death. . . .

It was Jordan who was the most pitiful victim of what happened here on the night before last. He had already written that during these Christmas holidays from his first year at college, he wanted to stay with us rather than at home, and before I met Paul for the last time I had written Jordan to tell him we would agree to have him here.

Honestly I had forgotten about his coming, with so many things on my mind. In the week following Paul's visit, I received two more brief letters from him, begging me to come to him while there was still time. I could hardly bear to read them, I was so torn with regret. Finally I wrote him a letter telling him that I felt obligated to remain with Beryl. For the sake of the children. For the safety of the child I was carrying. The fact that I loved him and would carry that love always could not dismiss me from responsibility. If Beryl were sincere in his desire to work out his problems, and it appeared that he was, then I must forget about the wishes of my heart because I made the commitment to him first.

It was harder to mail that letter than it had been so many years ago to hand the bulky stacks of wedding invitations to the postmaster. I held onto it for days and days before mailing it. I did not hear from Paul at all in response. I knew, since I had made that decision, there was nothing further for him to say to me. Yet I felt it was only fair to relieve Paul of at least part of the burdens he was carrying right now. Perhaps, if we had been given more time, everything would have worked out differently. There was no stopping the relentless march of war in Europe. There was no stopping the date on which Paul would leave for France, December 14. There was no stopping the daily changes becoming visible in my body as the child grew and flourished inside me, already making its own demands.

Then, early in December, Beryl went back to work in the shop. He did not take time off to go to the treatment center for alcoholism, claiming that he had already lost so much time that any further delay would be an "unafford-able luxury." For three days he was much the same as he had been since the accident. Then, on the fourth day, he began to drink again. For several days I did nothing but grow more nervous and watch to see what would happen. I kept hoping there would be some limit to this, that he really would not let it get out of hand again. And indeed, it did not seem as bad as before at first. Yet he began to come home later, and later still. And finally I had to face the fact that Paul had been right.

December 8. I sat down at my writing desk and tried to pen another letter to Paul, telling him I would come, after all. But I found I could not. I wrote a few lines, scratched through them, stood up, sat down and tried again. Every way I tried to phrase my feelings, I sounded foolish, confused, unsure of myself. I wadded up page after page. At last I leaned back in my chair and thought, I really am losing my mind. This is how it happens . . . inability to put clear thoughts down on paper . . . hardly able to sit still long enough to write anything down. I rose from my chair. There was at least one thing I was certain I could do, and that was talk to Neal.

We sat across from each other in his office that afternoon, and he let me express all my incoherent thoughts and feelings along with my tears before he responded. "It's all so overwhelming," I finally said, raising my hands. "I keep thinking of John, how puny he is. What if things are even worse over there than we believe, and I can't get him medicines when he needs them? What if I can't find proper care for the child I'm carrying?

"And there is Paul, with a family of his own to be responsible for, possibly to have to evacuate, an elderly uncle, an aging mother who is obstinate and demanding herself— Oh, I hesitate to think what she would say if I arrived with my brood at her doorstep; in fact, none of his family may accept me.

"I love Paul so dearly. I don't think I could do this to him, although I believe he would stand by me through anything."

Neal shook his head at last. "Elzyna, I could not in good conscience advise you to go to France now with Paul."

I felt enormously deflated. I don't think I had expected him to make such a final statement unless it were one I truly wanted to hear. I said nothing. I could hardly manage to get my breath.

"The truth is," he continued, "no one knows how bad it will get in Europe. I don't know what troubles you would have getting in there right now, or how easily you could get out if you needed to."

"Oh, you sound so—so full of doom and foreboding—"

"I'm trying to be realistic. I have an idea or two that might be more helpful."

"Yes, anything. What?"

He smiled gently. "I know how much you love this man, Elzyna. If not for the war in Europe, I would waste no time or motion getting you to him as soon as possible. But . . . did you ever think there may be a time yet? That it isn't the end of the world?"

I shook my head slowly. "Frankly . . . no. It seems like the end of the world."

"Here's what I would advise you to consider. I think you should write to him and tell him of your worries, just as you have told me. Tell him that Beryl has reverted to his old habits and you realize he was right in the first place.

"Tell him that you are eager to join him at the most advisable time, that he will have to tell you from his standpoint when that would be . . .

". . . and, more important, tell him in the meantime you are divorcing Beryl no matter what, and that if he still wants you, you will be free to join him as soon as the divorce is final." He looked at me in order to get my response.

I nodded without a pause. I was satisfied that I had done everything I could to save my marriage. I would never go back for any reason, my Catholic faith included.

"You know what it means going through, Elzyna. Are you certain in your mind that you are ready for whatever happens? Regardless of how dirty the fight for divorce becomes? Your mother alone will cause you untold grief."

"Yes. I am glad I have given Beryl this one last chance. I don't think I would have ever felt right if I had not. And . . . while there was a time when I would not have wanted to go through a fight in the courtroom, I believe now I could go through anything. The fact Paul loves me gives me that confidence."

"Even if you may not be able to spend the rest of your life with Paul?"

"Yes," I sighed. "Even so."

"Then I think Savoy will understand that you aren't simply looking for an escape hatch out of your troubles but that you truly love him."

I nodded again.

"And when the time comes, I'll do everything in my power to help you. If the war ends abruptly and he comes back, then that will be wonderful for everyone. If not, it may be a long wait, but if you love him enough and he loves you in return, it will be worth it. And remember that there may be a turn of events between now and the end of the war that will prescribe your going over there. . . . Elzyna, don't give up."

"I won't."

"I don't think you will either," he said, and smiled again. "I remember as though it were yesterday . . . you were recovering from your back injury, and when you found out Alvareda and I had troubles you wrote me a letter, determined to somehow get to me and straighten me out. I knew then that you had the kind of spirit that would overcome any adversity."

Hearing that from him bolstered me more than I could say. I smiled. "I'll write to Paul immediately."

"I have something for you," he said, and pulled out a check for twelve hundred dollars from his drawer—the balance owed on the sale of the property. "Let's go down to the bank and put this into a separate account right now."

And so we did. After I left the bank, I felt immensely better about everything. I would have given anything had I not written that first letter to Paul—I should learn a lesson: when something seems wrong, don't do it. The two biggest mistakes of my life had to do with putting things into the mail—but there was still time to write to him again, and now I knew I could put my feelings down in a logical order. I thought of what Neal said about an "escape hatch," and realized that was what bothered me while trying to write to Paul this morning. Oh, everything would be all right. Talking to Neal convinced me at last. Just before we parted, Neal told me to write down everything I could remember that might make my case in the divorce court completely convincing. "I could probably write a book," I told him.

He put an arm around me and said, "Something around the length of a three- or four-page letter will be sufficient to get the attorney started. Be as concise as you can."

A report the length of a letter would be enough to incriminate Beryl Farrish, I thought.

A letter. . . . How ironic that seems now.

I wrote a letter to Paul that evening before Beryl came home. It ran seven pages, but that was all right. I read it over several times, and felt I had finally expressed myself. "Till we meet again," I ended it. I folded it and sealed it in an envelope.

The next morning I walked out on the porch to see Senta and John off to school before I put it into the mail box by the front door. At the curb Senta turned. "Mommy?"

"What is it, darling?" I said. I was already slipping the letter into the box.

"I need a new composition book for arithmetic. I forgot to tell you yesterday. Can you get it today?"

"Of course I will. Go along now, and have a good day."

As she walked down the block I stood on the porch and looked at the street and the lawn. It was a beautiful day, sunny and warm. We were due for a cold front by the weekend, however. I gazed down at the shrubs and thought how dull they were getting to look. I would plant the four o'clock seeds as a border in front of them, and maybe even extend them up the walk. It would be good for me to have a reminder before me of Paul, especially if there were a long wait ahead. . . .

By the first of the following week I was expecting a response. Any moment the telephone would ring and Alvareda would say there was a letter for me at her house. Nothing happened. Others called—the butcher to tell me my order was ready, the alteration department at Levy's to say that John's winter coat was ready—but there was no word about Paul, and each time I spoke to the party on the other end of the line, my flat voice must have betrayed my feelings of disappointment. I began to think perhaps he had decided he did not want me after all. Or his mother had put up a fuss about me and he had decided the problems before us were too great. Yet, even if he could only say no, at least he could have written to me.

Well . . . perhaps he was still traveling, or just so busy, he had to wait till there was an opportunity to sit down and write a thoughtful letter. Perhaps the letter telling me he would wait for me forever if need be had already been mailed.

December 12, 13. Nothing.

The boat taking them to France left on December 14. Paul was not going to answer me. I do not believe ever in my life I have suffered a worse blow. Beryl had not injured me so much when he struck me to the floor. Even his calling me names and deriding me did not injure me as I felt injured now. I could not eat; I could not sleep. My back began to ache so that I could hardly get up the stairs part of the time. I took medicine. Inside me I kept trying to hope, even when I knew there was no hope. Beryl, I think out of deference to my pregnancy, did not bother me. I needed to write the report for the lawyer, but I could not summon the strength.

Yesterday morning I awoke feeling somewhat better. The medicine, I am sure, had finally taken effect. I had also come to realize that, even if Paul had not written to me before he left—perhaps my letter did not reach him in time for him to answer—he might still write to me, while aboard ship on his way to France, after arriving there, when he could send me an address where I could reach him. Any number of possibilities might be in the offing. I must hold myself together. I must not give up hope, just as Neal said. I must do something constructive about my report to the attorney.

Lately Beryl had hardly spoken to me. I had never known him to be so distant yet not openly hostile toward me. I did not know what changed him. I did not care. I had to think only of making plans, putting my thoughts together, remembering things that went all the way back to the beginning.

Before Beryl left for work, he asked me when we might expect the balance of the proceeds on the sale of the property.

I gripped the back of the chair nearby. "Soon, I hope," I lied.

"So do I. We still have a lot of bills to pay off," he added, and walked through the door.

After he was gone I sat down and began to write my report. I began to list things on one sheet of paper as they came to me. Later I could try and put them into some kind of order. I wrote down a couple of things, then stopped. How difficult to put the story of a marriage into the pages of a report. A look here, an inference there. A lie. I stopped again. A lie. I thought of the whole misrepresentation about Beryl's architectural career. Could I not say that from the beginning he married me under false pretenses?

Yes. I wrote that down. Then I thought. They would need more than that, surely. You needed dates, facts in a courtroom. I needed to look at that letter from Joseph West again, because if I did not do so while I had the opportunity, Beryl would take the letter and burn it. He might already have done so.

I went back into the room where he used to work. Most everything was in its place, many of his drawings showing signs of water marks at the bottom. After looking through three boxes, I finally found the envelope with the letter from Joseph West. I pulled it out and opened it to read. But something had been added, then erased. It was still clear enough to make out. There was an address written out in pencil, a California address, presumably Joseph West's new one. That did not seem overly significant. But there was something else —"$300 by May" was written down below that. Was that amount something owed to Beryl by Joseph, or the other way around? And May of what year?

I read over the facts in the letter and replaced it, then went back to my desk to continue my work. I kept thinking of the amount. Was it possible that Beryl was sending money to Joseph West on some regular basis?

Silly. Why would he do that?

I wrote some more, then stopped. On the other hand, why had Joseph West visited here really? Why had he stayed so long, when he was on his way to a new job? Why the long hours of talk between them, the drawings? Furniture. And then I thought: Maybe Beryl was taking money out of the bicycle shop business and sending it to Joseph West in order to put him into business designing furniture.

I rolled my eyes. How foolish. I wrote some more. Then I stopped again. The night Beryl had said he was leaving, the night I fled with the children in fright, I had assumed he was out of his head, speaking of murder, and perhaps suicide. But the next day he seemed to reflect on the evening as though he were quite himself. Leaving his own way, on his own terms, "leaving nothing behind," he had said that night.

I sat back and remembered his questions about the money this morning. Was he up to something I knew nothing about? I decided to look for further letters from Joseph West. It was very possible they would not be here, but instead up at the shop. Still, he might not have wanted any of his employees to know about his private business any more than he wanted me to. . . .

I went back into the room and went through the boxes again. I went upstairs and looked through his things. Nothing. He must keep correspondence somewhere else, if, that is, he has any correspondence. I tried to think. There was only one more logical place, and that was in his desk at his shop. How in the world could I gain access to that?

It was Jordan who provided the answer. He arrived around noontime, just as the sky was darkening and the air was turning chill. He was in high spirits at the prospect of being home from school for two weeks. He came in with his suitcase and brushed my cheek with a kiss before starting upstairs. "Do I bunk with old John, or somewhere else?"

"You can take John's room. I'll put him in with Senta."

"I stopped by the shop to see if I could use the Packard tonight. Gotta swell date. But Beryl wasn't there. Reckon I could use it anyway? I'll get it washed and shined for him."

"You know I can't give you permission. You'll have to wait and talk to him. . . . You say he wasn't at the shop?"

"Yep. They didn't know where he was. I'll give him a call in a little while."

I changed into a suit and hat, and went immediately to town. If Beryl should turn up, I would tell him I was stopping by on my way somewhere, to Levy's to pick up John's coat, that was it. And I wanted to see if Jordan could borrow the car.

When I got to the shop the employees were all in back, working on automobiles. Just as well they did not see me. I went inside. The counter and displays were dusty and looked neglected, but I supposed it might have been worse. I went into Beryl's little office. From there I could see anyone approaching either from the back or the front through the glass partitions. I took a deep breath and opened the drawer in the middle. I shoved a few papers aside and put my hand toward the back. I pulled a large envelope forward and looked in it. There were several letters from a California address. My cheeks were flaming. I looked up to be sure no one was coming. I pulled a group of letters out and read the most recent. It was dated mid-October. In it Mr. West reported that he had finally been able to arrange for Beryl to enter Stanford on a probationary basis this January. He was sorry it had taken so long to make this arrangement. Beryl would live in an apartment off-campus, "just a block from where I stay," and he must be prepared to bring tuition money plus living expenses when he arrived. He would need several hundred dollars in addition to that which he had already forwarded.

He went on to say that Beryl should arrive in California before the Christmas holidays if possible; then he named several things that needed to be done in the interim period before classes began on January 4.

That was all except for the closing but the message was clear. I started to go back through the earlier letters, now more curious than ever about how this evolved. But then I heard a door close in the distance and I looked up and around. Nothing, yet. . . . In a state of near panic, I crammed the letters back into the envelope and closed them in the drawer.

I quickly walked out. Thankfully, there was no sign anyone had seen me. No one was about. I kept going, through the door and out on the sidewalk, trying to look as though I had done nothing out of the ordinary, just in case someone were observing me.

There were things to do. Beryl must be planning to depart very soon. I had to get home. I had to think. How stupid of me not to see what was going on. He must have been working toward this since Joseph West visited here a year and a half earlier. And I had always credited Beryl with having the loyalty to at least continue to stay and provide for us.

What of Senta? What of John? The letter from Mr. West indicated no plans had been laid for Beryl to bring the children with him. Well, I could be thankful for that. But I could hardly believe he could so easily take leave of Senta, who loved him so dearly.

From the time I stepped on the streetcar until I got home again, I thought over the things he had said and done that led to this. Yet I had been too lacking in imagination to see. Finally I realized I had done the first sensible thing in my marriage when I took Neal's advice and opened a separate account in my name for the twelve hundred dollars. I had no doubt Beryl would find a way to get the additional cash he needed, but he wouldn't take off with my money.

By the time I walked through the door it was raining hard, and the temperature was dropping. The telephone was ringing. I answered, even then in some hope it would be Paul or some word about him. It was John's teacher at Kirby Elementary. He was not feeling well and I had to fetch him at once.

I breathed a sigh and hung up the telephone. I went to the barn, hitched up the buggy, and drove down to the school. When I touched John's forehead it was cool. I would watch him awhile before I called the doctor. One o'clock. I put him to bed upstairs in the spare bed in Senta's room and changed clothes again.

Jordan left "to go and see some old pals," and said he would stop by and see if Beryl was at the shop yet. I sat down at my desk again and pulled out the sheets I had begun. In the face of Beryl's abandonment of all of us, what did any of these things mean? My divorce would surely be an easy one now. He would not even be here to contest it.

Maybe, maybe all of this would soon be over. Oh, thank God. Thank God. Six o'clock.

John was still sleeping. I felt his forehead. Still cool. Perhaps he'd slept poorly the night before, and was simply tired. Jordan came through the door with a new suit and a new pair of shoes from Sakowitz. I wondered who paid for them. Mother, no doubt.

He put the packages down on the sofa and opened the lid on the Florsheim shoe box. "See these?" he said proudly. "What do you think of them?"

They were very nice, two-tone brown lace-ups. Expensive-looking. I told him I liked them.

"Guess who sold them to me?" he said with a sly grin.

"I have no idea. Who?"

"Gabriel Gerrard. Apparently he has a little vacation job in the shoe department at Sakowitz." He put the shoes away and laughed. "I made that rich jerk show me every pair of shoes he had in my size. Then I bought the most expensive pair of the lot. Showed him good."

I just shook my head. I had too many of my own problems to worry about Jordan's dislike of the Gerrards.

"Beryl finally showed up at the shop and he told me I could use the car," he said.

"Fine," I said, and thought, where he is going he won't be taking it probably. One could not drive all the way to California, could one?

Jordan said he was taking out a girl named Augusta Miller, whom he expected me to remember, but I did not. He planned to leave in an hour, and asked if I'd fix him some supper. He went whistling up the stairs, carrying his new things.

While arranging ham and lettuce and tomato on bread for Jordan, and warming up a little soup, I kept thinking of possibilities. What if Beryl had run up a great many expensive bills that I knew nothing about and would be left to pay? I gave the soup a stir and thought in frustration that he probably had. Well, I would just have to ask Neal how to deal with that. He would know. Oh, thank goodness for Neal. What would I have done without him through all this? Tomorrow I must tell him what I had learned. Or maybe it would be smarter to do it now. I turned off the stove and went to the telephone. The housekeeper answered. The Gerrards were gone for the evening. "No, no message," I said, "I'll call again tomorrow." Back in the kitchen I cut the sandwich and thought, of course. I would sell the car . . . that is, if he left it, and surely he would. . . . And what had he intended doing about his bicycle shop? Just abandon it, too? Well . . . that wasn't my worry, not for now, anyway. I must keep reminding myself of the positive side of all this. . . .

Beryl did not come home for supper, nor did he come afterward. Finally at ten o'clock I went upstairs to bed. I had already, in the most casual fashion I could, asked Senta if Daddy had said anything about taking her on a trip. She had looked at me for a moment, then said he had not.

The rain was still coming down but was reduced to little more than a drizzle. Tomorrow would be crisp and beautiful: a comforting thought. I dozed off now and then from exhaustion, though I was too wound up to really sleep. The thing to do was to stay calm and not betray the fact that I knew anything. Beryl would soon be gone, and I would begin to make plans to join Paul. Every day that passed, word from him might be speeding to me. I needed to be prepared. Oh, what pleasure to be able to report Beryl's abandoning us. Had I but known his plans sooner, everything would have been so much easier. Yet, I must not worry about that now. Everything was going to be all right. . . .

As I dozed off the last time, I felt that regardless of how Beryl behaved when he came home from work, he could not possibly rob me of the sense of well-being which grew as the hands advanced on the clock. Then around midnight, I awoke to hear music downstairs. Someone was playing ragtime on the piano in the library. I could hear the plinkety-plank notes of Scott Joplin's music. The roll of the bass notes and the tinkle of the treble. In between the songs I could hear the sound of voices. So it seemed Beryl was having a going-away party of sorts. I got up and checked to see if Jordan was home. His bedroom light was off, however. The children. I went toward Senta's room and pushed open the door. John was there. Senta was gone. I walked in and pushed the covers around on her bed. "Senta? Senta?" I called. She did not answer.

I went to the stair landing. The music was still going on. The laughing and talking continued. It seemed to me there were many voices down there. I took a few steps down and stopped. I could not decide whether to go on or not. Except for my worry about Senta, I would have gone back upstairs and tried to get through the rest of the night. I walked slowly down. When I got to the bottom of the stairway I stopped in the hallway and looked toward the library, where the party was transpiring. To my shock, there was Senta, in her gown, dancing on top of the piano. All around her were men drinking and smoking. I was livid. I walked in and ordered, "Senta, come to bed immediately." The man who had been playing the piano shot a sullen glance Beryl's way, and then lowered her down. I didn't want his hands on her. I stepped up and grabbed her from him. Senta was struggling. She didn't want to leave. She kept saying, "I hate you, Mommy. You spoil all the fun."

Several men at the dining room table playing cards looked in at the spectacle and laughed and made jokes. I could not understand what they were saying. I glared at Beryl and took Senta upstairs with me. I told her to go to bed, and if she came down again I would lock her in her room all the next day. She looked at me as coldly as I have ever seen her.

I went to bed and lay down. My heart was beating so fast, my breath came in gulps. Now that I had caused a spectacle, what would Beryl do? I had been so mad that I did not think. The idea of Senta entertaining those filthy men made me act without considering all the consequences.

The party must have been soon over. Within the half-hour I heard the front door open and close several times. Perhaps I had put an end to the party myself. I waited with my hands drawn tightly around my abdomen for the sound of Beryl's footsteps on the stairs. At last he came. He grabbed my shoulders and turned me toward him. "You bitch," he said. "I'll teach you to ruin my party for me."

I saw his arm go up in the air and I covered my face.

"All right, sweet Elzyna, here," he said, and I felt his foot right in the lower part of the center of my back. It was like a boulder hurled against me. He nearly knocked me off the bed, and at first I could not get my breath. I was, without even realizing it, curled up to protect the child I was carrying. He kicked me three times, my head rearing back in pain, then he went to the door.

"Why don't you leave now? Coward. Liar. Go see your friend Joseph West. I'm not holding you back," I said through clenched teeth.

He paused. Then he came forward and knelt down so that his face was close to mine. My whole body tensed with fear. "So I'm a coward, am I? I'm a liar? Then what is this, sweet pure Elzyna?"

He put a hand in his pocket and pulled out my last letter to Paul. I gasped, reaching for the letter. He put it in his pocket and raised his hand again. I buried my head. He came down with his knuckles across the back of my neck. The pain was so excruciating I slumped down in a heap on the bed. I think now that I lost consciousness. I do not know for how long. I opened my eyes and the house was silent. My letter, my letter, I thought desperately, and all at once I knew that Senta had purloined it for him. I had to get it, had to get it. Yet, for a long time I lay there, afraid to rise. There still were no sounds. I finally rose and walked to the landing. I do not remember any pain from the blows I had received. I know that I was not standing upright, but all I could think of was that I had somehow to retrieve my letter, no matter what resulted.

I waited for another half-hour, then I started down the stairs. At the bottom I stopped to look. Beryl was asleep on the parlor sofa. This was the epitome of his nerve, believing that he had put me in my place and that I would not dare cross him again. In that moment I felt a rush of hatred for him that was stronger than any I had ever felt. I went to the fireplace and picked up a poker. I would certainly not go toward him unarmed. I would try to slip the letter from his pocket and go back upstairs. Then I would dress, get the children up, and dress them. We would have to leave in order to avoid further violence from him. I walked toward him softly, the poker behind me. I thought he was into a deep sleep. I reached for his pocket and pulled out the bulky envelope. His eyes flew open and he grabbed my hand, suddenly, like a startled animal. He pulled me forward.

I raised the poker. He released my wrist. His eyes widened. The poker sliced through the air and came down upon him.

It must have been some moments before this that Jordan turned the corner several blocks up on McKinney and began to make his way in the automobile toward the house. He confessed later that he had had a few too many drinks while at the home of Augusta Miller, and when he started home, through the icy drizzle, he had difficulty controlling the automobile. He said that his bladder was full. All he could think about was getting home to the water closet.

On he came, past Dowling, St. Charles, and Live Oak. Past Milby and then, at last to our block. He saw the lights on in the front parlor when he got to the corner. He was thinking with surprise that someone was still up. He said he thought he might have been looking at the house, rather than at the street, when suddenly he realized a figure was almost directly in front of him. When the figure stepped off the curb, hands above his head, Jordan applied the brake. The automobile skidded and plunged right in the path of the man. He hit the car front on, his arms outspread as though he were being crucified. Jordan covered his face, afraid to look. He said that he waited several moments before emerging from the car. And when he walked around to look, the headlights revealed the figure to be Beryl.

I was still standing in the parlor, one hand wrapped around the poker, the other clasping the letter, my mind refusing to accept what I had just done. The screech of the automobile tires startled me to life. I looked through the front window. I could see the gleaming headlights at the curb, but could not make out the shape of the car in the darkness. It did not occur to me that either Jordan or Beryl had been involved. Some poor traveler . . . a neighbor, perhaps. . . . I must investigate. Someone might need to call an ambulance. I replaced the poker, then walked toward the door. I noticed lights coming on in neighboring houses, porch lights beaming up and down the street. I saw and heard others gathering at the curb. Then I saw Jordan, rushing up toward our porch.

When he told me what happened, I brought a hand to my mouth in horror. Jordan thought that Beryl might already be dead, but he wasn't certain; he was nearing panic. His frightened state helped to stabilize me. I told him to sit down and I went to the telephone to call first an ambulance, then the police. A sharp feeling of guilt and remorse rammed through me like a sword. Now I must tell the whole story. Everything must come out. As I ordered the ambulance, I rehearsed in my mind the words I must say to the police: ". . . you see, my husband and I quarreled violently; he struck me several times. . . . I was afraid he might harm me further, so I . . . ." I paused, one hand gripping the receiver. I lowered my forehead. I could hardly get my breath. What if . . . oh, God . . . what if they didn't believe me? I swallowed hard and looked at Jordan, who sat at the edge of the sofa, his head buried in his hands. I hesitated a moment longer. They would send me away . . . take my children from me . . . oh, I wanted to die; with all my heart, I wanted to die.

And yet . . . yet . . . as I finally found my voice to ask the operator to connect me with the police department, an instinct from somewhere deep inside me rose up like a wall. Suddenly I knew that I was not going to act on my guilt by telling the full truth. The Lord would judge me in a higher court, but no one, no one else would ever have to know. "Yes, this is Mrs. Farrish, 4001 McKinney Avenue. I want to report an automobile accident. . . ."

When the authorities came, the ambulance had already arrived. Within minutes Beryl had been taken to the hospital and Jordan had been taken to the station for questioning. A kindly man from the police department said that he was awfully sorry about the accident, and offered to drive me to the hospital and drop the children off somewhere.

"We have good friends out on Main Street. We'll take the children there," I told him evenly. I felt a deep sense of calm resolve, and I thought: When I return to this house, things will be different. The police officer's automobile was parked out at the curb awaiting us. I awakened the children, told them their father had suffered an accident, and that they would be spending the night with the Gerrards. We put on our coats and walked down the stairs together. When we opened the front door and stepped out on the porch Senta stopped and said, "Is my daddy going to get all right again?"

For a moment I could not speak. As many tears as I had shed through all the weeks just passed, that moment when I looked into my daughter's eyes and saw the love and concern for her father reflected there was the one moment in that tragic night when I came close to crying again.

"Yes, darling. I believe so," I told her at last. I could not bear to tell her that I had already been informed he probably would not live.

The clouds that had covered the moon were now moving quickly away from it, and it shone down upon us as we stepped off the porch. Senta took my hand. John stayed close to me. The man from the police department opened the rear door of his automobile, and the three of us walked down the stairs, down the front walk, and across the tiles that spelled out, B. FAR-RISH, 1906.

There is a great deal for which to be thankful, and I must remember this tonight and every other night, and go on. If I should hear the sound of a train rumbling down the tracks a few blocks away, I must be strong enough to cover my ears and look into the comforting log fire, and not think of New Orleans and all I cannot have, all for which hope is gone. I must think of the children who, thank God, have not been harmed or taken from me. I must think of this house, which I have loved since I was a child. These are the major blessings. And there are the small, daily things, like sitting out on the porch in springtime and watching the four o'clocks bloom, and not feeling afraid anymore.

Senta
1928–1940

PART 1

Chapter 1

If anyone knew of my connection with the tragedy that happened three hours ago, they would not believe I am at least partially innocent. How could I know I made a deal with the devil until I got caught in the middle of it? Now I wish, oh, how I wish, I could take everything back, all that I said, and all that I did, instead of just this one piece of evidence in my hand.

I was very young when I realized I could get anything I wanted badly enough, and at my seventh birthday party—right here on the front lawn of this house—I watched Gabriel Gerrard open the door of his father's automobile, cross the tiles and walk through the gate, come to fetch Lilly home from the party, and I knew that I wanted him. He paused to give my cheek a birthday kiss, and I thought surely he was the tallest, most handsome man in the world. As he left, carrying Lilly in his arms, with her waving at me over his shoulder, I wanted more than anything to go with them. I was suddenly bored with the party; bored with my presents. I told the other guests to go home, and I walked up the steps and into the house as they stared at me in wonder. At length Mother followed me, scolding me for rudeness. I told her it was a crummy birthday party anyway, and she could throw the presents in the trash for all I cared. Her feelings meant nothing to me.

All in all she ruined my childhood, hateful as she was toward my father and jealous of his love for me. She always favored John over me, pampering him as though he were delicate as a flower petal. Me, she scolded constantly.

My father said that if I would spy on Mother, let him know what she was doing all the time and sneak things for him to look at, he would not leave me behind when he went to California. Of course, Mother didn't know about anything I did, and I hoped she would never find out. The most daring thing I ever did was to take an envelope she had put in the mailbox just a few days before my father's accident. When he looked over the contents he gave a war whoop and swung me around in his arms. Of course I had no idea why it was so important. I had never seen him in such high spirits. We went for a spin in the Packard. It was the last time we ever did that.

I was devastated by my father's accident. On the night it happened, I cried myself to sleep as Lilly, lying next to me in her bed, held my hand to comfort me. I promised God that if He would spare my father's life, and let us go to California together, I would never, ever leave my father's side. Of course, it did not turn out that way at all.

I am sure that Mother was not sorry about my father's accident, and she was punished for how she felt—I could certainly see that. The next day John developed scarlet fever, and a few days later he died. I was saddened by his death, but not half as much as I was by my father's accident. Because John slept in my room on the night he was starting to get sick, Mother feared I might catch the fever. I did not. But Mother thinks that Laura, my sister, who was born the following May, may have suffered some consequences of the fever. I don't know because it seemed farfetched. But there was definitely something wrong with Laura, I'll never argue that.

My father, coming within inches of death, survived. He spent a long time recovering in a nursing home. I was never allowed to see him during that time. At last he was released, and the decision was made that he should live here in this house and that we would move out. He was crippled—his legs were useless, having been crushed under the Packard—and he sat in a wheelchair for the rest of his life. A woman was hired to come in and clean twice a week and prepare his daily meals. He never left the yard.

We moved to my grandmother's house. Lilly and I begged that we live with Lilly's family, but Mother would not consider imposing on them. Anyhow, Grandmother Leider was by then in failing health and Mother felt she should care for her since Grandfather was still seldom home. She would never say how long we would stay with my grandparents, but she always indicated we would one day return to our home on McKinney Avenue. In 1915, shortly after his release from the hospital, she divorced my father and renounced her vows to the Catholic Church. We became Episcopalians and attended Christ Church with the Gerrards.

After my father was settled in the house, Mother let me visit him now and then, taking me there and waiting as though she were afraid we might conspire against her if left alone. When I was older, I was allowed to ride the trolley out there by myself, and he would tell me about how it was to live there. The children in the neighborhood pretended the house was haunted and they thought he was a freak—he was able to get this information from the cleaning lady. They used to draw near the house and spy on him through the windows as though he were an animal in a circus cage. Once a pack of boys threw rocks into the beveled glass doors, and several of the panes fell out and shattered on the floor. I know it must have outraged him to be considered a crazy man. But he spent most of his time designing and paid them little attention. After several years he developed arthritis and finally lost the ability to draw.

He developed tuberculosis in 1924 and died in 1925 at the age of forty-three. His hair was almost entirely gray. I stood above his coffin and wept bitterly, for the waste of his life, for the way he was always misunderstood, and for the painful void I already felt because I would never again be able to see his eyes light up when I came through the door to visit him.

On the day of his death they opened Eastwood School, just blocks away where McKinney meets Polk. Such a short distance away, a school in the mission style—it looks much like the Mission San Jose in San Antonio—and he could not get out to see it, not even once. His funeral procession passed it by. How hard he had fought to get this style accepted in Houston; how cruel that when he could no longer appreciate it, the style began cropping up everywhere. I have long suspected that some of the architects in this city stole his ideas and designs.

My father was buried next to John in the Leider plot in Glendale Cemetery, located in what was then Harrisburg but now is just a neighborhood around the Houston Ship Channel.

After the funeral Mother announced we would move back into this house. The street was much the same, though the oak trees were larger and older. There were now homes a lot farther out than ours, and some of the older houses closer to town were gone. There were a few more businesses than there used to be—service stations and barbershops, drugstores and dry cleaners, and up at York Street by the railroad tracks, a café.

Our house was dilapidated by 1925, not having been painted for over ten years, nor new curtains put up. There were cigarette burns in many places on the furniture, and in the carpets. I don't think Mother had realized how thoroughly neglected—even abused—it was, because my father kept the curtains drawn and did not let the sunshine in. She forced him to live in a house which he had hated from the beginning. It served her right. I remember one afternoon after his death when we had come to make a list of repairs and things to be replaced, she sat at the dining table, which had little marks around the edges where cigarettes had been left to burn to the end, and after a while she began to weep. I watched her, and felt no pity. Why should I?

After a few minutes she realized I was watching her and she dried her eyes and looked at me. "Perhaps I'll meet someone . . . someone kind and loving . . . and marry again."

I continued to stare at her.

"Oh, never mind. I have work to do."

I told her I would be ashamed for my friends to see this house, and walked out on the front porch to wait for her. I must have stood there for a long time, looking out at the street. And I remember, all at once, something twisting up inside me at the thought of her being so downcast. I knew then that I could not hate her anymore. Although there were things for which I would never forgive her, that would keep me from ever feeling close to her or affectionate toward her, I didn't feel hatred anymore, either.

I believe it cost her most of her available cash to redo the house. She bought new carpets, and had the hardwood floors revarnished. She had the furniture repaired and the house repainted inside and out. She replaced the broken panes of glass in the French doors that up to then had been patched with plywood. She worked like a slave all spring and summer to get the yard back in order and the gardens thriving again. We soon had crepe myrtle bushes and roses, and four o'clocks, her favorites.

Mother designated that I would have the bedroom up above the front parlor, where she and my father used to sleep. She let me choose a flowered wallpaper and new throw rugs and sheer curtains, and she made some doilies for the dresser and let me keep the Tiffany lamp that had been beside the bed since I can remember. For Laura she remodeled the old nursery, because Laura liked that room best.

She made the spare room behind the parlor and next to the bathroom downstairs into her bedroom, because on the days she had back pain, she did not want to have to climb the stairs. Her back has bothered her more and more as the years have passed, even though she keeps her weight down faithfully, as the doctor prescribed, and tries not to strain it unduly. Her downstairs room was always the prettiest in the house. She bought a new pecan dresser and writing desk and a brass bed for it, and papered it in lavender with a print of violets and streamers. She had the fireplace and baseboards painted white, and put carpets in it with very light background and violets, greens, and golds in the floral pattern. She had shelves built above the fireplace for her collection of china figurines that the Gerrards had brought her from their overseas trips.

She never allowed Laura or me to go in there without her permission, but of course I didn't care. The only things I cared about were some drawings and personal belongings that were my father's, which she put in the attic. I was thankful at least she had not burned them.

I was finishing my course at business school and Laura, at the age of ten, was just beginning to show signs of being abnormal. I believe Mother felt if she got Laura away from her doting grandmother, she could deal with her better. Laura was a beautiful girl, with widow's peak and reddish brown hair, brown eyes and long lashes that always made me envious. But she was completely undependable. You could never tell what she would do next, and for many reasons she was a source of embarrassment for all of us.

Between 1915 and the first couple of years after we moved back home, I had rarely seen Gabriel, only now and then at family gatherings, being close to him just long enough to wish I could get closer and to nurture my dream of having him for my own. At first he was in school at Harvard, then he went away to the war for a brief period, then he returned and went to school at Texas University for a while. Finally he returned home and joined a big law firm.

It was maddening, never having an opportunity to let him know how I felt. Then my chance came. One night in April of 1928 when Mother and Laura and I had dinner at his parents' home, he was there, though he had had his own apartment since he went to work. I had had my hair bobbed that afternoon, much to my mother's dismay. It had grown down nearly to my waist, and I was tired of it beyond imagination. I was ready to look for a secretarial position, my stenographer's job at the gas company having become a bore. Therefore I wanted to look more businesslike. I was pleased with the effect of little fingertip waves above my forehead and short curls on the sides and in the back, and a spit curl right where the part began, above my left eye. I looked much older. Perhaps that is why Gabriel noticed me enough to say that he liked my hair.

"If I'd thought you would notice, I would have bobbed it a long time ago," I said and looked deep into his eyes a moment longer. Oh, he noticed that moment. There was more man in that six feet of Gabriel Gerrard than in any other man I've known. My whole face grew warm as he observed me in a new way. That was the night I had the idea of getting on at the law firm where he practiced, in the Esperson Building.

There was but one position open when I arrived in the personnel department. The director told me there had been many applicants considered, but most of them could not use the typewriter with the required accuracy. "Legal documents cannot have even one error," she explained behind bifocals. "It would be nice if you had a little experience as well," she remarked. I was directed into a little wooden booth to take a three-minute typing test. I was nervous that day, and made three errors. While I was trying to figure how I might correct them without being noticed, she grabbed the paper from my hand. "Time's up," she said. "Have a seat in the waiting area."

I nodded and found a chair, nervously clutching my handbag.

There was one other girl there and I decided it wouldn't hurt to get to know the competition. I asked her if she'd been looking for a job very long. She said no, that she had worked a year at Vincent Barton, but her boss left to go into practice in Dallas, and there were no other positions open in the firm. She was pretty, and also confident.

I leaned back, crestfallen. What chance did I have against her experience? She probably typed better than I did as well. If I could only have a look at the tests. . . . A few minutes passed and, miraculously, I had an opportunity. The girl left to go to the ladies room, and not two minutes later, the director left as well. I looked anxiously both ways, fearing someone else might come in, or the director herself return. . . . I drew in a breath. I had to do it now. The job meant everything to me. I rose and quickly stole into the director's office. I found the typing tests enclosed in our two folders on her desk. I scanned the other girl's and found no errors, then switched the tests from one folder to the other. Somewhere in the distance a door shut. I wheeled around and closed my hands behind me, my heartbeat a slamming in my chest. I waited breathlessly. One moment . . . two . . . No one appeared. I hurried back to the waiting room and sat down, hands shaking. In a moment the director returned, with my rival behind her. My mind raced forward. What if the girl went over the test with the director, and claimed it was not hers? I would have to be prepared, that was all. Not look the least ruffled if the question arose. The director must have mixed them up, that was it. Or someone in the office brushed by the desk and knocked the folders down. Oh, this was bizarre . . . what if I were caught?

Suddenly the director was calling my name. I followed her nervously into the office. She looked at my folder, then at me over her bifocals. "I am a great believer in experience before we hire personnel," she said. "But I have decided this time to let you through for an interview with Mr. Carney. He has just been promoted, and mentioned he has very specific ideas about how things should be done. Since the position of his stenographer doesn't pay handsomely, he would at least consider a girl with no legal experience. You seem to qualify.

"You can go up and see him now, Room 545, at the corner by the elevator." She called in her secretary and asked her to lead the way and take my file along.

As we walked out I saw my rival reading a magazine, no doubt confident she was about to be hired. But I knew that, unless the switch in tests were discovered, I'd get the job. I can handle men.

Mr. Carney was very tall and thin, with small round glasses in steel frames. He wore an awful printed bow tie and had a dowdy appearance. I checked his hand for a wedding ring. There was none. As soon as we bid each other good day, I told him how much I admired so young a man for having attained his position.

He looked across at me in surprise, and undisguised pleasure. He smiled and nodded slightly. "Are you a good organizer?" he asked.

"Excellent," I said, truthfully.

"Do you mind working extra hours if need be?"

"Not at all. I'm single, as you see, and can make my schedule according to my needs."

"What about transportation?"

"I ride the streetcar."

"And you aren't afraid to ride the trolley at night?"

"I'm not afraid of anything."

He observed me at length, as though trying to make up his mind. He drummed the desk with his pencil.

"By the way, do you know a Mr. Gabriel Gerrard?" I asked.

"Oh yes. His office is down the hall—is he a friend of yours?"

"Our families have been close for years. His mother and mine are almost inseparable. His sister is my best friend."

"Well, that's quite impressive. Gerrards are well known in this town . . . the well-established rich. Cotton, wasn't it?"

"Pardon?"

"The old man, Gabriel's father, made his money in the cotton business, didn't he?"

"I think so, yes. I'm not around Neal Gerrard very much. I think now he's just in banking, real estate, and so forth."

"Ah, yes. Well, I think the big cotton industry is virtually a thing of the past. Our economic base has become well heeled in the oil business. Once they opened the deep-water port and started building all those refineries, the cotton days began to dwindle."

"My uncle is in oil," I said. This was a stretching of the point, but I could see now what things impressed Mr. Carney and I wasn't going to let the moment pass. "I don't know much about his affairs, but he has drilled in all the important fields."

"Oh, what's his name?"

"Leider. Jordan Leider. His father—my grandfather—is in oil too, and now works for some company that sends him all over the world. We rarely see him. My grandmother still lives out in the family home on Main. Well, it's not so far out anymore, just four blocks from the Humble Building and surrounded by apartment buildings and business offices."

"And you live out on McKinney Avenue . . . is that far from where Magnolia Park used to be?"

"Not too far."

"My father used to take us out there to go canoeing nearby the pavilion. I kind of hated to see it chopped up into subdivisions. All those magnolia trees —ah, well, that's progress I suppose. Let's see . . ." he studied the file again. My blood was racing. I knew that he would hire me.

He looked up finally and said, "Call the personnel office tomorrow morning by nine. The director will have my decision by then. I have another young woman to interview. But I don't mind telling you, I think we could work together."

I smiled demurely and thanked him.

The next morning I was told to report for work on Monday. I put down the telephone and let out a screech of victory. Mother was rounding the corner. "Senta, what on earth?"

"I got him—got the job," I said gleefully, and pirouetted around and kissed her cheek. I ran up the stairs, thinking, this is it! This is it! In my room I threw open the closet door and ran my hand over the clothing, then narrowed my eyes and began to think. Monday would be the most important day that I had ever walked out of this house. What I wore had to be exactly right. . . . The trouble was, everything looked like the apparel of a schoolgirl. Pleated skirts, chemises, filmy boat-neck blouses and linen jackets, suitable for a day out on a boat, but not for a law firm.

Finally I knew. My Easter suit of light blue linen with a double-breasted jacket and large pointed collar. Or was it too dressy? No. Perfect. White stockings, white kid shoes, and Mother's long string of pearls.

I hardly slept over the weekend. On Sunday night I washed and curled my hair, and spent two hours pressing the suit and polishing the white kid shoes. I awoke at five o'clock on Monday morning and began the long ritual of dressing. I assumed, of course, that I would run into Gabriel first thing. I was mistaken.

I did not see him at all the first day, or the next, or even the next. In fact for the first month I was disappointed with how hard I had to work and how seldom I saw Gabriel. We might chance to ride the same elevator along with several other people, or stop at the water fountain at the same time. But he only spoke politely and rushed on. He always looked terribly busy and full of purpose. To think he might notice what I was wearing was almost laughable. But I did not give up. I bought a pale pink linen suit when the new summer things appeared at Sakowitz. I could not afford clothes from Sakowitz and did not ordinarily shop there, but Gabriel did. He was rich. He went around in Saybro suits and hand-tailored silk ties, and I wanted to be his equal. I spent my whole paycheck on the suit and part of another on the shoes and stockings and hat. The suit fell just below my knees—I was blessed with good legs, everyone said so—and was very straight and tailored except for four deep knife pleats right down the center. The jacket had a scalloped placket and a plain neckline, and a wide belt that fit just below the waist. The hat was floppy but not too large. It was the smartest thing I had ever owned in my life. I wore it one Tuesday, and as luck would have it, I did not see Gabriel.

But the suit brought me luck after all. I wore it again the next week, and because of a double work load and a big hearing coming up in court, I had to work till nine o'clock. My whole body was exhausted, especially my forearms and hands from pecking away at the typewriter—I had been rooted to my hard wooden chair since noon when I finally finished and handed Mr. Carney the sixty-seven pages to read. I waited impatiently as he proofed them and finally he waved at me to go, but then called out, "I won't be long. If you wait, I will drive you home, Miss Farrish."

It was a tempting offer, but I was soon thankful that I had turned him down. I walked out in the hall and started toward the elevator. Then, behind me I heard Gabriel's voice. "Slow down, kiddo. I'll ride down with you."

My heart leaped like a runner who just heard the "go" signal. I turned and smiled as he walked up. He had a confident gait, like most tall men. He carried his suit coat and had his tie off and his collar unbuttoned.

He never seemed as rattled with me as I felt with him. "You're leaving awfully late tonight," he said as the elevator arrived and we stepped in.

"Mr. Carney has a case in court tomorrow. I just finished typing a few minutes ago."

"Yeah, I know which one. The Dunbrad-Staton match. I did part of the research on that one."

"Oh? I thought clerks did all the research. Aren't you a junior partner?"

He smiled, probably at my researching him, and nodded. "But this firm is top-heavy with aging senior partners who are determined to stay around forever. There are three junior partners for every one of them, so we still get a lot of the dirty work. Test of our true humility. I keep telling myself I'm lucky to be learning so much."

"I've certainly learned a lot, in just a few weeks."

He looked surprised. "I didn't realize you had been here that long. Does Sid Carney keep you late often?"

"This was the first time, but I doubt if it will be the last."

"Well, he should have at least offered to drive you home, or did you drive a car?"

"No. I ride the streetcar, and he did offer but I turned—told him I'd be fine on my own."

He opened the building door and a wave of cool air hit us. It felt refreshing to my hot temples. "He should have insisted. Let me drive you."

"Really, I'll be fine."

"No, I'd never forgive myself if anything happened to you. My car is this way."

I could have dreamed all night about his last remark, if he said nothing the rest of the evening. His Buick roadster was new, and was the best-looking car I'd ever ridden in. It was a deep maroon color—I learned this later; it was too dark to tell that night—and the dashboard was of polished wood. The steering wheel was custom, he admitted—black leather with an ivory knob framed in gold—and the seats were deeply tufted leather. Boy, it must be nice to be rich, I almost said, but restrained myself just in time.

"How long you think it will take you to earn a full partnership in the firm?"

"Oh, I'm going to give it another year or so. If I'm still stuck by then, I'll go somewhere else."

Oh, don't go somewhere else, I begged silently.

"I'll bet you haven't eaten," he said suddenly. "Let me take you out for something."

"No, no. I ate a sandwich earlier. I'm not hungry," I said quickly. Had I not been so nervous I would have had sense enough to lie and say I was famished. It was too late now. And maybe it was for the best. In my present state all I could do was react to his attempts at conversation with dull, uninteresting responses. I kept wanting to go back and start over again, but the moments ticked by and soon we were speeding down McKinney Avenue. When we pulled up in front of the house he said, "You know, it's always been hard for me to look at this house and realize it is the old country place we had when I was a kid. It sure looks different."

"Does it? I never saw it any other way."

"Well it was way, way out then. Maybe it was because I was so young, but it seemed when we drove out here in my father's buggy that it took all day to drive here. And it was wilderness. Nothing was around here except trees and brush and wild animals—well, at least I pretended there were wild animals. My father predicted there would be houses and streets all the way to Harrisburg Boulevard and on all sides someday, and he was right."

All this talk seemed strange to me. It was a neighorhood like any other when I was a child. There were not as many houses, nor as many streets, and only Kirby Elementary School—which later became Rufus Cage—where John and I went to school for a semester in 1914 after Mother decided not to enroll us at Holy Sacrament. I hoped we would have time to get off this subject and onto another, more intimate one.

"Why don't you come in? Mother always waits up for me when I come in late, and always has coffee brewed."

He said that he would, and came around and opened my door for me. I brushed past him as I got out of the car. It was like coming within the radius of a strong magnet, and I was possessed of the almost overpowering urge I had had since childhood: to be held in the arms of Gabriel.

We sat in the dining room and had coffee and cookies with Mother. At first I was enjoying the nearness of him . . . watching his long fingers splay out above the table as he made a conversational point . . . watching his brown eyes shift from Mother to me, sometimes pausing for a prolonged glance in my direction as he said something about work in the law firm. My hands felt clammy and there was a ticklish sensation at the base of my ears. God, I wished Mother would get lost so I could have him to myself. . . .

Yet Mother and Gabriel never had trouble talking to each other, and soon were involved in chitchat about the family, leaving me out altogether. Mother asked if Clayton had written lately. He had been in Illinois continuing his study of medicine for two years.

"You know how Clayton is," he reminded her. "Becoming a surgeon is the only thing that matters to him. He forgets everyone and everything else."

Mother told him she wouldn't mind being attended by someone that dedicated to his profession. Gabriel asked if we had heard that Lilly passed midterm exams—all of us knew how hard a struggle Lilly was having at Rice

Institute. While she should be nearly finished by now, she had dropped out for a while, then returned, changing her major from math to English, and losing many of her academic credits as a result.

Alvareda and Neal were abroad and would be gone till sometime in May, a few weeks before Neal must get busy doing something for Jesse Jones for the Democratic Convention to be held here. Mother told Gabriel she had received several postcards—one from Monte Carlo, which sounded like the most romantic place in the world. Then she told Gabriel about the new drilling company Jordan had gone into with several partners. Mother was proud of this—it was Jordan's first real "break" in the world of business. He'd been working the oil fields since he quit school right after the accident in December of 1914. I was certain Gabriel would not care to hear about Jordan's business activities. Mother knew they disliked each other, and the fact that she brought up Jordan's name in front of him was no doubt because she was always hopeful Jordan would prove himself worthy of something other than disdain by the Gerrard family. Had she known what I did, she would have realized there was no hope for that. Last year, Uncle Jordan had asked Lilly for a date one Saturday night while Alvareda and Neal were out of town. Lilly accepted. I don't know all the details, because Lilly wouldn't talk about it very much, even to me. Apparently during the evening Jordan got fresh. They were somewhere in the vicinity of Gabriel's apartment at the time. She managed to get free from Jordan, hailed a taxi, and arrived at Gabriel's door in near hysterics, her blouse hanging open where a couple of the buttons had been ripped off. Gabriel, of course, was livid. As soon as he calmed her nerves, he left in his car to hunt Jordan down. When he found him, he beat the hell out of him. Lilly told me later she could not have predicted the extent of Gabriel's wrath when she fled to him. She said she thought if he'd had a gun he would have killed Jordan, and as she awaited his return she was even more frightened than she had been of Jordan's advances toward her. The incident was hushed up because Lilly didn't want to upset her parents. A week or so afterward, she received an envelope in the mail containing a statement from St. Joseph's Hospital, for emergency treatment to Jordan Leider that Saturday night. The bill was marked, "paid," by the hospital. There was a note scrawled across the front of it from Jordan, which said something to the effect that the score wasn't settled between him and Gabriel, and that one day he'd make Gabriel sorry for ever tangling with him. Lilly said that Gabriel didn't take the note too seriously, and apparently he was correct. Nothing ever came of it.

Gabriel now listened politely to Mother. I rose from the table to refill Gabriel's coffee cup, and there, lurking just behind the doorway like a little thief, was Laura. I was worn out from the long day and frustrated by the way the evening was going. I had no patience with a thirteen-year-old girl who behaved like a shy six-year-old. "Come out," I said. "Don't stand there eaves-dropping. Come now."

Mother and Gabriel looked around. "Hi, Laura," said Gabriel in his usual friendly manner. He got up and went where she was and took her by the hand. She smiled, and moved toward him silently. I noticed something then that I had not seen before. Laura was—physically at least—becoming a young woman. Her chest was beginning to show a slight contour and her waist seemed more of an indentation than before. Laura's build was similar to mine, neither of us taking much after Mother. And Laura looked more like my father than I did. Her hair was much darker than mine, and her facial features were sharp, her eyes keen and bright like my father's. Gabriel was talking to her as personably as though he had seen her the day before, and saw her every day of his life. She smiled and shook her head, and said nonsensical things. God, did he have a way with people! It was evident even then that he could charm people into doing anything he wanted them to.

Gabriel left at ten-thirty. When he walked out the door I thanked him again for giving me a lift. His answer infuriated me. "Anytime," he said. "A young girl shouldn't be out that late by herself."

He was almost down to the curb. "In case you didn't know, I am almost twenty-one," I yelled. I went through the door and banged it behind me. "Smart aleck," I muttered.

"Well, he is thirty-two, Senta. Perhaps that's why he thinks of you as a child," said Mother.

I glanced at her out of the corner of my eye. "It's time he changed the way he thinks." I turned to go up the stairs. Laura was close behind me, looking dreamy as though she'd just spent an evening with her first beau. "And why did you have to act so dumb?" I demanded.

Laura cut her eyes toward me and smiled mysteriously. She began to hum in that maddening way of hers, and padded softly by me up the dark stairway to her room.

Chapter 2

The fact that Gabriel still thought of me as a child came as a painful shock, though as I lay there in bed that night and thought it through, I realized I might have expected that. While most men—including Sid Carney—regarded me as fully mature, they had not known me as Gabriel had, a college man watching his sister and her best friend play with their dolls. Even if I had been telling myself for a lifetime that age did not matter between Gabriel and me, he had not known I felt that way because I had never told him or anybody else. It was one secret I had never shared even with Lilly. I would not take the risk of having Lilly or anyone else laugh at me for wanting a much older man. They would all know when I was old enough to do something about it, and then they would not be laughing.

What could I do to change his appraisal of me?

I thought and thought, tossed and turned, got up and paced the floor, then crawled into bed again. I walked to the window and looked out at the full moon, then thought with irritation, on such a beautiful night as this, I should be in Gabriel's arms. Oh, if only I could figure a way to skip this hurdle in the way of our relationship.

I had already bobbed my hair, gone to work down the hall from him, selected mature-looking clothes. What more could I do?

Suddenly an idea occurred to me. While in high school I knew a girl who was crazy in love with the captain of the debate team. But she was not as attractive as he was, and other girls in the school were after him. She feared she could not hold onto him, and as graduation neared and she faced the prospect of separation when he went away to college, she became more and more desperate. She did not plan what happened, but realized after it was done that all these concerns had played a part in letting him make love to her on the night of the graduation dance. That look she had as someone who had experienced the ultimate moment with a man kept going through my mind. Would Gabriel instinctively see me in a new way if I had that look about me? Whether or not I did, I'd be willing to bet that any girl he got serious about would have been around more than a little business school graduate from Houston, Texas, who'd never traveled farther than New Orleans. Those girls Harvard men went with must have gone all the way. They were so much more sophisticated in the East. You had only to look through an *Atlantic Monthly* magazine to realize that. Oh, certainly they didn't talk about it openly, but they knew what to do when the opportunity presented itself. . . .

As I pondered these things I realized I was not really prepared for what I had longed for all my life. I wasn't Gabriel's equal, no, not in a single way. The longer I thought about it, the more I felt small and insignificant when compared with him. What had I ever done that I should appear interesting to him? I reached no conclusion that night. And I remained preoccupied over the next few days with the finding of a solution.

I had never had any problem finding boys to go out with. Most of them were boring to me, and I only agreed to go out because there was a show I wanted to see, or a new place I wanted to go. There were several boys that I went out with now and then, one of them a fellow from my graduating class named George Deacon. I did not like George particularly, but I found him less boring and less difficult to put up with than the others. I often had to put him in his place when it came to pointing out just how far he could go with me, but then that was really nothing out of the ordinary. Men are men, aren't they? And they are easily aroused, and therefore easily manipulated.

George called me on a Wednesday evening and invited me to go with him to see *The Jazz Singer* at the Kirby. George was tall and had large hazel eyes, big earlobes, and a wide, slurpy mouth. In high school he reminded me of a broomstick but by now he had filled out some and looked a little better. He had always been a good dancer, and as often as not we wound up a date in one of the many dance halls on and around Main Street. Once in a while he could afford to take me to the Rice Roof Garden, but not very often. Usually we went somewhere with a small mediocre band and, as he knew a lot about music, he would often be the one to make a request from the floor to have a certain song played.

After the picture show we walked a block over to Travis and went to Schilling's Starlight Room, which was on the floor above a cheap dry goods store. Well, we didn't have a bad time as it turned out. The dancing was great and the Coca-Colas were icy cold and delicious. We left Schilling's about a quarter to eleven and George put the top down on his convertible and insisted we take a drive out along Brays Bayou. He put his arm around my shoulders and I felt relaxed and kind of . . . easy . . . comfortable, and let it stay. I didn't know where in God's name we were after the first ten minutes. George said he thought they were building a new subdivision out there somewhere but several times we wound up on a dirt road that led to a sawhorse and a "dead end" sign. It was at one of these that he stopped, rather than turning around immediately, switched off the ignition and began to kiss me. This sort of behavior from George was pretty standard, as I said, and usually I let it go on till I was bored with it, and told him to stop. But tonight I let him go a little longer than usual I guess, and when I raised my hand to signal him to stop, it was not as easy as usual. And he wasn't all that bad either. His big hands were kind of warm and moist and somehow felt good as they started to run in places they normally were barred from. With one hand on my knee and the other groping at my dress front I could not seem to get him to stop all of it at once. And then I realized the big black buttons starting at the bottom of my white linen skirt were being undone. I don't know what came over me. I started to push him away, but suddenly gave in, deciding at that moment that I was tired to death of wondering what this was all about. I shoved a hand down the front of his britches. I think he almost drew away in shock, but he recovered quickly. Very quickly then I was being laid down flat in the front seat and I felt him expand inside me. Lord have mercy, did that hurt. Maybe it didn't take him long, but it seemed forever before he was through and drew up looking at me as though he were not sure whether I had objected or not, unknowing whether I would begin screaming or reach up and kiss him tenderly. I smiled a little and pecked his cheek. He drew in a deep breath and sighed. Then he straightened his clothes as I did mine, put his arm around me, and switched on the car. I think he felt some sort of protectiveness toward me, but I didn't want that. He kept telling me how good it was, and I could hardly talk, feeling like I was splitting in two.

When we got home he kissed me again, and asked when he could see me again. "Oh, soon," I said hurriedly. "Don't bother coming to the door. We might awaken Mother." I slipped out of his reach and ran up to the porch.

I stood inside the door and leaned against it, breathing as hard as though I'd just run a block. Finally I collected myself and moved toward the library door. Mother had fallen asleep while listening to the radio. Good. What I had to do next she must not even suspect. I tiptoed through the hall and past the stairway, back through the breakfast room and into the bathroom. I prayed to God she had a douche bag somewhere. Taking a douche was something Sarah Nagel said she had not done after she was with Carl Odom. She wanted to become pregnant. That was the last thing I wanted from George. There was a large cabinet in the bathroom which had accumulated odds and ends over the years because Mother rarely threw anything away. All four of the deep shelves were practically running over with talcum powders and perfumes, near-empty bottles of shampoo, pieces of soap and bath salts, face creams and astringents. Once my clumsy hands knocked over a heavy bottle of OJ's Beauty Lotion, which went sailing to the floor and hit with a loud clap against the ceramic tiles. I froze in place and listened for Mother. One moment, two. Nothing. At least the bottle had not broken. I picked it up and replaced it on the shelf, then searched some more. I was growing panicky by the time I got to the top shelf and still had not found it. But it was there, way in the back and covered with dust. I seized it, shook it off, and opened it. Just my luck it will leak, I thought. I filled it with warm water, took off my stockings and panties, and stepped into the bathtub.

I used it five times, fearful it would not take. Then feeling somewhat relieved, I replaced it on the high shelf, confident it would not be touched again by anyone but me.

And maybe not even me, I reflected after I finally got into bed and turned out the lamp. The enormity of what I had done was just now beginning to dawn on me. Purity was treasured by most unmarried girls. If one—such as Sarah Nagel—lost control and lost her virginity in the process, it was usually because she loved a boy a lot, had been in close contact with him over and over again, and finally just gave in to natural desire. I had been almost cold-blooded . . . well, not completely. I always had kind of liked the touch of George Deacon. But that was the extent of it. If he continued to push me to go out with him and do it again, I'd have to somehow insult him so that he'd leave me alone. But then he might get mad and talk around his friends about me. Gad. I had not thought of that till now. They'd all think of me as "fast" . . . "easy." They might hang around me like alley cats.

Well, somehow I'd just have to avoid hurting George's feelings, I decided. Then I thought of Gabriel. It was for him that all this took place. The pain was still with me. There was a large spot of my blood that had to be washed from my underwear and from the white linen skirt. Like a badge for what I had done. A scarlet letter. All for him. What if he didn't appreciate it? How stupid of me not to think that his reaction might be revulsion.

On the other hand, why should he know? When we married—as I was certain we would—could he tell? Damn! I didn't know. No one had ever talked to me about that. Maybe if I didn't do it again, the place would tighten up. The way I felt right now it hadn't loosened although while we were doing it I felt the whole bottom part of my trunk was being drawn and quartered.

Finally I slept, and dreamed all night of being in the front seat of the car underneath George. The motion washed over me like big breakers against the shore, again and again and again. When I awoke to the sound of birds singing the next morning, the sunlight sweeping over the room, I felt achy all over my legs, arms, and shoulders. I lay there for a while, fighting down an urge to cry. It seemed worse in the morning than it had the night before, and more irreversible.

When I rose at last I walked over to the mirror above my dresser and looked at myself. Did I look more worldly . . . experienced? I could not tell. I only looked tired around the eyes. Perhaps I would not even get the desired effect from all this. I shimmied out of my gown then and looked at my body. It didn't look any different. My tummy was flat, my hips round, my waist small, and my breasts high. One thing I was certain of: I was as good-looking a woman as Gabriel was a man. He couldn't do a whole lot better than to choose me to spend his life with.

Chapter 3

It was around this time that the Democratic Convention became the most important topic of conversation. The fact that Houston was chosen to host the huge gathering was largely due to Jesse Jones. When he had made a bid for Houston during the meeting of the Democratic National Committee in Washington, he attached a personal check to his bid for $200,000, and promised the committee he would see that a convention hall with a seating capacity of twenty-five thousand would be ready when they began arriving. That was less than six months away.

As time drew near, the newspapers had long articles on the convention plans and building progress. A large ad with Al Smith's picture appeared, with a list of the names of supporters beneath, including Neal Gerrard, or rather his complete name: Clayton O'Neal Gerrard. The merchants up and down Main Street began to slant their advertising toward the convention, pointing out their shop was only a few blocks from Sam Houston Hall, or that people ought to buy white linen suits to be cool while they attended the convention. The Humble Oil Company put out a book called *Highways of Texas,* as a guidebook to the convention, and the AAA did an update of travel routes from all over the United States to Houston, to help motorists who would be coming to town.

Frankly I was growing tired of hearing about the convention and reading about it in the papers. I had not seen much of Gabriel since the night he brought me home, and my only consolation these days was that my monthly period began as usual, proving my one tentative journey out on a limb had not led me to disaster. What was more, I had received a telephone call from George that left me—and probably him—much relieved. He had been accepted into Duke University for the fall semester, and would be leaving before the end of the summer. I think he was trying to find out without actually asking outright whether I was expecting his baby, in which case maybe his college plans were all for naught. I wished him well and spoke to him as if nothing had ever happened between us.

One evening I came home from work to find Alvareda's big Chrysler in front of the curb, the driver snoozing behind the wheel. I walked in and found her and Mother having tea in the dining room. I was so hot my skirt was clinging to the back of my legs, so I poured a tall glass of lemonade and sat down with them. Alvareda never really looked her age. There wasn't much gray in her hair, although she was fifty-eight years old. There were few lines in her face, and she was still as slender as I could remember from childhood when Lilly and I played at her feet. Her friendship with Mother had always amazed me—after all, she was enormously wealthy, still lived in her massive home out on Main, traveled all over the earth for much of the year, and counted among her good friends most of the prominent people in Houston, including the Jesse Joneses.

Still, she often telephoned Mother, and visited here frequently. I liked to be around her because she usually spoke of Gabriel and Lilly. Today she fished around in her handbag and brought out a little box for me.

"Alvareda and Neal remembered you while in Italy," Mother said.

I noticed several boxes on Mother's side of the table, as I picked up the one for me and opened it. It held a brooch made of gold filigree and pearls, in the shape of an "S." "It's beautiful," I said, and thanked her. Alvareda and Neal had always been nice to me, and I liked them all right. Yet, somehow, I felt they would not want me to be involved with Gabriel, would not consider me good enough for him. Today I tried to be especially polite. I hoped that now I was so close to a chance with Gabriel, I could begin to encourage them to change their views. I asked about the trip.

"Oh, I was just telling Elzyna . . . it was nice. But Neal wasn't feeling well during the last three weeks. I was glad we were coming home, although if he gets busy with the convention, I am not sure he will be any better off. You'd think at this age he would slow down at least a little."

"What is he going to do at the convention?" I asked her.

"He's helping Mr. Jones with a lot of details right now, and I believe he is going to introduce some dignitaries during the meetings. He even has Gabriel involved in it."

"Oh?" My ears perked up. "What is Gabriel doing?"

"Neal said he's helping with the housing committee, and I think he'll be on that huge welcoming committee too. You know, there isn't enough hotel space in Houston for this many people. A lot of citizens are going to open their homes to the delegates, including the Gerrards."

"Not surprising," said Mother.

"Well, at least we live in a convenient spot and we have plenty of room. With just Lilly left at home we have no need for that kind of space, so in June we'll make use of it for a change."

"I haven't talked to Lilly in three weeks. How is she?"

"Oh, she's struggling so at Rice! I know she's unhappy but so far she's determined to stick with it."

It never seemed right to think of Lilly in college. She had not been aimed that way in high school. She met a boy named Stephen Sandock and from the moment they looked at each other they were in love. She talked of nothing but Stephen. After a year passed, when they were both about to become seniors, Stephen's mother fell ill and the family moved away to Temple so she could be near Scott and White Hospital. They wrote letters for a while, but the long distance relationship didn't keep and finally Lilly began dating others. I had always loved Lilly more than anyone in the world except my father. She is the only person I have ever known who was totally selfless. She always would do anything I wanted, and she treated her brothers and her parents the same way. She often got between Gabriel and Clayton—arch enemies—and settled quarrels. She adored them both, especially Gabriel, I think, because he was simply easier to adore than Clayton. But she always admired Clayton for his abilities and his bright intellect.

Lilly wore her auburn hair short—the best style for managing its profusion of waves. She had an infectious, giggly laugh and a winning smile that teased at the corners of her eyes before spreading across her bow-shaped mouth. She had a trim body—we often traded clothes because we were the same size. She was unendingly pleasant, I thought, as Mother and Alvareda continued to talk, and would die before disappointing her father—whom she all but worshiped—by dropping out of Rice a second time. He wanted so much for her to finish.

After Alvareda left that day I realized I had been stupid to become impatient with all the convention talk. If Gabriel were going to be involved in it, then I would somehow become involved too. Even if I could only manage to get a ticket, and to go to as many sessions as possible, it would give me something interesting to talk to Gabriel about, and if I could only interest him . . . stimulate him . . . then he would stop viewing me as a child.

It wasn't long before I realized tickets were very hard to come by. I had to figure out something in a hurry. At the first opportunity I walked down to the ticket counter they had set up at the hall, and asked what was left. The man shook his head and told me there was nothing available but the upper fringes of the balcony, and a few seats way back on the main floor. "Where could I get a better view, balcony or floor?" I asked him.

He shook his head again. "To be truthful, I don't think either one is really worth the price of a ticket. Why don't you stay home and listen to the convention on the radio?"

"Thanks," I told him, and walked off. All the way back to the office I thought bitterly of those people who really didn't need to go to the convention at all, but were going only because it was the most talked about event in Houston since the opening of the deep-water port fourteen years ago. Probably there would be people who would simply hold the tickets as souvenirs and never show up at Sam Houston Hall. My whole future with Gabriel might well hinge on my ability to witness the convention, and yet I was stuck without a ticket. I entered the doors of the Esperson Building and walked into the elevator. Two girls whom I did not know but had seen around the building were talking about their plans for attending. They had had their tickets for weeks, and were trying to figure out how to coordinate their plans with another girl who bought her ticket even earlier, and had a seat on the front row of the balcony. One said, "Janice will probably be all the way on the other side of the hall from us. With all those people, I think it's too much trouble to try and meet her at one of the doors. Why don't we just tell her to meet us afterwards at Patty's."

The other said, "We'll see. Let's go by now; maybe she's back at her desk."

On impulse I got off the elevator behind the girls and followed them. When they got to Room 358, they opened the door and one called, "Yoo-hoo, Janice, you back?"

I turned and hurried back to the elevator, and rode up to my floor. At my desk I pulled out the directory and scanned the list for a Janice located in Room 358. Dranke . . . Earl . . . Gandon . . . Ipscomb . . . Jones . . . Krelle. Krelle, Janice, 358. Telephone 951. I picked up the telephone and called. "Mr. McKee's office." I hung up. McKee . . . McKee. There it was, Gerald McKee. I was in luck. I had never heard of this attorney, and in the five months I had worked for Mr. Carney, he had never mentioned that name. The plan that had been formulating in my mind since I heard the girls talking in the elevator just might work.

As I rode the streetcar home that night, I determined that timing was very important. If I gave Janice Krelle too much time to investigate, she might find me out. It had to be a last-minute thing, to force her into a quick decision with no time to pause for reflection.

When I got home I told Mother I would be staying downtown late the following night, so that I could attend the opening session.

"Oh? I didn't know you were interested in politics."

"It—it probably comes from working in a legal firm. Everyone is talking about it."

"But will ladies be attending?"

"Of course they will."

Mother was so old-fashioned. Since my father's accident in 1914, she had never done much with herself, retiring like one who was much older than she was. She still wore her hair the same. Even Alvareda had never been able to get her to buy more than a couple of new dresses, and those she selected were dowdy-looking. Aunt Patricia, who had lived in Wimberley since Uncle George retired and bought a ranch there in 1920, came to visit a couple of times a year. She fussed at Mother for the way she had become, and tried to get her to come out of her shell, visit the ranch, meet "some West Texas men." It was futile. Mother's entertainment consisted of sewing, gardening, visiting with the Gerrards, and sitting out on the front porch quietly, lost in thought. Finally, after we moved back here, the Gerrards gave her a radio. She liked to sit in her cane-back rocker and have her morning coffee, and she never missed listening to the Victor Hour.

Well, I supposed she found it necessary to live quietly and hang onto the past. At nearly thirty-nine, she probably did not have much of a future.

"Senta, could you take Laura?" she asked at length. "Maybe just for one session? I think it would be good if she developed an interest in the making of history. That's what it is, you know; we're very lucky to have the convention here. Just think of the famous people you'll see."

"No, Mother, I have only one ticket," I told her, realizing that if my plan failed I would not be going myself.

"Oh, I see. Well, probably Laura is a bit young."

"Yes, and you know how Laura is. If I ever lost her in that crowd, there is no telling how I'd find her again. I wouldn't want to have to worry about that."

"You're right, of course." Mother still treated Laura as though there were some hope she would outgrow her queer ways. I thought it was because she could not bear to face the fact she was guilty of mistreating my father and therefore God was punishing her through Laura.

Would He punish me now, for tricking my way into the Democratic Convention? Perhaps He would, but for Gabriel I was willing to take the risk. And anyhow, it was far more important that I attend the convention than that Janice Krelle attend. I had far more at stake, no matter what her reasons for attending.

I did not sleep very well that night, for I worried all through the hours whether I would be able to get my hands on that ticket, whether I would be discovered, what I should wear, whether I would really see enough and hear enough to be able to talk with intelligence about the convention, or would I be better off to take the ticket seller's advice and follow on KPRC. Next morning I rose early and arrived at work thirty minutes ahead of time. I wanted to get some things done so that I wouldn't be cheated out of my chance to get the ticket. The day stretched out long in front of me. I worked through lunch, making certain Mr. Carney realized what I was sacrificing. Then finally, at four-thirty, I called on the telephone and explained my dilemma to Janice Krelle.

Right away I managed to get her thoroughly confused and unsure of herself. "Mr. who's secretary?"

"Mr. Carney. Sid Carney, of course. And you see, he just learned there is an important client in town—just arrived at three o'clock, unexpectedly—and he must have a ticket. Mr. Carney told me to comb the offices till I got my hands on a ticket. I only need one. Do you know of anyone who can spare a ticket?"

"Well, I—"

"Of course, I was hoping to go to the meeting myself, but I had to give up my ticket last week to some higher-up in the firm that I don't even know. Can you imagine these tickets being so hard to get?"

"Well, I suppose I could—"

"And apparently this man is very important. Has some oil firm, and might be swinging a big account our way. Boy, I'd hate to think he got mad and went elsewhere with his business because we couldn't even provide him with a ticket to the convention."

She paused at length. I knew then that I had her. The taste of victory brought a smile to my lips. Finally she conceded, "I suppose I'd better give him mine. I—I didn't really want to sit alone anyway."

"Oh, that's grand. You are a sweetheart, I'll send someone after it right now."

I hung up. Just in a split second I had realized it would be even safer if she didn't know my face. Lucky I thought of that. I called the mail room and asked for a messenger to get the ticket and bring it to me. Then I almost literally held my breath till, ten minutes later, he came walking through the door with an envelope.

Chapter 4

I was in no way prepared for anything that happened at the Democratic Convention. From the time I walked through the entrance door I felt as though I had been swallowed up in a sea of people. The number of people attending that had been published in the newspaper—twenty-four thousand —now, for the first time, seemed almost an underestimate. I have never been jostled so much, never been so overwhelmed by the smell of smoke from cigarettes and cigars, never had my ears accosted by so much noise and disorganization. How in the world could I have hoped this was a good idea?

At least my seat in the balcony had a fine view of the speaker's stand. I could not have made a better choice myself. Yet, even with the benefit of huge fans in the ceiling of the hall, it was hotter than an oven. People around me were using everything from palmetto fans to straw hats and folded newspapers to provide a breeze around their hot faces. Unfortunately I had not thought to bring anything, so I was soon bathed in perspiration and even more miserable.

After Miss Malvina Passmore opened the session with "The Star Spangled Banner," everyone sat down and made an attempt to hear what was to be said. The loud-speaker system left much to be desired, and half the time you could hear bits and chunks of what was said, but not entire sentences. Other times the talking was quite clear but you were not sure just who was doing it. People became restless and began to talk among themselves, and then you really couldn't hear what was going on.

It was a long time before I could even spot the Gerrards, not until a couple of hours had passed and Neal Gerrard stepped forward to introduce some delegate who was going to bore us with a lengthy speech about the state of the dollar. When Neal stepped back, I followed him with my eyes until he reached his seat. Gabriel was not with him up there. Damn. Surely he was somewhere near the platform at least. . . . At last I spotted him, recognizing his blond hair. He was ten rows away from the platform. Thank goodness, I thought. I watched him off and on for the next hour, almost forgetting that I had come to be informed about the convention proceedings.

At last I noticed the person next to him was a woman. My heart froze. I could not make out what she looked like from that distance. What hair escaped from under her hat brim was blond, as far as I could tell. Finally, at the end of the speech, she stood up with everyone else and applauded. She was wearing a deep blue dress. Well, maybe she was just sitting there by chance. Maybe she had nothing to do with Gabriel. Why should I just assume . . . Then Gabriel leaned over her way and, cupping his hands around his mouth, said something in her ear. Then they sat down. Damn! I murmured. From that point on I saw nothing but Gabriel and this woman, and forgot to listen to the next three hours of proceedings. Over and over I kept thinking, maybe he is just making conversation with a woman seated next to him. Maybe he never saw her before in his life. But somehow, I knew this was not so. I was fighting down jealousy. No wonder Gabriel had little to do with me. How could I have so naïvely believed he was not going with anyone else? Of course he was. How perfectly idiotic of me. Who was she? How well did he know her?

When I finally got home, close to midnight, Mother was still awake, listening to the radio in the library. "Tell me all about it," she said eagerly, and switched off the radio. "I heard that Alfred Smith was nominated for President. Does he look like his picture in the newspaper?"

I shrugged. "I guess. You probably got more out of the convention than I did. It was dreadfully hot, and noisy. The loud speakers sputtered and hummed. I'm exhausted."

"So you've had enough of politics?" she said, smiling.

"Oh no, I'm going back tomorrow night. I'll attend all four days if I don't suffer heat stroke."

This puzzled her. She shook her head in wonder, rose, and turned out the light. "Oh, I nearly forgot. Here, take my opera glasses tomorrow night. I thought of them after you'd left this morning, and dug them out."

"Oh, that's wonderful. Now I'll be able to see— Mother, do you know whether Gabriel is going with someone?"

"Alvareda hasn't mentioned it. I'm sure she would have said. She has about decided Gabriel will remain a bachelor. Why?"

"Oh, I just wondered. I saw someone near him tonight, and was curious, that's all."

I hurried upstairs. Sometimes Mother could look at me and figure out what I was thinking. I didn't want to betray my feelings for Gabriel now, not after I'd succeeded in keeping them secret all of my life.

Under the cooling breeze of the oscillating fan, I lay back on the pillows and thought. I had never even considered the possibility of Gabriel's falling in love with someone else until he was at the University of Texas. Then, during those years, I dreaded the thought. Each time Mother brought up his name, or Alvareda came to visit, I was fearful of hearing he was engaged to be married to some rich oil heiress he met while in Austin. When that did not happen, I stopped worrying so much. I felt as soon as we were both in Houston at the same time, I'd have my opportunity.

Yet it had not turned out that way at all. For three months my efforts had been foiled, and I had realized just how much distance there was between us, both in age and in social circles. He had grown up so differently from me. The Leiders and Gerrards started out in Houston on the same foot, but what happened after that varies depending upon who is telling the tale. According to my uncle Jordan, Neal shuffled my grandfather aside, using him as a stepping-stone for success. He refused to back my grandfather in the oil business in 1901 after Spindletop, and thereafter shunned him. The only social prominence left came from my grandmother Carlotta's side, and through the years, that dissipated. No one remembered March Bennett and his cotton domain anymore. My grandfather could never get a foothold on his life after Neal dealt him such a cruel blow, so now the Gerrard family was as prominent as anyone in Houston, and no one knew the Leider name at all.

Mother, of course, tells the story directly in opposition, and the truth is I don't really care who is right because it would have had no effect on me whatever. My mother had her own chance to make a name for all of us. Had she only backed my father instead of getting in his way, the Farrish name would be as prominent as the Gerrard, maybe even more so. Yet, that was not the way it was. I was just Senta Farrish, who lived out on McKinney Avenue and rode the streetcar to her job in a legal firm every day, while Gabriel Gerrard went around in his sporty roadster. His mother had a chauffeur-driven automobile; my mother rarely even left home except to go to the grocer or the hair salon. It was unfair. . . .

Yet, I was not going to give up so easily. If Gabriel had a girl friend it was apparently not serious at this stage. I didn't know who she was, but I would find out. And I would take him from her. It was as simple as that.

The next day I saw Gabriel on the elevator, and told him I'd been in the audience last night. "Oh, I didn't know you were a Democrat," he said, teasingly.

I just smiled. I was at a disgusting loss for words. Finally I said, "It was awfully hot, wasn't it? But I'm going back tonight. I wouldn't miss a moment of it."

"Me, too. Dad and I are going to a meeting at the convention offices this afternoon. We're trying to persuade Jesse Jones to take the Vice-Presidential nomination."

"Well, you can count on my support."

"Good girl," he said, winked and smiled, then stood back to let me out of the elevator first. As he disappeared down the sidewalk packed with people, I thought with dismay about his reference to me as "good girl." How in the world would I ever make him realize I'd grown up? Why hadn't I been able to figure out a way to ask him who he was with last night?

That night I was armed with a palmetto fan and Mother's opera glasses. Jesse Jones apparently did not want to be the Vice President, and Senator Joseph T. Robinson of Arkansas won the nomination. Once that was settled,

I focused completely on Gabriel and the woman. Now, with the opera glasses, I could see her much more clearly. She was very pretty, with that "society" look about her. Tall. Confident. Tonight she wore a red dress that followed the contours of her figure, with a small white straw hat with a red band around the crown. I still could not tell whether or not she was actually with Gabriel. If she was not, he spent plenty of time leaning over and whispering things to her. Perhaps he had only just met her last night, when they chanced to be seated next to each other. Maybe she was even married, and her husband was a dignitary seated near the speaker's stand along with Neal Gerrard and other important people.

I must have watched her through the opera glasses for the better part of an hour. Then, suddenly, right in the middle of someone's boring speech about the tariff, Gabriel shot up from his chair like a bullet and ran headlong down the aisle toward the speaker's stand. I followed him through the glasses. Neal Gerrard had collapsed, and the attention of the whole gathering of people was quickly being turned to the emergency situation, as more and more people in the immediate area rushed over to help.

I do not know whether the speaker paused in his presentation or kept going. Without really making a conscious decision, I was up on my feet and hurrying toward the scene of the incident. Never had a journey so short seemed so long—trying to get down the narrow aisles, getting by people, excusing myself as I bumped into one unwary person then another. I feared it would all be over before I arrived.

Finally I neared the spot, and now, in order to get by self-appointed guards, I repeated, "I'm a friend of the Gerrard family. I must get to Mr. Gerrard. Pardon, I'm a friend of—" By now there were two young men in white medical attire, lifting Neal onto a litter. Gabriel was there, anxious, frightened, trying to reassure his father. I pushed toward him. "Gabriel, how can I help?"

He looked up, startled. "Senta! Yes. Go and call Mother. Tell her we're taking him to Baptist Hospital just a few blocks away. Tell her I'll call her when I get there, not to worry."

I nodded and dashed off in search of a telephone, and ran headlong into Mr. Jones, who had been away from the floor and was just now learning of his friend's sudden attack. "Where is a telephone?" I asked him.

He turned quickly and pointed a long finger toward the aisle nearby. "Just there," he said, "about fifteen feet up on the left." Of course he had no idea who I was or what I was doing. He advanced toward Neal and I made my way through the crowd in the direction he had pointed. When I finally reached the telephone I had to push by six people waiting to use it while some long-winded fellow, bored with the convention, chatted with someone about dinner plans.

"I have an emergency call," I told him. "Please, let go of the phone." He looked surprised, and handed it over. When I finally reached Alvareda and told her the news she was instantly panicked. "I don't know what happened," I answered her query. "Perhaps the heat. It's stifling in here. But he is on his way to the hospital now. Gabriel will call you from there." Then I thought of something else. "Shall I call Mother and ask her to come and stay with you?"

"No, that's all right. Lilly is upstairs. Thank you, Senta. Thank you very much. I'll be right here by the telephone."

When I hung up the receiver it occurred to me that I had handled the situation well. I had remained level-headed and calm. I started to walk back to my chair in the balcony, but on impulse walked instead to where Gabriel had been seated. I drew up to the empty chair and spoke to the anxious-looking woman standing next to it, holding a pair of binoculars up to her eyes.

"Pardon me, are you a friend of Mr. Gerrard's?"

She lowered the binoculars. Her blue eyes were oblong and fringed with beautiful, thick lashes. "Yes, why?"

"I'm a friend of the family. I—I just wanted to let you know they have taken Mr. Gerrard to the hospital."

"Oh, thank you," she said. "Gabriel told me to stay here. I've been almost frantic. Yet I did not want to go down and add to the confusion. Is Mr. Gerrard going to be all right?"

How in the world would I know? I wondered with irritation.

"I expect so. Have you a way home?"

"Yes, no, that is, I'll call my father and he'll send someone to pick me up."

I envisioned a chauffeur-driven automobile awaiting this woman at the curb. Clearly she was wealthy. From close up it was obvious she was dressed expensively. She was also as pretty as she had appeared through the opera glasses, with a clear complexion and a small upturned nose. Her hair had not been bobbed. It was pulled up underneath her hat. Suddenly I wished I had not bobbed my hair. Before I clipped it short, it was much prettier than hers, surely.

We stood there silently for a few moments, then suddenly she said, "Excuse me for failing to—my name is Louetta Hemphill."

"Senta Farrish."

This did not ring any bells with her. At once I knew she was not yet well acquainted with Gabriel. And her next statement confirmed it. "I haven't known the elder Mr. Gerrard very long, but he seems such a nice man. And he looks young for his age and healthy. I hope he'll be all right."

"Are you new in town?"

"Yes. My father has an interest in a business here."

"I see. How did you come to know the Gerrards?"

"My father is a client at the law firm where Gabriel works."

"Oh, how nice." I stood there silently raging. My job, my whole effort to get to know Gabriel better through working around him seemed so puny. I did not want her to know I was a working girl at all. When finally the last round of applause began and the crowd dispersed to go home, she asked me if I were with someone.

"No. I came alone."

"Could I give you a lift home?"

"No, thanks. I have a way."

I watched her walk away. Little society cream puff. Surely Gabriel could not be interested in her. Obviously a man with an important future, he needed someone strong and reliable. Someone who could take charge of matters without notice. While Louetta stood up with her binoculars, watching helplessly the scene of Neal's attack, I had acted quickly.

On the way home, while gazing out the streetcar window and enjoying the breeze on my face, I thought of the times my father and I had gone down to City Park when I was a little girl. There was a tall sliding board there. I would insist on climbing to the top and going down alone, though I was much too small. "By golly, Senta, you've got nerve," he'd say. "I'll bet you can do anything you set your mind to." And when he would ask me to spy on Mother, and I'd bring him the information he wanted, usually not knowing why he wanted it or what it meant, he'd praise me, and tell me I was smart. He was right. I was smart, and I could get anything I put my mind to.

By the end of the week I knew that acting to help Gabriel that night had been a step in the right direction. He did not come to the office for several days, and I learned from Mother that Neal had suffered a mild heart attack but was expected to recover fully. On Friday Gabriel caught up with me from behind as I carried some files down the hall. "Mother was so grateful," he said. "She told me you were very reassuring to her."

"I'm glad that Neal is doing better."

"Yes, aren't we all. . . . Say, it's almost noontime. Let me buy you lunch today. That is, if you're not busy."

My heart took a broad leap forward. "Oh, nothing that I can't get out of."

"Good. I'll meet you downstairs at twelve straight up."

"Fine," I said, and smiled. He disappeared down the hall. I felt weak. My arms were shaking so much I could barely hold the folders any longer. To think, this was what it took to make him notice me. Or, maybe he just hadn't known how to break the ice before.

For what remained of the morning, I was too preoccupied with the prospect of lunch with Gabriel to be of much use in the office. Where would he take me? Probably one of the exclusive clubs. Maybe the Rice. Earlier I had spilled a tiny amount of coffee on the skirt of my yellow linen suit. The spot now seemed to grow in front of my eyes, becoming more and more apparent. My fingernails needed filing. They had not looked too bad this morning when I left, but now they seemed to be glaringly unkempt. I should have washed my hair, instead of waiting till tomorrow. I should not have forgotten to wear the filigree "S" that Alvareda gave me. I'd hurried off this morning, having overslept. Why did this have to happen, when on almost every other day for the last three months, I had been prepared for Gabriel to invite me out?

At twelve o'clock I met him, and within moments I was to realize Gabriel's choice of dining rooms would have been suitable for the building janitor. Gabriel had a long stride, and was oblivious to the amount of effort I had to put out to keep up with him. After five or six blocks, I finally said, "Slow down, will you?"

He stopped abruptly and looked at me. "Sorry," he said, smiling. "I forget how small you are."

This made me angry. "Does *she* have an easier time keeping up with you?"

"Who?"

"Louetta—Miss Hemphill, isn't it?"

"Oh, I guess so. I haven't really been with her that much. Here we are."

We were a half block from the tall spire of Annunciation Church, at a coffee shop called, the Apple Blossom. I seemed to remember coming in here years ago, one morning after early mass on some holy day or other, and eating a sugar doughnut. It was not exactly my idea of a nice luncheon spot. There were but four booths and the long narrow counter with round stools. Two short-order cooks flipped meat patties on the sizzling grill, and one waitress wrote down orders in a little book and chewed gum. Along with all its other attributes, the Apple Blossom was noisy with the sound of voices and the clatter of plates and flatware.

Gabriel directed me to the only unoccupied booth. "It isn't fancy, but the food is good, and usually I don't have much time for eating." He surveyed the menu on the wall. "How about a sandwich? American cheese, ham, goose liver? Or maybe some Irish stew?"

"Oh, a cheese sandwich, I guess, and some tea," I said. In truth I didn't think I could swallow a bite, I was so overwhelmed by being this close to him.

The waitress came. He ordered the same for both of us. I had not realized before that Gabriel really had very little interest in food. I supposed that when you had lived all your life surrounded by luxury, there were a lot of things you didn't pay attention to.

"Well, what did you think of the convention?"

"Oh, it was . . . it was exciting. A bit hot, but exciting."

"I just hope Al Smith wins in November, but frankly I don't think he has much of a chance over Hoover."

"I didn't know till just lately you had an interest in politics."

"My dad got me interested. I think he would have been a good public servant, but it's too late for him now."

I had to think quickly . . . say just the right thing. "It takes a lot to succeed in politics, doesn't it? I mean you have to have the right people on your side, lots of important friends . . ."

I was speaking of his chances, but he assumed I was talking about Neal. "Oh, he had all that," he said. "I think he just never really found the right time. I know he'd like for me to be in politics. Nothing would please him more."

"Is that what you're hoping to do?"

"Certainly that's part of it. I would probably do just about anything he wanted me to, when it came right down to it. But I must admit I get a thrill out of all the commotion, all the excitement."

I smiled and tried to look worldly. "You know, you're lucky."

"Me? Why?"

"Because you can be whatever you want to be. You're not limited by—by things."

He studied me for a few moments, then asked, "What would you like to be, Senta?"

"Oh, I don't know. I guess it's pretty much a man's world, isn't it? When I was a little girl I wanted to be a dancer. Now . . . well, to be honest, I think I have a lot to offer. And I wouldn't mind being married to someone that I could help." Then because I feared I was being too transparent, I added, "You know my mother never helped my father at all. She just pulled him down."

He did not respond to that. I knew that he had heard the tale differently. "No one understood my father," I went on. "He was bright—probably too bright for his own good. He had no patience with people who couldn't see the obvious. He could have been a famous architect. He certainly had the talent."

He shifted in his chair. I knew I was making him uncomfortable. Lightning quick, I shifted the subject a degree. "It is interesting to me that you're so close to your father. I mean, I always thought males were closer to their mothers. My little brother John—do you remember him?—Mother was crazy about him, and he clung to her. I was just the opposite. I wanted nothing more than to crawl up in my father's lap and be held by him. I do believe if he were alive today I'd still feel that same way."

He smiled and changed the subject. "I hear you are a remarkably competent secretary. Maybe you'll move right up in the firm, work for a senior partner one day. That is, if Sid Carney will let you go."

"Oh, he won't hold me back. No one holds me back."

He was still smiling. "Yes, I expect that's true."

Chapter 5

When we parted that day, I was convinced Gabriel had at least begun to think of me as an adult. Whether or not he was interested beyond that, I could not tell. If not for a mishap that happened soon afterward, I might have been left to wonder for a long time.

The Glendale Cemetery in Harrisburg had gone to ruin over the past few years. It had always been customary—since the first bodies were buried there after the Texas Revolution—for individual families to look after their grave sites, or hire someone to do it. For years this had worked out fine, but many families had moved away from Harrisburg since the early 1900s, and those loyal relatives who had taken care of the family plots for years had begun to die away themselves. What once had been a beautiful, secluded spot at the foot of Magnolia Street, filled with tall oaks and pines, moss-hung and stately, now suffered the ravages of neglect.

I remembered well that when John was buried there, when I was seven years old, the cemetery was well maintained and beautiful. By the time my father was buried there in 1925, the opposite was true. Only plots of several families, such as Milby, Tod, Allen, Cane, and Leider, were kept up. I recall my mother hiring some men to go out there and mow and clean up before we buried my father because, even though her family plot was perpetually maintained, others around it were not and the burial procession at my father's funeral would literally have to plod through weeds and snarly underbrush to get to the grave site.

It seemed that since 1926, when Harrisburg was annexed to Houston, we more and more often heard stories about another portion of fence having fallen down around the cemetery, or as was often the case, being pulled down by mischief-makers, who then entered the cemetery and did damage of one kind or another. The most remarkable of the reports was that a group of marauding youths rode horses through the cemetery and pulled up a few markers with lassos.

Within a few days after my lunch with Gabriel, we learned that my father's gravestone had been pulled out and turned over, and scribbled with paint. Mother and Alvareda were talking about this when I came in from work one evening, and Mother was very upset.

"I'd ask Neal to go and have a look at it, but he's only been home a couple of days and I don't think—"

"Oh, I wouldn't dare have him do that," Mother protested.

"I'll go out there," I offered. Had it been anyone else's grave I probably would not have. But I was incensed that anyone should have desecrated my father's burial place.

"I wouldn't go out there alone," said Alvareda. "No telling what those hooligans might do." She thought for a moment, then added, "I know. We'll get Gabriel to go with you. And while there he can check on our family plot as well."

I was ready to jump with glee at this unexpected opportunity to be with Gabriel. Before going upstairs to change, I said, "Ask him to pick me up at ten o'clock Saturday morning."

I was ready five minutes early. I'd been up since seven to wash my hair and fluff it out—it was growing out again and I was seriously considering letting it grow to my collar line at least. It had enough natural wave to look good at that length and if Louetta Hemphill could wear her hair longer than was stylish, then I could too. . . .

I pulled on a filmy plum-colored blouse and a beige skirt, and walked to the window of the little sleeping porch above the front door so that I could watch for Gabriel as I tied a long plum and blue scarf around my neck. At a few minutes past ten, the roadster pulled up to the curb with a screech, and Gabriel in his white linen slacks and white shirt, alighted from the car and crossed the tiles, then reached for the gate. It was just then that Laura—coming from nowhere it seemed—appeared on this side of the gate. She held him up for the longest time, talking about heaven knew what. Laura could be so engaging if she wanted to be. I stood there watching her dominate his attention, seething with jealousy. After a few moments I realized she might be inviting herself to come along to the cemetery. Thereupon I all but ran down the stairs to head off certain disaster. On my way out the door I heard Mother call, "I've got hot biscuits and orange butter. Tell Gabriel to come in for a few minutes."

"We don't have time," I told her, and shut the front door behind me.

Gabriel, with his top shirt button undone and his sleeves rolled up almost to his elbows, looked as though he were ready for a day of sailing more than an investigation of the cemetery.

"Laura wants to go with us," he said now.

"She can't," I said quickly, then added, "She has some things to do for Mother this morning. Go on in the house, Laura. We'll be back in an hour or so."

Laura pushed out her lower lip. "Let me ask," she demanded.

"Go on," I said firmly. "Go!"

"We won't be long, Laura," said Gabriel kindly. Laura moved sulkily back toward the porch, and Gabriel opened the car door for me. It was a fine, windy summer morning. As I lifted my foot to get in the car, the wind whipped up under my skirt and it billowed out behind me like an accordian. Startled, I grabbed the skirt and glanced around. Gabriel was getting an eyeful of my legs. I smiled, then made a face at him, my heartbeat tripling. It couldn't have gone better if I'd planned it, I rejoiced, and slid into the plush automobile seat.

He slid in beside me and smiled. "Well, I guess we're off. I hope we didn't hurt Laura's feelings. I wouldn't have minded—"

"Spare me two hours with Laura. She drives me crazy," I interrupted.

"That's how I used to feel about Clayton," he said with a chuckle. Then he paused before adding, "In fact, I still do."

Gabriel started the motor and we roared off. He really wasn't much of a driver, racing too fast and stopping too abruptly. The roadster purred like a kitten once he got it into gear. I sat not more than a few inches from him, my long scarf blowing in the wind, my hair plastered back against my head, thinking that I had not felt so exhilarated since my father used to take me for a spin in the Packard.

As much of a talker as he was, Gabriel now seemed content to drive along in silence. I searched for some subject that would interest him. Finally I asked, "Why don't you and Clayton get along?"

He shrugged, and pushed the hair out of his eyes. "We're like daylight and dark. He lives in fear he'll get his hands dirty," he said. "He has always been that way. I used to throw mud pies at him just to get him mad."

"Sounds like you—drove him—crazy."

"I guess I did. But it's a good thing he is going to be a surgeon. His bedside manner can't be very comforting. He hasn't cracked a smile more than a couple of times in his whole life."

"Well at least he has some future. That's more than I can say for Laura."

"But Mother says Laura is very creative, that she plays the piano and sketches."

"Laura doesn't have a fraction of the talent my father had. I don't care what my mother tells your mother."

He said nothing for a few moments. We crossed Dumble and turned down Harrisburg Boulevard. Then he said, "You know, I've never understood why Laura is supposed to be so strange. She seems perfectly normal to me."

"Oh, sometimes to talk to her would make you believe that. But she's— well, she never matured past the age of six. She is completely irresponsible and totally gullible. I can't tell you how many times Mother has packed her school lunch only to have her let someone smarter talk her out of it. We've lost more lunch boxes than I could count, not to mention scarves, coats, caps, jewelry, and the like."

"But there isn't anything unusual about that," he insisted.

I was growing impatient at all this talk about Laura. It seemed Gabriel had taken more notice of her than of me. "It is at the rate Laura does it," I argued. "She makes horrible grades—just above the failure mark every year. Mother nearly pulls out her hair trying to help Laura. She just doesn't open her ears. She lives in a completely different world all the time.

"I've taken her to movies only to lose her while waiting in the ticket line. She can't get on a streetcar alone because she couldn't tell anyone where she's supposed to go or how to get there.

"And now . . . now she has begun asking if she can learn to drive Mother's car."

"It's a little early for that, isn't it?"

"Yes, thank God."

What is it about a cemetery that causes one to want to linger, to become quiet and reflective? It is as though a fragile net of time-stood-still forms a canopy above this small bit of earth reserved for the dead, even though it is obviously in the open air. As soon as we crossed the little wooden stile and entered the gate, our moods were affected.

"Which way?" Gabriel asked.

"Oh, I'm not sure," I told him. "Toward the back. But listen, let's stop by your family plot first," I added quickly. Suddenly I did not want to face my father's disturbed grave.

"All right. This way," he said. The only sound was that of our footsteps swishing along the weeds and vines and the occasional flapping of bird wings above us. Being here made me nervous. I felt vulnerable. Maybe someone would take a pot shot at us or throw a rock. Yet, it was incredibly quiet. . . .

"Here we are," he said. He took my hand while I stepped over the low fence surrounding the plot. By far the most imposing monument was that of Samuel Cane, Alvareda's father. The others were quite small beside it. "It looks all right," said Gabriel. Then he smiled. "Probably there isn't a kid in the whole area who would dare bother my grandfather's grave."

"Why is that?"

"Oh, he was mean. A regular tyrant."

"I didn't know that."

"He ruined the life of Mother's sister, Olivia—ran off every suitor—and he almost kept my mother from marrying Dad."

"Really? How could he do that?"

"Things were different then. If a young woman couldn't get permission from her father to marry, she usually didn't do it. The penalty in Mother's case was disinheritance."

"How ridiculous. I'd never let anyone tell me whether or not to marry."

He laughed. "You're a whole different generation, twice removed from that one," he said.

"How did she manage to change his mind?"

"She didn't. She ran away. And my grandparents in Galveston took her in until the wedding could be arranged."

"How romantic!"

"I guess so. Although it probably didn't seem so at the time."

"And she had nothing to do with her father after that?"

"It was the other way around. She never gave up on his forgiving her till he died."

"And did he forgive her?"

"No."

We stood there at Samuel Cane's monument for a few moments longer. Finally Gabriel said, "Well, he's powerless now, isn't he? Let's find your plot."

The paths between grave sites were so overgrown that walking through the cemetery was much like walking through a forgotten maze. We had not gone far before I felt a thorn tear at my stocking. I stopped and looked down. "Damn."

"Here," he offered, and knelt down to remove the thorn. I watched from above, the sunlight glancing off his blond hair. For an ever so brief moment, his hand lay on my ankle as he wrested the thorn from the stocking. It felt so exciting I wanted it to keep coming up—

"There," he said, and raised up. "I'm afraid you'll have to chalk off one pair of stockings."

"Oh, it doesn't matter," I lied. In fact the stockings were brand new, and if not for the opportunity of that moment with Gabriel touching me, I would have been furious.

We walked on. I wondered how families could become so indifferent to anyone they had once loved. I would never let this happen to my father's grave. "Here, I think this is the one," I said.

All the headstones were intact except that of my father. It was not only pulled out of the ground and turned over, but a big chunk was broken off one corner. I felt as though someone had punched me in the stomach.

"Looks like you'll have to replace this one altogether," said Gabriel.

"Oh, why would anyone do such a thing?" I said.

"Beats me. I guess there's a lack of excitement in Harrisburg these days."

"If I could get my hands on them, I'd kill them."

"Don't take it so personally. I'm sure they had no idea who Beryl Farrish was."

"That's the trouble. Thanks to my mother, no one knew who Beryl Farrish was."

"Come now," he said, as one will to a fretful child. "You can't blame Elzyna for your father's misfortune."

"Can't I? If she had been any kind of wife, he would have been successful.

Those big tall buildings going up downtown nowadays would have been his designs, not Cram or Finn."

There was a note of indulgence in his sigh. I felt tears of frustration behind my eyes. Always my father was blamed for everything. Always he was made the villain.

"And now this," I said. "Did you know the cleaning woman found his body? He was all alone when he died. God, what a waste!"

Gabriel came closer and put a hand over my shoulder. "Don't cry, Senta," he said. "This can be fixed. You'll get another marker, maybe a better one."

"Oh, go away. You think I'm a foolish child. What could you understand about my feelings? There is nothing in your family's background to cause you shame."

"I'm sorry," he said, and lifted his hands in futility. Then he pulled out a handkerchief and wiped my cheeks with it. "Come on, let's get out of here," he said. He put an arm around my shoulder again, and this is how we walked back to the car. Having him that close was almost enough to make the whole incident at my father's grave worth the anguish.

When we drove away he said, "I know what. Let's go dancing tonight."

"You don't have to take me dancing," I said. I felt like a child offered a lollipop after a visit to the doctor's office.

"You sure are hard to get along with! I want to take you dancing, okay?"

"All right," I said, and playfully held up the scarf under my eyes like Theda Bara's veil in *Cleopatra*.

When we got home, Uncle Jordan's late-model Franklin was pulled up to the curb. I had invited Gabriel to stay for lunch, and to my delight he had agreed. As soon as he realized Jordan was visiting, however, he looked at his wristwatch and said, "Oh, gosh, I hadn't realized the time. I have a golf game out at Houston Country Club at two. I still have to pick up a club at the repair shop. Sorry."

"It's all right," I said dourly. "But about tonight—"

"I'll pick you up at seven."

"Where will we go? I have to know what to wear."

"Any place you like. Wherever they have a good band. I don't go dancing much, so you probably know better than I do."

I had hoped for the Rice Roof, but I couldn't suggest such a fancy place if he didn't bring it up. "Well, the Arragon on Main above Liggitt's is nice."

"Fine. I'll walk you to the door."

"Don't bother. You must be in a hurry."

I slipped out and closed the car door behind me, then turned around and leaned over. "Thanks for going this morning . . . and for putting up with me."

He smiled and winked. "See you tonight."

Inside the house I could hear Mother and Jordan talking about oil drilling.

Jordan was telling her something about a property he and his partners had just picked up in East Texas. Jordan could really go on bragging if you let him, and today I didn't care to listen to him. I stole upstairs before they knew I was there. Then I walked up to the sleeping porch and looked down. To my surprise, Gabriel's roadster was still parked out front. Laura was leaning over the doorframe talking with him.

"Damn," I muttered. I didn't know whether to call down to her or not. She was maddening. I waited a few moments, then just as I was about to open my mouth, she moved away, and Gabriel waved and started up the engine. I ought to give her a good talking to, I thought, but I was tired and I wanted to be fresh for tonight. I went to my room, shut the door, switched on the fan, and lay down for a nap. I had a crazy dream that my father came and sat down beside my bed and asked me to take him away from that house. In the dream I got up and took his crippled hand. We walked down the stairs and went out on the porch. And there, at the curb, was a long line of automobiles pulled up behind a hearse. My father nodded his approval. I knew he would climb into the casket and ride to the cemetery to be buried. But we never got that far. At the curb he suddenly produced a shovel, and began throwing dirt upon the tiles that bore his name. And then, instead of that, it was as though someone changed the picture in front of me. We were at my father's grave, and the grave diggers were piling dirt upon the opening.

I woke up. I felt clammy all over.

The weather was hot and muggy that evening. Rain had been threatening since the afternoon, but still the sun shone and the humidity gave everyone's skin a spongy feeling. I wanted to look as alluring as I could, and would try on everything early so I wouldn't be rushed. I pulled a peach-colored jersey blouse with a boat neck and a matching skirt from the closet. For underneath I chose a low-cut brassiere and the sheerest slip I owned—the whole top from the waist up was thin lace; the bottom was almost transparent. I pulled out a pair of beige Constance pumps with a slender heel and strap.

I put it all on and stood in front of the mirror, considering. Finally I shook my head. I lifted off the blouse, took off the brassiere, and pulled on the blouse again. Better. Mother would die if she knew I sometimes wore almost no underwear, but I had the right shape of bosom for it. And the nipples were exactly symmetrical—some girls weren't so lucky—and firm, firmer still whenever I was near Gabriel.

At five o'clock I washed my hair again and borrowed Mother's pearls. I manicured my fingernails and painted them with peach enamel. At six forty-five I stood in front of the mirror again and turned slowly. Then I leaned over slightly. The boat neck of the blouse fell just enough to reveal the curves of my breast, and you could get just a peek of the lace if you were interested, which I hoped Gabriel would be. I put just a little essence of jasmine right at my throat—it was a light, airy, slightly floral scent: my favorite. I replaced the perfume bottle, humming. Then I opened it again and put a spot about six inches lower. Mother was knocking at the door.

"Come in."

"My, you look pretty," she said, and sat down on the edge of the bed. "Going out?"

"With Gabriel."

"Oh?"

"Don't be so surprised, Mother. Why shouldn't Gabriel want to take me out?"

She inclined her head first one way then the other, and I wondered if she was speculating about my lack of certain under apparel. Finally she said, "He's so much older . . . yet, in many ways I am certain you are even with him or perhaps ahead of him."

Immediately I wondered if she had found the telltale douche bag and figured out the rest. I admitted nothing. "Well . . . I'm certainly mature for my age."

"You always have been."

"And there were several years between you and Father when you married. Not that I would use that as a measure for right or wrong. Too, I know Neal Gerrard is ten years older than Alvareda."

"You sound serious—I mean, speaking of marriage."

I gazed in the mirror and patted my hair, then pulled out the box of lip color. Luscious Coral. That would do. "Oh, when two people are interested in each other, nothing is outside the range of possibility."

A cloud of displeasure seemed to settle on her face. I had the feeling it was not because she felt Gabriel was unsuitable for me, but rather the reverse.

"I came up to ask you about the grave site. What do you think we should do?"

"A corner is broken off the gravestone, and Gabriel didn't think it could be fixed. In my opinion we ought to order a new one. And maybe something a little nicer than the old one."

"Markers are not cheap, Senta. I think the old one was appropriate."

"You asked my opinion. Now that I am working, maybe I could help out on the difference in expense."

"That's kind of you, dear. I'll look into it," she said, and then the telephone rang and she went down to answer.

When I came down shortly after, afraid it might be Gabriel canceling our date, Mother said Alvareda had just invited us to spend Sunday at their house on Trinity Bay. "I thought I'd fry a couple of chickens and make an angelfood cake. We would leave right after church and spend the whole day. Unless it rains of course."

"I don't know," I said, wondering if Gabriel would be there. Probably not.

He didn't live at home anymore; he had his own life apart from his parents. "I'll let you know when I get home, or in the morning."

Mother paused for a few moments, then said, "It's nice of Gabriel to take you dancing, isn't it."

"Yes."

"I'm a bit surprised—"

"Here he is, Mother. Don't wait up for me."

Gabriel wore a pair of light brown trousers and a tan silk shirt, open at the neck, and dark brown brogans. I loved the fresh woodsy smell about him, the almost breathtaking maleness that emanated from him. As he walked me down to the car he smiled and said, "You look terrific, Senta." And I thought at once that all three hours I spent preparing for this night were worth it for that one remark.

We drove in the open car down McKinney to Main, and parked a block away from the Arragon. Along the way I found I was almost too nervous to carry on a conversation with him. I began to wonder if I should have worn a brassiere after all, because maybe I'd be so worried all night about having done the wrong thing, I'd mess everything up.

"I'm probably not as good a dancer as you are." He cut through my thoughts.

"It doesn't matter. I can follow anyone," I said breathlessly. I felt like someone about to board a canoe and ride down the rapids.

"One thing about you, Senta, you are sure of yourself."

Getting less so with every moment, I thought, but did not say so.

As it turned out, everything was right about the night. As soon as we walked into the Arragon, I could sense other men looking in my direction and that bolstered my confidence back up to where it should have been. The Arragon was large and had big fans in the ceiling to keep the place cool. The Coca-Colas were always cold, and the band was excellent. The mood of the musicians, in fact, seemed to capture the mood of the dancers because they started off with such light tunes as "Toot, Toot, Tootsie," and "If You Knew Susie," and as the evening wore on, played nothing but waltzes.

That was when I was first aware that Gabriel was finally becoming aware of me in the way I wanted him to be. I guess you can't be in someone's arms over a period of an hour or two without feeling either that you wished you could be with someone else, or that you would like to be much closer, to feel much more. He held me close during the first waltz, and although I did not want him to know quite how excited I was, I think he sensed it anyway. I believed that soon he must have made some sort of decision about me because at the end of one dance he pulled me even closer and held me there just a moment longer than the music played, and looked into my eyes. He didn't say any of those tired old phrases like, "You're just the cat's meow," or anything. He just looked at me in a new way. And after that, when we danced he seemed to be concentrating more on me. He held me tighter still. He must have been able to feel every curve of me and every point through the peach jersey, and he liked this, I knew he did.

Finally the dance hall band announced they would play one more song before closing down. And they played the old Fanny Brice song "My Man." I knew this by heart and I sang it in Gabriel's ear. At the end he held me closely again and this time I knew for a fact I had finally aroused him from the swell that pressed against me right around the base of my abdomen.

I pulled away and smiled. "Don't ever feel you don't measure up on the dance floor," I said.

When we drove home that night there was a circle around the moon. "Now the rain will come," said Gabriel.

"Oh, by the way, are you going to Trinity Bay tomorrow?"

"I might. You?"

"I was considering it."

"You like to swim?"

"Yes." I almost told him I was an excellent swimmer. But it seemed I was always telling him I was the world's greatest at something.

"I'll come if you will."

I thought my heart would pop open. "Why don't you pick me up around eleven?"

We pulled up to the curb and stopped. I looked over at the house. The library light was on. Mother had probably fallen asleep listening to the radio. Gabriel had had an arm wrapped loosely around the seat behind my shoulders. He pulled me toward him and kissed me. It was a kind of tentative embrace. Controlled. He could have had me right there, but he did not know that. In gentlemanly fashion he released me, and opened the door.

He did not kiss me again on the porch, possibly because Mother had the porch lights on each side of the French doors brightly shining. "You know, you're much too young for me," he said.

"You're probably right. But it doesn't matter to me if it doesn't to you."

"See you at eleven tomorrow."

I nodded and walked through the door. I stood there for a few moments, holding the knobs tightly and breathing deeply. I smiled and hummed to myself, the ringing in my ears making that just barely possible. At last I walked into the library to wake up Mother, and turned off the radio. She looked young as she sat there sleeping. She reminded me of the way she looked when I was a little girl. Most of the time I thought of Mother as being past any opportunity for a life of her own. Now, maybe because I was feeling so enthusiastic about my life, that seemed a premature assumption.

She woke up. "Oh, Senta. Did you have fun? What time is it?"

"I did. It's after midnight."

"Did you decide about tomorrow?" she said, stretching her arms and rising.

"Yes. I'm going with Gabriel."

"Oh?"

"Good night."

Up in my room, with the moonlight shining through the window, I gazed out at the shadows in the yard below, knowing all my efforts were not in vain. I would have Gabriel.

On Sunday morning before I left, I did something that was more out of obedience to a sixth sense than any conscious plan. I told Mother that Gabriel and I might not show up at Trinity Bay, that we might go somewhere else instead, and if we didn't come, not to worry.

"All right," she said slowly. "But try and make it, will you? We've prepared a nice picnic, and you could go boating, or swim."

"We might," I told her, then the doorbell rang and I turned to go. I'd purchased a new Catalina swimsuit in navy blue early in the spring, and a cotton skirt and blouse to go over it. I had a scarf tied in a ring around my hair, to keep the wind from blowing it so much. Gabriel said, "You always look as though you just stepped out of a fashion magazine. I hope you won't be ashamed to be seen with me. My swim trunks are three years old, and they look even worse than that."

"I could never be ashamed to be with you. Even if you can't swim—can you swim?"

"Yes. I learned in the Kirby's natatorium when I was seven years old."

"My father taught me to swim when I was four. He was a natural athlete."

He shut the door on my side and climbed into the car. "You know, the swimming isn't much good at the bay. I wonder if the surf's up at the beach."

"Galveston?" I asked, hopefully.

"No, I was thinking of Sylvan Beach at LaPorte."

"Sounds fine to me." Anywhere that we could be alone sounded fine to me.

The wind blew a gale, but the sun continued to shine most of the day. We laughed and chatted all the way down the bumpy, dusty road to LaPorte, with Gabriel driving dangerously fast and honking the horn every time a car approached us on the other side of the highway. I loved his lightheartedness, his absolute confidence in the world. It was infectious.

Halfway to Sylvan Beach Gabriel confided that Clayton had come in on the train last night for a month's visit, and he would be at Trinity Bay. "That's one reason I didn't want to go. I'd as soon attend a funeral as go to a party with Clayton."

"And was there another reason?" I asked, coyly.

"I just hate fried chicken," he said, and I pinched his arm. We started to laugh again, and behind my laugh I could feel my heart pounding.

We arrived at Sylvan Beach before noon, and Gabriel pulled the car up not too far from the big dance pavilion which stood on wooden stilts above the shoreline. I asked Gabriel if he had ever gone dancing there. "A time or two," he said. "You?"

"Only once. I liked it because the breeze off the water keeps you so cool."

"Well, if we're around that late tonight, maybe we'll go for a spin. You nearly wore my legs out last night, though."

"I have always loved to dance," I told him. "When I was a little girl, when my father had his friends over, he would come get me out of bed and I'd put on my tapping shoes and go down with him. Someone would play the piano and I'd dance on top of the piano while the grown-ups cheered." I didn't tell him of the night that Mother caught us, and mortified me by making me come down off the piano and go up to bed. And later I overheard her and my father quarreling, and then, the accident that put an end to those nights with my father's friends. . . .

"There's the bathhouse," said Gabriel. "I'll meet you in the surf."

The whitecaps were beautiful, high and powerful, sending great sprays of water ahead of them. I loved the water when it was like this, not on the days when it was tame and boring. I shimmied out of the skirt and blouse and pulled the scarf out of my hair. Something about the ocean made me even more daring than I was the rest of the time. I stopped to take a quick look in an old broken mirror that was hanging on the bathhouse wall.

Gabriel was waving to me from the surf when I got out there. He looked even taller and thinner than usual in his black knit swimsuit, but his shoulders were broad and apparently he'd already spent some time outdoors because his arms were already suntanned. I wondered suddenly if he took Louetta Hemphill to the beach. From then I felt even more desperate to bind him to me.

Oh, the water was so exhilarating that day! There were others around us, swimming and stopping to picnic and rest on the beach, but we were nearly oblivious to them. We swam out as deep as Gabriel would allow me to go. "Oh, don't be afraid," I told him, and plunged in. He grabbed my ankle and pulled me back. "It's too far," he said, obviously distressed.

"What's the matter? Afraid a big fish will eat me up?"

"No, it's just the undertow. This is far enough." The water there, not counting the waves, was chest-deep for me, waist-deep for Gabriel. He let me ride on his shoulders, then dive off into the waves. We did this several times, then I slipped, lost my balance, and turned to grab him out of instinct. He had both arms around me. I lifted my face and he kissed me, not like the last time, but with a promising hint of passion. His arms pressed hard against my ribs. Yet, abruptly he released me. As he did I pretended to be overcome and fell back in the surf like a fainting damsel. He grabbed for me, and I spun around and lunged ahead into the water, laughing.

He was standing there looking at me, hands on hips, as though uncertain what to do next. The murky water was almost to my neck. I reached down with one hand and pulled the swimsuit off one shoulder, then the other. I pulled it down, and slipped it off. Then I raised it up over my head, like a triumphant Indian brave with the scalp of his victim.

Now as I look back I see myself as a poor little frantic marionette, trying desperately to get the attention of its audience. I did so many things for Gabriel on impulse, trying so hard that often I did not think how it made him feel. He looked at me in astonishment, then practically yelled, "Senta, no, put that back on. You can't do this. I can't believe—" then he turned and splashed back to the shore.

I felt as though my hands had been slapped. I was so ashamed, I could have drowned myself. I put the suit back on—no easy job—then plunged through the surf and up on the beach. Gabriel was picking up the towels. "Get changed, we have to go," he said coldly.

I retreated to the bathhouse like a banished puppy dog.

We were in the car—it seemed like it all happened so quickly—driving home, before he ever said anything else. "We have to stop this," he said. "You don't realize—you're getting in above your head with me, just like you tried to go too far out in the water."

I looked away, for if I had looked at him he would have seen the tears welling up in my eyes. "I think I can be the judge of that," I said. I started to tell him there were some things he didn't know about me, but decided not to. I didn't want him to think I was an easy target for every man who came along. All my life, my only design had been to get to him.

"I don't understand you," I continued. "You lead me on, then you stop."

That wasn't exactly true, and I knew it. He didn't say anything for a long time. Then finally he said softly, almost to himself, "You must know that I want you, Senta. But it isn't—I can't—"

"What? Why not?"

He shook his head and pressed hard on the accelerator.

Around two o'clock we arrived at the house on McKinney Avenue. No one was home. The windows had not even been lifted. We sat very quietly at length. I could hear the sound of thunder in the distance and the sky had begun to change. Menacing clouds, gray and heavy with rain, scurried across it. Finally I said, "You don't hate me, do you, just for being crazy about you?"

He looked across at me and smiled. "Of course not." His voice was now gentle. I think he feared he was leading me astray, that at my age I should be totally innocent, unworldly, unsophisticated. "Senta, you're one of the most exciting people I've ever been around. I've had more fun with you than with anyone in a long time. It's just that—"

"I know. I'm too young for you," I said, then looked at him sidelong. "Well, kiss me once more, then I'll know you really don't hate me."

"Silly," he said, and kissed me on the cheek. I rose up on my knees, put my hands around his face and kissed him on the mouth, forcing my tongue between his teeth and rotating it until I felt his tongue swirl in response and then press hard against mine, moving back and forth over it. I broke off the kiss, though God knows, I didn't want to. I had to make him come after me. I lowered myself slowly down against his chest so that he could feel the hardness in my nipples and know that I was not kidding, that I'd live, die, kill for him. Then I pushed away and looked at him. His face was hot, his cheeks red. I could see the muscles tensing in his jaw. His brown eyes were wide and wet. He looked almost crazy. Let him try and turn away from me now, call me a child. "I'll show myself in," I said. He went on looking at me. When I closed the car door he was leaning toward it, one hand gripping the steering wheel knob, and one hand on the back of the seat.

I backed up to the gate, paused a moment, then turned and slowly opened it. I stepped in and paused again. I walked up to the front porch, and turned around to look at him once more. The thunder rumbled and splinters of rain began to fall and make blotches on the concrete. The smell of rain was everywhere. The door was locked. I fumbled in my handbag for the key I seldom used and, finding it, shoved it in the keyhole. Once inside I closed the door behind me, and pushed the damp hair back from my face. I don't believe I took a breath.

I threw down my things and walked toward the stairs. I turned and looked out the beveled glass of the front doors. The roadster was gone. I swallowed hard and took another few steps. Then something made me stop and turn again. The hair on the back of my neck stood straight. I waited. And then, as though in answer to a prayer, the car pulled up again. I heard the brakes squeal. I heard the door slam shut. One hand flew up to my throat, and the other gripped the banister. I don't believe I knew what to expect. The thunder cracked and the rain came down in torrents, as though someone had pulled a chain and released it. I saw his figure approach the porch, his mottled figure dressed in damp white linen through the beveled glass. I ran my tongue over my lips. His hand reached for the door and opened it. I stood there looking down at him. He came forward and reached for the banister. We looked at each other. One moment . . . two. . . . I moved up a step backward; then another. He came toward me. We moved up the stairs in this manner, never taking our eyes off each other, slowly as two cats squaring off for a match. At the landing I stopped and turned and ran for my bedroom. I backed up against the door and waited. I heard his steps two at a time up the rest of the stairs. I smiled and closed my eyes. Yes, come and get me, come and get me. . . .

I opened my eyes and held out my arms.

He grabbed me and kissed me and ran his hands up under my blouse, under my skirt, searching me everywhere. God, it was awful; Christ, it was wonderful. My hasty fingers reached for the buttons on my blouse, helping. He pulled it off and flung it aside. He jerked and unfastened until there was nothing left but me. He caught his breath. His eyes widened. I reached down and tore at his trousers and buried my face against him. He lifted me in his arms, kicked open the door, and carried me in to the bed. He threw me down and took off his trousers. I raised up on my elbows and watched him emerge, taking in big gulps of air. When he was naked, he fell on me. He closed his mouth over one breast then the other, sucking and licking the nipples until moistness sprang from my vagina and lodged in the hair around it. God, Gabriel, God. . . . His fingers swept down my trunk and parted my legs. He saddled me with his warm hand, and stroked and played me with his fingers till the whole lower part of my body convulsed with pleasure. He lowered his head down between my legs and closed his hands around my thighs, and licked me again and again while I shuddered and moaned ecstatically. My hands reached out for him, grasping at his arms. He raised up above me, cradled my hips in his hands, and thrust himself deep into me, again and again. The thunder clapped and the rain beat hard upon the roof outside the window. I could not believe how close to violence he came. I felt I was being consumed.

I have never known such excitement.

Chapter 6

In January of 1929, Stephen Sandock returned to Houston and his return had an effect on all our lives. The fact that Neal Gerrard did not want Lilly to marry Stephen was understandable—he could not offer her the kind of life Neal would have wanted his daughter to enjoy—but he had only himself to blame when the two of them came back together after a separation of more than six years.

Neal's schedule was now as active as before his attack and one day as he walked along the corridor of the Gulf Building on his way to a board meeting, he passed by a young man who was gold-leafing the letters on the frosty glass of an office door. Realizing the man was Stephen, Neal struck up a conversation with him and wound up inviting him home to dinner. Neal may have been a stickler for Lilly's education, but he also had the soft heart of a father. Lilly's life was miserable, and her father found a way to bring some bright light into it. Little did he realize he was starting something that could not be stopped.

Alvareda encouraged Gabriel to join them for dinner that night, and Gabriel in turn invited me. Though no one ever said as much in front of me, I never felt any more accepted by the Gerrards than Stephen did. It certainly did not matter to me then. Gabriel and I were inseparable, and Gabriel was far past the point of having to answer to his parents about the girl he chose to be involved with. Whether or not they realized just how serious we were, I had no idea. Gabriel was about to move from his old apartment into the new Isabella Court at Main and Isabella. Having a natural affinity for the Spanish Colonial style of the apartments, with their courtyards and balconies and lofty tile roofs, I had offered to help him decorate his one-bedroom unit. We had spent several Saturdays looking at furniture at Stowers, not to mention hours spent considering carpets, lamps, pictures, and small objects from ash-trays to bookends. Once he had shaken his head and observed, "You sure know how to spend money."

"You've got plenty of it, so why not?" I told him. I did not say that I expected to spend as much time there as he did, so I might as well fix it up to suit myself. We did not discuss any terms of our relationship. It was under-stood, or so I thought, that it would one day end up at the altar. In the meantime I stayed overnight with him whenever I chose, and Mother did not say a word. I know she wanted to, but she also realized it was futile to try and tell me what to do.

In front of the Gerrards we exercised the proper decorum. That is more than I can say for Stephen and Lilly on the night we all met for dinner in the second, less formal dining room of the Gerrard home on Main. Alvareda had gone to some trouble to make the table festive, with a huge urn of hot-house roses of yellow, pink, and white, and tall candles in the center of the table, a fabulous crocheted tablecloth, and china and sparkling crystal.

There was some time spent on appraising Neal's state of health, then Ste-phen was urged to tell what he had been doing over the past several years. Stephen was shorter than Neal and Gabriel, probably around five feet, ten inches tall. He had dark eyes and hair, and a kind of mysterious look. I remembered from high school days that he was rather shy, and wanting when it came to long conversation. Except, of course, with Lilly. He did not feel comfortable with large crowds of people or even among a roomful of impos-ing guests. It was probably out of deference to his feelings that Alvareda kept tonight's dinner party on a small scale.

He told us that after his mother died, he had left home with his box of paints and tools, and traveled all over West Texas and down into Central

Texas painting signs for a living. He smiled and said, "I pretty well wore out two old Fords, and went through gosh knows how many sets of tires."

Here Lilly smiled and looked across the table at Stephen with unabashed adoration. "Oh, I think it's wonderful to be that self-reliant, all on your own," she said. Lilly's voice was soft and gentle. She looked so pretty that night, in a turquoise taffeta dress with a broad white lace collar. Her cheeks glowed—no doubt with excitement. She wore almost no makeup as a rule.

Stephen looked at her as though she were the only one sitting at the table, and said, "Oh, it was a lot of fun, but awfully lonely."

Lilly looked down at her lap and started to toy with her handkerchief. Just at that moment, for the very first time, it occurred to me that those two were meant for each other, that something about their feelings for each other had endured over the years apart as though there had been only minutes in between. They must marry, I thought. It is the only chance for happiness for either of them. Surely the Gerrards can see that.

Gabriel said, "And you just walked into a little town and asked somebody if you could paint them a sign?"

"That's about right," said Stephen. "You can look around and tell when someone needs something better than what they've got. A lot of times you can point that out to them, and they'll hire you on the spot. Then there were lots of times when I'd go in with someone else and paint a brick wall on a building, maybe a Coca-Cola sign needed redoing or maybe a Purina Feed advertisement. I could pick up maybe five dollars or so, then I'd go on my way."

"And where did you sleep?" asked Lilly.

"Sometimes in the car, sometimes out in the open."

Alvareda was beginning to look uncomfortable. "Well, that's a good life for a young single man, isn't it?" she said. "Of course—"

Gabriel interrupted her. "Boy, you said it. I'd give anything for a year or two of just roaming around the countryside. What a life!"

"It's kind of nice to be back in Houston again," said Stephen. "I guess I got my traveling out of my system."

Alvareda was visibly relieved. Even if Neal sat there listening quietly without drawing any conclusions about his daughter's future, Alvareda was sensitive to every look between Stephen and Lilly, even to the sparks that filled the air above the candles between them.

The evening lasted till after eleven, with Lilly and Stephen still completely engrossed in each other. When Gabriel and I left they were still sitting alone in the parlor talking quietly. On the way to Gabriel's apartment I said, "Did you notice how Lilly and Stephen looked at each other?"

"Hm? No, how?"

"Oh you know, as though they'd been in love forever," I said, then paused long enough to gather courage before I added, "Have you ever felt that way about anyone?"

"Oh, I don't know," he said. "Tell you one thing though. I never wanted a woman as much as I want you." He winked at me and pulled me close to him. "All the time. Even during dinner tonight."

I smiled and kissed his fingers. "Listen, can you hear my heart beating?" I asked, then I shoved his hand down inside my blouse and placed his palm right where he could feel it.

"God, Senta, I've still got to drive another four blocks," he protested.

Lilly and Stephen began to court immediately, and almost as soon, Lilly's grades at Rice took a plunge. Now on weekends, when she used to stay behind the closed door of her bedroom studying, she went with Stephen on outings. Sometimes Gabriel and I went with them, but most of the time they did not request a double date. Stephen might pick up Lilly at nine in the morning on a Saturday, bring her back home at ten o'clock that evening, and be back again right after church on Sunday, to be gone till late that evening. Lilly was like me—too old to be supervised by her parents. And once Stephen came back, she ceased to care very much what anyone thought. She confided to me, "I am going to marry Stephen, I don't care what anyone says. School can go hang."

It was very unlike Lilly Gerrard to be rebellious, and as far as I knew this was the only time she had actively set out to disobey her parents' wishes.

"When are you going to get married?" I asked.

"As soon as Stephen asks me," she laughed. I knew it was only a matter of a short time before he would do that, and one afternoon when I came home from work Alvareda was in the library visiting Mother. It was apparent she was thinking along the same lines.

"The thing that bothers me is that it is obvious Stephen hasn't got the need to roam out of his system. How do I know he won't quit his job at Eagle Sign Company and strike out again? With Lilly in the car with him? What kind of a life would that be, sitting in a car for hours, waiting for your husband to get work as a sign painter somewhere out in the middle of nowhere? For one day?"

"Now, now," Mother was reassuring her. "I'm sure if Stephen is as nice as he seems to be, he'll be ready to settle down if they marry."

"I wish we could be certain. Lilly is too blinded by her feelings to make a good judgment. She'd marry him on any terms."

As a matter of fact, Alvareda was more right than even she must have expected. Stephen took a long time to ask for Lilly's hand in marriage. And when finally he proposed, presenting Lilly with an engagement ring with the tiniest diamond I have ever seen, the proposal was qualified by the ultimatum that Lilly give up her inheritance. Stephen, we found, was as proud as he was independent. Perhaps it was no surprise that Lilly accepted immediately. The

Gerrards were outraged. They asked Gabriel to try and reason with her, to get her at least to complete her education first. If anyone could persuade her, it would have been Gabriel. But Lilly wouldn't listen even to him. She could hear none but Stephen's voice.

They set a date in mid-June, and she wrote to Clayton asking him to come home for the wedding. Stephen called his father in Temple and told him all about it. They arranged to be married not in Christ Episcopal Church where Lilly had grown up, but in a small church that Stephen had attended while his family lived here. What preoccupied me more than anything was my hope that now, with the excitement of wedding bells in the offing, Gabriel would be moved to suggest a double wedding.

Toward the end of April Lilly asked me to go with her to choose her wedding dress. "Not a dress, really, not in the usual sense. I want a simple linen suit, with kidskin pumps to match, and a pretty hat. I'm going to wear the string of pearls Mother and Father gave me for graduation."

"You aren't going to wear Alvareda's gown?"

She shook her head. "Mother's wedding gown was borrowed from my Aunt Josephine. And anyhow, this is going to be a simple wedding. A suit is more appropriate."

"It doesn't seem you are doing anything except if it is Stephen's way. That's all right, but are you sure you shouldn't compromise at least a little, for your parents?"

"No. I'm going to be Stephen's wife. We'll do things our way."

I shook my head in wonder. I'd never seen her so determined to have her way. She was behaving more like me than ever.

"And, Senta, would you stand up with me? Be my maid of honor?"

"I—well, of course I will."

She hugged me tightly and I thought, sweet Lilly, I just hope you will be as happy married to this sign painter as you think you will be.

The next Saturday we trudged up and down Main Street for hours, stopping in Levy's, Hahlo-Harris, the Fashion, so many stores I lost track after a while. It was after four o'clock when we finally found just the outfit—a dressier suit than she had set out for, of off-white Irish linen with reappliquéd lace and tiny lace ruffles around the long sleeves at the wrist. As soon as she buttoned it up, we knew this was the perfect one. She looked positively beautiful. The saleslady walked in and clapped in satisfaction. Lilly turned round and round as we spoke excitedly of what sort of hat would match, and the need for just the right gloves and shoes. Then the saleslady left and Lilly suddenly switched moods. Tears filled her eyes. She sat down on a little stool.

"Whatever is the matter? Don't you like the dress?"

"No, it isn't that, I love it," she said, sniffling. "I was just thinking, I shouldn't have robbed my mother of this moment with me. That was cruel.

I've been so determined to do it my way, I know she has been very hurt. So has my father. . . . Oh, I'm wicked, Senta. I'm ashamed of myself."

"No, you're not, Lilly," I said, holding her hand. "It's your life, your future, isn't it?"

"Mine and Stephen's," she corrected me. "Senta, I haven't told anyone yet, but I'm failing two courses this semester. I had a hard enough time before Stephen came back, but now I never open a book. I'm afraid my parents are in for two blows, rather than one."

"Well, where would your courses at Rice get you, anyway? What would you do with them after you marry, regardless of who you wind up with?"

"I suppose that's true. Oh, Senta, I wish I were as smart as you are. You're the one who should have gone to college. All that work is wasted on me."

"I'm not so smart. If I could get Gabriel to propose to me, I'd consider myself fairly bright. I don't seem to be able to accomplish that."

"Gabriel just may be a confirmed bachelor, though he wants a political career. Seems like politicians usually have families, doesn't it?"

"I wish you'd try telling him that."

"Senta," she asked, "don't you stay over with Gabriel sometime, in his apartment?"

I must have turned white. "Who told you that?"

"No one. I just sort of arrived at that conclusion."

"What would you think of me if I told you you were right? Would you think I was terrible?"

"No. As a matter of fact, Stephen and I—well, we have for a long time—I guess off-white is okay for my wedding dress, I mean—"

"Lilly! Not you. You are teasing me!"

"No, I'm not. Stephen isn't exactly the most patient man I've ever gone out with. We spent about a week holding each other away. But after that, one night, we just gave way to nature."

I just sat there and gaped. I couldn't believe it.

"Anyway, it doesn't matter. Stephen knows he is the only one, ever. And we're going to be married. So, why wait?"

I rolled my eyes. I could not say any of these things for myself and Gabriel, though I still hoped one day I could. I looked at my watch. "It's getting late. We still have to shop for a hat, unless—oh, you look tired all of a sudden. Are you feeling all right?"

"No, I'm just fine," she protested, then admitted she had had a headache all day. When she arose, she blinked and grabbed her forehead. She nearly lost her balance.

"Sit down, Lilly. What's wrong?"

"I just felt dizzy—sick all at once, and my head really hurts. I'll be all right."

Considering our conversation, I said, "You don't think you're—expecting —do you?"

"No, probably just tired from the excitement. This happened once about a week ago, too."

"Maybe you ought to see a doctor."

"No, I don't have time. Promise you won't tell Gabriel. If you do, he'll tell Mother, and she'll tell Father, and you know how that goes."

I promised, but somehow I had a very uneasy feeling about it. I did not talk to her for the next few days—she was in the midst of exams and was cramming in the hope of at least getting by and not completely disappointing her father. As far as I knew, she had no further dizzy spells. Then in early May, she and Stephen and Gabriel and I went to see *Showboat* at the Queen. Gabriel was a few minutes late picking me up, and when we met Stephen and Lilly at the theater, the line was already halfway around the block. Therefore we had a lot of standing ahead of us. People crowded together, as though that would get them to the ticket counter faster.

We were among the last dozen or so people to get tickets before the theater was sold out, and we hurried in with the rest of the mob and found four seats together right at the back. It was very stuffy, and as we sat through the first hour of the movie it became hotter and hotter.

Lilly and I were sitting next to each other between Stephen and Gabriel. After another quarter of an hour passed, Lilly leaned near me and said, "I've got to get out of here. Come with me to the ladies lounge."

We rose and scooted past the long row of spectators' knees, out through the aisle and through the lobby. "I just had to get some air. My head is killing me," said Lilly. Her face was pink and her forehead had little beads of perspiration on it. It seemed forever before we made it to the lounge. We opened the door and she sat down on the sofa and took deep breaths. I went to the sink and wet my handkerchief, then dabbed her face with it.

"Lilly, does Stephen know about these—these spells?"

"Don't call them 'spells,' Senta. I'm just a bit overwrought, you know, with school and the wedding coming up."

"And you haven't said anything to Stephen?"

"No. There's no reason to. I'll be fine."

"I really think you should tell him."

"No. No, I couldn't. He'd worry too much." She smiled and added, "Anyway, I've got you to take care of me." She reached for my hand and squeezed it. There was something so vulnerable about that little gesture. I felt tears behind my eyes.

After a few minutes she said, "We'd better get back. We're missing so much of the movie. I'm sorry to have caused the fuss."

"It's all right. But get up slowly. Take it easy."

When we got back into the movie it was almost over. There was a lot of singing and dancing going on, which I didn't think was all that wonderful. I kept thinking of Lilly. She was the only good friend I had ever had. Without knowing why, I felt there was something onerous about these things she didn't want to refer to as "spells." I was tempted to tell Gabriel, in order to force the issue so she would see a doctor. As it happened, I was saved the trouble. When the movie was over, everyone rose at once to leave. We filed down the aisle and merged with the hundreds of others trying to get through the lobby. We ought not to have hurried so fast, and waited instead till the theater emptied, but not one of us thought of that before it was too late. As we arrived at the door leading out to the street, Lilly collapsed, going down like a flower that had been snipped at the stem. "Lilly," Gabriel cried, then Stephen said, "Clear away, everyone, give her some air, please."

We could not revive her. It seemed a very short time before the manager appeared and said he would call an ambulance. Gabriel and I hovered above, while Stephen cradled Lilly's head in his lap, looking like a frightened boy, till finally two men in white arrived with a litter to take her to the hospital. They would not allow more than one other person in the ambulance, so Gabriel and I rushed to the car and followed. All the way there Gabriel hardly spoke. He seemed almost oblivious to the fact that I was there. In the distance I could hear the dreadful sound of the siren.

Chapter 7

Lilly's private room at Baptist Hospital was banked from end to end with flowers. Neal sent a bouquet every day she was there—a full week—and friends and relatives showered her with more flowers, baskets of fruit, and presents gift-wrapped at such places as Sakowitz and Battelstein's. Stephen came by three times a day—once in the morning before work, then again to spend the noon hour, and again in the evening. Neal and Alvareda were there every evening, and in between, friends came in great collections. The nurses finally complained that Lilly had too much company.

"But I feel fine," she protested. And indeed she looked completely well. The doctor would tell her nothing while she was put through a number of tests. Once when I came in her doctor was just leaving, and she made a face at him.

I laughed and gave her a hug. "Well, at least you don't have to go to school."

She giggled. "I've been ordered not even to study while I'm up here, just to rest. As though anyone can rest when they wake you up at all hours, prod you with needles, and tell you it's time for another enema."

We both laughed, but then she became serious. She took my hand. "Why is it I feel as though something terrible is wrong? Maybe if they'd tell me something—anything—I'd really be able to rest, with some peace of mind."

"Maybe it's better. Perhaps it would be too confusing to go on just part of the information."

"That's what Clayton says. Mother calls him every day to tell him about me, though I can't think what she could say to him that he doesn't already know."

"Don't worry, then."

"I try not to. Oh, listen. Today I went down to the children's ward. They have this little playroom down at the end of the hall, with things to climb on and big stuffed animals. The children are so precious. You would never know any of them were really sick, except of course the ones that have to lie in bed. I stayed an hour just visiting. If you could come earlier one day, you could go down with me. I promised to come back every day, as long as I'm here."

I could not imagine wanting to be around children in a hospital, but I just smiled. Obviously she felt differently.

"I'll be so glad when I have one of my own, or two or three—as many as we can have. Stephen wants lots of children. He was lonely growing up. And I was too, in a way. The only girl, and four years younger than Clayton."

"I saw Gabriel this afternoon. He said he'd been up to see you this morning. I'm going over this evening to cook dinner for him."

She smiled at me and raised an eyebrow. "I wish I were going to cook Stephen's dinner. Or, as far as I am concerned we could skip dinner."

"Lilly!" I said, and she laughed. Her laughter was always so bubbly and light.

"You know what I wish?"

"What?"

"That instead of going to Rice, I had gone to nursing school. I love talking to the student nurses all over the place. They come into my room in groups of three and four."

"Are they the ones in the dark blue uniforms with white aprons criss-crossed in front, and little drawstring caps?"

"Those are the ones. But all I really want to do is marry Stephen. I told Dr. Creighton he had to let me out of here because I had things to do for the wedding. We still haven't picked out your dress."

"There's plenty of time," I told her.

On Saturday Dr. Creighton came by to visit with Lilly, and report on the results of all the observations and tests. Shortly after that I arrived, and she reviewed what he had said. "I'm perfectly healthy, with a couple of serious exceptions," she began, her eyes red from crying. Her blood pressure was way above normal, "dangerously high," as the doctor put it. Even with a week of rest and hospital care, and restricted diet, the pressure remained a source of grave concern. Dr. Creighton told her she must continue to eat carefully and come into his office regularly to have a reading taken. They had given her the only medication available—the name she could not even pronounce for me—and he wanted to keep her on it, though so far it had been completely ineffective.

That was only the first blow. Since Dr. Creighton had known Lilly all her life, and knew of her upcoming wedding plans, he took the opportunity to do a gynecological examination. "I'm sterile," she said flatly. "Frankly I wondered . . . I haven't done anything to prevent pregnancy in these months with Stephen. I guess I should have realized something was up." Her eyes filled with tears again. "Oh, Senta, Dr. Creighton said that considering the level of my blood pressure, the fact I cannot bear children may be a blessing in disguise. Unless some way were found to control it, pregnancy would have been very dangerous for me."

I could not think of anything to say. I thought it was the most unfair piece of news I had ever heard in my life. I took her hand in mine and patted it. I could hardly bear to see Lilly disappointed about anything. It was almost as though it were happening to me.

Lilly dried her eyes. "Otherwise, he says, I can lead a completely normal life. Normal! What can be normal about not bearing children?"

I could not truly understand why bearing children was so important to most women. My only reason to would be to please my husband. Otherwise I had no desire for brats running all around me. And I certainly would not be tied down by breast feeding a child. I still remembered Mother being hindered by feeding Laura, and how large and cumbersome her breasts were. I was ashamed of her, and didn't want people to know she was my mother. . . .

"Lilly, try not to upset yourself," I said. "Things will look different when you get out of here and back to the usual routine. It's depressing to sit in this little room, that's all." I knew my remarks were inadequate, but it was all I could think of to say.

"Stephen will be here in an hour," she said. "Oh, I wish he wouldn't even come. I can't bear to tell him."

"Look, I'll go now. Take some time to get your face fixed up, comb your hair. Try to be calm when he gets here. If he knows how upset you are, it'll upset him too."

"Yes, you're right. I will, Senta."

I hugged her and kissed her cheek. "See you tomorrow."

I knew I must be reassuring to Lilly, but as soon as I left her I gave way to depression. Why did it seem things always turned out so rotten? So many people never got what they wanted. Lilly had money, loving parents, a man who was crazy about her, yet she was to be denied the one basic thing that meant almost as much to her as all these other things put together. Why couldn't it be me who was sterile? I'd probably wind up with six kids, just my luck . . . of course, if they were Gabriel's I'd have twelve, if that's what he wanted. Trouble was, I was beginning to wonder just what he did want. When would he ask me to marry him? Or did he not want me? Oh surely not that. I shook my head hard, as though the motion would dissolve the notion. Maybe he expected me to nudge him like I did when I wanted him to go out with me. Well . . . I had to snap out of this. It was just concern over Lilly that made everything seem wrong, or at least I hoped it was. . . .

I arrived home around five-thirty, with just enough time to bathe and change before Gabriel picked me up at seven. Shortly past six-thirty the doorbell rang. It was Stephen.

I slipped into my dress and combed my hair, put on my stockings and shoes, and a little makeup. When I got downstairs Laura was showing Stephen some drawings she had done, and he was just polite enough to be kind and solicitous. "Laura, leave us alone," I said.

She looked up and said, "I'll only be just a moment, Senta."

"Go on," I said. "Stephen came to see me. He doesn't have time—"

"It's all right, Senta," Stephen said kindly. "And I think there are some real signs of talent here." He made some remarks to her about the drawing. Laura looked at me with hatred. Or I suppose that was what she felt. I had never seen her look like that before. She's now fourteen, I mused . . . beginning to be rebellious. Stephen handed the drawings back to her and said he'd like to see more of her work sometime.

When finally we got rid of Laura, I closed the library doors and let Stephen talk. "Lilly has broken the engagement," he said. "I tried to tell her that children don't matter to me enough to give her up. I told her we could adopt some one day if she wanted to, I didn't care as long as she would marry me.

"But she won't budge. You know how determined she can be. She said she wouldn't see me again, that she wanted me to find someone else." He looked at me with such a pained expression, I was afraid he would break into tears. "You know I've never loved anyone but Lilly. I don't want anyone but her, and I never will."

I was shocked that Lilly would go this far. I nodded understanding of his plight.

"I was wondering—you're so practical and have such a level head, and she thinks the world of you—could you just talk to her, try to bring her around?"

"I'll try, Stephen. I think she may just need some time to think this through. Having children means so much to her, and she has some idea she's letting you down by denying you the opportunity to have a houseful."

He placed a hand on his forehead and leaned back. "I wish we'd never even discussed the subject. You don't think of the possibility that you won't have kids unless you're suddenly faced with it. You just assume all that will come naturally."

"And are you sure that the marriage would be the same for you without children? I mean, are you being honest with yourself?"

"Yes, of course I am. The reason I made an issue of having several children is because I grew up so lonely. But I didn't mean I'd feel slighted if we had none. Please talk to her, Senta. I'll be in touch in a day or two if I haven't heard from you."

As he went out the door Laura came down the stairs with another drawing. "Is he gone?" she said. "I wanted to show him this."

It was a macabre-looking sketch, with some sort of black skull in one corner and some other things that I couldn't identify. "That's ghastly, Laura. I should think you'd keep that one hidden. Get out of the way. I've got to finish dressing."

"You never took me to see *Showboat,* and now it's gone," she yelled. "You never do anything nice for me."

I ignored her and shut my door.

That night I told Gabriel about my conversation with Stephen. "Imagine, all this over having kids!" I said.

He was thoughtful for a while, then he said, "Lilly must get that from Mother. Mother was afraid she'd never have any more kids after she lost the first one. She always made out as though having children was one of the major accomplishments of life."

"Times have changed, though, don't you think? People don't think like that anymore."

"Oh, I don't know. Obviously Lilly does."

"How do you feel about children?"

"Oh, I'd like to have one or two when the time comes."

I wanted so much for him to personalize the conversation, yet I could not think of the right way to bring him to it. In a moment he added, "How do you feel about it?"

"Oh, it makes no difference to me, one way or the other. I'd do it for my husband if I loved him enough."

It was the wrong response. "How strange you are," he said. "Your instincts always surprise me."

He might have said "disappoint me," yet he did not. We made love that night, but a cloud hung between us and robbed us of the usual excitement. While Gabriel was sleeping, I thought how mistaken I had been. All these months, I'd been faithful to the count system most of the time, and otherwise just damned lucky, all because I thought Gabriel would not want to be saddled with a kid, that he would hate me if I turned up pregnant. Now I wished I hadn't been so careful.

On Sunday I spent almost two hours with Lilly, trying to accomplish what

Stephen asked of me. She was at home now, resting in her room. She was, however, as determined not to marry Stephen now as she had been to marry him just a week earlier. "I'm going back to Rice and finish this term. If I don't pass, I'll just have to make it up," she said. "I will not place limitations on Stephen's life."

"But that's just what you're doing," I said.

"When he finds someone else, someone who has been blessed with good health, and marries her, and has children by her, he will love her as much as he loves me. And they'll be happier than we could ever have been."

"But, Lilly, what about you?"

"Oh, it doesn't matter about me. If I can't marry Stephen, I don't want to marry anybody. If I can get through Rice somehow, I'll be a school teacher I guess."

It seemed a pitiful compromise for anyone's life, especially Lilly, and my heart ached for her and Stephen. I thought rather naïvely at the time that I would never compromise my future as she was determined to do. Only a small voice inside me warned I might be forced to.

At the end of May we had flooding rains: more than five inches in less than a week. All the bayous rose and the bridges were out. Downtown we were high enough that there was no threat of flooding anywhere except possibly in the basement. But water was high in the streets. One by one the streetcar routes were closed. The newspapers said that if not for the ship channel and the widening and deepening of Buffalo Bayou—allowing the flood waters to drain into Galveston Bay—the disaster would have been much worse.

The last day I went to work was Wednesday, the twenty-ninth. After that the water pressure in our building was so low that the plumbing was affected and all the employees of the law firm were told not to come back until the situation was better. That afternoon Gabriel took me home. It was the last I would see or hear from him for more than a week. The whole area nearby the Gerrard place on Trinity Bay was cut off from any communication except telegrams and light planes. Food and drinking water were flown there and on one of these short trips, Gabriel and Neal rode along. Their house had just been opened up for the summer, and Neal was afraid the whole house might be under water.

I couldn't complain that Gabriel didn't contact me while they were away, for there was no way that he could. Yet just being separated from him that long made me anxious and I found my confidence ebbing away like the flood waters receding outside. What if he was thinking of someone else? What if he wasn't really there, and instead hiding out somewhere in order to avoid me? Oh, silly. Yet, I couldn't help myself. As long as he was present, I knew he wanted me. When we were apart, I could not trust him for a minute. What if Neal was trying to sway him against me, trying to get him interested in someone else . . . Louetta, for instance? I dug my fingers in my hands, and wished this whole damn weather nuisance would be over and done with. At least if I could go to work, I'd be able to keep my mind busy. If I had to stay at home and look at the walls much longer, listen to Laura banging on the piano, and listen to Mother remind me to conserve the water she'd collected in jugs, I'd go absolutely mad.

It was after Gabriel and his father returned, having found three feet of water on the first floor and most of the furniture ruined, that I first noticed a real change in Gabriel. On Friday night he called and said, "This has been a hell of a week. How about dinner tonight? There's a new seafood place in Kemah."

My heart went through the roof. He picked me up at seven o'clock, and the whole evening was almost like old times. We laughed and chatted about all kinds of things, stopped at the beach and ran barefoot along the sand. He lifted me off my feet and kissed me. "For God's sake, let's go home," I said.

"Oh, don't make me wait, Senta," he said.

So, laughing, we went and hid behind a big pile of debris and driftwood doubtless washed up in the recent rains. We shimmied out of our clothes. Then we looked around and laughed again at our foolishness because there was no one there. We went spattering naked into the water and made frantic, hurried, grasping, achingly good love, and I thought that he could not find anyone as responsive to him as me, and that he would never look at another woman, that I was everything to him.

We were tranquil and full of peace for most of the way home under the moonlit sky. In a thoughtful mood, Gabriel said, "Last weekend when we were at the bay I realized just how delicate my father's health has become. He was short of breath, and stopped to rest every few minutes. Yet he wouldn't go home. I'm really worried about him."

I got close to him and held the hand that was draped around my shoulder. He forgot his cares for a moment and said, "Um, you always smell so good, Senta. I love your scent."

"Even now, when I smell of salt water?" I laughed.

"No, it's below that, something always with you."

I shoved my hand down and felt of him.

"God, you're an animal, Senta Farrish. You're going to kill me."

"Are we almost home?"

"I certainly hope so." In a moment he was moving his hand from around my shoulder, shoving it up under my skirt and inside my pants to fondle me and make me wet with pleasure while I assured myself again that I had been dumb to worry about his feelings for me, God, look how he couldn't keep his hands off me.

At his apartment we raced up the stairs, fell into bed, and made love again. Somewhere around one o'clock in the morning we both fell asleep in each other's arms. It was the best sleep I had had in two weeks. Yet, about the time the sun came up I awakened to find Gabriel lying there with his eyes open. He said he had been awake for a long time.

"Something the matter?"

"No. Nothing, really. Just thinking."

"About your father's health?"

"That, and other things," he said, but would not elaborate further. Soon he rose and said he had to go to the office. "I'll take you home first."

"I could go with you, maybe be of some help."

"No, there isn't anything for you to do. Mostly I need to get some reading done on a case coming up next week."

His spirits were low. We hardly talked all the way to my house. He kissed my cheek absently before he drove away, and I stood there looking at his car disappearing down the avenue, telling myself that he was preoccupied by a lot of things, that was all, and there was nothing wrong between us.

Chapter 8

On the day after Christmas, Neal was taken to the hospital in an ambulance following a serious heart attack. This time he rallied a couple of times, and once Alvareda—she had been with him around the clock from the moment he went into the hospital—even thought she might be able to bring him home. Then one night as he lay sleeping with his hand around hers, she realized that he had awakened and was smiling at her. Then his grip suddenly tightened, then relaxed, and she later said she knew that it was at that moment the life passed out of him. She reached up and kissed him.

She said that he had been signaling her almost from the time he regained consciousness after the initial attack that he was not going to get well this time, not come home again. They talked a lot about the days gone by, and I guess there was a lot to talk about over forty-two years of marriage. He had said good-bye in many different ways, yet only once, that last time, did she get a clear understanding of what he meant.

Of course this was not said directly to me. I overheard her telling Mother sometime later.

Gabriel said that morning he felt she was well prepared for Neal's death, though not necessarily for the long aftermath. She called him herself from the hospital, at two o'clock in the morning. I was with him when the telephone rang and I knew before Gabriel lifted the receiver what had happened. Alvareda sounded calm, and said she was going to try to reach Clayton at school, after phoning Lilly.

He pulled on his trousers and buttoned his shirt. When I rose to get dressed, thinking I would go with him, he paused and said, "No, Senta. Stay here."

After he was gone I lay back on the pillows. Of course, how silly of me to think I would be included in this event in the lives of the Gerrards. If I showed up at the hospital with Gabriel his mother would know how intimate we were. That would be upsetting to someone as stuffy as Alvareda, and also insulting as she did not consider Gabriel and me on the same level. I was not good enough for her golden boy, I thought bitterly. So now, when Gabriel, not to mention Lilly, needed me most, I was to be shoved aside like an old pair of shoes. I got up and called a taxi to take me home.

I was astonished at how hard Mother took the news of Neal's death. I had no idea how much he meant to her. When I shook her awake to tell her, she gasped, and brought a hand to her mouth. Tears sprang to her eyes. I was uncomfortable seeing her like that. I told her I was going back to bed. She nodded and said she would be all right. I went upstairs and fell sideways over the bed. Before I fell asleep I heard the bathroom faucet turned full on. Then shortly I heard the sounds of her fussing in the kitchen. That's what she always did when distressed. She was still up, and still in her robe, when I came down for breakfast at six. Her eyes were red and she kept sniffing as she forked up the bacon and put the eggs on my plate.

"Mother, why did you cook so much? I can't eat half this."

"What? Oh, I'm sorry, Senta. Just eat what you want," she said distractedly. She poured two cups of tea and sat down across from me.

"You're awfully upset," I observed.

She paused before responding. "Is it surprising?"

"Well, I know he's a friend of yours, but after all he was what—around seventy years old? And you can't say he had not had a good life. God, I should be lucky enough to live so long and be happy doing it."

"You're right, of course, Senta. But it doesn't make it any easier when you love someone. Neal was more a father to me than my own father ever was . . . when I was a child he treated me as though I were his own. And later, when I was having problems . . . after I married . . . he was supportive and understanding. Enormously helpful."

I could not respond to Mother's last statement without getting into an argument. Her eyes soon filled again, and she sat there staring at her tea without drinking a sip of it.

Finally I rose from the table. I felt I should say something, but I didn't know what to say. It was another of those times when I was reminded by circumstances that she really was not very old. One always thinks of one's mother as being old, I guess, until someone much older dies, giving you a new perspective.

"Are you going to the Gerrards—to Alvareda's?"

"I suppose so. I don't know if I should call, or wait for her to call me. What do you think?" She looked up at me, perplexed as a child who cannot make a decision because of inexperience.

"I don't know. Do whatever you think is right."

She blew her nose and looked around, sitting straight in her chair again. "I think I'll wait. I don't want to tie up the line should Clayton call, or should they be awaiting a call from Neal's family in Galveston. Meantime, I can be baking some things. Let's see . . . I just bought flour and eggs. I'll make an angelfood cake . . . Neal always liked my"—here she sighed, with sudden resignation—"and I can bake a chicken to take over there."

"Oh, Mother, are you sure that's necessary? I mean, who'd want food at a time like this and anyway, the Gerrards have a cook. They don't want your food."

I didn't mean for it to sound hateful, but the truth was I was edgy from lack of sleep, from feeling that I had no real place in all this, from observing that no one seemed willing to acknowledge my importance to Gabriel at this moment in time.

Mother said, "It's the only thing I can do. If no one wishes to eat it, I don't mind. I just can't go over there empty-handed."

"Well, if you go, give Lilly my love and tell her I'll be in touch as soon as I can get off work."

"All right, darling. I just wish Neal could have lived to see Lilly happy, not in the state she has been lately. You know I think Lilly was his favorite of all the children."

I was my father's favorite too, I thought later while riding the streetcar to town. Before he died, I had great plans for changing his life once I was working and on my own. Death comes at no convenient time, I realized now, not for my father, not even for someone who has exercised control over his life like Neal Gerrard. Dangling out there, something left unfinished, was Lilly's direction in life. . . .

Thanks to Laura, I was robbed of the opportunity to see the Gerrards that night. Mr. Carney had no reason to be sensitive to my feelings that day, though everyone including him was talking about the death of Neal Gerrard. He kept me until after six, typing then retyping a contract that had to be ready the next morning. When finally I left, I reminded him that the Gerrard family were close friends, and I would have to take time off to attend the funeral. "Of course, Senta," he said with his eyebrows raised, as though he had only just realized I was directly affected by what he'd been hearing about all day.

I rushed to catch the streetcar, planned what to wear, and gazed impatiently out the window till finally I arrived on our doorstep at a quarter past seven. To my surprise, the house was dark. Inside, the gas heater in the living room had been left on—something Mother never did. I went through to the dining room, feeling spooked, turning on lights along the way. If Mother left me a note, it was always on the dining room table.

Tonight was no exception. She'd written it at one-thirty in the afternoon, just before she left to go to the Gerrard home. "I've told Laura to stay in the house and wait for you. Then the two of you can come together. I'm going to take a taxi and leave the car for you."

"Oh, damn!" This was not at all the way I had things planned. I didn't want Laura to be around. I certainly didn't want to drive that old car over there, to park alongside Chryslers and Cadillacs. And now I didn't even know where Laura was . . . "Laura! Laura, are you up there?"

I went up the stairs and looked in her room. Nothing. She wasn't in my room either. Oh, this was just grand. There was no telling where—

The telephone was ringing. I hurried down to answer. It was Mother. "I've been calling for an hour," she said. "I thought you and Laura would be here by now."

"I can't find Laura. I've a good mind to just leave without her."

A moment or two of silence. "No, don't do that. I talked with her after she got home from school, and told her again to wait for you. I can't imagine where she is."

"Neither can I," I said with sarcasm.

"Please find her, Senta. I just can't leave Alvareda at this time."

Again, I felt shoved aside. It seemed there was no one less important than I was right now. "I'll see what I can do," I told her, and hung up.

It was pitch dark outside now. Even the streetlights were not much help. First I walked up and down the block, calling to her. Damn, it was cold. I hugged my coat around me and shoved my frozen hands down into the pockets. She picked a hell of a time to pull a disappearing act. Having no luck, I finally turned around and went back home to get the car. I had no idea whether she'd struck out toward town, or the other way. I pulled out of the driveway and turned toward the direction of Eastwood School. I figured I'd go as far as where Telephone Road began, and if I hadn't found her, go back toward town. I began to feel uneasy. It was getting near eight o'clock. I pulled into the entrance drive to Eastwood School to turn around and head back in the other direction. When my lights flashed on the long drive ahead, I thought I saw a movement. Who would be on the school grounds this time of night?

I decided to drive in a little farther. When I came nearly to the entrance I saw a man's figure dart across in front of me and disappear into the bushes. If I had frightened him, he certainly had frightened me. I threw the car into reverse and backed all the way out the driveway, then pulled out into the

street and headed back up toward McKinney. I was about two blocks from
our house when I caught up with Laura, running toward home. I shoved on
the brake and rolled down the window.

"Where have you been? Get in the car, you little brat."

Like a child who's been caught cheating on a test, she lowered her eyes and
got into the car. She sat quietly and folded her hands.

"Tell me what you were doing. Mother told you to stay at home. What
were you doing?"

She looked out the side window and said softly, "Nothing. Just taking a
walk."

"At this time of night? In this weather, without a coat? And that was no
walk, sister. Why were you running?"

She shrugged and ignored the question. As we arrived at home I began to
put two and two together. Back in the house I took her by the shoulders and
made her look at me. "You were with someone, weren't you?"

She smiled a little and looked down.

"Who were you with, Laura? I'll slap your face if you don't tell me. You've
ruined all my plans for the evening. Tell me."

"I don't have to," she said, and pulled away. I followed her into the library
where she sat down on the piano bench and began to run the fingers of one
hand over the keys.

"If you don't tell me, I'll tell Mother and she won't let you take driving
lessons next summer like she promised. If you don't tell me, I'll see you stay
locked in your room after school for a week."

She sighed in resignation, banged the keys with her fist then threw back her
head and looked at me. Oh, she could be so defiant if she wanted to. I wanted
to strangle her. "I went for a walk with a boy," she said.

"A boy! Who? Which boy?"

"You don't know him. I met him in school."

"Did you walk with him to the school grounds?"

"I—I—" she faltered.

"You did, didn't you? And when you saw the car lights, you got frightened,
both of you, and separated. Isn't that right?" I grabbed her shoulder and held
tight.

"Leave me alone," she said. "I want to go to my room."

"And what did you do while on the school grounds?"

She looked at me. Her face was growing pale.

"Come on. Did you let him kiss you, Laura?"

She shrugged again.

"Is that all?"

"I never said that, you said it," she remarked triumphantly.

"Oh, go upstairs to your room," I finally said. "You better be careful about boys. You might be in for more than you expect, taking walks after dark. Don't ever do a thing like this again."

Of course I had no reason to expect she would obey me. It was one of those times when I realized that because of her sheer lack of common sense she could get in a great deal of trouble, and because of her willful nature she would not listen to reason. I did not know whether Mother had discussed with her the real possibilities of what could happen between a boy and a girl. When someone behaves like a six-year-old, you forget sometimes that her physical development goes right on and with it the natural desires and instincts. All we needed was to have Laura involved with boys. God, I wish we could just put her away, I thought. All I longed for now was a hot bath and an early bed. I was exhausted from head to toe, and it was much too late to try and get to the Gerrards'.

I had not seen Clayton Gerrard more than half a dozen times in my life, and over the past five years since he began medical school I had not seen him at all. When Gabriel spoke of him so negatively, I simply thought that was typical rivalry, expressed way out of proportion to the truth. After we met again—at the funeral home on the night before Neal's funeral—I spent much time reflecting on Gabriel's remarks, realizing they were no exaggeration.

Beginning with their physical appearance, Clayton was so opposite from Gabriel, it seemed impossible they were brothers at all. Oh, they were both tall and slender, like their father. But Clayton's hair was dark, almost black. His skin tone was pallid—he looked as though he never got out into the sunshine, and possibly as busy as medical school kept people, that was the truth. But for whatever reason, he had an unhealthy look about him. His smile was faint, his handshake limp, his voice low and lacking in vigor. He might have been considered handsome, except that he was lifeless. When he stood next to Gabriel, greeting people who came that evening, it was as though he was darkness; Gabriel was light. I remember thinking after our very brief exchange that evening that he seemed out of place as a Gerrard. None were like him. Perhaps he was like Alvareda's tyrant father. One thing was certain: he was the only man who ever frightened me.

I did not stay very long at Fogle-West that night. Gabriel was so busy greeting others that he had no time for me. Lilly was surrounded by people and while she asked me to stay near her, the number of people wishing to pay their respects was so great that I finally gave up. I did not sign the register until just before I left, and as I looked over the page of signatures above mine, I noticed Louetta Hemphill had been there earlier. I was furious, seized with an urge to pick up the pen and scratch all the way through her signature, eradicating it. Only the fact that someone was waiting behind me to sign the register forced me away. After that unpleasant shock, plus meeting Clayton, which cast a pall over my spirits, I walked out into the cold January night feeling desolate.

Of course, Louetta Hemphill did not have to work for a living. She did not have to wait to leave an office, go home and change, before making an appearance at the funeral home. She probably slept till ten, went to an afternoon tea, maybe spent a couple of hours shopping, then came home at four-thirty to take a long luxurious bubble bath before having her car brought around at five-thirty, and speeding over to the funeral home by five forty-five.

Well, at least Gabriel did not leave with her. That was some consolation. Of course he might be going over to her house after leaving the funeral home tonight. At the thought I stopped and considered. Maybe, rather than going home, I ought to go to Gabriel's apartment and wait. No, perhaps he wouldn't like that. I pulled my coat tight around me and went home, frustrated by having no control whatever over the events now surrounding Gabriel. I would be so glad when all this was over and we could get back to normal.

Neal Gerrard's funeral was probably one of the largest Houston had ever seen. The obituary in the newspapers on the previous day occupied a quarter of a page, and among the pallbearers listed were Jesse Jones and John Kirby, and other recognizable names like Cleveland and Cargill and House—names my grandmother Carlotta used to mention regularly when speaking of cotton men and other important people. The floral sprays had filled the large state room at Fogle-West yesterday; this morning they were quadrupled in number at least. The automobiles in the procession were parked up Texas Avenue from Christ Episcopal Church four or five blocks, and around the corner on Fannin as far as the eye could see. The church itself was packed, and as there were a number of people who could not be seated for lack of space, I felt for the very first time somewhat special because Mother and Grandmother Carlotta and Laura and I were seated in a special roped-off section for close friends of the family, just behind the pews designated for relatives. My grandfather, David, was in Germany, and could not get home in time. My uncle Jordan simply did not show up. He was now doing well in the oil business. He drove a new Franklin 137 and spent a lot of time traveling, so there was no telling where he was today.

I looked around me out of the corner of my eye and found Stephen three rows from the front on the opposite side. I was surprised to notice how upset he looked.

I have never seen Alvareda Gerrard look more beautiful or more stately. She was the last to come in, on the arm of Gabriel with Lilly behind them on Clayton's arm. She wore a black wool suit that had long sleeves and a cape that reached to her elbows and a little stand-up military collar that accentuated her slender neck. She wore a simple black hat with a veil and a pair of black opera pumps. She seemed composed as they were seated, but of course you really could not see her face behind the veil and she was carrying a small white handkerchief with a black border in her hand. How strange it must seem, I thought, to have lived with someone all those years and now to face going on without him. If . . . no, when . . . Gabriel asked me to marry him, I would not want to think that I would ever have to say good-bye to him like this. . . .

The Episcopal funeral service is not very long, and, with closed casket, not terribly conducive to emotionalism. When the church had emptied out and we all made our way to the waiting automobiles, a curious thing happened. Before stepping into the limousine, Alvareda suddenly stopped and looked back at the church, as though she'd heard someone call her name. She said something to Gabriel, who was waiting to help her in the door. Then she walked back into the church. Gabriel waited for a few minutes and, finally, as the whole procession was being held up, he walked back in to fetch his mother. It was still another few minutes before they both walked out together, got into the car, and the final drive to Forest Park Cemetery began. I later asked Gabriel what the sudden return to the church was all about, and he said, "Mother wanted to sit for a little while in the back pew. She said she felt Dad's spirit wanted her there right then. It was where he first kissed her."

"That gives me the shivers," I said.

"Why? My parents loved each other above anyone else. No two people were ever more meant for each other than they were. I wish—"

"What? Wish what?" I asked.

"Nothing, nothing."

I sat there, helpless and frustrated, my hands closed into fists.

It was one of many conversations between us in the weeks following that seemed to wind up at a dead end. It was as though he wanted to express something he could not quite do. There was a restlessness in him, a new impatience, which I sensed. He was more serious than before, yet did not seem to be able to get focused on anything, in his work or anywhere else. One day out of the blue, he called up Stephen and invited him to go for a weekend drive.

"Where are you going to?" I asked.

"Anywhere. I don't care. I just need to get away and see some different scenery."

"Maybe you should become a sign painter," I said, and smiled. I was only kidding, but he took it seriously.

"I need to do something; I need to become something."

"But you're doing well in the law firm—"

"Ah!" he groaned, and shrugged.

When I was with him he never seemed relaxed, rarely laughed. Then after a month or so, he said, "I think maybe we shouldn't see so much of each other. I'm—I'm not very good company right now."

Fear shot through me like a rabbit through the woods. "But it's all right. I don't care. I just want to be with you. Please, Gabriel, don't push me away."

"I've decided to give up my apartment. The lease is up pretty soon. I'm going to move home with Mother and Lilly. I don't want them living in that house by themselves. I'm going to sell the house if I can talk Mother into moving. You know, there's nothing out there where she lives but businesses and apartments. It isn't a decent neighborhood anymore. Main Street as a residence address is part of the past."

"But where will you go?" I asked. My voice was barely audible. I felt like someone was choking me.

"River Oaks, I think. I'm going out there to pick a lot pretty soon, to build on. They're developing a new section now."

River Oaks! That was the kingdom of the very rich, a whole different world. He might as well move to Canada. "Your mother will never move," I insisted hopefully.

"You may be right, but I hope she does. Lilly's for it too. And Clayton approves. You know, he's coming home this summer. He'll begin his internship at Baptist Hospital this fall."

I didn't know what to say. All the things I'd come to depend on were changing just because someone died. It wasn't fair, not at all, but I was as powerless to stop it as I had been to keep my mother and father together so long ago. I was like a ship without an anchor, drifting helplessly. I couldn't eat, couldn't sleep. All I could do was stay at home and listen for the telephone to ring, for Gabriel to show some sign—any sign—he couldn't do without me, regardless of where he lived.

When Mother noticed I was spending a lot more time at home, and Gabriel wasn't coming around, she asked if we'd broken up.

"No, of course not," I said quickly. "He is just . . . well, he's busy right now. He was out from work some after Neal died. And . . . and he has a lot of responsibility."

She looked up from her sewing and turned down the radio. "You know, Senta, sometimes after a person loses someone close, he needs time to get straightened out. It's better to leave him alone for a while."

Did she know I'd begun calling him, but receiving no answer? "Certainly that's right. He just needs some time, that's all."

She went back to her sewing. I went up to my room and lay across the bed. I felt I was about to burst open at the seams. I wanted to scream, I wanted to run, I wanted to beat on somebody. I could do nothing.

Gabriel's move transpired, but not exactly as planned. One night there was an attempted burglary through a downstairs window in the Gerrard home on Main. This, even more than Gabriel's masterful persuasion, convinced Alvareda to do as her son directed. She now did not want to wait to have a house built, and they decided to buy a John Staub home which was up for sale on DelMonte. Mother told me that much. It was days later, however, that Gabriel filled in the rest. At least he had the decency to come over one Saturday—unexpectedly arriving at three in the afternoon. We sat down on the front porch. He did not look at me, but looked ahead at the passing cars.

"We've found a two-story with a detached cottage for Mother," he said. "Lilly has made up her mind to enter nursing school, so she won't be living there. And"—he paused, and drew in a deep sigh—"I'm going to be married in July."

Chapter 9

I gaped at him, the life draining out of me. No words would come. At last I looked away and cleared my throat. A fleeting hope this might be some form of proposal to me lingered in the back of my mind. "Oh? And who is the lucky girl?" I said, almost in a whisper.

I think in that moment he knew relief. He took in a deep breath and said, "Louetta Hemphill."

I knew it, I knew it; every syllable of her name pricked me like a needle. I turned toward him. "What in the world would you want with her? That little pansy who's been carried around on a pillow all her life? What possible interest could she be to you?" But I knew of course. She was exactly the kind of wife someone like Gabriel would choose. Someone with the "right" back-ground.

"Don't speak that way of her, Senta. You can be angry with me, but not with her. She doesn't know anything about us."

The news rallied me. . . . I sensed a door opening. . . . "Oh? And what would she say if she did?"

"I—I don't know," he said, and looked away again. I took some joy in the confirmation I'd happened upon his vulnerable spot. I wasn't going to touch it, not yet.

"Shouldn't you think about this some more? I mean, since your father's death, you've been a little off-balance, haven't you? Before then, you seemed to know what you wanted. But lately you've been confused. Is this a good time to make such a decision?"

"My father's death shook me up, yes. It also brought me to my senses. I'm thirty-four years old. I've got to settle down, begin building for the future.

There's . . . there's no one out there between me and the rest of the world anymore."

"I can understand that. But surely you realize how much I believe in you. I always thought one day you'd see me as a part of your future."

He paused, and lowered his head for a moment. "I know, and I'm sorry. And in a way I'm nuts about you, but I don't think we're really suited, and—"

"And you are better suited to her?" I shifted the words.

He nodded. "I knew it almost from the first time I met her, but I guess I wasn't ready to start thinking of a lifetime commitment."

Lifetime commitment. . . . The words were like a deathblow. What I had longed to hear him say to me, all my life, he had said to someone else. My voice quivering, I pleaded, "Those are lofty words, but you never said you loved her. You never said she excited you, not the way I do."

"There's a difference, Senta. I never met any girl who excited me the way you do. But I do love Louetta . . . in the ways that you need to love a person you intend to marry." He sighed. "I understand now what Dad meant when he explained how he felt about Mother."

"Are you doing this to please him? Because you think he would choose someone like her for you?"

"No. I'm marrying her because it's what we both want. Maybe I'll always want to win my father's approval, deep inside. But he never said anything to me about Louetta. He never really had a chance to get to know her."

"I see. And he wouldn't have 'approved' of me, would he? It seems no one approves of me. I'm the black sheep, just like Clayton."

"No, Senta, that's not true of either of you. Well, at least not you. It's just that you're young and you don't yet know what you want. I can tell that by talking with you. I don't believe you and I would be good for each other."

"And when you met Louetta, you weren't ready to get serious, so you had a little fling with me first, while you kept her on the string," I snapped.

He paused before responding, as though trying to figure how best to express his feelings. "It certainly seemed to be what you wanted."

I took in a short breath. "It takes two, doesn't it?"

"Look, I've got to get going. I'm still moving things out of my apartment." He stood up and looked down at me. "I'm a jerk for letting you down, but when two people break up one of them has to be the heel. I wanted to tell you myself, before you heard it from someone else."

I knew he was through talking now, through listening to my arguments. My heart was squeezed with panic, and tears were boiling behind my eyes. I couldn't let him know he was tearing me apart. "I'm sure I'll be reading about it in the society page, and I know that you'll be making the rounds of boring parties, talking to dull people. . . ." I said.

He shrugged. "Maybe you're right about that part of it. I'll always be grateful for the fun we had together, and I hope one day you'll realize that all this is right because you'll have found someone who is right for you," he said gently.

"I certainly intend to keep the excitement in my life, with or without you," I said with a lift of my chin.

He nodded a farewell and walked away. I watched him until he'd gotten in his car and driven out of sight, my trembling fingers drumming my lips as my mind fought down acceptance. I sat there for a long time, staring out into the street, the traffic swimming in front of my eyes. This wasn't really happening. He couldn't leave me; no, he loved me, I knew he did. He'd come back, just as he did before, not able to help himself. Any moment now . . . Tears rolled down my cheeks. I wiped them off with the back of my hand and sat waiting.

Finally, Laura walked up. "Where's Gabriel?" she said. "I wanted him to see me in my new dress."

"Why would he want to see you?" I barked, and looked at her. She was wearing a filmy jade green dress, with a neckline that came up high in the front and dipped down low in the back. She turned around to model it. "Where are you going in that getup? You look like a little whore."

She glanced at me and smiled. I realized she'd heard the conversation that just went on between Gabriel and me, and was loving every moment of my torture. She began to hum under her breath and with an exaggerated sway of her hips walked back through the door. I watched her, thinking God, she'll turn up pregnant before she's sixteen.

Then I looked forward again and wished I could turn up pregnant. That would certainly change things for Gabriel. Then he'd have to come to his senses and marry me. I thought of him now, packing away things that we'd picked out together in his apartment . . . maybe he'd give them away, shoving them out of his life just as he had shoved me out. Yet . . . why had he made a point of telling me that was what he would be doing? Could it be he wanted me to follow him? Or, even without really being conscious of it, that he wanted me to come to him? If I did, now, that would ruin his engagement. Anything that happened before the proposal was off-limits to Louetta, but not something that happened afterward. That was a different story. I rose and went inside. "Mother? Mother, where are you?" I called.

Mother came out of the kitchen, wiping her hands on her apron. I told her I wanted the keys to the car, that I had an errand to run.

"They're on the sideboard in the dining room. Senta, why do you have to behave so rudely to Laura? She just told me what you said to her out on the porch, and—"

"Laura gets on my nerves," I said. "And I've already told you about that night she disappeared and I found her on the school grounds. You'd better watch her. She's in for trouble."

"Oh, I really think you exaggerated that, and anyway, if you call her names, you'll have her convinced that is what she really is. I know from experience . . ."

Her voice drifted off as I rushed out the back door and headed for the garage. I had already figured out what to tell Gabriel when I arrived on his doorstep. He'd apparently forgotten—or perhaps he really hadn't forgotten at all—that I still had a key to his apartment. Damn him! How could he just abandon me like that, as though I meant nothing? He simply could not intend to go through with this. He loved me, and I knew he did, even if he'd never said it in so many words. And he knew I was to be taken seriously, or he should by now. I kept the accelerator pressed to the floorboard, whizzing by cars and pedestrians, daring anyone to stop me. I had to get there, the sooner the better. . . . The car raced no faster than the blood coursing through my veins.

I arrived at the Isabella Court around five o'clock. I knocked on Gabriel's door and waited. No answer. I knocked again, harder this time. So, he'd lied about coming home to pack? Damn. At last I decided to shove the key in. The door opened easily. I walked in and closed it softly behind me. There were boxes from one end of the living room to the other, paintings propped up on the floor, carpet rolled up. There was a bucket of paint and a ladder in one corner. Apparently the apartment owners would be redoing the unit. I walked back toward the hall, and then I heard the sound of the shower running.

I pushed the door of the bathroom open and walked in. The room was steamy. I could see his blurred figure behind the curtain. I am not sure at just what point he realized I was there. I stood by the lavatory and took off my shoes, pulled down my stockings, shimmied out of my dress and slip. He became very still, as though not quite sure whether he'd heard something or not. Then he continued with his bathing. I pulled the shower curtain back and climbed in. "Senta, what are you—"

"I brought your key back," I smiled. "Hand me the soap, will you?"

"You can't do this," he said, the hot blades of water swilling down him and the steam rising up around his face.

"You mean you want me to keep the key?" I asked. I grabbed the bar of soap and slowly glided it in a figure eight around both breasts and in a line down my stomach and between my legs. I leaned over and looked up at him while I hiked one leg on the side of the tub and continued to slide the soap up around the inside of my thigh and down, along my calf and around my ankle.

He paused. "You know exactly what I mean. Now, stop it. I can't believe you—"

"Hm?" I said lazily, and as he watched I put both arms behind my neck and moved the soap around the back of my shoulders. He stood there, saying nothing, his eyes locked on me, his chest full of wet swirls of hair, rising and falling. Finally I put the soap aside and said, "Wash me off?" Then before he could respond I pulled up against him and shimmied down his front, my hands stroking, working down his sides and then along his hips and thighs. I could feel his body trembling. I closed my mouth around the hard bulge of him, then drew away and looked up. "Should I stop?"

One moment . . . two. . . . Something close to a smile of resignation crossed his lips under a strange, angry look in his eyes, and he whispered, "You monster."

"Say you don't want me, say it."

He turned and switched off the shower, then looked at me again. Then he closed his hands around the back of my head, fingers pressing hard, pulling at my hair, and, still with that puzzling look on his face, said, "Shut up." He reached down with one arm and jerked me up against him, his clutch hurting my ribs. He closed one hand tightly around my face and kissed me, his tongue first rotating deliciously inside my mouth, then suddenly, pushing so hard underneath my tongue, I thought he'd tear it loose. His mouth moved away from mine and slid down my face and along my neck, down inside the crevice of my throat, lingering a moment while I felt the wetness of my own desire empty out. Oh, Gabriel, I can't wait, I can't— His mouth moved down then, scaling over and around and between my breasts, then biting so hard on one nipple I let out a stifled cry. I blinked at him, all at once afraid. Looking into my eyes he reached down with one hand and forced me wide apart with his fingers; then it felt almost as though his whole hand closed like a fist and shoved into me. My fingernails traced down his back like a rhapsodic music score. I thought I would come in two, yet he could not, could not hurt me enough to make me stop wanting him. "Gabriel, Gabriel," I murmured in his ear. He lifted me up and carried me through the bathroom door and dumped me on the bed. I wasn't through, not nearly through, this couldn't be all, "Gabriel?"

He grabbed my shoulders and turned me over so that my face was against the pillows. "No, wait!" I cried, but he ignored me. From behind he covered me with his body and pinned my arms against the pillow with his hands. He forged deeply into me again and again, until he flooded the inside of me like a river gone wild. At last he raised up, panting, and turned me over to face him. He looked at me for a long moment, his eyes like hard beads. Then he fell back against the bed, his elbows drawn behind his head, his chest heaving. I didn't know what to say; I didn't know what he meant. I felt used up, abandoned. I lay there, eyes wide, unable to say anything at all.

Presently he rose from the bed, dried off with a towel, and began to dress. I watched him, every muscle in my body still tensed up, waiting for him to say something to me, afraid of what he might say. He buttoned his trousers and sat down on the edge of the bed to pull on his socks. I could see the marks I made along his back. I bit my lip. He put on his shoes, then stood up in front of the mirror, buttoning his shirt and putting on his necktie. "This doesn't change anything," he said.

"Oh, doesn't it?" I said faintly. I was half angry; half perplexed.

He glanced over at me, then picked up his coat. "No. And don't confuse what just happened with 'love.' "

That wounded me more than anything he had done. "You're still going through with the marriage?"

"Yes."

"What if I get pregnant?" It came out before I was sure whether I meant it as a threat or an appeal.

He stopped and turned. If ever I saw him unmistakably furious, that was the moment. He narrowed his eyes at me. Finally he said, "We'll cross that bridge when we come to it. Now I have to go, before I'm late."

"You'll just leave me here, like this?"

"It was your decision to come in that way."

"You bastard!"

He walked out of the bedroom, through the apartment, and slammed the front door behind him. I could have ripped up the sheets, slung paint all over the place, slashed up the paintings with a kitchen knife, torn the apartment to shreds. Instead, for a long time I lay there, my face buried in the pillows, crying my eyes out and cursing him.

Much later, as I finally rose to get dressed, I had another idea. I would simply report, just as I had done as a child. Words, I had learned then, were far more powerful than tantrums. Tomorrow I would pay a call. . . .

The Hemphills lived on Inwood, a wide, meandering street in River Oaks. Their large home, which looked like a French chateau, was perched far back from the street among the trees, and surrounded by wide ribbons of blooming pink azalea bushes. I had dressed in the very best outfit I owned, yet when the maid answered the door and surveyed me from head to toe, I felt suddenly tacky and out of place. It was a searing jolt, and one which I would never forget. I told the maid my name and she nodded quietly and asked me to wait in a room to the right of the big marble entrance hall.

I walked in and sat down on a sofa. I looked around me at the mahogany moulding along the walls, the deep maroon silk wallpaper, the dazzling crystal chandelier above, and the plush carpet below. Just the furnishings in this room—the paintings and china figurines, the oriental urns and the candleholders—must have been worth more than my mother's house and property put together. Oh, I hated our house, with more passion now than ever.

The door opened and Louetta Hemphill stepped in. She was smaller than I remembered, not any less tall, but more delicate in build. She was wearing a very pretty light blue dress that brought out the blue in her eyes and offset her blond hair. Her hair was no prettier than mine, only longer. "You wanted to speak to me?"

"Yes," I said, and smiled sweetly. Then I sat down and told her all about Gabriel and me, about how I'd practically lived with him over the past year or so. With every word, her face blanched a little more. Finally she looked down and said, "Well, I suppose what Gabriel did before we became engaged is really none of my business." She looked across at me then, and I continued with yesterday's event, leaving out all the details which were none of her business anyway. All she needed to believe was that I still had Gabriel wound around my finger.

She sat back and looked off to the side, picked up a pillow and smoothed a hand over it. Her fingers were long and slender. She did not wear Gabriel's engagement ring yet. There was a blue sapphire surrounded by diamonds on one finger. "Is that all?" she asked weakly.

I told her it was.

"Well, good day, then."

I rose and pulled on my gloves, studying her face expectantly. She threw the pillow aside, and kept sitting there as though she had suddenly forgotten I was around.

When I walked out the door I did not have the feeling of triumph I expected. Oh yes, she grimaced and flinched a few times, and looked quite at a loss as to what to do. But she didn't show any signs of real anger as I might have expected, nor did she declare Gabriel Gerrard to be a scoundrel as I'd hoped. I could only believe she would save those expressions for him.

Within the week I learned enough to figure out the rest. Mother told me, in her somewhat timid way, that the engagement of Gabriel and Louetta was being announced at a party that Saturday night, and would be in the Sunday papers. I just sat there, staring blindly ahead. She must have realized she had knocked the wind out of me, for she sighed and folded her hands. "Senta, I know how you must be feeling, and I'm sorry. But don't think you won't find someone else, maybe even someone better suited to you."

There were those despicable words again, hurled at me like a baseball. "By 'better suited,' do you mean, someone more of my station? Someone who grew up in a house like this, rather than one comparable to the Gerrards'?"

"No," she said, as though surprised. "That is not what I meant at all." Then she paused and added, "Or maybe it has something to do with that—with the different backgrounds you and Gabriel have had—after all.

"But whatever, you'll meet someone else, you'll see. You're a beautiful, bright young woman. The last thing you want to do is spend your lifetime with someone who loves someone else, or, at least, doesn't share your feelings. Believe me, I know."

Now I was livid. I could feel the blood rising in my cheeks. "What do you know? If you'd been any kind of wife to my father, everything would be different. My father would be alive today. He'd be designing houses and buildings that would win him the fame he deserved. We'd be living somewhere besides this heap, and Gabriel Gerrard would be lucky to have me look his way.

"Oh, but don't think I'm giving up. I'll show you and I'll show him. One day you'll all be sorry for doing this to me."

I stomped away, paying her no more respect than I ever paid her before. How I wish now I'd heeded her advice.

Chapter 10

It is about this point—the middle of 1930—that I can look back and see how every decision I made led inevitably toward the events of today. First of all, the decision to quit my job as a legal secretary and become a registered nurse. When Lilly enthusiastically suggested it—we would enter training at Baptist Hospital together, "It would be such fun!"—I refused to take the idea seriously. But then it did have a certain appeal. As Lilly said, I had the kind of cool, efficient personality that would make me good. Also I was strong in the subjects of science and math—almost a must for a nurse. The three-year course was free, the uniforms furnished, and at the end of it all I would be a "professional," with initials after my name. That was a lot better than being a secretary.

All these were good arguments. Yet in the end, it was something else entirely that decided me. Clayton would be doing his internship at Baptist Hospital. I was still angry enough at Gabriel that the idea of having his despised brother become interested in me . . . maybe one day even get serious about me . . . was worth entertaining. The more I thought about it, the more right it seemed. But I wouldn't rush it. That was my mistake with Gabriel. There would be plenty of time, three years. . . .

On a Friday afternoon at the end of August, Lilly and I went for an interview with Mrs. Jolly, the director of nursing. Mrs. Jolly was an attractive woman of around sixty, with perfect skin and soft, gray hair pulled back in a knot with a deep wave over her forehead. She had a discerning gaze that made me uncomfortable. She warned us that nursing was hard work, and that training would be the most demanding experience of our lives. Her standards were very high. She asked many questions, wrote down many observations, and when she had satisfied herself we were acceptable, she put her pencil down and folded her hands. "Now, you may bring as many belongings as you like, but be aware there is only limited space in the dormitory—"

"I won't be living here," I interrupted.

"I'm afraid it's compulsory. You'll understand, once you're in training."

"But I can take a streetcar every morning—" I protested. I had not counted on the sudden usurping of freedom all this would mean.

"Of course, if you have problems at home, perhaps it is best—" she began, and I feared she was going to call it off.

"No, no," I said quickly. "I—I guess it can be arranged." I could not imagine how to tell Mother about this. She depended on me to help look after Laura. . . .

"I'll expect the two of you back at four o'clock on Sunday, for orientation."

In the first few weeks of training, I felt I'd been swept away by a hurricane force. Mother did not give me the expected trouble about moving out; I suppose she was sympathetic about my losing Gabriel, and did not want to get in the way of my starting something new. However, something else happened that put me behind before I even began. On the Sunday we were due to arrive at school, my grandmother Carlotta died suddenly. Mother was very upset, especially because Grandfather David refused to come home from overseas to attend the funeral, and Uncle Jordan was hanging around to put in his bid for Grandmother's house out on Main (he did not win; Mother finally had to inform him that everything went to Grandfather according to the terms of the will, and no amount of pressure was going to change that). On top of everything else, Aunt Patricia and Uncle George came for the funeral, bringing several of their family members. I was kept busy with all the arrangements, greeting people, trying to pretend to be sorry about losing someone who was about as lovable as a hickory stick and every bit as rigid, and everything else connected with the funeral. Not till the middle of the second week of classes did I arrive at school. I barely had time to get my breath before I was presented with assignments that all of my classmates had already done, plus new ones.

If I thought I had been busy working for Sid Carney, it was nothing to compare with nursing school. We were up before dawn—shortly after 5 A.M. —dressed in our blue uniform, white kerchief, black stockings, and lace-up shoes before 6, most of us fastening on our name pins as we rushed out the door and hurried to the chapel at precisely 6 A.M. At 6:30 we were dismissed with the Lord's Prayer and marched through the tunnel to the dining room for a breakfast big enough for a hungry farmhand. We arrived on the hospital floor for duty at 7. Our days were twelve hours long. They included classes and lectures and labs, as well as the floor duty. At the end of the day, after the dinner hour, we adjourned to study. Curfew on "in" nights—Monday through Friday—was ten o'clock. On weekends it was ten-thirty. I usually fell asleep as soon as my head rested on the pillow.

Gabriel had been appointed to work with the Texas Railroad Commission, prosecuting offenders of the ever more restrictive oil and gas production laws. He would be maintaining homes both in Houston and Austin for the duration of his appointment. Anyone could easily deduct that this was the beginning of a political career, I observed upon reading about it in the newspapers.

One day I looked out the window of the dormitory to see him talking to Lilly down at the curb. He was dressed in a suit and tie, leaning against an expensive new navy blue Cadillac Town Brougham with canework appliqué on the sides. Apparently he had given up his sports car along with the light-hearted side of his nature.

I moved aside to be sure he didn't see me. I had not come face to face with him since the last time we were together. I had not attended his wedding with Mother and Laura. I was so embarrassed by everything, especially my foiled attempt to turn Louetta against him, that I couldn't bear to see them marching down the aisle of Christ Church together. In a few minutes, Lilly reached up and hugged his neck. Then he got in the car and drove off, a good bit slower than he used to drive his roadster.

I wouldn't want him anymore, I thought, but I knew that wasn't true, and when Lilly told me that evening that Louetta was expecting their first child, I felt frustration rise in me like acute indigestion. If only I'd had sense enough not to be so careful about getting pregnant during the time I went with Gabriel. . . .

I went to bed that night too upset to fall asleep. I could not keep my mind off the vision of Gabriel and Louetta, in bed together, conceiving the child. Was she as good-looking naked as I was? Did she arouse him as much? Did he . . . did he sometimes think of me when he was making love to her? Even though I could answer these questions and others along the same line to suit my own satisfaction, it didn't help much. I lay there for hours, listening to the clang of the streetcar as it rounded the corner outside, digging my fingernails into my hands, and all the next day I walked around distracted while Mrs. Jolly eyed me suspiciously.

I rarely saw Clayton Gerrard, and for a long time even the sweet prospect of getting back at Gabriel through him seemed lost to me. The interns lived in their own quarters on the top floor of the hospital, and with all the rules governing our relations with them, they might have lived at the South Pole. Nursing students were forbidden to fraternize with either doctors or interns. There were a couple of girls dating interns on the sly, but it was next to impossible to get to know a doctor or an intern well enough to go to these lengths to be alone with him. Every time you turned around, there was an old maid nurse—the hospital was full of them—looking down her nose at you. If you so much as looked interested when a man in a white coat walked by, you stood the risk of being reported. While I assisted Clayton now and then as he made rounds and read charts, he never showed any interest in me. In fact if there was any one intern I could name that was especially aloof—and the other girls would have readily agreed—it was Clayton Gerrard . . . Dr. Gerrard, to be more correct.

With Lilly he was the same, or more so. While on duty, he spoke to her as though he had never met her in his life before they both entered training. One night I heard a student tell another that Dr. Gerrard was a cold fish. And I thought: I'll bet I could warm him up, if I could just get near him.

After a little time off at Christmas, we returned to a full spring schedule of training. Thanks to the abundant food at nursing school, and Lilly's refusal to follow doctor's orders, she was ten pounds heavier than when she entered the school. Certainly she was not fat, but she was teased a lot about being chubby. It was in early February that she first began to suffer from headaches and dizziness. I noticed that she would hesitate before getting up in the morning, sitting on the edge of the little bed as though to steady herself. If I asked her what was wrong, she'd say it was nothing, that she had always been that way. I knew better, but left her alone.

Then one night in late May, while on floor duty, she blacked out at the desk. I was grateful, felt it was so lucky, that I was around and no one else was. It was easy to pull her just a little farther into the small supply room and elevate her feet with an extra pillow nearby. I picked up the phone and asked for Clayton. It was a big mistake.

He came down at once, obviously concerned. She was coming to when he got there. She seemed all right now except for some numbness in her fingers. He measured her blood pressure, took her pulse, did all those things a physician does efficiently and coolly. Then he looked up at me. "You realize what this means, don't you?"

"She probably needs some time off."

He looked down at her again. "I'm afraid your nursing days are over, Lilly."

I couldn't believe my ears. I stared at him, then at Lilly, then back at him again. He had sealed her fate right there, her own brother. I had called him thinking he would be discreet, not tell Mrs. Jolly about it. He might have somehow gotten her a few days' rest without bringing about her dismissal. She'd almost made it through the whole year. For weeks she had talked of nothing except earning her cap. In a month she would have been wearing it: the insignia of having completed one third of her training. Now, thanks to my error in judgment, she had just forfeited all of it. I slumped down next to her and took her hands, "Oh, Lilly, I—I'm so sorry. . . ." Tears were streaming down my face.

Clayton wasted no time in telling Mrs. Jolly that Lilly must drop out. A week later, as I walked down the hall toward a patient's room, downcast because of the new empty bed where Lilly once slept, Clayton approached me from behind. "I hope you understand that what I did was for Lilly's own good."

I looked at him bewildered.

"When she had that attack some time ago, I'd be willing to bet she suffered a slight cardiovascular accident. This time, there is no doubt at all."

As far as I knew, the doctor who treated her before never said that, yet I had always wondered. Surely now, since there was no damage, she could just take it a little easier. She wanted this so much—

He had a pleasant expression on his face. "I have heard you are very efficient. I must compliment you on your ability, now that I've seen you in action, Miss Farrish."

Miss Farrish! With that remark he turned from me and walked briskly down the hall. I stood there gaping at him, fighting down the urge to cry. He had just signaled the end of the most important thing in Lilly's life and he almost seemed to enjoy it.

Chapter 11

I came home one weekend in late September to find Mother very much changed, and entertaining a visitor for tea. Ordinarily I probably would not have taken her gentleman caller seriously. His name was Walter Brubaker, and except for the fact that he was apparently a successful attorney, there seemed no reason for him to capture the interest of any woman, even Mother. He was probably in his fifties, balding, and perspired so heavily that under the arms of his white linen suitcoat were wide damp rings.

Mother called to me from the library, and behaved as though there were nothing for me to look surprised about. She introduced her friend. "Mr. Brubaker is handling Mother's estate, and now that Father has surprised everyone by remarrying over in Europe, the estate matters are a little complicated."

We had received word of the remarriage of my grandfather through the wire service two weeks ago. It seemed obvious that what little was left of my grandmother Carlotta's money was to be denied him if he remarried. But there were other complications to be settled pertaining to properties passed down by previous generations. Personally I had to hand it to my grandfather for having enough gumption to marry again at his age.

I spoke to Mr. Brubaker politely and went back to the kitchen, dying to have a moment alone with Mother. I heard them resume their conversation.

Mother said, "My mother was simply using that as an instrument to keep a hold on my father. She had been doing that for years, through the Church—"

"Yes, but perhaps it wasn't unwise in this case. That aging countess or whatever she is, that he has taken up with, has no money of her own—we've already found that out—and she'll probably outlive him and take what your mother had left if she's allowed to." Mr. Brubaker had a slight lisp, and a soft, conciliatory voice. Just the kind of person Mother would like.

Since Neal died she had not had anyone whom she really trusted to counsel her about investments. After my father's accident Neal had taken some of her money—part of which were the proceeds from the sale of my father's business—and begun investing it for her. Then later, after my father died, Neal had invested part of the life insurance money. I was never told the details of these investments, but the income had enabled her to live comfortably and of course she knew no extravagance—not till today, anyway. Now, I guessed, Walter Brubaker would be helping her with her financial affairs. Maybe, from the way she was dressed up, she hoped he would become something more than a business associate. I could stand it no longer. I pushed open the door to the dining room and said, "Mother, I can't seem to find anything in your kitchen anymore. Could you come here for a moment?"

As soon as she walked into the kitchen I said, "What are you up to? Your hair—"

"How do you like it? I've been thinking about having it bobbed ever since you had yours done, but it took me all this time to get up the courage."

She had parted it down the side with little finger waves over her forehead and curls close to her head. It was fairly becoming I guess. "Did you have it lightened?"

She looked somewhat guilty and patted it with her fingertips. "Just a lemon rinse. The hairdresser swears by it. My hair was getting so dull and lifeless, not at all the way it used to be."

"Well, as long as you didn't dye it."

She laughed. "Oh, for heaven's sake, Senta. This is 1931. And I'm forty-two years old. Give me some credit for good judgment."

"Mr. Brubaker seems nice. Is he married?"

"Why, Senta, how you do rush on!" she said, then with a look approaching coyness, she added, "He is a widower, actually."

"My, my," I said, smiling. I knew she'd never admit to me she liked him, but time would tell. He might just be ordinary enough to find her charming. "That's a new dress, isn't it?"

She sighed. "Yes. I was afraid the floral print would be too busy, but the sales clerk assured me it was becoming. What do you think?"

"It's all right, I suppose. As long as you don't put on any weight."

"Senta, you sound exactly like my mother used to. You know very well I haven't put on an ounce of weight in twenty years. In fact, I'm down five pounds more now than when—when your father had his accident. I really have to get back to Walter—Mr. Brubaker—now. What was it you couldn't find?"

"What? Oh, skip it. I'm going to take a nap."

She stopped at the door and turned toward me. "I'll be spending a lot of time at the law office over the next few weeks, so if you need to reach me and I'm not here, keep calling back."

"What about Laura?"

"Laura's a big girl now. She isn't nearly the bother she used to be. She's doing quite well in her art lessons."

I shook my head in wonder. Stephen Sandock entered Laura's work in an art contest some time ago, and she won. The lessons were the prize. They were not, however, any special sign that she was grown up. Mother was so naïve when it came to Laura. Or perhaps, this time, she was too smitten with her new gentleman friend to pay much attention.

Not long after that, I was reminded of my own words. Lilly and Stephen soon eloped. This came as no surprise to anyone. She told me that she had finally come to her senses and accepted the fact that he truly loved her for herself, and that was all that counted. And to Stephen's credit, he had not seriously looked at another woman and claimed he would have never married anyone else.

They settled near Rice Institute in a little cottage of their own, which Stephen bought with his savings, and which Lilly quickly fixed up like a doll house, with crisscrossed organdy curtains, flourishing pot plants in every sunny corner, and a gas log fireplace in the living room flanked by two easy chairs. Stephen had worked at the Metropolitan in the art department since shortly after they broke off their engagement, and now he got Lilly on as cashier for the theater. It was of course a sit-down job in a cool place that was free of stresses except during normal busy theater hours, or when some special movie was showing or a famous entertainer was on stage.

Now that Lilly worked at the Metropolitan, Mother felt it was safe to let Laura go to the movies there unaccompanied. If she had a problem, help was only as far away as the ticket office in front where Lilly sat. Laura could ride the trolley up McKinney Avenue to town and walk half a block over to the theater. As Mother said later, she felt it was a good way to force Laura to become more independent, to grow up. But it backfired. While Mother was busy at the law office one late afternoon, having ridden to town on the trolley herself, Laura returned from school and helped herself to the car. She went to the Metropolitan to see *Cimarron*, and stayed through two showings and the stage show as well. Lilly might have worried earlier had she realized Laura was there without Mother's permission, and also with the car.

Around nine o'clock, Laura walked out. Lilly was selling tickets to the next showing, and noticed her leave. Within a few minutes, Laura returned in tears. She could not remember where she parked the car. Lilly could not leave the theater yet, and she immediately called Mother to let her know what had happened. Mother did not answer. Stephen was out of town visiting his father, who had been hospitalized a couple of days earlier. So Lilly was not certain what to do, and at the same time she was frantically busy selling tickets to impatient theatergoers. Finally she thought to call Gabriel. Gabriel drove up in less than a quarter of an hour and picked up Laura to search for her lost automobile.

It was nearing midnight when they finally got home—Gabriel insisted on following Laura in his car after they found Mother's car parked over on Dallas. When they finally got there, Mother had just arrived, never having known her daughter was missing.

It was much later before I learned all this. Lilly had not called me because she knew there was nothing I could do—I had no car at nursing school and obviously someone was needed who could search the many blocks of downtown Houston with the aid of lights in order to find the missing automobile. When I did learn of it, I was horrified at Mother's allowing Laura to get so out of hand. It was nothing, however, compared with the crisis that shortly followed.

Near the close of October, Mother became concerned about Laura and took her to a doctor. Following an examination, he called Mother in to break the news: Laura was around two months' pregnant. Mother called me home from school on that Thursday night. I do not believe I have ever seen her so distressed. When I walked in she and Laura were sitting across from each other at the dining room table, and Mother was, in as forceful a manner as she was capable of, trying to reason Laura into telling her who had fathered the child.

I knew that Laura was maddening at times. Tonight she was in top form. I arrived breathless and worried. When I heard the news I took Laura by the shoulders. "Look at me, you little slut—"

"Senta, please," Mother begged. "Sit down and let's try and keep calm."

Laura looked at me through the bright eyes of victory.

"Just tell us, Laura," Mother cajoled. "If we know, then we will have a better idea of what to do next."

Laura looked down and turned her hands over in her lap. "I—I don't know."

"Who are the—young men—you have been with, then?"

"Name one or two," I said sarcastically.

"I haven't been with anyone for a long time. I don't remember."

"Do you even have any idea what makes a girl pregnant?" I asked.

"Yes, I think so."

"Then, who have you done that with?"

"Lots of boys. It's fun."

Mother leaned back and wiped her brow. "It's late," she said. "Get some rest, and we'll talk again in the morning."

"How can you rest at a time like this?" I demanded.

"I don't know, but this isn't getting us anywhere, obviously. I probably shouldn't have called you home, but I was in such a panic."

"I told you you shouldn't let her run free the way you have. But you wouldn't listen to me. Now look what has happened." I rose. "And if you don't know who the father is, and she won't tell you, what are you going to do? Pretty soon she'll be showing."

"I'm aware of that."

I probably should not have been speaking this way within Laura's hearing, and I certainly should not have said what I said next. "You ought to send her away, and put the baby up for adoption."

Laura turned in her chair and looked at me fearfully. "Don't send me away, please. Mother, you wouldn't send me away, would you?"

I realized we had finally hit a sensitive cord. I knelt down beside her. "Not if you tell. Maybe we'll let you stay here."

Mother rose. "Stop terrorizing your sister," she said. "Laura, I don't know what to do at this point. Let's take one thing at a time."

I shook my head and walked toward the stairs. If Mother was going to go on protecting Laura, we'd never find out anything.

That night I lay awake a long time, listening to Laura sob in her room. She had been a problem since birth. I always knew something terrible would happen to her. If I'd had my way, we would have institutionalized her years ago. But she was always just sane enough to convince Mother she was eventually going to turn normal. I could not understand how even a mother could so deceive herself about her child. And now this. Laura had probably been hiding in bushes with boys since she was fourteen. Yet even that first time I caught her down at Eastwood School, Mother insisted I was jumping to conclusions. Well, it was her problem now. I wasn't going to stay around and watch this happen. Thank goodness I lived elsewhere. Maybe if Mother was lucky enough to find out who the father was, she could arrange a hasty marriage, that is, if he was stupid enough to marry Laura.

I turned over and thought some more. Who the hell could the father be? Unfortunately I had not been here to see who she was going around with, and obviously Mother did not have her eye on Laura, so there was no telling. Laura had always put on a show around men. Even when Gabriel and I used to date, she hung around him, kept him from leaving. . . . And he had seemed to like her, not that she gave a person much choice. Gad, what if? I wondered, then dismissed the idea. That was too long ago.

I slept late the next morning, and when I went downstairs Mother and Laura had already talked out the matter and Mother had reached a decision. Mother poured a cup of coffee for me and began. "The boy, as near as I can tell, was a classmate last year. But there were two boys that she was apparently . . . well, that she had been with, so it would be difficult to know who is responsible. Therefore, I must take the brunt of responsibility. I've decided to keep her here and give the baby the Farrish name."

"What? Mother, do you realize what you're saying? Everyone will know. It'll be the scandal of the neighborhood, not to mention a tremendous embarrassment for me."

She looked at me coldly. "You don't live here anymore. If you want to avoid coming home on weekends for the next few months, you are welcome to do so. I'm tired of having my life dictated by others."

"And you are just going to keep the baby—raise it?"

"Perhaps I will. There is plenty of time to decide on that. Laura is terrified of going away from me. I can't force her to. And I am disappointed you fail to realize what seems an obvious fact. Granted Laura is gullible and naïve, she is no different from you when it comes to certain things, just not quite so discreet."

I looked away, feeling my heart beat a little faster.

"If you're ashamed to be part of this family, well maybe it's just as well you will soon finish nursing school and be out on your own. You don't ever have to come home again," she said.

I stared at her. I couldn't believe she could so cavalierly dismiss me.

"Now, I have groceries to buy. I'll be back shortly."

When I went back to school that afternoon, I was determined to take Mother at her word. In a way she had kicked me out of my own home. And I might have guessed it would come to this. She always favored the others over me, John, while he was alive, then Laura in her turn. If not for my father, I would not have had any devotion at all.

On a Sunday afternoon shortly after that, Mother paid me a visit at the school. I had not heard from her since our quarrel, and was very surprised to be told she was awaiting me in the parlor.

Maybe she had packed up all my belongings and brought them in exchange for my housekey, I thought as I walked downstairs. . . .

Yet she was smiling when she saw me, and her words were conciliatory. "I've been thinking, and I realize you're right. Laura should go away. I—"

"Well, it's about time you came to your senses. Where are you sending her?"

"I'm not sending her. I'm going with her. She . . . I couldn't bear to force her to go through this alone. We're going to New Orleans. Alvareda has friends there, from the days when we visited New Orleans frequently. Laura and I are going to stay with the family until after the baby is born."

"Then what?"

"There is a possibility these people may take the baby, but I'm not ready to make that decision as yet."

"Well, I think you should seriously consider it," I told her. "No one would ever have to know then. There would be no embarrassment or shame. . . ."

She looked away as though to dispense with my opinion, then looked back at me again. "We're leaving in a few days. I've written the name and address here, so you can contact me if you need to . . . or, if you want to."

Laura's unpredictability had not lessened. As Mother was saying, "Come to the car and tell Laura good-bye," Laura suddenly appeared at the door. This time she had at least had sense enough to ask someone to show her where we could be found. I reached out to give her a hug to please Mother, and realized she was beginning to show. Her belly was rounded just enough to make her skirt a little tight. I was mortified to think that others around the dormitory would notice this and begin gossiping. I dispensed with the two of them as quickly as possible. When they were gone I read the piece of paper. Captain and Mrs. B. W. LeCourt, 2505 Prytania, New Orleans, Louisiana. The name and address meant nothing to me.

Chapter 12

My revulsion at Clayton's treatment of his sister Lilly had taken the edge off my interest in him, though after a short while I had to allow the possibility that he was not quite as cold as he seemed, when out of uniform. Now I was so self-conscious about what Laura had done, my questions about the kind of person Clayton was became overshadowed by his possible doubts about me and my family. After all, the Gerrards had no soil on their pedigree. Alvareda might be treating Mother and Laura with special kindness, but that was only because Alvareda and Mother had been close friends for years, and this certainly wasn't the first time Alvareda had come to Mother's aid. I could not fathom Clayton's overlooking an illegitimate child in the family of someone he chose as a girl friend, not to mention a wife. But for a conversation I had with Lilly that fall, I might have abandoned my pursuit of Clayton forever.

I had never told Lilly of my designs on Clayton. She knew so much about me and Gabriel, I just didn't want her to know my real motive was a strong desire to get back at him that lingered in me still. Now I said, truthfully, "I'm glad you and Stephen got together. Frankly I thought Clayton double-crossed you. I wondered whether he had any real feelings for anyone."

"Oh, Clayton's really very fine . . . and he has such a great sense of responsibility that it makes him seem . . . hard . . . at times, especially when it comes to anything involving medicine."

"Well, he ought to be a great surgeon. He certainly doesn't pay any attention to anyone—anything else."

She looked at me for a long moment, then her face lit up with a smile. "Senta! Why didn't you tell me you like Clayton?" She sat back in her chair. "I've got to get busy."

She invited us both to her home for dinner one Saturday night. It was a nice November evening, crisp and chilly. I arrived before Clayton, and while Lilly and Stephen were busy in the kitchen I stayed in the living room and looked over the array of baby pictures of Gabriel's son, Alexander, born last spring. Obviously Lilly was very proud of her only nephew, judging by the amount of snapshots she'd collected. I was trying not to let myself think about the special meaning of these photographs for me . . . of what I lost out on . . . when I saw car lights through the window nearby. I peeked through an opening in the Venetian blinds and watched Clayton get out of the car and approach the house. In a couple of moments he rang the doorbell and Lilly hurried in from the kitchen to answer.

Clayton was wearing a navy wool sweater, rather than a coat, gray pants, and a pair of leather loafers. He carried a bouquet of flowers and a gift for the newlyweds. I remarked to myself that he looked almost human.

I stood back as Lilly hugged his neck and kissed his cheek—she had to reach on tiptoes—and made a fuss over the gift of a crystal pitcher and matching tumblers.

He seemed quite pleased with himself over it all. In the past I would have said always that Clayton lacked the charm of the other Gerrards, and the style. Tonight there was just the slightest hint of both, and I felt my pulse quicken a little as he turned and greeted me. "Well, Senta, you look different without your blue uniform and kerchief."

I smiled. "I wasn't sure you would remember my first name."

"Nonsense. One of my early surgeries was performed on your doll. Lilly dropped her on the floor and she was decapitated."

We all laughed, and Lilly said, "Hurry up into the dining room. We have tomato aspic and it'll be slush in a few minutes."

I've been wrong about him, I thought. He pulled out my chair at the table. As he sat down, I noticed that in profile he resembled his father. I had never thought of him as bearing any resemblance to Neal or anyone else in the family.

The dinner conversation was light and gay and I enjoyed myself for the first time since the days with Gabriel. Lilly had a great talent for bringing people out, and making them feel comfortable. That, I realized too, was part of being brought up by very social parents.

After the meal she took Stephen into the kitchen to help clean up and make the coffee, leaving Clayton and me to ourselves. We sat on the couch and talked about life at the hospital. I told him he had all the student nurses terrorized. He seemed surprised and said, "I guess I don't have much of a sense of humor at work. And I can't tolerate any noise in the operating room"—he looked at me and smiled—"so be well advised when you wind up there with me next year."

"You don't have to worry about me. The first thing I learned was never to question a doctor about anything, so I keep my mouth shut. If he makes a mistake, that's his tough luck."

"Interns are the same next to full-fledged doctors. A week ago Dr. Kerwin —he's awfully shaky, you know—severed an artery during surgery. I was standing right there, and I knew it was coming. But I couldn't say anything. Luckily the patient didn't suffer serious damage from his ineptitude.

"Someday all that will change."

"You mean, you will be able to talk back?"

"No, I mean that I'll be chief of staff and I'll get rid of surgeons like Dr. Kerwin. I'm watching all of them now."

Something about that statement sent a chill through me. "That sounds awfully cold-hearted," I murmured.

"That's how it is in medicine. The only thing that counts is curing the patient. Feelings don't matter."

His reasoning seemed twisted. I sensed that he would be the same if the patient were an automobile in need of repair and he were a mechanic. But I told myself he was just a serious young doctor who wanted to be a fine surgeon one day. Clearly he was ambitious. I had always found that attractive in men. Even when Gabriel was footloose and without a care, you still sensed that there was an underlying seriousness that would one day come to the surface. I just wasn't prepared for it to result in my being left in the lurch.

At nine-thirty Clayton received a call from the hospital, so the evening was cut short.

"Can I give you a lift?" he offered.

"No, thanks. I've got an hour and a half till curfew. I don't want to spend any more of the evening in the dormitory than I have to."

He surprised me by saying, "Maybe we could get together again sometime. I enjoyed talking with you."

I smiled coyly. "You know the rules. I'm not allowed to fraternize with the interns."

"That's a problem for you all right. However, it isn't for me. Mrs. Jolly knows better than to tell me what to do."

"You mean, you don't think she'd say anything if we—"

"Not to me."

That lets you off the hook, doesn't it? I thought.

In that one evening of conversation, Clayton sent me clear signals about his personality; signals that I ought to have heeded, about his cold disregard for others, his almost rigid intolerance, and his alarming lack of depth. He was like a well-sharpened steel knife. But Lilly was there from the beginning, reminding me of Clayton's good points, making him seem like the man who was misunderstood by almost everyone, kinder than anyone realized. That night she lay back on the couch and propped her stinging feet up in Stephen's lap for a tender massage, gleeful over the way things turned out, especially Clayton's bid to see me again.

"But I gather that if I'm caught, he'll let me shoulder all the blame with Mrs. Jolly, and pretend he was just an innocent victim of my designs."

"Oh, bosh, Senta! Clayton wouldn't do that. He is just afraid to make a commitment to anyone. I know him. He's my brother, for heaven's sake."

That night I lay in bed thinking until the clock struck two. I knew now chances were good something would develop between me and Clayton.

Yes, it all seemed to be right somehow, in ways I had never before imagined. What a piece of luck it would be to wind up with Clayton Gerrard . . . Dr. Clayton Gerrard. Wouldn't Gabriel just be eaten up inside to have to think of me spending my nights in the arms of the brother he despised, while he was stuck with a wife who was probably as cold to the touch as her diamond wedding band. . . .

From that time on I tried to convince myself that I liked Clayton, felt warm toward him. As the months went by I tried further to convince myself that I had fallen in love with him. My feelings were all on the surface, running no deeper than a minor skin abrasion. I never fooled myself about that. Yet it didn't seem so idiotic at the time. Marrying for love of a man would not be my destiny. I knew that as soon as I lost Gabriel. Therefore I had to look at everything else and weigh it dispassionately. Probably with almost any other man, it would not have been so big a mistake. With Clayton it spelled disaster.

To the extent he was capable, I believe Clayton loved me, at least for a while, and he mistook my reticence for modesty becoming to a young woman in her mid-twenties. Our courtship may have been secret from Mrs. Jolly and covered admirably well by my roommates at school, but otherwise it was not so secret. We spent a lot of time with Stephen and Lilly, on outings or at home. We even spent an occasional evening with Gabriel and Louetta—never just the four of us; always at some cocktail party or dinner held for political reasons. If someone connected with the hospital happened to attend, Clayton would simply point to me as a long-time friend of his family. That was the truth, of course, so it did not call for any special risk on his part. Gabriel was on several committees for the Texas Democratic Party, and was actively involved in fund-raisers to swing the Texas vote in favor of Franklin Roosevelt in 1932. His parties were attended by some of the most important people in Houston. One could easily see that Gabriel himself was now a full-fledged rising political star.

Clayton was quiet and reserved at the functions thrown by his brother and sister-in-law. Once I asked him as we drove away why he bothered to go.

"Oh, it doesn't hurt to give your brother a hand," he said, and changed the subject. His real feelings toward Gabriel were so far a mystery to me, and I never pressed him very hard to explain them. He was away at school during the time I went with Gabriel, and he knew almost nothing about that period other than that I had dated his brother while we worked at the law firm. That was the way I wanted to keep it.

As for Clayton's experience with other women, I knew almost as little. I gathered he had been too busy studying for most of his adult life to bother much with dating. And certainly there had been no serious romances. In fact he treated me more like an old buddy than a girl friend. It was not until another intern—Dr. Isaaks, who was a year ahead of Clayton—asked me out, that Clayton indicated he was really interested in me, on Valentine's Day of 1932. He had not remembered me with a card, much less a bouquet of flowers or a box of chocolates. Dr. Isaaks had been glancing in my direction since the first of the year and frankly I could have done worse, regardless of the vast difference between his Judaism and my Episcopal upbringing.

Clayton was stunned at the news that I was unavailable for the evening. After much questioning about who I was going to see and why, much pacing up and down, he turned and said, "I just don't want you to see anyone else, Senta. Please."

"Why not? I don't seem to be getting anywhere with you."

"I don't . . . don't mean to be so distant. That's just the way I am. I do care about you. Surely you realize that I don't have time to see any girl unless she means something to me. . . ."

"Keep talking."

He walked up to me, looked both ways to see if anyone was coming, then he pulled me to him and kissed me. It was the most passionate I had ever seen him, and it wasn't all that bad if I didn't compare it to Gabriel, and didn't discount the fact I held back a little so I'd appear modest. There was a certain kind of timid urgency about the way he brought my mouth to his and held it there.

"Promise me you won't go out with Isaaks."

I could not suppress a smile of pleasure. "All right, Clayton. If it means that much to you. But you ought to try showing your feelings once in a while. Anyone would think you don't have any."

Mrs. Jolly suddenly rounded the corner at the end of the hall and Clayton immediately lost the slight look of vulnerability he had assumed. "And let me know as soon as there's any outward sign of change in this patient," he said, and walked off.

"Yes, Doctor," I mumbled. "Afternoon, Mrs. Jolly."

"Straighten your cap, Farrish."

"Yes, ma'am."

Two months later Clayton said, "I can't give you a ring yet, for obvious reasons. I don't want to jeopardize your nursing career because you're too good. But, if you'll have me, I'd like you to be my wife as soon as you graduate."

I was not surprised, and felt only a slight tingle of excitement as I accepted —I don't believe it was much more than a smile and a nod—and he kissed my cheek and hurried away, due to be back at the hospital within a few minutes. I felt pleased in a way you do when you learn you've made an "A," on a test you were not worried about because you had spent much time preparing for it.

At that moment I had sealed my future almost casually. It was not until I lay in bed that night that I realized I was to be a Gerrard. I turned over and hugged the pillow, seeing myself as Clayton's bride . . . yes, he'd make a handsome groom. . . . I tried to envision him naked. His shoulders were less broad than Gabriel's, but he had the long slender Gerrard trunk. . . . I wondered if he was built anything like his brother below the waist. Then my imaginings were suddenly halted as I realized I was probably not at all what he was expecting. I tried to convince myself it didn't matter. He'd never know.

Chapter 13

I had never taken particular joy in sharing things with Mother. While she was around, I kept most of my thoughts and a lot of what I did to myself, not wanting her interference, not wanting to risk her disapproval. But now that she wasn't around, I found it frustrating.

We had not exchanged more than a half-dozen letters since she left for New Orleans. When she wrote, her letters were full of news about how Laura was doing in her pregnancy, and how nice the LeCourt family was. She obviously enjoyed being back in New Orleans again after so many years, and she said she often walked around the French Quarter, finding many of the shops unchanged from nearly twenty years before. She said the food was as rich as ever, the LeCourts had a wonderful Creole cook, and she found it most difficult to keep her weight down.

I was usually tardy in answering her correspondence, and my notes were short and to the point. I was in charge of overseeing the house, and I went by regularly to be sure there were no signs of vandalism, no leaks after a rain.

Thankfully this was not the season for yard work. While she had always loved her garden, didn't mind mowing the grass or trimming or raking, I detested such miseries. Now that she was away, the yard would not be touched until her return. To be sure she didn't even suggest I do anything to the house, inside or out, I always made a point in my letters of how busy I was at nursing school, lest she forget.

On the afternoon following Clayton's proposal, I sat down and wrote her a long letter. I may not have been bursting with happiness about being engaged to Clayton, but I did feel triumphant about the accomplishment of landing a Gerrard. I told her we preferred a small wedding with only family and close friends invited. (I did not say, though this was uppermost in my mind, that if she decided to bring both Laura and the baby home to live on McKinney Avenue, I'd rather die than to draw attention to any of us by having a large to-do.) I told her Clayton knew about Laura, I had told him everything, and he took it equably. I did not tell her that he suggested the father be found and forced to take responsibility for his actions. His point was not that the scoundrel should be punished, nor that Laura and the child deserved the benefit of wedlock, but that as the kid grew up, there might be a medical emergency in which facts about the father's heredity would be vital. I assumed Mother would not sympathize with Clayton's concerns.

I almost signed the letter, then realized I had not told her the wedding would take place in August of 1933, after the completion of my training. I reread the letter. It lacked the tone of a happily engaged young woman. It read more like a business letter. But what did it matter? What was marriage, anyway? You just lived in the same house together and shared the same bed. Maybe sex was exciting; maybe not. If not, you just faked it. You had to clean house and learn to cook, but Clayton wasn't much interested in food. Anyway, we'd surely have enough money to hire a maid to clean and a cook to prepare meals. We would be very nicely set with Clayton's inheritance plus his income as a physician. And if I got too bored staying at home, I could always go to work in the hospital, or maybe do private-duty nursing. It couldn't be such a bad life, even if you didn't really love your husband. And I knew how to work Clayton, just like everyone else in my life. He was easy in a way because all he cared about was medicine, and he was happy—no, not happy, you could never describe someone that serious as being happy—but content, as long as you didn't interfere with that.

Mother wrote back within a week. "Are you sure this is what you really want? I wish you would give yourself more time to be sure. Your training has been so demanding. Don't take on new responsibilities yet. . . ."

Regardless of Mother's apparent misgivings, I know I would have gone on feeling confident about the marriage if not for Gabriel. He came home from Austin in May and heard the news from his mother. I had gone home for the weekend, to begin readying the house for the return of Mother and Laura and perhaps the baby, though I still hoped very much they would have sense enough to put it up for adoption in New Orleans. I was sitting out on the front porch enjoying the breeze on Saturday afternoon when Gabriel drove up in his Cadillac.

Except for the different automobile, he might have been the Gabriel who came to court me four years earlier. He slammed the door and came bolting up the walk toward me, his white shirt unbuttoned at the neck and his sleeves rolled up. For the length of time it took him to reach the porch, my heart stood still. Could all my dreams be coming true? Was he coming back for me? Gad, he looked so good, he could have pressed me down and made love to me right there.

As it happened, I hardly had time to open my mouth to speak. He hiked a foot upon the porch step. "Is it true, you're going to marry my brother?"

I leaned back on my elbows, and tried to sound unruffled. "Oh, so that's why you came. You have a better suggestion?"

"You don't love him."

That made me angry. I shot him a hard glance. "What's it to you?"

He paused, then said, "I do care about you, Senta. I never said I didn't. And I'm begging you not to make this idiotic mistake."

My spirits collapsed as I realized I could kiss my fantasies good-bye. I looked at him. "It's my life. And Clayton's. Why are you so sure it won't work?"

"Because I know him—and Senta, you don't know him at all. He's cold and cruel. He doesn't really give a damn about anyone but himself. He'll make you miserable."

"What if I did love him, not that it's any of your business. Would you tell me the same thing?"

"You could not love Clayton. You're not the sort who could go for him, so don't try to convince me you do."

"And what 'sort' am I, Gabriel?" I asked, thinking I might enjoy this conversation after all.

He sat down next to me. It was a while before he answered. "First of all, you like to be in control."

I laughed under my breath. "I certainly couldn't control you, especially the last time we were together."

He sighed. "I know I behaved like a bastard, but you asked for it, and you know it. I don't think I've ever been that angry in my life."

"You certainly let me know it," I said, and looked away.

He shook his head. "I'm sorry about that, but listen to me." He turned my face toward him, and, half smiling said, "Damn you're headstrong."

I looked into his eyes. Suddenly I knew that he really did care about me— from the way he looked more than what he said—and I felt better in that moment than I had since that day in his apartment. I began to listen to him and weigh what he was saying.

"Senta, you're so exciting . . . and you're attracted by excitement. You are passionate . . . easy to touch off. Can't you see that Clayton for you will be like a dead socket?"

I drew up my shoulders. "How could you really know anything about Clayton as a grown man? He has been away at school for about a third of his life. I think you're being unfair."

"Clayton has always been as cold and painstaking as a bank clerk. If he was normal, he wouldn't make you wait out a year, playing hide and seek. For God's sake, you've already gone with him for six months. If he had any passion at all, he'd marry you now and hang the consequences. That is, unless . . ." His voice drifted off. I knew now what was bugging him, but I wasn't going to tell him unless he had guts enough to ask. Finally he said, "Are you sleeping with Clayton?"

My heart skipped a beat. I looked away and said, hoarsely, "How could we be? He lives on the top floor of the hospital. We're lucky to meet in the hall once a day."

"That's what I thought. And how do you suppose he'll react on your wedding night, when he realizes you aren't a virgin?"

Now I was furious. I stood up and put my hands on my hips. "What makes you so sure he'll know? Just guessing isn't foolproof, or didn't you know that?"

"You know that if he ever thought for a minute that you had been with me, you'd have hell to pay."

"Well, I'm not going to tell him. And Lilly certainly won't say anything. Your mother doesn't know how . . . involved . . . we were, and mine would never say anything. So who's going to tell him? I'm not worried. Are you?"

"I don't give a damn what Clayton thinks about me. It's you I'm concerned about." He folded his hands and bowed his head. I sat down again.

"I feel so responsible for you, that's all."

"Well, don't. I have always loved you. I simply went after you when I was old enough."

"But you weren't old enough. I shouldn't have given in to you," he said, then paused before adding, "I've caused so much grief already—please, let me stop you from making this mistake. Don't marry Clayton. Call it off. Find someone else. I know lots of people who'd give anything for—"

"I don't want anyone else," I argued, tears coming to my eyes. "Don't do me any favors. The only way to keep me from marrying Clayton is for you to give up everything and marry me."

I turned to him. He said nothing. For just a moment I felt hope rise in me again. "Will you, Gabriel? If you would, then nothing would matter. We could run away today, to hell with everybody else." I lifted my palm and moved it slowly up his back. His hand reached around and gently moved mine away. He rose and stood back from me, looking down into my face. "I'm sorry, Senta. What was between us was over a long time ago."

I leaned back on my elbows again and gazed up at him. "Was it really? Tell me Louetta is as good as I am in bed. Tell me she's more to you than a stepladder into politics. Tell me that. Look me in the eye and tell me."

He looked as though I'd slapped him across the face. After a moment he said, "I don't have to tell you anything at all, Senta. My wife is kinder toward you than she should be, a lot more than you deserve. I can hardly believe the extent of your hatefulness."

I knew then I'd overstepped myself and felt panicked. I lifted my hands. "Gabriel . . . I'm sorry . . . I only meant—"

He turned and walked back to his car and drove away, not looking back at me.

"Damn you to hell," I mumbled again and again. Then I sat there with tears rolling down my cheeks. I felt as I did that last time we went to bed together: abandoned, shunted aside. With all my heart, I wanted to make him come back to me, but all I could do was sit there and drive a fist into my hand.

Thereafter I viewed marriage to Clayton with the feelings I imagine someone has just before she slits her wrists and watches the blood rush out. I began to consider ways I might graciously back out. Then something happened that put everything into new perspective.

Chapter 14

On the first Monday in June of 1932 I received a telephone call at school from Mother. Laura had died following the birth of a baby girl the evening before. I have never heard my mother so despondent. I didn't feel anything except shock. I could not take it in. My mind flashed from one question to the next. First I wanted to know what had happened.

"She began hemorrhaging a few hours after the baby was delivered. They could not get the uterus to contract. It happened so quicky, and nothing could be done."

"But I don't understand—with all those doctors and nurses around? I assume she was in a hospital?"

"Of course she was. It was at night, sometime after midnight. I—I don't think Laura realized what was happening until too late. When a nurse came by to check on her, she was already semi-conscious. It was too late to do anything to help her. She had lost too much blood. Everything possible was done, but there just wasn't time."

"And you? Where were you all this time?" I demanded.

"I—I was at home," she stammered. "I had been with her till she went to sleep around ten o'clock. I'd planned to come back in the morning. They called me around three."

She said she could not talk about it any further, that it was too upsetting. She probably was afraid I would remind her that if she had listened to me long ago, this might have been prevented.

The baby was apparently healthy, and within a few days Mother would bring her home. Her name was Robin. She had blond hair and, from early appearances, blue eyes. She weighed nine pounds at birth.

"You're . . . you're going to keep the child?" I asked.

"Yes," she stated. There was more force behind that one word than any she had uttered during the conversation. I was furious at her stupidity—didn't she know what that would do to her life, how she'd be lassoed with responsibility, how much explaining she'd be doing? I started to vent my feelings. But she cut me off before I had time to tell her my viewpoint. She ordered me to make the arrangements for Laura's funeral. Alvareda had been contacted already (Mother called her first, I observed, even before her own flesh and blood, and probably talked an hour), and was standing by to help in any way possible.

"And when should I plan for it to be held?" I asked her.

"Let's have the service on Saturday." She gave me the name of the funeral home in New Orleans that would be coordinating from that end. She said she preferred a simple graveside service, and was contacting Forest Park about a site near where Neal Gerrard was buried.

After we hung up I sat on the telephone bench for a long time, still unable to take it in. I tried to remember if Laura ever showed signs of being a free bleeder. I couldn't think of any, but that might not be significant. And the baby was large. . . .

I kept shaking my head. I felt numb because I just could not accept it. It was too sudden. Exams began tomorrow. I would need to arrange to take mine later, after this was over. Then I would have to go home. I had a long list of details to look after. Mother had instructed me to get the crib from the front bedroom across from mine, where some of Grandmother Carlotta's things were stored. I had to stop at the Colombian and get some linens. And doubtless there would be other things that Mother had not thought of in her haste. As soon as I could reach him, I told Clayton what had happened. He said that he was sorry, and would be glad to do whatever he could. We did not talk long. He was due back in surgery in a few minutes. I thought of what he had said about the baby's father taking responsibility. He had been so right. If the father had married Laura, then she would not have had to hide away in New Orleans all these months. The baby could have been born right here at Baptist, where I could have looked after Laura myself, and Clayton would have been nearby to handle any emergency. No telling what kind of second-rate hospital Laura wound up in. Oh, I couldn't believe Laura was dead. I could not feature her dead.

I drove home on Tuesday afternoon. The first thing I did was to go into Mother's bedroom and look at Laura's picture on the wall. It was the only recent studio portrait of her that I knew of. She looked so young, so innocent. So . . . vulnerable. I began to cry, and then to sob harder and harder. I had been so mean to her, so impatient. She had always gotten on my nerves. I never thought she'd die. People don't die at seventeen. Yes, women sometimes hemorrhaged following childbirth, and sometimes died, but not Laura. Not my sister. If only she had been here. . . .

I passed the next few days in a state of suspension. The telephone rang constantly. Lilly came over to console me. Louetta called to express regret for her and Gabriel. Gabriel was not in town, but would be here for the funeral on Saturday. No one knew what to say. There were no comforting words. You couldn't say Laura had a good life, for she didn't. Unless living in your own little world could be considered a good life. Maybe it was. Maybe people who were slightly mad had a special, enchanted existence that none of us understood or participated in. I thought of all the grief Laura had caused us, her irresponsible ways, her prevailing immaturity. She was like a little pet dog who would never grow into a state of self-reliance. She would always need to be taken care of. And Mother had certainly tried her best to do everything for her, to protect her.

I was glad Mother had not sent Laura away to a home of some kind. At least she spent the last few months of her life knowing her mother loved her.

And now here was this product of her complete gullibility about life's most basic instinct. Robin Farrish. There would be a story of some kind made up for this child growing up in her grandmother's home. How would she fare, no mother, no father? How queer. None of it seemed right. All of it seemed strange.

I picked up Mother and Robin at the train station Thursday night. It was raining like crazy; you could hardly see the street in front of you. Mother was dressed in black—perhaps this was proper when accompanying a body home on the train. The baby was wrapped in fragile knitted blankets. When they got off the train I took the baby and held her. She had a perfect little head and face. She opened and closed her hands. She yawned and stretched. How unexpecting she was. She did not know she was in for a life without her mother.

Mother put her arms around me and wept. She looked as though she had not slept in three weeks. Her face was pale and her eyes drawn. I thought for the first time how devastating this must be. Laura was the second child she had lost. Surely there could be nothing more painful for a mother than this.

I bundled them both into the car, and drove home down the wet streets through the heavy traffic. Mother held Robin and hummed a lullaby in her ear. She did this for a while, then wept, then she hummed some more. She had very little to say to me. At home she sat in her rocker in the library and fed Robin a bottle of warm milk. The child took a very long time sucking her bottle. Every few minutes Mother would put the bottle down and put Robin up on her shoulder, and hold her there, patting her back, till she burped. Then the process of sucking would begin again. I was so dreadfully exhausted. I could not stay up any longer. I kissed Mother and went up to bed. The baby would be put in the waiting crib next to Mother's bed downstairs. Mother would raise another child. From this day forward she would no longer have the status of matron finished rearing her family and able to live a life of freedom. The little girl was beautiful, but why on earth must she bring her home to raise?

I was allowed to see my sister Laura at the funeral home on Friday night, and from that point on I was haunted by her. She was so beautiful in death. Her cheeks were pink, and her dark red hair longer than I'd ever seen it, draped around her shoulders. Her little upturned nose and her long lashes made her look so young, so trusting. She wore her baby pearls around her neck and a white ruffly blouse. Mother reached over and kissed her. I could not. I was terrified as I have not been since childhood. When someone young dies, it seems that all of us are suddenly more vulnerable. With grief is mixed fear. Suddenly, all I could think about was how glad I would be when all this was over. If I did not soon get that picture of Laura in death out of my mind, I would go mad.

On the night following the graveside service, I finally had some time to myself. I lay in my bed, thinking of the future. I was thankful I had not been too hasty about breaking my engagement to Clayton. I sensed I had finally figured out his true nature. He simply did not care about impressing anyone. Gabriel did not understand him. Clayton would do what he felt was right, and to hell with what people thought about it. He had been right about having Lilly dismissed from nursing school, even if it seemed cruel at the time. It was probably because of his good sense that she wound up with Stephen, which is what she truly wanted in the first place. Now he had been proven right in his early analysis of Laura's predicament. Yet, through all the aftermath of her death, he had never once boasted about it. He was, it seemed to me, as good a person as Lilly always insisted, and I was now attracted by the strength he had exhibited.

Unfortunately, I was the poor unsuspecting moth, dazzled by the flame.

Chapter 15

If I had confided in Alvareda Gerrard, she might have offered a key to the strange personality of Clayton. After all, as Gabriel once said, Samuel Cane was a tyrant. Perhaps if I had asked her to tell me more about her father, I would have learned that Clayton simply inherited his grandfather's traits.

Yet I never chose to talk to Alvareda about her father, and I told myself Gabriel exaggerated his remarks about Clayton in order to make an impression on me. Therefore I took the name Gerrard, vaguely aware that I was marrying the one person who did not live up to the Gerrard family image, yet unaware of how serious would be the consequences. Had his life been opened up with the same adroitness with which he made a surgical incision, exposed to light as bright as that in the surgical pavilion, then Lilly, Alvareda, Gabriel —all of those who called themselves Gerrard—would have hidden in shame.

Clayton was a madman.

I did not fully realize this from the beginning of my marriage to him, but gradually the truth dawned. At first I thought it was his disappointment in me, but actually I only provided an easy target for a derangement that was, till then, unfocused. I believe that any wife he married would eventually have suffered as I have. And God help a child we might have brought into the world.

As an engaged couple we had not delved into each other's past. I had not asked him about other women at any length; he had not probed into my experiences with other men. And of course if a conversation ever began to edge toward my involvement with Gabriel, I quickly made light of it and got Clayton on the more comfortable subject of medicine. During my third year of training, in those months when I was on operating-room duty and on call twenty-four hours a day, I had many opportunities to observe Clayton at work, many ways to get him involved in the one subject he truly loved, and although I could not see it at the time, I was frequently using our experiences together in the operating room to steer him away from less favorable subjects.

He was gifted, just as I always believed. I have never seen anyone to equal him as a surgeon. In that last year of my training, he came to admire me more and more because I was able to work with him in the quick, precise way that he demanded. He behaved like one who had more authority than he did, but none questioned him. One simply looked at him and knew that he would be a highly successful practitioner.

I imagine that, even then, a lot of the doctors resented him, and this created a stumbling block for him later. But then I only saw what I wanted to: our future together, the envy of all who knew us, the pride of the Gerrard name.

In June of 1933 I graduated from nursing school, in July passed the state Board exams, and finally gained the right to wear the long-awaited black stripe on my cap and the full white uniform. The state Boards, which were administered over a three-day period at the Galvez Hotel in Galveston, were not as hard as I expected. Nonetheless, after it was all over I was relieved.

With a sense of excitement the following week, I approached Mrs. Jolly's office and finally related the words to her that I had so long held back: "Dr. Gerrard and I will be married in August."

I will never forget how she looked, sitting there in front of her rolltop desk. She raised an eyebrow in surprise. "I see. . . . Well, I hope you will be happy," she said without conviction. "Will you be nursing, or retire to house-wifery?"

"I am not certain yet. I may go into private duty."

"Well, a wife belongs in the home. And yet I despair seeing so many young women finish training only to marry and retire. You forget so much if you don't use it soon. You're an excellent nurse, Senta, especially in surgery. There is always a great need for good nurses."

"Thank you, Mrs. Jolly," I said, and walked away, wondering why the moment seemed to belong to her after all, making the victory empty for me. . . .

Clayton and I were married on August 12. Only a few people attended. There was Mother, of course, accompanied by her attorney friend Walter Brubaker, and Alvareda, who, according to Mother, dabbed her eyes all the way through the ceremony. There was Gabriel, who looked stunningly hand-some—the sight of him with Louetta on his arm nearly broke my heart—and there was Lilly and Stephen. Stephen was Clayton's best man. Lilly stood up for me.

I wore a white linen dress with a lace jacket and a white hat with a wide brim. Mother gave me her long string of pearls, which I wore knotted in front and hanging down below my waist. As a bride she had worn them wrapped around her neck in choker fashion. I believe the pearls were a peace offering. I don't know why she could never just give up on having any sort of decent relationship with me, always trying to reconcile after a quarrel. I did not really care all that much then, though I would later. She lived her life and I lived mine.

Clayton was a handsome groom. We had spent at least a little time swim-ming at the beach that summer, so he had more color in his face than was usual for him. He had needed the time off. Next month he would be a full-

fledged physician, joining a surgical group practicing at Baptist—now re-
named Memorial—Hospital.

We left the church that night through a cloud of rice and confetti and
motored to Galveston for a short honeymoon because we would be leaving on
Monday for Boston where Clayton would attend a week-long seminar. It was
during that hour-long drive to the island that I began to worry seriously
about his expectations of me as a bride. I wasn't afraid of pretending to be
enthralled by my new husband. I was afraid that Gabriel might prove correct
after all about Clayton's perception in the bridal bed.

That night, before we drove up to the entrance of the hotel and were met
by smiling bellboys and an oh-so-delighted-by-the-happy-couple desk clerk, I
remained determined not to say anything, but take my chances. In our room
there was champagne and flowers from Alvareda. We made a toast and still I
felt reasonably certain I could fool him.

But later, when I opened my suitcase and looked at the white peignoir with
its pink ribbon encircling the waist, something told me I had to be truthful,
that to get it out from the beginning would be the best idea. I will never know
whether that would have made any difference as opposed to his finding out
the truth for himself.

I dressed in my nightclothes and walked into the sitting room of the suite.
Clayton was attired in pajamas and dark blue satin robe. When I walked
through the door, he smiled expectantly. I thought my knees would give way
under me. I sat down in a corner and said, "I think there is something I ought
to tell you now," then proceeded to tell him the fateful truth but to lie about
the circumstances. I told him I had been seduced in high school, but that was
the only time. From then on I had not been seriously involved with a man. I
tried to make it seem as though I had been innocently used.

He stood there, his glass of champagne poised in the air, until I finished.
Then he walked near me—I did not take a breath for fear of his reaction—
and threw champagne into my face. He raised the back of his hand, ever so
slowly, and brought it back full force against my temple. "You little bitch,"
he said. "My brother had you, didn't he? I always suspected that. I ought to
kill you."

Never in my adult life had anyone dared to strike me. The swift biting pain
and the almost unbearable ache which followed it were not as cruel as the
astonishing truth facing me: Clayton was exactly the person Gabriel tried to
tell me he was. And now I was his bride.

I crept over to the bed and lay down, shivering with fear and shame. He
did not hit me again. Presently he got dressed and left the room. He did not
come back till morning.

And that's the story of my wedding night.

PART 2

Chapter 1

It seldom snows in Houston.

When it does, unless people have some very important reason for driving, they stay off the streets and build a log fire at home, pop corn, and make hearty soup for supper. On January 22, of this year, 1940, the snow flurries started at five in the morning and continued until dark. By late afternoon, the broad oak trees along both sides of Mother's street were covered with snow. The heavy limbs that reached across to form an arcade above the avenue were laden with white. It was a beautiful sight, like the lofty ceiling of a Gothic cathedral, and children, kept out of school by the weather, were busy building snowmen and tossing snowballs at each other, giggling and cheering, falling and rising and shaking snow off their heavy coats and caps.

How normal it all seemed. One could imagine that, whatever went on inside the brightly lit windows was as safe from danger or sadness as the scene of children frolicking outside. The youngsters themselves had no more reason to believe they would grow up to lead abnormal lives than I did at their age.

Yet, that is what happened to me, and that is why I was driving to Mother's on that snowy afternoon regardless of the hazardous road conditions. Even if I were killed in an accident, it could be no worse than what I escaped at home. I pulled up at the curb and went inside. Mother was in the kitchen teaching Robin how to make gingerbread men. Robin had flour all the way to her elbows and Mother had a white spot on the end of her nose. The smell of ginger and cinnamon and cloves pervaded the whole downstairs. Almost from the time Robin began to talk, she called Mother "Nana." An early attempt to pronounce "Elzyna" came out with only the last syllable of Mother's name, doubled. Mother quite obviously enjoyed every moment with

Robin. I'd never seen her so content, and it was a certainty that Robin was better off in her care than she would have been in anyone else's. If the neighbors gossipped now and then, it didn't seem to bother Mother a bit. And of course, Robin was still too young to know the difference.

I offered my usual excuse for unexpected appearances, and went into the library to warm up by the fireside and think. It was likely I would soon be asking Mother if I could move back here, and if so, I would have to tell her what the past seven years had really been like, how much worse than she imagined. . . .

I lifted my cold hands toward the warmth given off by the smoldering logs. I had never liked living in this house, not in all the years I did so. Yet now I viewed it as a peaceful haven. When Clayton and I quarreled—which was often—and I feared for my sanity if not for my life, it was to this house I came. Sometimes in the middle of the day, sometimes in the dead of night. I always told Mother that Clayton had to go to the hospital for some emergency, and our house was too lonely and I could not sleep. Whether or not Mother believed my story, I do not know. On the surface Clayton and I looked as happy and content as any married couple around. We lived a block off Montrose in a two-story house that had been owned by a doctor before us and was, if not as ostentatious as Gabriel's River Oaks home, at least large and comfortable. I was not limited in my personal spending—I shopped at Sakowitz and Battelstein's, wore expensive clothes and good shoes—and Clayton and I were often photographed together at social functions that were reported on the society page, me wearing the appropriate fur hat and coat, with tastefully expensive jewelry and a huge flower corsage on my shoulder, and Clayton in evening wear and the appropriate smile.

Like most prosperous couples, we had a regular cleaning lady who cooked the evening meal before she left, and never once witnessed any of our frequent arguments. So if I said I came to Mother's out of loneliness, there was no reason for her to suspect otherwise. Once I had a bruise above my eye where Clayton struck me, but I told Mother that I raised up under a kitchen cabinet door. I have spent a lot of time thinking up plausible explanations for visible scars of my marriage.

More than a few times, I would return home to find Alvareda visiting, or awaken late the next morning, exhausted, to find her having coffee with Mother. She cared for Gabriel's son Alexander while Gabriel and Louetta traveled, or simply were busy here at home.

From the time Alexander was around five and Robin nearly four, the two of them played like best friends. Alexander is as good-looking a youngster as you might expect, with deep blue eyes and golden curls. Robin is . . . well, admittedly she is pretty in a way, though she has always been shy. Whenever Alexander arrived on the porch with his grandmother and rang the bell, Robin would scamper up the stairs and wait to be summoned. Then, when he called her name, she would rush down as though he were some important dignitary. I've often thought that when she gets older, I'll teach her not to pander to anyone named Gerrard; to do so will bring her more misery than it's worth.

Up until now, though, Alexander seemed to have installed himself as her great protector. They took long walks together, sometimes were driven or walked up to Eastwood Theater for a movie during Alvareda's visits, and when there was nothing else to do, he would push Robin in the swing under the big oak tree out front. I have seen them from the window, their heads together, Alexander talking and Robin listening raptly.

On that snowy January day, I was determined as never before to give up everything for the sake of my peace of mind. The last time I approached the idea of having our marriage dissolved was four years ago. Clayton's response then had been, "Oh no, you aren't going to ruin my career as well as my personal life. You will stay married to me just as the ceremony states: 'Till death us do part.' "

"And what if I tell how you treat me?"

"I'll expose you as just what you are—a whore—by simply telling the truth. See how much sympathy you'd get then. Don't start something you can't stop, Senta. I can be a lot nastier than you can and I've got a lot less to lose."

I stayed overnight at Mother's on January 22, and through the next day. Whenever I would open my mouth to talk with her about my marriage, something would hold me back. Whether pride or shame, or perhaps not being quite as ready to give up the superficial comforts of marriage with a Gerrard as I had thought, I could never speak to Mother of my plans. I would watch her move about the room, fluffing a pillow, winding the clock, and I would remain silent.

Then, around four-thirty, when I stood in the front parlor and peered through the window at the glistening carpet of snow, Clayton drove up and parked at the curb. As soon as I saw him, my stomach burned like a furnace. I believe the thing that angered me more than anything about Clayton was that he still could frighten me as much as when I first saw him after Neal Gerrard's death.

I didn't know what he might say or do in front of Mother, so I flung on a coat and went out to meet him. We stood there in the middle of the front walk, the cold air that made our breaths frosty as we talked no colder than the feelings we had for each other. "You have to come with me," he said. "We have to be at Gabriel's for dinner at six. I tried to call but the phones were out."

"I don't want to go, thank you," I said. "And I can't imagine why you would want to go either."

"That's my business," he said. "Get your things. We'll drop off your car at home, and go together from there."

I was furious at being forced to go with him, and I envisioned myself standing up in front of everybody at the table and lifting the lid on our marital problems, then flinging my drink in Clayton's face.

I wonder what course our lives would have taken if I had done that? If I had told the whole Gerrard family that Clayton was a cold, uncaring animal of a man who routinely knocked me around after starting an argument just to provide the necessary excuse? What if I had said that we rarely went to bed together, that I recoiled from him in a way I would never have imagined? What if I told them that he suspected my intimacy with Gabriel even before we married, but said nothing and that, after he had it confirmed, he did not even confront his brother, instead taking out his antagonism on me?

Oh, I could have said so much that would have indicted him, and I wish to God I had. Yes, it would have ruined Gabriel's plans, by creating a nasty divorce scandal in the family, but it would have been better for him in the long run.

As a rule, we did not see very much of Gabriel. I could not remember when we had last been in his home except for the traditional gatherings at Thanksgiving and Christmas, which we all observed in deference to Alvareda and which would have been stiff except for the presence of Lilly. She managed to coax everyone into a party humor, even Clayton.

I did not think of Gabriel a lot either. When something happens as painful as losing him was for me, you have to somehow discipline yourself to forget, or you'd wind up crazy. Once in a while, even after all these years, a memory could still take hold of me and send warm chills from my head down to my toes. But whether it was of something he had once whispered in my ear, or some special way he aroused me in bed during those feverish months we shared, I stubbornly quelled it because it hurt like a bee sting. By the time we gathered around Gabriel's table that January evening, I had succeeded in constructing a high wall around myself behind which I survived fairly well; not much hurt by Gabriel; not too badly injured in an emotional way by Clayton's hideousness; not feeling much at all. Until that night.

There was a big log fire in the dining room, and the long table was set formally, as though some very special event were to take place. The candle-light from the long tapers banked at the center reflected in the large hanging mirror behind the sideboard. Reflected there, too, were all of us who surrounded the table: Alvareda, Gabriel and Louetta, Stephen and Lilly, Clayton and me, plus a friend of Gabriel's from law school days whom I had never met before named Bill Hansen. Bill was short and rotund, with only a fringe of brown hair left, and a boyish face and smile.

All through dinner Gabriel made nothing but his usual animated conversation about things in Austin, the work of the Railroad Commission, and how he and Bill Hansen had gotten to know each other and stayed in touch, though Bill practiced law in Dallas and had a ranch in Taos, New Mexico. I thought how confident Gabriel seemed when in front of people, even more now than when he was younger, and also how handsome he was still, maybe even more so. I found myself thinking of more intimate details about him, and swallowed a big gulp of wine to chase the thoughts away.

After dinner, Bill produced a bottle of champagne from a hidden place in the sideboard. He passed everyone a glass and then rose beside Gabriel and said, "I'd like you all to toast the next governor of the state of Texas."

Only Louetta had been advised beforehand. Alvareda put a hand on her chest and said, "Oh, my goodness!" She looked like a young girl who'd just been given her first kiss. Clayton, I think, had suspected some sort of political campaign in the works, and smiled and gave his brother a handshake that was probably warmer than usual. Lilly approached Gabriel from behind and threw her arms around his neck. Louetta gave him a kiss, causing me to make a tight fist in my lap. I quickly nodded and smiled at him, not surprised but not able to speak for the lump in my throat. Everyone joined in the toast three or four times.

Gabriel told us that Bill Hansen would be coordinating the campaign, and then he explained that he had called us together not only to make an announcement, but also to ask our help. "I'd like this to be a family endeavor," he said. Stephen had entered a partnership in the outdoor advertising business a year ago, and Gabriel wanted his help with advertising material—picture posters, circulars, etc. This Stephen was only too happy to do. Before he turned from the subject of advertising, Gabriel hooked a thumb in his vest pocket and cocked his head playfully toward Stephen. "Do you think you could doctor up the picture a little, and make me look like Clark Gable?"

Stephen laughed. "I'm sure I could, but it won't match unless you dye your hair and grow a moustache."

Gabriel seemed to consider this, then said, "Well then, how about Leslie Howard?"

Everyone laughed and I thought: As though you needed to look like anyone else.

Lilly was asked to keep the campaign records. She said, "Great. I'll set up shop at home."

Gabriel nodded. "All receipts, expenses, contributions, and so forth have to be recorded. There is some reporting necessary by state law, and I'll get all that information together for you."

Next he turned to me. "Senta, I need someone to pave the way for appearances all over the state, and I was hoping you would help Bill with this—letters to be written, calls to be made, maybe some traveling."

"Of course," I agreed. To my irritation, my voice was not quite steady. Why was it he could affect me that way just by speaking to me directly? And worse still, I knew I wouldn't make any trouble for him now by exposing Clayton . . . knew I'd never do anything in the world to hurt Gabriel, regardless of what I had to put up with. . . .

Next he turned to Clayton and said, "I don't have anything specific to ask of you at this point"—and, I thought, he is afraid of being turned down. "I need your support in any way you could offer it. Talk to people—you know lots of prominent people who could be helpful—and later there will be more for all of us to do. I'll get to that in a minute."

Clayton nodded.

"Louetta will be holding ladies' luncheons and teas, receptions and so forth, and Mother will help her, right, Mom?"

"Oh, that sounds fun," said Alvareda. "I'll get Elzyna too; she'll want to help."

"Now, here is what we are up against," Gabriel began, and warned that the incumbent governor—Pappy O'Daniel—a former flour salesman and hillbilly singer, was popular in spite of his ineptitude at handling government business. "Trying to get anything done in Austin during his administration has been next to impossible. Pappy is busy handing out amnesty to anyone who butters him up, and that means that the job of prosecuting cases against hot oil running and overproduction has almost come to a halt. He has a lot of people fooled into believing he's just a good old honest country boy with deep religious beliefs, in spite of the fact that he made campaign promises with no plans for finding the revenue to back them up. . . ."

He'd begun to walk around the table as he spoke, pausing behind one chair, then another, as he made several more points about O'Daniel's irresponsibility. At last he was standing behind me. He tapped the high back of the chair, then ran his fingers along the velvet piping, saying, "So don't think for a minute he isn't going to be able to summon plenty of support . . ." I felt my heart squeeze up, then gradually loosen as he moved on. I suddenly noticed Clayton's face in the mirror, observing me with interest. I looked away, feeling my cheeks redden.

". . . What we have to do is convince people we need intelligent government in this state, and I think we can if we make them aware of the dangerous waste of our greatest natural resources." He paused. "Now, we have just six months before the primary, and my name will be among several others. What I'm hoping for is a good showing. Pappy will probably win."

"Then?" someone asked.

"I will go on an independent ticket in November."

Clayton looked nonplussed. "But the Democrats always win the Texas governorship."

Gabriel glanced at him. "There was one exception, eighty years ago. And now there will be another."

He went on to explain some ideas he had for streamlining and cutting waste on the state level, and improvements in the highway system to meet the increasing state population, and I thought how silly for him to do all this. He's wealthy; his name alone can obtain almost anything he desires that he doesn't already have. . . . Yet, maybe that would be the key to his ability to succeed in political office. O'Daniel might have a lot of voters out there, but people all over the state knew the Gerrard name not only because of Gabriel's effective record with the Railroad Commission, but also because of Neal's many civic and business connections during his long lifetime. Then I remembered something Sid Carney once told me, "When a man has wealth, he yearns for power."

We were at the Gerrard home until almost midnight. Gabriel and Louetta saw everyone to the door. Everyone was still congratulating him. Stephen said, "Well, you certainly have what it takes to make it. We'll do all we can to help."

"You can count on all of us," Lilly piped up, then her eyes lit up and she said, "You're going to win. I just know it!" She reached up and hugged Gabriel again.

Of course, surrounded by Clayton and Louetta and everybody else, I could not say what I felt, that I'd give up anything to make this work, even if he didn't deserve it. I just had to shake his hand and say something stupid like, "We'll give it all we've got."

Outside the weather was drizzly; the wind was deathly cold. Clayton drove carefully along the icy streets, the only sound between us that of the windshield wipers and the purr of the car heater. The car hit a chughole right after we turned on to Montrose—they are as numerous in Houston streets as are the mosquitoes that breed in them after a heavy rain—and Clayton remarked, "Too bad Gabriel doesn't get into city politics. Instead of worrying about improving the state highways, maybe he could do something about city thoroughfares."

I didn't answer. I was busy thinking. If I had to continue putting up with marriage to Clayton, perhaps there would be some other consolation . . . some other opportunity. Certainly Gabriel owed me something, even now. . . .

I took an uneasy breath when we walked into our house, half expecting a tirade to pick up from where our last argument left off two nights ago, when I had failed to pick up Clayton's white shirts at the dry cleaners.

Instead, Clayton sat down in the living room and rested his head back on the sofa. "Like a drink?" I asked him.

"No, I think not."

I sat down across from him. "Do you really intend to help Gabriel in his campaign for governor?"

"Of course I do, why?"

"It just surprises me, that's all. I can't imagine— Well, nothing."

He sat there a while longer, and then he told me his reasons. "It looks like there will be an opening for a new chief of staff pretty soon. Reddon is going to retire at last."

"Oh? And you think you'll be picked?"

"Frankly I don't think I have much of a chance as matters stand. I may be the best surgeon on the staff, but I've never been one to make friends, not like my fair-haired brother."

You're telling me, I thought.

"If I help Gabriel now, I can call on him to help me later."

I almost blushed. My own thoughts had closely paralleled his. "How?" I asked.

"The hospital is already pretty deep into debt, and there is some talk about building a new wing. It would require a lot of money, and a lot of the board members don't like the idea of going deeper into debt. The trouble is, the hospital is groaning at the seams, turning people away for lack of sufficient beds."

"They could do with a new building for the nurses in training, too."

"Yes, though that is secondary."

You would think so, I thought, but said nothing.

He turned and looked at me. "You know, Gabriel holds the purse strings on the foundation set up after my father's death. For the most part, Mother lets him decide what charity lucks out."

"I see. And what you mean is, if you help Gabriel get elected, you can hit him up for a big donation to buy a new wing for the hospital, and thereby become very attractive as a prospective chief."

"Well, maybe not enough to finance the whole project, but enough to cut the cost way down to size."

I raised an eyebrow. "Well, it looks like the governor's race is as important to you as to Gabriel."

"I'll stop at nothing to get him elected, and I'll expect you to give it all you've got as well," he said, then paused, and a queer, twisted little smile crossed his face. "I'm sure you will have no trouble putting your heart into it, Senta."

I quickly looked away. Could he see with what excited hope my eyes were filled, he would certainly find justification for slapping my face.

Chapter 2

Within a week after Gabriel officially announced his candidacy, the Houston *Chronicle* ran a long article about him with a photo of him with his family at the top. The article was favorable toward him, as though the newspaper wanted him to run and to win. It told about his background, growing up in Houston as the son of a "hard-working, enterprising" cotton factor who started from scratch and built a fortune in investments. Gabriel was quoted as saying, "My father taught me the value of making my own way and doing something worthwhile." It told about his family rallying to help run his campaign. Three columns were devoted to Gabriel's platform. Even if the details on his beliefs and plans did not get the attention of voters, the photograph above would have endeared him to many. It was taken a year ago in the backyard of his home in River Oaks, near the terrace. In the background you could see the great old trees that graced the lawn all the way down to the edge of the bayou. Louetta was dressed in a long satin gown with beaded bodice and sleeves, which was one of her favorites. Her long hair was pulled back from her face and hung softly at her shoulders.

Gabriel stood behind her in his dark, double-breasted suit and white shirt, one hand resting on the back of the chair where she sat. Alexander was in front of them both on the lawn, his blond locks tumbling down his forehead, his sailor suit neatly pressed and straight.

The portrait as it appeared above the article had a slightly blurred effect, as reproductions in a newspaper often will, and it made them all look as though they were in some sort of dreamland. I stared at it for a long time, thinking how much better it would be were I in Louetta's place.

Put it away, I thought. Soon you'll have an ulcer.

The article and the photograph—in spite of its dreamlike effect—made the whole prospect of Gabriel's campaign for governor seem suddenly more real than before. And there was something else that I noticed beginning around that time that had a similar effect. Clayton, as though in an earnest attempt at keeping up the "solid front," treated me more amiably. He seemed to try hard to steer clear of domestic fights. I said nothing to him of my relief at the change in him. I felt that he had such a stake in this political race, that he did not want to take any chance of ruining it.

Regardless of the fact that Gabriel himself predicted he would not win the Democratic primary, I believe all of us worked toward that point in the election process in the hope it would bring him overwhelming victory; that, following the casting of the ballot on July 27, our work would be accomplished and we could approach the fall confident of Gabriel's inauguration after the first of the year, having no worry about the general election in November.

Through the spring I spent most of every day writing letters, making telephone calls, coordinating with Bill Hansen (usually by telephone or letter or wire, because he went all over the state with Gabriel) on travel arrangements, train schedules, interviews with the press and on radio. I found my job easy because people wanted Gabriel Gerrard. I nervously called KPRC radio one Monday afternoon to get him an interview on the "Chuck North Evening Hour," and learned to my surprise the producers had been trying to reach me in order to accomplish the same goal.

And whether speaking before a group of railroad workers or war veterans, longshoremen or professional businessmen, Gabriel came across as warm and charming, sincere in his views. He appealed to the intelligence of his audience, just as he vowed he would, and gently led them into the realization that they had been fooled by the incumbent, but were not stupid because they had made the mistake. He was very persuasive. In radio interviews his voice was calm and resonant. He spoke like one who had never lost at anything, and therefore he elicited confidence.

I always came away from listening to him thinking: This was Gabriel's destiny. He was meant for this from the time he came into the world. He will go far, far past the governorship. He has only just begun.

Clayton, to be sure, had a busy surgical schedule, so he was not able to do as much as the rest of us. He did, however, host a large dinner party in Gabriel's honor that was attended by forty couples from attorneys to bankers to doctors and other medical personnel (I scarcely realized he knew so many people), all of whom had the means to contribute money to Gabriel's campaign. He also joined with several other supporters to throw an ice cream social at the San Jacinto Battleground in later spring, which was attended by well over two hundred people. I remarked to Mother, who was helping serve ice cream alongside me, that I had never seen so many women at one gathering. When Gabriel stood up to speak, there was a sea of floppy hats and cotton dresses below him.

"I noticed that," Mother said. "The number of women voters will probably be higher than ever when July comes."

I began to realize that Gabriel's chances at winning were much dependent upon his being seen and heard and I don't mean being heard to talk about the issues, I mean just being visible to people. The charm I had recognized since childhood was so apparent that I sometimes doubted that people paid any attention to what he told them, though his campaign promises were reasonable and his ability to relate them was eloquent.

During our family's meetings with him, he continued to prepare us for his less than adequate showing in July. None of us could imagine it. We had seen so many people persuaded by him. His appearances all over the state had been so well attended, the press releases so favorable. Contributions had begun to trickle in in March, and by the end of May they were plentiful. Gabriel had estimated he would spend around a hundred thousand dollars during the course of the campaign, and by the end of May one third of that had been contributed by supporters, and posted in what we affectionately called, "Lilly's Ledger."

Thanks to Stephen, the advertising side of the campaign was more comprehensive than anyone could have hoped. Big advertising boards all over the state, and concentrated in the larger cities like Dallas and San Antonio and El Paso, wore giant posters with his picture and campaign motto, "Vote for good sense in government . . . elect Gabriel Gerrard . . ." Campaign circulars were spread out through the state like confetti during a parade, and we all felt certain that our combined efforts had acquainted the voting public with Gabriel.

"Heaven knows, I've shaken enough hands between here and El Paso to be elected governor" Gabriel said one night. "But I just want you all to understand that the worst fight is still ahead. That home-grown hillbilly could talk a farmer out of his crop. He still has a lot of people fooled."

"How about Thompson?" someone asked.

"He'll do all right. If I can edge in behind him, I'll be happy."

"Nonsense. You'll take them all by a landslide," said Lilly, and from the back of the room where he had stood quietly, Clayton murmured, "I certainly hope so."

On the way home I told Clayton his remark seemed to carry a lot of doubts. "Don't you think he'd have any luck as an independent?"

"Not a Chinaman's chance if you ask me. What do you think?"

"Oh, I think he can win in July and we won't have to worry about it. He's going to be well enough known, and he has a well-known record for his work in state government up to now, so it isn't as though he doesn't already know the ropes in Austin."

"Well, for all our sakes—especially yours and mine—I hope you prove me wrong. Still I don't have any real faith you will."

I thought it was a pretty sorry statement, and I told him so. I'd grown more brave now that he was being nicer to me. "How does it feel to use your brother, pretend you love him when you never did?"

He took the remark without batting an eye. "You should know all about using him," he replied.

"What do you mean? I have nothing to gain—"

"Maybe just his undying gratitude. I'm sure you could use that if you really wanted to."

You jackass, I thought. Yet in truth, of course, he was partially correct. After a long while of wondering just what opportunity might be open for me —at first all I could think of was the job of his personal secretary once he was elected, and of course the chance of Louetta or even Clayton allowing that was zero—I had just lately given some thought to asking instead for another, less intimate position. I was doing a good job as a public relations person for him. Why should that not continue into his term as governor? There would be no big to-do, of course. But I would move into the position quietly and it would be understood that I would be commuting back and forth from Austin to Houston on weekends in order to be with my "devoted" husband. I would be able to live in peace at least a good portion of the time, only having to face Clayton two days a week . . . maybe even one sometimes . . . or none at all.

As it turned out, Gabriel's political instinct was far better than ours. Pappy O'Daniel won over five hundred thousand votes in the primary, with Ernest Thompson some three hundred thousand behind. Gabriel was not too far behind Thompson, with a total of slightly over one hundred thousand. The other contenders were not even close.

I was downcast—I felt a sense of betrayal, as though all those people who appeared to support Gabriel had not kept their word. I was amazed at the incredible amount of votes cast for O'Daniel. Even more than he got in the election of 1938. I felt angry. I wanted to retaliate, shake people by the shoulders. It was one of the most frustrating feelings I had ever had. There was no one to strike at.

"The incumbent always has a forceful edge, no matter what his failures," Gabriel said. He met us at Lilly's on Sunday afternoon, looking more tired and deflated than he would admit. He was like a cheering squad in front of a losing football team. "Now, here's what we do next. We have to circulate petitions with signatures of at least 1 percent of the total vote cast for governor in the last election. It will be somewhere in the neighborhood of 3,700 and must be only names of people who did not vote in the primary."

"Oh, that'll be easy, we can get that many in Houston," said Lilly with that enthusiastic smile that made anything seem possible and would have pulled anyone out of the doldrums.

Gabriel went on to outline his new strategy of picking up votes of the candidates who dropped out. The plan would include almost a constant round of appearances.

Clayton was silent all the way home that night. Finally I said, "I guess you were hoping to approach the Board of Trustees next week and tell them you would help bail them out."

"That's the way it goes, I guess," he said. "They're talking now about getting a bond issue. Of course, I can always present them a check in November. They'd be as happy to get it then as now."

"Oh, so you think Gabriel might win after all?" I said, more out of eagerness to hear someone's positive statement than a true assessment if it were bleak.

"Frankly, I don't. He should have done much better in the primary."

It was not long before Gabriel had the needed petitions, and the newspapers were lifting him high as a contender. There were interviews in both papers, in which he spoke of his unwillingness to give up his aims regardless of what party "name" he had to run under. And four of the other candidates had already endorsed him. Thompson had not really commented except to respond with a "no," when asked if he'd consider switching political parties and staying in the race.

I was encouraged by what I read, felt we hadn't missed a lick after all, and was eager to continue what I had started in January. But then as bad luck would dictate—or what I assumed at the time was bad luck—I was to be robbed of the opportunity to do anything for anyone over the next month.

Gabriel was scheduled to speak on several college campuses during the early fall, and it was my job to be sure that final arrangements were completed and his tour went smoothly. In most cities he had three or four appearances, only one of which was on campus. Rice Institute in Houston was already set up, Bill Hansen was handling the University of Texas in Austin, and I worked with people in the northern direction, Sam Houston State Teachers College and Southern Methodist University, plus a stop at Texas Christian University in Fort Worth at the end. I left on a Monday afternoon to travel by car to the three cities along the tour, the back seat piled high with circulars and pamphlets, posters and photographs of the candidate.

I arrived in Huntsville in time for a four o'clock meeting, and was tied up until six-thirty. The people I met with—two ladies and three men—all begged me to spend the night in Huntsville rather than head for Dallas. Yet I had an 8 A.M. breakfast meeting at Southern Methodist University on Tuesday, and a room already booked in Dallas for overnight. I was not afraid to drive the distance after dark.

I should have been. I had probably done as much driving as the next person, but I had never driven in that area before, and I soon found what was easy to navigate in the daytime was almost impossible at night. There were no lights along the narrow, two-lane roads and the stretches between one town and the next were long. By seven o'clock it was fully dark, and I felt as though I were driving through a long tunnel. For a short while I had at least the company of the car radio, but not too many miles north of Huntsville, the transmission was almost totally one of rude static. Finally I turned it off. I have never known such quiet. The full moon above was the only continuous source of light; seldom did I pass an automobile on the other side—such a comforting sign that all was well and normal and that others were traveling the same road as I was. By eight-fifteen I was becoming more and more fearful I had missed a turn somewhere. Surely by now I would have gone through the town of Fairfield, or, was that the mere interruption in the road twenty miles back that I did not even take to be a town at all?

"I've got to get hold of myself," I murmured aloud, and the sound of my own voice, speaking into nothingness, made me even more nervous. I laughed at my foolish nerves, and thought this must have been how Ichabod Crane felt on the night of his fateful journey. . . . Lest Gabriel be elected to the governorship and discard his ideas for improving state highways, I would be there to remind him of the importance of the issue.

A railroad crossing but no sign of a train.

A gas station closed up tight, with a large light bulb above the door, illuminating the sign in the door, "CLOSED."

A tourist court up on the right, back from the highway. Abandoned for lack of business apparently. No one about. Lights on the building probably to keep people from driving into it.

How can it be, there are no cars on the road? Is no one else driving to Dallas tonight?

My eyes were getting tired. And on top of everything else, I needed to go to the bathroom, worse by the minute—too many cups of coffee at the Huntsville meeting. Finally I could see the approach of a cluster of lights. I had no idea what town it was, but at least I could get my bearings there. I breathed a sigh and drove on, more relieved with every yard. But then as I reached the city limits, I passed a sign that announced bad news. I had reached Crockett, Texas, not on my route. Damn. I drove on into the town and at last I saw a café open on the right. I pulled in, grabbed my road map and handbag, and went in. There was no one in the place except the balding proprietor, who looked around at me in surprise as he untied his apron. "We close at nine," he said, as though correcting a wayward child who'd broken a rule. "That's five minutes from now. I don't cook anything after eight-thirty."

"I don't want anything," I told him. "Just tell me how I went wrong. I'm trying to get to Dallas."

I opened the map and he peered at it. He soon tapped it with one finger and said, "Most likely you took off to the right at Centerville. It's a common mistake out here at night. Go back up here to the highway, and on back to 75. I believe there's a sign, but I'm not sure. Hardly ever go that way myself."

"How far is it?"

"Oh, thirty miles, give or take."

I must have looked as deflated as I felt. "I don't have no more coffee, but I could brew you some tea."

"Thank you, no. I'm already way behind schedule." I folded up the map and picked up my handbag.

"These highways are poorly marked. It's better if you travel in the daytime."

I nodded and walked to the door, then I thought of something. I opened my handbag and pulled out a leaflet. "Here. Vote for this man. He's going to improve the highways as soon as he takes office. You can count on him."

His mouth opened and he blinked in surprise. As I walked out I thought well, at least maybe I picked up some votes in Crockett. When I reached the car I realized I'd failed to stop at the ladies room. Damn. I turned back toward the café. Just then the lights went out. Oh well, I'd just hold on. It couldn't be too much longer, now that I knew where I was going.

For the length of the drive back to Highway 75, I felt more confident. But after I turned at the sign and traveled another few miles, I felt as alone as before. I was therefore not unhappy to notice the lights of another car behind me. For probably around ten or fifteen minutes the car lights were at a reasonable distance. At least there seems to be one more person in the world headed for Dallas, I thought. But then suddenly the car began to come closer to me, as though the driver was impatient at my speed and wanted to pass. Now I know this is probably the silliest thing I did on the whole trip, but I didn't want the car to pass because if it did, then I'd be alone again on the road. I decided if the driver wanted to go faster, I would go faster to accommodate him. Then maybe he'd stay put and I'd retain my road companion. I increased my speed to fifty, then fifty-five. Still he rode dangerously close to the rear of my car. The lights were brighter and brighter behind me. I wasn't finding his companionship so comforting anymore. Or hers, or theirs, who could say? Hell, if he wanted to pass there was nothing to stop him. Still he rode near, for probably another mile or so. I had a hard grip on the steering wheel. My teeth were clenched tightly. I felt an alarming sense of having lost control, as though he could make me go faster and faster until I crashed into . . . I swallowed hard. Exercising supreme effort, I made myself slow down. "Go on, pass me," I pleaded to no one but myself. When I slowed down, however, he slowed down, and kept following me with the tenacity of one magnet on the tail of another.

Then it happened. He sounded his horn and edged up behind me and to my left, and to my absolute horror, there he stayed, edging closer to me, forcing me to the right. It must have been seconds, though the realization was painfully gradual, before I realized I was headed off the road. Just before I lost control of the wheel, I remember thinking, I've got to see who it is, what kind of car. Unfortunately, I did neither. All ahead of me was black. I brought my hands to my face. I was certain this was the end of my life.

I felt my bladder release a warm flood. That was the last thing I remembered.

Chapter 3

I awoke in a small hospital in Palestine, a small town fifty miles southeast of Dallas. I had a nasty cut on my forehead and three broken ribs, badly bruised elbows and knees. Upon waking I attempted to raise my shoulders. I have never known such pain. It felt as though my collarbone came unhinged. I moaned and slumped back against the pillows. A nurse standing by touched my arm, and said, "Sh, dear. Don't move now," and proceeded to tell me that my car had been discovered by the highway patrol within minutes of the accident, and pulled out of the ditch. "Your husband is on his way from Houston now."

"What time is it?" I asked weakly.

"One o'clock in the morning."

"Ugh . . . I've got a meeting at eight o'clock in Dallas."

"You aren't going anywhere for a while. Try and relax. Forget your cares," she admonished, and left the room.

Forget your cares . . . easy for her to say. All I felt then was anger at having been interrupted in the midst of an important errand. Who would take my place in making the arrangements for Gabriel? No one could easily pick up where I left off. At least, I didn't like to think anyone could.

The longer I lay there, the more I was convinced what happened was no accident. The driver of the other car had deliberately run me off the road. But why? What was to be gained by doing a crazy thing like that? I wanted with all my power to strike back, but I could not. While I lay up here, injured within a hairsbreadth of my life, he went scot-free. I didn't even have his license plate number.

. . . Unless it had some connection with the campaign. The fact I was making this trip was well known. What if someone wanted to hurt—not to mention kill—me, in order to threaten Gabriel? There had been threats on the lives of politicians before, even murders. Maybe this was some kind of warning. . . . Every time I closed my eyes I could see that car edging closer and closer, but I could not see the face of the driver and could not have identified the car.

"Farfetched," Clayton called it. He arrived at five o'clock, looking unruffled and unconcerned. X-rays had already been taken. He wanted to look at them, to be sure there was no internal damage. "Then we can get you out of here. You'll be on your feet in a few weeks."

"Oh, that's wonderful," I said with sarcasm. "In time to go to the polls in November, I hope."

"Don't exaggerate," he said, looking over my chart. "Long before then," he said. "In the meantime, someone can fill in for you."

"What a hell of a time for this to happen," I burst out, then collapsed in pain.

I was taken back home in an ambulance and, as Clayton's hours were so long at the hospital and there was no one to care for my needs at home except the cleaning lady, I decided to go to Mother's until I was up and about again. Mother insisted upon giving me her bed downstairs. On the evening of my return there I had a visit from Gabriel. Mother peered at us uncertainly from the door as Gabriel hurried into the bedroom and sat down beside me on the bed. He brought red roses and a box of chocolates. He took my hands. "Are you all right? Imagine, fallen in the line of duty. I'm so sorry. You must forget all about the campaign and get well," he said tenderly.

"I won't forget the campaign, but I will have to take some time to get well. I told Clayton to call the people in Dallas to let them know. Did he do it?"

"Yes, and Bill's going to cover for you until you're up and about again."

He rose from the bed and walked to the fireplace. He looked so handsome that day in his dark gray dress suit and white shirt. God, my life is such a disappointment, I thought. I would have given anything to be able to pull him into the bed at that moment—

"Clayton says you think it may have been deliberate," he was saying. He leaned on one arm against the mantelpiece.

"Oh, probably my imagination. Don't worry about it."

"Tell me how it happened," he said.

He listened attentively while I went all through it, even telling him about the detour to Crockett and the man in the café.

"Then you think someone might have been waiting for you in Centerville?"

"Oh, I did at the time I was telling Clayton about it, but it's probably ridiculous." I was anxiously trying to get him to forget about what happened, in case he might decide to insist on my dropping out of the campaign for good. Then everything I hoped for would be ruined again.

"Well, I guess you may have confused the other driver by speeding up, then slowing down. Or maybe you made him mad. Or maybe he was drunk, in which case there is no telling what made him decide to do what he did. . . . Anyway, I feel terrible about it."

"It wasn't your fault."

"Yes it was, because I didn't keep up with what you were doing—I mean, your schedule. I would not have let you head for Dallas at that time of the evening if I'd known. And certainly not alone."

His sincere concern melted me. I had almost forgotten how much I loved that quality about him. I smiled. "I'll know better next time."

He said he had ordered the hospital and other expenses sent to him. Then, before his next remark, he walked to the end of the bed and placed a hand on the brass rail. He looked away from me. I think he had wanted to ask me for a long time but didn't quite know how to phrase it. "Clayton treating you all right?"

"I—he—" I stammered. "Yes, lately. That is, yes. Fine."

He looked at me in puzzlement.

"We're just fine," I assured him. "Your question surprised me, that's all. The thing is, he isn't home very much. He's mostly involved in the hospital."

I came close to telling him what Clayton planned to ask him for when all this was over, but decided not. I did not want to say anything that would hurt him then.

Before he left, he leaned down and kissed my cheek. The nearness of him was almost overpowering for me. I held my breath till he was out the door, then big tears trickled down my cheeks. It was the first time I had felt the release of tears since the accident. Over and over I anguished at how close he could be, yet how remote from me because I couldn't have him, he wasn't mine. I had to watch him walk away, knowing he would go home to someone else and that I was only accorded the attention of a dear, long-time friend. I cried and cried, and refused dinner when Mother brought it to the door.

I stayed with Mother for four weeks, until a new set of x-rays proved I had mended well. Whereas during the period of recovery I had been reasonably content to read and listen to the radio, once home I felt confined and impatient. I decided to run some errands and drop off the dry cleaning. I went through Clayton's closet to see what needed to be taken, and after finding three suits that needed cleaning I pulled out a fourth. This one he did not wear very often, but it could stand at least a press job. I dipped my hands into the pockets, and found a slip of paper. In Clayton's handwriting were three items: a date, January 5; a dollar amount, $20,000; and a place, Elk Grove.

At first I assumed it had to do with money for the new hospital wing— maybe someone had offered a donation. Yet . . . Clayton would have told me that. Anyhow, Elk Grove was in Illinois. A big hospital was there. Well, there was probably a simple explanation.

I started to put the paper on Clayton's dresser and take the suit to be cleaned. Then I changed my mind. If it was something I was not meant to see, then he'd probably fly into a rage when he realized I'd found it. Best to leave it alone. I picked up the other clothes, and as I started to leave, the telephone rang. It was Lilly. "Got some exciting news," she said. "There is going to be a big rally for Gabriel right before the election in front of the new city hall on Hermann Square."

"Great. How did that happen?"

"I don't know exactly. Daddy had lots of friends in city politics and of course he was on the Chamber since the days when it was the Houston

Business League. Anyway, it seems a terrific way to wind up the campaign. Oh, and Bill said he'd be in touch with you about some of the arrangements."

I told her that would be fine because I couldn't wait to get busy again. After that I was preoccupied with what she said and forgot the note. I needed to make a list of things to be done, and when. No speaker could have a better setting, and Gabriel would look marvelous there. . . .

A week later I had an appointment with my gynecologist for a regular checkup. When I finished at ten forty-five, I stopped down the hall at Clayton's office to leave him a note. Bill and his wife had invited me to eat supper with them while we talked about the city hall affair, and I wanted to let Clayton know he ought to stop off somewhere to eat, for I didn't know what time either of us would arrive home.

I searched his desk for a piece of paper to write on, and noticed that number again—$20,000—scribbled on a sheet near the telephone. Now I was curious. I left his office and walked up to the floor desk. "Is Dr. Gerrard due out of surgery soon?"

The secretary looked up. "Oh, Mrs. Gerrard—no, I don't think so. He's booked through the afternoon. Can I give him a message?"

"No, that's all right. I'll leave a note on his desk."

Feeling relatively safe, I went back down the hall to Clayton's office and opened his filing cabinet. I found nothing in it except folders on patients and ordinary hospital correspondence. I turned to his desk. In the top right-hand drawer I found an unmarked folder. Inside it was a group of letters from a Dr. Danfield, administrator at Elk Grove General Hospital. All five letters in the folder were in response to letters written by Clayton, of which there were no copies. Yet Dr. Danfield's letters were explanatory enough. Clayton was seeking the chief of staff position in that hospital. The first letter from the Illinois doctor was dated August 5 of this year. As the correspondence went on, it was apparent that that hospital was considering several physicians at this point and would be getting back to him with their final decision. He specified a salary of twenty thousand dollars.

The most surprising, not to mention chilling, phrase in all the letters was the final line on the last letter, written just over a week ago. "How unfortunate about Mrs. Gerrard. I was so terribly sorry to hear of your tragedy."

What had Clayton told him about me? Maybe he mentioned my accident. Yet, if that were true, had he not added something about the fact I suffered only minor injuries? Surely that information would not have prompted such an expression of sympathy.

It was almost as though he wanted to lay the groundwork for my demise. . . . No, that was ridiculous. Or was it? I wondered, uneasily. I hurriedly went through the other drawers in the desk, but there was nothing else. I grabbed my handbag and went quickly out the door and straight home. There were two puzzling facts. One without the other would not have seemed odd at all. Had Clayton discussed the matter of taking a position in Illinois with me, then I would not have found the last line of Dr. Danfield's letter so onerous. If there had been no reference to me, then the fact that Clayton had not discussed moving with me would have seemed unusual, but not . . . not threatening.

The worst part was that I could say nothing to Clayton without giving myself away. Then, if there were a plausible explanation, he would consider it reason enough to attack me. If there were not, it might be even worse. In all my years of marriage to Clayton, I had never felt so trapped. At home I fixed a strong drink to calm my nerves. I looked through Clayton's dresser and closet, but found nothing beyond the original slip of paper that started all this.

I returned downstairs and fixed another strong whiskey. I sat in a chair in the living room for a long time, thinking. I had not had anything to eat since a piece of toast early this morning. My thoughts became more and more tangled as I drank and sat. The significance of the date of Dr. Danfield's first letter finally dawned on me. Clayton began this correspondence a few days after the Democratic primary, at which time he lost hope that Gabriel might win the governorship. Evidently he was paving the way for a job elsewhere, certain he would not win the chief of staff position at Memorial because he would not have the money to buy his way into it. In one sense I had to agree with him. He was anything but popular among the staff at Memorial. Without the advantage of a check to present in his bid for the job, he probably would not even be considered.

I canceled my dinner plans so that I could be waiting for Clayton when he arrived. Then I'd do some "fishing" to see what I could find out. But I would have to be careful. The last thing I wanted him to know was that I had been snooping around his office. If he figured that out . . . even suspected it . . . I shook my head. I simply had to be careful, that was all. I fixed another drink, and sipped it while I waited for the sound of his arrival. My hands around the glass were icy. Six-fifteen . . . six-thirty. I had almost emptied the whiskey glass again and took a mental count of how much I had consumed. Three. Or was it four? I'd better not have anymore. Seven o'clock. Through the window I saw the beam of headlights snake up the drive. I tightened my hands around the glass, rehearsing how I was going to handle this conversation. . . .

I drew in a deep breath as the back door opened, and as soon as Clayton entered the living room I felt a sudden pierce of anger that he should have me so cowed. God, how I despised him. He pulled off his tie, unbuttoned his shirt, and joined me in a drink. So innocent. I asked him to make a refill for me. He took one look at my face and said, "Haven't you had a few too many already?"

I smiled my insistence. My lips were trembling slightly.

He returned with the drink and sat down, curious. "What's up?"

"I've been thinking. When this campaign is over, I'm going to register with the agency and do private duty. I'm bored at home."

He shrugged. "Do whatever you want."

"Would that look bad for you, if you get the promotion? Having a wife who works outside the home?"

"You can forget about the promotion. I have."

"You still think Gabriel will lose?"

He put down his glass and sighed as though impatience threatened to overtake him. "Listen, Senta, I know you think Gabriel could sprout wings and fly if he took a notion, but there has never yet been a governor of this state who won on an independent ticket, and only once or twice has a Republican even taken the office. So face facts."

"What'll you do if that happens, if he loses?"

He did not bat an eye. "Just keep going as usual, I guess. Why, what's it to you?"

I took another swallow of whiskey. "Maybe nothing; maybe a hell of a lot. I just think I have a right to know, that's all." I was aware my voice was straining, thanks to the drinks. How loud was I talking? I couldn't tell. I felt numb.

He considered a few moments, his whiskey glass between the palms of his hands. I felt safe, as though there were a barrier between us through which he could not penetrate. I kept staring at him, and I loved making him uncomfortable for a change.

Finally he rose, saying, "You ought to cut back on your whiskey, Senta. There's nothing more unattractive than a drunken woman."

"Unless it's a lying man," I said, though I'm not quite sure I meant to. I could not seem to weigh my remarks before I made them.

He glared at me. "What are you talking about?"

"Does Elk Grove ring a bell?" Again, I spoke before I thought. That was not what I'd planned to say. I couldn't keep the questions in sequence. I was beginning to feel as I had that night just before my car was run off the road.

He sat down, searching my eyes. Finally he hedged, "I don't know what you're talking about."

"Oh, Clayton, don't bore me," I blurted. "You're hoping to go there as chief of staff on January 5. All I want to know is whether your plans include taking me." That was it. I was in it now . . . no going back. . . . I sipped the whiskey, every heartbeat before he replied a swift whack in my chest. Hold on . . . hold on. . . .

He had not taken his eyes off me. At length he said, "How did you find out about that?"

"Quite by accident," I said, and was aware the whole phrase was drawn out with a slur.

"What sort of 'accident,' Senta?" he challenged, and came to stand above me. The false bravery was draining away from me like rainwater down a gully. Yet I could not let him know that. I lifted my head back and told him about the suit jacket. He seemed to be making a mental note, as a doctor would when a patient lists a group of symptoms, then he said, "And what else?" His eyes were blazing.

"That was all—" I began, but I knew he'd seen through me and I felt panicked.

"No it wasn't, you bitch," he snarled. "You helped yourself to the files in my desk, didn't you."

"I— No, I—" I choked.

"If you ever set foot in my office again, I'll beat the hell out of you and kick your ass all the way back down to McKinney Avenue."

The words snapped me in two. Through all our stormy married life, that was the cruelest remark he had ever made to me. All I felt in that moment was a consuming outrage. I wanted to jump at his throat and was all the more angry that I could not physically stand up to him. When I spoke my voice was like the hiss of a cat. "If you intend to divorce me, then go ahead, but if you intend to get nasty, you better hope you get that job in Elk Grove because before I'm through they'll know all about your plans at Memorial, and see what happens to your career then."

At once I wished I could recall every word. He looked as though he would like to kill me. And I thought, if he touches me, he better kill me. This time I'll tell, regardless of anything.

After a long moment he rose from his chair and walked toward me. I wanted to shield my face. It took every ounce of courage in me to keep still and stare back at him. He looked at me as though he had not decided what to do. Then, to my surprise, he turned and picked up his coat. He walked out the door and slammed it shut.

I took off my shoes, tucked my feet under me, and sat in that chair as though paralyzed, staring at the door, until the clock struck twelve. Shortly after that I fell asleep. When I awoke the next morning, with a start, the sun was shining through the windows. Clayton had not come home.

Chapter 4

From that night on, life with Clayton was like a boiling kettle about to explode under a tight lid. Again and again I wished I had never said anything; often I wished he had reacted to my statement in his usual way. Instead he behaved as though the conversation had never happened so that I had, in effect, drawn myself into a box from which there would be no escape for the next six weeks, till Election Day. Several times I came near talking to Gabriel about it, but each time fell just short of going through with it. Oh, if only I had done that, it might have saved tragedy. Twice when I gathered the courage, he had just left for another out-of-town appearance. Louetta's voice on the other end of the line put a special distance between us and I hung up and discarded the idea for a few days. I did not want to bother Gabriel at this stage of his campaign. Yet there was a more basic motivation that sucked at my courage: I detested admitting to him that he had been right, that I should have never married Clayton in the first place.

I wonder now how I could have possibly believed anything might change for the better after the election. Yet it seemed there were so many reasons to hope. If Gabriel won and Clayton got the promotion at Memorial Hospital, he might find, after holding the position for a while, he could quietly divorce me without causing scandal. If Gabriel lost, he could go forward with his plans to move to Illinois, and an immediate divorce would have no effect on him because it could be played down, perhaps not even mentioned at all. He could go on with his life, and never bother me again.

Under the circumstances, I would be in a position to negotiate a nice financial settlement.

The disturbing thing that kept coming back to mind was that queer phrase at the end of Dr. Danfield's letter. ". . . so terribly sorry to hear of your tragedy . . ." Unfortunately, the only person who could explain that peculiar selection of words, aside from the doctor himself, was Clayton. I'd have died before asking him.

In the first week of October we went to a cocktail party in Gabriel's honor at the River Oaks Country Club. The champagne flowed from a marvelous ice sculpture in the shape of Texas, flooded with colored lights. The hors d'oeuvres ranged from star-shaped little garlic toasts and cheese spreads shaped like Texas boots, to stuffed mushrooms and mounds of spicy meatballs.

The party began at eight, and lasted till nearly midnight. I probably sampled at least one of every variety of food on the enormous table, and had four or five glasses of champagne. We returned home at 1 A.M., and at 4:30, I awoke doubled over with the worst kind of stomach pain I had ever experienced. I threw an arm over to awaken Clayton soon after. He turned on the light, took my pulse and heartbeat, then picked up the telephone and called the hospital to tell them he was bringing me in. My forehead was perspiring, my whole body felt clammy. The convulsive pain seized me relentlessly, like shock waves.

It seems to me in retrospect, Clayton took an especially long time getting dressed. At the time I was in too much pain to count the minutes. Every second was an eternity for me. But I remember that when we reached the hospital and I looked up from the stretcher as we passed the clock on the wall, it was nearly six. Shortly after, the door was closed to the examining room and a doctor I'd never seen before, attended by a nurse and an intern, proceeded to pump out my stomach. I would almost have preferred to live with the pain. It was the most dehumanizing, horrible experience I have ever had. I felt I'd been obliged to swallow the whole Gulf of Mexico.

By nine o'clock I was resting comfortably in a private room. The nurse on duty was one I had gone through training with. She told me they had checked with the River Oaks Country Club to see if anyone else had gotten sick after the party, and so far no one had reported illness. "Probably something you got at home that didn't cause mischief till the next day. You rest easy," she added, fluffing the pillows. "The doctor wants you to stay until you get some color back in your cheeks, then you can go."

Something I ate at home. . . . I went over what I had eaten. It did not amount to much—a bowl of cereal at breakfast, a half sandwich made with leftover baked ham and some raw vegetables at noon, no supper, then the party. Oh yes, and a drink before I left. A whiskey and soda, prepared by Clayton. With an addition of lemon juice. He never fixed whiskey and soda with lemon, and when I asked him why, he said, "Oh, just to perk it up."

Perhaps I was too tired to begin to put things together up to that time. I had slept only about three hours overnight, and had suffered the rude experience of a stomach pump, plus an interruption by the nurse at the time I might have dozed off. I fell asleep not too long after that, and awoke at noon to look into the face of someone I had not seen in a very long time.

"Uncle Jordan!"

He strolled over and kissed my forehead. "You don't mind if I have a cigar, do you?" he said, biting the tip off one and fishing for his lighter.

My stomach flipped over at the idea. "No, I guess not . . ." I said discouragingly. "I'll tell you if it makes me sick. How did you know I was in here?"

He was already drawing on the cigar, exhaling smoke toward the window. "I called Elzyna this morning, and she told me," he said. "She wasn't dressed yet but she'll be over after a while. I was coming to town anyway—got some business in the Humble Building—so I thought I better stop by and see about you."

It was the kind of thing he would have done, not caring enough to go out of his way, but willing to make the gesture if it was convenient. In a way I had always liked Jordan. For one thing, he was always ready to have a good time —we had had many laughs together during the years I was growing up—and for another, I always knew what to expect from him. In any situation, Jordan looked out for himself. That was as sure as a pebble, thrown into a pond, sinking to the bottom.

I hardly had a breath in which to say thanks, before he sat down and began to tell me about his latest venture. Jordan's ventures were as flashy as his clothing—today he wore a light blue suit with a horrible maroon tie with a palm tree on it, and a diamond stickpin, two-tone oxfords, and dark green socks. His light hair was parted down one side and he had the well-tanned look of someone who stays outside a lot. He wore an expensive-looking gold wristwatch that I had never seen before.

He'd been up in the Conroe fields working a deal with some partners in a drilling venture. Now he was trying to get financial backing, and therefore would be staying with a girl friend over the next few weeks, here in town, before returning . . . "Hopefully, with all the loot I need."

On and on he talked, about how he'd been cheated by two partners in a deal last year, how he knew of some good properties in Conroe if I wanted to invest a little money, how he had this new car in mind—"a real honey, maroon convertible with black interior—" and as soon as he had the money he was going to buy it.

These were stories typical of Jordan. I had heard them all my life, while sitting around Mother's dining room table, or while being taken on "joy" rides in Jordan's latest automobile. He would spend his last dime for a flashy car. He lived as a nomad, never staying in one place very long, going from one oil field to the next as soon as he got wind of a big strike about to happen. I had heard since childhood that my grandfather David had got a serious case of oil fever with the Spindletop discovery in 1901, from which he never recovered. Apparently Jordan was likewise infected.

He was always beginning anew; he never seemed to finish anything he started. He was always running out of money, always starting new drilling companies with new partners. Time and again he had appeared at Mother's doorstep, asking for a little help, just to tide him over till his well came in. Mother never received any money back, as far as I know, and for the past few years, he had not stayed with her anymore. Yet, she felt responsible for him, especially since the night in 1914 when my father wound up fastened to the front of the automobile Jordan was driving. On top of that, Jordan wound up without any inheritance. What was left of my grandmother Carlotta's estate eventually found its way into the hands of my grandfather, and when he died of a heart attack four years ago, already divorced from his "countess" wife and never having returned from Europe, there was nothing left. Mother had sold the house on Main to cover some of the Leider debts. It was now a piece of commercial property like everything else up and down South Main. Not surprisingly, Jordan was bitter.

"Hey, according to Elzyna, you haven't had the best of luck lately. What was that you were driving when you got run off the road?"

"A staid old Chevrolet sedan; nothing you would find interesting."

He shook his head. "It's what you get for working in the campaign. Just letting Gabriel use you, that's all. And what for? He won't win. People in the oil business consider him to be dangerous as snake poison. Pappy O'Daniel may be a hick, but at least he leaves us alone."

I didn't feel like arguing with Jordan this morning. I just lay back on the pillows quietly, knowing he'd eventually run out of steam and leave. "Oh, I know how it is with you," he was saying now. "I can't say I blame you for getting hooked up with the Gerrards. I hate the fuckin'—'scuse me—bastards but I sure don't have nothing against their money. I would have done it myself if I could. There was a time a long while back when I might have gotten on with Lilly. So I know how you think, Senta. You think just like me." He smiled. He had ugly teeth, yellowed from a lifetime of smoking. Something about the way he looked just then made me uneasy.

He took my silence to mean I did not know about his aborted date with Lilly, and explained, "Of course, she was just like the rest of the family, thought she was too good for me."

"Oh?"

"Yeah, the little prick teaser ran off and tattled on me to Gabriel, and he came after me, the son-of-a-bitch."

"Oh," I said, innocently.

"But that's all right, my day will come. Besides, I figure I came out ahead on that one."

"Why is that?"

"Well, I wouldn't want anything to do with someone who turned out to be sickly like her, no matter how much money she has."

"No, I'm sure you wouldn't," I said.

I lay there silently again, thinking how he'd spent a lifetime waiting for his "day to come," for fortune to drop into his lap. Presently he stood up, and smushed his cigar into an empty bowl on my bedside table. "Well, I gotta get going. Don't want to be late. You take care of yourself. If I didn't know better, I'd think someone had it in for you."

As soon as he was out the door, the nurse came in, made a face, took the bowl with the cigar in it, and left again, holding it out away from her. I lay there thinking about what he said. First the incident outside of Centerville, then the food poisoning episode. Added to that Clayton's failure to lash back at me over meddling in his private affairs, plus his adding lemon juice to my drink, then, when I was so sick, taking so long to get ready to take me to the hospital. I remembered now that he had said to someone at the hospital over the phone, "No, don't send one [presumably an ambulance], I can get her there faster myself." Yet he hadn't hurried at all. An ambulance would have been much faster.

Oh, nonsense.

Yet . . . after all he had done, why should I think him incapable of looking for a means to get rid of me? I would find it hard to believe him a murderer, but I wouldn't rule it out either, not if I was really in his way.

". . . so terribly sorry to hear of your tragedy . . ."

I had a sickening feeling in the pit of my stomach now, and it had nothing to do with food poisoning.

As the days went by, and I began to feel better, the fear created by Jordan's casual remark dwindled. All my "grouping" of the various events in my life lately had become diffused again. I simply had had a bad automobile accident. I happened to get hold of something that made me very ill. My husband was obviously making plans without me, but so what?

Two weeks later I received a jolt that convinced me I was really in danger from Clayton. Since I had left the hospital, he had made a point—so unlike him—of being solicitous about my feelings. He made frequent references to the fact that I did not seem to be as cheerful as usual (no one had ever characterized me as "cheerful" before, and certainly not Clayton). I looked a little pale still, he said. Was I eating right? Still no appetite? Well, I must not let the experience get me down. Why not go shopping, buy a new dress?

These were the kinds of remarks Clayton made to me daily. They were puzzling at first.

Then one evening as I sat at home and alone and listened to Gabriel in a radio interview, the radio went dead. Ordinarily I would not have bothered to try and fix it myself, but since I was so anxious to hear the program I just had to give it a try. I needed a screwdriver to get the back off the radio, so I went out to the garage in search of Clayton's toolbox, which he rarely opened. Cursing under my breath because I was missing so much of the interview, I finally found the box in a corner behind some yard tools. I released the catch and threw it open. Right in the center was a small pistol. I felt the hair rise on my neck.

Gingerly I picked it up and turned it over in my hands. I knew nothing about guns and had no idea if it was loaded. I looked through the toolbox, and found a small box of bullets. I could not tell if any were missing. I put the gun back and closed the box. I tried to tell myself there was a logical reason for its presence there. It may have been there for a long time . . . years even. . . . But why? I wondered uncomfortably as I walked inside again. In case of prowlers? Maybe. . . . Yet, as far as I knew, we'd had no prowlers on this street. Anyway, as much as I stayed alone, if the gun had been purchased to ward off prowlers, surely Clayton would have told me it was there in the event I needed it. And he wouldn't have left it way out in the garage. How long had it been there? I asked myself again and again. . . .

I sat down in the living room, forgetting about the radio interview. The longer I sat, the more frightened I became. I finally went back into the garage, reopened the toolbox, and counted the bullets in the box. There were supposed to be fifty, according to the box. There were only forty-nine. With heavy steps, I went back inside the house. God. What was I to do now? Be afraid to sleep for fear of being shot? Afraid to walk through a door? Step out of the shower? For what other reason would Clayton have a gun around?

I jumped up and paced the floor. I would never know any peace in this house again. What could I do? Casually mention that I found the gun while looking for a screwdriver, to alert him I knew it was there? No. Then he would lie. He probably already had an excuse made up. He would move the gun, perhaps to a place where I would never find it.

And what plans did he have for it? Kill me now? Or if not now, when?

Nervously, I went over everything again. I remembered all the remarks of the past few weeks about my paleness and lack of "cheerfulness." Then I realized what was about to happen. It was to look like suicide. Of course, he'd never shoot me and risk being caught. How stupid. He would make it look as though I had done it. The question was not how, but when. A sudden vision of myself lying dead on the floor shot me through with fear. I had to think, I had to think. I sat down and drummed my fingers on the chair arm.

I considered for a long time before I realized it would be after the election. Clayton could say that I had not been myself since the automobile accident. That I had counted so much on Gabriel's victory. Of course, he might then say I had been in love with Gabriel, and that might bring scandal, but it would bring so much sympathy for him that scandal would soon be forgotten. And within a few weeks Clayton would quietly move to Illinois and take up a new life, trying to forget his grief. . . .

I knew I must tell someone, but who would believe me? Just a handgun in the garage. I had no solid evidence that Clayton ever meant to harm me. In front of people we seemed content. Because I did not want to admit our failure to Gabriel, even he did not know the truth of our marriage. And even if he thought his brother cold and hard, he might not believe him capable of murder.

Perhaps he wasn't. Perhaps this was all in my imagination. At midnight I went up to bed. Clayton would probably not return until at least three in the morning. He had been called to the hospital for an emergency following a three-car collision involving several seriously injured people. I took a bath, conscious of the sound the running water made, conscious of the sound of the wash cloth coursing over my body, ears keened for the sound of the garage door closing, the back door opening, hardly able to function for fear I had not guessed correctly about the timing, and that Clayton might try and murder me tonight.

Murder me! When I got out of the tub and toweled off, I looked at my image in the vanity mirror. My face was white, my eyes wide with fear. Something took hold of me then. I was suddenly furious that I should be manipulated into a trembling little fool. No one had ever manipulated me in this way.

I had to take command, somehow. I had to tell someone. And in the event Clayton succeeded in killing me, I had to leave evidence proving his guilt.

Finally I went to bed and lay back on the pillows, my thoughts muddled from sheer exhaustion. I couldn't figure out any sensible answer right now. At last I fell to dozing off now and again, then waking with a start. Around two-thirty, I heard the sound of the back door opening. That was the first sound I heard, so I had no idea how long was the interval from the time Clayton pulled into the driveway, parked the car, and came into the house. Long enough to open the toolbox and get the gun?

I rose from the bed and, weak-kneed, stole across the hall to the extra bedroom before he reached the stairway. We kept books in that room, and I could always surprise him from behind, with the excuse I'd had trouble sleeping and went after a book to read. I grabbed one from the shelf, leaving the door open just enough to peer through the crack and see if he had anything in his hand. I paused. I could hear his footsteps on the stairs now. I ran my tongue over my lips. By the time he reached the upstairs landing my heart was threatening to pound through my chest. As he passed I thought his hands were empty, but I could not be absolutely certain because of the constricted view. When he'd gone into our bedroom I came forth and followed him. I could barely breathe. "Clayton?" I said timidly.

I'd startled him good. He jerked around. "What the hell?"

"I didn't mean to surprise you. I was across the hall getting a book."

He sighed and crossed the room, pulling off his tie. I slipped into bed, quivering. I opened the book to a page and began to watch the words. I was far beyond the point of being able to read. When he had finally gotten into bed and turned over to sleep, claiming he had never been so exhausted, I switched off my light and lay there very still, my feet and hands icy cold. It was near dawn when I finally slept and after ten o'clock before either of us awakened.

At the first opportunity I went to Mother's house. Here I accomplished two things: first, I left a long letter explaining my fears for my life, indicting Clayton positively should he manage to do away with me. By the time I wrote the message I had figured out the perfect place for it. By long custom, Mother took up the carpets and washed and polished the hardwood floors twice a year. She had done this since she moved into this house, and even though she now had a lady to come and help her, the project would still be done right on schedule. The next time she did it would be the early part of January. I slipped the letter under the library carpet near the fireplace. This was always the first carpet to be pulled up. If all of this proved to be an error on my part, I would simply remove the letter at a later date.

That made me feel a little better, a little more in control. In fact, I later mused, if Clayton pointed the gun at me I could always tell him evidence indicting him was already at hand, planted where it would certainly be found.

Afterward I asked Jordan to meet me at Mother's. I told him everything I suspected, right from the automobile wreck. I knew he would not be afraid to tell me if I sounded foolish; nor would he be eager to jump to Clayton's defense. Strangely, from a man who had lied and deceived all of his life, the chances were good I would get an honest appraisal of the situation.

He listened more attentively than usual, puffing on his smelly cigar at the other end of the wicker swing on Mother's porch. Finally he said, "There's only one reason for having a handgun, and that's to kill someone. You can't hunt game with it."

I had never thought of that before. The finality of the statement was terrifying. "You know of anyone else he might want to kill?"

"No. He may feel like murdering Gabriel, but I know for a fact he wouldn't do that, certainly not before the election anyway."

We both sat there for a while. Finally I said, "What should I do?"

He thought about this for a moment or two, then said, "It's kind of like being out in the field and watching a snake slither up. If you don't get him, you can be damned sure he'll get you."

The picture he portrayed shocked me. I brought a hand to my breast. Protecting myself had been the only thing I had considered before now. "You mean, murder Clayton? Surely you can't be serious—"

He cast an indulgent look my way and said, "Here you are in a life-threatening situation, wondering if you ought to take the first step to defend yourself."

"But what if I'm wrong?"

"What if you're right?"

"But I don't think I could just point a gun or a knife, or whatever, and kill someone. No, I couldn't." I shook my head.

"You just remove yourself from it. You get someone else to do it. There are people for hire, you know, and there's never a trace of evidence found."

Oh, God, I thought in horror . . . I didn't know that.

I told him I'd think about it. He rose from the wicker swing, smashed his cigar in a flowerpot, and walked toward his car. I sat rigidly on my end of the swing for a long time. I could hardly believe what had just taken place. It was such a peaceful, beautiful fall day. The grass was still green, the trees still heavy with foliage. Mother's crepe myrtles were still blooming. . . .

Mother walked out on the porch. "What was that all about?"

"What? Oh, I just needed to talk to Jordan about something," I said. My voice was dull and lifeless.

She paused at length. "Is he coming back?"

"No, I don't think so. Did you need him for something?"

"No. Certainly not."

She turned and went back into the house. I wondered if there had been a falling out between them. She hadn't sounded pleased about his being here. Maybe she was tired of his antics.

In a few minutes Robin came outside, wearing a new corduroy dress with a big yellow flower appliquéd on the front. "Aunt Senta, would you button my dress? I can't reach the last two."

She turned around. As I fastened the dress in place she said, "I asked Nana to do it, but she just walked right by. Is anything wrong?"

"With Nana? No, I don't think so."

"How do you like my dress? Nana just finished making it." She pivoted around to model it.

She looked adorable, but I didn't want to fool with her anymore just then, so I told her to leave me alone. She went back into the house.

I sat there awhile longer, thinking about the conversation with Jordan. For another three or four days, and sleepless nights, I thought about it more. Every time Clayton walked in empty-handed I first felt relief, then a brand-new realization that every day the election drew nearer. October 15, 16, 17. After November 5, my life might not be worth the price of one of Jordan's cigars.

At last I began to contemplate the alternative.

A widow. I would live in the house—not home—we once shared, only no longer in fear, but in confidence, with plenty of money to support me and young enough to find another husband should I choose. Plenty of prestige— at least Clayton had bought that for me. No one to worry about except myself. No worry of being beat up or yelled at, accused and held in contempt. A peaceful life from here on in. Yes . . . a widow. . . .

I shook my head. No, I simply could not do it. This was all crazy, the whole thing. Clayton was no threat to me. He was a Gerrard, for God's sake; how could he be a murderer? And yet . . . and yet . . . so much evidence now weighed in favor of the fact that he was about to become one. I wished there were somebody I could talk to, someone who knew enough about Clayton to assure me one way or the other. I felt as lost in this mélange of possibilities as I had felt that night on my way to Dallas. I stayed as busy as I could, making telephone calls and writing letters for Gabriel, and when there was nothing else to do, raking the few early autumn leaves in the yard. One afternoon I spent two hours out in the yard, working like a slave, and it occurred to me as I folded my hands above the rake, if Clayton could see me doing this he would know something was up.

Still, I could not make up my mind. I was now drinking up to five or six highballs every evening, just to keep from coming to pieces. Finally, I sat down with a drink one night and began to cry, then to sob so hard I held my arms around my quaking abdomen. And soon I found myself wailing, "I'm losing control; I've got to hang on; I'm losing control; I've got to—"

I sat still and drew up my shoulders. Control. I remembered what Gabriel had said of me so long ago, that I wanted to be in control, inferring that with Clayton I would not be. Gad, he could not have known how right he was. Control. That was it. The very word was like a taste of sweet nectar on my tongue. I knew what to do. Even if I canceled everything before it was over because somehow I was proven wrong about Clayton's plans to do away with me, and I hoped to God I would be, I would still be prepared, still be in control.

"It's simple," Jordan said a few days later, when I asked him how one goes about hiring a murderer. We were sitting on Mother's porch again. "The element of surprise is the whole thing. The best way is to pull it off when there are a lot of people around, creating confusion."

It seemed so dangerous, regardless of his opinion, regardless of my resolve. I shuddered. Today the weather was bleak; the first chill of fall was in the air. Everything, in this weather, seemed more threatening. I shook my head.

"It's happened more than a few times right after an oil strike . . ." he was saying now.

"You mean, to a friend of yours?"

"One time I knew the guy. They never convicted the murderer. He was just one of the crowd. No one even saw the gun."

"Well, that's out," I sighed, relieved in a way that murdering Clayton might be impossible. "Clayton is never in a crowd, except maybe at a party. We have no more party invitations between now and the election. The largest group he ever has about him otherwise is during a surgery at the hospital. No stranger would be allowed in there."

"There are other ways. A hired killer knows what to do. You leave it to him."

I took in a breath. "Could you—could you find someone and set it up for me?"

He laughed. "Hold on a minute, girl, this is your party, not mine. I could get you a name. But that's all."

"But I could pay you. I don't know how much, but I'm sure I could make it worth your while."

He thought about this for a moment or two, then expelled the smoke in his mouth and shook his head. "Naw, it's too much of a risk. Here I am about to make it big for the first time in my life—it looks like we'll get the backing we need to drill—and I don't want to screw it up."

"I guess it's off, then. If you can't even do that much for me." A wave of relief swept over me again.

He raised his hands in supplication. "Look, Senta, why don't you get a gun of your own? Or take that one out of the garage and hide it someplace, or dump it."

"I've already thought of all that. If I take his gun he'll just get another. And I would be afraid to have a gun for fear he'd find it, and use it on me."

He stood up. "I'd like to help you, Senta, but you can see my point, can't you? If you decide to talk to someone, I'll get you a name and number. But that's it."

I sat there in the swing, my forehead in my shaking hand, the sense of relief leaving me; the feeling of being lost and out of control overtaking me again.

You couldn't really blame Jordan, I realized later. Jordan always looked out for himself first, last, and always. If you wanted him to do something for you, you had to make it profitable enough for him to risk it. At this point, I could not do that. People made millions in the oil fields daily. I could not dream of making him that rich even if I gave him Clayton's whole estate. And there was just enough doubt in my mind about Clayton's plan to kill me that I wasn't willing to give away everything I had to gain as his widow.

In the newspaper on Sunday, October 20, there was a big article about Gabriel's campaign—the biggest ever—stating that Gabriel's chances of winning the governorship were increasing. "Gerrard now has many important organizations behind him, and he has charmed the women voters right out to the polls on Election Day, many believe."

That was an endorsement if ever I had seen one. It left me tingly with excitement. And in addition, within the week, major newspapers in Dallas, San Antonio, Fort Worth, and Abilene all expressed the same views. As much as I had believed in Gabriel's ability to win at the beginning, it did not compare with my absolute certainty of his victory now. Just a few months hence I might be moving to Austin. . . .

That is . . . if I were still alive. Would Clayton still want me out of his life, even if Gabriel's victory brought him the coveted position at Memorial?

Fear shivered through me. Of course he would. And why be forced to go through a costly divorce, when there was a much simpler way . . . a way that would gain sympathy rather than scorn from others? A suicide might not be so easy to explain but, perhaps, an accidental death of some kind?

Was my fate now sealed, one way or the other?

Chapter 5

Shortly after that, Jordan called me from Mother's and said he wanted to talk to me. When I drove up, his new maroon convertible with black interior was parked at the curb. If he just wants to take me for a spin in his new car, I thought with irritation . . .

"Get in, we'll go for a ride," he said.

"From the looks of things, you've met with success," I told him. The seats were plush and comfortable. The engine hummed quietly as we rode down McKinney and turned south on Main. "In a way," he replied. Then he laughed. "Hell, it don't take much to make me happy—just a couple of gushers with my name on 'em and a new car." His yellow teeth showed. He pulled out a cigar and bit the tip off it.

"I've been thinking," he said. "I saw that article in the papers last Sunday about Gabriel, and I came up with a good idea. That rally down at city hall on November 2. Did it occur to you that would be the perfect time to get Clayton?"

I looked away nervously. "Get Clayton." It sounded like a hunter going after a deer. "No. How could that be?"

"He'll be there, won't he, along with Gabriel?"

"Yes . . ." I said slowly. "We'll all be up there on the speaker's platform."

"The killing would look like an attempt on Gabriel's life. Now that he is getting so close to victory, it's a natural."

"You mean, it might look like Governor O'Daniel—"

"Naw, naw," he shook his head impatiently. "Just a political sympathizer. Plenty of people hate Gabriel for what he has done to oil men. All those regulations telling people how much oil they can drill and when. Nobody paid too much attention to them till he came into the picture, pushin' his weight around. Tell you one thing. He wouldn't dare set foot in an oil field unless there were plenty of witnesses around.

"What I mean is there's always one or two lunatics who might take a shot at him at a rally. The police will be busy till Gabriel runs for office again trying to figure out who did it."

"Oh, but that's too dangerous," I said. "Someone else could be hurt, or even killed."

"Not if it's done right. You'll be up there, won't you? Would I let anything happen to you?"

I shook my head, less convinced than I wanted him to know. "I'd have to think about it. It seems too risky."

"It's the safest plan we got, and it may be the only chance at such a perfect setup. Listen, I ran into someone the other night, and—"

The words jackknifed in me. "You mean, you've already told someone about this?" I gasped.

"Don't worry, Senta. I opened the door for you, but I didn't shove you through it."

"Thank goodness for that."

"The thing is, time is short. If you don't act fast, pretty girl, you're liable to be dead before an opportunity comes around again."

"Shut up, Jordan, shut up. This is tearing me to pieces inside. You have no idea."

He laughed and accelerated speed. "Don't tell me you're queasy, Senta. Hell, I've known you since I could hold you on my knee. You were never afraid of anything that I can remember."

Being reminded of that, I suddenly felt a lot more daring, and as we wheeled our way down toward Rice Institute and all the way back again, we fell into chatter about the days when my father was alive and Jordan would stay with us, lifting Mother's pin money off her dresser behind her back, never to be caught.

Before we parted that day Jordan said, "Let me know by tomorrow. After that it'll be too late. This is the twenty-fifth, you know."

"I know. I'll call you."

All the remainder of the evening and the next day I thought about it. If there were just some way to be sure about Clayton . . . yet there was not. If he were not already the beneficiary of so much wealth, I might call and find out if he'd taken out a life insurance policy on me in the last few months. But, why should he take that kind of chance when there was no need to? Just to be sure, I called our agency. No, there had been no new policy issued, not since the initial insurance we bought when we married. The clerk asked if I wanted to buy an additional policy.

"No, of course not. I was just checking, that's all," I said, and hung up thinking that was a stupid thing to do. What if, when all this were over, some investigator got curious about me, and began to ask questions?

Oh, it was dangerous no matter how you looked at it.

I believe I might have dropped the matter right there, but for an incident that happened the night of the twenty-sixth. Clayton had no late surgery scheduled that evening, and no one called from the hospital to say he was delayed with an emergency case. Yet he did not come home on time. When he failed to show up by eleven, I got worried. I called the hospital. He had left at six-thirty.

I lay awake till half-past one in the morning, afraid to go down and check on the gun in case he drove into the garage while I was looking through the toolbox. Finally I could stay awake no longer, and dozed off. At two forty-five I awoke with a start. I had failed to hear the garage door, or the back door open and shut. All I heard were footsteps on the stairs. I raised up in bed and looked toward the bedroom door, my whole body rigid with terror.

There was silence. He had stopped. At the landing? At the door? I waited, unable to move. Finally I called out, "Clayton, is that you?"

The door opened slowly. It was him. "I was afraid I'd wake you," he said.

"Where the hell have you been?"

"None of your goddamned business," he said. He slammed the door again and went back downstairs. Now I had the pleasure of wondering what he was doing for the rest of the night, afraid that he might be coming back up the stairs, this time with the gun. Maybe he had not brought the car all the way home, instead parking it around the block and walking home so that it would not look like he had been here. Now he could kill me and pretend he had not ever been here, that I had apparently heard a prowler, or thought I did. Or . . . oh, this was a hell of a way to live. Suddenly the years of misery and fear which had plagued my life with Clayton seemed to engulf me with anger. I would endure it no longer. The next morning I called Jordan and gave him the go-ahead.

"All right, hold on. I'll get the phone number. It's in my other suit."

"Wait! I want you to arrange it. I just can't. And if anyone should see us, it would look too suspicious. Please, please do it for me," I begged.

"I don't know . . ." His voice drifted off.

I felt as though I were about to drown, begging to be tossed a life buoy. Somehow I had to persuade him. "Jordan, please—" I began.

"Remember your old uncle," he interrupted. "He never did anything for free. You'd find it cheaper to do it yourself."

"I'll pay you," I said nervously.

His voice became lower. "All right. The gunman will charge you three grand. Fifteen hundred tomorrow, fifteen hundred after he completes the job. You'll have to get cash and give it all to me. In advance. Plus seven-fifty commission for me."

Gad, it was ten times more costly than I'd imagined. "I—I'll have to pull it out of savings . . . what if Clayton finds out?"

He paused momentarily. "Make the check out to the Fitch and Leider Oil Drilling Company, like it was an investment in the new well we're getting ready to drill up in Conroe. Put . . . let's see . . . for one-sixteenth share of well number three. I'll take care of the rest. Got it?"

"Yes, I think so . . . well number three, one-sixteenth. Okay."

"Get it to me tomorrow by four o'clock, and also a copy of the agenda, and the seating arrangement. I'll take care of the rest."

"But if Clayton finds out I took the money, he'll be—"

"Don't worry. It won't be the first time he was mad, will it?"

"I guess not. But, Jordan, I just feel so—Jordan? Jordan, are you there?"

He was off the line. The dial tone was droning monotonously.

On Wednesday morning, four days before the rally, Bill Hansen called and asked me to meet him and Gabriel at city hall to have a look at the way the platform was to be set up and talk over last-minute plans.

Around two-thirty I pulled up to the curb on the McKinney side of the building. Bill and Gabriel were already there, having come from an earlier meeting. They had picked up Alexander after school. I joined all three of them out on the big front lawn, and as I walked up Gabriel smiled and said, "Well, it's good to see you walking upright, kiddo."

I smiled, but his calling me kiddo made me feel like I used to when I was trying so desperately to make him notice me as a grown woman. Alexander wore a new pair of long pants that made me realize he really was growing up. "Hello, Senta, I was hoping you'd bring Robin," he said.

"Sorry. We don't live together, you know."

He drew nearer to Gabriel then, having dispensed with any possible interest in me. He really did look a lot like his father, except he was going to be an even better-looking man, you could already tell that.

The city hall building stood between McKinney and Walker. It was composed of a large central tower of ten stories, with a clock face on all four sides and a flagpole in the center. Facing off from this tower were two shorter wings of graduated height on either side, so that the structure resembled a stack of blocks. But I'm not faulting it. The building was a lot better-looking than any of the previous city hall buildings had been, and its beauty was offset by a large rectangular reflection pool that stretched out over the square toward Smith Street.

Around the edge of the majestic grounds, a fringe of spindly young oak trees were planted.

It was between the building and the reflection pool, on a wide promenade, that the speaker's stand would be constructed. Bill said he had already talked with KPRC radio about the microphones—the rally was to be broadcast—and he wanted to be sure about the number of chairs needed. I told him we needed two rows of chairs, five on each. Gabriel reminded Bill about having a pitcher or two of water and some glasses. "My mouth gets dry when I talk very long."

The obvious retort was begging. "Maybe you ought to cut your speech a little shorter, kiddo," I teased.

He turned and laughed, then said, "You could be right." God, here I was supposed to be all ears about the setup for the rally, and all I could think about was how much I wished I could get the old days back, when Gabriel could not wait to get me alone. I did not think I would ever get over him, no, if I worked with him for the next thirty years while he went from governor to

United States senator to President, for that was where he was headed, I was certain of it, I would still be waiting and hoping we could start over. . . .

When we left that afternoon Gabriel opened my car door for me and then leaned down to say good-bye through the window. "It's almost over, Senta."

"Yes," I said, and looked ahead. I could not face him. If I did I would start crying.

"I want to thank you for everything you've done. You've been just swell. Senta—I may not win, you know."

"Of course you will."

"Whether or not, it's only the beginning. I know now this is the direction I have always wanted to go, and I'm like a boy who just had his first taste of cotton candy. I'm not going to stop, no matter what happens."

"I know that. There is no reason why you should. You're going all the way."

He reached in and kissed my cheek. "Bye, kiddo."

"Oh, shut up," I said, and turned on the ignition. All the way down the street I drove through a blur of tears.

That night I suddenly did not think I could go through with all this, felt that it would be better to take my chances with Clayton in the feeble hope that maybe I was wrong about his plans for me. I went to the telephone and tried to call Jordan. He had already told me, when I delivered the check to him, that we should not contact each other again. Yet I felt that if I called, surely he would know that it was important enough for me to break the rule he imposed. There was no answer at the number he'd given me. At one of our earlier meetings I'd asked him to tell me where the girl friend he was staying with lived, but he had evaded the question. No doubt on purpose, I now thought bitterly. How stupid of me not to insist on having that information.

I called Mother. She said she had not heard from him, and she did not know where he was staying. "If you hear from him, ask him to call me," I said. I tried not to betray the urgency I was feeling, but did not succeed.

"What's the matter, Senta?"

"Nothing. Just ask Jordan to call me."

He never called.

By Thursday night the weather had turned nasty. The winds howled as I had never heard them before. Rain pounded down on the roof. I was at home alone, answering the door to hand out candy to the few kids who braved the weather to go "trick or treating." Halfway through the evening I called Mother to see if Jordan had been in touch with her. He had not.

"Isn't this weather something?" she commented.

"Yes," I said impatiently. Who cared about the weather? But then she added, "If this keeps up they might have to cancel that rally on Saturday."

I had not thought of that.

"I surely hope not. I have a feeling it will be very important to the voting next Tuesday."

"Yes, you're probably right," I said and thought, Maybe the rally will be canceled. Maybe all of this can be called off by a simple act of nature.

Before I went to bed I tried to call Jordan again. This time the line was dead.

This morning, Saturday, November 2, 1940, dawned crisp and beautiful. Sheets of white cloud stretched across the blue sky like angels stretching after a long nap, and the temperature rose no higher than forty-nine degrees. Thanksgiving weather.

I rose at seven and sat alone in the living room with a cup of hot coffee and the newspaper. Weather news eclipsed the headline space that I had hoped would be extended to Gabriel's rally, but he still received a fair share of bold headlines, beginning about halfway down the front page. Until around four o'clock on Friday afternoon, when the weather changed, it seemed as though the rally would have to be canceled. What was now termed a "Halloween Windstorm," beginning on Thursday night, had blown down signs, torn up roofs, uprooted trees, and left a great deal of debris in the streets. I was not sure whether to be glad Gabriel would have this one last chance to pick up the needed votes, or frightened for what had already been put into motion. What if something went wrong?

I tried again to call Jordan, but our telephone was still dead.

The rally was scheduled to begin at three in the afternoon. A high school band would play Texas songs for the first fifteen minutes, then Gabriel's speech would last half an hour. Another concert would follow as he walked among the crowd shaking hands. I'd done the seating arrangement myself, in order to be sure Clayton was placed at the end by the steps. I'd given all this information to Jordan, emphasizing that the shots must be fired during the second concert following Gabriel's speech. It would be so easy then: just at the point Gabriel started down the stairs, the shot would be fired and it would look like a mistake when it was Clayton who was hit. The sound would be muffled by the loud notes of the brass and wind instruments, and the pounding of the drums.

I had not told Jordan that I was pleased the crowd would hear all of Gabriel's speech before the shots were fired. Hopefully then, his chances at victory would not be marred by what occurred afterward. Maybe he would even win votes of sympathy that he would not otherwise have gotten. Maybe the event would even swing the election in his favor. Yes. I had not thought of that. Something to dream on.

Clayton had a busy day at the hospital, and would come home just in time to change and pick me up, then we'd go together to city hall. Special parking places had been set aside for those of us to be on the podium.

I was so nervous I could not finish even one cup of coffee. I spent the morning running errands, picking up Clayton's suit for today at the dry cleaners, grocery shopping, thinking that these routine chores would be useless by tonight. I could scarcely take a breath and my hands trembled as I wrote out a check at the grocery counter. I went to a pay phone and called Jordan. The line was working, but there was no answer. Damn. I did not know if I would have told him to call it off. I only needed to hear his voice . . . to know I still could. Perhaps by now it was too late already.

At one o'clock I filled the tub with hot water and took a long soaking bath. Sprinkling in bath salts and sitting with eyes closed, knees above the water, leaning back, I listened to the clock by the sink, ticking, ticking away. One forty-five. Two o'clock. I had a curious sense of calm. It was out of my hands now.

I allowed myself too little time to dress, and was hurrying into my stockings when Clayton walked in and began to undress for a quick shower. I shimmied into my black slip with the lace top and sat down at the vanity to put on my makeup and comb my hair. From the bathroom Clayton said, "Hey, guess what I heard? Gabriel unearthed some evidence on a drilling company that he has been after for more than a year. He's going after them hell-bent for leather after the election. Guess whose company it is, or was; it has been dissolved for months."

"Hmm? I don't know," I said absently, picking up my lipstick.

"Jordan's."

My hands went down on the table before me. I turned white in the mirror's reflection. "The tie-in hasn't been made public yet, but the principals of the company were subpoenaed about a week ago. Louetta called me at the hospital this morning—apparently our phone is dead. She was worried about the fact he's your uncle. I told her I didn't think it would hurt your feelings any."

I felt as if my temples would burst through my head. I turned around and clasped my stomach. What time was it? Nearly two-fifteen. How could I find Jordan now? How stop him? No, I should have known. How stupid. How perfectly idiotic not to realize Jordan was using me to trap Gabriel, not to see through his sudden willingness to cooperate. God. What was I going to do? How was I going to stop this?

Clayton walked in, toweling off his hair. I jerked up from the bench as though I'd been sitting on a firecracker. "Are you almost ready?" he said.

"Uh . . . I don't think I can go. I—I feel so sick all of a sudden," I stammered. "Nerves, I guess." If I could get out of this, maybe I could find Jordan and force him to call off the killer. "Gad, what if my stomach is kicking up again? Maybe I ought to—"

"Oh no, you're going," he said rudely. "We're in this thing all the way to the end. You'll go if I have to carry you."

"All right, all right," I said. There was nothing I could do from here, having no idea where Jordan could be found. In fact, I now realized, he probably left town to divert suspicion from himself. Of course . . . that was why I couldn't get him on the telephone. I ran my tongue over my dry lips and collapsed on the vanity bench again, staring into my cloud-white face. I had to think of something. Oh, God, I had to do something. Yet, it was too late. Damn Jordan; damn him.

At twenty minutes before three we got into the car and hurried down the street. We weren't more than five minutes from city hall. All the way there I searched for a way. Yet there was no way out now. . . . Unless . . . unless I could warn Gabriel. Yet, if I said anything I would be incriminating myself as well as Jordan. Jordan knew that . . . he knew that. Damn him. No, it wouldn't work. My mind slammed up against one useless idea after another.

We were getting closer. I could now see the clock tower on city hall. Less than ten minutes to three. How could I stand up there helplessly and watch this happen? I felt I was going to come apart inside. Then, all at once, I knew. I would have to find the gunman. Mention Jordan's name and he'd know. Fringes of the crowd, Jordan had said. I'd have all the way through the first band concert, then the speech, to find him. Surely in all that time I could locate him and pull him off to the side, tell him the deal was canceled, to forget it and go home. If that did not work, then I would simply have to interrupt the rally and alert Gabriel, worry about the consequences later. Or pretend to have spotted the gun and . . .

"God, look at the people," Clayton said. They seemed to be heading toward Hermann Square from all sides.

We drove up to the curb on Walker and parked. I kept thinking how stupid I had been. All of his life Jordan had hated Gabriel Gerrard, had been jealous of him, envious of his money. Why did I not realize I was playing with fire by involving him in my troubles? Stupid. Stupid. Now I had to find someone I could not even recognize. I got out of the car and looked around. The clock on the huge central tower of city hall registered two fifty-five exactly. I looked down at the speaker's stand with its red, white, and blue bunting. In a few minutes we'd all walk up there in a line. The crowds were gathering. I had never seen so many people: people carrying signs, mothers pushing babies in their strollers, young people, old people, more and more. Reporters with their boxy cameras and flash equipment. There was no space whatsoever around the reflection pool or in front of it, between the speaker's stand and the pool itself. And as the moments ticked by, there was less and less of a fringe in the crowd. It looked like solid people to me. One thing for certain, however, the gunman would have to be somewhere near the front.

I would go up on the stand first, with everyone else, and have a look around to see what possible person might be the killer. Then, when the band began to play, I would tell them I could not stay any longer, that I was ill. All through the concert and through Gabriel's speech, I would walk among the people, hoping against hope I would find the person surely consigned to murder the wrong Gerrard.

Those of us on the back row would be seated before the front row. Alvareda wore a black dress with a big white collar and a small hat. Clayton helped her up the stairs first. Then came Bill Hansen's wife, then Stephen and Lilly before myself. When I saw Lilly my heart contracted. I thought of that night, so long ago, when Jordan made a pass at her and she ran to Gabriel. . . . Jordan's own words just weeks ago, that I had misunderstood, marched across my mind now . . . "My day will come." For what Gabriel did in Lilly's defense, plus what he was planning to do to Jordan now, plus all the hatred and jealousy centered on him and compounded through the years, he was about to be murdered . . . unless I could stop it. . . .

Next the front row: first Bill, then the mayor, then Louetta. She looked stunning today, in a deep brown coat with a leopard collar and matching leopard hat, and pretty brown pumps. Gabriel helped her up the steps. He wore a dark blue suit and blue tie flecked with maroon. His blond hair picked up the sun like a halo. She smiled and squeezed his hand. I could not look. I fiddled in my handbag for a handkerchief while Gabriel came up on the stand, then, at last, Clayton.

I could see nothing from my place on the second row.

When the band, grouped over to the left of us, struck up "The Eyes of Texas," I turned and said, "I'm going to be ill. I've got to get down from here."

"Go with her, Stephen," said Lilly.

"No, no. Just leave me alone. I'll be all right." I rushed down the stairs and tried, myself, to disappear in the crowd. I could not make out any special face. They all looked like people out to see the candidate. It seemed with every step I took, some reporter flashed a picture. I passed by lone men standing on the edges. One thought I was making a pass at him. He smiled and raised his hand. The hand was empty as far as I could tell. I went around the back pushing by people, excusing myself. It was just like at the Democratic Convention all those years ago, when Neal Gerrard became ill, and I was trying to push through the crowd. Then I was trying to help save a life. Now I was trying desperately to do the same thing, but it was all my fault, all my fault. . . . The other side, in front of the wing to the left of the speaker's stand. Faces, faces, so many of them, none looked strange. I looked down and up, up and down, down and up. Hands, pockets, suit coats with bulges. Sunglasses, scarves, handbags, gloves. I could see nothing clearly. There was a terrible glare produced by the band instruments.

The band stopped playing. I stood still while the mayor introduced Gabriel. That took two or three minutes. Then I watched Gabriel walk forward, proudly, confidently. The crowd threw up a great cheer. The bright sunlight glanced off his golden hair. Tears sprang to my eyes. I watched him fiddle with his notes. The wind was gusty, threatening to blow them off the stand. I kept thinking of all that he was, all that he could be, how much I loved him still . . . I had to stop this . . . must do something.

I let him get started, then when everyone was spellbound by his words, and they were, oh, they were entranced by him, you could feel it in the air, I began to poke about again, looking and looking everywhere, as desperately as someone trying to find his way out of a deep forest at nightfall. I looked back at the speaker's stand now and then, and once I saw Clayton walk up and help Gabriel hold down the flapping edges of the paper. Very unobtrusively. How thoughtful. . . . I wiped tears from my eyes. I could not let myself feel anything now, had to hold on. . . . There was still time. I could stop this, even if I had to interrupt Gabriel's speech. I looked up at the clock face on the tower. He'd only been talking five minutes. When the hands were pointed at three forty-five, I would make my way back up to the speaker's stand and stop everything. But I still had twenty minutes. Surely in that amount of time. . . . I looked some more. I saw someone who looked like a possibility. His left hand was shoved down inside his coat pocket. Yes. I watched him. The pocket bulged. I looked up at Gabriel again, licked my lips. I was sure that was him. I started toward him. . . .

And that was it. From a place I had not even looked, the shot was fired. From up above one of the building wings, the sniper had taken his aim, and before anyone else, I saw who it was. The blond head of Jordan was just barely recognizable above the rooftop.

It was all so very quick. Two, three seconds at most. My hands flew to my chest. I looked down at the speaker's stand again. Gabriel fell forward, his arms outspread. I could see the pain and shock on his face, the tight grimace across his mouth. My mind refused the shattering image before it. Screaming, "No, Gabriel!" Louetta reached out toward him. The pages of the speech pitched up into the air and fluttered sideways and down. There followed a second shot, and Clayton was flung to the left, slumping down against his brother. His right arm went out and upset a pitcher of water. The water flew out in a spray across the table and the pitcher rolled off and crashed to the ground. I looked up. Jordan was gone, my soul with him. Could he have tossed me the gun, I would have killed myself.

There were people, so many people, now swarming on the victims. All I could hear were the continuous sounds of my own screaming merged with all the others. And in just a few moments, there was the sound of the ambulance sirens.

Robin

1960

Chapter 1

It is four o'clock on Tuesday afternoon. Outside the sky is cloudless and blue, but the wind is chilly and persistent. Now and again it startles the bare limb of the tree near the window and causes it to scratch the glass like fingernails. I am sitting in the middle of my bedroom floor, with the gas heater flaming nearby, and whenever I hear the scratching I stop and look up and listen. As a child, I sat in this place many times and listened for the voice that I cannot help but listen for now. Then, I was paying for the mistakes of others; now I am paying for my own, because I never learned to stop counting on some things and some people.

At least now I know the truth, after having been lied to all my life. Certainly that is worth a lot, and when I leave here this time I won't be leaving any questions about my father, why he did such a terrible thing yet was spoken of with such kindness. That was the mystery that drove me away, or part of it. The other part was, who was he anyway, and why should his name be kept from me?

These things together would have driven anyone away, and especially someone like me. But the reasons went beyond the shroud of secrecy around my father. For one, it was terrible to live here in the house in the neighborhood best known for the crazy man who occupied it up until the mid-twenties. Some of the neighborhood parents remembered vividly how he stared through the windows at them when they walked past the house with their school books and lunch pails. His frightful visage caused them to quicken their steps. If someone chanced to ask, "Wasn't he your grandfather?" I would argue with the lie he was not, that he was just someone who rented the house from Nana while she lived elsewhere.

The exterior of the house embarrassed me. Even though Nana kept it painted and fixed up as well as she could, it was still old-fashioned, and the tiles at the curb were buckled and broken in places. Inside the house was furnished with old things, from carpet to furniture. In the kitchen was a cookstove that stood on legs, which Nana had been using since 1925. In the bathroom we had a footed tub, and the light fixture hung from the tall ceiling by a cord and switched on at the bulb. The bathroom tiles were white hexagon, broken in spots. There was only one girl friend—my next-door neighbor Charlotte Lang—whom I could invite over without feeling ashamed. Her house was not as old as ours, but it was old. After it burned to the ground one night, her family moved to a new house over in Idylwood by the Forest Park Cemetery.

I sometimes wished our house would burn so we could move to Idylwood, but Nana would never have moved as long as her house remained standing. Nana herself was the other source of my unhappiness. It was not that I didn't love her—I did, and trusted her, too, for a long time—it was only that other kids had a mother and a father, brothers and sisters, and I had only Nana for a while and, later, Aunt Senta, whose presence only made things worse. The only grown-up man who came around was my great-uncle Jordan Leider, and he did not come very often or stay very long. My memories of how Uncle Jordan looked are vague but I was frightened of him, I know that, and for reasons I could not identify. Nana seemed to be watchful of him, as though she expected him to steal something, or do something terrible. Well, I guess my instincts were sharp when it came to him.

For the first eight years of my life, there were two major consolations: one was my friendship with Alexander Gerrard, and the other was my dream that someday my father would return and take me away with him.

Alexander was someone whose devotion I never doubted, and whose frequent visits I assumed would go on forever, no matter where I was, even when my father took me away to live with him. In fact, I was certain that when my father returned, he would take me to live in a house as fine as Alexander's, and as I assumed all the beautiful houses that existed were in Alexander's neighborhood, then it followed that when I moved to my father's house, I would see Alexander even more often than before.

As though it happened yesterday, I can close my eyes and see the long Lincoln sedan approach the curb: I am seized with shyness. I run up the stairs and wait in my room, hardly taking a breath until I hear Nana bid Alexander and his grandmother Alvareda welcome. Then she says, "I believe Robin is upstairs, Alexander. Why don't you call her while I put some cookies on a plate?"

He comes to the bottom of the stairs and calls, somewhat impatiently, as though it is incomprehensible that I should be up here when he is down there, "Robin, are you up there? Come down!"

Filled with joy, I rush down the stairs to meet him.

To me Alexander was a prince with blond curls, who would someday grow up to be a king. And I would sit beside him on the throne in an imaginary kingdom where there was nothing but happiness. After all, he lived in a palace in the enchanted kingdom of River Oaks, and his house sat in a yard so great that you must go up a long, curved drive before you saw it at all, back among the tall trees, and then its massive size, its deep roof and shining mullioned windows, its beautiful setting of bright flowers and thick green grass, made you feel you had been transported into another world, a fairyland people read of in storybooks. At his birthday parties, there were long tables with white cloths, china and silverware. The birthday cake was always as tall as a wedding cake, and we were usually entertained with a real circus clown who could juggle and do acrobatics.

And then came November 2, 1940. On that Saturday afternoon Nana sat in her cane-back rocker in the library and turned on the radio. Together we listened to Gabriel Gerrard deliver his speech, his voice deep with authority. Suddenly Nana's hands went to her chest; her face was stricken. "God have mercy," she cried. And it was very hard to connect that moment with what I was later told. Uncle Jordan had murdered Gabriel Gerrard, had nearly killed and seriously injured the brain of Aunt Senta's husband Uncle Clayton, then had been fatally shot while escaping from city hall.

Alexander did not come over anymore, and the few times I saw him after that, he was different. Our friendship was shattered by things we could not control. But that was not all that was shattered for me. A short time later, I came home from school one day to see Nana crying. I thought she was upset because we had just learned that the property next door where the Langs used to live would soon be occupied by a drive-in grocery store—an icehouse. Nana had been worried that there would be people loitering and drinking beer within "a stone's throw" of our house. She did not hear me come in because of the noise created by the cement truck at work outside, and I stood at the dining room door and watched her for a while, uncomfortable at the sight of her pushing the iron across the board with one hand and dabbing her eyes with the other. When she saw me she propped up the iron and came toward me. She put her arms on my arms and said, "Robin, I have something to tell you. I have just received word that your father died . . . some time ago. I'm sorry." She hugged me and cried some more. I stood rigidly in her grasp, looking out at the rising dust off the white shell paving, too stunned to shed a tear.

Nana had never said anything that prompted me to believe he was ever coming back for me, and I am sure she did not realize how deeply I nurtured that dream. I had always been told that he had left my mother Laura shortly before I was born in New Orleans, that they had been living there together because he worked on a boat that docked at the port. Nana never spoke my father's name, but if I questioned her about him she always said he was a good man, kind and gentle. Even a child can arrive at the conclusion that such a nice person must have had some reason to leave his family, and I concluded that most likely he went off to seek his fortune, as people do in books, and would be back as soon as he found it.

Now, I reasoned that night as I lay in bed, I am like Alexander. My father will not come home again. Never in my life can I remember feeling so completely alone. I cried so long and hard that Nana heard me and came to hold me in her arms.

Around that time Aunt Senta came to live with us. She had tried remaining in her house off Montrose Boulevard after the tragedy in November, but she could not walk out into the yard without someone staring at her. She could not go to the grocery store without people whispering about the terrible event. She did not have a lot of money (and no hope for much in the future, I later learned, because Uncle Clayton's estate was put in trust for his hospital care and at his death it would revert to the charity endowment begun by his father Neal Gerrard decades earlier), so she decided it would be best to move in with us.

She soon went to work as a private-duty nurse. Her hours were from eleven at night to seven in the morning, and they were part of the resentment I felt toward her. Because she slept during the day, I was under the strictest instruction to be quiet. I walked around in my stocking feet most of the time, and especially upstairs where our bedrooms were—by then I slept in the room across from hers.

Aunt Senta was strict and harsh. On many occasions when she scolded me, Nana came to my aid and told her she wasn't ever to treat me the way she had "treated Laura." Nana put up with her, I think, because she felt sorry for her. Aunt Senta was a beautiful woman, and her life was empty. It consisted of going to visit her husband at St. Vincent's Home once a week (she never talked of those visits with me, and never took me with her), and working. She rejoined the Catholic Church about the time she moved in with us, and seemed determined to live out her faith. I still remember watching her nail a crucifix upon the wall above her bed. She kept a rosary and a Missal near at hand. She went to mass on Sundays and all holy days. She often made me go with her, on days I was not in school. She would come home in the morning from her nursing case, change clothes, and get me out of bed. We'd catch the bus at the corner and ride down to Annunciation Church. She talked to me about adopting the Catholic faith; it was as though she felt obligated to look after my spiritual development lest my soul be in danger. Yet I would not, because she tried so hard to force me.

I can remember only one occasion when Aunt Senta seemed to look kindly on me. When I was just turning thirteen, starting to develop curves and to experience the monthly menses, she came into my room one day—I had just bathed and was letting my long hair dry while I looked at a magazine. She took my face in her hands and said, "Robin, you're going to be a beauty . . .

no, look at me, don't be shy. Don't make the same mistakes that I did. Don't use your looks to get your way." Then she began talking to me again about becoming a Catholic. I stopped listening; I was thrilled by the compliment. Just for a little while, I could believe she might be right.

Through all those years of growing up lonely, in an environment that was different from the way other children lived, I often let my mind dwell on my fantasies about my father. I knew, or thought I knew, so much about my mother. I had seen her drawings, had touched her clothing, her hairbrush, her few pieces of jewelry, and the other things she left behind. On the wall of Nana's bedroom there was a portrait made of her at the age of fifteen, and so I knew how she looked, that she was pretty in a less showy fashion than her older sister Senta, and resembled her brother John. I knew that Aunt Senta bullied her a lot, that she was shy and retiring, loved to draw and sometimes to play the piano. For me she had a past, a chronicle of her short life. And her death was real to me because I knew she died giving birth to me, and because I could visit her grave at the Forest Park Cemetery and see the whole cycle of her life engraved on a marker: "Laura Farrish, 1915–1932."

Except for her married name. When I asked why she changed her name back to Farrish, Nana said that my mother preferred it, that she did not want to carry the name of a man who abandoned her and her child. I believe it was from the moment I heard that statement that I first began to wonder about the contradictory stories of the kind of man he was.

More and more I was impatient with Nana's only answer to my questions about him: that there was much she wanted to tell me someday, but I was not yet old enough to understand. If I asked when I would be old enough, she would say she was not certain, but whenever the time arrived we would sit down together and have a long talk. Aunt Senta would tell me nothing. She always said I would have to "get it from Nana." Then she would go back to filing her fingernails or putting on her lipstick.

And so I waited, trusting Nana to come through with the answers. If I had not depended on Nana so much, I know the argument that finally erupted between us would have taken place much sooner than it did, and I might have been saved from more than one serious mistake.

Chapter 2

From the time I entered Stephen F. Austin Senior High School, it seemed obvious Nana wanted me to have a better life than she had, and that she was putting a great deal of effort toward that. Sometimes she told me the reasons behind the decisions she made for me. Other times I sensed her decisions were based on her hopes. She seemed to feel that my high school years would be a sort of make-or-break period in my life, and looking back I suppose she was right.

That summer of 1947, she had a lot of work done on the exterior of the house. She had all the trim painted, had a new roof put on, and ordered a new wicker swing for the front porch. She hired a man named Mr. Nickleby (he frequented the icehouse next door, and came looking for work one day) to care for the yard and tend the gardens because her continued back pain made yard work impossible. Part of the time she used a cane, especially when climbing the stairs.

She frequently asked my opinion about such matters as a color of paint or the shape of a new planter for the porch. But when it came to the tiles at the curb, she was unyielding to my wishes. Long ago she had ordered two of the blue tiles removed from the letter "B" to form an "E." Now she abruptly refused when I asked her to remove them all.

"But nobody has these old things on their front walk anymore."

"I don't care," she said. "They've been in that spot since I came to live here, and as long as I am alive, they will remain."

I did not argue further. After all, this property was her wedding gift from the Gerrard family in 1906, and even before that, when it was no more than a wilderness, she had spent time here. She had always loved every part of it.

After a few moments, she put her arm around me. "They don't really look so terrible, do you think? I know how important it is for a girl your age to be proud of her home."

And thus she conveyed the reason for all the work in the first place.

That was not all. One night she came to my room while I was reading, and said there was a little money left over from the house repairs. We could use it to redecorate my room.

I had moved into the big bedroom opposite Aunt Senta's as a child, when I began to find it difficult to breathe in the nursery. Nana had surmised the ventilation was not good because the nursery was at the back of the house and had only one double window in it. She also assumed that my frequent night-mares of being suffocated, which began around the same time and from which I would often awaken screaming, were caused by the fact that I could not breathe. The doctor bore out this theory and said that my nasal passages were not very large and I probably grew congested easily.

I had no problems breathing once I moved into the big front bedroom, and the nightmares did not recur.

Nana now walked from one end of the room to the other, full of questions about what colors I would prefer in wallpaper, bedspread, curtains, and car-pet. When she had paused to sit down in the rocker and hear my thoughts, her eyes were bright with enthusiasm.

"Anything you want is fine," I said. "It doesn't matter." I did not think the changes she suggested would help much to relieve the severe look created in the room by the massiveness of the furniture, left over from my great-grand-mother Carlotta's estate. Yet I didn't mean to sound so uninterested.

I was trying to think of something nicer to say when she drew in a deep sigh, raised herself with her cane from the chair, and took my face in her hands. "Robin, you break my heart sometimes."

"Why? All I meant was—"

"You are so very much like me at the same age. I have hoped, for all of your life, that you would be . . . gay . . . confident of yourself. You are such a lovely girl, you know, much prettier than I was."

I shrugged and looked away. How could she expect me to be any different?

Undaunted, she awoke me early on Saturday morning so that we could catch the bus at the corner and be downtown by the time the stores opened at nine o'clock. There is much about that day I will never forget. I dressed more quickly than she, and went downstairs to sit on her bed while she finished her face and hair. Except for my own room, I had always liked her room the best, with its white woodwork and lavender prints and sheer curtains over the big windows. Today as always she entertained me with stories about the various figurines upon the shelves above the mantel, which had been brought back from all over the world by her good friend, Alvareda Gerrard. She was very proud of the fragile figurines. She would always end her monologue with the encouragement that I should travel when I grow up. "If you could go abroad just for a while, you would be fortunate," she would say, and once I asked her which foreign country she thought would be the best to visit. She ran her finger along the edge of a little ballerina from Paris and said, "France. If I could go to France, I believe my life would be complete."

She would not tell me why.

Otherwise, I liked Nana's room because in here was kept the portrait of my mother. Now while Nana fashioned her gray hair into the proverbial twist and dabbed Chantilly—her favorite cologne—on each of her wrists, I looked at the portrait for a while, then said, "Nana, when we redecorate my room, could we put Mother's portrait on my wall?"

She turned as though I had surprised her, then reached for her face powder. "I guess you could," she said. "It's just that it's the only one I have and if it's up in your room I could not enjoy it so much. You can come in and out of here any time you please."

"She was my mother, though," I said defiantly.

She turned to me again. "She was my daughter."

I looked away. "Nana, you know that picture of you and my grandfather in the album, the one taken when you got married?"

"Yes . . ." She went back to powdering her face.

"Did my mother and father have a wedding picture made?"

She stopped, but did not turn. "No."

"Why not?"

"Because . . . because it was during the Depression. There was no money for niceties then."

That was disappointing. I was built like my mother—according to Aunt Senta—small-boned, with high breasts and slender hips and legs. Yet I did not look like my mother in the face, and of course my eyes were blue, my hair, blond.

"I wish I could see just one picture of my father. Do I look like him?"

She turned to me now and smiled. "Yes, Robin, you do."

"How? Is it my face, my hair, or what?"

"Oh . . . it's hard to describe. Listen, if you want the portrait of Laura in your room, maybe it is your turn to have it for a while." She picked up her purse. "Let's go. It's almost time for the bus to come by."

We shopped all morning, up and down Main Street. We picked out figured wallpaper with blue cornflowers and a pretty border around the top. We chose a floral upholstery material for the rocker seat with blue, pink, and purple snapdragons on it. We ordered a beige rug with muted trellis design, and we bought sheer lace panels for the windows. We bought a new lamp with a tulip shade for my bedside, and a blue cotton spread and pillow shams for the bed.

After all these errands, Nana looked more energetic than I had ever seen her. "I just love shopping downtown," she said.

"But you almost never come."

"That's because I don't like to come alone. I like to have a shopping partner. Tell you what. Let's go to James Coney Island for lunch, shall we?"

I had been there many times before, with Aunt Senta, but I did not want to spoil her joy by telling her. We waited in a line that snaked around and outside the door to the noisy lunch room—they were always crowded at noon. Above the loud clatter of wooden chairs scraping across the tile floor, we ordered two hot dogs each with Fritos and Dr. Peppers. Nana looked at hers, then eyed me guiltily and handed her plate back to the man behind the counter. "More onions, please."

The server was already taking the order from the next person in line but he plunked another spoonful of onions on each hot dog. Satisfied now, Nana winked and smiled at me. "You mustn't be afraid to demand what you want," she said. "Come along, and let's eat upstairs where it's less noisy. I need to talk with you about something important." Seeming to have forgotten her painful back, she trooped up the stairs in front of me, with her cane swinging from her arm. As we passed up the narrow staircase, I saw a girl from school eating with a friend downstairs. She nodded hello, then whispered something in the ear of her friend. I wanted to go through the floor. Why did I have to see one of the most popular girls in school when I was trailing behind my grandmother?

Neither of us spoke through the first hot dog. I was already feeling guilty for my embarrassment at being seen with her. Finally she wiped her mouth and said, "You know, Robin, this is the best day I've had in a long time. It has given me a real lift."

"You look like a young girl," I said, attempting to salve my own conscience.

"Do I?" she said, and suddenly her eyes filled with tears. She paused to wipe them.

"What's wrong, Nana?"

"Oh, I expect it's the onions," she said with a laugh, then with a look of resolution on her face she said, "No, that isn't it. I just want so much for you to be happy. There are so many things I wish I could have given you."

"What?"

"Oh, things you could not understand—"

"About my father?" I asked hopefully.

"No. Most of all, my youth I guess . . ."

"Oh, you're not so old, not for a grandmother."

In fact, she would soon celebrate her fifty-eighth birthday. Yet her skin was good, her face almost youthful. While her breasts were large and grandmotherly, her figure was slender for a woman her age. She looked as though she might start crying again, so I changed the subject. "While we're shopping, why don't you buy a new stove?" The bottom of her oven had rusted through in a small area, and I hoped that would prompt her to replace it at last.

"I wouldn't think of it. That old stove has been warming my kitchen for too many years. It still makes the best angelfood cake in town." She paused. "Does the stove embarrass you?"

"No, no, of course not," I lied.

"Good. Now, I want to talk with you about . . . well . . . about . . ."

I looked up. "What?"

"I'm concerned about you. You have so few interests for a girl your age

. . . you hardly go anywhere, or . . ." She sighed. "I know you've never liked the house, and I'm hoping that with the changes we're making you will invite people over a little more often. But I've been thinking of something else, something that will really give you a boost as you begin high school."

I couldn't imagine what she was talking about. I had already decided not to join the band as Charlotte planned to do. I was considering the debate team . . .

"I want you to join the Scottish Brigade."

The idea took me by surprise. The drill team was a very prestigious group. I had never thought of myself as becoming a part of it. The girls were popular, outgoing, they—

"I've been talking to Mrs. Eldridge over on Walker. You know, her daughter graduated last year and she was a brigadier.

"Anyhow, Mrs. Eldridge thought it would be good for you. Scholarship is uppermost in Brigade, and you've always made excellent grades. It would give you a chance to meet new friends. It would help you gain some self-confidence." She paused. "Honestly, Robin, you have so much in your favor yet you just hide away and don't try to develop any social life at all."

I had never looked at it that way exactly. Maybe she was right. Still, the idea of trying out for something like the Scottish Brigade was a little frightening. What if I didn't make it?

"My back problems be hanged," she was saying, "I'd have belonged to a drill squad if there had been such a thing when I was your age. It might have changed . . . well . . . a few things about my life."

Over the next few days I thought about it. It seemed to mean so much to Nana, and she had already gone to so much expense to fix the house in my behalf, I felt I owed it to her to give it a try. I vowed to resign after summer practice if I didn't like it, and she agreed. "That's fair enough."

I decided to try for the Drill Corps—the girls who danced the Scottish dances to the tune of the bagpipes. Over that summer, wearing my white shorts and cotton shirt, I found I could pick up the steps and rhythms easily. By fall I was as thoroughly steeped in the strict rules and traditions of the drill team as anyone else, and I began to excel. By the end of the first year I was promoted from the reserve unit to the regular corps, and was issued the proud uniform of plaid woolen kilt and green gabardine coat, granny shoes with white spats, and black hat with plaid ribbon and green feather. For the first time in my life I really felt proud of myself, and Nana was filled with joy. She took rolls of pictures of me at each half-time football game performance and every parade.

I developed many new friendships. I began to have girls over for slumber parties after Friday-night performances. Nana made dozens of cookies, tuna fish and pimento cheese sandwiches, dips for potato chips and Fritos. She boiled and chilled pounds and pounds of shrimp. She iced down cases of

Coca-Cola. Because of her efforts, my friends in Brigade loved coming to our house for slumber parties. And they were intrigued by the house itself. It was more interesting than where they lived. My bedroom was a great place for sitting around in the dark telling ghost stories. It was great, too, for sitting around talking about boys.

During my first year at Austin I had very few dates, and most of these were blind dates arranged by other, more popular, Brigade friends, and were less interesting than staying home and reading a book. I felt vaguely disappointed. I did not think of Alexander with any regularity anymore. The last time I saw him was at one of his extravagant birthday parties years before, when I was eleven, and I felt clearly that I had no business being there. The other kids were not like me, and Alexander paid his attention to another girl instead of me. I went home early and cried because of that and because I felt I had looked so foolish. Yet I still had romantic hopes that a boy as swell as he had been at one time might turn up and invite me out. Only it would be someone not so far above my social level, now that I had come to know what that was. McKinney Avenue was a long way from River Oaks in some important respects. That I would ever belong in a place like the one in which Alexander lived had been a silly dream that was shattered with the death of my father.

My second year was different. I dated two boys, both of whom I liked. Winston Carlson was a bright boy who wore glasses and participated in the debate team. He was a year ahead of me in school. His dream was to be an attorney someday, and his family had no better means of financing his education than mine did. I suppose what drew us together was a mutual love of books, and it always seemed like an important fact that we had a lot to talk about while we were together. Nana seemed to approve of him, and remarked that he was the most serious-minded boy for his age she had ever seen, with the exception of Clayton Gerrard. I felt no great physical attraction for Winston, and he was not what you would call aggressive when it came to that subject.

The other boy, Roy Kingsley, was another story. Roy had only recently moved into the East End. His family bought a house in Country Club—the nicest neighborhood in the area—which reflected the prosperity of his father, who owned a restaurant-supply business. Roy was good-looking. He had brown hair, which he kept very short, and beautiful brown eyes and long lashes (for which he received much kidding). He was not more than average height, and had a big chest and shoulders. He looked like a candidate for the football team, but he intended to become a doctor, following the wishes of his father. When he asked me for a date, I was excited in a way I had never been excited about Winston. He was more possessive, too, than Winston, and it was not long before Winston was shoved aside. Certainly Nana could not but approve of Roy. That Roy's parents did not approve of me was not apparent at first.

By the end of our junior year, Roy had been voted class president. I had been selected drill major—one of the top offices in the Scottish Brigade. Thus we were catapulted into the status of most admired couple of the senior class. We must have been carried away by the force of success. I had never been happier in my life, or busier. Everyone knew me. I was in all the clubs, from the Senior Sub-Debs to the Honor Society. My life was a constant swirl of Brigade performances, sock hops, club meetings, slumber parties, and dates with Roy. The physical attraction was strong between us. Often I pushed him away right at the point of surrender, and so of course it seemed logical to talk of marriage. I could not think of anything I wanted more. We became engaged, though Roy planned to give me my engagement ring on the night of graduation. I had applied for and won a scholarship at Baylor in Waco, where Roy was going. Roy believed his parents would support us both as we completed our college degrees. Maybe they would not have, under any circumstances. But as it happened they found an easy out.

Just before graduation, Roy came over one afternoon and said, "Could I talk to you?"

I sat out on the porch steps looking up at him as he stood nearby. "I—I'm afraid I'm going to have to break our engagement," he said.

The announcement hit me like a fist. "What? I don't understand," I exclaimed. "Why?"

He bowed his head. "I'd rather not say . . . it's what my parents want."

I was floored at the sudden realization they did not like me; I had always thought they did. "But there must be some reason," I insisted. "Surely they owe us some explanation," I added, still hanging onto the hope that it wasn't what Roy wanted, and therefore we were on the same side.

He hesitated a moment longer, and put his arm out on the porch rail. "It's about your mother."

I felt a pricking at the back of my neck. "What about her?" I asked.

He looked away from me, then back again. "It isn't what I think, remember. Only, my parents hold the purse strings on my college education. If I expect to become a doctor I have to have their help, that's all. They've put it to me this way . . . ."

"What about my mother?"

He hesitated then began, "My mother was talking to someone who has lived in East End for a long time. The woman said that your mother was— well, she called her a bad name."

"Tell me."

"She said she was a—slut. She said you were illegitimate . . . that no one could say for sure . . . who your father is."

My heart collapsed. I could not speak. He sat down beside me. "I told her that was crazy, that it wasn't true."

"Well, you're right. It isn't," I said defensively. My voice shook with outrage. Yet all at once I knew that somewhere, at some time in my life, I had heard my mother called that name, and that the tag for me was appropriate as well.

". . . but there isn't much I can do about it, unless somehow my mother was proven wrong."

"Well, I'm sure she will be. We'll just talk to my grandmother about this right now."

He backed away. "I—uh—I have to go to Oshman's right now, but I'll be home later this evening." He turned and hurried down the walk.

I stood up. "Roy? Wait. Will you call me?"

He got into his car and drove off. I stood there, gaping at the empty space where his car had been parked, unable to believe this could happen to me. He would call me back tonight, of course he would, and all this would be over. We loved each other . . . surely he couldn't just walk away. . . .

I rushed inside and found Nana at the dining room table. She was busy cutting strips of ocean green satin for the flounces on my prom gown, the prom that Roy and I were to have attended together a week from now. "I want to talk to you," I said, and told her what had just transpired.

The change in expression that gradually overtook her face betrayed the fact that she had expected something like this to happen. When I finished, she looked away from me and put the scissors down.

"Why would anyone say a thing like that?" I demanded. "Is it true?"

"Of course not. That's the ugliest thing I have ever heard."

"Nana, it isn't the first time someone has said that."

She looked at me, her eyes wide. "What are you talking about?"

"I don't know. I just know someone has said that before."

She shook her head. "That's nonsense."

"What would have given anyone that idea, though?" I asked. There was something about the way she was handling this that made me feel as though the ground were dissolving under me.

"I—I don't know. Laura was one of the sweetest souls in the world. That's a cruel thing to say about her, especially when she is defenseless."

"Tell me the truth about my father now. I want to know. I can't go through life not knowing. If I had known the truth I could have set the record straight. But I had to sit there like an idiot because you have never told me.

"Am I? Am I illegitimate?"

She looked at me for a long moment, then she said, "That anyone could say that about you is abominable. If ever a child was wanted or loved by both her parents, it is you."

"Then, tell me the truth. I'm old enough. Why would you wait, now, when my future with Roy depends on it?"

"If you try to force the issue now, in order to hold on to this boy—I don't care how wonderful you think he is—you are foolish. If he does not love you enough to want you for yourself, then you are far better off without him."

I was infuriated. She wasn't going to wriggle out of this now. "If you don't tell me right now, I swear I'll find out for myself," I warned her.

Her face was hard, yet she spoke very softly. "I can't tell you now, Robin. I just can't. I'm not ready. Not yet."

I glared back at her. "I'll make Aunt Senta tell me. She knows."

At first she was silent, and there was something in her expression that I could not identify . . . something close to fear. I had never seen her look that way before. At last she said, "Senta knows less than she thinks. Whatever you might learn from her would only confuse you because she doesn't know the truth either."

I searched for the adequate words to hurt her. "I'll never trust you again, Nana, I don't love you anymore."

She looked as though I had destroyed her. Tears flooded her eyes. She drew up her shoulders and walked unevenly away from the table. A long strip of green satin material slid off the table and collapsed in a heap on the floor. I sat there with tears running down my face. I felt my life was over. The whole past three years had been one enormous bad joke played on me. I had thought I was someone special at last, had felt the world was open to me. Now I felt that I never wanted to step foot out of my house again, for fear of what people were saying about me.

That night, Roy did not call. Nana sat out on the porch and rocked and wept. I had not seen her do this since Alvareda Gerrard died years earlier. I sat in the library and agonized. She held my future in her hands, and she didn't care. Whatever the truth about my parents, it could not be worse than what I had heard today. Yet she would not tell me. I hated her. Somehow I'd get back at her.

On the night of the senior prom I stayed up in my bedroom and wept. I moved through the graduation exercises like a stone. That summer I began to go out with Winston Carlson, and before fall we ran away and got married. I was never to see Nana alive again.

Chapter 3

Even in the beginning I don't believe I intended to cut myself off from Nana forever. I only wanted to prove that I did not need the precious secret she withheld from me in order to be happy, or to make my life complete. That I did not see her at all between that time and this was due to the way my life evolved. I never reached a point when I could go back and face her and say truthfully that I had been right in leaving. I sent her my address whenever it changed, and occasionally she would write. But she never made any indication that she was ready to apologize and have the talk I had waited for during the first seventeen years of my life. I did miss her. At times I would have given anything to go home and be held in her arms. My own scorching declaration that I did not love her haunted me more and more; the look in her eyes as she heard the words tortured me; yet I could not rescind what I had said, not in a letter, not as a peace offering. I was determined to go back home on my own terms. Then we could have a new beginning. . . .

For a while Winston and I got along all right. I never told him that the real reason for my marriage to him had nothing to do with love. Perhaps he sensed it from the beginning. We spent our wedding night in a nice motel out on South Main, near Playland Park. I can remember the disappointing lack of passion that left me feeling so let down. We were both completely inexperienced at sex, yet I felt even then that surely there ought to have been at least a kind of joy. It was all so quick, as though he were ashamed of himself, or me, or us, and didn't want to draw it out. Maybe it's like this for everybody, I reasoned uneasily.

Sometime before midnight I awoke. I got up and walked to the window, and looked out across the street at the glowing neon signs in front of the park. They had always reminded me of big toothbrushes upended. The great ribbons of lights on the roller coaster were burning brightly. I could hear the squeals of the people riding in the open cars as they slowly crested the heights of the amazing network of crisscrossed bars, then plunged almost straight down. And I thought: It should have been that way, making love with Winston, should have had that excitement . . . that sort of . . . daredevil release. . . .

I looked back at his sleeping face and thought, I don't love you. That was the first time I had ever really stopped to articulate my feelings, and I wondered whether Winston loved me, or just loved an ideal he had seen in me while we were in school together.

We kept our commitment to each other for a long time. Winston had been accepted his second year of college into S.M.U. in Dallas, and had acquired some scholarship money and some money from the government because his father had been killed in the war. It was not enough to live on, and I worked in order to help support us while he went to school year round. I first had a job as a filing clerk in a title company office, and eventually went to business school at night so that I could get a higher-paying job. I hated every moment of it, the typing, the shorthand, the bookkeeping machines. But I always held on to the hope someday I would be able to do what I wanted, to teach English. My own scholarship money at Baylor had been revoked of course, but I was not smart enough to worry about that at the time. Our plan was for Winston to obtain his degree, then to support us while I obtained mine. Yet by the time he had his law degree, he was no longer committed to me or my education. He had done very well in school, was considered a promising young attorney, and I think he suddenly blossomed as people will, and wanted to put his old life and his old way of looking at himself behind him. I was a living reminder of those years he wanted to forget. During the first summer after he finished school, he fell in love with a secretary in the firm where he worked, and asked me for a divorce.

At first I self-righteously refused. I had not been so devastated since the day the terrible argument erupted between Nana and me. Thus began a long period of conflict with him. I did not answer any letter that came from Nana —I could not move the pen across the paper I was so distraught, not even when she told me Aunt Senta had cancer and was not expected to live out the year. I was so caught up in my own problems, I failed to imagine how hard it must be for Nana to care for a seriously ill daughter, the physical as well as the emotional trials she was certainly put through. Her letters dropped off completely after a while. I did not hear from her until after Aunt Senta's death, and I knew she had not called me home for the funeral because she was embittered that I had given her no support during the ordeal. I am sure, too, that she took my neglect as a sign that I never intended to mend my relationship with her because she never wrote again. I felt no great affection for Aunt Senta and did not have any real regrets I had not seen her before her death or attended her funeral. I can hardly believe now that I was that cynical, but I was and now it is too late to rectify my failures in that and in many other areas.

In the end I gave into divorce as any one eventually would. I changed my name back to Farrish, like my mother before me. Winston promised to help me with the expense of going to school, and he gave me our house, which I sold for a small amount of equity. I entered college in the fall of 1956, and took a very small efficiency apartment near the campus. The next four years were the hardest ever because there was never enough money to get by on. I took part-time jobs here and there, now and then, but never allowed a job to interfere with my full academic schedule. And I thought of Nana often, every time one more semester passed and I was brought closer to obtaining my degree. I finished at the end of the summer of this year, and started to write her. But then I decided it was so near Christmas that I would wait. I would go home and see her, and tell her I had made it on my own. And maybe then she would consider me mature enough to tell me what I had really never given up wanting to know.

I did not admit to myself then that I was now almost frightened of going home, for I had let so much time pass and had flagrantly injured her feelings. Maybe she would refuse to see me. Maybe she would not tell me . . . well, there were other things to do, good reasons to wait and go home during the holidays. One was the fact I was driving the same car that Winston had bought used while he was in school. I was not sure I would trust it for the two hundred and fifty miles to Houston. I would need to save money for transportation, and besides that, I needed clothes and shoes. I needed—well, virtually everything.

I learned just a few days before the fall semester began that I had been chosen for a position in the English Department at St. Paul's Academy, an expensive and well-respected private school in Dallas. I was chosen over four other applicants. I would be teaching the gifted English students. When I found out about it I was ecstatic for the first time since I won the office of Drill Major in the Scottish Brigade in high school. Salaries were above average at St. Paul's, and by Christmastime I would be able to save enough money for the trip home. How perfect, I thought, that I had waited until I had this good news to report to Nana. She would have no choice but to admire me.

In October I moved into a new apartment near the school. It was in a large complex and my efficiency unit was to be upstairs, looking down at the swimming pool. On moving day I learned the unit of my choice had developed a leak in one of the walls, and would have to be repaired before I could move in. I did not have time to wait, as my old apartment lease had expired. The new apartment manager showed me another efficiency far from the pool, and I decided to take it, though I did not like the location as well. It was twenty dollars a month cheaper, and I certainly could use the extra cash. I needed to write Nana of my new address, but I put it off. Christmas holidays were coming up soon and I was very busy with my new job. . . .

Then, the week before Thanksgiving, I received a wire from someone whom I would have never expected to contact me. Alexander Gerrard sent the message of Nana's death that morning of November 15. He asked that I call him immediately in Houston.

The words pierced me like a sword. My mind struggled with the realization that time had run out for Nana and me . . . that she was no longer as I had envisioned her for years, sitting quietly in her library, awaiting my return. I felt a deep wrenching inside. I gave Alexander's number to the long distance operator.

"Robin? Is that you? I'm awfully sorry—" he began. At the sound of the grown-up voice, resonant with the strength that as a child I had instinctively known was there, I sat down on the telephone bench, a tightness in my chest and throat that made it almost impossible to get any words to come forth. Finally I asked him if he knew what had happened, and he had more information than I would have expected, even in my distracted state.

"She had not been ill," he assured me. "Her heart was weak—she had known this for a while—and at the end, it simply failed."

I gripped the receiver . . . weak heart . . . broken heart. . . . "Nana, I don't love you anymore. . . ." Tears were now stinging behind my eyes.

"There is a burial policy that covers everything necessary for the arrangements," he was saying now. "If you want, I can reserve a time for the service. Just let me know when you can get here."

I considered at length. Right then I was having trouble remembering what day it was. At last I told him I could come the next day, and we could have the service on Friday.

"All right," he said. He told me I'd need to call the funeral home and give them the information for the obituary. "And they need the names of six pallbearers."

Pallbearers. The term brought me skidding into the reality of all that awaited doing. I had no idea where to begin—"Would you be one?" I asked.

"Of course. I'd be glad to. Will you be flying down, or driving?"

"I—I'll have to fly," I told him, wondering whether I would be able to afford the plane ticket.

"Let me know your arrival time and I'll meet you and your husband at the airport. The weather down here is really nasty."

"I'll be . . . traveling alone. I'll wire you the details."

"Is there anyone you want me to contact?"

I had not even thought of that. I considered a moment. Aunt Patricia. I still had her address and phone number somewhere, at least I hoped I did. "Not unless you think of people that your family knows too. I'll call Aunt Patricia."

"Okay. Do you have a pencil? Write down my address and telephone number. . . . Say, I had a hard time finding you."

"Oh?"

"Elzyna had given her attorney an address and phone number for you that is apparently outdated by now. Luckily she also gave him the name of the firm your husband was with at the time, so I finally traced you beginning there."

"Oh yes, I—I'm sorry for all the trouble." I started to explain about the divorce, but decided to wait.

"I'll see you tomorrow."

"Thanks, Alexander."

Having an immediate purpose must be the most powerful weapon against grief, and I was aware that I was using it almost from the time I hung up the telephone. As long as I stayed busy, I could avoid dwelling on things that were horrible to face, especially my own failings. Nana, I don't love you anymore, my thoughts echoed. I closed them out. I hurriedly searched through my box of papers—one could not distinguish such a collection by calling it a file—until I found an old book with Aunt Patricia's telephone number. It would be a miracle if this were current. I dialed "o." I had not stopped to prepare myself for what I had to relate to Aunt Patricia. I had not seen her since I was thirteen or fourteen. Several years after her husband George Stanley died, leaving her quite wealthy, she married a man they had known in Wimberley. Her name was now Baughman. That was all I knew about her. The telephone was ringing. Someone younger answered and called her to the phone.

When I told her about Nana she was silent briefly, then said in a kind of resigned way, "All right, when is the funeral?"

"Day after tomorrow, I hope. Forest Park is handling it. I'll call you from there and let you know the details."

"All right. Should I bring anything? Will there be a reception afterward at your house?"

Oh, Lord, had Nana told her nothing about my leaving? I said I didn't think so, and told her about Alexander helping with arrangements.

"Is he one of the Gerrards?" she said.

"Yes, ma'am." I asked her if I should arrange a place for her to stay, or would she like to stay at Nana's house? I was not sure what I would find there, and told her so, explaining I had not lived there for a long time, nor had I been home.

"Oh yes, that's right. Elzyna said you left. I'd forgotten. The older I get, the less I can depend on my memory. Just a minute."

She was away from the phone for a long time, and when she finally returned she said, "My family will bring me down. Susan has a new Imperial that's road-worthy. I don't drive anymore, myself. Can't see well enough."

I had no idea who Susan was, and did not want to ask.

She continued, "We'll probably stay with my nephew on George's side, so plan for us to meet at the funeral home."

I told her that would be fine, and that I was sorry we would have to meet under these circumstances. I'm sure it sounded phony, but I really meant that.

"Elzyna did not have much joy in her life, you know. Her marriage was not happy like my first one was. I used to try to get her to come to Wimberley and stay with me awhile. I have a big old house, plenty of room. But she always claimed her back gave her too much trouble to do any traveling. I regret now I let us drift apart. I haven't talked to her more than a few times since Senta's death. And of course I was ill and couldn't come to the funeral."

There was nothing I could say. If she felt guilty for her absences, what would she think of me?

Next I dialed Trans-Texas Airlines to make a reservation for a morning flight. I was disgusted with myself for saying I would fly. If I had been talking to anyone else, I would have said I'd take the bus. Yet even now, after all these years, I had a subconscious wish to impress Alexander. How absolutely stupid to be ashamed to tell someone you couldn't afford to travel by air.

I was pleasantly surprised to learn the airline was offering a special fare till the day before Thanksgiving, for anyone who had never flown Trans-Texas before. My ticket would be only twenty-five dollars, round trip. Feeling relieved, I went to the closet to see if my navy suit was clean, and to figure out what else to pack for the trip to Houston. At every turn I thought of Nana, then tried to close her out. I was torn between my anger that she had died without keeping her promise to me, and my anger at myself for having abandoned her. "I don't love you anymore. . . ." Yet, what could she expect? While polishing my navy shoes I stopped, cloth and shoe in mid-air. Hadn't I done to her what I always believed my father did to me? Left to seek my fortune? And, like him, I had waited too long to return.

That night I slept fitfully, dreaming I was with Nana in various settings around her house. In the dream I was aware she was dead, but she was still talking to me, moving around as though alive. We would be sitting at the kitchen table, having angelfood cake, or we would be in the dining room with the lace tablecloth between us. We would be in her room, while she dusted the figurines, or in the library, with her seated in her cane-back rocker and me on the floor at her feet. That was the final one, the one in the library, and she was interrupted when the Seth Thomas clock on the mantelpiece began to strike the hour. I opened my eyes. The alarm clock was buzzing.

The dream had almost banished the awful truth that Nana was really dead, and would not be moving around ever again, anywhere. I was seized with depression, as though I had just learned of her death all over again.

I boarded the plane just before ten o'clock, feeling as though I had not slept at all. The dream kept repeating itself in my head, and I struggled to remember anything she might have said about the identity of my father. Of course, there was nothing, only the titillating prospect that she might, at any moment, announce his name. Oh, this was cruel. I must stop. Dreams can't make magic, can't produce information that was never there. . . .

Alexander had reported that the weather was nasty in Houston. He sounded confident and in control. No doubt he was married, and had two or three kids. Maybe his wife would be waiting with him at the airport when I arrived. She'd be wearing a fur from Ralph Rupley and have a diamond on her finger as big as a doorknob. She'd be in a hurry to make a Junior League luncheon at the River Oaks Country Club. And as we drove away from the airport she and Alexander would chatter about some dignitary they had met at a reception last night, in order to avoid the subject of Nana's death or my divorce, which they would learn of as soon as I arrived and explained. Then, if we were in the car long enough, she would produce pictures of their children. I was fortunate that my marriage failed to produce children. . . .

I could remember in that brief period when Winston was finishing up his education and had not yet started looking elsewhere for female companionship, I longed for a child. I could not understand why, month after month, I failed to get pregnant. Yes, I knew that I had my years of study ahead, but I still wished for a child in that remarkable, impractical way that one wishes for something basic and natural. I went to a doctor, who, finally, after many tests, concluded that my failure to conceive was psychological, resulting from the death of my own mother at my birth. According to him, I had a deep subconscious fear that the same fate would be mine.

"It's just that simple. You're too frightened to relax."

Well, at least I knew that much about myself. Perhaps because of my own stubbornness, more than that of Nana, it was the most deep-rooted secret I would ever learn about myself because now she was dead, and it was too late for talking. Unless . . . unless . . . What if she left something, maybe a letter or a document of some kind? Perhaps she might have put something in the custody of her attorney, or even left something for me in her house. Yes. Of course. She must have. Even though she did not suffer a long illness, she was getting old, her heart was weak, and she surely realized she would not live very much longer. She wouldn't just ignore my need for answers. . . .

How easy it was, then, to catch hold of this thread of hope, that Nana was not too hurt by what I had said and done to forgive me . . . to overlook my long silence. I felt warmed by the prospect of going through her house . . . searching . . . .

Chapter 4

Until the last few minutes of the flight, when the pilot announced we were nearing Houston, I was too preoccupied with Nana to give any more thought to Alexander. Under any other circumstances, I would have been nervous about seeing him again. Well, perhaps now that I thought about it, I was a little nervous, but I mustn't let him know that. He had said, over the telephone, that Nana was in contact with his mother before her death. His calling me was, no doubt, a result of that. Which made it another case of a Gerrard lending a helping hand to a Farrish, just as they always had done.

In all my childhood dreams that Alexander would one day return to me, I would never have imagined it would be under these circumstances. I wondered how much Nana had told him and his mother about my breaking away from her. What must he think of me? Someone who had become the man of the house at a very early age, who had always done exactly what he was supposed to, would no doubt be impatient with a rebel like me.

Impatience. Alexander was impatient, quick to anger. Once, long ago, it must have been the summer before his father was killed, I went with him and Alvareda to visit relatives in Galveston over a weekend. The people we visited lived in a huge old house close to Broadway that was raised high off the ground. We played under the house in the sand, along with cousins who were around our age. One little boy was rude and shoved sand in my face. Alexander jumped on him and began to beat him with his fists. I was more terrified of that than of having sand in my eyes. I ran into the house screaming. The adults had to come out and pull the boys apart. Alexander was my hero. He never let me down . . . he was always the champion of right, even if it got him into trouble, as it did that day in Galveston.

I remembered when I was in high school, Nana cutting out a notice in the newspaper about Alexander being accepted into the School of Engineering at M.I.T. Where else? And while he was no doubt making the dean's list every semester at one of the most prestigious institutions in the country, I was typing letters in some business office or other, having given up my scholarship money in order to get vengeance on the person who loved me the most in the world. I was glad, at least, I had finally earned my degree, and had a good teaching job. He would have to respect me for that.

I believe I would have recognized Alexander anywhere. He was waiting at the gate, wearing a full-length black coat over his suit, holding a big umbrella. He still had blond curls, still a boyish face and smile, and except for the fact that he was tall and slender, he looked much as he did when we were children. He put an arm around my shoulder as we walked the long distance to the baggage pickup and said, more than once, "Boy, it's great to see you again."

In spite of all my talking to myself, my heart leaped in a way it had not done since the days he came to visit me at Nana's house.

I told him I was glad to see him too, and that I appreciated his coming to get me.

He smiled. "You look just like your picture—the one in Elzyna's house."

"Oh, you've been over there already?"

"Yes," he said, "I went as soon as I heard about her death. Her attorney called me."

"Why would he do that?"

He hesitated. "She named my mother executor of her will, and Mother is out of town. Robin—"

I was astonished. "Your mother? I didn't realize that. Nana must have made a new will, after Aunt Senta died."

"Yes."

"I wonder why she didn't name me executor. I mean, since I was her close relative. . . ."

He didn't answer.

Of course, it wasn't his problem. "Well, I guess that's what I deserved," I told him. "Do you know if she left anything for me—a letter or something?"

"Not that I know of," he said. He seemed relieved to be off the subject of the will. "Were you expecting one?"

"Not exactly," I told him.

"Here's the baggage counter. What color is yours?"

"Ah—it's, well—mixed," I said. I felt an unexpected pang of embarrassment, as though I had just discovered my dull white slip was showing out from under my skirt hem.

As he pulled down the luggage from the conveyor rack, I noticed his hands were long, his fingers narrow, hands like one would expect to see on a pianist. . . . I noticed, also, that I needed to stop thinking about how he looked. "Yes, that's the lot," I said of the luggage.

Alexander drove a white Mercedes, with a JFK for President sticker on the rear bumper. He was quick to tell me that the car was ten years old, that he had purchased it from a student at Rice last year. "The bumper sticker is new," he quipped.

"Are you studying at Rice?"

"No. I'm a teacher in the architecture department."

"Oh. I thought you were an engineer."

"I was, but I switched. Do you work?"

I had to smile at the oversimplification. "Oh yes, I'm an English teacher," I told him, then decided I might as well get the rest of the story out of the way. "I have to earn my own living—I'm divorced. In fact, I was in the middle of a crumbling marriage when Aunt Senta died. That's why I didn't come back." I looked at him to gauge his reaction, not so much to my divorce, as to my failure to return for my aunt's funeral. I did not want him to think I was irresponsible.

He paused momentarily, then said, "I was in Italy at the time, so I didn't hear about her death until Mother wrote to me later. Now Mother is in Montreal—snowbound, from all I can gather—and probably won't get home for Elzyna's funeral."

"Nana always liked Louetta. I guess I'm not all that surprised she named her executor of the will. Has your mother ever remarried?"

"No. But she stays busy. I spend a lot of my time taking her back and forth to the airport because she travels so much. In January she's going to President Kennedy's inauguration. She worked very hard raising money for him in Houston. One of her prized possessions is a picture of herself with him and Jackie at a dinner in Washington last spring."

He sounded as though he were very involved with his mother. I had noticed he had no wedding ring on and, while that was not always significant for a man, I wondered now if he were married. I asked him.

"No," he said. "I was engaged, but she—well, we decided to call it off."

Inside I was cheering, but I reminded myself that brought us no closer together.

"Elzyna didn't tell me you were divorced," he was saying.

"I didn't inform her."

"I see . . ." he reflected, as though that illuminated something for him.

"How did she look before she died? Did you see her recently?"

"The last time I saw her was a few months ago. She came to visit us one day. She looked just fine, then. . . . Robin, I don't understand—" he began, but I interrupted. I knew what he was going to ask me, and I felt panicked at the thought of talking about it, especially to him.

"Who found Nana, after she died?"

"A man who does the yard. Apparently he had come by to see if there was anything he could do for a few bucks—"

"Mr. Nickleby, no doubt. In the wintertime he has trouble supporting his drinking habits."

"Anyway, he saw her sitting in the library, but she would not answer the doorbell. He realized something was wrong, and went to tell someone at the little store at the corner. They called the police, and so on."

So she was there, just as I had always pictured her. . . . Awaiting my return? I wondered. All at once I felt so thankful her death was quick and she did not suffer. Heaven knows she had suffered enough in her lifetime.

We were at the funeral home for an hour, making the arrangements for the service. Alexander had been correct about her preparedness. She had purchased a plot with four lots when my mother died and Aunt Senta had been buried in the second of the four. We telephoned the rector of Christ Church Cathedral on Texas Avenue, where she had attended services for years, and arranged to have the funeral in a small chapel. I selected a casket and a shroud, which did not upset me as I might have imagined. All these arrangements seemed sterile and independent of the event that brought them about, perhaps because I had not seen her beforehand.

As we left, Alexander put an arm around me again. I know he kept looking for the moment when I would dissolve into tears. "You all right?"

"Fine, thank you." I smiled up at him.

"Would you like to stay in Mother's house while you're here? I live in the cottage where my grandmother lived, so you'd have complete privacy except for Mother's maid, Janice. She'll see to your every need."

"No, thank you. I think I'd like to go home now. I suppose I could stay there till I leave Saturday or Sunday," I said. I couldn't imagine myself in a more incongruous setting than Louetta Gerrard's home.

Alexander had already told me I was to meet with Nana's attorney on Friday, after the funeral, about the will. I assumed there was nothing left in the estate except for the house. At this point I had no idea what I would do about disposing of it. I was not ready to think about that.

"Let me take you to lunch first. It would give us a chance to talk."

Again, I sensed he was going to quiz me, and headed it off. "Thank you, but I don't think I could eat. I'd like to be alone for a while, and tonight I have to be at the funeral home."

"I'll pick you up and take you there."

I looked at him for a moment. "You know, you really are nice. You needn't bother with me. I can get a taxi," I said, then remembered something. "Nana had a car, an old one. Maybe it's still in the garage."

He shook his head. "She told us when she visited that she did not drive anymore, and had sold her car a while back."

"Oh, I see. . . . Well, anyway I can still take a—"

He smiled. "Let me pick you up, Robin. I want to."

His remark pleasantly unsettled me, and I continued to enjoy its effect until we arrived at 4001 McKinney Avenue. At the sight of it, my spirits fell. As we got out of the car, I looked at Alexander, wondering if he had any idea why the property was in such a poor state. He shook his head in response. It seemed that nothing had been done to the house since I left. The shrubs that formed a fence around the property, once so neatly kept, were now tall and bushy. The iron gate had been taken down altogether. The grass had been allowed to grow over the front walk in places so that it no longer cut a neat pathway up to the porch. There were no gardens anymore, only unhealthy shrubs around the perimeter of the house. As we walked up to the porch I could see the roof was rotted in spots. The paint on the house trim, the beautiful doors and the window facings, was peeling. The wicker furniture on the porch needed painting, and there were several leaks in the porch ceiling. Suddenly I felt angry. "What has Mr. Nickleby been doing around here all this time?" I demanded. I imagined Nana's vision growing poor as the years went by . . . her failure to realize she was paying for work not done.

Alexander shook his head and unlocked the door. I braced myself for something even worse. The interior, however, looked better at first glance and more than anything else, I felt relieved. It was as cold inside as out, so Alexander went about the task of lighting the gas heaters in the parlor and library while I looked around.

I have heard it said that sometimes when a person dies, the spirit lingers briefly. I don't know if that is true, but as I walked around, I felt Nana was always a step or two behind me. Perhaps it was only because the whole atmosphere of the house was pervaded with signs that she had occupied it for so many years, and not only that, but had exercised care and control over every inch of it. Not a room failed to evidence that this was the home of Elzyna Leider Farrish, and that it had never really belonged to anyone in the way it belonged to her.

As I stood in the doorway to the library, I felt her presence even more. The rocker . . . the empty rocker near the window. It was as though she would, just any moment now, approach it and sit down with her coffee, first stopping to turn on the radio. How many times had I sat at her feet, my head in her lap? I could remember the smell of her starched apron. I felt tears pricking my eyes.

Alexander distracted me. "Well, that's one down," he said of the glowing library heater. He rubbed his hands together.

I nodded, drew in a sigh, and walked into the dining room. The lace tablecloth she loved so much was spread over the oak table. Her soup tureen and china serving bowls were still on the sideboard. In the kitchen was the same old stove that had always been there and that used to shame me so. Her apron hung on a hook by the door. I went through the hall and to the huge bathroom—it seemed even larger than I remembered—past the footed tub with the rusted place near the drain where the water always dripped, and the light bulb that was suspended on a cord from the ceiling. Last of all I entered the bedroom she had occupied since she returned to the house in 1925. The bed was made up. I had never known her to fail to make up her bed when she rose in the morning. Her writing desk in the corner had a stack of mail upon it, and her writing pen was in its place nearby. On the wall above her desk hung the studio portrait of my mother Laura, the one that I had borrowed to hang in my room. I had come close to taking it with me when I left home, had even removed it from the wall and put it in my suitcase. But Nana had always made a point that the portrait belonged to her, that she was letting me hang it in my room but not giving it to me. I wanted it very much, but I felt like a thief, so I replaced it. I did not pause to study it now. On Nana's dresser was the linen and lace doily that had always been there, her bottle of Chantilly cologne and her bowl of hairpins and face powder. There were two framed photographs on the dresser: a very old snapshot of herself out in the front of the house with blond-haired Senta and little John nearby, the sun causing all of them to squint at the camera. The date on the photograph was 1912. Next to it was my high school graduation picture, my face smiling confidently as though the world awaited me to take it.

I believe I would have been all right if I had not turned then and seen her cane hooked at the foot of the brass bed. I reached out and ran my hand over it, and burst into tears. Hearing me, Alexander looked through the door, then came and put his arms around me. That sympathetic gesture just made me cry harder, and I was thankful suddenly that he was there, and that he still cared about my feelings. He stroked my back and told me that he knew it was hard, losing her, and murmured other comforting phrases in my ear.

After I had soaked his shoulder with tears, he pulled out his handkerchief, still holding me. "I'm sorry for doing that. I'm all right now," I said.

He smiled. "You look just like you did that time when you dropped your doll on the porch and her head broke into pieces."

I laughed. "I'm surprised you remember that."

"Look, are you sure you'll be all right? Why don't you stay at Mother's, just for tonight?"

"No, I really want to stay here. What time will you pick me up?"

He released me. "How about seven o'clock?"

"Fine. That gives me time for a long nap. I promise I'll look better tonight."

He smiled at me again, the smile I remembered from childhood, that made me feel that I was special to him. "You look wonderful. Oh, and I took your bags upstairs and lit the stove in your old room, so it'll be cozy."

As he drove away, I thought how kind he was, not stuck-up as I had expected, and how warm and secure it made me feel to be around him, how good it felt to be in his arms. . . . I shook my head. It would be foolish to dwell on that, and I was determined not to. As nice as he was, he was still a Gerrard, and I had known for many years there was more than one reason not to waste my time wishing for him to come back to me.

I heard a noise on the porch, and went to the door. The postman, a black man, was about to stuff the mail in the box. Seeing me, he tipped his hat and handed me the mail. "Where is Mrs. Farrish?" he inquired.

"She passed away yesterday," I told him.

He frowned and shook his head. "That's too bad. Are you her daughter?"

"Granddaughter."

"Well, I'll miss Mrs. Farrish. She was a nice lady." He shook his head again, tipped his hat, and started down the porch stairs. Then he turned. "I wonder, did she get that package mailed she was so concerned about?"

"Package?"

"Yes'm. I told her I'd take it on my truck and I'd bring her a ticket for the postage. But I was down sick for three weeks. Maybe the carrier who took over my route carried it for her."

"Maybe so. She didn't tell you what it was or where it was going, did she?"

"No, ma'am. I asked her did she want to insure it, and she say no, she'd thought about that, but she didn't know how to put a value on it."

I shook my head. "I'll look around and see if it's still here. Thank you."

"You'll let the post office know where to send her mail, won't you?"

"Surely. Thank you again."

I closed the door and looked through the mail. Light bill, flyer about Foley's Christmas selection, gourmet cheese catalogue, and water bill. Just that little bit reminded me that life goes on as though no one died and nothing changed. There would be a great many details to look after. I walked through the downstairs rooms, looking for a box wrapped for mailing, but found nothing. My first guess was that she had done some holiday baking and sent a currant cake or maybe some cookies to a friend. She often did that this time of year. By now the package was probably long-since delivered and its contents consumed.

Three o'clock. I was too exhausted to think of getting anything done right now, and went upstairs to my old bedroom to lie down. I looked into Aunt Senta's old room first, and found it the same as I remembered. My room, too, had been left as it was, and thanks to Alexander it was now toasty warm. I crawled under the covers and fell asleep.

I awoke a little past five-thirty. Darkness was quickly gathering outside, and the only light in the room was from the gas heater across the floor. I got up from the bed and stood in front of the heater to warm myself. I had forgotten how good that always felt, growing up, how I'd warm my front side first, then turn around and warm my back. When you are ashamed of the place you live, you don't stop to consider the little things that sometimes make it nice in spite of age. If I had been certain it was safe, I would have built a fire in the fireplace. Yet there wasn't time. I pulled some clean underwear from my suitcase and went down to bathe. I turned the switch on the bathroom bulb and lit the gas heater in the corner. Every motion brought back the memory of having done all this before. Out of long habit over the years I lived here, I put my bath towel on the stool close to the heater to warm it up. I turned on the faucets in the tub—one for hot, one for cold—and put the stopper in the drain. There was always plenty of hot water, and always the tub filled quickly. I pinned up my hair, undressed, and slipped into the tub. I had forgotten how much deeper this tub was than the modern built-in tubs such as that in my apartment in Dallas. You could really luxuriate in this bathtub, forget all about the passing of time . . .

I knew that I did not deserve to expect Nana to have written a letter to me about my father, since I abandoned her, but I still could not help hoping she might have softened toward the end of her life, realizing time was surely running out for her. I did not think there would be any other kind of evidence about my father in the house. After all, I was born in 1932 and lived here till I got married. Nana had not kept the contents of her desk hidden from me, nor her dresser, or anything else. If there had been some hidden evidence, I would have discovered it before I left home. Or would I? While here, I intended to look around carefully. I could stay till Sunday night if need be. Surely by then . . .

I pulled out the stopper and reached for the towel; then I remembered about the package and felt a thrill of hope. What if Nana was mailing me a box of things that belonged to my father, or to both my parents? Sometimes people have an inkling their own death is near. I could just see her picking out a good sturdy box, and some strong twine to tie around it. She'd put it on top of the dining room table and carefully pack the things that would be significant to me. . . .

As I switched off the bathroom light, I realized a package sent to me would have reached the wrong address. Damn. Yet, the post office in Dallas had a forwarding address for me so surely it would have gotten to me eventually, or at least have been returned here.

Mrs. Sobel, who lived in the apartment next to mine, would be home from work by now. She was not a close friend, but she worked in the office at St. Paul's Academy, and we had already begun riding to and from work together. When I saw her out in the hall before leaving that morning, she had offered to pick up my mail. I had left her a key.

I dried off and threw on my robe. I ran upstairs to get her phone number out of my purse, then back down again to the telephone in the hall. My anxious hands were shaking as I dialed the operator.

After three rings, Mrs. Sobel answered. "Was there by any chance a package in my mail today?" I asked her.

"No, no packages. There wasn't much. I left it on the table inside your door."

Damn. I sat there in silence.

"You want me to see if there's a yellow slip in the stack? If the package was big, the postman would have taken it back to the post office."

"Oh, would you mind? I'd really appreciate it."

"You want to call me back?"

"No, I'll just hold if you don't mind. I'm getting ready to leave for the funeral home."

She was gone for what seemed an eternity. With every second my hope lifted higher. Finally I heard a noise, and then her voice. "No, Robin, I don't see anything. You want me to call the post office tomorrow?"

"No, thank you," I said, deflated. "It's probably too early. I won't be home till Saturday or Sunday, though, so I'll check with you again tomorrow, if you don't mind."

"Surely," she said, and started to ask about the funeral arrangements. The doorbell rang. I looked up. Alexander. Confound it all. I told Mrs. Sobel good-bye. Poor Alexander. I hadn't even thought to turn on the porch light. I opened the door. "Come in, I'm awfully sorry," I began. He was wearing a dark blue suit and tie, and a baby blue shirt. He looked so handsome . . . I felt like an idiot. "I hope I'm not too early," he said with a grin. His eyes swept all over me.

"Sit down for a few minutes. I overslept," I told him, and hurried back up the stairs, thinking of the magnetic quality about Alexander . . . it seemed almost unfair for a person to have everything, plus good looks. Gad, how he made me feel . . . all lit up inside.

As I dressed I was suddenly more aware of how I might look to him. . . . I would wear one of my only two good suits tonight—a plum-colored wool with pale blue piping on the sleeves and wide collar, and a pale blue silk blouse with a small jabot underneath. He'd probably think I was trying to match up with his clothing. . . .

I brushed my hair out and combed it back from my face, letting it fall around my shoulders. I had worn it this way for such a long time . . . maybe he liked short hair better. . . . I put on some plum-colored lipstick and brushed a tiny bit of blue eye shadow on my lids, then mascara to lengthen the lashes. I looked at myself. I wondered whether he could tell how much he affected me simply by appearing. I sprayed on a little Chanel No. 5 —a purchase I'd allowed myself to indulge in as soon as I found out I'd gotten the job at St. Paul's—and grabbed my handbag.

He was awaiting me at the foot of the stairs, just as he used to. He smiled approvingly, said, "You look lovely," and took my arm. He smelled of something faintly herbal, not too spicy. I loved it, whatever it was. I felt I was being courted almost, and I could not help regretting all the years we'd missed, held away from each other. Still, he knew how to use a telephone. . . .

I had not attended many funerals in my lifetime, and even fewer times had I paid a call to a funeral home. The death of Alexander's father Gabriel, twenty years ago, was my most vivid memory of the sequence of events surrounding a funeral. At the funeral home there were great crowds of people —so many you could hardly get through them. So many that Alexander barely spoke to me before turning to some adult who hugged him and made a fuss over him. He looked so overwhelmed, so lost. Then at the funeral it was the same. Christ Episcopal Church had been packed. And the line of limousines and fine automobiles that progressed out to the cemetery seemed endless. At the grave site there were more flowers than I had ever seen. Tiers and tiers of arrangements encroached on other graves as well. By virtue of the fact that Aunt Senta was married to Gabriel's brother, we sat behind Louetta and Alexander and Lilly and her husband during the burial service. I saw Alexander look up at his mother trustingly; she smiled at him, and her black-gloved hand reached for his and held it till the end.

With the death of Nana, it was different. Tonight the funeral home was quiet, devoid of crowds, and there were many fewer flowers. The funeral director approached. "Mrs. Farrish is in the blue room. Won't you follow me?"

As we drew near, I had almost to force myself to look at Nana. Why should her death have been so frightening to me? Was it because in the face of her lifeless body might lay the last hope of answers to my innermost questions, as well as the knowledge of her forgiveness toward me? I do not know, even now, but I am so glad that I gathered the courage to look at her. She looked, if I could describe her in a word or two, to be at peace. Her hair was a little grayer than I remembered, but otherwise she looked very much the same. I had chosen a petal pink silk shroud with high collar and lace down the front and around the cuffs of the sleeves. I saw now that it was right for her. Her face in death was beautiful. I thought of all the worries she had suffered in her lifetime, from the beginning of her marriage and maybe even before. I was sure there was much I had never been told. But whatever the sum total of her experience in life, she looked as though she faced death with confidence, and with the strength that characterized her nature. I would never have thought I would reach down and kiss her forehead, but I did.

When I moved back, tears were running down my cheeks, but I did not feel sadness as much as I felt a kind of sheltered warmth for her. Standing behind me, Alexander looked as though he was about to cry as well. "She makes me think of my grandmother Alvareda," he said. "They both had such dignity."

I smiled up at him, surprised and grateful.

I believe that was one of the nicest remarks anyone ever made about Nana, and it reminded me that our families were inextricably tied through that long friendship. I couldn't speak just then. I caught his hand and squeezed it.

Several people came by the funeral home that night, and there were a dozen or so funeral sprays and arrangements near the casket. A huge spray of pink roses had been sent by Louetta and Alexander. I went around looking at the cards, and found a number of them from people I had never heard of. It was a good reminder that Nana had a life exclusive of me. One card, however, was a pleasant surprise—from Mrs. Clifton B. Lang—Charlotte's mother. I had not heard from her in years, not since before I left home. It had never occurred to me that, once a neighbor of Nana, she might have kept in touch. Or perhaps she only saw the obituary and wanted to pay her respects.

When we got back home that evening Alexander said, "I really hate to leave you. I wish you'd come home with me."

"No, I want to stay here," I said, and felt a little guilty for not telling him I had searching to do. He put his arms around me and hugged me tightly, and kissed my cheek. He looked at me for a long moment before letting me go.

I watched him from the doorway till he'd walked to his car and driven away. It would be so easy to fall for him again, lock, stock, and barrel. Tonight when we were together, it seemed as though we had never really been apart. He put his arms around me as though it were a natural gesture. There was no awkwardness about it. It felt so good being that close to him again. There was that quality of strength about him that was hard to put into words, but that made me feel that, as long as he was around, everything would be all right.

Yet, Alexander no doubt regarded me as a kind of long-lost sister and, being a Gerrard, he felt obligated to look after me as Elzyna's granddaughter. That was all.

I took a deep breath and locked the door. I was wide awake now, and suddenly famished. I went to the kitchen and opened the refrigerator. There was some baked ham inside and some cheese as well. In fact from the looks of the refrigerator, Nana had shopped shortly before she died. There was milk— still fresh—and lettuce and tomatoes. I felt quite elated suddenly. That she had felt so well to the end of her life was wonderful. I opened up the bread box and found half a loaf of bread. I made myself some supper, and carried the plate to the table.

Earlier today when Alexander and I passed Eastwood School—now Dora B. Lantrip School, according to the sign—I could not help but observe the neighborhood was even more run down than it had been when I left. The apartment house across from the school was a shambles, and many of the houses up and down the street were dilapidated as well. Some of the people now living around here hung linens out on the front porch to dry, and parked their cars in the front yard. Even still, I felt at home. The drugstore nearby was still in business, and so was the washateria next to it. Austin Senior High School, which we had driven by at my request, was still very much the same. It would be nice, I thought, to be able to go back and visit some of the places I remembered. It would be nice, even, to think of returning someday to live here again.

Silly. . . .

Yet now that I was here, it felt natural to think of that.

Of course, it would cost a lot of money to fix up this house again, and I could not even think about it for years. But I could keep the house in the meantime, and rent it out . . .

Nana would like that, I thought. Again, I felt almost as though she were near, and I had the most delicious feeling that she loved me still, and had forgiven me. I washed the dishes and began to look around for some visible evidence that I was not mistaken.

Chapter 5

I soon found there were a lot more places to look than I expected. There were two major storage areas—one in the large closet underneath the stairs, and the other in what used to be the nursery at the back of the house. Doubtless there were things in the attic as well, but you did not store valuables there where they might be eaten up by roaches and rats, or water-damaged if the roof leaked. Likewise, the garage. I would save these places for later, and concentrate now on the easily accessible places on the first and second floors.

The obvious place to start was Nana's desk. She might have written me a letter and left it in a drawer. There were two drawers on each side and a lap drawer in the center. I found nothing in any of them except bills marked "paid," her check register, and letters she received of an obvious business nature. Her address book was in the top left-hand drawer, but as I flipped through its pages I found nothing that seemed significant. I looked around her dresser, and pulled open the drawers. Nothing except the scarves and handkerchiefs that had been there always. I turned and looked above the mantel—nothing. Then I realized the collection of china figurines was gone. That seemed odd. Had she given them away? Surely not. They were too dear to her. Maybe she had moved them to another place.

Next I thought of my own room. Maybe she left a note in there, where I obviously would look should I return home. Again, I was disappointed. I had taken most everything in my dresser when I left, and there was no message for me here. I looked in every other spot I could think of in my room and in my closet, but found nothing.

Next I tried Aunt Senta's room. This was less disappointing than it was unsettling, for all of her things were still in the drawers and in the closet. On her dresser were her nurse's cap, starched white with a black stripe, her graduation pin from nursing school, and her lozenge-shaped name pin. There was also a photograph of her with Lilly Gerrard, the two of them in their student uniforms, arms around each other, smiling broadly as though the person with the camera had said something very funny. Also on the dresser was a wooden frame that opened like a book. One side held a picture of Lilly. The other side held a photo of Lilly's husband, Stephen Sandock. He was a handsome man, with dark, deep-set eyes and hair combed straight back. My aunt had always been selective in the people she cared about, and there were few of them. There was no photograph of her husband, Clayton, and though I had never been told they were unhappily married, I always sensed it because she never spoke of the things they did together, never said she missed him.

In the dresser drawers were nylon lingerie, hosiery, scarves, and jewelry. She had exquisite taste. I used to admire her looks if not her personality. It was difficult to imagine her body ravaged with cancer. In a way I was glad I had not lived with her through that. There were no messages in here, not any that would help me, at least. I opened her closet. There were the dresses she wore, and several white uniforms, all starched and ironed as though ready for duty. On the shelf above were rows of shoe boxes three deep and a half dozen, side to side. Sakowitz. Andrew Geller. I. Miller. I opened one. The shoes had never been worn. They were chocolate brown leather with a gold chain T-strap. Others were also unused. She always took advantage of Sakowitz and Battelstein's shoe sales, buying sometimes a dozen pair at a time. She must have made a shoe-shopping pilgrimage just before she got sick.

I wondered why Nana had never gotten rid of these things. Sometimes it seemed as though she was in complete control of her mental faculties to the end; other times, I wondered. . . . One thing for sure—she left nothing I was intended to find, unless I had overlooked it thus far.

Next I opened the door to the nursery, the room I had disliked as a child.

Surely my problems with this room were not as great as they seemed. Yet it was close, musty. I could not seem to breathe very well in here, even now. I poked around some. Most of the things I ran across belonged to my great-grandmother, Carlotta Leider. Lamps, linens, a couple of small chairs, a little table, a few boxes—one containing men's shoes that belonged to no telling who. Most of the stuff ought to have been thrown away.

I opened the closet door and looked through the clothes hanging inside. Some looked like they had belonged to Aunt Senta. There were some boxes on the shelf above, but I decided to leave them for now. I didn't want to stay in here any longer. The room made me feel depressed somehow. I started out, then noticed a box of drawings behind the door. Outside in the hall I looked through them. Some I recognized. A pot of flowers on a ledge; a duster and straw hat hanging on the back of a door; something more abstract that looked like dancers in tutus circling on a stage, or maybe it was a crown of laurels. A sailboat on the water; no, a witch's hat, maybe. All these had the faint etching of my mother's name at the bottom. Strange, and also saddening, to think that her drawings were the most significant material evidence that she had ever lived. There were more of them than photographs of her, even though the snapping of pictures was such a pastime of the lives of those around her. It almost seemed, when you got right down to it, that she was an object of shame, whether or not for the reasons the neighbors were apt to claim. The one snapshot that I owned was actually taken of Aunt Senta. My mother was just at the edge of the porch, in kind of a blur as though she were trying to move out of the photo's range before the camera snapped, but did not quite make it.

I went down to Nana's room, for I wanted to see the tinted portrait again, and I stood and gazed at it for a long time. Laura Farrish was a fetching girl, with auburn hair and a widow's peak. She had a kind of—what was the word, alluring?—look in her eyes. Teasing. Her mouth was small, her nose up-turned. I had always considered her to be prettier than her sister Senta. I stepped back and sighed. To her grave she took so many secrets. Perhaps I would never know them all. I was grateful at least I knew who she was and what she looked like. That was more than I knew about my father. I took the portrait down and put it in my suitcase. This time it would not matter if I took it home with me.

The obvious places had yielded nothing, and maybe I should not have expected them to. Nana probably resented me too much to care about my feelings, especially after I offered no help during Aunt Senta's illness. I would give anything now if I had not been too concerned with my own troubles to wake up to the fact she might have needed me. Had I done so, she certainly would have felt inclined to tell me what I so wanted to know, deserved to know, before it was too late.

After that I started looking for items not intended for my inspection, pulling out drawers here and there, in the kitchen, in the dining room, in Nana's bedroom, the dresser and the lingerie chest by the bathroom door. On through the parlor, and from there into the library. I looked around. The bookcase. I had not thought of that. I opened the glass doors and ran my finger along the spine of the books. A set of encyclopedias, long since outdated, a world almanac, a huge Webster's dictionary. Farther down, on the third shelf, a group of books I had never heard of before, on the subject of architecture. My grandfather's no doubt. Then, at the end, Nana's album. Why had I not thought of that before?

I flipped through it. There were news clippings, photographs, and a few handwritten notes. I turned back to the beginning. There was an inscription inside the front cover that said, "To Elzyna and Beryl—with best wishes on your wedding day, December 15, 1906." It was signed, "With love from Patricia and George."

On the first page was a wedding picture of Nana and my grandfather that I had not seen for many years. I had known all my life that they had an unhappy marriage, though I did not know why. Children hear only a few bits and pieces of information adults happen to drop their way. The only glaring evidence of the unhappiness was the fact of her divorce from him, even after he was an invalid. It was also testimony to her determination. That determination I was only now beginning to comprehend fully.

Hard to believe they could have been unhappy, when he was so dashingly handsome and, according to Aunt Senta, very gifted. I had never seen any of his designs or drawings and now, I remembered, they were consigned to the attic. My eyes lingered on the photo. Nana's wedding gown was beautiful, but obviously she was not a match for her groom's good looks. In fact, it seemed to me now, Nana became prettier as she grew older. More slender, too.

On the following page were several portraits of Aunt Senta as a little girl. In one she wore a dress of lace tiers and a beautiful ruffled French bonnet. Her sausage curls peeked out from the bonnet. She had on white lace gloves and long stockings, and she had a charming smile on her face. She held a Missal in one hand, with a rosary draped around it. "Senta's First Communion," was noted at the bottom, and also a note, "Dress designed and made by M. Savoy of New Orleans."

There were some photos of Senta and her brother John. He was a frail-looking little boy, with large eyes and hair that must have been light brown. Buster Brown haircut, too, as all boys and many girls wore in those days. He looked like a sweet child, but then so did Aunt Senta and I had heard she was a little dickens.

There followed many photographs and news clippings, in chronological order to a great extent, and most of these were of Gerrards.

I turned a few pages over and found a newspaper photo of my mother Laura with Stephen Sandock. From the caption, he had sponsored her in an art contest of some kind in which she won a series of lessons at the art museum. I did not remember ever having seen this before. She and Stephen were facing each other, holding her certificate of award. Stephen was employed at the Metropolitan Theater art department, according to the caption. On the next page was the certificate itself.

After that there were some clippings about Aunt Senta and Lilly Gerrard in nursing school, and one photo story about Dr. Clayton Gerrard joining a group of surgeons who practiced at Memorial Hospital. There was next a picture of Alexander—an early school picture—pasted on a red valentine and, to my surprise right next to it, a picture of me in a similar frame. Underneath was written, "Valentines, 1939. Alexander and Robin." I remembered us sitting at the dining room table one rainy afternoon, making these. I felt the blood rise to my cheeks. I'd be embarrassed for him to see them now.

The last Gerrard picture was clipped from a newspaper at the time Gabriel was about to run for governor. He and Louetta were out on their back lawn, all dressed up. Alexander stood in front of them in short pants. I flipped the page. Nothing, until the album began to be an exclusive chronicle of my school years, especially those at Austin. Here was evidence of every time Nana pulled out her camera, at performances, at installations, at slumber parties. There were many girls in the pictures whose names I could no longer remember. When I thought of all the love and effort Nana put forth to make those high school years happy ones for me, I felt a wave of sadness that brought tears to my eyes.

That was about it. I flipped through the remaining empty pages. Not far from the end, placed there but not yet glued down, were two news clippings. One was a photo story of Alexander. He had a beard, and looked much different. According to the caption, Alexander O'Neal Gerrard was about to leave for Italy, "for extended studies in architectural history." It said that he was already degreed in mechanical engineering, and was now working on a master's in architectural history, and had spent some time in Greece and Spain. This was dated 1956. I thought again how faithfully the press followed anyone named Gerrard.

The other photo story was more recent. Alexander was without his beard, posing with a pretty dark-haired girl named Frances Newhouse. She was the daughter of Oscar Newhouse, it said, long-time official of the Houston Fat Stock Show and Rodeo, and Chairman of the Board at Newhouse Energy. His wife was a patron of the Houston Symphony. Bluebloods. There was a biography of Alexander: "son of Mrs. Louetta Hemphill Gerrard and the late Gabriel Gerrard, graduate of Massachusetts Institute of Technology School of Engineering . . ." and so on.

The caption said the two were engaged, giving no wedding date, and that he was joining the firm of Cooper, Lebanorta, and Crisse, architects in Houston. Also mentioned was a party held the previous evening, to honor the pair, in the Emerald Room at the Shamrock Hotel.

Much ado about an engagement that never wound up in a trip to the altar. Much ado about a new job that wound up in a departure, and apparently soon. Why would someone like Alexander wind up teaching, even if it were in a distinguished institution like Rice? Maybe he enjoyed the mobility, since teaching offered long vacations and sabbaticals, leaving him free to travel frequently. Certainly he didn't lack the financial backing to make that possible.

I stared at the girl Frances Newhouse, remembering the birthday party for Alexander when I was eleven, when he had paid all his attention to the other girl. She had worn an expensive red dress, of sheer material. When she leaned over the table, I could see she was beginning to develop breasts. She saw me looking at her, and stared at me with a triumphant gleam in her eyes. I was so embarrassed. I, of course, was flat as a tabletop, with no sign yet that I would ever be otherwise. That was when I decided I could not bear to stay any longer. That was when I realized I failed to interest Alexander anymore. I was not rich and I was not . . . not mature.

I smiled now at the thought of that party, but had that feeling of inadequacy ever left me? No. Not even now. Frances Newhouse might be the party girl all grown up and still dazzling Alexander . . . at least until the recent past.

Why had his engagement been broken? I wondered. Maybe he was too attached to his mother and Frances felt she was about to marry more than just Alexander . . .

Finally I closed the album and put it away. I looked at the clock above the fireplace. Nearly midnight. I turned out the gas heaters downstairs—we never left them on through the night for fear of fire—and turned out all the lights except the one in the hall, which was also our custom. Upstairs in my old room, I turned up the flames in the gas heater, to make the room still warmer. Then I got into bed and, too exhausted to read, turned out the lamp and fell asleep. In the night I had a dream. My father came and sat beside the bed to talk to me. I do not know what he said, nor what he looked like. Throughout the dream I struggled to try to see his face, but I never could. I had a safe, peaceful feeling while he sat with me, and it seemed to last a long time. Finally he vanished. He did not tell me good-bye and kiss me the way a father should. He simply disappeared. In the dream I closed my eyes and lay back on the pillows. Sometime after there was a click, like a door being softly shut. The warm, peaceful feeling was displaced by an ominous one, and in moments I felt something cover my mouth. Someone's hand, strong and unyielding. Quickly I awoke and sat up in bed. I looked toward the door, not certain I had really dreamed. The door was open as I had left it. Still, someone could be in the house. Stupidly, I called out, "Who's there? Who is it?" and the sound of my own voice, alone in the silence, frightened me more. I sat there for several moments, heart pounding, not sure what to do. I opened the drawer of the bedside table. There used to be a flashlight kept there. Finding it, I flipped the switch hopefully. No luck, the batteries were dead. I rose and put on my robe. I couldn't sit there and wait to be attacked again. Starting with my own bedroom I went from room to room, throwing on the lights, glancing fearfully into closets. Nothing. I went downstairs, repeating the process. With every room I passed through, my confidence grew. No one had come into the house. It was, after all, a nightmare. When I got back to my bedroom I turned down the gas flames. The room had grown too hot, I reasoned, and caused the dream. Curious, after all these years, that that nightmare would recur. I couldn't recall if there was a person suffocating me in the childhood dream, but whether or not there was, the dream was no less terrifying. What a horrible way to be—what?—murdered?

I awoke very early, before daylight, feeling as though I had not slept at all and anxious for a cup of coffee. I put on my robe and went downstairs. I had not thought about how icy cold it would be without the heaters lit. Nana had always done that, rising early each morning; so by the time I came down for breakfast, the rooms downstairs would be warm except for the floors. They were always cold. The open-ended house shoes I wore now were not to compare with the furry ones I always wore when I lived here. Every Christmas there would be a new pair under the tree.

I lit the heaters and went to the kitchen. The percolator once used to brew coffee in the morning was not in its usual place. I opened a cupboard door and found a jar of instant. I lit a burner on the stove and put the tea kettle on to boil. I could remember so well the sight of angelfood cake sitting on the stove shelf, golden brown on the outside and five or six inches high, peeking up from the tube pan. I could see Nana standing here in her apron, looking up and patting the cake gently with her fingertips to see if it had cooled enough to remove it from the pan.

I turned around and sighed. I was cold through and through. My thin house robe—so perfect for a small, cozy apartment—would not be adequate for sitting comfortably with a cup of coffee in Nana's house. I went into her bedroom and opened the closet in hopes of finding a chenille robe. She always had one. There it was, hanging on a hook inside the door, rose-colored. When I put it on, it brushed the floor and the sleeves reached below my wrists, but I did not care. It was invitingly warm. My eyes wandered up to the shelf above the clothes. There was a stack of boxes there. I pulled them out and put them on the bed. Only one, the heaviest, contained anything of interest. The box itself, too large to be for lingerie, but small for a dress box, was white and bore an inscription down in the right-hand corner, in gold lettering: "Savoy Fine Lace and Linen Company, New Orleans." The same name as Nana had written underneath Aunt Senta's photograph in the album. I removed the lid and found a huge collection of letters. They were grouped in stacks of ten or so, with ribbons binding each. The tea kettle began to sing. I picked up the box and took it to the kitchen.

I had a wonderful feeling of anticipation as I started through the stacks. Then I realized that most of them were from Alvareda, written much earlier than the year of my birth, 1932. Many of them were from back in the years previous to World War I, written from overseas during her travels. Her handwriting was difficult to read—a cross between script and printing. Personally I had no real interest in Alvareda's letters, but it occurred to me that as well known as her family was in Houston, the library officials might be glad to have them.

While drinking my coffee I scanned a few. Most were not very long, and were chatty and enthusiastic, telling of a place she and Neal had visited that day—a museum in London, the cathedral in York, the Champs Élysées in Paris, the Eiffel Tower. I could remember the stories Nana would later tell me, and realize it was through these letters she enjoyed Alvareda's world travels, while tied down with the everyday concerns of young children and a house to keep, a husband to take care of. . . .

After five or six, the letters seemed to run together for me, and I began to dig for later postmarks. Many letters no longer had their envelopes with them. And of those which had no envelope, only a portion of them had a date at the top. Often times she would note, "Tuesday afternoon—" then begin, "Dearest Elzyna." I poked around until I finally found some with later postmarks, 1923, 1927, 1928. Then I found a black-bordered envelope which held a long, black-bordered note dated January 1930. It was a thank-you for Nana's kindnesses following the death of Neal Gerrard. The phrase that stood out from the rest was simply, "You of all people know that the best part of me is gone." That seemed to me a considerable tribute to pay to someone who died. There was not much left after that. A couple of letters in the bottom with no envelopes. I opened one, which mentioned the name "Laura," but I could not make out anything except that Alvareda was sending some article to her, and that "Prissy and Wallace are fine people who can be trusted." Trusted for what?

The other said more. "The feelings you were having when you last wrote were understandable, and also I appreciate what you said about not wanting me to share any of this burden. But I want to—it is the only way I know of that I can help—and Neal would have been the first to agree. As family, we all must share in the responsibilities of each other. More anon. Your own dear friend, Alvareda."

There was no envelope for this one, but it was dated January 2, 1932.

I read it over again. I would have given anything to see the letter from Nana that precipitated this reply. As it was, I had no idea what Alvareda referred to. There were no other letters in that late period that I could find.

At the bottom of the box was a layer of dark tissue paper, and a little gold seal that apparently once held it together. I shook out the box, to be sure I had not missed anything. Only one other article fell out, a gift card that probably was in the box in the first place. "For Elzyna, to help you hold the memory—Joyeux Noël. Alvareda. 1913."

One thing was certain. If this card were enclosed in the Savoy gift box as appeared to be the case, Alvareda shopped at Savoy Fine Lace and Linen Company too. I put all the letters back, and put the box away in Nana's closet. I could think of no where else to look.

Outside the sun was shining. It would be a good day for the funeral, and I would have to forget about all this for a while and begin preparing myself. My hair needed washing, and required a long time to dry. I had to do my nails and sew a button on my suit blouse. Alexander would pick me up at one, and I had no idea how long it would be before I got back here this evening. The meeting with the attorney might take a while, and then—I stopped. The most obvious notion occurred to me. Maybe the attorney was holding some items Alexander did not know about. There might well be a surprise awaiting me in his office that afternoon, I realized. And, in fact, there was.

Chapter 6

Sometimes on the way to a funeral, passengers riding in a car together adopt a certain tone of voice, and make attempts to express words appropriate to the occasion. I do not know whether Alexander was truly sensitive to what he assumed were my feelings about attending Nana's funeral, or he was simply trying to figure a reasonable way to put off the conversation that must inevitably take place between us. He said it was so fortunate that Elzyna and his grandmother both had such long lives, and were both in relatively good health almost to the end. Then he said, "Of course my grandmother began to fail soon after my father was killed. At her age, it was a horrible thing to have to go through. Not that it would have been easy for anyone, at any age."

"How old was your father?"

"Forty-four—nearly forty-five."

We rode on in silence. For years there had been something I wanted to say to Alexander, but the circumstances never drew us together and allowed me the chance. I was now aware the moment had arrived, and even though I knew it probably would not help to close the gap created between us in November of 1940, I still felt an overpowering need to say it. "I would give anything in the world if I bore no relation to Jordan Leider," I told him. "I've always wanted you to know that."

I held my breath. The words seemed to bring the old tragedy back to life . . . and seemed even more inadequate than I'd have imagined. For a while he did not respond; then he said, "I don't think anyone really would want to claim him. And certainly no one in my family associated what he did with the rest of you."

Thank God for that, I thought, relieved.

"I guess in every family there is a misfit. Grandmother said she could see evil in Jordan from the time he was a child, and that he always seemed to have it in for my father."

I let out a breath. "I'm thankful for your attitude, really I am." I patted his hand and looked out the window. Still, I wondered if he really could be as objective as he claimed. He continued, ". . . the tragedy of my father's death was that he had such potential. Could he have only lived out his life, I don't think there was anything he could not have become in time, regardless of whether he won that election for governor. He was a pretty dynamic fellow."

I studied his face. "You're awfully proud of him, aren't you?"

"More than anything. There have been times in my life when the memory of him . . . well . . . got me through a bad situation."

I wasn't sure what he was referring to. Maybe his broken engagement. Somehow I didn't feel I could ask him just then. "It's good you and your mother have had each other," I said.

"We've depended on each other a lot. . . . I remember as though it were yesterday, that morning my father was killed we had gone outside to walk around the yard and see what damage the wind had done. You know, there had been that terrible windstorm. He was wearing a red sweater, a pullover sweater with long sleeves.

"By noon I was running a fever, and didn't get to go to the rally—everyone always said that was so lucky. I don't know. I've never really gotten it sorted out—but anyhow, that evening when my mother finally got home, I had been asleep. I awoke and heard her crying in her room. I walked up and pushed the door open. She was sitting on the edge of the bed, holding that red sweater and weeping. I'll never forget that. At once I wanted to protect her. I grew up feeling very close to her. And I guess I always will."

"Was that why you didn't get married?"

He looked uncomfortable. "No. That was something else entirely."

Obviously he did not want to talk about it now. I retreated to a safer subject. "Just be glad you've looked after your mother. I wish now I had never left Nana."

We were turning into the drive leading to the funeral home, where we would board the limousine for Christ Church. Suddenly he looked toward me. "Why did you leave?" he asked, as though my answer would unlock some door for him.

"Because Nana—well, it was something I don't believe you'd understand."

He looked as though I had hurt his feelings by not trusting him enough to be honest, so I added, "Someday I'll tell you about it, when we have more time. But I've been in that house now—how long? Not even twenty-four hours—and it seems almost as though I never left. I expect to see Nana around every corner. Everything I see, every time I touch something, it brings back a memory. And I find I am appreciating the house in a way I never could before. I think maybe someday I will move back there."

Now he looked truly surprised. An official in dark suit with a white carnation in his lapel was signaling him to roll down the window. "Family?"

"One—" said Alexander. I leaned across and told the funeral official that Alexander would be riding in the limousine with me. He smiled and waved us on.

"Robin, it wouldn't hurt my feelings to drive my own car, really."

"No. You've been kinder than anyone else and I want you to ride with me."

Inside Aunt Patricia was waiting, surrounded by a collection of family of varying sizes from a little girl in a pink pinafore and Mary Jane shoes to Susan (a niece, apparently), a grown woman, and three fine-looking young boys. Their names meant nothing to me. I did not know whether they were family by her first husband or her second. Aunt Patricia herself was heavier than I remembered. She had on a black dress and dark hose and black shoes. Her calves and ankles were thick. Her hair was iron gray, and her eyes under black brows were snappy and keen. When she saw me, she burst into tears and hugged me. I smiled politely and hugged her back. How could she feel any emotion for me? But then this was a very emotional time for her. I felt almost numb.

There were about seventy-five people in attendance, only a few of whom I knew—Mrs. Lang, and some other neighbors on Walker, some people who knew Nana through church, the attorney Mr. Brubaker, who stayed somewhat apart as though quietly observing, even some of Aunt Senta's nursing school friends. One of them said, "Mrs. Farrish used to cook the most delicious things and bring to us at the dormitory. Everyone appreciated her. She was very kind."

Mrs. Lang told me they still lived in Idylwood, and Charlotte lived in Biloxi, Mississippi, with her husband and four boys. I promised to call and get Charlotte's address so that I could write.

The Episcopal service, with the casket closed by tradition, was comfortably impersonal. It was not until I stood above the grave site that I felt a sadness that brought tears to my eyes again, and this was not really so much for Nana's death as it was for the tragic order in which her children had been buried: first John, the youngest, who at age five was buried in Glendale Cemetery, later to be joined by his father, Beryl Farrish. Next, right here before us, Laura Farrish, 1915–1932. Then Senta Farrish Gerrard, 1907–1955. And at last, the open grave over which the Episcopal priest now tossed the ceremonial dirt, ". . . earth to earth, ashes to ashes, dust to dust; in sure and certain hope of the Resurrection unto eternal life . . ." Imagine a mother having to suffer the loss of all three of her children. The thought of it broke my heart, and as though in punishment, my words echoed again: "Nana, I don't love you anymore."

When it was over and people were departing the cemetery, Aunt Patricia insisted we all go to eat together. I did not want to, but of course I could not turn her down. So we drove in two cars to Kaphan's—she rode with Alexander and me, so we could "visit," and the others rode in the big white Imperial. Once there, we sat through a long-drawn-out meal and I listened to incessant talk about family and other people I had never heard of, straining to remember things she felt I should know. At a quarter to four, Alexander whispered that the appointment with Mr. Brubaker was at four-thirty. I realized Aunt Patricia should be told about it so that she could be there if she wished.

"No, you can call me if there is anything I need to know. We're due at Robby's by five-thirty."

More than grateful, and with a splitting headache, I told them all good-bye and we hurried to Alexander's car. It was freezing cold and the sky was clouding over again. When we were in the car I said, "I'm so glad that is over." I took off my shoes, and settled my head back against the seat.

"You held up better than I expected," said Alexander.

"I know. But I feel like I've been dealing with Nana's death since I got here and went into her house. The funeral did not seem to have anything to do with her, not until the end."

He sighed. "Robin, I don't know how to tell you this. I've been trying to find the right moment since you arrived, but I could not seem to do it. You've got to know before we walk into Brubaker's office."

I looked at him.

"Some time ago, Elzyna called Mother. She had decided to leave the house to our family—well, to me."

I was flabbergasted. I wrenched around toward him.

"I don't understand—I can't believe—"

"It wasn't out of any special regard for me, it's just that I'm the last of the Gerrards, and since the house had belonged to my grandmother first, and had been given to Elzyna, she decided it should come back into our family after she died.

"I—think she had decided you didn't want it, or maybe she would not have done that. When you started talking about your feelings toward it today, I didn't know what to do. Or what to say."

I was flooded with anger. I felt betrayed. "What the hell do you need with it? Haven't you got everything you ever wanted? And you knew, all the time, but you led me on—"

He threw me an icy glance. "No, I didn't lead you on. If you hadn't been so thoughtless as to abandon your grandmother all those years ago, I'm sure she would have willed the house to you."

The remark was like a slap in the face. I could not keep my voice down. "What do you know? How would you have any idea of my problems or the reasons I left? It's easy for you to say, when you've grown up in a normal household." Too late I stopped.

"Not exactly," he said. "I didn't have a father."

I could have killed myself but I was too angry to let him know it. "I didn't have one either," I said. "Not even for the first nine years of my life."

He sighed at last and said, "Robin, you've just been through an emotional experience. Maybe you should just try—"

I interrupted him furiously. "That wasn't what you said five minutes ago. You complimented me on getting through the funeral so well. Don't try to pull that nonsense on me now . . . oh, she'll get over it and behave." Then I thought of something else. "Aunt Senta used to say that if it came down to a choice between a Gerrard and one of Nana's own, we'd be left out in the cold. Now I understand exactly what she meant."

I folded my arms. We both fell into silence for the rest of the trip.

I kept going over it again, like a tongue rubs over a sore ulcer in the mouth. How could she have done that? Was the extent of her bitterness toward me that great? Oh, I shuddered at the realization that indeed it was. Then I went over it all again and wondered how she could wield such a cruel blow to me.

Walter Brubaker looked to be around Nana's age or older; he was almost completely bald and had heavy jowls and a rotund waistline. He spoke softly with a slight lisp. After he invited us into his stuffy little office in the Esperson Building with its pine-paneled walls and mahogany furniture, he sat down and paused to say a few words about "dear Elzyna" and how long they had known each other. "She was a fine woman," he said. "I've handled her legal business since her mother died." I drew in a sigh and shifted in my chair. Alexander sat rigidly, drumming his fingers on the chair arm. Mr. Brubaker hesitated, then looked from one of us to the other. "You two have already talked about this, I take it?"

"Could I see a copy of the will, please?" I said dourly.

He handed us both copies, then began to explain it as though we had not the ability to read it ourselves. "It's pretty simple. Mrs. Farrish explained to me that she had nothing left of any value except the house. She did not specify about furnishings. Robin is the beneficiary of a small insurance policy. Probably when she took it out years ago, it seemed like a lot. It will yield around twelve hundred dollars. I have it here."

I looked over the two-page will. "Is that all? She left nothing for me, a letter or something?" I asked with just a seed of hope taking root.

Alexander glanced at me, puzzled. Mr. Brubaker did not pause. "I'm afraid not," he said. "She did not think you wanted the house or anything in it. And since you were married and settled elsewhere, I guess she felt it might be a burden for you to worry about disposing of it. I really can't say—she had her mind made up and didn't want to discuss it much."

I could just see her, shoulders high, mouth drawn up . . . I had seen that look myself. I should not have been too proud to let her know my life was a mess, I admitted. Still, the house should have come to me in any circumstance. "I could contest this will, couldn't I?" I asked.

"On what basis?"

"That—that I'm the only rightful heir."

He shook his head. "Not sufficient. You'd have to prove that Elzyna was not in her right mind when she drew up the will, or that she was unfairly influenced by the beneficiary."

Again, I felt I'd had the breath knocked out of me. I looked at Alexander. He would not face me. You dirty rat, I thought. You're going to let this happen. You don't care anything about me. . . . Suddenly the airless room, put together with the events of the past two days, converged on me. I felt nauseated, and as Walter Brubaker made some further conciliatory remarks, the nausea redoubled and my palms and forehead grew moist. I knew I could not sit there any longer or I would faint. Abruptly I stood up. "I've got to go, Mr. Brubaker. Thank you," I blurted out, and hurried into the hall.

It was cooler there. I leaned against the wall and took deep breaths, feeling a little more steady. Alexander soon emerged with my coat. He put a hand on my arm.

"Are you ill?" he asked. "Here, let's find a place for you to sit down."

I pulled my arm away. "I'm fine." I reached for my coat and started down the hall. He followed me.

"Robin, I'm sorry, I—"

"Sure you are." I pressed hard against the elevator button. When the door opened and we stepped in, I said, "I'll vacate your property immediately."

"It isn't all that urgent."

"What are you going to do with it?"

"I'll put it on the market as commercial property. There isn't much else you can do with a place so close to town."

What I was going to return to and take care of and make into a home one day, he was going to convert into office space. I felt completely whipped now.

"Take whatever you want from the contents," he said. "I have no use for them. Some of the furnishings are obviously good pieces. Maybe you could use them in your home."

"My 'home' is an efficiency apartment that isn't much larger than the library in Nana's house," I corrected him. Not that he would have any concept of that, having grown up in a mansion.

"I'll see if I can get a plane back to Dallas tonight. What I want from out of there I'll take with me. It won't be much. Obviously, Nana didn't want me to have anything."

We were at the front door of the Esperson Building now.

"All right. If you like, I'll drive you back to the airport."

"I'll take a taxi. In fact, I'll catch one right now."

"Whatever you wish."

On the way home I was still near the boiling point. The quarrel had been like a flash of lightning. Yet, if I had it to say all over again, I would still feel the same. I should have seen this coming. Since I arrived at the airport yesterday, Alexander had given me plenty of clues. Nana had changed her will after Aunt Senta's death. Obviously, at a time when she was disappointed in me, wouldn't it follow she changed not only the executor but the beneficiary as well? I could see it all now, Nana hurtfully explaining that I wanted nothing to do with her or her home, that I never bothered to write or call. The Gerrards had always treated her with more kindness than her family. So it seemed perfectly logical . . . if not vindictive . . . to give them back their house.

And the household contents. She had said there was nothing of value, that she would not specify what was to be done. That was convenient. Just let her good friends have everything. Robin didn't matter. I felt as though she were manipulating me all over again. Alexander probably did only what he had been doing all his life: just stood still and let everything come to him, the way it was supposed to. I was too infuriated to want to cry. I wiped salty tears away from my cheeks like one pushes away an annoying gnat.

At Nana's house I made some tea and sat down with it. Yet I could not relax anymore. I was no longer comfortable here. Six o'clock. I thought of calling Mrs. Sobel again about the package. Then it occurred to me the package may have contained Nana's collection of china figurines. She had told Walter Brubaker there was nothing of value except the house itself. Those figurines must be valuable. She might have intended to send them to someone . . . maybe even to me. At least that would be something. Yet, if so, she could have arrived at a value for insuring them. But perhaps she found more sentimental value in them than anything else and would not have been able to view them in a practical way at all. Oh, who could say what she was thinking? I realized in exasperation.

Mrs. Sobel reported there was nothing in today's mail except a bill from a bookstore. I thanked her, and told her I'd probably be home later tonight.

Something inside me would not give up. I hung up the telephone and did some figuring. Even if Nana had not mailed the package until the day before her death, it would have arrived by now, four days later. Yet packages took longer, especially out of town. Maybe Monday. But maybe . . . I dialed Alexander's number. When he answered I said, as calmly as I could, "Did Nana give you her collection of china figurines?"

"No. Why?"

"I just wondered. The postman told me she wanted to mail a package and the collection is missing. I was just trying to put two and two together."

"Maybe she was mailing the collection to you."

"I doubt it," I shot back. "I don't seem to have been on her hit parade before she died. Thanks anyway."

I hung up and dialed Trans-Texas Airlines. I wished the postman had not told me about the package. He could not have imagined what effect his few little words had on my hopes, for proof about my father, or for proof Nana had forgiven me, for the proof she loved me.

I reserved a seat on the eight o'clock plane. I needed to leave here within half an hour. I rushed around picking up my own belongings, then called Yellow Cab. The only thing that I would take with me was the photo album, although now I thought bitterly, there was more in it pertaining to the Gerrard family than to mine. Other than that, I'd need Nana's check register in her desk drawer and the collection of bills that needed paying. Perhaps I was not the one to take care of these odds and ends. Yet the insurance policy named me as beneficiary, having been taken out soon after my birth, so some responsibility fell on me.

I walked back into my apartment at a little past ten, tired to the bone and having had no peace on the airplane because the woman sitting next to me talked incessantly about her grandchildren. It seemed I had been away for months. The apartment seemed small and cramped. I poured a glass of brandy and sat down on the sofa to relax. I had not been there long when certain thoughts began to come together and make sense for me. First of all, the letter written to Nana by Alvareda in early 1932, and the other that was not dated. If the two went together as it appeared because Alvareda used the same color ink and the same stationery for both letters, then Nana must have been away for a while. I knew that long ago people sent notes to each other locally, rather than picking up the telephone even if it were available, because of well-established habit. But by 1932 surely Alvareda would not be sending Nana a note in town. Nana had to be away. And where? Did she stay with my mother for a while before I was born?

That was possible, even probable if my father took off, and especially if my mother were having problems in the late months of her pregnancy. Yet Nana had never told me that. All right, so it didn't seem important to her. Maybe for a long time she did not talk about it because of the unpleasantness about my father's leaving. Yet Nana never said anything unkind about him. Maybe it was my mother who caused the marriage to break up. I realized now that I knew little about my mother. Nana said only that she was gifted, difficult to know, kept to herself. But she was also sweet and loving. Aunt Senta just didn't talk about her at all. Doubtless after her death, Aunt Senta felt guilty about having been mean to her.

I poured another glass of brandy and thought some more. I remembered vividly the day Roy Kingsley told me his mother had talked to someone— who, I wondered still?—and had been told my mother was a slut, and I was illegitimate. Nana said it was not true, and certainly I had not ever believed it either, though I had heard her called that before, by who? The same party?

My father was supposed to be the villain. The only way that made sense was if my childhood image of him going off to seek his fortune were correct. Yet, if it were, would he have never contacted me in all those years before he died, sent a letter to me, a birthday card, anything? Of course, he may have learned my mother died at my birth, and out of guilt and anger stayed away from me. I had never thought of that before.

I thought again about the day Nana told me of his death. I could see her as though it were yesterday, standing at the ironing board by the dining room window, crying. And, seeing me, she walked up and put her arms around me. . . . But she never said how he died, or where. And I was too young to ask such questions, or if I did, I was not answered. I was certain of that.

The problem with all this was that it did not add up. Surely after his death, there would have been no reason for his identity to be kept secret. Yet it was. Why? To protect my feelings? Or . . . to protect someone else? I leaned forward. The letters. Oh, why had I not brought them with me? What had they said? Something about responsibility for family . . . those names I had never heard of, what were they? Prissy and somebody . . . Wallace, that was it . . . Alvareda insisting she help.

"Your mother was a slut. You were . . . illegitimate."

God. A Gerrard.

I swallowed hard. I felt chill bumps pop out on my arms. If you looked at it from that perspective, many things made sense. Go back and consider it all, from the beginning, putting a Gerrard in the place of the father. Laura Farrish . . . a pretty girl, talented, keeps to herself. Up comes a good-looking man known to the family. They get involved, she gets pregnant. To save the family embarrassment, she is taken away. To New Orleans. To stay with friends named Prissy and Wallace. From the letter, Alvareda's friends instead of or as well as Nana's. They make up a story that Laura married a man and lived in New Orleans. He abandoned her. She died at my birth. Nana came home to raise me.

No one would know. No one would know.

"If there was a choice between a Gerrard and one of us, we'd be left out in the cold."

Was that how it happened? Was I the one left out in the cold? And if so, which of the Gerrards? Gabriel? Uncle Clayton? Probably not Clayton, unless Nana lied about his being dead. Yet she might have struggled with it and decided that was best all the way around because of his condition. Damn, I wished Aunt Senta were alive. I would call her up right now, and ask her when Uncle Clayton came to study in Houston. Suddenly I remembered that expression on Nana's face during our quarrel, when I threatened to ask Aunt Senta for the truth. Why was that so upsetting? I shook my head.

The album.

I rushed to my suitcase and pulled it out, hurried through the pages. The notice about Clayton was dated 1933. Still, he might have been there during his internship. Surely interns, busy as they were, had some time off duty. I looked at his picture. Dark hair. Mother's hair was dark, also. And me blond. That, too, was not impossible. Yet . . . Gabriel Gerrard, a blond. And by 1932, already headed for a political career. A doctor certainly did not need an illegitimate child lurking like a skeleton in his closet. But less so a political hopeful.

I sat down again, leaned back, and talked myself into it and out of it, again and again. It could not be, yet it almost seemed certain. And either of the Gerrard brothers was a possibility. Gabriel was around our house more, earlier, while he dated Aunt Senta. Clayton, however, was probably around more later, nearer the time I was born.

All the evidence stacked up, I still could not believe what stared me in the face. Finally, much later, I went to bed and fell into a deep sleep for several hours. Then, just at daylight I awoke with a start. I was thinking of that day again, when Nana told me of my father's death. I was almost certain it was around the time of the murder of Gabriel Gerrard. It had always been connected that way in my mind, because I had thought that now Alexander and I both did not have fathers anymore. Nana might have waited awhile after the murder, unable to gather the courage to tell me my father was dead. She said, "He died some time ago."

Did that mean she had just learned of it, or that only now was she telling me about it? And the continuing secrecy after his death would fit perfectly. Why hurt Louetta by letting the truth escape?

Why hurt Alexander?

Alexander . . . the boy of my dreams. Was he, after all, my brother?

Chapter 7

By morning I was bursting with ideas about what to do next. The only trouble was that, while I could pursue a few of them via long distance telephone, many of them required that I be in Houston, and I could not get there until the holidays, and even then I would be short of money. There were the insurance proceeds from Nana, but I did not know how long it would take to get a check, and I also had no idea how much of it would have to go to paying her bills. Already due was over a hundred dollars to Forest Park for items not covered by the burial policy. Sometime in the near future I would have to choose a headstone for her grave and it would not be cheap. One point in my favor was that the holidays from school would be especially long this year because Christmas fell on Sunday. I could leave here on Friday, the sixteenth, and would not have to be back until Monday, January 2, and be ready for school to resume on the third.

Obviously I had to get back into Nana's house. There I could look at those letters again. Also I might find something about Uncle Clayton's activities when I was conceived in 1931, in Aunt Senta's things. I'd visit him if need be. There might be some things he remembered. I had no idea what shape he was in because I had not seen him since he was injured.

There was always the slim chance I could even get Uncle Clayton to tell me the truth . . . and what would I do if he sat down and told me quite rationally that he was my father? I shook my head. I could not envision it. Then another thought occurred to me and I began to make a list. Telephone Memorial Hospital in Houston and see if they had information about Clayton's internship among their records. Telephone the bureau of birth records in New Orleans. It occurred to me that the doctor's name would be on the certificate. Maybe he had something in his records. Twenty-eight years later, it was truly a long shot. The doctor was probably dead by now. But at least I could check. And at some point I might contact him, or her, go to New Orleans . . .

Find out when the icehouse on McKinney was first opened. It was under construction when Nana told me my father was dead. Mrs. Lang might remember.

And one final item. Find Stephen and Lilly Sandock. They probably were not in Houston any longer, or Alexander would have mentioned them. They would have attended Nana's funeral. I checked long distance information. No listing.

That this was Saturday infuriated me. Should there be a package too large for the postman to deliver, I would have to wait until Monday to get it. Probably I could get nowhere with Memorial Hospital archives on Saturday, and certainly not with the city of New Orleans. Oh, how I wished I could question Alexander about Stephen and Lilly's whereabouts, and a lot of other things. Yet I had alienated him, no doubt. I realized now that I had been wrong to attack him the way I did. He was right about my emotional state. I did not feel so angry with him today. It was not his fault Nana willed her house to him, and besides, he probably felt he had as much right to it as I had. I still felt he should have let me know earlier than he did, but then I was the one who made myself scarce before Nana's death and perhaps he really did find it hard to tell me once I got to Houston.

I owed him an apology, and I certainly would have to extend it if he were ever to help me. By the time I got back to Houston a month from now, he could have already sold the house and dumped all its contents. And if he did not hear from me, he probably would. Yet, on the other hand . . . why should he want to help me find my father under any circumstances, and especially if my quest might lead me to the doorstep of his family?

I could not let him know what I was doing, at least not until I had something really solid. He would more likely prove an obstacle than a help. It was not that I distrusted him exactly, it was just that his own image of his father or his uncle would be threatened and, worse, his mother's feelings were involved and he had already stated he would do all he could to protect her. Imagine finding out Gabriel Gerrard fathered a child and managed to get by without detection. All these years she had revered his memory, never remarried. It would be awful from her standpoint to learn now he had betrayed her. Maybe worse now than earlier. No . . . I could not let Alexander know what I was about. Somehow I had to persuade him to leave the house alone until I went through it again. There might be still other things I failed to find before. I started to pick up the telephone and call him, then thought not. What if my voice betrayed me? He might ask a question that would prove awkward to answer. Better to write him a letter, and say I had decided to come home at Christmastime to pick up some items I left behind, so please hold off any sale of the property until then. Or maybe not say anything about the sale. It sounded too urgent. Might tip him off. I had already made it known that I wanted to discover the identity of my father on more than one occasion while we were together. If Alexander had an inkling I was tying this to his family, he'd probably set the house afire before I got back there. He would conclude I was after revenge because of the house, or after Gerrard money—a claim to part of the inheritance—or both. And that was not right at all. Yet it did occur to me that it sure would make good leverage for getting him to relinquish Nana's house to me. Leverage. I hated the sound of the word. I sat down and buried my face in my hands. I had never thought like that before. What was I becoming?

Before the morning was over I called Memorial Hospital in Houston. Just as I feared, the department I needed was closed on Saturdays. I pulled out the insurance policy and called Information in Dubuque, Iowa, to get the phone number of their claims department. First I learned the insurance company was now defunct. Their policies, however, had been sold to another insurance company in Fargo, North Dakota. A call there revealed there had been still another sale, to an insurance company based in Arlington, Virginia. Finally, after filling up a note pad with telephone numbers, I reached the right place and talked to the Claims Department. It was immediately apparent my word would not bear any weight. The woman said they would have to have a copy of the death certificate and several other items I had never heard of before.

"How long will all this take?" I asked.

"Six to eight weeks, usually."

I breathed a sigh of exasperation and hung up the telephone. I would be doing well to pay my own telephone bill after all this was over.

Next I called the Metropolitan Theater on Main in Houston. The assistant manager—the only official on duty that day—sounded as though he was not much older than I was. Theaters did not have art departments anymore, he told me.

"I realize that, but I thought someone at the theater might remember Stephen Sandock and know where he went to work following his employment there."

"That long ago? Hm . . . let me see. Hold on a minute." I heard him ask someone if "Bubba" was around. In a few moments the answer came back and he returned to the telephone. "We have a custodian who has been here a long time. He's a pretty old fellow. He might know this Mr. Sandock," he said. "But he's upstairs mopping the balcony floor right now. I'll have to go and get him," he added discouragingly.

"Would you please?"

A sigh of irritation. "Hold on."

Another wait, this time a very long one. Finally the old man picked up the telephone. I explained what I was after.

His voice was scratchy as an old recording. "Well, I was around at that time all right, and before that. I don't remember names very well, though."

"Do you know where any of the art department people went after the department was closed?"

"No. Maybe into sign painting, you know, them companies that puts up highway signs. Like for cigarette ads and such."

"Oh, I see. All right. Let me give you my telephone number, and if you happen to think of anything else, you could call me. Collect."

"All right, miss. Are you interested in old posters? We got a few in a storeroom in the back, I could show you."

"No, thank you. I'm just interested in locating Mr. Sandock."

I did not even know where to begin without a Houston telephone directory. I pulled out the Dallas Yellow Pages and found "Outdoor Advertising." There were several listings. I called each of them. The last one, the Federal Sign Company, was the most help. The man there told me the names of three Houston firms for outdoor advertising, where there were people who had been in the business a long time. Perhaps one of them might know Stephen.

"If he has been in the sign business very long, someone will know him. I'll keep your number and let you know if I hear anything," he offered.

Of course I was operating on a very thin shred of evidence. I did not know if Stephen stayed in the advertising business. By now he might be a used car salesman for all I knew. Again I was frustrated and angry with myself for cutting off all ties ten years ago. As a high school graduate I didn't have sense enough to know the world is ever changing and would not stand still while I grew up. In the past four days, more than ever before, I had been forced to look at my own remarkable immaturity when I ran away and afterward.

I dialed the Neon Electric Company in Houston, and was referred to a person called "Fitz." Short for Fitz—something, I assumed.

"Yep?"

I explained my mission for what seemed the twentieth time. He listened patiently, then answered, "No, I don't know him myself. But wait a minute, let me get something." In a few moments he returned with a directory of the state association for the outdoor advertising trade. He looked through it, but found no one by the name of Sandock. "Tell you what, though. I have a friend over at State Neon who knows everybody from one end of the state to the other who ever painted signs. Just ask for Frank. Wait, here's the number."

I copied it down and thanked him. At that point I was ready to stop. I could not afford much more long distance investigating. I walked away from the telephone, hesitated, then walked back and picked up the receiver. Oh well, just one more, then I'll stop this and write a letter to Alexander.

"State Neon."

I asked for Frank.

"This is he. May I help you?"

I told him my name, and that a man named Fitz from Neon Electric Company referred me to him. "I'm trying to locate a man named Stephen Sandock . . . he's a friend of my family and it's very important that I locate him. Do you know him by any chance?"

"In fact I do, and I'll be glad to help you."

"Oh, thank you," I said, and my voice broke. I had not realized I was close to tears until I heard a note of kindness and sympathy in the voice on the other end of the line. I felt so stupid. I must have sounded like a little girl who just lost her daddy, which was not far from the truth at that.

"I've known Stephen for years. We used to paint signs together, and we worked together at the Met," he was telling me. "He's in Temple now. I'm just looking for his number here."

"Oh, he is? I can't believe it." Tears were running down my cheeks. You idiot, stop this, I kept thinking. I sniffled.

"Here it is." He recited the number, then insisted I repeat it to be sure I got it right.

"I don't know how to thank you. I didn't think I would ever find him."

"You say he's a friend of your family?"

"Yes, sir. I don't know him personally, but I'm hoping he might know something about my father."

"Oh, sure 'nough? Well, Stephen's a fine man. You know, he lost his wife some years ago."

"No, I didn't know that."

"I believe it was shortly after that he moved back to Temple. Now, he doesn't stay in his shop too much. If he takes a notion to leave for a week or two, he does it. So I can't guarantee you'll be able to find him today. But if you keep trying, you'll find him directly."

"Thank you so much. This means so much to me."

"I have two daughters—one married and the other in high school. I'm always grateful to people who treat them kindly."

I hung up the telephone and blew my nose. He was the nicest man I had ever talked to. Boy, were his daughters lucky. If I could just know my father had been that nice a man, maybe it would be enough.

I looked at the kitchen clock. It was nearly one. Well, maybe I'd hit it lucky twice in one day. "Operator, I'd like to place a call to Temple . . ."

Stephen Sandock had a soft, low voice. When he answered the telephone I was so elated that finally I was getting somewhere, I blurted out my name and told him I was trying to learn the identity of my father.

Dead silence.

I realized I must have sounded like someone in hysterics. I started over more slowly, explained about my mother's pregnancy, the story I was told, the sojourn to New Orleans. "The trouble is, now I'm beginning to find things that make me believe I was told a lie. I'd very much like to find out the truth."

Another exaggerated pause, in which hope rose and fell in me two or three times.

"I don't know that I—I just—"

He knew something. Now I was certain of it. A thrill of excitement went over me. Maybe he would rather not talk over the telephone. "Could I come to Temple and see you? I could come tomorrow, and I wouldn't take very much of your time."

He hesitated, then said, "Yes, of course." He gave me his address and directions from the highway.

I told him I would be there by noon. Temple was just over a hundred miles away. "Be careful. The roads get iced over this time of year," he cautioned. Then he said, "By the way, how did you find me?"

I told him about the grapevine of the sign business, and about talking with his friend, Frank, in Houston.

"Oh, is that right?" He sounded more pleasant, more relaxed. It suddenly occurred to me that he might be involved in a pact of silence for the benefit of the Gerrards, so I told him that my grandmother Elzyna had passed away and I had been in close contact with Alexander since then. I hoped he would gather I already knew so much he might as well answer my questions. Yet . . . what if he reported my call to Alexander and Louetta? I wondered uneasily.

After I hung up the telephone I surmised he might well do that, but I'd just have to take the chance. I would also have to take a chance my car would hold out through the trip. If I got stranded somewhere and could not get back for school on Monday morning, I might find myself out of a job.

Except that his hair was a little thinner, Stephen Sandock looked very much like the man in the photograph I'd seen. He was of slight build and had a trim waist for a man his age—he would have to be in his mid-fifties, I had calculated. His coloring indicated he spent a good portion of his time out-of-doors. I recalled what his friend Frank had said about him. He was wearing a pair of khakis, a tan shirt, and a brown ribbed sweater, and when I drove up in front of his brick cottage, he walked out on his front porch to welcome me.

He took my hands and looked into my face. "What a beautiful girl you are, Robin. Come in, come in. I'm so glad to see you." I was surprised to be greeted so warmly. He seemed to like me already.

He invited me to sit down in the living room while he fixed hot cocoa in the kitchen. I looked around me. The living room was modest, and had been decorated many years before. The fireplace had a gas log heater which made the room cozy and warm. On the windows were ruffled curtains, crisscrossed and tied back at the corners. There was a mahogany tea table in front of the sofa with copies of *Field and Stream* and *Signs of the Times* and *Life*. Above the fireplace there was a Seth Thomas eight-day clock that was almost identical to that on the mantel in Nana's library. On the wall behind the sofa was an oil painting with Stephen's signature at the bottom. A landscape, with a lonely farmhouse at the edge and a windmill. There were lots of dark blue and green tones, and it looked sad and forlorn. Otherwise, the room was dominated by framed photographs of Lilly, some of them just her, and others of groups including her. One, right across from where I sat, was a group photo apparently taken during Gabriel's gubernatorial campaign, for in the background was a speaker's stand with streamers and bunting. From the left to right, Aunt Senta, Uncle Clayton, Stephen, Lilly, Louetta, and Gabriel. They were all dressed up, the ladies in hats and gloves, the men in suits.

I had learned more from old pictures than any other source. I picked it up to get a closer look, and was still holding it when Stephen came back through the door.

"I'm not much of a cook—Lilly spoiled me. But I do make good cocoa. Careful, it's hot."

I thanked him and took the steaming mug with marshmallows on top. He sat down across from me. "That photo is one of my favorites," he said. "The months of Gabriel's campaign were among the happiest in our lives. She had her first major stroke shortly after that."

"Her first?"

He nodded. "She had several. She was in a wheelchair for the last six years of her life—she died in 1953 of kidney failure. But she was cheerful and uncomplaining right to the end."

"Frank said that was when you left Houston."

"Yes, but I didn't settle down immediately. I put our house up for sale and packed my brushes and paints, and drove off to—well, to anywhere and nowhere. I just had to keep going. It was the only way I could keep from breaking down.

"I painted signs here and there, like I did in my younger days, and now and then I'd hire on somewhere for a few months, then quit and move on again. I lost touch with practically everybody. And finally I just got tired of moving and came back here. I lived here before, you know, as a young man. We moved here so that my mother could take treatments at Scott and White. This was the only place that had no connection with my wife, and so I thought it might be a good place to stop."

His gaze circled the room. "At first I didn't have all these pictures around. It took me a long time before I could bear to have any reminders around me. Now the house is furnished with things that were ours, and pictures that help me remember that I was lucky to have had as many years with Lilly as I did."

He stopped and shook his head. "I'm sorry. I didn't mean to get off on that subject. But I haven't talked to anyone from the family in such a long time."

I could not help believing him, and felt relieved that this trip might prove an opening of doors, rather than the encounter of more blockades. "I was hoping you could remember something from 1931 and 1932 that might help me. My grandmother told me a story of my father that I believed all my life, until just recently. And of course I have to allow for the possibility she was leveling with me. It's just that, I can't understand the reason for all the mystery, unless she was protecting someone who might be hurt if the truth were known. I was supposed to believe he and my mother divorced shortly before I was born, but I was also expected to believe that he was a good man, kind and—"

I stopped in mid-sentence and blinked.

"Robin, did you ever think it might have been me?"

"You?" I breathed, my heart in my throat.

He was reaching for my hands. "Wait," he said. "Let me tell you a story. . . ."

Chapter 8

The mugs of cocoa were empty. The clock on the mantelpiece struck three. Stephen had chronicled his first courtship of Lilly Gerrard, had told of the long period when they had been forced apart by his own mother's illness during the 1920s, all the while assuring me at every pause of his love for Lilly, his devotion to her. Now and again he stopped to say that he hoped I could be patient with him, for going through all this, but that I had to understand a lot of things if I were to understand the point he would make at the end. Through it all I sat completely still, following him with my eyes as he walked to and fro, his hands behind him, sometimes remembering things and going back. I was afraid to imagine where all this might be leading, was afraid to let myself think my search could be over—my mind was like a combination lock, fingers turning the dial toward the final number that would open it.

"When Lilly broke off with me because of her illness, I did not think I could bear it. I could not make her believe that it didn't matter about children, not to me. All I wanted—all I had ever wanted—was for Lilly to spend her life with me."

He sighed. "Well, some months after that, after she'd gone into nurse's training, and I had to face the fact she was really not going to change her mind, I began to pay some attention to Laura."

I felt my heart contract, and gripped the edge of the chair arm. Stephen sat down to continue. Now he would not look at me. He turned his face toward the little gas log fire as though he were too ashamed to look into my eyes. "It didn't just happen as it might have with someone else, someone different from Laura. I had been admiring her talents since the first time I was in Elzyna's home, back when Lilly and I and Gabriel and Senta used to pair up and go places. She was very gifted, but because she had some sort of—well—mental problems, I guess, no one took any notice of her. Everyone shoved her aside.

Especially Senta. I liked Senta, you understand, but she was ugly to Laura, really ugly."

I told him I remembered hearing that from my own childhood.

"Personally I think she was jealous because Laura inherited their father's artistic talents. Gabriel and I both felt sorry for her. I saw an ad in the *Chronicle* about a contest for young artists, and the prize would be a four-month series of free art lessons at the Museum of Fine Arts. I felt if she won, the instruction there might help her talent, and also help her gain some confidence in herself. So I persuaded her to let me enter one of her drawings.

"Well, I guess you probably know, she won the contest. I really think it was the only wonderful, exciting thing that ever happened to her. We went down to the *Chronicle* and had our picture made together for the newspaper. The classes began soon after that, and were held in the afternoons after school. I was working at the Met then, and sometime in the early fall of 1931, Elzyna called me to ask if I would mind picking up Laura from art school and taking her home. She had some business to take care of—I think it was something to do with her mother's estate—and she usually got away by five o'clock, so I told her I'd be glad to see that Laura got home safely. The lessons were twice a week, and I did this for Elzyna over a period of three or four weeks. There were a couple of times when I got away too late, and had to contact the museum and tell them to be sure Laura got on the bus. But anyway, we were thrown together, by ourselves, several times."

I kept trying to imagine them together . . . he was so kind and caring . . . how wonderful to find I was a product of that union. . . .

He paused before continuing, as though he were not sure how to go on. "Laura was a fascinating girl. If she ever got away from her sister, she was much more talkative and unafraid to say what she felt. She looked at everything differently from anyone I'd known. I actually think she had a brilliant mind. Sometimes I could not keep up with her."

I remembered hearing that my mother was dumb in school, made horrible grades, was always in trouble with the teacher. I had never questioned that, always accepted it as I had everything else. . . . Now Stephen was saying things I'd never been told before, even by Nana. I suddenly felt proud of my mother, for the first time in my life. . . .

"She simply did not communicate with most people very well. I could see easily that she was way ahead of most people up here"—he tapped his forehead—"but had no common sense at all. Her art teachers thought she was one of the most gifted pupils they had ever taught. Can you imagine someone her age not being reliable enough to make it home on the bus by herself? Poor thing . . . I think Senta completely undermined her confidence for her whole lifetime, convinced her she was an idiot. At least I suppose that's right. Something frightened her. I know that.

"Well, I guess you can figure out the rest. Laura was so . . . so grateful to me. I guess no one had ever paid her that kind of attention before. And you know how easy it would be for someone that age to become infatuated with a man who was kind and believed in her." He paused again. "And not only that. Almost from the beginning, I realized she was—well—somewhat experienced with boys." Now he looked at me. His voice tight, barely audible, he said, "Laura was the most seductive creature I have ever known. And one night, just one, I—we were together."

Stephen had tears in his eyes. I swallowed, and nodded my understanding, thinking how sad my mother was, what a curious, helpless human being, for all her talents.

After a while he went on. "When her pregnancy was discovered, Elzyna called me. I had recently been reunited with Lilly, and we had gotten married. Alvareda, Elzyna, and I met together one day. Aside from concern about Laura and the baby, a matter of utmost concern of course was Lilly, that she never find out. I felt I must tell her, that it was the only honorable thing to do. But Alvareda looked at me. I had never seen her look that cold—maybe determined is more the word—and said, 'That may be the best thing for you, Stephen, but it could prove disastrous for Lilly with the state of her health being what it is. If you love her as much as you claim to, then you'll try and do the kindest thing you can for her, and learn to live with your guilt without forcing her to live with the knowledge of what you did.' Her eyes softened a little after that. She reached across the table for my hand, and said, 'I know you love my daughter, Stephen, and don't think I'm sorry the two of you married.'"

He took in a breath. "The tentative plan was that the baby would be given up for adoption. Elzyna did not seem to be settled on what to do for the duration of the pregnancy. She said she might just keep Laura at home. Laura kept to herself anyway, and she wouldn't show very soon because it was a first pregnancy, and so forth. Alvareda suggested they investigate the possibility of a private home where Laura might stay for a while. But the issue wasn't settled in that meeting. Later, probably about a month afterward, I was told that Alvareda had close friends in New Orleans who would put Laura and Elzyna up until the child was born, and she had persuaded Elzyna to go there. From my understanding, someone there was considering the adoption of the baby."

"So in the letter I found from Alvareda to Nana, she was referring to you, rather than one of her own sons?"

"That letter was dated when?"

"In January of 1932."

"Yes. That would be right."

"And Alvareda sent money to help Nana?"

"Yes."

"Then after Mother died, they changed the story so that Nana could bring me home and raise me, in hopes I would have an 'acceptable parentage'?"

"I gather that, yes. I imagine, having lost her daughter, she did not want to give up her daughter's child as well. But wait, that isn't all. I—I can't help wishing it were, just at this moment.

"When Elzyna was on her way back to Houston with you, and of course, Laura was dead, Alvareda called and asked me to come to her house because she needed to talk to me. When I got there she apologized and said that I was not your father after all."

I felt my hopes collapse. "What? I don't understand."

"She would not tell me much more, though I begged her to. Just that, apparently, Laura had confessed that it was not me but someone else; she was a little farther along in the pregnancy than she at first gave anyone to believe.

"I remember Alvareda stood up and walked over to the window, and looked out. She was a tall, thin woman. She wore a black suit—it seems to me she was still mourning her husband, that she did for a long time. Finally she looked around and folded her arms. 'I wish you had fathered Laura's child,' she said. 'I can assure you, the truth is quite the most distressing thing I've ever heard. . . . I feel so angry, and so helpless—"

I felt shaken up and overwhelmed, like a mountain climber must feel, when she has fallen down the side of a cliff, grasped onto the rope, and now starts the difficult task of coming up again, hand over hand, every yard a struggle. "Then who were they trying to protect? And why?"

"I don't know. But I must tell you I seriously doubt it was either Clayton or Gabriel. Yes, they were both in town—at least Clayton was, and Gabriel, too, part of the time. But Gabriel's only responsibility was for encouraging me to enter Laura in that contest. As I said, he felt sorry for Laura, too. If not for that, many things would not have happened."

"We would not be sitting across from each other now, I guess," I told him. Somehow I wanted to reach out for him, to hold on to him because he was so close to what happened.

He smiled. "I'm so thankful that we are. I'm only sorry I could not be of more help. I—I somehow feel we came so close to belonging to each other," he said, echoing my thoughts.

"You know, I hate to admit this, but when you called I actually entertained the idea of letting you believe I was your father. I get very lonely sometimes. . . . I'm glad I didn't now. It would not have been fair to you. But I hope we can still be friends."

"I'd like that. Yes, I'd like that very much," I said, and smiled.

Before I left that evening, Stephen and I talked of many things. I told him about the circumstances of my running away, and all the reasons I stayed away so long. He seemed to understand this, and related it to the fact that he had dealt with his grief over Lilly's death in much the same fashion. The hour grew late and darkness fell. He made more cocoa and turned up the blue flames in the gas log fire. I had never talked with anyone more accepting before, and thought what a shame it was that he had no children of his own and must be left alone with his memories. I told him about Nana's death and about her willing the house to Alexander. I told him of the quarrel.

"I've often thought of him and wondered what sort of a person he turned out to be. I can't imagine a more horrible thing than losing your father the way he did," he said. Then he thought for a few moments before adding, "You know, it's just possible he isn't mad at you as much as he's trying to get back at your family for what happened."

"You mean because Jordan Leider was my great uncle?"

"Yes. He doesn't have anyone to fight. The house could be a viable weapon from his point of view."

"I never thought of that. I did talk to him—very briefly—about the fact I was ashamed to have to claim Jordan Leider as a relative. He didn't seem to hold that against me. Of course, we had that conversation before he admitted the house was to be his."

"Well, maybe I'm wrong, but it seems it would be awfully hard not to have some really strong feelings against Jordan's family. Of course, what happened was twenty years ago."

What he was saying now had the unmistakable ring of truth. From the time I was old enough to realize people held grudges, I had felt certain that was the way all Gerrards must surely view our family. I was thankful all over again that Alexander did not know what I was up to. The fact that his father's image was subject to a little tarnish was bad enough. To have to accept a descendant of his father's murderer as a sibling surely would be the bitterest sort of medicine.

Finally I sighed and leaned back. "I wish I knew where to go at this point. I know you don't believe my father is a Gerrard, but Alvareda's reaction seems to point to that, don't you think?"

He shook his head. "I have to admit you're right. I just can't help but feel in all those years between 1932 and 1940, I would have found out. Someone would have let the truth slip out down the line."

"Oh, I don't think so. And it could be true that the person responsible was not even told. Remember, with my mother, Laura, dead, it would be so easy. Nana never gossiped a word in her life, and Aunt Senta didn't know anything to tell.

"But what about Uncle Clayton? No one knew much about him, did they? My only memory of him was of a cold, forbidding person, but obviously he had the normal instincts for a man. I mean, he married my aunt Senta."

Again he paused to reflect. Finally he said, "I never met anyone like Clayton Gerrard. It was as though there were certain elements of his personality that were missing. If he tried to be personable, he came off a little phony. Lilly and I used to discuss him a lot. She only saw the good side of him. But then, that was how she saw nearly everybody. But you know what?"

I shook my head.

He leaned forward. "I found him as frightening as you did. I really didn't like to be around him, and only put up with him for Lilly's sake. To imagine him having anything to do with a girl like Laura is just—"

"Yes, but remember you said she showed a completely different side of her personality around you. Maybe Uncle Clayton was different around others."

He smiled. "You're awfully perceptive, Robin."

"I believe I'm going to try to visit him. I know it sounds crazy, but he might know something. Or I might get him to betray something without realizing it. Did you ever see him after—afterward?"

"Yes. Lilly and I went to see him fairly often. But he didn't even recognize us. He always thought Lilly was someone else. Most of the time I'd wait out in the hall while she visited. I just couldn't take it."

"Well, I'm going anyway. At least now I know that he was around at the time. I can't tell you how much you've helped me. I never dreamed I'd be going through something like this. There just isn't anything to go on. I was so stupid for wasting my chances by cutting myself off from Nana. Do you realize I could go to my own grave without knowing?"

He shook his head and a faint smile crossed his lips. "Somehow I have a feeling you will find out. Let me know if there is anything else I can do."

All the way home I thought about the details of our conversation. In retrospect, the strongest impression was that of Alvareda saying what she did after my mother's death. "The most distressing thing I've ever heard. . . ." she had said. She had said she was angry, and that she felt helpless. The longer I thought about it, the more convinced I was that my father was one of her sons. And what would I do if it were true? What would I have? Either a father I could not ever be close to because he was incapable of being close to anyone, or a father who had been dead for twenty years. Suppose I wound up beating Alexander with his own weapon, and regained the house from him? Then I would have a house. But I would still have no one. . . .

Except for Stephen. I felt now I would always have his friendship. Perhaps that was as much as I would ever gain from this whole search. If so, then I would have to be grateful for at least that much. Yet . . . with the same natural desire as a child has for its mother's breast, I wanted more than anything I had ever wanted to find my father—dead or alive. It might take years. It might cost me all my money, however much or little that might be. But I was going to keep searching until there was nowhere else to look.

Chapter 9

The following month was the longest in my life. I seemed always to be either waiting out the time or facing still another disappointment. The bureau of birth records in New Orleans confirmed the confidentiality of records of adoption. They would be glad to send me a copy of my birth certificate "currently on file," but not until I sent them a money order for two dollars, and then waited eight weeks for it to be processed and mailed.

I awaited a package in the mail. Monday, Tuesday, Wednesday. Finally I gave up and wished again I could forget I had ever heard the postman speak about a package.

In less than two weeks I received a reply from Alexander. "Let me know when you're coming, and I'll meet you with a key." That was all he said. Did this mean he intended to stand over me while I looked around? Swell. Now I'd have to figure out some way to get him off my back. And what if he had already listed the property, without the house being emptied? People did that every day. I had not even thought of that. People coming through, talking about the good and bad points, checking for termites, opening up the closets . . . how awful.

There was one other serious preoccupation that troubled me over the weeks before Christmas vacation: my money situation. None of the airlines that flew between Dallas and Houston were offering price breaks now. I could not afford a round-trip plane ticket. Moreover, I might not have a place to stay in Houston. I could not afford a motel, not for more than a few nights. I wouldn't feel right asking Alexander for permission to stay in the house. I did not want him to know anything about my financial situation, especially now. Nor would I go begging a loan from my ex-husband, although by all rights I should. He had been extremely uncooperative about the tuition money he promised me, especially near the end of my years in college. If he meant to teach me there was a limit to his obligations to me, he had been more than successful. And I wouldn't be a bit surprised if he were in a squeeze for money himself by now. A year ago he built a fine new home in an exclusive part of nearby Arlington; now he commuted back and forth to a high-rise office building in Dallas, which he owned with several partners. I could see myself knocking on his door . . . . no, I couldn't.

I would just have to make do. Cut back on household expenses over the next few weeks. That would help some. I would ride the bus to Houston, and while there use the local bus system to the extent that I could. St. Vincent's Home was near downtown. If I went to see Charlotte's mother, which I had considered, then I could ride the Lawndale 7400 bus as I had many times. If I could get by without asking Alexander's permission to stay in the house on McKinney Avenue, I would. I could always behave as though staying else-where had never entered my mind and naturally in order to save time and be out of the way soon, I would find it easier to stay on the premises. . . .

I still hoped every day there would be a notice a package had come. Daily my fingers searched for a yellow slip, even though I knew the chances were zero.

Classes were dismissed at two o'clock on Friday, December 16. I bundled up the essays I had to grade before school resumed, plus all the information I needed for making up the final examinations, and put them in the briefcase given me by my homeroom students for Christmas. The briefcase was made of leather and bore my initials in gold. It must have cost a great deal of money. I thought of my incongruous need for hard cash. I smiled and shook my head.

My bus would leave at 4:05. Because of a number of stops, it would not arrive in Houston until eleven o'clock. I would have to bear the expense of a taxi ride to McKinney Avenue and I had written Alexander and asked him to leave a key in the mailbox because I would arrive very late. That seemed an ingenious way to keep from having to face him.

I did not mind the long bus ride very much, although the driver kept the coach too warm, apparently overlooking the fact that every seat was filled and everyone on the bus had on warm clothing. I took off my coat and my woolen scarf and pulled out a few of the essays I needed to grade, but I did not get very far. Before seven o'clock we stopped in Corsicana to pick up passengers, and three high school kids sat down near me. I began to listen to them talk and realized these kids were from the Oddfellow's Home for Chil-dren in Corsicana. They were all bound to visit relatives for the holidays. Suddenly I felt very sad for them, and I began to think that I could have easily grown up in someone else's home, or in an orphanage, in Louisiana. Far away from Nana. She must have loved me a lot, to raise me by herself, knowing she'd be old by the time I was grown—she was almost forty-three when I was born. I could not remember thanking her for that, not even once. Suddenly I missed her very much. I put the papers away and closed up the briefcase. I wiped a circle of frost off the window glass and gazed out into the empty night. The group of kids from Corsicana began to sing Christmas carols, their voices mellow and harmonious, as though they did this fre-quently and were comfortable with each other.

As they crooned the old familiar melodies, I bit my lip and fought back the tears. If Nana had just lived a little longer, I would be on my way to see her right now, instead of on my way to an empty house. The Christmas tree lights would be glowing in the window when I approached. . . . I'd go into her arms, and bury my head in her soft bosom, tell her I didn't mean what I'd said, that I did love her, that I always had . . . oh, Nana, just to be able to touch you again, feel your hand in mine. . . .

As we neared Houston, the weather outside worsened with every mile. Icy rain smacked at the window like frozen darts, and my spirits dropped even lower.

Not until almost midnight did the bus pull up at the station, and I spent the few minutes of the taxi ride to Nana's house trying to talk myself out of the doldrums. Now I could go forward with my search. There were the letters which I could reread tonight, perhaps finding more information than I first discovered. And over the past month I had noted several other places to look. In the morning the sun might be shining. The wind might not be blowing hard, the rain not coming down sideways.

"Here we are, lady. Two dollars, ten cents please."

The lights were on in the house. Alexander's car was parked at the curb. I had not expected this at all, and was not certain whether to be happy or not. All that I felt for him, all that I had tried not to feel, was now suspended in the middle of the confusion my life had become. I didn't feel angry with him anymore. In fact I was ashamed of myself for treating him so badly; he didn't deserve it. None of this was his fault.

"It's nice to go home for Christmas, ain't it?" said the driver. "Up till five years ago, we always went to San Antonio where my folks lived. But they're both dead now. Let's see. Ninety cents is your change."

"Keep fifty. Thank you. And Merry Christmas."

"Take your bags up?"

"No, thanks, I can manage."

Alexander emerged from the house with an umbrella, and took my bags. "How did you get here?" he said.

"I, uh—I flew, of course."

"No, you didn't. You were coming from town. I saw the cab drive up."

"All right, so I took the bus. I had a lot of papers to grade, and needed some time to do it." He looked genuinely puzzled, but said nothing.

Inside, the house was invitingly warm. "Good thing you wrote when you did. I was about to have the telephone disconnected," he said, putting down the luggage.

"It was kind of you to wait about that. I'll finish up as soon as I can and get out of your way. I probably won't make any long distance calls, but if I do I'll ask for time and charges so I can pay you." I paused. I hadn't meant for that to come out as a snide remark.

"You don't need to bother," he said. "How long will you be here?"

"Oh, a couple of days probably," I lied, trying to sound casual. "Will you be in town over the holidays?"

"As far as I know. We have classes through next Wednesday, so I'll be at school until then." He reached into his pocket. "Here's the key."

I sighed. "You really didn't have to do all this, but I appreciate it."

When he was gone, I locked the door. He had been fairly nice. Not overly friendly. I thought of what Stephen said again.

I had not eaten since noon, and was famished. I went to the kitchen and opened the refrigerator. Someone—Alexander presumably—had emptied it out. I looked in the cupboard. There were Vienna sausages and crackers. I pulled some out, and made instant coffee. Before sitting down, I went to Nana's closet and found the box of letters again. This time I went through each stack of letters more carefully than before. If there had been just one in which Alvareda said more. . . . Nothing. At the bottom of the box I found the gift card again. That was no help. However, at least now I could check the names "Prissy" and Wallace. I put the box away and went through Nana's address book for a telephone number. Page after page, nothing. Most of the telephone numbers did not name a city. I could only presume those few that were for people who lived elsewhere would say so. I looked up Patricia Baughman. Wimberley was enclosed in brackets. So that was how she identified out-of-city numbers. . . .

Early the next morning as I ate breakfast, I went through the pages again. This time I found one written differently: Genevieve Reneau, then seven numbers, rather than two letters followed by five numbers. That was odd. Like some sort of secret code. It might be a Houston exchange. I went to the telephone and looked at the dial—5-2 was JAckson. I dialed the number. The operator cut in.

"What number are you dialing, please?"

I repeated it.

"I'm sorry, but that is not a Houston number."

"Would you have any idea what city it is?"

"No, ma'am."

"Thank you. Oh, operator, would you try New Orleans, please?"

"I'll connect you with long distance—"

As it turned out, the number itself had been a working number in New Orleans, but was no longer in service. It also might work in any number of cities with a JAckson exchange. It was probably nothing, but I would keep it in mind. I would also take Nana's address book home with me, as I should have done the first time.

After cleaning up my dishes, I went to the dining room and opened up the sideboard cabinet. Nana used to keep her tablecloth in the box when it was not on the table. I wondered if it were from Savoy Fine Lace and Linen. I found the box. Another Savoy.

Somehow that caused a thrill to run through me, but I couldn't say why except that anything remotely connected with New Orleans seemed hopeful, even if the timing was off. She may have made friends in the early part of the century who were still her friends later. She may have been in touch with them when she went back. Of course, Savoy was just a shop and maybe only a catalogue order house at that. I might be able to find out through long distance.

I listened to the soft pitter patter of rain on the roof, a cheerless day. I thought about the Savoy shop. There was only a remote chance of any connection, yet I could not let go of it in my thoughts, any more than I could let go of the hope a package might arrive that would enlighten me about the identity of my father.

Maybe Alvareda said something in her earlier letters that would give some idea. I pulled out the box once again and took it into the library. If there had been just one more person in the world besides Alvareda who Nana talked to about her problems . . . and if by some remote chance that person were still alive . . .

December 1913. February 1914. "We'll talk when I return, but I wanted to let you know the dates for the spring meeting are April 22–25, and Neal has to be there one day ahead, on the twenty-first. You know how much your happiness means to both Neal and me. You must to go N.O. with us as often as we go. I could not live with myself if I thought for one minute I had let anything stand in your way."

I read it over again. The Savoy shop might be a catalogue order house, but it seemed apparent Nana went to New Orleans more than once. It seemed to be awfully important to her—but why? New Orleans is not so far away by train. Not like New York or Boston. "I could not live with myself . . . ." Weighty words. From the tone of the letter, it seemed vital. Or maybe Alvareda was a bit overdramatic. July 1914. "I found this in a little shop in W" —something, I couldn't make out the word. "It isn't much, but I think the center is val lace, isn't it? It made me think of you in New Orleans. Affectionately, A."

I found no other correspondence from 1913 or 1914, and was not sure there was any point in going farther. Since Nana was expecting a child in a good portion of 1915, I knew she would not have been traveling. I sat back and sipped my tea, thinking. Why Alvareda's grave tone? I wondered. . . . If Nana's marriage was so unhappy, maybe the trips to New Orleans really were her only moments of happiness. Yet . . . somehow it seemed more than that, this preoccupation with New Orleans, with lace. Why would all this mean so much, unless— I sat forward. Unless Nana had a lover there. Oh, surely not. Not my Nana. Never was there anyone more conservative, more prim and proper. Couldn't be.

But. But. If it were, then my own mother might have been her lover's child. Lord, I had never thought of that. I hurriedly went through the packets until I found a group dated 1915. The fourth was dated January 30, 1915, and began,

"My dearest Elzyna. First of all, I am so sorry for having had to leave you so soon following all the tragedy, especially John's death. But Neal is in a conference already, and I have several hours to prop myself up on the pillows and write to you of things that I truly believe will help to make you feel at least a little better.

"You must never, never think that in John's death there is punishment for you and what you have had with Paul . . ."

A lover named Paul. I could hardly believe what I was reading. I tried to envision him. Paul who? What was he like? How exasperating—just a first name. I read on.

". . . God would not be so merciless or lacking in compassion. I want to tell you a story, Elzyna. Before you were born, I had a little girl who was stillborn. She was my first child, and I was devastated at losing her. I was certain that because of something I had done I was being punished. I don't think I could have made it without Neal's loving guidance and understanding. He kept telling me again and again that I was wrong, that no matter what I had done this was not punishment.

"Years passed before I found out for certain he was correct. In the coming years you, too, will see that there is meaning in John's precious life and even his early death that God has yet to unfold for you.

"There was meaning in the loss of Alice Marie Gerrard. And that was my deep love for you. Soon after her stillbirth, you came into the world. The first time I held you in my arms I felt a special kinship with you that has been a great blessing in my life. I still remember your little heartbeat, your warmth. Could I have stolen you from your mother, I would have! As it turned out, you have been like my first daughter. I think you know that no one of my children has ever taken your place in my heart."

I looked up from the letter. I had not known any of this. The bond between them made more sense to me than ever.

". . . Remember now that each of your children has a special place. The child who is growing inside you needs you more than anything in the world, so take care of yourself. If need be, live for a while just for the baby. I would give anything if you could have had a living product of your love for Paul, but it simply was not to be. Hold onto all the memories, all the things you can keep and look at to remind you of him.

"And again, remember how much Neal and I adore you. I will call you the moment we return. Alvareda."

I read the letter again, and yet again. It was the most beautiful expression of love I had ever read. No wonder Nana loved Alvareda so. And it confirmed Nana had a lover. At least for a while, someone who made up for her poor marriage. I read over that part of the letter again. Certainly there was some sort of unhappy ending to the affair, I realized. Poor, sweet Nana. . . .

Who was Paul, and what happened to him? Was he killed in the war? At least my question about the child Laura being his was answered. I would not have to go back even farther to search out my beginnings. Yet now I felt I was suspended between 1915 and 1932. Could anything that happened so early have affected anything much later? Could this lover named Paul be alive? If so, might Nana have seen him while in New Orleans? Might she have confided to him the secret of my father's identity?

I paused. The last question sent my hopes up like balloons above a carnival. Yet . . . the chances did not seem too favorable, when I thought about it further. He might have abandoned Nana, not from neglect or the letter would not have treated him favorably. But he may have been married already when they met and in the end forced to honor his marriage bond. If so, Nana probably would not have looked him up all those years later. And maybe he was already dead when Alvareda wrote the letter. Well, certainly the Savoy shop was a place to begin looking. I fished through the box until I found the gift card from the shop again. Royal at Conti Streets. I went to the telephone and asked for long distance information in New Orleans. Savoy Fine Lace and Linen Company. The operator took the shop name and also the telephone number on the card. I waited one minute, two.

Finally, "I'm sorry, but there is no listing for Savoy Fine Lace and Linen Company at any address in New Orleans."

My heart fell. "All right, thank you."

Another dead-end, I thought.

I returned to the box of letters. Alvareda's letter seemed like a finale, but there might be something more, some mention—1916, 1917, 1918, 1920. Scant correspondence in these years, and little through the twenties. Nothing that seemed at all significant. I was about to close the box when I heard a noise out on the porch. I looked toward the window. A man, looking inside at me. Startled, I jumped up from the chair, disturbing the box and knocking its contents to the floor. Then the man called me. "Miss Farrish? Is that you?"

Mr. Nickleby. It wasn't that I recognized him. I just had to assume it was he. I went to the door and opened it slightly. His coloring was like cardboard. He was unshaven and his hair needed cutting. His coat was rumpled and old. He was wearing a pair of lace-up boots, one of which was coming undone at the toe. Had he always looked this raggedy?

"Yes, Mr. Nickleby, what can I do for you?"

"You are Mrs. Farrish's granddaughter, ain't you?"

"That's right."

"I thought you'd come back."

I remembered he was the one who first discovered Nana after she died. I asked him about it.

"Yes'm. I come over to the window there, and tapped like I always used to do. Thought she might have some work for me. House needs a coat of paint, don't it? Anyhow, she was still and didn't answer. I knew she must be dead. I went next door and told 'em at the store, then I ran and hid."

"Why?"

"I's afraid they might think I killed her. I didn't think of that till I already told. Mercy, I never ran so fast. I looked in the papers for a few days to see if anythin' was said about her bein'—well, you know, killed. And when it didn't, I decided she must 'ha died natural."

"Yes, she did. But where were you for all the months beforehand? No work seems to have been done in a long time."

"Oh I caught me a train up to Oklahoma City, to see my sister. I stayed up there for a year or so. Come back finally. It was too cold up there and I couldn't find no work. Can't find none here either. That was why I come to see Mrs. Farrish. I—I'm awful sorry about her dyin'. She always treated me kindly."

"Thank you, Mr. Nickleby."

"You think, now that you're here, we could maybe work out somethin' for me to fix the place up again? It used to be real pretty when I worked on it."

"I know that. But I won't be living here. The house is to be sold. If you'll come by when Mr. Gerrard is here, he might let you look after it until someone buys it. He drives a white car."

"Oh, I seen that car here last night. I didn't want to come up here then, 'cause it was so late, although the lights was on. I thought it must be your car."

Hardly. "Well, you come back when you see that car here again," I told him, pushing the door a little. Maybe he'd go.

"Oh, Miss Farrish, I wonder if you could spare me a little money. I been out of work awhile, and I sure could use—"

"I'll give you a dollar. That is the most I can spare right now."

"Much obliged."

I went to my purse. He'd be surprised to know I wasn't a whole lot better off when it came to hard cash than he was. But giving him a dollar would probably be wise. Best to stay on his friendly side. I remembered how Aunt Senta used to loathe Mr. Nickleby. She always claimed he stared at her whenever she passed through the yard. Nana would say, "Oh, he's harmless. And I always know where to find him when I need him."

The icehouse. I pulled the dollar out and took it to the door. "Oh, Mr. Nickleby, I wonder if you know when the store next door was first opened."

"Oh, I dunno. Been a long time, though. I first come in there after the war."

"Not before that?"

"No, ma'am. I didn't live around here till then."

"I see. Well, good day to you."

I watched him until he turned at the sidewalk and went toward the icehouse, and went on gazing out the window after he had passed out of view. Finally I picked up the letters spread out over the floor and put them back into the box.

So Nana had a lover prior to World War I. That was difficult to imagine because Nana was Nana, and I would probably be remembering things and puzzling over her for a very long time. But that really had nothing to do with what I wanted to find out. Outside of a slight possibility she might have retained a friendship between 1914 and the year of my birth, someone who could now tell me the truth, I was still back to where I had been at the beginning, and all evidence still pointed to either Clayton or Gabriel, and more likely Gabriel because he at least knew my mother well enough to have sympathy for her (so why not fascination as well?), and because of the simple physiological fact we were both blond, and my mother Laura's hair was dark red, almost auburn.

While here I would look about for more letters and other documents that might help me, but I also needed to begin moving in a forward direction. In this house, I could go on speculating forever, and I did not have the luxury of unlimited time here.

I made two telephone calls. The first was to the nursing home about Uncle Clayton. All I wanted was general information about the visiting hours, but apparently at that place they dealt on a patient-by-patient basis. I was told by the nurse at the desk near Uncle Clayton's room that I could come over the weekend anytime. That was when most visitors came. I did not want to do that. I imagined that Alexander and Louetta visited there some weekends, and I did not want to run into either or both of them.

"Could I see Mr. Gerrard on Monday?"

"Well, I suppose you could. If he's doing all right. Are you a relative?"

"His niece. I live out of town, but I'll be here next week."

"Well, you call before coming, then. I would like to prepare him a little so that he'll feel at ease. He doesn't have many visitors."

"All right. Where are you located exactly?"

"Out the Katy Highway, going towards San Antonio. You know where Howard Johnson's is? It's about five miles farther than that."

I did not know there was anything but woods out there. "Is there bus service from town?"

"No. I'm afraid there isn't. But it's pretty out here, kind of a country setting with lots of trees and squirrels and jackrabbits."

I told her I'd call one day next week. Then I called Mrs. Lang. I caught her just before she left for an out-of-town trip. "I won't be back until Sunday night. How about Monday?" she said.

"That'll be fine. And Mrs. Lang, what year was it you moved over to Idylwood? I was trying to remember the other day, and I couldn't."

"Let's see . . . 1941. In the summer."

"Was that soon after your house burned on McKinney?"

"Well it was a few months. We rented for a while, over on Rusk, while the new house was being built."

"I see. Well, I'll check with you Monday morning."

I thought of the day Nana told me of my father's death. Could it have been very early, say in January or February of 1941? That might fit. Or even, December of 1940, or earlier. Yes, it fit. Perhaps it wasn't much, but it was the best I had so far.

Mrs. Lang lived in a pretty stone house at the top of a hill above Brays Bayou.

She was silver-haired and wrinkled. She looked like the grandmother she was, with a brooch on her dress lapel and a hankie pushed down inside her belt. She brought cups of coffee and a little plate of cookies. I listened to tale after tale of her grandchildren before I was able to get to the reason for my visit.

"You know that my mother Laura died at my birth. And I was never told the truth about my father . . ."

She listened while I explained the circumstances, leaving out names that would mean nothing to her anyway. "I wonder if you remember anything about the situation shortly before I was born." No sooner did I close my mouth than I thought surely this was a foolish errand. Mrs. Lang wouldn't know anything helpful. Just a neighbor—

She was thoughtful for a while. Then she said, "That was a long time ago and I don't remember a lot. But . . . I always kind of worried about Laura. I can remember once, when she was still in Eastwood School, she came over one afternoon because her mother wasn't home and she couldn't get in. Laura was like a frightened kitten. She paced up and down in front of the window, until we saw Elzyna's car come up the driveway. She darted out of there without saying, 'Boo' to me.

"Well, that was just a little thing, but after that I told Elzyna to have Laura always come over after school if she wasn't going to be at home. And for years, until high school I guess, Laura did just that. But she usually seemed awfully nervous. She wouldn't take anything to eat or drink over here. It was as though if anything threw her off, she didn't know how to cope with it and became—well—upset, you know."

I nodded. I wanted to get her to a later point, but my instincts told me that by going through the early events, she might remember the later ones better.

After a while she said, "Elzyna came over and told me she and Laura were going away for a few months, and asked me to keep an eye on the house and so forth. I knew what was going on, of course. It didn't take a genius to figure it out."

"But why?"

She looked at me sidelong, probably pondering whether to continue with her recollections. I reassured her. "It's all right. You won't hurt my feelings regardless of what you say."

"Well, Laura was popular with the boys." She frowned. "I'm not saying she was a bad girl. More naïve than anything else. But my Joe knew her in high school . . . and . . . things were said about her from time to time. I always told Joe he was not to talk ugly about Laura, that I'd punish him good if he ever did."

"Did you ever see her with anyone special?"

She rubbed her forehead. "I wish you had come to me ten or fifteen years ago, Robin."

"Me, too."

"There was a gentleman who visited from time to time before they went away. I probably would not have noticed, and I'd forgotten till you asked, but he had such an impressive-looking automobile. Sporty, if I remember right. But then I'm not sure about that. My husband knew more about cars than I did."

"What color was it?"

"Dark. At least that is the best I remember. You know, the neighborhood over there was modest. Not many people had expensive cars. So you'd remember if you saw one parked at a house more than once or twice."

"And the man. Did you ever get a look at him?"

"Seems to me he was light-haired. I didn't see him up close."

I drew in a breath. "Did he come when Nana was not at home?"

"Now, that I don't know. I never paid any attention."

"Just one more question—you understand how important all this is to me. Did Nana leave you an address where she could be reached?"

"Let's see. . . . No, I don't believe she did. She gave me a number for one of her friends in Houston, said the woman'd come over right away if anything happened."

I couldn't help feeling disappointed.

"Well, thank you very much. You've been very helpful. If you think of anything else, I'd appreciate your calling me. I'll be at Nana's house over the holiday. . . ."

Surely the truth was glaring right at me. Gabriel Gerrard was the visitor in the expensive car. The problem was one of solid evidence. I needed to search the house carefully, in case there might be something, anything that would help. Other than that, the only thing left was to try and find out about the people in New Orleans. And for that I would have to go through Alexander or Louetta. Even they might not have what I needed . . . they might not admit to having it, either, if they had any idea of where this was leading.

On the way home on the bus, I went over our conversation again. Mrs. Lang confirmed what Stephen said about my mother's "experience with men." She was "popular with boys . . . I told Joe he was not to talk ugly about Laura, that I'd punish him. . . ."

Slut . . . illegitimate. It suddenly occurred to me that if my mother were that promiscuous, my father could be anybody. I stopped. A chill went up my spine. Your father could be anybody. Where had I heard that before? Somebody said that to me. But who? I tried to remember. Someone told me that in a vicious way. I could remember the tone, the inference, but I could not remember who said it or when. Was it before Nana contrived the story of my father as having been married to my mother, or after? I could not remember the first time Nana told me the story. For that I drew a complete blank.

Your father could be anybody. Laura was a slut.

I leaned forward and held the back of the seat. That was it. Those two phrases joined together. I tried again to remember more, to put a face on that person who told me, even a voice. Was it a man? A woman? Finally I shook my head. The voice was like a whisper, haunting . . . terrifying. The thought of it seized me with panic. I wanted to run and hide.

I shuddered and sat back. Probably nothing, or if so, I may have overheard an adult talking once. Still . . .

I tried to reconstruct what must have taken place over that summer of 1931. Gabriel Gerrard had known my mother before, when he dated Aunt Senta. She interested him then, but possibly nothing happened . . . or maybe it did. Two years later, they saw each other again, perhaps meeting the first time by chance. When she became pregnant, she may or may not have known who the father was. She may have at first told Nana it was Stephen because he had not been married at the time they were involved. Maybe she thought that would have been more acceptable, get her in less trouble. It was difficult to tell how she reasoned. Maybe somewhere down the line she panicked and told the truth. And if she was farther along than it was at first believed, that tended to prove the fact it was not Stephen but Gabriel. There was no questioning the strong desire to cover up the truth, either way, because a Gerrard was involved. Lilly, if Stephen were the father; and Gabriel's whole career if he were. I truly felt at this point Clayton could be ruled out. Too much evidence—including what Mrs. Lang just told me—pointed away from him. There was no way he could be mistaken for having light hair, assuming she remembered correctly. Alvareda's reaction was indicative of the collapse of all her hopes and dreams. And certainly all her hopes and dreams were centered on her firstborn son.

Everything fit, from the letters to the conversation with Mrs. Lang. Everything except that I just could not think of myself as the daughter of Gabriel Gerrard. Not without irrevocable evidence. Perhaps I was frightened of getting my hopes up, or even because, face it, I had feelings for Alexander that would not, under any circumstance, fit into this puzzle. If not for all this, I could so easily let myself care for him with all the intensity I had felt as a child who wanted to be swept away to a magical kingdom with her Prince Charming. I would never, ever admit that to him. If I lived to be—

The bus lurched to a halt. One more stop to go. I made my way to the front of the bus and stood by the door, looking out the window. When we drew near Nana's property I saw a big beige Cadillac parked in front and two men standing out on the front lawn, talking and gesturing toward the house.

When I approached one turned to me in some puzzlement. Neither of us was sure who was intruding. "I'm Mack Purvis, Purvis Real Estate." A folksy man, with sagging belly and curly hair.

My heart sank. "Robin Farrish. This is my—I'm staying here for now."

"Oh," he said, even more surprised. "This gentleman is down from Oklahoma—"

"Richard Lassiter. Pleased to meet you." This man was taller, immaculately dressed, and obviously impatient. He was rolling up a large piece of drawing paper.

"I don't understand—"

"Mr. Lassiter locates service station sites for his company. The property has been bought for that purpose."

Service station site, I thought fearfully. Alexander never told me that. He didn't even tell me he had listed the property. There was some mistake. Surely the icehouse was the building to be torn down. This was all some kind of mix-up.

"You—you mean to tear down this house?"

"Yes, ma'am."

I felt he had just swung the wrecking ball at me. I had never been so crushed.

"We're looking to close on the sale before the end of the month, and they'll have a wrecking crew in here by the middle of January," he assured me. "It's gonna be a real nice station. What did you say your name was again?"

"Robin Farrish."

"Oh, you're related to the woman who owned the house?"

"Granddaughter."

"So I guess you're a friend of Alexander Gerrard's?"

"We're acquainted," I corrected him.

"Oh." A shifting of feet, adjusting of the waistband of his trousers. "I have been telling Mr. Lassiter here that they ought to sell those doors and that transom. Those pieces would bring a lot, with all that cut glass and all."

"No doubt you're right," I said, lifelessly.

Another pause. "We're about to finish up here. We didn't have plans to come today, it's just that Richard—Mr. Lassiter—could not get a flight out of Tulsa sooner because of the weather."

"I hope we didn't get in your way," said Mr. Lassiter.

When they were gone I turned on my heel and started for the house. Get in my way! My hands were shaking so I could hardly turn the key in the door. Shit. Finally I managed and pushed it hard. I walked to the telephone and opened the directory. Rice Institute. No, it was Rice University now. I picked up the phone and dialed. "Alexander Gerrard, please."

"Which department is he located in?"

"Architecture," I insisted, almost in a yell.

"One moment."

"Hello." A man's voice.

"Alexander? I want to know—oh. Let me speak to him, please. Yes, Alexander Gerrard."

"Just a minute. I'll see if I can find him."

I stood there bursting with impatient fury, my pulse racing. Bastard. How could he? Who does he think he is? "Yes?"

"He's on a jury right now. It'll be out at three."

Damn it, why was it just when I needed to talk to him most, he was not available? "Have him call me please," I asked, trying to calm my voice lest the person taking the message discard it for spite. "Robin Farrish. Yes, that's right. He knows the number. Thanks, you've been very helpful."

I hung up the telephone. I felt trapped. I could not possibly go through all this stuff in less than two weeks. I had no money to have it moved out, and if I did, where would I send it? Where would I store it, and how pay for the storage? Damn. I got up and walked around aimlessly. Suddenly the amount of things in this house seemed more overwhelming than ever. And what of the attic? The garage? What if something were in a place I had not checked? Something really valuable? It took time to figure out what to look for. Look how long it had taken me to realize I had to look for more letters. There could be anything yet uncovered. Anything.

I went into the library and sat down. I had to calm down. I could not think or plan in this state. I got up and made tea. I sat down again. Finally, right after four-thirty, the telephone rang.

I yanked it up. "Alexander?"

"Robin?"

"What the hell is going on?"

"What are you talking about?"

I told him about the men.

Long silent pause. Finally, "I'm sorry. I didn't know they were coming out there."

"It's a good thing they did. You don't ever seem to tell me anything."

"You didn't ask," he barked. "And besides, it happened very quickly. I put the house on the market the last week in November, and Mack Purvis already knew these people were looking out in East End. As soon as he showed it to them they wrote up an earnest money contract and sent a higher-up to approve it. They've got the money. There was no reason to wait. You said you didn't want anything. And even when you changed your mind, you didn't indicate you intended to take a long time looking through."

I tried to steady my voice. "Look, you've got to hold off. I need some time. I can't go through all this overnight."

A pause. "I'll be free after Wednesday. I can come over and help if you like."

"No! No, I don't want your help," I said, and gulped. In a moment I'd give myself away. . . .

"Listen, I'm sorry, but a deal like this doesn't come along every day."

"I thought someone was going to make an office out of the house. I didn't know you were going to demolish it. Oh, Alexander, how could you?"

"Damn it, Robin. Quit trying to make me out to be the villain. You were the one who walked away from it."

I wanted to swing my fist at him. "I'll find a way to stop you," I said, and slammed down the receiver.

I looked around me. In my wildest imagination, I would not have thought of this house as not being here anymore. I had gotten used to the idea of its being an office building of sorts, its interior changed, but not this. Not gone without any hope of ever being converted back into a house. Everything here had existed for such a long time. How could someone just destroy it?

I remembered again what Stephen had guessed about Alexander. Well. The thing to do was act quickly. At least I had to save the significant contents, whatever they were. I rose and walked around, wondering how to organize my search. Perhaps what I ought to do is just find the boxes which held papers, put them aside somewhere, and go through them all. But then, what if something aside from papers was important? You couldn't always find everything written down, and something else might jar an important memory, such as the memory of the day Nana told me my father was dead. Still . . . I found a flashlight and went up to the attic. I walked just inside and moved the flashlight around. End to end, it was covered with a myriad of objects. I closed my eyes and walked out again. I went back downstairs, outside, and opened the garage. There wasn't so much in here, from the stacks of things picked up by the light. Good. I closed the door and started back toward the house. Then I remembered the closet under the stairs. I went to it and opened the door. Boxes and boxes. I approached and pushed open a box. Check registers. I opened another. Check registers and old bank statements. Another. Old bills long since paid. There were many others, but I could not reach them easily. I closed the door. All these things could be important, and from the number of boxes it appeared Nana had saved personal records since the day she moved in, in 1906. So much had happened here since then. And now all record of its existence would be destroyed. In one swift blow of the wrecking ball—

I called Wald Transfer and Storage, and asked about the possibility of moving and storing the contents of the house. The man told me the charges were based on weight, and when I got through telling him what there was, he said, "It isn't possible to estimate over the telephone. I could come out and look."

"Could you just give me some idea?" I begged, no one, no one seemed to realize time was running out, I thought desperately.

"From what you say, I could only guess you'd be talking somewhere in the neighborhood of three to four hundred dollars for moving. And probably twenty to thirty dollars a month storage. Again, that isn't a firm figure."

"Thank you."

Maybe that wasn't reasonable. I called two other moving and storage outfits. One estimated more. One estimated about the same. I made tea and sat down in the kitchen to drink it. All my life, everything of any great importance had been hard to come by. Granted, it was my fault I lost my scholarship money. It was my decision to cut myself off from Nana. And these hasty decisions had cost me a lot. Yet, every important decision I had ever made resulted from the fact that I could not get at the truth about my father. Surely, if I could only learn that one piece of information, my life would be different from that point on.

I started to cry. I shook my head. I had to pull myself together. The thing now was to decide whether to try and get in touch with the people in New Orleans, and possibly go down there, or to stay here and do more hunting rather than risk losing at least two and maybe more days on a wild goose chase. I sat for a long time in a state of indecision, thinking all the time how unfair this was. Then I thought of Stephen again. It was possible he might loan me the money to pay the storage people—that is, if he had that kind of money.

Oh, I hated to ask him. It would be a long time before I could repay him. Yet . . . he had been in on this from the beginning. He also understood my viewpoint. I decided to try and reach him. That would be the deciding factor. If I could get the money from him, I would put off going to New Orleans until the spring. If I could not, then I would not let another day pass without calling Alexander and involving him, the thing I had most wanted to avoid all along.

I had two numbers for Stephen—the one at home, the one at his shop. I called them both, over and over, all afternoon and evening. Finally, when I failed to reach him at nine o'clock, I dialed Alexander.

Chapter 10

I told Alexander only that I wanted very much to find out who my father was, that it was all I ever really wanted, and the only real evidence I had were the names Prissy and Wallace, which Nana had written down as friends of the Gerrards.

He listened attentively and said at last, "My grandmother did not have quite the penchant for saving things as Elzyna. But there are some things in the attic of the cottage that belonged to her. I could check through them but not until Wednesday night. Until then I'm going to be busy trying to finish before the holiday."

"You realize that, thanks to you, I'm quickly running out of time," I retorted.

He recognized the same argument coming and decided to let the remark stand. "I'll be glad to look and if I get a break before then I'll do some fishing. Is that all?"

Again, the total disregard of time. "Unless you can think of anything else that could be helpful," I said dourly.

"I don't know anything. I'll see if Mother does."

"All right. Call me as soon as you can, and—and, thank you," I said. I felt frustrated by my own mixture of feelings. I couldn't help getting angry at him, yet I could not stay that way either.

At least I did not have to be idle while awaiting his call. And obviously he had not guessed this might all be leading right back to his family. I was relieved about that. I spent all day Tuesday and Wednesday moving things around, opening boxes and drawers, trying not to look just for written documents but instead to be open to finding anything that might trip a memory. I went through the entire closet under the stairs and found nothing of real help. Nothing was conveniently identified as having to do with the stay in New Orleans. There were no check stubs of money paid to a doctor during the period previous to and after my birth. Nothing which carried any notation of the people named Prissy and Wallace. Nothing to the Savoy shop except a check identified as payment for Senta's dress and bonnet, in 1913. Presumably Nana paid cash for the tablecloth, for there was nothing that documented its purchase. There were statements from a variety of stock purchases and other investment items covering a long period. From all I could gather, Nana eventually sold all her stocks long before she died. I found a small box with a copy of the original deed of the house when the Gerrards made a gift of it to her in 1906. As I read over it, I realized that Neal Gerrard, or his "heirs or assigns" had first option on any part of it outright. I knew long ago before I was born, she had sold all but the house and the lot it sat on.

I sat back on my heels. If this were still in force, then she need not have given the house back to them now. They could have bought it from me. Then I could have enjoyed the proceeds. Was she further insulting me, then? Or did she truly feel I was doing so well in Dallas I would not want to fool with it?

I read some more. I found nothing to document exactly when the lots changed hands, and that made me think of other things I had not discovered, such as her marriage license, her divorce decree. I would never understand her sense of organization, I realized in frustration.

Late Wednesday night while I was sitting in the middle of the living room floor surrounded by boxes, Alexander telephoned.

"I finished early today and came home to look. I've found something that might be helpful. Could I bring it over?"

A thrill of anticipation went through me. "Of course. Now?"

"Well, it's nearly ten."

"That's all right with me," I assured him.

"I'm on my way then."

I rushed upstairs, combed my hair and put on some makeup. I kept thinking, excitedly, this is going to be it. If there was nothing further in my way of making a connection in New Orleans, I just had to be close. The people who took my mother and my grandmother into their home simply must have been told the truth. And it was only twenty-eight years ago, so surely the possibility was good at least one member of the family would be alive, hopefully Prissy or Wallace.

When the doorbell rang I remembered again how thrilled I used to be when Alexander would come to this house to see me, and I thought it was sad that we had become friendly adversaries because I did not really want to be angry with him, not at all. When I opened the door and saw his solemn face, I knew he had figured out more than I thought. "Well, I've found an old address book with some New Orleans people in it. But there's something I'd like to ask you."

"Come in and sit down."

"Yesterday Mother went out to see Uncle Clayton, and the nurse at the desk told her a woman who said she was a niece from out of town called about coming to visit him this week. I could only assume that was you."

I could have gone through the floor. I sat down. There was no way to deny it. "I thought he might know something that would help me find out about my father."

"And you would go to question someone not in his right mind instead of coming to me or my mother?"

I nodded.

"May I ask why?"

"I was afraid you wouldn't—wouldn't be able to help me."

"What would make you think that, Robin?" The question was edged in distrust.

I couldn't look at him. "I just—after the argument over the house and everything—" I said faintly.

"But I was happy to let you come back and stay here, to go through Elzyna's things. Why didn't you tell me what you were after?"

"None of your business," I replied nervously.

"Oh, I think maybe it is my business. I think that you've decided my family is somehow involved in what you're trying to find out."

I looked at him. I felt almost relieved to have it out at last. "Well, maybe I have."

"And what made you gather that? Just the fact that my grandmother's friends in New Orleans helped out your mother in some way?"

I shook my head. "It was more than that."

"Do you mind telling me what? I think I have some right to know."

I felt a wave of sadness again, for how much pain this was causing him. I paused, "Is that the price on that little address book?"

"It might be."

"All right, I'll start from the beginning. At least then you will understand that I came into this with a completely open mind. . . .

"First of all, I was lied to by Nana. She contrived a story about my mother and father divorcing before I was born, while they were living in New Orleans."

"That's what I was always told."

"Well, I've found things that indicate something quite different," I said, then I told him about everything I'd learned so far, including what Stephen had told me, and also Mrs. Lang. With every sentence I studied his face . . . I wanted so badly not to hurt him. I could see the little boy who held his mother's hand while they buried his father. . . .

Alexander was soon shaking his head in wonder.

"Apart from all that, I learned that Nana, too, had connections in New Orleans from back in 1913 and 1914. Actually she had an affair with someone there."

"An affair?" he repeated.

"Yes. It took me by surprise as well. I was thinking that maybe Nana might have been in touch with the man—his name was Paul, but I don't know what his last name was—when she went back to take my mother into hiding during the pregnancy. Trouble is, I can't find out anything about that unless I can get in touch with the people Alvareda referred to in her letter. And there is an even better chance that the people—Prissy and Wallace somebody—would have been told the truth. After all, they opened up their home to Nana and my mother." I stopped. "Does any of this make sense?"

"Yes, it makes a lot of sense. And I can see why you drew the conclusions you did. But I'm certain you are wrong if you think my father was to blame. He would not have done anything like that."

I lifted my arms in futility. "Oh, Alexander, would that make him a monster? After all, he was flesh and blood just like the rest of us."

"Granted, but he would have never taken advantage of a poor, simpleminded girl."

The phrase pierced me with insult, though I knew it wasn't intended. "Simpleminded is not my term. Who called my mother that?"

"I—I don't know. It's what I've always been led to believe."

I told him what Stephen said about her creative gifts. "Let's just say she was a bit eccentric," I corrected him.

"All right. But I don't believe my father would have covered it up. He would have done the honorable thing. Not like— He would have done what was right."

"On his way up the political ladder? With a wife and a son? You don't think under those circumstances, he might have been anxious to sweep me under the rug?"

"No, no, he wouldn't. He just wasn't that kind of man."

I sighed. "Well, I'm open for suggestions."

"I don't have to offer any. I don't have to do anything about this."

The remark made me feel as though I'd just been shifted back to the starting point. "I knew you would take that attitude. That's why I didn't contact you in the first place."

"What does it matter anyway, after all this time?"

I scowled at him. "It matters a hell of a lot to me."

He sat there for a few minutes, thinking. "There just has to be some explanation, that's all. I don't care what it looks like. I just don't believe it."

Alexander's blind refusal was throwing me into a tailspin. I had to take this slowly. . . . "One possibility occurred to me . . . do you suppose—say it was Gabriel, or even Clayton—and Alvareda didn't want to tell? I mean, she was very much involved in hiding this. If, say, your father was guilty but not aware of it, and anyway, it was pinned on Stephen until afterward, your grandmother might just have kept quiet."

He appeared to consider this, then just to block it out. "No. No, it just isn't true."

"Were you aware your father once dated my aunt Senta?"

"Yes. I heard about that."

"He would have had ample opportunity to get to know my mother. Of course, Clayton would too."

He hesitated for a few moments, then said, "To be perfectly honest, I could not see Uncle Clayton doing that. Frankly, I think he was cold to women. I don't mean he was queer. I just think he was . . . well . . . without feeling for anyone, really."

"That was how Stephen saw him, too, I gather."

"Did Stephen think my father—"

"No. He did not. He was as certain as you are."

This seemed to relieve him. I asked him if he thought it would do any good to visit Clayton. He shook his head. "You can if you want to, I wouldn't stop you. But honestly, Robin, he's not in touch with reality at all. The doctors have said it is a miracle he has lived this long—he has a steel plate in his head —but I don't think it's a miracle. I think it's a damned curse."

I drew in a breath. "All right. I'll think about visiting him some other time maybe."

He looked up at me. "Robin, you aren't doing this just to get back at me, are you? I mean, it seems that it all started after you found out about the house."

I looked away quickly. I could not bear to see the hurt in his eyes. "No. It doesn't really have anything to do with that. I know how hard it is for someone like you to imagine. And I won't pretend what you are saying has not occurred to me. I am angry about the house. But I'm really more angry with Nana than you. Anyway, I will go on searching until I find the truth, regardless of what happens to the house. It is something that has never once been out of my thoughts, and it has already cost me a lot. Including more than five wasted years in my marriage."

"Could I think about it? Just let me get myself straightened out."

"Alexander, I understand how you feel, but you've got me boxed in. I have neither time nor money to wait."

He rose. "I'll be in touch soon, I promise. I'm really trying to understand your side, but it's hard."

At the door I asked, "Will you leave the book?"

He didn't look at me. "Not now. I'm sorry. I've got to think this through. Then I'll be back—we'll work out something."

I was crushed. Work out something. Sounded like a business deal. Perhaps that was how he viewed it already.

I shrugged. "All right."

After he was gone I felt really crummy. The truth was as obvious to him as it now was to me. Tonight he looked as though I were driving a stake through his heart. I couldn't stand hurting Alexander, no matter what he had done. Damn it, I had never wanted to hurt anybody. I felt tears of frustration welling up behind my eyes. I went back and sat on the floor again, and looked through another stack of papers. Then I got up and went to bed. I was so very tired of trying to read between the lines of my grandmother's life.

I did not hear from Alexander all the next day. I finished the boxes from the closet underneath the stairs. I kept putting off going into the old nursery room. I kept listening for the telephone to ring. At seven o'clock I called Mrs. Sobel to see how things were at the apartment . . . to see if I'd gotten a package. No, she said. A few Christmas cards had come.

I hung up the telephone. Christmas. I hadn't thought about it since that night on the bus. This was Thursday. I ought to trim a tree. Except that I didn't have any way to get a tree here. I forgot about it for the moment, but as I cut up an apple for supper, I began to think about Christmas when I was a child. Nana always bought baskets of apples and oranges, and pierced them with cloves. When I was old enough, I helped her do it. And the tree. She always had a small but, as she termed it, "a stately fir." It sat on the table in the middle of the library, and the lights were made of clear glass, shaped like candles, and inside them was a colored liquid that bubbled. Many of the ornaments had been given to her by Alvareda, from various parts of the world, and Nana packed them away very carefully in cotton. Where were they now? If I could find them, I certainly would want to keep them. A small Christmas tree was one of the few things that Nana loved which would be sensible in my apartment.

I tried to think, but could not remember. I walked through the downstairs rooms, opening cabinets and closets. I remembered the cardboard box that held them all said General Electric on the side. A radio had come in it. Finally I went upstairs to look. As soon as I reached the landing, I remembered. They were a part of all the things that had once been stored in my bedroom, and were moved out of there and into the nursery to make room for me. I opened the door. It was stone cold in there, naturally. It wouldn't take long to find such a formidable box, however. I walked around, moving things out of the way. Finally, in the corner, I saw it. It was only a matter of moving a few things off the top of it and scooting it out. As I placed my hands on an old blanket to move it out of the way, I had the strange sensation that someone was in the room with me. I stopped, looked behind me, fear pricking me like needles. Nothing. I listened. There was no sound except that of the wind whipping around the house . . . a lonely sound that made you feel . . . vulnerable. Finally I shrugged it off. I could see the box clearly. I put my hands back on the blanket and pulled. I suddenly felt very sick to my stomach, and couldn't get my breath. I put my hand at my throat. Damn it, what was this?

I hurried out and closed the door. There was perspiration on my forehead and above my mouth. My heart was pumping hard. Maybe I had not eaten enough, and was empty. All the excitement, all the events of the past few days. Everything was getting to me. That must be it. I felt giddy. I hurried to the kitchen and made myself some hot cocoa.

As I sat at the table drinking, I thought of that room and its odd effect on me. My mother Laura had used the room all of her life. She never wanted to be in the larger, nicer bedroom across from Aunt Senta. Perhaps as mean as Aunt Senta was, she wanted to be as far away from her as possible. I could not remember anything ever happening in there except that I had trouble breathing because of the poor ventilation. But that wasn't so tonight. Maybe deep inside me I still associated the breathing problem with that room, and the nightmares that resulted. Nightmares of being suffocated. The night I spent here in November, before the funeral, I had the same dream. But I wasn't in the nursery then. I shook my head. I was probably making something out of nothing. It must have been coincidence. I'd probably never know if there was anything else significant about the room because pretty soon there would be no more nursery, no more house.

Still, my mind searched for something to connect it all.

I went to bed at ten, bone-tired and relaxed from the cocoa. I fell asleep immediately. Sometime in the night I had the dream again. Perhaps it was not long in duration, but it seemed to last for hours. I know that in the dream I was in the nursery. I don't know how I knew this because I could not see the room in the dream. Again, the clicking of a door, then the sensation that someone was holding me down, with a hand over my mouth. I kept trying to turn my head, but the grip was like a vise. The hand was large. It pushed so hard. I could not utter a scream because the whole bottom portion of my face was covered. Then there was a light. Not the light of the ceiling fixture, but a bright, bright light, like that of a flashlight. A voice whispered something. I opened my eyes in the dream and could see nothing but the piercing light. I could not breathe, nor could I scream. I kept looking at the light. The whispers continued, but I could not understand the words. I wriggled and writhed, but could not get free. And all the while the light and the hand on my face, keeping me from breathing or making a sound.

I shot up in bed and opened my eyes. I screamed and screamed, until I realized that I was alone in my own bedroom, and the only light was the cheerful blue flame of the gas heater across the floor.

I lay awake the rest of the night. I have never been so terrified.

I rose on Friday morning with a curious sense of foreboding. The dream was as vivid as though it had only just happened. And for the very first time, I had a strong feeling that the dream had some connection not only with my feelings about the nursery, but also with my father. But why?

Alexander called at ten and said he would like to come over.

"All right," I said, uncertainly.

"Something the matter?"

"No, of course not. I just didn't sleep very well, that's all. I'll put the coffee on."

My spirits were at zero level, and I could not shake the feeling I had, nor could I identify the reason for it. Just a dream. No, not just a dream. I sat at the table and stirred my coffee. I wished suddenly I had told Alexander to wait. I didn't feel like getting dressed, nor did I really care what I looked like. Finally I ran water in the tub. A hot bath would surely help. And yet as I lay soaking in the water I kept thinking of the dream in which someone obviously was trying to kill me, and after a while, for the very first time, I suspected Nana may have been trying to protect me, rather than my father, and that the truth might be something dreadful in nature.

I sat up in the tub, water dripping off me. Could it be that what I was about to bring down on myself was far worse than the frustration of remaining ignorant? I hurriedly finished my bath and climbed out.

Alexander, in spite of his concerns, was in better shape than I was when he arrived. At least he was prepared to accept the worst. "I've decided that I'll never stop wondering if I don't somehow put this to rest. The only thing I must make you promise is that you won't ever do anything that will alert my mother—that is, if what we find out should affect her feelings. I won't have her hurt anymore."

I nodded my understanding.

"Otherwise, I'll do anything you want, give you anything that I can, though I'm not at all sure I can stop what is to happen with the house. I could be sued for breach of contract if I back out. But I am not going to worry about that just yet. I'm not at all convinced what you speculate is even near the truth."

I wanted to remind him that he could probably pay off a breach of contract suit with pocket money, as wealthy as he was. But I did not want to alienate him further. In fact, at that moment, with a small amount of persuading, I would have put a stop to the whole investigation. Maybe not forever, but at least for now. I had never felt so awful. I wished I had not gotten Alexander involved.

"Let's get to work on the telephone," he said. Then after a pause, "What's the matter with you, Robin? You seem to have lost all your enthusiasm."

"Oh, I'm sure it will pass. I had a nightmare last night."

"Want to tell me about it?"

And so I did, explaining that this wasn't the first time. "The weird part is that I just have an overpowering feeling that it has something to do with my father. There is no rhyme or reason for that, I know."

"You mean, you think something once happened in the nursery, and triggered the dream?"

"I honestly cannot think of anything at all. If so, wouldn't I remember something that horrible?"

"I don't know. Not necessarily, I don't think. I don't know very much about the subject of dreams. But if that was your father who paid you a call, he doesn't sound like Mr. Personality."

I shook my head. "Let's forget it. I'll be all right. A few more cups of coffee . . . an hour or two . . ." He was pulling the directory from his pocket.

As we sat together and turned the pages, I had a slender hope that maybe Genevieve Reneau was in New Orleans, as I had first suspected, and was also a friend of the Gerrards. Yet there was no name, first or last, that looked possible. Nor was the telephone number repeated here. However, we did find four different listings for New Orleans friends, and apparently Alvareda kept in touch with them over a long period because the telephone numbers, and sometimes the addresses, were changed two or three times. Of course, Alvareda herself had been dead nearly twenty years. We found no Wallace anything. No Prissy either.

"Here's one for a Stratton. But the number can't be any good. There aren't enough digits. Still, we could try information. John and Isabel." He went to the telephone and began. "Yes, operator, that's correct." A long pause. Then, "Well, how many Strattons with that initial are listed? Um-hum. All right." He cupped his hand over the phone and turned to me. "There is a John W. and even a J. W. Stratton. Could be Wallace."

I nodded.

"All right, um-hum, I have them. One more thing, check the Stratton listing for a Wallace Stratton, or a W. something else, please. Yes, I'll be glad to hold."

Another long silence. Finally he jotted down something else and thanked the operator, then pressed the receiver button and began to dial. "Couple of W. somethings but not a Wallace. Look through the directory to see if any of those listings look different. My grandmother's handwriting wasn't all that great. Maybe we misread."

I looked through again. One listing had been changed to a different address, in Metairie. The names were Ernest and Mathilda Ross. By the revised listing there was no telephone, just an address. I could not see much hope for finding a Wallace and Prissy in that. Another was for a Rose Penwald. Nothing had ever been done to change that one. Apparently she was a spinster, or maybe a widow. The other listing did not look very promising either. This was a Captain B. N. and Olive LeCourt on Prytania Street. The number had been changed once, but not the address. I could understand Prissy being a nickname, but not Wallace. I flipped through some more. Alvareda had written in tall, lavish capital letters, and lowercase letters that followed were a scrawl. All examples of her penmanship were somewhat on the extravagant side, and from the appearance of this book, perhaps became more so as she grew older. Maybe she didn't control her pen as well, and that would account for it. I could hear Alexander negotiating with the parties on the other end of the line, without any luck. Now and again I would look toward him when he made a hopeful sound. But again and again he shook his head. I began to feel a little more alive, and welcomed the feeling although it might be short-lived, that he had taken charge. He wore a pair of dark gray pants today and a gray argyle sweater with maroon and navy in the weave. His shoulders were broad and firm-looking under the sweater. His long hands were expressive, and shifted and splayed out as he talked with first one party then another. I wished I could stop feeling so damned attracted by him, especially now. . . .

I turned all the way to the Z's (there were not any) and flipped over to the last page, the one entitled "Notes." No one ever made notes in these kinds of books; these were the spaces for doodling, I mused. Then I came upon something interesting. There was a name written down that looked like N. A. (Nilly) Perkins. Nilly? Then I looked closer. That was not an "N." It was a "W." W. A. (Willy) Perkins. I flipped back to the listing for LeCourt. Captain B. N. and Olive LeCourt. It could well be Captain B. W. and Olive, and probably was. Suddenly hopeful, I looked up toward Alexander. He had at last reached someone and was listening earnestly. I could not make out much except she was apparently quite old and was reminiscing about his grandparents. "Yes, ma'am, they certainly did," he said, more than once, and then "No, ma'am, my grandfather passed away in 1930." "Yes, ma'am. I'm sure they did. Those cotton people really stuck by each other."

He looked toward me and lifted his eyes. "Yes, ma'am, well, thanks anyway. I'll be in touch if I think of anything else. Yes, ma'am. Thank you. Good-bye."

He put the receiver down. "She was eighty-four," he said with a sigh, and laughed. "Poor old thing. I gather she doesn't get many calls."

I smiled at him. I thought of Nana, alone during her final years, no one to talk to except the postman and the drunk who came by to take care of the yard when he was sober enough. "I might have something here," I said, and showed him the listing for LeCourt. "Why don't you sit this one out and drink your coffee before it gets cold."

I dialed the long distance operator again. "I'm looking for a listing on a B. W. LeCourt at 2505 Prytania Street."

"Spell that last name, please."

"Capital L-e-Capital C-ourt."

I waited. In a moment she came back on the line. "I have no one by that name on Prytania Street, or any other."

"All right. How about a Wallace LeCourt?"

"One moment."

When she returned she said, "I find no such listing, but there is W. S. LeCourt on South Rampart. Would you like to have that number?"

"I certainly would. Thank you."

I pressed the receiver button and turned to Alexander. "This could be at least a relative, if we're lucky." The telephone was ringing. Shortly a woman answered. I asked her if this was the Wallace LeCourt residence.

"Yes it is. Who did you want?"

"I am trying to reach a Captain B. W. LeCourt."

"That's my husband's father. He's dead."

"Oh, I see. Well, may I speak with your husband?"

"He isn't here right now."

I took in a breath. "Could you just answer a question or two? I'm not at all certain I have located the right family. The people I'm looking for were friends of a Houston couple named Gerrard. Mrs. Gerrard referred to the man and his wife as Prissy and Wallace. I was—"

"That's my husband's parents, all right. But they're both dead, and have been for—oh—let's see—nearly ten years."

"Oh, that's wonderful—I mean, I didn't think I'd ever locate the family. The initials B. W. threw me."

She laughed. She had a friendly voice, and like all people from that area of the South that I have ever talked to, she flattened her "r's," especially at the end of a word. "Well, with a name like Beauregard, what would you expect? And if you had known Prissy, you could see why she was called that instead of Olive from the time she was ten."

"Mrs. LeCourt—"

"That's pronounced LeCour, with a silent 't.' "

"Oh, excuse me. Do you think I might be able to reach your husband now?"

"Yes. Wallace is semi-retired, and works at the Cotton Exchange twice a week. I don't think he works very much, but don't tell him I said so." She gave me the telephone number.

"Thank you very much."

Alexander was standing right over me. I looked up. "I think we may have it, but Prissy and Wallace are both dead. The only hope is if their son knows something. Even he is already semi-retired." I gave the number to the operator. Two rings. "New Orleans Cotton Exchange, Wallace LeCourt here."

My heart skipped a beat. "Mr. LeCourt, my name is Robin Farrish, and I'm calling from Houston. . . ." I told him I was trying to locate information about my father, and that I believed my mother and grandmother may have stayed in his home during 1931 and 1932.

"You see, your parents were friends with Alvareda and Neal Gerrard, and the Gerrards were close friends of my family."

"I remember the Gerrards all right. Their son, the one who was killed, was about my age."

I looked up at Alexander. "Uh—yes, that's right. Do you recall the name Elzyna Farrish, or Laura Farrish?"

". . . No, frankly I don't. But you see I was not living at home by that time. I was married and living in Baton Rouge, let's see, from '29 to '35, when we moved back here to New Orleans.

"My sister might know something. She was studying at Mississippi State at the time, I believe, but she came home on most weekends. She also has a better memory for names than I have."

Genevieve Reneau, I thought excitedly. I held my breath while he fished around for her telephone number, recently changed. Finally he said, "I have it now. That's Mrs. Ruthellen Mitchell. She lives around the block from Commander's Palace, by the cemetery there. Are you familiar with the area at all?"

"No," I told him. He repeated the telephone number, and I thanked him and hung up. "One more name," I told Alexander.

"Good," he said, and smiled. "At least I can see a little color coming into your cheeks. Maybe that means we're close."

Again I dialed long distance. "Line busy. Do you wish to try again?"

"Yes, operator. Try again in ten minutes, and call me back, please."

I went back in the parlor and had another cup of coffee.

"Feel better now?" Alexander asked.

"A little. Just a few minutes ago, I thought I really was going to have all the ends tied up. I just knew Mr. LeCourt was going to tell me his sister's name was Genevieve Reneau."

"Who's that?"

"A real mystery lady. Her name was in Nana's address book, with a telephone number of all digits and no initials. I don't know why it was written like that."

"What was it?"

I went to get the book from my things upstairs, and brought it back. "It's 526-4311."

"That's J-A, or could be," he said.

"I know. I tried to get such a number in New Orleans, but it was not in service. And there was no Genevieve Reneau listed. The Information operator said there were rows and rows of Reneaus in New Orleans, and wouldn't offer to try each one of them for me."

He shook his head. "I'm just beginning to develop an appreciation for what you must have been going through in the last month."

"The trouble is, I don't seem to be getting anywhere. Even last night, I went to get Christmas decorations upstairs. When I finally located them, I had that weird experience of not being able to breathe and getting nauseated in the nursery. So I had to abandon that project."

"Oh, that's what you were doing in the nursery last night, before the dream?"

"Yes. And that may be what tripped it."

"I'll get the box of decorations for you."

"Oh, thanks. They're in the General Electric box in the corner. There's a blanket folded on top—"

"I'll find it."

He was back in a few minutes, and placed the box on the floor.

"Did you—uh—feel anything odd up there?"

"No. It's cold as an icebox. Are you going to decorate a tree?"

"I thought I might, but I don't have any way to haul one over here from the tree lot, and anyway, after last night I'm not sure I really want to anymore. I don't feel much like Christmas this year. It might be better if I skip it."

"I'll take you to get a tree, but I have a better idea. Why don't you spend Christmas with us? We're not doing anything special. Mother has an open house every Christmas Eve from three until six, and we usually go to Christmas Eve services at St. John's, but you could do all that with us. How about it?"

I wanted to say yes because it was very hard to say no to him. He reminded me of himself as a child, when he would suggest we walk to the Eastwood Theater and see a great movie, or to the drugstore for an ice cream soda. There was a spontaneity about him that had always been there, that allowed him to think up something fun or nice without first considering the possible complications. I really loved that trait about him, and was glad it had survived. But I didn't think I would be comfortable spending Christmas in his mother's palatial home, with his mother and all her society friends.

"I appreciate it, but I don't think so. Maybe another Christmas." The telephone was ringing. "I'll get it."

Ruthellen Mitchell was a good bit more help than I expected. Once she understood what I was after, she paused momentarily, then lowering her voice, said, "At the time all this happened, I was bound to silence. But I suppose it would not do any harm to tell you now, now that Mrs. Farrish is dead. . . ."

I was trying so hard not to get my hopes up just to sustain another disappointment. Yet, as she talked I found myself rising off the telephone bench, gripping the receiver more tightly. . . .

"My parents were born and bred New Orleans people, very stuffy and proper, so I was not told a lot. Most of it I gathered from what I saw when I came home on the weekends. And I think, to be truthful, that my college money may have come from Mrs. Farrish."

"I don't follow you."

"Well, my parents owned a large home in the Garden District. By the time your mother and grandmother came to stay, my father had lost a fortune in the stock market. They had no servants at the time—it was in the servants' cottage in back of the house that Laura and her mother stayed.

"Don't get me wrong. I'm not talking about a slave's cabin. The cottage was very nice. Mrs. Farrish paid for room and board there, and because of that, my parents were able to afford to send me to school in the style I would have expected. Of course I didn't figure all this out at the time. You know how kids are—they live in a dream world. And too, my father eventually regained what he lost, so it was a temporary inconvenience, as the saying goes. . . ."

It occurred to me that Ruthellen Mitchell was just a little stuffy herself. She told me that she would see mother and daughter occasionally when she came home from school, and that for a while, they took their meals in the main house with her parents. Finally she said, "Of course I was taking final examinations when you were born, and came home soon after that. I remember waking up one morning and looking through my bedroom window. Mrs. Farrish was getting into a taxi, holding you in her arms. She was all dressed in black, head to toe. She had you all wrapped up in white blankets, with lace trailing down. She got in the taxi and away it went. And I thought how sad it was, all those mourning clothes when it should have been such a happy time, with a brand-new life in the world." She paused, then said, "I never saw either of you again."

"And no one ever mentioned the name of my father to you, or anything about him?"

"No, absolutely not. I was very sheltered, you understand. My parents told me nothing."

I breathed a sigh. It seemed we had reached a dead-end at last. Then I remembered something. "Mrs. Mitchell, do you remember if anyone came to visit my family while they were there—perhaps an older man, or woman, anyone?"

She thought. "You know," she said finally, "I would not have thought of this if you hadn't asked me specifically. But when I came home for a holiday —I believe it was Christmas—yes, it was. A lady came to visit your family and she brought my parents a cake she had baked. It had almonds in it, and whiskey. I was very impressed that I would be allowed to eat something made with whiskey. A very thin sliver, mind. I guess that's why I remember it. Anyway, she and my mother talked in the parlor for a little while. She was a local, I think."

"Do you remember her name?"

"No. I'm awfully sorry. I didn't participate in my parents' conversations very much. It just wasn't done in those days, at least not in our house. I just remember the cake. And, I remember she was a very pretty woman, with dark hair and a slender figure. Seems to me she had a coat with a lot of fur around the collar and a little fur hat."

"Could it have been Genevieve Reneau?"

"I—I'm sorry, I really don't know. The name doesn't ring a special bell. Of course that's a fairly common name."

"All right, I understand. You've been very helpful. If I could leave you my number, the one here and the one in Dallas, perhaps you might call me collect if you should remember anything else. Thank you again."

I hung up the telephone and shook my head. "There's nothing left to do, at least from here. Assuming Genevieve Reneau is the woman who visited in the LeCourt home, I'll have to go there to find her. The only other avenue left is with the city birth records. I might be able to find out something from the doctor who delivered me, if I can find out his name on my birth certificate. I've ordered a copy sent to me, but I gather I can look for it sometime near February."

"When do we leave?"

My heart took flight. "You mean, you'd go with me?"

"Of course. And we'll talk to every Reneau in New Orleans if we have to."

I threw my arms around his neck, and he lifted me up and swung me around, both of us laughing with glee. It was the happiest moment I'd experienced since Nana's death.

"We might start by tracing down the owner of this lace shop where Nana and your grandmother used to buy a lot of things before the First World War. You know, shops in those days were more personal than now, and sometimes people got to know each other a little better. . . ."

Chapter 11

We arrived in New Orleans at five o'clock, and went immediately to the French Quarter in hopes we might find out something about the Savoy Fine Lace and Linen Company before closing hours. Streets are narrow in the French Quarter, and even the ones on which traffic is allowed are difficult to negotiate, so we parked the car and went on foot from Canal up Royal to Conti. I do not think I have ever been so cold. The icy wind cut down the narrow streets between the gaslights and iron lace balconies, rattling the Christmas garlands, and setting the little signs hanging from the balconies to swinging on their hinges. I had not expected to find the Savoy shop still in operation, but I was still a little disappointed when we found the address and looked in the window. An antique dealer. Inside there were crystal chandeliers and dark polished paneling.

The bell above the door tinkled and a lady behind the counter looked up. She looked to be in her sixties. "May I show you something?"

When I told her we were looking for information about the Savoy Lace Company she shook her head. "We've been at this address since 1946. I don't know anything about a lace company. Just a minute." She went through a small doorway at the back of the shop and spoke to someone in there. Shortly she returned. "I thought my husband might recall. There is a perfume shop up in the 300 block of Royal. He suggested you try there. That shop has been in existence in the Quarter for a very long time. It's on the same side of the street as this shop."

Out on the icy street again, I told Alexander, "Appearances can be deceptive. The French Quarter looks as though nothing ever changed here." We found the Bourbon French Perfume Company at 318 Royal and walked in. The tall shelves were lined with bath salts, perfumes, potpourri, soaps, and all manner of related things. The mixture of many spices and herbs gave the shop a heady aroma. The lady behind the counter was very pretty, with clear skin and gray hair parted down the center and pulled back. "May I help you?" She looked at Alexander. "Some special perfume for your girl friend's Christmas stocking, perhaps?"

I went forward. "We're looking for information about a shop that was here at least until 1914 or 1915. . . ." She listened. "Let me think. I know of the shop, but I don't know what happened after it was sold. That was wartime, you know, and so many changes took place during the next few years. Madame Rapho's used to clean and restore lace. Madame Rapho was over on Bourbon Street for—oh, let's see—the shop was there for at least three quarters of a century. But even Rose Devlin has been dead, about ten years."

"And there are no other lace shops in the area?"

"No. I don't think so."

"I wonder what would have happened to employees of a business of that kind," I said. I was thinking of the defunct art department at the Metropolitan Theater in Houston. Employees had to go somewhere—

"Well . . . let's see. I believe people still go in for elaborate christening dresses and layettes, that sort of thing. There is a shop over on St. Charles Avenue, Vivian's is the name. My granddaughter has a bonnet from there. Just a second." She pulled out a telephone directory and found it. "Let me call, to be sure they're open." She dialed the number and waited. Finally, "This is Mrs. Caro over at the Bourbon French Perfume Company. I have a couple here looking for information about a lace shop that used to be in the Quarter, oh, back before the First World War. Is there anyone around who might know something? No, not Madame Rapho. Savoy—" she looked at me. I handed her the gift card. "Savoy Fine Lace and Linen Company, Royal at Conti." She paused, cupped a hand over the telephone. "She's checking. There is an old woman there who used to sew for a shop here in the quarter. Oh, she does? Yes. Good. Well, let me ask." She turned to us. "Can you go over there now? They're open till six."

"Yes."

"They'll be over shortly. It's very nice of you. No, I'll give them directions."

We hurried down the street once again and gratefully stepped into the car. "You know, it isn't normal to think of New Orleans as a winter place. You think of summertime and blooming things, and hot, humid weather like something out of a Tennessee Williams play."

"I came here once, for Mardi Gras, and the weather was just like this."

"Well, it's romantic anyway, isn't it? I wish I knew something about the affair Nana carried on in this setting. I wonder how she met the man Paul."

"You haven't discovered anything about all that in her things?"

"Nothing. Maybe there was nothing in the first place, or, if there were love letters or something like that, she burned them so that her husband wouldn't see."

I was amazed at the short distance we covered. From what the woman said, I thought we'd be in for a much longer drive. Yet in less than five minutes, I saw the sign.

"Look, in the center of the shops. Vivian Layette and Linen Company," I said excitedly.

The proprietress had gone home and left a young employee to wait for us. She wore her dark hair flipped up like Jacqueline Kennedy, and her pink sweater had lace around the collar and sleeves. "I'm sure Mrs. Caro explained that Manette is very old," she said. "She used to sew christening dresses when she lived out in the country, and later she worked in a shop in the Quarter, monogramming. We think it is the shop you're looking for.

"I'll bring her down."

"Oh, but we could go up if it's hard for her to make the stairs," I suggested.

"No, it's time for me to take her home anyway."

While she was gone I looked around. It was more modern here than in the French Quarter, and much roomier. Obviously the shop catered to the wealthy people in the city. There were little girl's bonnets—I saw one that looked like Aunt Senta's in her photograph—and dresses, baby shoes, and knitted receiving blankets. Smocking, embroidery, lace inserts were in evidence. I was reminded of some of the clothes Nana used to sew for me. I realized now I had not seen any of them in the house. . . .

They were coming now, the young clerk patiently directing. The ancient woman was tiny and hunched. She had braids wound around her head, and wore a dark navy dress with a neat white collar. "That's it, Manette. Careful now. Take your time. There, almost got it. There."

The old woman looked at us. Her skin was very dark, a succession of deep wrinkles. Her hands were somewhat twisted—arthritis, probably—but not, apparently, severe enough to keep her from sewing. Her knuckles were enlarged. The clerk was explaining about us. Then she turned to me. "Speak loudly. She's very hard of hearing. And go slowly, please."

Manette's expression never changed as I told her what we were looking for. At last she nodded. She spoke with a very thick Creole accent. "I work for Monsieur Savoy twelve—maybe fifteen years. Before he leave for overseas."

"Overseas?"

She nodded. "His family in France. He go there to be sure they are all right. Not come back after the war."

I took a breath. "Did he have family here, or do you remember any employees of the shop here?"

She thought. Then, "One daughter came back to live here. She come by now and then to shop for something here. Genevieve Savoy."

"That's it!" I exclaimed so excitedly that the woman's eyes widened. "I'm sorry. Do you have any idea of her last name now? Could it be Reneau?"

"I don't know."

At that point the young clerk spoke up. "Oh, I didn't know that was who you were talking about. Mrs. Reneau comes in pretty often."

"Do you know where I can reach her?"

"She has an account with us. Just a minute, I'll pull the card. I—I guess it would be all right."

While she was in the back, Manette spoke again. "Savoy a fine man, you know, good to people. He not put up with anything except the absolute best. Anything that go out of his shop had to be passed on by him personally." She pulled out a hankie and wiped her lips. "After de war, everything change. People don't want lace anymore like they did once. And most of it made on machines, not by hand anymore."

The young clerk returned with a telephone number for Mrs. Reneau. "You can call her from here if you wish."

"Thank you. Thank you very much."

The telephone rang four times before a voice said, "Reneau residence."

"Mrs. Genevieve Reneau, please."

"Mrs. Reneau is not here right now. May I take a message?"

"When will she be there?"

"Tomorrow."

"Not until then? Can I reach her?"

I believe I had offended the person on the other end of the line. She said, "No, you may not disturb her. She will be calling me later, and I can ask her to get in touch with you then."

"I don't know where I'll be—" I looked at Alexander.

"We'll have to go to a hotel. Tell her you'll call back from there."

"Yes. I'll call and give you a number. Yes. My name is Robin Farrish, from Houston. I'd like very much to talk to Mrs. Reneau as soon as possible. Yes, Robin Farrish. Thank you."

I turned to Alexander. "This has to be the woman who visited Nana and my mother while they were here. Why else would Nana have a phone number written down in her book?"

We thanked the old woman and the young clerk, and hurried out the door.

When we got into the car I said, "You know, this really could be farfetched. It's very likely she doesn't know anything either."

"It's worth a try anyway. And it's so late now, we can't get to the city records. In fact, since Christmas is Sunday, it's a safe bet they won't be open again until Tuesday."

"I hadn't even thought of that. Boy, it's hell to have to work up from nothing, isn't it? Just be thankful you were smart enough not to mess up your life the way I have. That you never made a mistake that could not be undone."

Alexander was silent.

"Listen, I don't think we're accustomed to traveling in the same style. When I came to Houston, I wasn't expecting a side trip to New Orleans, and a night in a hotel. Is there somewhere we can stay that is decent, but not too expensive?"

"I was thinking of the Chateau Bourbon, where I stayed last time. A travel agent found it for me because most of the hotels all over New Orleans were booked up for Mardi Gras. It's nice but not very large, or expensive. If you don't have the money, let me pay for it and you can pay me back sometime."

I thought how nice it was to have so much money at your disposal that you could afford to be generous without having to count the cost. That must be what people were talking about when they referred to people who were so wealthy they were unaware of money altogether. "Alexander, you've already been nice enough to drive me here and go around with me, and to buy me lunch—"

He laughed. "That was a hamburger at the Dairy Doodle, and besides I ate half of yours."

"Oh heavens, the Dairy Doodle."

Then we both got tickled and were still laughing when we pulled up to the entrance of the Chateau Bourbon.

The hotel was small as Alexander claimed, but tastefully furnished. There were deep, luxurious carpets over a parquet floor in the lobby, and velvet-upholstered Chippendale furniture. Great pots of all kinds of flowers were placed on top of tables. Everywhere from elevator doors to ashtrays, there was highly polished brass, and tall gilt-framed mirrors. I realized Alexander's idea of "not too expensive" was quite a bit different from mine. We were put in adjoining rooms on the third floor, and as soon as I walked into my room I called Mrs. Reneau's residence and left the hotel number with the woman I talked with before—apparently the housekeeper. Then, as the weather had turned even worse than before, and the rain was coming down in torrents, Alexander suggested we have dinner in the hotel dining room.

"Around eight o'clock?" I suggested. "I need time to bathe and change."

I could not seem to get warm enough. I turned up the heat in the room and bathed in water so hot I could hardly stand it. I pulled on a white wool dress with long sleeves and a belted waist and a little white-fringed shawl. This isn't a date, I told myself, but I still felt like it was.

On the way down Alexander said, "I think this building may be a James Gallier design, but I'm not sure. If I had more time, I might look around. I'd like to see some examples of his work."

We were seated at a small table in front of a window on Bourbon Street, where we could watch the rain and see the few people passing by. The table was set with a white linen cloth and had a small hurricane lamp with a candle in the center, and a small pot of roses nearby. Alexander ordered wine, and I thought what a truly romantic place this was, how easy it would have been for Nana to fall in love with someone here.

"Alvareda wrote the most beautiful letter to Nana, after her love affair was over. Remind me to show it to you sometime."

"What did it say?"

"Oh, mostly she told her not to feel she was being punished, not to feel guilty."

"I wonder if Beryl Farrish stepped in and brought the affair to a halt."

"I wish I knew. Maybe Genevieve Reneau has the answer."

"Beryl was an architect, wasn't he?"

"Yes."

"I understand they can be very temperamental individuals," he said with a smile. "Look at Frank Lloyd Wright—one of the world's greatest prima donnas. He pushed everybody around, including his clients."

"Maybe my grandfather was pushy, too. I don't think Nana would have found it very easy to put up with that. Grounds for her divorce, maybe."

"You're pretty headstrong yourself. Was your husband pushy, too?"

I was surprised at his opinion of me. I'd never thought of myself as being headstrong . . . pushy. I smiled sheepishly. "I guess I had that coming. I've been pretty terrible, haven't I?"

He took a sip of wine. "Well, there have been moments, lady, when I felt like putting you over my knee. But what about your husband—"

"If you mean, is that why I divorced, the answer is no."

I explained about having run away to get married. "It was pure romance on the rebound, too," I said. "My first choice didn't approve of my lack of pedigree—or at least his parents didn't—and when Nana refused to set the record straight, I was infuriated," I told him, then paused. I needed to talk about all this suddenly. "You know, that quarrel has been the hardest thing of all for me to deal with. I've never told anyone this before, but I said some awful things to Nana. I don't think I'll ever stop being ashamed."

"Would you like to tell me about it?"

"It's just—I—I told her I didn't love her anymore . . . and I never ever took the statement back, never apologized." I swallowed the lump in my throat and waited for his response.

He reached across and patted my hand. "Don't you think she must have realized you didn't mean it?"

I shook my head. "I don't know. I hope so," I told him, grateful for his understanding.

"So, after that you—"

"I went back to another fellow I had dated, and got married just as soon as I could. Can you imagine such stupidity? Taking your future out on your grandmother?" I said, then something occurred to me.

"What is it? You look troubled."

"I was thinking of that day we argued about my father. It never occurred to me then that maybe the truth was so . . . so awful she didn't think I was mature enough to handle it."

"If so, she was probably right, I take it?"

"Yes. I suppose she was." My mind drifted back to the dream . . . the piercing light . . . the hand covering my face.

"And you were not happy in marriage, though she thought you were?"

"What? Oh yes. Winston used me, that's all. I put him through school and then he dumped me. I lost my scholarship money—and had to struggle through school. But I made it. And now I have a job that I really love. Maybe I wouldn't have gotten such a good job if things had worked out differently. Something good always comes out of tribulation, I guess. . . . But to be fair, I used Winston too. I didn't love him when I married him. I used him to hurt Nana. All I wound up doing was hurting myself."

"What will you do if it turns out we're on a wild goose chase?"

"I don't know. Try to figure out some other avenue to follow, I guess."

He leaned forward. "What if the answer simply cannot be found? Would you let that rule your life?"

"What do you mean?"

"What if you . . . fell in love with someone that you had known in childhood? Would you turn your back on him on the chance he might be related to you?"

The question cut right to the bone. I must have blushed. I looked down. "I hadn't really thought that far ahead."

"Well, think about it now. Will you go all the way through life letting these questions dominate your decisions?"

I looked up at him. "I don't know . . . I don't see much danger in falling in love with anyone who might—" I stopped. He was staring at me, testing my answers. Damn him. "There just isn't any chance of that," I said, and took a big sip of wine. He just kept sitting there, looking at me. I wasn't about to admit I had any feelings for him. "What about you? You have a big stake in this too."

"If I don't learn anything that completely proves otherwise, I'll always stand by my convictions."

"You really don't think we're going to wind up at your father's doorstep, do you?"

"I'd be willing to bet my life on it."

"And Clayton?"

He shook his head. "I'm almost as certain about him."

"But why?"

"There is something I haven't told you about him. I didn't think about it until we were on our way here. I wanted to confirm it with Mother, but I couldn't reach her when we got to the hotel."

"What is it?"

"I think, but I'm not sure, that I was told once Uncle Clayton is sterile. He—"

"Sterile?" I repeated.

"Again, I'm not sure if I'm right, or have it confused in my mind with someone else. What made me think of it was that on the way here I was reflecting on the fact he and Senta never had any kids. Again, I'm not sure so don't get your hopes up yet. I shouldn't have mentioned it until I've talked to Mother. But then we got on the subject—"

"What do you mean about getting my hopes up?"

"Well, who'd want to think they had a man like him for a father?"

"I don't understand what you mean. He may not have been charming, but—" I stopped. "You're thinking of the dream again, aren't you?"

He paused. "If something like that really happened to you, what kind of a man would do that to his own child?"

"Do you really think he might?"

"I don't know. He was so obsessed with his career. If he thought for one minute something might be threatening to it, he might have done most anything."

"I see." I shook my head. "I wish I knew whether that dream was based on reality."

"So do I. If it is, I hope it wasn't Clayton. You can wind up in jail for beating the hell out of a mental patient."

The waiter brought huge crusty loaves of bread and salads built up like crowns on bib lettuce and spinach leaves. I felt frightened again. When the waiter was gone I changed the subject. "Well, now that I've bared my soul to you, tell me why you broke off your engagement."

He picked up his salad fork and said, "Oh, it just didn't work out. I was luckier than you, finding out beforehand. Let's eat. You must be starved."

Throughout the meal Alexander managed to escape telling me anything about himself, while being absolutely charming at the same time. Perhaps his fiancée grew intolerant of that part of his nature.

As we walked out again he said, "It's too early to go in. Let's go hear some jazz." And so huddled under his big umbrella we walked several blocks up the street to a place from which we could hear jazz music through the doorway. "Sounds pretty good, anyway," Alexander said.

Inside it was not very crowded, yet the air was heavy with smoke and the jazz band was wound up as though to play for a stadium crowd.

There were chairs and tables on three sides, and a bandstand and small dance floor on the far wall. After a few songs the band stopped for a break and recorded music for dancing began. We were both halfway through our second drink and Alexander said, "Let's dance."

The suggestion almost panicked me. I didn't trust myself to get that close to him. My hesitation was long enough that he said, "You look like I asked you to go to bed with me."

God, would you lay off? "Oh, it's just—I haven't danced since high school," I said with a nervous laugh. "I'd probably step all over your feet."

He winked. "I won't bite if you do. Come on."

And so we stepped out on the floor—no one else was out there, just the two of us. From that point on the evening was happy with a kind of sadness around the edges because there was no getting around the fact that we still had feelings for each other, even after all this time, after having been worlds apart, yet how could we allow ourselves those feelings now? Just as before, when we were children, there was an obstacle in our path that was no fault of ours, yet over which we had no control. At least that was what I sensed, and for the moment I let my guard down and allowed myself to believe that Alexander felt the same way I did. It was the wine and the whiskey, I cautioned myself. But it felt good, being taken in his arms and maneuvered around. I kept seeing the children we were, remembering how I used to love it when he pushed me in the swing, so high, and when I'd come down he was there. How could I have had such feelings at that age? Perhaps puppy love was not so far from the real thing when you came right down to it.

I looked up at him and smiled. "I've always loved the way you look at me," he said.

The music went on for a long time. They played all kinds of tunes, some old, some new. Most of them I did not recognize. Then they played the theme from that movie *Picnic,* and it sounded very pretty and also, I thought, there were times like this when a saxophone was very sexy. I did not say this to Alexander. Instead I said, "Did you see that movie?"

He said that he did.

"Did you like it?"

"Yes. I liked the way it turned out."

"Oh, that was what I didn't like. I just couldn't see it, you know, her going off with him on the train like that. How would they make it if she got pregnant? If they did a sequel, can't you just imagine them down and out with six kids to be fed?"

He threw back his head and laughed. "My, how cynical you are."

"Am I? Maybe I am. But that's what I thought, anyway."

"Stop ruining my image."

"I'm sorry. You're a romantic, aren't you?"

"Incurable."

The music played on. He held me closer. We looked into each other's eyes, and I thought about everything, about how we were coming into focus together in one way, and we might find out pretty soon that we were something quite different. I believe, that night, if I had not been so preoccupied with that, he would have forgotten it altogether. At the end of the last song we danced to, he kissed me. Not on the cheek, but first playfully underneath my ear, then full on the mouth, easing his tongue inside so that it seemed to capture my tongue and toy with it. Desire for him ached in the pit of my stomach. God, I can't fall in love with you, I thought, and pulled away. "We ought to go. Tomorrow will be a full day."

He nodded resignedly. I picked up my woolen shawl off the chair, my fingers trembling and cold. We said nothing else all the way to the door of my room in the hotel, and when I reached in my bag for the key, I thought he was going to kiss me again. I put a hand on his arm. "We can't do this."

"Why not?"

"You know why."

"Could we, if things were different?"

"Of course we could. Oh, you're mean, Alexander. You shouldn't put me through this. Let's just try and get through tomorrow."

"What if we never find out?"

"I don't know. I don't know. Let's just not give up yet." I put my hands on his face and kissed his cheek. "Good night."

He sighed. "Good night."

I closed my door behind me and took several deep breaths. Damn. I wanted him so much my pants were filmy inside. I went to the bathroom sink and splashed cold water on my face. I tried to urinate, but gave out short, abbreviated trickles. Don't be dumb, Robin. He doesn't really care about you. It's just that New Orleans is such a romantic city. When all this is over, he'll go away from you again, just like before, and find another society dish. I walked into the bedroom.

The bed had been turned down, the pillows fluffed. A chocolate mint candy wrapped in gold foil and shaped like a coin had been left, along with a little form which could be checked and left on the doorknob if you wished morning coffee and a newspaper at a specified time. I picked up the mint, then noticed a message had been left by the telephone, to call Mrs. Reneau's housekeeper, Mrs. Blanch. It had been written at nine-fifteen. When I reached Mrs. Blanch she said that Mrs. Reneau had tried to call me before nine, from the hospital. But when she could not reach me she left a message at the house.

"Is she ill?"

"No, no. Mr. Reneau had minor surgery this morning, and she's staying the night with him. She could not call out of the hospital after nine, because the switchboard closes then. She asked me to tell you to come here at ten in the morning, 619 Esplanade. She has some very important information about your father."

Oh, praise God, I thought, and tears came to my eyes. "All right. I'll see you then, and thank you very much."

I dialed Alexander immediately, and told him. First a pause, then, "Wonderful," he said. "One of us better order a wake-up call."

He had not sounded enthusiastic, but then how could I expect him to? He had almost as much of a stake in this as I had. I took a very hot shower, in hopes it would relax me. Now the room was too hot, stuffy. I turned the heat down a little and put on a royal blue nylon gown with spaghetti straps.

It took me a very long time to get to sleep that night. The prospect of having someone tell me what I had always wanted to know, on top of the evening with Alexander, left me with boundless nervous energy. Had I been at home I would have cleaned out all the cabinets and rearranged the bookshelves, anything to keep busy. The only thing I could do here, however, was try to read myself into drowsiness. I kept telling myself that if I was in for bad news, surely Mrs. Reneau would not have relayed a message phrased in the way that she did. She would have covered somehow, said that she had some information to tell me, something she wanted to explain. And this train of thought kept me from dwelling on the possibility that I was in for a terrible shock until I finally dozed off around one in the morning, still going over everything I knew for a fact and speculating on what I did not know. Just a few more hours. . . .

I slept soundly for a while, and then I had the dream again. It was the same as before: first, the click of the door, then the awareness of having a hand over my face, being held down, struggling to breathe, struggling to scream, and then the piercing light and finally, the threatening whispers.

I raised up, frantically pushing my hands at the air, screaming, "Go away, go away, no, go away, please, don't hurt me!"

Or at least that was what Alexander heard me shouting when he stood outside my door trying to get in. I awoke to the sound of him pounding on the door and yelling, "Open up, Robin, open up!"

I fled to the door and opened it. I had never been so glad to see anyone in my life, and I threw my arms around him and held on. In a moment he lifted me up and carried me back to the bed. He sat down and took my hands. "What happened? I heard you screaming like crazy. I thought someone had broken through the window." He gently pushed the hair back from my face.

"It was the dream again. Someone is trying to kill me, but I don't know who or why." I held his hand. "Oh, Alexander, I'm almost afraid to find out about all this. I wish I'd never started it."

He put an arm around my shoulders. "Listen, it's all right. Whatever that woman says tomorrow, it happened years ago. No one can hurt you now, I don't care who they are. I won't let anyone hurt you. Come. Lie down again and try to go back to sleep."

I didn't want to let go of his wonderful, comforting hands. He kissed my cheek and pulled the covers around me, then after a few moments he walked back to the door. I watched him go, in his pajama bottoms, without his shirt on. Poor Alexander, having to go through all this. In a moment he'd be— "Alexander, please don't go. I need you, I really do."

He turned back and looked at me. It was the most beautiful face I had ever seen. I raised up and held out my arms. When he walked toward me, I did not see anything but him, did not care about anything but him. I had awaited this moment all of my life, and it was the only thing that mattered now. . . .

He knelt down before me and searched my face. "Robin, I know now. I—"

I touched his lips. "It's all right. Don't say anything now. Just love me."

He took my hands in his and lifted me to my feet. He put his hands around my face and kissed me very gently on the mouth, then pulled me against him with one arm. He began to kiss me on my neck, his mouth straying down farther until he reached my shoulder. "Oh, Alexander," I breathed, kissing his face, his neck. He paused and looked into my eyes, then with his fingers moved both straps of the gown off my shoulders. The gown slid down to the floor. He held me away and looked at me. His eyes were moist. "Oh, Robin, you're so pretty . . . so very pretty. . . ." I pulled his hands to my breasts, feeling I was ready, could not wait, but he was enjoying this as one enjoys a very long awaited pleasure, and would not be hurried. My mind flashed back to my wedding night with Winston, the sterile haste of that futile exercise that brought us no closer and left me so empty, and at once I understood that only now was I being made love to. One hand cupped under a breast, Alexander leaned his head down and kissed the nipple and rolled his tongue gently around it. Excitement boiled all through me. He pulled me up against him and moved his mouth over my breasts, softly sucking at them, making me wait longer still, and now I loved the waiting, took joy in it. My arms were around his neck, stroking along his shoulders, and up again. He knelt down and moved his long lambent fingers inside my pants, pressing them down until they lay on the floor and I stepped out of them. I felt his thumbs move my legs slightly apart, then he put his mouth on the pubic hair and moved his tongue around until he found the hard clitoral point. I felt a wild sense of release like a burst of fireworks inside me and, grasping at him, moved down and shoved my hands inside his pajama trunks and pushed them down. My heart thrilled at the sight of him. I crouched down, pressed my hands against his groin, and closed my mouth over his erected penis, delighting in the warm, sweet taste of him. After a few moments, he put his hands up under my arms and lifted me back into the bed, telling me again and again that he loved me, adored me, that I was all he had ever wanted. Not yet . . . not yet. . . . He covered my body with wet, feverish kisses until I could not wait a moment longer and closed my arms around him, begging him, "Now, oh please, now!" I brought my hands around his hips and pulled him forward, wrapping my legs around him. When his flesh pierced mine I held on tight, and felt that wonderful, shattering release again and again before the warm, welcome flood of his semen emptied inside me. I wished suddenly, with razor-sharp poignancy, for a child.

We went to sleep just before dawn, lying on our sides, me in front of him, one of his arms around my breast and the other like a pillow between my legs. I couldn't believe this was happening to me, that being made love to could be this good, that the childhood dream of being carried away to some magical kingdom by Alexander could have translated into this. I wanted to hold back time . . . wanted to stay here, like this, forever. . . .

The ringing telephone awakened us. Sunlight was streaming through the window. Alexander reached over me to answer the wake-up call. Then he put his arms around me again and lay back on the pillows, lifting my hair and kissing my neck. I turned toward him and smiled. Then, abruptly, reality hit me and I lay back, seized with guilt.

I could not look at him for a long time. Finally, I said, "They should not have let us be together when we were children. If they had not, none of this would have happened, but you know I've loved you all my life. Damn."

"So you're still convinced we're blood-related?" he asked, his voice playful.

"I'm scared to death of the possibility, aren't you?" I could not see how he could take all this so casually.

"I was trying to tell you last night that I know now you are wrong. I finally got in touch with Mother, about Clayton. She said it was Lilly who was sterile, not Clayton."

I took in a breath. "Oh, so it could be, we're only first cousins," I said dourly.

"Listen. Mother told me the answer without even realizing it. She said that Elzyna would have been pleased that you and I were together. I asked her why she thought that. I had to press her pretty hard about it. Finally she said she didn't want to tell me because she hated for me to know how disgusted she had been at the moment. It was right after she found out about the breakup of my engagement. Elzyna said she had wished when we were children that we would wind up together someday, that she would have been proud to have me in the family.

"She would not have said that if she hadn't known that neither my uncle nor my father were responsible for your being in the world."

I felt a great weight lifted off my shoulders. "That's right. Oh, that's wonderful. I can hardly believe it, but it's so simple. I can't believe I didn't ask your mother in the first place."

"Well, it certainly doesn't solve the mystery, and it doesn't explain the dream, if it is based on a memory you've managed to lock away."

I sat up. "Why didn't you tell me as soon as you knew?"

"I tried to. I called, but you didn't answer. I thought you might already be asleep."

I thought for a moment. "Oh, I took a shower. But I was awake for a long time after that."

"I . . . didn't try again."

"Why not?"

"I was afraid."

"Of what?"

"That you might not share my feelings, as I hoped you did, and that without anything to stop us, you might still not want me."

The modesty of the statement warmed me through. I smiled. "Well, it's nice to know you can be honest if you want to," I told him. "Heaven knows, that's the first time you have ever told me anything about yourself."

"Oh, I have all sorts of fine, upstanding traits."

"Name one," I told him, laughing.

"I love you very much for one thing. You make me madder than hell sometimes, the way you jump to conclusions, but I still love you. I knew it the minute you stepped off that airplane in November. And I thought to myself, you jerk, you missed the boat. She's already married. She was too smart to wait around for you."

"Did you ever think of me, in all those years?"

"Yes. Now and then, especially if I happened to be out in your neighborhood. But you seemed so far away from me."

"I couldn't have said it better myself."

"Listen, Robin, I'm not far away anymore. Don't be afraid of the truth. Whatever it is, I'll be there."

I lifted his hand and kissed the palm, then held it to my face. "I believe I could face anything as long as you were there," I said. "It's funny, after all these years of wondering, to be so nervous when the time comes. I had always believed my father was a great man, and now I have such a strong feeling he was anything but that.

"I guess we ought to be going. It's nearly nine o'clock."

His eyes swept over me. "You shouldn't sit there like that, not if you're in a hurry. Come here."

I lay down beside him and put my arms around his neck. He laid one hand across my abdomen and said, "You're like something wonderful that I found under the Christmas tree. I want to play with you all day." I loved the way his warm hand felt against my abdomen, loved— "Alexander, I loved the way you didn't hurry last night," I said suddenly.

"It isn't that I didn't want to," he said, "but to hurry through lovemaking with someone you adore is like . . . well . . . like scarfing down a good, expensive brandy. You miss so much of the pleasure . . . and you are all pleasure, Robin, from head to toe." He winked.

"I love your hands," I said.

He looked surprised, as though his hands were not something he thought remarkable. Then a mischievous look came into his eyes and he walked his fingers down lower, asking, "Where do you like my hands? Up here, or down, oh, about here?" His hand lodged between my legs, igniting me.

"I love the way you really are outrageous," I giggled, and kissed him.

Genevieve Reneau's home on Esplanade was described by Alexander as a "shotgun house," with two stories and balconies across the narrow front, which disguised the commodious size of the structure. In the door glass was a frail-looking lace curtain. When we stopped at the curb I said, "If you hadn't known what Nana said about us last night, would you have made love to me?"

"I don't know," he said thoughtfully. "I'm glad I don't have to worry about that."

I looked out the window. "I was irresponsible, but I got so tired of listening with my head, I just didn't care. Have you ever felt that way?"

"Of course I have. Why do you think you always have to be the strong one?"

"I don't know. I don't feel very strong right now."

Genevieve opened the door. "Robin?" she said, and took my hands. "Elzyna has died, then?"

I nodded, bewildered at her greeting.

"I'm so sorry, but I am so relieved you've come. And this is Alexander? Good. Come in both of you and sit down. We'll have coffee and beignets."

She was a beautiful woman, dark hair interspersed with gray, deep green eyes, and a very well-maintained figure for someone who had to be nearing sixty. She obviously had more than adequate means. The house and all its furnishings had been inherited from her grandmother, she told us. There were three exquisite stained-glass windows in a graduated row beside the stairway. The carved fireplace before which we all sat down was one of the most beautiful I had ever seen. Over the tall windows were ornate wooden valances, from which hung very sheer lace draperies. While pouring cups of coffee she explained that the house had been built for Grand'mère by her second husband when they married in 1870. Even when the family returned to France in 1914, the house was not sold but rented. "She died in 1920, but of course I didn't claim the house until I moved back over here several years later. As a child I detested it because it was so old, and more than that, because Grand'mère was so stern . . . downright hard. My father made me come with him on Thursday afternoons every week, and on all holidays, and

I hated every minute of it." She smiled. "He didn't like it very much either, but honored tradition anyway. There. Have a beignet. They're still warm from the stove."

She sat back in her chair and lifted her eyes. "I have so much to tell you. It is hard to know where to start. The story begins a very long time before you were born. Just before the First World War, Elzyna Farrish visited here several times. She met my father at his shop in the French Quarter, and they became acquainted. . . .

"My father was a widower when he met Elzyna. He soon came to adore her—not since the death of my mother had he cared deeply for another woman. She was not here but a few times, and in between they corresponded by mail, through your grandparents, Alexander. My father begged her to go away with him when war came to Europe. He did not want to leave her behind. But she felt she must stay. Her husband was apparently very cruel to her, perhaps you already know about that, but from what I have been given to understand, he was a violent man, a drunk, who beat her and attacked her viciously with words."

"No, I didn't know that. She never told me that." I felt sick inside at the thought of anyone being so horrible to my Nana.

"Well, you can be sure she found a different sort of person in my father. He was the gentlest, kindest human being there ever has been in the world. And he would have done anything to spend the rest of his life with Elzyna, and protect her.

"He could not convince her, however. She had this loyalty to her husband, and at that time, her Catholic faith, and of course the children. She was expecting Laura when war came and we had to leave for France. My father was distraught. It seemed there were worries both here and over there, and once we arrived, oh, it was so dreadful. It was a long time before we found— well, that's a different story. Let me get back to the point.

"We stayed in France for many years after that. My father owned a fashion house near Paris, and was very successful. He eventually remarried, because of me more than anything. My sister Renée was grown up and a practicing physician with a family of her own. He felt I needed a mother. He was not happy in marriage, and felt it had been a mistake, but he continued with it anyhow. His wife was one of those people who are 'sickly,' yet she outlived him.

"I married in 1928, and my husband and I moved back here. Renée and her family stayed in France. In 1931 my father came to visit, for a couple of months. It was the first time he had been back here since 1914. He decided to pay a visit to Elzyna. He contacted her, and went to Houston for three weeks.

"While there, they found a rekindling of their feelings for each other— and—" She stopped.

"What is it?" I asked her.

"Robin, you are not Laura's child. You are the daughter of Paul Philippe Savoy and Elzyna Farrish."

I leaned forward, not absorbing it.

"Yes, it is true," she nodded, and repeated the statement.

Alexander's hand closed around my shoulder. I glanced at him, then back at Genevieve. I could not speak. It seemed that all feeling, all emotion inside me was suddenly crystallized.

Genevieve continued, "You were the most important thing in the world to Elzyna. She wanted me to be the one to tell you about her and your father." She paused and dabbed at her eyes with a handkerchief. "No one knew. And I'm afraid the rest of the story is not as happy as that part. Laura became pregnant around the same time as her mother. Elzyna contacted me and said they were coming to New Orleans, and she wanted to talk to me. When she first arrived, I don't think she knew what to do. She would not let me tell my father. She did not want to destroy his marriage. She felt enough damage had already been done because of their first encounter. He died without knowing about you, Robin. And I've always been so sorry about that. He would have loved you so—"

All the childhood fantasies of my father now flooded me, and I realized suddenly, joyfully, that he had not abandoned me. Tears sprang to my eyes. There was so much I needed to know. "When did my father die?"

"In January of 1941. I went over there when he took ill, and when he died I wrote to Elzyna."

That was just weeks after the murder of Gabriel Gerrard. Yet Nana was not referring to him that day as she told me. . . . I remembered Nana crying so hard . . . as much for herself, I now realized, as for me . . . oh, precious, sweet Nana. . . . I was now weeping profusely. Alexander gave me his handkerchief.

"When Elzyna came here in 1931, I begged her to let me take her child and raise it. I had not been able to have any children of my own, and as it turned out I never did. She appeared to consider it, although I know she wanted you desperately. She would only say that we would discuss it later, after the babies were born. I believe there was some thought that Laura's baby would be given up for adoption. They could have returned to Houston as though nothing had happened, and could have gone on with life, at least all things would have looked the same on the outside. As it turned out, however, both Laura and her child died. When that happened, I could not have even dreamed of asking to raise you. I accepted her decision to bring you up as Laura's child without argument. All things considered, she felt it was the best alternative at the time. And she always planned to tell you the truth when you were older."

So there were two children, not one. Two fathers—"Did Nana tell you who was the father of Laura's child?"

"No. She did not. But let me go on. . . ."

I looked at Alexander. He was silent. I picked up his hand and held it.

". . . I did not hear from Elzyna very often after the two of you left here. Now and then she would write something about you, to keep me informed, and she sent me pictures. But then, a few months ago, she called me. She said that you were not living at home anymore, had not been for a long time. She explained the source of unhappiness that made you leave. She said that she had made a new will, leaving her home to Alexander, and that she was getting her affairs in order. She wanted me to have some things that belonged to her, from my—from our father, and would send them to me. I told her that I would be happy to take care of them, and to keep them, but I felt she should leave them to you. I encouraged her to write to you, at least give you a chance to make amends.

"I sensed that she really wanted to, and perhaps only needed someone to put it into words. Still, she would not agree to it at that moment. I did not hear from her for a long time. Then one day some time later, I heard from her again. This was only a short time ago, mid-October. She had written a letter asking you to come for a visit so she could talk to you."

"But I never got it," I quickly protested.

She nodded. "It was returned to her. She said she found no listing through the long distance operator for your telephone number in Dallas either. She could only assume you had left the area and perhaps . . . well, anyway, she could not find you. That was when she told me she'd like to leave her secret in my custody."

If ever there was one moment when my own stupidity came crashing down over me it was now. I had never realized that all the twists and turns of my life could lead Nana up a path that would dead-end. Winston's name was no longer in the Dallas white pages, and she would not have known to look for me under Farrish, for I never told her about my divorce. Then there was the mix-up in my apartment situation that I had never even thought about till now. I had not informed the post office of the change in unit number till the end of October, and apparently her letter to me got caught somewhere between my old address and my new one. Had I only realized that time was of the essence when it came to Nana . . .

Genevieve continued, "She said she had been gathering things and was going to put a box in the mail to me."

"When was that?"

"Let me see. Around the first of November I believe. Yes. It was All Saints' Day, and I had just gotten back from the cemetery when she called."

The package, the one I was so hopeful might have been on its way to me. "And she sent it?"

"Yes, it is here." She called for Mrs. Blanch to bring it in. "I have not opened the box, Robin, and I don't know what it contains. I think she included a letter. If you have any questions, I'll be more than glad to help you in any way I can. Certainly I can tell you all about your father."

I suddenly felt a warm sense of kinship with Genevieve. My sister. . . . All those years of growing up, I had family who loved me even aside from Nana. "Have you a picture of my father?" I asked.

"Yes. I've selected several for you. I'll go up and get them while you look through the box."

"Thank you, Genevieve, thank you very much."

The box wasn't terribly large—about four feet long and a foot deep. Alexander snipped the rope around it with a pocketknife and I tore open the top, and pushed aside some dark paper. There was, taped to the top of the contents, a letter to me. I grabbed it and tore it open.

"My dearest Robin,

"As I write this letter, I am still in hopes of locating you. I have never wanted to write any of this down. I always hoped we could talk about it together one day, so that I could answer any questions you might have, so that I could be sensitive to the expressions that cross your face as you learn the truth.

"I must allow for the possibility that you and I may not see each other again in this life. If not, I want Paul's daughter Genevieve to be the one to sit down with you and tell you all about your wonderful father. I am enclosing this letter along with the things that are most important to me. If these treasured items cannot be in your hands, they surely belong in hers. If I do not find you soon, I will write a note, directing you to Genevieve, and put it here in the house or give it to Louetta Gerrard for safekeeping."

She would have left me the key to all this, I realized with a sharp pang of regret. She simply ran out of time. . . .

". . . The fact you are reading this letter proves you have already learned the greatest—the happiest—part of the secrets I kept from you. I would give anything if the whole story could be a happy one.

"But before I get into it, let me first explain my reasoning behind the decision to leave the house to Alexander Gerrard. I know you do not have the attachment to it that I have, and I understand your feelings. I felt it should be returned to the Gerrard family, since it was their gift to me so many years ago. When I talked to Louetta about this, she told me that Alexander had had some troubles and I thought giving it to him might be a fitting way to pay back a few of the many favors his grandfather did for me. As to the contents, I'm too old and tired to go through everything here. I've sent everything of any real value to me in this box because I like to think of it as surviving me. As to all the other, there is really nothing of any value outside of the sentimental kind. Alexander can do with it whatever he wishes, and you won't have to bother with it.

"Now, to the other things that you deserve to know.

"To begin, I've made only one mistake in my life that I truly regret, that I feel had unending ramifications for all of us. On the night of December 16, 1914, my husband Beryl and I quarreled violently. I struck him—more than once—with a poker from the parlor fireplace nearby. He fled from the house, out into the street, and was hit by his own automobile, with Jordan at the wheel.

"At the time I felt this turn of events was something of a blessing. Everyone assumed Beryl was hurt at the scene of the accident, not realizing that he had been injured before. It was a sign, I thought. I would let Jordan shoulder the full blame of Beryl's tragedy that night. I knew that if I were to be charged with harming him, and put into prison, I would be leaving my children without their mother. Perhaps it would not have been such a horrible thing, but it seemed to me then that the lesser of two evils would be to say nothing and hope the truth never surfaced.

"As it happened, it did not. And Jordan knew no more than anyone else. But my feelings of guilt about letting him suffer for something I had done were almost crippling. I let him take advantage of me whenever the opportunity came. I gave him money, which he never repaid. I let him stay in my home whenever he was in town. My actions led to more tragedy.

"In 1931, when Paul visited here for three weeks, I was for the first time neglectful of Laura. I thought of no one and nothing else except Paul and being with him for as long as I could. And I might tell you now for I'm sure you don't know this, I prayed nightly I would become pregnant. When my prayers were answered, I felt a happiness inside me that I had never known. You were probably the most wanted child who ever came into the world, Robin, this you must understand."

Oh, Nana, sweet, sweet Nana, I whispered, as I realized for the first time in my life that I was truly wanted, from the beginning.

". . . Shortly before I learned I was pregnant, I learned that Laura was expecting a child as well. When Senta and I questioned her—Senta brutalized her sister to the point that she was very upset and frightened—Laura told me a lie. She said that Stephen Sandock had fathered her child. I do not know whether she would have told me the truth if Senta had not attacked her so cruelly; perhaps not. After I learned of my own pregnancy, we made arrangements to go to New Orleans and stay with the LeCourt family. I told Senta nothing. I would never trust Senta with a secret if at all possible, for reasons you'll come to understand.

"Three weeks before the expected arrival of Laura's baby, she became panicky about having lied. One night she called me into her bedroom and, in a state of upset that broke my heart, she told me the truth. She had been forced into sexual relations with her uncle Jordan Leider beginning a long time before. Probably from around the time she was fifteen. After the first time, he had repeatedly approached her. He threatened her life should she tell, and she never did, not till then."

I felt my stomach contract as I read the words. I could see the face in the portrait . . . the pretty girl . . . lost inside herself. . . . I thought of Stephen's remark that something had frightened her. God. I clasped a hand around my abdomen. Jordan: the man who gave Laura her "experience with men," the blond man who often visited in the "expensive car." I looked at Alexander. "It was Jordan," I said. "Jordan fathered Laura's child."

His mouth opened in shock. He looked as though he found that more awful to accept than that his own father might have been at fault. I read on. . . .

". . . I have never known such rage as I felt that night. I called Laura's doctor the next morning to discuss it with him. What he told me about the chances for that child she was carrying were almost more than I could bear. I did not know what to do. The baby was due so soon. I told Laura what the certainties were about her child, that it would be retarded, unhealthy, I did not know to what extent. This frightened Laura more than I could have expected. She went into a state of depression over the next two weeks. The day before you were born I found her lying on the bathroom floor. She had taken her own life."

I looked away from the letter, the whole bizarre incident closing in on me as the pieces fit together. Finally I resumed.

"I did not ever confront Jordan. Laura and the child were dead, so what evidence to incriminate him existed? I did not know what he might do if I told him, and of course I would have had to explain about you. I would never have entrusted that information to him."

I realized now, with a jolt, exactly what the dream was based on; I remembered it perfectly. One night, I do not know how old I was, Jordan found his way into the nursery where I slept. He covered my mouth so that I could not scream out. He shone a flashlight in my face so he could look at me. He asked me what people had told me about my father. He was, I think, trying to assure himself that I was not his child and it must have been difficult from what he knew of the frequency of his intimacies with Laura. He got no information from me, of course. At last he told me if I told anyone about his coming in there, that he would hurt me, and he spat out, "Laura was a slut, anyway. Your father could have been anybody."

The memory sent cold waves of revulsion over me now. My hand closed into a tight fist and I brought it to rest against my mouth.

"What is it?" Alexander asked.

I shook my head and reached out for his hand.

Nana's next words confirmed the memory. ". . . Jordan did not come around very often, and I think he had begun to suspect his part in the tragedy of Laura. One night when he was here along with some other guests, he stole up into your room. I remembered something I needed upstairs, and when I started up, he was coming down. I could tell by the look on his face that he was up to something, though he made some excuse about being up there. I got past him and fled into your room. To my great relief you were sleeping soundly, and nothing seemed to be amiss.

"However, the next morning you told me you had had a dream of a man holding you down and talking to you. As well as I could question you without frightening you, I probed to find out if he had harmed you in any way. I was satisfied he had not, but when you began to have the breathing problems and the recurring dream, I realized he had done more harm than I thought. After that I simply took even greater care to be sure he did not get near you.

"I struggled many times over the years about whether to tell you this, and the only reason you need to know what he did to Laura is because of what he did to you that night. If some day you remembered part, but not all, you would be haunted for the rest of your life about the reason for his rude entry into your room, and that would surely be an unnecessary source of grief.

"Laura, as you know, was returned to Houston for burial at Forest Park. Her baby, unknown to anyone before now, is buried in Babyland at Forest Park as well. The records are at the cemetery office.

"Of course I lied to Senta about the circumstances of Laura's death. On that day, so many years later, when you demanded I identify your father, one of my purposes in refusing was to save you from a drastic mistake. The other was that, with Senta living under the same roof, I was very much afraid she might somehow learn the truth from you, and that would have opened up the question of Laura all over again. I had no idea where that might lead. There were still so many people who could be hurt by the speculations she might have shared, I would have been compelled to silence her with the truth. And I did not think I could live in the light of Senta's judgment of me for letting so terrible a thing happen to her sister Laura. At the worst, Senta might have used the information to turn you against me. I could not bear to take that risk.

"Certainly I could understand your reaction, yet I waited such a long time for you to have a change of heart. I want you to know that I forgive you now, and that I know your words to me were merely expressing the anger you so rightly felt at that moment."

I read the words of her forgiveness again and again as tears rolled down my cheeks. She could have given me no greater gift than this, like warm sunshine after a cold, rainy day.

"Robin, you must know how very deeply I love you and that I hope you will only dwell on the good part of your beginnings—the only part that really has anything to do with you at all. What I told you about your father time and again, about his kindness, his patience and caring, is all true, more than I could say. In this box I have left you some examples of his work, and his dear, precious letters written to me.

"Above all, please know that I shall go to my death, whenever that may come, at peace, as long as I am certain you are happy and have made something good of your life, with or without my being near. It is what any mother wishes for her child. Please remember that you have always been wanted, and that you have been the most cherished and least deserved blessing of my life."

"Nana"

I held the letter to my breast. It was as though something inside me, long held in check, was released, and I cried hard for a very long time. When Genevieve walked back into the room, I went into her arms and we cried together. Then I handed the letter to Alexander, and as he read, I went through the box of my mother Elzyna's treasures. . . .

Chapter 12

Of the three pictures Genevieve gave me of my father, there is one I like best. It was taken in the courtyard behind his shop around the time he met my mother. He leans against a little table, his arm resting on the shoulder of Genevieve. His other daughter, Renée, stands behind them, with her chin lifted in a whimsical way. Both girls have on dresses with lace flounces around the bosom, and Genevieve has a big bow at the back of her hair. My father has on a business suit, and his measuring tape dangles in the front. I can almost see myself in the picture, and it is a good feeling to know I am part of this family. But more important, when Alexander looked at the snapshot for the first time, he said, "Oh yes, I can see you in Monsieur Savoy. Your smile is just like his—can you see it?"

Beneath the letter addressed to me in the box which I must have by some queer instinct known was coming to me, there was a white blouse with lace inserts that must have belonged to Nana, and the dress made for Aunt Senta's First Communion, along with the French bonnet with its rows and rows of lace ruffles and satin tie strings. There were two dresses Nana had made for me as a child, in which were inserted strips of what Genevieve identified as val lace, from the Savoy Fine Lace and Linen Company. In the midst of all this were, carefully wrapped, the china figurines. In a separate stationery box, there was a group of letters addressed to Elzyna Farrish in care of Mrs. Neal Gerrard. As we drove back down Esplanade on the afternoon of Christmas Eve, I waved to Genevieve, who stood on the porch, waving back until we could see each other no more. Then I turned and began to read the letters from my father to my mother. And as I read, I began to see the chance she missed at happiness because of her strict loyalties. I was at first impatient with her for continuing to turn away from my father, until the time at last ran out. But then she was a young woman of another time, I had to remember, one in which there was little understanding by society of following the needs and desires of the heart. Then, of course, too late she changed her mind. The letter which was never mailed to my father was included in the stack of his letters to her, and before we left Genevieve explained what she and our father both learned in 1931 about the purloined letter.

I read it through twice, then folded it. "Aunt Senta was really a monster. She must have taken after her father."

Alexander said, "Senta was a determined individual. She nearly ruined my father's engagement to my mother in her attempts to get him back. Mother told me about it a long time ago."

I looked at him. "And what happened to your engagement, Alexander? Did it have anything to do with what Nana said about you in her letter?" Even as I asked the question, I thought Nana must have far underestimated the extent of Alexander's wealth.

He shook his head. "I certainly wasn't expecting her to mention that in the letter. But to answer your question, yes, it did. You see, the Gerrard estate is categorized—some for my mother, which I wouldn't touch, a big portion for charity, a trust for my uncle Clayton's care, and my own personal inheritance, all of which I squandered."

I waited for him to continue, and when he did not I said, "Is that all you're going to tell me? When I've trusted you with so much about myself, won't you trust me with anything about you?"

"It isn't that I don't trust you. Not that at all. It's just that—well, remember when you told me I ought to be thankful I'd never made any mistakes that could not be undone?

"I'm afraid I have. A lot of them. First of all, when I was eighteen or nineteen years old, I had this idea that I was really somebody. I was a 'Gerrard.' My father died a hero of sorts. Everyone knew who I was. There was nothing I could not have if I wanted it. I blew money right and left. I went all the way through M.I.T. just short of being thrown out."

"You're kidding," I interrupted. I remembered the newspaper photo in Nana's album. . . . Alexander going off to M.I.T. with great fanfare.

He continued, "One night when I was drunk I rammed a new red Corvette into the fence behind one of the buildings at school, and did several thousand dollars' worth of damage to the property as well as totaling the car and nearly killing myself."

I was shaking my head in wonder. I could not imagine anyone so steady . . . so responsible as Alexander coming to that.

"You might say I 'bought my way' back in after that. My grades were just barely good enough to get by. I really wasted the whole four years I spent up there."

"Was that why you went back to school and studied architecture?"

"Not exactly. I became interested in architecture while studying the design of ships. But I shoved it aside because I thought the great thing was to become an engineer. Then, just before I finished I—I got this girl up there pregnant.

"She wanted me to marry her, but I was not that responsible . . ."

I thought of Gabriel, his father, and realized now why it was so difficult for him to accept the possibility his father had made the same error.

". . . It was nasty for a while, but she finally agreed to an abortion . . ." His voice drifted off, and I sensed he was more regretful about that one situation than about all the rest put together. I could see now what he meant about the seriousness of his mistakes.

"I bought that, too," he continued. "And I gave her the money to leave me alone. But after that I began to feel like a jerk—exactly what I was . . . you wouldn't have liked me then at all. As I told you, even my mother had a hard time liking me for a while.

"So I graduated, not exactly with honors, and the most painful memory I have was that of a professor of mine telling me how pitiful I was, and how I had wasted my potential.

"I came home for the summer. I began to think about my father, what a fine man he was and how disappointed he would be if he could see me. And that, plus the infinite kindness of my mother, got me turned around. You know, it has occurred to me over the last week that if you had approached me then with the prospect that my father had done what you said, I would have had a nervous breakdown.

"Anyhow, I registered for the study of architecture at Rice. What money there was left that I hadn't already wasted, I spent going back to school, and because I felt it was truly important to be good at what I wanted to do, I traveled to Italy and Greece, and to Egypt—well, I spent months traveling, but this time I wasn't goofing off.

"When I came back I met Frances Newhouse. I don't think I ever really loved her. She was spoiled and immature. But everyone thought it was such a good match. What my family had not done, hers had. I got carried away with the idea and asked her to marry me. It wasn't until afterward I got up the nerve to tell her I was broke, but that I was not given to staying that way forever, and I was determined to make it on my own."

It was obvious that Alexander would one day inherit great wealth again, but I didn't remind him of this. I felt it was not really money at the base of his concern. "What did she think of that?" I asked him.

"She broke the engagement."

"And you were about to go to work for an architecture firm?"

"Yes. I backed out."

"But why?"

"Because it seemed to me that I landed that job based on my name, not my talent. They hardly even looked at my portfolio. It didn't seem important when I accepted the job, but later when I thought about how Frances had not really loved me for myself, and I was about to go to work for people who didn't hire me for myself, I just didn't want any part of it."

I felt that showed great strength of character, and I told him so.

"So I took a fellowship to teach at Rice, until I could decide what to do with myself."

"And you're still deciding?"

"Yes."

"Are you a good teacher?"

"No. I think I'm a good designer, and my teachers felt I had a lot of promise. But I'm only passable as a teacher. And I can't spell worth a damn."

I laughed. "Only English teachers have to spell perfectly."

"Well, now you know all about my shady past. I didn't want to tell you before, because I didn't want you to be disappointed in me, too. But it looks like Elzyna fixed that in her letter."

I rode along silently for a while, thinking of the many times I had felt Alexander could not understand me because of his limited life experience, how many cruel things I had thought and said.

Finally he said, "Well? Are you disappointed?"

"No, not anymore than I am in myself. We both wasted a lot. You know, I wish so much I could have known my father. But just as much I wish I could get those years back that I spent away from Nana—I guess I'll always call her that. Yet—and I've never admitted this to anyone before—I used to wonder why I felt so detached from Laura. When we visited her grave, Nana would often weep. I never could. I always thought it was because I didn't know her in my lifetime. I was certain Nana would scold me if she knew how little I felt for Laura, but of course, she never did.

"I feel more of a bond with that pitiful soul now than I ever did. The thought of what Jordan Leider did to her turns my stomach. What in the world do you think made him such an animal?"

He shook his head. "I just don't know, and long ago I gave up wondering."

I looked at him. "You are one of the most well-adjusted people I've ever met. I wish I could be like you. Every time I think of him coming into my room, interrogating me, I just get a cold chill. He must have been the devil incarnate."

"My grandmother, Alvareda, helped me deal with Jordan Leider. She was a good therapist."

I remembered what Stephen said about her reaction to the truth about

Laura's child. Then, all those years later— "How could she be that objective?"

"Experience taught her, I guess. She lived nearly three years after Jordan killed my father, and we were very close during that time. My attitude was worse than yours, and I think that worried her because she was afraid I'd grow up full of hatred and vindictive, like her father, Samuel Cane. She'd always remind me, 'Jordan Leider is dead. God will judge him. Don't let hatred rule your life because if you do, then Jordan has won a victory over all of us.' It took me years to see her wisdom. I really think her one purpose in living was to make me see that."

For a long distance, we rode in silence. Then, I said, "You know, I've realized something just now. When I was a child, I contrived all these fantasies about how my father had gone away to seek his fortune, and that when he came back for me, he would be rich and he'd take me to a place to live that would be like your house, near you. I couldn't see before today that I was trying to make my father into someone acceptable to you and your family, to fit into your structure. Isn't that crazy? But it's true."

He looked surprised.

"I feel differently now . . . not in the way I look up to you and your family, but in how I look at mine. I think my heritage is something I ought to be proud of, don't you?"

"I certainly do," he said, then he studied me for a moment and observed, "You look so tired. Why don't you try and sleep for a while?"

"Oh, I'm much too wound up to sleep," I protested, but at his urging, I lay down with my head resting on his thigh and put my feet up in the seat. He began to stroke my back and it must have been no more than a minute or two before I was enjoying the best, most peaceful sleep I had had since Nana's death.

When I woke up we were just at the edge of the Houston city limits. He didn't have much to say, yet I thought nothing of it because we soon hit the traffic resulting from last-minute Christmas shoppers. I felt warm and comfortable, confident. In just a few short weeks my life had turned around in every single way. . . .

It was almost dark when we drove along McKinney Avenue and pulled up at the curb of 4001. I gazed lingeringly at the house, with all its years of memories locked up behind the beautiful French doors. It looked stately somehow, and full of character, as the last rays of sun disappeared and bathed it in soft, muted light. My mother Elzyna's home. Could it ever have belonged to anyone else? "I'm sorry I acted so ugly about the house," I said.

"Well, I guess I could have been a little more patient, too. Look, if this deal on it closes, I'll split the proceeds with you. Oh hell, you can have it all. God knows you deserve it."

Now that I knew the true extent of his generosity, I couldn't think how to express how deeply I appreciated it. I put my arms around his neck and hugged him. "No, it's yours now," I said. "I think Nana was right."

He held me just a moment, then pulled away and looked into my eyes. He seemed sad. I searched for something to make him feel better. "You've been swell," I said. "I could not have made it through this without you. Even when I was mad at you, I was so glad you were around to be mad at."

For some time now, my mind had been preoccupied with what he would say to me when we reached this point. I thought he would offer some commitment to me. Instead he asked, "What are you going to do now?"

"Oh—oh, I don't know," I told him, trying not to sound deflated. "I do have this burning desire to go to France. And I ought to learn French first. Why I went through four years of Latin I'll never know. . . . What are you going to do?" I asked him. My heart was now lodged in my throat.

He looked at the steering wheel and said, "I'm not sure." Then he looked at me. "You must be bushed. I'll light the heaters for you."

"Yes, that would be great," I said, trying to smile. This was it, then. He was just going to walk right out of my life again. . . . He unloaded the car. I stepped up the walk, carrying my box from Nana in my arms, my right hand with the key in it, shaking. No, I argued then, as soon as we get in the house, he'll say the words I've waited for all my life. He loves me. He said he did. I adore you, he said. I pushed the key in and opened the door.

The house was dark and cold. I turned on the light switch by the door. The Seth Thomas clock was just striking the hour of six. Alexander put the bags down and lit the heaters in the library and parlor, then went upstairs to light the one in my bedroom. I stood there like a little urchin who hopes for a handout from a kind stranger in the street, every moment hope ebbing away.

At last he came down the stairs and went to the front door. He turned around and said, "I've got to scoot; I have some things to—"

"Sure," I interrupted. "Listen, I really appreciate your taking me to New Orleans. I think you know what a . . . a change in my life all this has made."

He didn't respond to that. "Will you be all right?" he asked.

"Sure. I've got plenty to do between now and the time I leave to go back to Dallas."

"You won't change your mind and spend Christmas with us?" he asked, his voice tentative.

I would have, would have gone anywhere with you, even River Oaks, if I thought you loved me. "No, I think not. It's going to take all the time I have left to get squared away here."

He kept standing there, his hand on the doorknob. "Robin, I—"

I looked at him expectantly, hoping against hope—

"Merry Christmas."

I let out a breath. "Yes, you too. And uh . . . give my best to Louetta."

He nodded, then he walked out the door. Not so much as a kiss good-bye.

I went and stood in front of the gas heater in the library. I felt the same way I did all those years ago, when I went to the birthday party at Alexander's house, and he paid attention to someone else. I had been so sure this time, as much as I tried to fight it at first; I let myself believe in him . . . let myself fall for him from the moment I saw him that day at the airport. And all the way through these weeks, always I thought that, even though things were a mess, he cared about me. And then last night, that one, beautiful night in New Orleans, I felt so completely loved. . . .

I looked at the box from Nana, now sitting on the piano bench. Suddenly a brand-new emptiness had replaced the old one. I let the tears run down my face and dry by the heat rising in front of me.

On Christmas Day I awoke feeling a little better. I had decided to take my father's name. I would be Robin Savoy. Nana would like that. I began packing things into boxes, discarding things, making decisions as to what to have sent to me in my tiny apartment, and what to leave behind. For the whole first part of the day I tried to count my blessings. I was going to be all right; I'd survived a broken marriage; gotten myself through school; landed a wonderful job. I now had two new people in my life that would always be there—Stephen and Genevieve—and family that I had not even met in France. I would begin immediately to save up money to travel there. As I realized after Nana's death, having an immediate sense of purpose is the best weapon against grief.

But I could not keep Alexander out of my mind, could not stack up all the blessings against the pain of being rejected by him, and I spent the better part of the afternoon sorting out things in old boxes through a blur of tears. Late in the evening I decided to call and wish him Merry Christmas. Just to hear his voice, one more time. Then I decided not to, that that would be stupid. Obviously he was not as serious about me as he seemed for a while, and did not want to hear from me. . . . But even if all that were true, he had been so good to me, through all this, when much of the time it was very hard for him.

Shortly before ten, I walked to the telephone and dialed the number. I was seized with anxiety and almost hung up while it was still ringing. What a dumb, schoolgirl thing to do.

Then Louetta answered. Her voice was warm and friendly. "Alexander is at the airport," she soon explained. She could not have said anything that surprised me more.

"Oh, I'm sorry. I hadn't realized he was leaving town." He probably has a girl friend out of town. Stupid, stupid Robin. . . .

"To tell the truth, I hadn't either. But that's how he is when he makes up his mind. As soon as he walked in the door last night, he locked himself up with the telephone. The next thing I knew, he said he'd been talking to an architect friend out in San Francisco, and that a partner from the firm had agreed to meet him for an interview Monday morning."

"Oh, that's wonderful," I said, for truly I thought it was. She began to congratulate me for all that had happened in New Orleans. "I hope you don't mind Alexander sharing it with me. He was so happy for you."

"Yes," I said, almost in a whisper. It would have been so much happier if the trip hadn't ended the way it did. "Well, Merry Christmas, Louetta. I've got to get back to packing up things."

I hung up the telephone. Bastard. Life goes on, doesn't it?

All day today I have gone in and out, taking boxes to leave by the curb for the garbage truck to haul away. And now I'm sitting on the floor of my old room, surrounded by scrapbooks and school yearbooks, old dried-up corsages and other keepsakes, and I am trying to decide what to take and what to throw away. I feel as if I have been doing this forever and will never finish.

Then I stop because I've heard the front door open. I bring a hand to my throat, fearing an intruder has walked in. I should have locked the door—

"Robin, are you up there?"

Alexander.

I hurry out to the landing and look down at him, almost afraid to take a breath for fear this will not be true. He is dressed up in a suit, his hair wind-blown, his tie loosened. He has never looked so good to me. I can't seem to make any words come forth, and he starts up the stairs. "Robin, you can't take someone to France on a teacher's salary, and besides, I couldn't ask you to spend the rest of your life with me if I didn't do something with myself. Will you marry me?"

If he says anything further, I don't hear it. Just as it used to long ago, when I was a child and knew that I belonged with Alexander, a thrill goes through me and I am rushing down the stairs to meet him.

It is a beautiful spring day, a perfect time to keep a promise to my daughter and return to this place of my memories. At the age of twelve, Elzyna Genevieve is the youngest of our three children, the only girl. She is, like Nana, quiet and dignified. She is also inquisitive. She has been hearing stories of her grandmother for years, and for a while she has seemed more introspective. I sense she is near the point of wanting to know things I have not been ready to convey. This time when she learned we were to visit Houston, she insisted I had delayed bringing her here long enough. As we turn into the drive, I am still not certain I am as ready as she is. . . .

The absence of the house at 4001 McKinney Avenue is startling to me, even though I've known it is gone for years. After the original sale fell through, Alexander placed it on the market again. During the cold winter of 1961, when we were already far away and the house stood vacant, a transient broke through the kitchen window to take refuge from the weather. He built a fire in the old stove, not knowing there was a place at the bottom of the oven that was rusted through. He may have been sleeping nearby when the blaze took hold and the house began to burn, but he did escape. No human remains were found. I have always suspected the transient was Mr. Nickleby. When we came back to view the charred skeleton of the house with its tall brick fireplaces standing like sentinels over a graveyard, I went over to the icehouse and asked about him. Mr. Nickleby had not been around since the fire.

That was the last time I was here.

I linger now at the wheel of the car, but my daughter is impatient to have a thorough tour and tugs at my hand, so I step out and walk up the driveway with her. My eyes follow the remains of the front walk all the way up to the point where the porch used to stand, and I can see a clear indentation in the ground of the configuration of the porch and the outer edge of the house as well. We walk from place to place, and I point out where each room used to be. From this vantage point, it seems to have been much smaller than I remember and I confess this fact to my Elzyna. She remembers the tiles, and we go to the place where they used to be, but they are not there anymore. The grass has grown over the spot. One section we find up in the middle of the yard, as though wrested from its place by a giant hand and hurled aside. We can make out the edge of the broken white and blue tiles, and the first initial, the capital E, is almost completely intact. She asks what caused the rearrangement, and I have to shake my head for I don't know.

The huge oaks still provide shade to the yard. I point out the oak near the walk and tell her that a swing hung from the big limb reaching toward the house, and that her father used to swing me when we were children. I can still remember the breeze across my face and the welcome feeling that he was there. Where is the swing? What became of it? she asks me next. Again, I shake my head. That was something I never learned because I left, and when I finally came home it was gone. There are many things I lost in that one hasty indulgence in rebellion. It occurs to me there may be more new questions opened on this day than old ones answered.

To the right of the property, at the corner of Cullen Boulevard, the icehouse survives. It seems possible that the owners of that establishment now own the Farrish property as well, because there are wooden tables and benches placed where the stables and, later, the garage, used to be. There are also two refuse cans nearby, and some of the contents have spilled into the yard. The breeze is pleasant but perverse, and blows a potato chip wrapper across a table and farther on, until it stops at just about the spot where the library windows used to be. I close my eyes. The house that once stood here and all that happened in it seem close enough for me to reach out and touch. . . .

I suddenly feel ready to pour out the whole story of Nana, but I realize that I cannot do it here. And anyway, her own letters and keepsakes, which I have not been ready to share, will tell much more than I could say. When we are home again, I will open the box at last. . . .

The visit is over. As we walk arm in arm toward the car I notice the street sign no longer says McKinney Avenue. Now it is simply McKinney Street, like any well-traveled artery near downtown at the foot of which great buildings rise. The word Avenue no longer applies. As we drive away Elzyna asks if there will ever be a house there again. I shake my head. How can I say? It seems to me that this spot is as much a wilderness now as it was in the beginning. Yet, perhaps, only for a time.

R.S.G.